THE PENGUIN SPORTS LIBRARY
*General Editor: Dick Schaap*

THE UNFORGETTABLE SEASON

G. H. Fleming is a baseball aficionado and historical expert by avocation; vocationally, he is a professor of English literature at the University of New Orleans. He has published scholarly books on the Victorian novel *(George Alfred Lawrence and the Victorian Sensation Novel)*, the Pre-Raphaelites *(Rossetti and the Pre-Raphaelite Brotherhood* and *That Ne'er Shall Meet Again: Rossetti, Millais, Hunt)*, and the American painter James Whistler *(The Young Whistler)*.

# THE UNFORGETTABLE SEASON

## G. H. FLEMING

Foreword by
Lawrence Ritter

PENGUIN BOOKS

Penguin Books Ltd, Harmondsworth,
Middlesex, England
Penguin Books, 625 Madison Avenue,
New York, New York 10022, U.S.A.
Penguin Books Australia Ltd, Ringwood,
Victoria, Australia
Penguin Books Canada Limited, 2801 John Street,
Markham, Ontario, Canada L3R 1B4
Penguin Books (N.Z.) Ltd, 182–190 Wairau Road,
Auckland 10, New Zealand

First published in the United States of America by
Holt, Rinehart and Winston 1981
First published in Canada by
Holt, Rinehart and Winston of Canada, Limited, 1981
Published in Penguin Books by arrangement with
Holt, Rinehart and Winston 1982

LIBRARY OF CONGRESS CATALOGING IN PUBLICATION DATA
Fleming, Gordon H., 1920–
The unforgettable season.
Includes index.
1. National League of Professional Baseball
Clubs—History—Addresses, essays, lectures.
2. New York Giants (Baseball team)—History—
Addresses, essays, lectures. I. Title.
GV875.A3F55  1982     796.357′64′0973     81-21167
ISBN 0 14 00.6273 4          AACR2

Printed in the United States of America by
R.R. Donnelley & Sons Company, Harrisonburg, Virginia
Set in Bembo

# THE PENGUIN SPORTS LIBRARY

The purpose of this series of sports books is simple: It is to make available in paperback, at a reasonable price, some of the finest books that have been written about sports, books that otherwise might not be in print. There is only one basic requirement for a book to be considered for this series: It has to be good. It has to be pleasurable reading. It can be fiction or nonfiction. It can be a play. It can be angry or funny or, better yet, a blend of both. The author can be famous or obscure. He can be an athlete or an academic. He can write about the beauty of boxing or the brutality of chess. He can be a cynic or a cheerleader. He can be anything except dull.

A secondary requirement for a book to be selected for this series is that I must read it. This is my pleasure. The wonderful thing about reading and rereading the truly outstanding books about sports is that they are about so many things besides sports.

—Dick Schaap
New York City

To Muggsy and Big Six,
To The Iron Man and Turkey Mike,
To The Chief and Laughing Larry,
To Pancho and Pep,
To The Rajah and Irish Emil,
To Highpockets and The Fordham Flash,
To King Carl and Prince Hal,
To Fat Freddy and Master Melvin,
To Frisco Lefty and Memphis Bill,
To Leo the Lip and Eddie the Brat,
To The Barber and The Kid Who Said, "Say Hey!"

and to every other New York Baseball Giant
this book is gratefully dedicated.

# FOREWORD

If the expression "Truth is stranger than fiction" did not originate in 1908, it should have. Because not even the most imaginative of story-tellers could have dreamed up what actually happened that memorable year as the Pittsburgh Pirates, New York Giants, and Chicago Cubs schemed and clawed their way in quest of the elusive National League pennant. More than seven decades have passed since that extraordinary season, but the years quickly melt away as we fall under the spell of G. H. Fleming's masterful reconstruction of one of baseball's most sus-penseful pennant races; and before we realize it, the day-to-day tides of battle become as immediate and dramatic as a late-breaking news flash.

The changing fortunes of war, favoring first one team and then an-other, build up a tension that is compounded even further by a marvelous cast of characters. Baseball in those days, like America at large, had more than its share of idiosyncratic personalities, many of them reflecting the regional and individual differences that still characterized the nation at the turn of the century. Today, ball players are named Willie, Jim, and Tom, just like everyone else. But not then: Dummy Taylor, Iron Man Joe McGinnity, Turkey Mike Donlin, and Three-Finger Brown were *sui generis.* Not to mention McGraw and Matty of the Giants, the great Honus Wagner of the Pirates, and the Cubs' fabled Tinker, Evers, and Chance—names that have become legendary with the passage of time. All of these, and more, come to life once again in the pages that follow.

Luther (Dummy) Taylor, for example, was a deaf mute from Olathe, Kansas, whose pitching skills helped the New York Giants win over 100 games in the early years of the century. Despite his handicap he was an integral member of the team, off the field as well as on, because Manager John McGraw insisted that all the Giants become proficient in the deaf-and-dumb alphabet. McGraw often gave his on-the-field signals that way, spelling out S-T-E-A-L on his fingers so plainly that anyone who knew the system could read his instructions. When Taylor retired from the game, he joined the faculty of a school for the deaf in Kansas.

(Iron Man) Joe McGinnity, another of McGraw's pitchers, came from Rock Island, Illinois. Winner of close to 250 games during his ten-year big-league career—seven times winning at least 20 games and twice more than 30—McGinnity became famous by pitching both halves of doubleheaders, a feat he accomplished on five different occasions in the major leagues. Three times he won both games. The 1908 season was his last in the major leagues, but he continued to pitch for many more years in the minors. In 1925, at the age of 54, he notched 6 wins and 6 losses with Dubuque in the Mississippi Valley League. That year McGinnity, who was also the team's manager and part owner, said: "I have to pitch because it's the best way I know to protect my investment."

Another of McGraw's favorites was Turkey Mike Donlin, one of the hardest hitters and most popular players of his day. He hit .351 in 1903 and .356 in 1905. But Mike's heart was not in baseball. A fine singer and raconteur, the life of the party, Mike was not overly devoted to abstemious habits. He married stage star Mabel Hite in 1906, and thereafter played only one more full season (in 1908, when he hit .334). Increasingly Donlin turned to vaudeville, where he and Mabel were tremendous box-office attractions, and wound up spending most of the rest of his life making movies in Hollywood.

For their part, the Chicago Cubs countered with Mordecai Peter Centennial (Three-Finger) Brown—his parents threw in the extra middle name because he was born in 1876. A farm boy from Indiana, Brown joined the Cubs in 1904 and won 20 or more games every season from 1906 through 1911. As a youngster he had an accident with some farm equipment, which necessitated the amputation of most of the index finger on his right hand (his throwing hand). The same accident also rendered the little finger of that hand useless. Nevertheless, his pitching hardly suffered; indeed, he always claimed the injury gave his sinker ball that extra something no one else could duplicate. In crucial Cubs-Giants games it was invariably Three-Finger Brown vs. Christy Mathewson on the mound—and 13 out of 24 times the decision went to Brown!

Even so, it was generally acknowledged that the greatest pitcher of his generation was Christy Mathewson. To a large extent it was Matty, more than anyone, who changed the public image of baseball and elevated it into the mainstream of American life. Until the turn of the century, professional baseball was looked upon as a rowdy sport, played mainly by roughnecks. Few women attended games, and even many fathers would think twice before taking their sons to a professional game. Matty helped change all that. Handsome, well educated, reserved, he was the very embodiment of the all-American boy, and his entrance into the sport gave it a big push toward respectability and middle-class acceptance. Born in Pennsylvania, the son of well-to-do parents, he played football in addition to baseball at Bucknell—where he also found time to join the glee club and the literary society. Later, he gained fame as checkers champion of half a dozen states. Indeed, his passion for checkers was so great that some suspected it ranked above baseball in his priorities. All of which would have been irrelevant had he not also been the best pitcher of his time, perhaps of all time. In 1903, '04, and '05 he won 30, 33, and 31 games, respectively, and then went on to his most remarkable season, in 1908. It is doubtful if any baseball player has ever been cited so often as a model of deportment to errant offspring by fathers and mothers the length and breadth of the land.

The Cubs also had shortstop Joe Tinker, second baseman Johnny Evers, and manager–first baseman Frank Chance (the Peerless Leader), whom newspaper columnist Franklin P. Adams, a rabid Giant fan, immortalized with his lament over their double-play skills:

> These are the saddest of possible words—
> Tinker to Evers to Chance.
> Trio of Bear Cubs and fleeter than birds—
> Tinker to Evers to Chance.

Frank Chance had become manager of the Chicago Cubs in 1905, when he was but 27 years of age. He had been attending Washington College in California in 1898, planning to become a doctor, when an opportunity arose to try out with the Cubs. He made the club as a second-string catcher—never having played a day in the minors—and became a star when he was shifted to first base several years later. His intelligence and leadership qualities were so obvious that it was no surprise when he was appointed playing manager after having been a regular for only two years.

So far as the population of Pittsburgh was concerned, however, there was only one star in the firmament and his name was Wagner. Close to 6 feet tall, a solid 200 pounds, bowlegged as a pair of parentheses, Honus

Wagner's ability was exceeded only by his modesty. He hit .300 or better for 17 consecutive seasons, led the National League in batting 8 times, and stole over 700 bases during his career. He remains the greatest short-stop who ever lived and possibly the greatest baseball player of all time (rivaled only by Babe Ruth and Ty Cobb).

And last, but far from least: 19-year-old rookie Fred Merkle. Because the Giants' regular first baseman, veteran Fred Tenney, developed a bad back, the inexperienced Merkle replaced him in the starting lineup for a crucial late-season game. As fate would have it, Fred Merkle inadvertently played a larger role in the pennant race—at least in the eyes of the press—than any of the more established stars.

In those days, long before radio and television, the daily press played a distinctive role in disseminating baseball results to an eagerly awaiting public. The day's scores were published, almost inning by inning, in special late afternoon and early evening editions, and a newspaper's reporters became as identified with particular teams as radio and television play-by-play announcers are with teams today. By virtue of their unique status and long tenure, many of the reporters—like some broadcasters today—had no hesitation about expressing their opinions on topics only remotely connected to the game they were supposed to be covering. Indeed, racism and anti-Semitism turn up in the sports pages of the era in ways that would now be considered shocking. It is sobering to realize that prejudice and bigotry were evidently as American as apple pie back in those idyllic "good old days" of yesteryear.

G. H. Fleming's skillful reconstruction of the 1908 season brings that exciting pennant race alive as though it were taking place today. In the process, it also provides a jarring glimpse of an America that was not quite as tranquil and serene as nostalgia would generally have us believe.

—Lawrence Ritter

# —— ACKNOWLEDGMENTS ——

While I worked on this book, numerous people assisted me. I received valuable suggestions and answers to questions from Betty Cook, Stanley Coveleski, Ashbel Green, Carl Hubbell, George (Highpockets) Kelly, the late Richard (Rube) Marquard, Eddie Mulligan, Larry Ritter, Wilfred (Rosy) Ryan, Arthur Schott, and Horace Stoneham. At the National League headquarters, in New York, I was hospitably received by Katy Feeney and her colleagues, who directed me to useful material in the league files. At the Newspaper Division of the New York Public Library I was helped by members of the staff. From the Pittsburgh Baseball Club I was given two excellent glossy photographs of Honus Wagner and Fred Clarke. At my home base of operations, the New Orleans branch of Louisiana State University, I was helped in various ways by Elizabeth Ashin, Jody Blake, Rayza Caballero, Evelyn Chandler, Anna Lloyd, Raeburn Miller, Jean Montero, Gregory Spano, and Nita Walsh. After completing the first draft, which was too long for publication, I was excellently advised by Jeffrey C. Smith on how to reduce it to manageable proportions. To all of these persons I extend thanks.

# PREFACE

On Sunday, November 10, 1907, the sporting section of New York's most widely circulated morning newspaper, the *American*, startled readers with this banner headline: BRESNAHAN TO SUCCEED M'GRAW AS MANAGER OF THE NEW YORK GIANTS. John T. Brush, the Indianapolis textiles tycoon who had owned the Giants since November 11, 1902, was reportedly ready to sack his manager, John J. McGraw, in favor of his catcher, Roger Bresnahan. This was New York's most electrifying baseball news since July 1902, when this same John McGraw, already famous at the age of 29 after a decade with the legendary Baltimore Orioles, became the Giants' manager. Buried in the National League cellar, from which they had not strayed far in seven years, the Giants were a local embarrassment, almost a national joke. McGraw had had scant opportunity to elevate the 1902 team, but in 1903, with 67 victories by the greatest of pitching pairs, Christy Mathewson and (Iron Man) Joe McGinnity, the Giants rose to second place, just 6½ games behind Pittsburgh. And in 1904, finishing 13 games ahead of second-place Chicago, they won the pennant. In two and a half years McGraw had raised his team from the basement to the penthouse. The 1904 season ended, however, on a sour note. Even though the Boston Red Sox had won the initial interleague championship in 1903, John Brush refused to recognize what he regarded as the upstart American League, and so there was no World Series in 1904. But never again would a club owner be able to act thus peremptorily, and after the Giants had repeated as champions in 1905 they defeated Connie Mack's Philadelphia Athletics in the World Series four games to one, with Mathewson pitching his probably never-to-be-equaled three shut-outs.

The Giants now ruled the sporting world, and in 1906 no one doubted that they would win a third straight pennant. No one, that is, but Frank Chance's Chicago Cubs, who finished the season 20 games ahead of New York. In 1907, McGraw's Giants suffered a total collapse, finishing

25½ games behind Chicago and also trailing Pittsburgh and Philadelphia. Fourth place would have been a pleasure palace for the old Giants, but it was intolerable for John T. Brush, especially since his manager often seemed more interested in horse races than ball games. And so, it was rumored, McGraw might soon be left free to follow the horses.

But McGraw was not discharged, and partly because of his continuing control of the Giants no one who took even a remote interest in baseball then would ever forget the National League season of 1908. "The game," McGraw wrote prophetically not long before his death, "will never know another battle like that of 1908."

Viewed from the perspective of McGraw's Giants, that battle, which a later *Spalding's National League Guide* called "unparalleled in baseball's history," is the subject of this book. Hardly anyone alive remembers that distant season, but in the following pages we can vicariously relive those memorable days. The narrative, however, is not mine. The story will be told by those who saw and heard all that happened. I have read every relevant issue of New York's twelve daily newspapers of 1908, as well as the Brooklyn *Eagle*, three daily papers from Philadelphia, two from Boston, two from Pittsburgh, three from Chicago, two from St. Louis, and one from Cincinnati, along with the two baseball weeklies, *The Sporting News* and *Sporting Life*, and I have selected, edited, and reproduced the most vivid, provocative writings on the activities—inside and beyond the field of combat—of players, managers, owners, umpires, spectators, and ordinary citizens. Through the eyes and ears of those who were there, we shall thus restore this vanished culture, and, day by day, in all its significant details, we shall again experience the excitement of that unforgettable season.

Play ball!

—G. H. Fleming

# THE PLAYERS

THE 1908 NEW YORK GIANTS: 1, Bresnahan; 2, Tenney; 3, Seymour; 4, Mathewson; 5, Devlin; 6, Snodgrass; 7, Wiltse; 8, Brain; 9, McGraw, Mgr; 10, Merkle; 11, McGinnity; 12, Needham; 13, McCormick; 14, Crandall; 15, Doyle; 16, Taylor; 17, Donlin; 18, Herzog; 19, Barry; 20, Ames; 21, Bridwell; 22, Marquardt; 23, Wilson; 24, Durham; 25, Beecher; 26, DeVore.

*Pictorial News Co. Photo., courtesy New York Public Library.*

John J. McGraw, manager of the Giants (below, coaching at third base). *Photoworld.*

Christy Mathewson, the great "Matty."

Roger Bresnahan. *Culver Pictures, Inc.*

"Iron Man" Joe McGinnity. *Photoworld.*

Mike Donlin and his wife, the actress Mabel Hite. *Library of Congress.*

Fred Merkle. *Culver Pictures.*

Larry Doyle.
*The Bettmann Archive.*

Luther "Dummy" Taylor.
*Library of Congress, Baine Collection.*

Honus Wagner, "The Flying Dutchman." *The Bettmann Archive.*

THE 1908 PITTSBURGH PIRATES: 1, Shannon; 2, Clarke, Mgr.; 3, Wilson; 4, Phelps; 5, Brandon; 6, Moeller; 7, Leever; 8, O'Connor; 9, Camnitz; 10, Leifield; 11, Thomas; 12, Kane; 13, Vail; 14, Phillippe; 15, Leach; 16, Abbaticchio; 17, Maddox; 18, Starr; 19, Wagner; 20, Gill; 21, Willis; 22, Storke; 23, Gibson. *Pictorial News Co. Photo., courtesy New York Public Library.*

THE 1908 CHICAGO CUBS: 1, Zimmerman; 2, Reulbach; 3, Fraser; 4, Pfeister; 5, Durbin; 6, Steinfeldt; 7, Lundgren; 8, Campbell; 9, Moran; 10, Overall; 11, Brown; 12, Howard; 13, Kling; 14, Evers; 15, Chance, Capt.; 16, Tinker; 17, Slagle; 18, Sheckard; 19, Schulte; 20, Hofman.

*Courtesy New York Public Library.*

The great infield double-play combination of the Chicago Cubs: "Tinker to Evers to Chance." *Culver Pictures.*

"Three-Finger" Mordecai Brown. *Photoworld.*

Frank Chance, the "Peerless Leader"
of the Chicago Cubs. *Culver Pictures.*

# THE
# UNFORGETTABLE
# SEASON

"Johnny McGraw will not be manager of the Giants next season. He is too fond of the race track, and doesn't seem to want to give it up. He will at best have to make a choice quickly."

A man prominent in baseball circles and personal acquaintance of President {John T.} Brush, of the Giants, made this statement yesterday.

Roger Bresnahan, the Giants' famous catcher, was named as possible successor.

President Brush and Secretary {Fred} Knowles are dissatisfied with McGraw's conduct and the consequent wreck of the Giants, he said, and have decided that a change is necessary.

McGraw's contract has not more than a year to run, so it will be possible to remove him without involving too great a financial sacrifice.

The utter failure of the Giants last season to make anything like a good showing is supposed to have wiped out the last of President Brush's patience. McGraw had a wonderful array of ball players, all the material necessary for a great team {but} the play of the Giants became listless and their teamwork fell away to almost nothing {they finished in fourth place}. There were frequent rumors of internal disturbances and quarrels, and McGraw was often seen at the track during the Summer meetings.

Neither President Brush nor Secretary Knowles could be located last night, but it is probable that no official announcement will come until the change is put into effect.                    —New York *American*


───◇ MONDAY, NOVEMBER 11 ◇───

Whenever John J. McGraw has been asked why the Giants made such a poor showing last season, he said that the umpires would not let him get out on the coaching lines and "pump ginger" into his players. This really is a weak excuse, for McGraw could have stayed on the coaching lines as long as he wanted to if he would only restrict himself, but Mac usually got into a row with the umpires and was ordered off the grounds.

—New York *Evening Journal*

## ◇ WEDNESDAY, NOVEMBER 13 ◇

President John T. Brush has by this time been asked point blank a dozen times whether McGraw is to go, and in no case has he availed himself of the simple denial.

There are just two possible explanations of the attitude that President Brush has taken. The club may be seizing this opportunity to get a little off-season advertising, but this can be thrown out. Undenied statements that a manager as well known as McGraw is to be hurried out of his job so he can have more time to devote to the races is not healthy advertising for any club.

The only other explanation is that McGraw is to be let out, and that the time for the official announcement is not yet. Impartially reviewing McGraw's record as a manager in the last two years, there will not be a great deal of surprise when the announcement comes.

The shopworn references to the glory of the world's champions and the injustice of fans who want pennants all the time have lost their punch. Fans don't want pennants all the time, but they want good, sincere baseball and a team that is "up there." Finishing fourth in a league as poorly balanced as the National cost the ex-world's champions many a friend.

—New York *American*

## ◇ THURSDAY, NOVEMBER 14 ◇

John McGraw of the Giants has quit the race track.

The leader of the local National League team has not been seen at the Aqueduct course since the announcement that his devotion to horse racing had put his job in jeopardy.

McGraw also failed to turn up at his usual haunts on Broadway yesterday, and as the men at the head of the club maintained silence on the subject, the McGraw mystery is as deep as ever.

—George Sands, New York *American*


After all the recent hysterics about John J. McGraw being released as manager of the Giants, the fact that he is still the manager and will continue to be so as long as he wants the job should go a great way toward calming the hysterical ones.

McGraw will be manager of the Giants next year and {New York catcher} Roger Bresnahan will not.

Roger possibly has managerial aspirations, but he is altogether too hotheaded to be given full authority to dictate to a team of players who know as much if not more about baseball than he does.

McGraw is a born leader of ball players, and there is not a Giant or any other player who has ever played under him who did not appreciate the value of his leadership and the results he obtained by his thorough knowledge of the game.

—Sam Crane, New York *Evening Journal*


———◇ **TUESDAY, NOVEMBER 19** ◇———


Big, awkward, conscientious, good-natured {Pirate shortstop} Hans Wagner, steady and strong in his years of baseball lore, this year established a new record for long batting success on the diamond, this being the fifth year that he has held the National League title. He won the batting championship with a mark of .350 and the base-running honors with 61 stolen bases.

No one ever saw anything graceful or picturesque about Wagner on the diamond. His movements have been likened to the gambols of a caracoling elephant. He is ungainly and so bowlegged that when he runs his limbs seem to be moving in a circle after the fashion of a propeller. But he can run like the wind. When he starts after a grounder every outlying portion of his anatomy apparently has ideas of its own about the proper line of direction to be taken. His position at the bat is less awkward and the muscular swing of his great arms and shoulders is strong enough to drive the ball farther than most batters who hit from their toe spikes up.

There is no question that Wagner is the greatest all-round ball player of this or probably any other season.    —New York *American*

──◇ **SATURDAY, NOVEMBER 20** ◇──

Mike Donlin will be the field captain of the New York Giants, Secretary Fred Knowles informed the baseball public yesterday. Knowles and McGraw decided to give Mike a little responsibility, for it would be, in their opinion, a good thing for him to have to maintain the dignity necessary to the character of field captain.

Mike will have to watch everything carefully that takes place during a contest, as it will be up to him to do the official talking. Knowles and McGraw feel that the honor of the position will cause Mike to quit his kidding ways and make him an example to the rest of the team in deportment.    —New York *American*

Nobody knows what Frank Chance draws as manager of the Cubs, but President {C. Webb} Murphy has stated for publication that he gets more money than any other player ever did. His salary as a player is large, for he is one of the stars of the game. Added to that is his salary as manager of the club, and besides this are the dividends he receives for the 100 shares of stock he holds in the club, presented to him by Charles P. Taft when the club was originally purchased from James A. Hart.

   —*Sporting Life*

──◇ **TUESDAY, NOVEMBER 26** ◇──

CHICAGO, Nov. 26—Mike Donlin is again a Giant.

Last night the great outfielder and batsman, who was formerly the star player of the New York National club, signed a contract for another season with the Giants. Secretary Fred Knowles, who has been here for several days, concluded arrangements with Donlin, who has promised to be good and redeem himself in the eyes of the New York fans.

Secretary Knowles has been in communication with the swell hitter for some time. Knowles came out here ostensibly to see the Carlisle-Chicago football game last Saturday, but in reality he was after Donlin. Donlin wanted a wartime salary and he finally got it on condition that he keep in trim throughout the season of 1908, refrain from all intoxicants and make the Spring training trip to Texas with the team. {The term *wartime* refers to conditions that had prevailed a few years earlier when the National League would not recognize the status of the newly formed American League, and the two leagues competed with each other for the services of players.} —New York *Evening Journal*

## ———◇ MONDAY, DECEMBER 9 ◇———

Beginning tomorrow and for nearly the balance of the week magnates of the National League will be in session at the Waldorf-Astoria, where they will do some baseball legislating, but possibly more posing around the round tables in the big cafe.

It was President Harry Pulliam's pet idea for the magnates to break away from Broadway and hold forth at the more exclusive Fifth Avenue hostelry. {Opened in 1893, the Waldorf-Astoria was then located on Fifth Avenue between 33rd and 34th streets. Earlier meetings of the National League had been held at a comparatively modest hotel on Broadway.}

There does not appear to be any desire on the part of the magnates to change the present playing rules. The general feeling is that it is better to leave well enough alone. The past season was one of the most successful financially in the history of the organization, and every club made money.

Possibly that is why the Waldorf-Astoria was selected as the place of meeting. —Sam Crane, New York *Evening Journal*

## ———◇ TUESDAY, DECEMBER 10 ◇———

PITTSBURGH, Dec. 9—Hans Wagner, the Pirates' veteran shortstop, will not be in the game next year if he takes his doctor's advice.

"Big Honus" went to see his doctor yesterday. They had a powwow over the big fellow's rheumatic shoulder, and the man of medicine gave his verdict—quit baseball.

Wagner is almost crippled with the rheumatism, which has settled in his right arm and shoulder.

"I'm comfortably fixed financially," he said, "and I'm ready to quit. My old friend, the M.D., settled it for me yesterday. I am out of professional baseball for good." —New York *American*

───◇ **WEDNESDAY, DECEMBER 11** ◇───

Owners of the National League baseball clubs who may have come to New York to trade players made little progress yesterday. Rumors were thicker than drops of vapor in a Southern cloud, but there was little to give encouragement to the reports.

Much of the business transacted yesterday was purely routine. Mr. Pulliam recommended that the sale of liquids in bottles be prohibited at all baseball grounds and that no intoxicants be sold in grandstands. He also went on record against mutually arranged seven-inning games where doubleheaders are to be played. He would also make it compulsory that postponed games be played on stipulated dates in the future, taking from the home club the right to announce a date satisfactory to itself. Under that provision whenever a game is postponed the future date of its playing will be immediately known. —New York *Herald*

President C. Webb Murphy, of the Chicago club, does not do anything by halves. He is the whole Swiss cheese at this meeting—holes and all. He came here like a conquering hero and really he is the whole show. Charley showed this in a most appealing way by buying two rounds of drinks before the Waldorf-Astoria bar.

—Sam Crane, New York *Evening Journal*

───◇ **SATURDAY, DECEMBER 14** ◇───

The Board of Directors voted to advance Harry Pulliam's salary by $2,000. The president of the league, with that advance, will receive not far from $10,000 a year. —New York *Herald*

By one of the biggest deals in the history of National League baseball, Manager McGraw last night succeeded in materially strengthening the New York club for next season.

After a long conference between McGraw and Joe Kelley, Boston's new manager, it was announced that {Dan} McGann, {Bill} Dahlen, {George} Browne, {Frank} Bowerman and {Cecil} Ferguson had been traded to Boston for {Fred} Tenney {the former manager}, {Al} Bridwell and {Tom} Needham.

The Giants' infield will be greatly strengthened by the addition of Tenney at first and Bridwell at short. The two working with {Arthur} Devlin and {Larry} Doyle will form a fast combination which should prove a winner. Needham will be valuable as an assistant to Roger Bresnahan behind the bat.

For a long time McGraw has contemplated the separation of Bresnahan and Bowerman. Ever since the world's championship series of 1905, when Bresnahan caught every game, there has been friction between the two receivers.

Charley Murphy, president of the Chicago club, was not backward in saying he hoped McGraw could pull off a deal with Boston that would strengthen the Giants, for he felt it essential to the prosperity of the league that New York have a first-class team in the next pennant race.

—Sam Crane, New York *Evening Journal*

———◇ **MONDAY, DECEMBER 16** ◇———

Still "The Talk of New York" is the big deal pulled off by John McGraw. The acquisition of Tenney is regarded not only locally, but everywhere else, as an excellent thing for the McGraw combination. Harry Pulliam characterizes the eight-player swap as one in which both clubs got the better of it, while Ned Hanlon {manager of four National League teams, 1889–1907} said McGraw had made a ten-strike in landing Tenney.

"Fred is one of the hardest men in the country to pitch to and makes the man in the box put them over for him. He can sacrifice beautifully and also can change tactics on a second's notice and carry through the hit-and-run play. Tenney is certainly a nice Christmas present for the Giants."

In Pulliam's estimation New York got a live asset in Al Bridwell, Harry C. thinking that McGraw will correct the youngster's indeterminate style at the plate and make a first-class hitter of him. Baseball sharps agree that Bridwell is a beautiful fielder, who is fast on his feet and knows intuitively what to do with the ball.

Few players stay so long in one city as Tenney stayed in Boston. Fred went there in 1894 from Brown University {a member of the class of 1894, Tenney was the first college graduate to achieve baseball stardom}, and has been a Beaneater ever since, save for about two weeks during his first season, when he was sent to the Springfield farm, where he acted as backstop for John Dwight Chesbro {famed spitball pitcher who competed for Pittsburgh, 1899–1902, and then for the New York Yankees}. {Frank} Selee, managing Boston then, liked Fred's style, and a left-handed receiver was no novelty, as Jack Clements was backstopping for Philadelphia. The new Giant caught and played in the outfield in his first season with Boston, and was windpaddist {catcher} and suburbanite {outfielder} during the following two campaigns. In 1897 Fred became a first baseman.

In thirteen full years in the National League, Tenney has played in 1,598 games, and his grand batting average is .308. As a fielder Tenney for the last seven seasons has topped all National League first-sackers in the number of assists.

Bridwell is a juvenile. He was with Atlanta in 1903, Columbus in 1904, Cincinnati in 1905 and Boston in 1906 and 1907. Bridwell's National League batting average is .230.          —New York *Press*

─────◇ **WEDNESDAY, DECEMBER 18** ◇─────

With nearly all of the Giant pitchers greatness is a memory, not a reality. Three years ago {Christy} Mathewson, {Joe "Iron Man"} McGinnity, {George} Wiltse and {Luther "Dummy"} Taylor won games almost before they went into the box. They were believed and believed themselves to be invincible. But that is no more.

In 1906, after his great year of the championship, Mathewson began to slip. "Antitoxin for the nasal diphtheria," said the wise ones. "It'll die out and he'll be all right next season."

Next season found Mathewson even easier to solve. He no longer inspired fear. Teams that formerly threw away their bats when he stepped into the box slammed his favorite slants all over the lot. Mathewson is by no means a "dead one," but no stretch of the imagination would place him as the best twirler in the league. And he is kingpin of the staff.

Of the others, McGinnity and Taylor seem pretty nearly past the days of big league usefulness. And that is no shame to either. Both have done noble work at the Polo Grounds for years, but their performances last season could hardly be rated first class.

Wiltse is plainly a second-class man now. {Leon "Red"} Ames would be a great pitcher if he had any knowledge of the direction likely to be taken by the ball after he lets go. This wildness has been a chronic weakness with "Red" for so long that it·is idle to hope he will get over it.

The Giants' pitching staff is now very much second class, and unless it is refitted there will be no National League ribbon at the Polo Grounds next Fall. —New York *American*

———◇ **THURSDAY, DECEMBER 19** ◇———

Did Joe Kelley hand McGraw a lemon? Tenney, a back number; Bridwell, a poor hitter; and Needham, a minor league catcher, handed over for Bowerman, Dahlen, McGann, Browne, and Ferguson. If that isn't sure enough quince, I will admit that McGraw has more brains than all the judges in America. While Tenney is still a good player and is greatly the superior of McGann, it's no cinch that Tenney will help the Giants. But cutting Tenney and McGann out of it, it's a joke to think Needham can fill one of Bowerman's shoes, while Bridwell, at shortstop, will look like an amateur in the absence of the heady Dahlen, even though Dahlen has gone back. Ferguson doesn't count. Browne, outside of Beaumont and Kelley, is a better man than any of the Boston outfielders last year. —Joe Vila, *The Sporting News*

———◇ **SUNDAY, DECEMBER 22** ◇———

Practically completed are all arrangements for the Spring training trip of the Giants, who will get into condition at Marlin Springs, Tex.

This will be the Giants' first trial of Texas as a training place. Manager John McGraw likes the climate of California, but says that the journey to and from the Pacific coast is too long. Texas suits the Little Napoleon as a training camp, and he thinks he has picked the most available place in Marlin Springs, about forty miles from Dallas.

Since 1902 the Giants have taken training trips, visiting Savannah in 1903 and 1904, Birmingham in 1905, Memphis in 1906 and Los Angeles last Spring. Previously the Giants trained at the Polo Grounds, in Lakewood and in Jacksonville, having a record now of training in seven states—California, Tennessee, Alabama, Georgia, Florida, New Jersey and New York. Texas will be the eighth.          —New York *Press*

──◇ MONDAY, DECEMBER 23 ◇──

While Fred Tenney at present seems assured of holding down first base for the Giants next season, he will have to play up to a high mark to hold the place, for he has a young, ambitious rival in Fred Merkle, the Toledo High School boy. In fact, the struggle of the youngster to supplant the veteran will be an interesting feature of Spring practice, and the battle will probably be waged throughout the year.

In Merkle, Tenney has a rival that would worry any veteran. Although but nineteen years of age, he has already shown major league caliber. He played with the Giants at the tail end of last season, and the way he whipped the ball over to Dahlen and Doyle aroused the enthusiasm of local fans. Merkle is also strong at the bat. The youngster is six feet in height and is splendidly proportioned. Best of all, he has plenty of nerve and a cool head.          —New York *American*

──◇ WEDNESDAY, DECEMBER 25 ◇──

PITTSBURGH, Dec. 24—It will not be a merry Christmas for Hans Wagner, the big shortstop of the Pirates, nor will it be a merry Christmas for the person who sent out the fact than Hans is suffering from rheumatism, if Wagner gets his hands on him. Wagner feels bad enough with his occasional twinges of rheumatism in his right shoulder, "but," he sobbed this evening, "it isn't half as bad as to have every old woman and every quack in the country hounding the life out of you."

Since the public came to know that Wagner has rheumatism, every mail and every express wagon brought him hundreds of remedies, and this evening all the medicines were sent to West Penn Hospital, whose superintendent was told to do what he pleased with them.

—New York *American*

WASHINGTON, Dec. 25—John Heydler, secretary and treasurer of the National League, in this city spending the holidays, has no hesitation in saying that he disapproves of any changes in the rules which have for an object increased batting.

"I cannot believe," said Heydler, "that there is any necessity for changes at this time. The cry that the public wants more batting is not borne out by existing conditions. If the rules were not satisfactory the attendance would certainly prove it, and attendance is improving every year.

"I am in favor of the rules remaining as they are. Why break up a winning combination? If it is essential to have more batting, there is a way of doing it without changing the rules. Have the manufacturers of the ball increase the amount of rubber in it, and the batting can easily be increased. A ball can be made so lively that a batting average of .500 will be commonplace."

—New York *Evening Journal*

───◇ **THURSDAY, DECEMBER 26** ◇───

It costs more to run a major league baseball team than a fair-sized racing stable. Frank J. Farrell, owner of the Yankees, can vouch for it. Farrell enjoys the unique distinction of being one of the most prominent men in two big professional sports. He is a power in baseball, and every racing man knows of his turf operations.

On the two sports he spends at a conservative estimate $138,000 a year, and of this close to $98,000 is spent on the team that is managed by Clark Griffith. The cost of running his ball team is about as follows: salaries of 25 players, $40,000; traveling expenses, $11,000; hotel bills,

$6,375; Spring training trip, $5,000; incidentals, clerks and attendants, $15,000, making a total of $97,375.　　　—New York *American*

───◇ **MONDAY, DECEMBER 30** ◇───

Among wishes for the new year by John McGraw, Christopher Mathewson, and followers of the New York Giants will be that in 1908 the Giants will be more successful against Mordecai Brown of the Cubs than in the past, and particularly will there be a wish that the Polo Grounds combination will be able to beat the Three-Fingered Wonder when he is opposed by the Bucknell boy. {Known as "Three-Finger" Brown, the Cub pitching star gained his nickname from a youthful accident when his right hand became caught in a piece of farm machinery and he lost most of his forefinger as well as the use of his little finger. This mishap enabled Brown to give a peculiar, frequently puzzling twist to his curve ball.} The Miner {Brown had been a coal miner} and the Collegian {for three years Mathewson had played baseball and football at Bucknell University} have hooked up eleven times since they have been big league rivals, and Matty has gone down before the man with missing digits seven times.

—New York *Press*

───◇ **TUESDAY, JANUARY 7, 1908** ◇───

McGraw will leave for the coast in a few days. He received the signed contract of McGinnity yesterday and said that he was having no trouble over contracts with the veterans.

"It is the new men that think they are getting the worst of it," said McGraw. "We send them a contract for $1,200 or $1,500, and they think they are worth a great deal more. They are worth more when they are good, and after they have proved that to our satisfaction we always give them considerably more than the contract calls for.

"These young fellows are unable to understand the position of the club. If we signed them for $2,000 or more, and failed to find a place for them on the team, it would be very difficult to dispose of them to minor league clubs at such a high figure."　　　—New York *American*

Joe McGinnity will be a Giant next year, and the good old "Iron Man" will again endeavor to twirl the horsehide in a way that will put the Giants in the running. {Contrary to popular belief, McGinnity did not gain his nickname because during a single month, August of 1903, he pitched and won three doubleheaders. The name derived from his employment, prior to entering professional baseball, in an iron foundry.}

Manager McGraw received a letter from McGinnity yesterday, in which the redoubtable "Iron Man" wrote that the terms offered him were eminently satisfactory, and he was greatly pleased to be back with the Giants.

McGraw said yesterday, "McGinnity's letter showed the right spirit. He is one of the best Spring pitchers any club ever had, simply because his control is so perfect. He never showed up with a lame arm, and he has been one of the most willing workers I ever had."

—Sam Crane, New York *Evening Journal*

---

## ——◇ THURSDAY, JANUARY 9 ◇——

McGraw left yesterday for Los Angeles, where he will have the chance to watch the horses run at Arcadia for at least a month before he goes to Marlin Springs. McGraw has evidently decided that further deals for players are unnecessary.                    —New York *Sun*


Secretary Knowles received a letter from a Massachusetts genius who claims to have invented a pitching machine that can do everything a star twirler can and a great deal more.

"These fellows will never learn," said Knowles, "that a perfect pitching machine is of no use, for it would lack the very human weaknesses that it is necessary for a batsman to learn and anticipate. One of these inventions has turned up every season for several years just before Spring practice. They have been tried and found wanting. I am sorry for the men who waste their time inventing them."

—New York *Evening Journal*

—◇ **THURSDAY, JANUARY 16** ◇—

McGraw will stand pat. He should have made a big effort to strengthen his pitching, in addition to securing a competent second baseman, but he ignored all suggestions in this respect and said he was satisfied with the Giants as they are. It's a little early for predictions, but I'll take a chance with the prophecy that Chicago, Pittsburgh, Philadelphia, Brooklyn, and Boston will finish ahead of the Giants this year.

—Joe Vila, *The Sporting News*

—◇ **SATURDAY, JANUARY 18** ◇—

New York baseball "fans" {short for "fanatics"} missed one treat last Fall, a chance to see Merkle play first base. He joined the Giants in the West, and when the team returned to this city, the season was over. He remained with the players and went through Pennsylvania with them on their barnstorming trip. Every player who returned to New York for the Winter was loud in his praise of this Toledo boy. What surprised the old fellows in regard to Merkle was the boy's wonderful speed. McGraw says he is the fastest man to touch runners and to touch the base he ever saw. He made two plays in Chicago so quickly that {Charles} Rigler, the umpire, lost both of them, and after they were explained to him admitted he had decided wrong. —New York *Evening Telegram*

—◇ **FRIDAY, JANUARY 31** ◇—

The identity of the umpire who won the championship for putting players out of games has just been made public. Charles Rigler, Pulliam's new fighting "ump" from Massillon, Ohio, was the boss banisher of the year, for he evicted 37 men. He was the only man on the staff who had trouble with all eight clubs. Billy Klem is entitled to a crown for favoritism, for he scored 14 put-outs against the Giants. Altogether 111 men were ejected.

Men indefinitely suspended were Al Bridwell of the {Boston} Doves, now a Giant, Frank Chance of the Cubs and Manager John McCloskey of the Cardinals. Brid and Jawn J. {John McGraw} got back after seven-day layoffs while it took Pulliam eight days to investigate the pop-bottle incident in which Chance figured. {In Brooklyn, Frank Chance threw back into the bleachers a bottle that had been hurled at him.}

John McGraw stood No. 1 on the list of players chased, being told to skiddoo seven times. Other Giants ejected were Dahlen, 4 times; {Sammy} Strang, 4; McGann, 3; Bresnahan, 2; {Danny} Shay, 2; Mathewson, 1; McGinnity, 1; Devlin, 1.                                    —New York *Press*

———◇ SATURDAY, FEBRUARY 1 ◇———

The first gun of the baseball season was fired today with the departure of Groundkeeper John Murphy, of the Polo Grounds, for Marlin Springs. Murphy sailed on the *Nueces* for Galveston, Texas.

Murphy had the Giants' bat bag with him, filled with enough "Louisville sluggers" to break all back fences in the National League, scraped and sliced to a finish. Before McGraw left for Los Angeles he went down to the cellars of A. G. Spalding & Brothers and selected six dozen bats that spell base hits. When he selected the bats, he said, "It is the bats that tell the story and make ball players. Pitchers may be all right, but give me the bat I want—the one that feels good to me—and I will make the other fellows extend their grounds."

—Sam Crane, New York *Evening Journal*

———◇ WEDNESDAY, FEBRUARY 5 ◇———

Unless there is a change for the better, Frank Chance, manager and first baseman of the Chicago Cubs, may not be able to play ball again. Chance, in California, is suffering from neuritis in the left foot, which began to develop last year from a bruise. The best specialists on the coast are trying to avert an operation by using every possible treatment, but it seems as if Chance would have to submit to the knife to be entirely cured.

—New York *Sun*

## ◇ THURSDAY, FEBRUARY 6 ◇

Bridwell, the Giants' new shortstop, can't hit an airship with a shot-gun charge.

—Joe Vila, *The Sporting News*

## ◇ SATURDAY, FEBRUARY 8 ◇

The advocates of Sunday baseball playing still believe they will be able to play games on the first day of the week during the coming season in Greater New York, particularly in Brooklyn. {Sunday baseball was prohibited in New York as well as Boston, Philadelphia, and Pittsburgh.} The Baseball Managers' Protective Association has taken the matter in hand, and the first steps to be taken will be to amend the bill which now lies with an Assembly committee in the Legislature {so that} games may be played between 3:30 and 6:30.

—*Sporting Life*

## ◇ MONDAY, FEBRUARY 10 ◇

The origin of the "spit ball," used by nearly all the star pitchers now-adays, has been a matter of endless discussion. Billy Hart, a veteran boxman {whose career ended in 1901}, has just thrown some interesting light on the subject: "I notice they claim Chesbro and {Elmer} Stricklett were the first to discover the 'spit ball.' Well, back in 1896, when I was pitching for St. Louis, I met Catcher Bowerman, who was with Baltimore that year. Calling me aside in St. Louis one day, he took the ball and requested me to get back of the catcher and watch his curves. I did so and was surprised to see how the ball acted as it neared the catcher. I asked Bowerman what made the ball act so. He explained that he simply spit on the ball, held onto it with his thumb at the seam and let it go. The odd part of it was that there was no speed to the ball that Bowerman pitched, whereas today they claim that the 'spit ball' can only be delivered with speed. I mastered it after a while, but found that it injured my arm, as it brought into play muscles not generally used. I advise any pitcher with good speed and curves to let the 'spit ball' severely alone. It will ruin an arm of steel in due time."

—New York *Sun*

Four young Giants sailed today on the Morgan liner *Creole* for New Orleans, from where the party will go by rail to Marlin Springs, Texas. At the pier a horde of baseball fans wanted to see the youngsters. John O'Brien, the big outfielder, got many a handshake. Indeed, he said that if he could stay here another day the hand shaking would almost put his arm in condition.

W. J. (Bill) Malarkey, a new pitcher, took well with the crowd, and John McKinney, the "Rusie of Oyster Bay," had to break away and hide in his stateroom. (Charley) Herzog, the young infielder, was labeled O.K. by the crowd. {A legendary Giant pitcher of the 1890s, Amos Rusie won more than 30 games in each of four seasons, and gained 233 victories in eight years.}                    —J. J. Karpf, New York *Evening Mail*

This is the Summer of "Larry" Doyle's prosperity or discontent. Doyle played so streakily last year that it was almost out of the question to get any fixed line on his ability. One day he would be a dead wall which nothing could pass, and the next he wabbled on every hit that came to him, like a boxcar on a coal railroad. Some days he could hit the ball on both sides of the seams, and on other days he missed all sides.

Some baseball men are confident that it is merely a question of time when Doyle will establish himself as a sterling, dependable player. If they have failed to read the signs right they are willing to be sentenced to eat five dozen hard boiled eggs and eighteen caviar sandwiches as punishment.                    —New York *Evening Telegram*

With the Giants, off the coast of Florida, Feb. 14. Everything is lovely on the steamship *Creole*, except for a little seasickness. The young fellows early this morning looked over the rail, and when no one was looking batted a few out to the fish. The war correspondents (Sid Mercer and Sam Crane, the two baseball writers who would cover the Giants' spring training) are helping things along wonderfully. They are doing so good that the fish come right up to thank them.

—Sid Mercer, New York *Globe*


Bresnahan will chaperone a second bunch of Giants to Marlin from St. Louis next Tuesday. It was McGraw's plan to keep the old-timers away till early March, but he has changed his plan. He considers it necessary to have a good catcher with him, one that can coach the young pitchers, and he is using excellent judgment. When coaching young pitchers it is absolutely necessary to have a veteran catcher to steady them.

—New York *Evening Mail*


———◇  **SATURDAY, FEBRUARY 15**  ◇———

Unless Manager McGraw is mistaken in his estimate, the Giants will have a grand shortstop in Albert H. Bridwell. Bridwell always has been rated as a clever fielder, but fans belittled his abilities because he did not knock down fences when he swung at the ball. At that, Bridwell last year hit eleven points better than the man he succeeds—Dahlen—having a stick credit of .218. McGraw thinks Bridwell will be a .275 whaler with the Giants, and considers the former Bostonian one of the most promising players in the business.  —New York *Press*


———◇  **MONDAY, FEBRUARY 17**  ◇———

Baseball magnates will take a step in the right direction if they put in effect the suggestion of Clark Griffith and Frank Chance to prohibit a pitcher to soil a new ball. The custom of a pitcher getting down on his knees and rubbing a new ball in the grass has long been an irritation to patrons. The practice causes delays and should be stopped.

The pitcher rubs the ball in the grass to wear off the gloss, which enables him to get a better grip on the sphere.

—New York *Evening Mail*

Roger Bresnahan said he would certainly use his big shinguards again, but he denied any intention of using headgear. He said he had been hit in his time and wasn't in the least afraid of being hit again. {In 1907 Bresnahan had been the first, and only, catcher to wear shinguards.}

—New York *American*

──────◇ **THURSDAY, FEBRUARY 20** ◇──────

{Because only two baseball writers, Sam Crane and Sid Mercer, were with the Giants in Marlin Springs, virtually all spring training reports will come from the pages of the *Evening Journal* and the *Globe*.}

MARLIN SPRINGS, Tex., Feb. 20—After being on the road a few hours over a week, the four Giant recruits, McKinney, Malarkey, O'Brien, and Herzog, with Trainers Richards and {John} Leggett and party consisting of nine persons in all, arrived yesterday afternoon. They were enthusiastically greeted by Groundkeeper John Murphy.

"By gum, Sam," Murphy said, "McGraw has picked out a great place for training. Wait till you see the grounds. They are as level as a billiard table, a bit sandy and a skin diamond {a hard, dirt diamond with little grass}, but as smooth as a floor. It's luck they sent me down ahead, for the grounds had been given up to steers, stray pigs and horses, so I had my work laid out to fix things right."

The boys are quartered at the Arlington Hotel, a swell hostelry in appearance. I know the rooms are all right, and Murphy tells me the "feed" is O.K. too; and Murphy knows something besides corned beef and cabbage.

The players will have the benefit, and it is a great one, of the bath house run with the hotel. The water used in the baths comes from the same hot springs used for drinking, and Murphy says the baths and drinking combined will make new men of the whole bunch. Marlin is a typical Texas town in appearance, with low, one-story stores and one main street. Saddle horses and mules are tied in front of the offices and stores, while the broad-brimmed thatched owners saunter around the streets and transact their business.

The people here are all anxious to see the prominent players and the whole town turned out at the depot this afternoon. The Giants' visit has caused a sensation all through this part of Texas.

—Sam Crane, New York *Evening Journal*

MARLIN SPRINGS, Feb. 20—Marlin is a pretty little city of 8,000 inhabitants, situated on a broad prairie. There is a little excitement now and then. On Tuesday night a Texan used his artillery on three colored persons. The white went on his way unharmed and the colored gentlemen were taken to the hospital for repairs.

—Sid Mercer, New York *Globe*

{A comment by former St. Louis Cardinal pitcher Eddie Murphy:} Donlin is a fine fellow. His mother was killed in the Ashtabula Bridge horror, Mike found in his mother's arms. His brothers and sisters were placed in orphanages. Mike was taken into our home and we became chums. While still quite young we decided to go out and see the world. We struck out and drifted South, but soon after going to New Mexico I decided to return home. Mike kept going. He finally reached California and the next thing I learned he was playing ball out there. A year or so later he was picked up by the St. Louis Nationals and he has been in the limelight ever since. Just because he makes a lot of noise on the field and has a peculiar stride, people look upon him as rowdy.

—*The Sporting News*

———◊ **FRIDAY, FEBRUARY 21** ◊———

MARLIN SPRINGS, Feb. 21—Real business was started yesterday. Training stunts were gone through, but footballs were brought into play to do the limbering up. There was any amount of leg work in kicking and chasing the leather sphere, and arms and shoulders were loosened up in throwing the ball around in the college style of passing the pigskin.

It was Winter weather for this part of the country, for thin ice formed on water in the gutters and was enough to set the natives to shivering and turning up their coat collars, while the poorly clad negroes hunted the sunny sides of their shacks and longed for watermelon time.

—Sam Crane, New York *Evening Journal*

───◇ **SATURDAY, FEBRUARY 22** ◇───

The time-worn cry of "more hitting" is heard again, and to help along the slugging several members of the joint rules committee will try to make a change that will bring the pitcher's box on a level with the home plate. Just now the pitcher hurls from a mound fifteen inches high. This, say committeemen who want the rule changed, gives the pitcher just enough advantage to cause the so-called falling-off in batting.

—J. J. Karpf, New York *Evening Mail*

───◇ **MONDAY, FEBRUARY 24** ◇───

MARLIN SPRINGS, Feb. 24—With the arrival of Manager McGraw the Giants' training camp seems to ooze pepper and ginger. Roger Bresnahan has done wonderfully well during the short period he had the youngsters in charge, but it remained for the big boss himself to pull the work out of the boys Sunday, yes, Sunday.

Contrary to all precedent, McGraw ordered the entire bunch for morning practice, and would doubtless have done the same in the afternoon, but the bath house was closed.

—Sam Crane, New York *Evening Journal*

MARLIN SPRINGS, Feb. 24—One subject that always crops out when fans discuss the Giants is the probable arrangement of the infield. Devlin and Tenney are conceded third and first base, but there is much uncertainty about Bridwell and Doyle. There's going to be so much rivalry for short and second that the lucky individuals finally chosen will squarely please the Polo Grounds patrons. Bridwell and Doyle have the inside track, but their positions are not guaranteed, and Fred Merkle and Charley Herzog will have to be reckoned with. Merkle has been doing most of his work here at second and short, and is a fellow who uses intelligence in everything he does. The only thing that will stop Herzog is his brief experience and lack of an infield opening.

—Sid Mercer, New York *Globe*

———◇ **TUESDAY, FEBRUARY 25** ◇———

Fred Tenney is the originator of the type of fast left-handed first baseman. He instituted the idea of clever and rapid double plays from first to second and back to first, through his ability to field the ball perfectly and snap it with sufficient speed and accuracy to second to permit a return throw to first.

The new Giant is in the best of physical condition. During all his service on the diamond he has been a member of the conservative element, devoting all of his time to baseball and little to frivolities. He is abstemious in his daily life, his sole indulgence being tobacco. "I suppose I could get along without that," he remarked last Winter, "but like a great many other athletes I like to chew something while I am at work, even if it's only a toothpick. Keeps my nerves settled."

—New York *Evening Telegram*

———◇ **WEDNESDAY, FEBRUARY 26** ◇———

The spit ball has been a source of a great deal of annoyance to catchers. Because of the quick and unexpected shoots that this delivery takes it is most difficult to gauge its course, and many a finger has been broken and shin bruised because of the inability of a catcher to intercept the ball with his mitt. {"Nig"} Clarke, of Cleveland, however, believes he has solved the problem by inventing a new mitt, which, he claims, will make handling a spit ball as easy as a fast or curve ball. Just what this mitt is like is being kept secret by Clarke.  —New York *Evening Mail*

MARLIN SPRINGS, Feb. 27—All the training paraphernalia, such as medicine balls, a new home plate, bases, balls, uniforms and the big pushball came yesterday from New York, and a variety was added to the regular routine. The pushball, a new institution to the young players, was the source of much amusement and excellent practice. The embryo stars of the diamond ran the big leather sphere from one end of the grounds to the other, playing "follow the leader" in leaping onto and over the ball as it rolled over the field.

The pushball was of infinite interest to the spectators, especially the "chocolate babies" delegation, the darkies rolling over and over on the grounds in paroxysms of laughter whenever a player lost his balance while on the ball and pitched forward on all fours or floundered flat and hard onto the field in a sitting position.

—Sam Crane, New York *Evening Journal*


How can any sane person believe, for an instant, that the Giants have even a slight chance to win the pennant? Why, boys, don't overlook the fact that McGraw's pitchers are weaker than Griffith's ever were, and Larry Doyle is a failure as a second-sacker.

Barring Mathewson, the Giants haven't got a single up-to-date twirler. McGinnity began to hit the toboggan in 1906, after he had pitched his arm off the previous year. Last season his efforts at times were painful. Luther Taylor was all in early last Spring and was a joke thereafter. Ames (who wants to be called "Red") cannot be depended upon because of his erratic work and his temperament. Wiltse lost his grip in 1906, because he was overworked.

Will anybody say it is good managerial judgment to go all Winter without picking up a couple of first-class pitchers and a second baseman? Instead of letting Bowerman, McGann, Browne, Dahlen, and Ferguson go for Tenney, Bridwell and Needham, why didn't McGraw make a deal for a pitcher? If Merkle is the coming first baseman, as McGraw says, why was the deal made for Tenney?

Take it from me, gents, the Giants will slide down pretty close to the second division simply because of these weak points. There's nothing to it, and by the time Memorial Day rolls around you'll be ready to take off your hats to me. —Joe Vila, *The Sporting News*

## ◆◇ FRIDAY, FEBRUARY 28 ◇◆

There was a joint meeting of the major leagues' rules committee yesterday, and it was agreed that the words "except the pitcher" after "player" in section 4 of rule 14 should be stricken out. This means that the pitcher must not discolor a new ball by rubbing it on the ground. {Prior to this amendment, Rule 14, Section 4 read, "In the event of a ball being intentionally discolored by rubbing it with the soil or otherwise by any player except the pitcher, the umpire shall, upon appeal by the captain of the opposite side, forthwith demand the return of that ball and substitute for it another legal ball and impose a fine of $5.00 on the offending player."} —New York *Sun*

MARLIN SPRINGS, Feb. 28—Texas ladies drive to the grounds in carriages, and some come on horseback. One beautiful young lady rode to the grandstands in a most fetching costume, which included a wide-brimmed hat, and she attracted the attention of players away from their practice. The equestrienne stationed herself along the first-base line. It was remarkable how badly the players wanted to play the initial position. She sure was a peach.

Card playing is a diversion that ball players are accustomed to on Spring training trips, and what some of the old-timers will do to pass away their leisure time here is a question, for Texas laws on card playing are very strict. Gambling of any kind is a State's prison offense, and card playing, whether for money or marbles, is not allowed even in one's own home.

Dominos are allowed and that is the game played by the boys in the hotel. This with weird ragtime music played and sung by a quartet of darkies, is the only amusement here. The streets are deserted after dark and there is not a thing in town to distract or lure the players from their training.

That is one reason why McGraw likes the place so much as a training camp. But it is slow, oh, so slow at times. One can't spend a picayune after dark if he wants to.        —Sam Crane, New York *Evening Journal*

───◇ **SATURDAY, FEBRUARY 29** ◇───

The mooted question as to the wisdom or folly of Southern training camps and extended Spring exhibition tours has received its usual Winter threshing—without changing conviction or methods; and so, as usual, all major league teams will start their rehearsals for the Big Show of 1908 in the so-called Sunny South. Following is a list of training places:

| NATIONAL LEAGUE | AMERICAN LEAGUE |
|---|---|
| Chicago, Vicksburg, Miss. | Detroit, Pine Bluff, Ark. |
| Pittsburgh, Hot Springs, Ark. | Philadelphia, New Orleans, La. |
| Philadelphia, Savannah, Ga. | Chicago, Los Angeles, Cal. |
| New York, Marlin Springs, Tex. | Cleveland, Macon, Ga. |
| Brooklyn, Jacksonville, Fla. | New York, Atlanta, Ga. |
| Cincinnati, St. Augustine, Fla. | St. Louis, Shreveport, La. |
| Boston, Augusta, Ga. | Boston, Little Rock, Ark. |
| St. Louis, Houston, Tex. | Washington, Galveston, Tex. |

—*Sporting Life*

───◇ **SUNDAY, MARCH 1** ◇───

By far the most pretentious training season undertaking will be that of {Charles} Comiskey's White Sox. Last night a special Pullman train departed from Chicago conveying 32 players and many relatives and friends of the club to Los Angeles. It is the first time that a baseball club has had its own train for a Spring trip. A year ago the White Sox went to Mexico in special cars, but they were attached to regular trains.

—New York *Times*

## ◇ TUESDAY, MARCH 3 ◇

MARLIN SPRINGS, March 3—A broad-shouldered young man walked into the Arlington Hotel at noon yesterday, set down his grip, and in a neat hand wrote S. Strang Nicklin on the hotel register. The cub Giants spotted him for a ball player, but the name on the register puzzled them. Mike Donlin walked up, seized his hand, and said, "Hello Strang." "No more Strang, please," replied the man from Tennessee. "That fellow has been waived by all clubs in all leagues, and has retired.

"Allow me to introduce myself, Capt. Donlin. I am Strang Nicklin."

"Turn over on your back, you're dreaming," replied Mike.

"This is straight goods," said Sammy. "I have decided to use my real name. Not long ago I was thinking I would like to meet some of my old friends whom I knew in my college days. They don't connect Sammy Strang with Strang Nicklin, and a lot of them don't know that I am playing ball. If there is anything coming to me in my career I want it credited to my family name."

And so it will hereafter be Utility Man Nicklin. {Nicklin had played in the National League during nine seasons, for four teams, under the name Strang, used because of the low status formerly given to professional baseball players.} —Sid Mercer, New York *Globe*

## ◇ WEDNESDAY, MARCH 4 ◇

MARLIN SPRINGS, March 4—All the Giants regulars are here now. The party that left New York by the steamer *Momus* arrived yesterday afternoon. Luther Taylor arrived at noon, and could not get out to the ball park quick enough to get into the afternoon practice.

Taylor on every training trip I have been with him has been the life of the camp, and yesterday he was more full of life, good nature and ginger than ever. Bresnahan began to spar with him at once, but Luther {a deaf mute} is pretty good with his hands, and knocked off Bresnahan's dicer the first crack out of the box. This pleased the amiable Luther immensely, and then there was more finger lingo than could be furnished in a deaf and dumb asylum. All the old players are adept at the deaf and dumb language, especially Bresnahan. Needham tried to break in with it, but Luther looked at Tom's knotted digits and spelled out on his fingers: "Another Bowerman; I'll bet he has a brogue."

—Sam Crane, New York Evening Journal

## ——◇ THURSDAY, MARCH 5 ◇——

MARLIN SPRINGS, March 5—{Spike} Shannon, Tenney, Donlin, {J. Bentley "Cy"} Seymour, Bresnahan, Devlin, Doyle, Bridwell and Mathewson—this will be the Giants' batting order this season. And allow me to whisper it is as nifty a bunch of slapstick artists as there is in the country. Just try to pick out any weak spots.

What looks good to me, too, is the spirit shown by the players. They all seem imbued with an inspiring confidence that presages winning results. One of the most prominent players said: "Yes, the old winning spirit is there all right. It is the same feeling we had three years ago, which we lost after winning the world series."

—Sam Crane, New York Evening Journal

## ——◇ FRIDAY, MARCH 6 ◇——

MARLIN SPRINGS, March 6—Marlin yesterday showed the Giants what genuine Southern hospitality really is. Thirty prominent merchants met the players after the day's practice with buggies, carriages, traps, automobiles and other vehicles and drove them to the Falls of the Brazos, a beautiful resort about four miles from town.

Luther Taylor can ride a horse like a Texas cow-puncher, but this can't be said about Mathewson. The big pitcher has been desirous of learning, and he was induced to straddle one of the broncos in making the trip to the Falls.

Matty's long legs made his pony look like a goat. Taylor took extreme delight in making Matty's life miserable, and would dash by him at a fierce gallop, which caused Matty's mount to coast wildly. All hands arrived safely all right, but it was noticed that Matty took his barbeque standing up.

Social affairs were not allowed to interfere with daily practice. Mathewson and McGinnity warmed up together, and I don't remember ever seeing two pitchers show better form so early in the season. Matty fairly made the ball talk, and had almost perfect control. McGinnity appeared to have more speed than ever. Joe has developed his "Old Sal" so that he can make it take an inshoot as it raises. {McGinnity called his favorite pitch, which he is credited with inventing, Old Sal. It was also known as a raise ball because, delivered underhanded, it rose as it approached the batter.} He said of this new delivery, "I have been practicing it this Winter and think I have it down fine enough to be effective. Us old pitchers must dig up something new, you know, to keep in the game."

The ball looked to me as if it took an incurve, but Joe still persists that no right-hand pitcher ever got an incurve to a ball.

"It is not possible for a right-hand pitcher to so twist his hand as to curve the ball in. It would require a man without any bones in his fingers to do it," said Joe. "Matty's fadeaway does not curve," continued Joe, "no more than this raise ball of mine."

—Sam Crane, New York *Evening Journal*

———◇ **SUNDAY, MARCH 8** ◇———

{On this day Sam Crane left Texas to join the New York Yankees, with whom he spent the remainder of spring training. Until their return to the Polo Grounds, Sid Mercer would be the only New York writer covering the Giants.}

DALLAS, March 7—The Giants played their first real game of the season today, defeating Dallas of the Texas League, 2 to 0. McGraw gave orders that McGinnity, Ames, and Mathewson, who trotted out in turn for a three-inning stint, could depend on speed as much as they liked, but so far as bending them or putting on the "jump" or any other twist was concerned, there must be absolutely nothing doing.

—New York *Times*

## ———◇ THURSDAY, MARCH 12 ◇———

MARLIN SPRINGS, March 12—The other day at the dinner table Luther Taylor wrote on the back of the menu and passed it to McGraw. "This is a quiet town," was what the manager read. Coming from Taylor this is surely a recommendation of Marlin's virtues as a peaceful resort.

—Sid Mercer, New York *Globe*

## ———◇ MONDAY, MARCH 16 ◇———

DALLAS, March 16—Manager McGraw has decided that Marlin as a training point is about the best place in Texas, but as a headquarters for a team playing exhibition games in larger cities it is inconvenient, on account of bad train schedules. He will therefore move his big squad this week and establish headquarters in Dallas. —Sid Mercer, New York *Globe*

PITTSBURGH, March 16—Every indication is that Hans Wagner will never again play baseball. Satisfied that no ordinary contract would receive a second thought, Pittsburgh mailed him an offer of $15,000 a year and agreed to permit him to cut the Spring training trip, but the largest salary ever offered a ball player was turned down. Another, signed by the club, but with the salary line left blank, then was sent him. It was also refused, Wagner saying that there is not enough money in the world to induce him to play ball this year. He told a friend recently that his private business had grown to such proportions he can't afford to play.

—New York *Evening Mail*

## ———◇ WEDNESDAY, MARCH 18 ◇———

One big item in the annual expense list of a big league ball club accrues from traveling over the circuit throughout the season. The sixteen teams will travel 188,287 miles between April 15 and the first week of October. The American League teams will cover 95,772, while National League clubs will cover 92,165 miles. At the rate of two cents a mile, each club carrying an average of eighteen men, the expense for railroad fares alone figures close to $68,000. And this does not include expenses for berths, meals and other incidentals.

One of the most remarkable features of traveling by baseball teams is the way in which they steer clear of accidents. In recent years there has been only one bad smashup in which players have figured. This was when a special train, carrying the St. Louis and Cleveland Americans to St. Louis in 1904, was wrecked. A few players were cut up, but the game the next day was played as scheduled.     —New York *Evening Mail*

## ———◇ FRIDAY, MARCH 20 ◇———

DALLAS, March 20—This city looks as big as New York to the Giants, who quit the bush league circuit after one day's experience. The discomforts attending the game at Calvert yesterday {in which the Giant regulars defeated the colts (rookies), 5 to 3, with McGraw umpiring} and the hotel accommodations were almost the limit. The players were so anxious to get out of the place they accepted upper berths in two sleepers without grumbling. Anyone who has ever heard a diamond star roar when an upper is handed him can appreciate how anxious the McGrawites were to get out of Calvert.

The town turned itself inside out to attend the game, all stores closing at 4 o'clock. The game was not started until all the school children had arrived {at 4:30}. The players rode to and from the game in a hay wagon and played on a field surrounded by strips of coarse bagging stretched on fence posts. The boys on the outside saw through this easily, but their elders paid cheerfully to get a look at the Giants.

                                        —Sid Mercer, New York *Globe*

## ———◇ SUNDAY, MARCH 22 ◇———

Recent developments had led fans to believe that Chicago, the probable pennant winner, is not so sure of the flag, and that Pittsburgh will have a hard time finishing in the first division.

Chicago stock has depreciated since news came out of Vicksburg,

Miss., that Manager "Husk" Chance had to leave for Chicago to see about his injured hoof. Men who know assert that Chance will be lucky to play ten games in succession at any stage of the race. With Chance out, the world's champions will lose an aggressive, enthusiastic leader, who is one of the best pinch-hitters in the business, a grand base runner and a splendid fielder. {In this context a pinch-hitter is a batter who is dangerous in crucial situations.}

Hans Wagner, the Demon Dutchman, always has been considered the backbone of the Pittsburgh outfit, and if he persists in his determination to keep out of the game, the Pirates will be greatly weakened.

—New York *Press*


"You can't win without pitchers," is a baseball axiom. John McGraw expects the Giants to win this year. So he must have pitchers.

Known all over the country, Christy Mathewson returns for his eighth year at the Polo Grounds. He is easily the star of McGraw's staff. Over six feet in height and weighing about 190 pounds, he has an ideal build for a pitcher. "Matty" is a right-hander, and last year he played in 41 games, won twenty-four and lost twelve, and led his league in strike-outs with 178. He is one of the best fielding pitchers in the league. "Matty" is a warm-weather pitcher, reaching his best form in the Summer.

Luther (Dummy) Taylor is the oldest player with the Giants in point of service, this being his ninth year. He is also right-handed. Last year he won eleven games and lost seven, with three shut-outs. The "Dummy" is always ready to take his place in the box, and is one of McGraw's most useful men. He is a great favorite with fans because of his antics on the diamond.

Joseph "Iron Man" McGinnity begins his sixth season with the Giants. He is 5 feet 10 inches and tips the scales at about 175 pounds. The bulk of the work fell on his shoulders last year. Several seasons back he made the great record of winning both games of four doubleheaders within one month. {The month was August of 1903, when McGinnity won three, not four, doubleheaders.} McGinnity is a right-hander, won eighteen and lost same number of games, and struck out 130 last year.

"Red" Ames starts his fifth year as a Giant. Last year he won ten and lost twelve. He needs a steady man to catch for him, as he is inclined to be wild. Although he struck out 146, he also gave 108 passes. Ames is still young, and McGraw expects this to be his best year.

The last of the veteran pitchers is George Wiltse, a southpaw, who wears a New York suit for the fourth year. He is 6 feet tall and weighs 170 pounds. Last year his health was poor. Out of 25 games he won thirteen, five of them shut-outs, and struck out 79.

Of the youngsters trying to win places as pitchers the most promising at present are {Roy} Beecher, Malarkey and McKinney.

—New York *Tribune*

———◇ **TUESDAY, MARCH 24** ◇———

JACKSONVILLE, Fla., March 24—Today Nap Rucker {of Brooklyn} sprung the new-fangled knuckle ball, which seems to be causing a considerable stir in professional ball. It had the opposing batters guessing all the time.

—New York *Evening Mail*

The knuckle ball is what its name implies. It is thrown with the hand all double, not unlike a pig's knuckle, and merely floats to the plate without a twist or turn. No speed can be put on it, the cramped position of the hand preventing that. It is safe to use only with a change of pace from a swift ball, and then when a pitcher has the batter in a hole.

—New York *Evening Journal*

———◇ **THURSDAY, MARCH 26** ◇———

DALLAS, March 26—To show how busy McGraw is it is only necessary to outline a day's work. Yesterday, for instance, he put the Dallas players through signal practice and infield work for two hours. Then his own players arrived on the field, and until nearly 1 o'clock McGraw worked with them. After a respite of an hour and a half, during which the Giants had dinner at the Hotel Oriental, McGraw had them out again. The game with the Dallas team started at 4, and was over at 5:30. When the last man was out, McGraw sent his colt team out to practice, and kept them at it half an hour. He finished his supper at 7:30 and still seemed as fresh as a daisy. —Sid Mercer, New York *Globe*

It is seldom that a minor league recruit in his first year in fast company shows enough class to win a regular position, but this may be the fortune of Charley Herzog. He covers considerable ground around short position, is a sure fielder, and a fast and accurate thrower. He also has the knack of touching a base runner without getting spiked or cut up, and is clever at the bat and a good base runner.

Doyle and Bridwell have shown up well in their respective positions, but they have nothing on Herzog in fielding; besides he outclasses them with the stick. McGraw is puzzled just what to do, as he says the youngster is too good to be kept on the bench. —New York *Globe*

————◇ **SUNDAY, MARCH 29** ◇————

When the Giants open the season New York baseball enthusiasts will watch with much interest the working of the infield. John McGraw has made many changes, and the biggest have been in the infield.

At first base, where Dan McGann reached for wide ones and scooped up low ones for years, Fred Tenney will be in command. The veteran Boston player is a left-hander and one of the best first basemen in the game. Though a fast man in the infield, he is at his best at bat and on the bases. All the fine points of the game are at his command, and he is a past master at advancing a runner.

At present it is undecided who will cover second base. It lies between two youngsters, Larry Doyle and Fred Merkle. In build they are entirely different. Doyle is short and stocky, Merkle tall and lanky. Doyle played second with the Giants in sixty-odd games last year. He was green, but his work was satisfactory. Since he has been in the South he has shown much improvement. Merkle plays best at first base, but that position is well covered. McGraw likes Merkle. He will find something for him to do, and second base is the weakest point on the team. Therefore Merkle is getting his chief practice there. Doyle will probably be the regular and Merkle general utility man.

Al Bridwell will play shortstop. In the territory where Bill Dahlen held forth so many years the young Boston player is expected to do some fast work this year. He outclasses Dahlen in every department of the game. Bridwell is coming, while Dahlen has almost reached his limit of usefulness.

The only veteran Giant in the infield will be Arthur Devlin, at third base. For steady, reliable playing he has few superiors. This is his sixth year in a New York uniform, and he is faster than ever. Devlin is a hard worker, and his playing is filled with ginger.

—New York *Tribune*

─────◇ **MONDAY, MARCH 30** ◇─────

The shinguard is to be the fashion this summer among the big baseball men. The latest from the South is that {Kid} Elberfield {New York Yankee shortstop} and {Harry} Niles {Yankee infielder} are to decorate their legs with the guards, wearing them under the stockings, of course. Elberfield is always colliding with a base runner's spikes because he is so aggressive he will take all sorts of chances to get a runner stealing. Niles, too, has had sad experiences with spikes, and believes the guards will prevent further injury.     —New York *Evening Mail*

─────◇ **TUESDAY, MARCH 31** ◇─────

Chance has joined the Cubs again in the South and believes he will be able to continue practice with them and report in Chicago in good order to begin the season.

A special shoe has been made for his injured foot. The spike plate has been taken off the sole of the shoe, and in its place is a special arrangement of nails on the edge of the sole which do not press upon the affected portion. Eliminating the plate, it is believed, will put an end to his suffering. Its rigidity prevented the shoe from giving, and whenever he ran briskly and threw his weight upon his foot the pain was so intense he sank to the ground and had to give up completely.

Someday somebody will come along with an arrangement which will do away with the old-fashioned shoe plate. More men have been seriously hurt by cuts resulting from shoe plates than by almost any other source in baseball.                              —John B. Foster, New York *Evening Telegram*

───◇ **WEDNESDAY, APRIL 1** ◇───

ATLANTA, April 1—Many contradictory stories have been published on why Honus Wagner has been holding out, but Frank Chance says the correct story has never been given the light of day.

According to the "peerless leader" of Chicago, Wagner's refusal to play was due to trouble with Fred Clarke, the Pirates' manager. Chance got this information from a Pittsburgh player.

"All this talk about Wagner quitting on account of rheumatism, chicken farm and other things is incorrect," said the boss of the world beaters.

"According to my information the whole trouble started over a play at the Polo Grounds last summer. Wagner has always been known as a player who worked for his individual record more than for the welfare of his team. In that game Clarke is said to have told Wagner to make a play in a certain way to help in getting a much-needed run. Honus at first refused, but when ordered to do so went to bat, made one effort as directed and then did exactly opposite from what Clarke told him. His effort failed, and Clarke called him good and hard.

"From that day to this they have been enemies. I understand that Wagner at first refused to join the Pirates unless Clarke was released, and held out until a few days ago. That Clarke wasn't going was a cinch; it was only a question of what could be done to placate the ire of the big German. That something will be done is evident, and I expect that President Pulliam is taking a hand in getting Wagner in line."

—New York *Evening Mail*

───◇ **MONDAY, APRIL 6** ◇───

MCALESTER, Okla., April 6—For the first two weeks of the season at least, and perhaps much longer, the Giants must struggle along without the services of Joe McGinnity {who was suffering from a severe fever}.

McGraw does not believe that Mac will be out for more than three weeks, but it is the opinion of several players that the Iron Man will be lucky to report by the time the team reaches St. Louis on the first trip West.                                              —Sid Mercer, New York *Globe*

————◇ **WEDNESDAY, APRIL 8** ◇————

Players are learning to take almost all kinds of hits so that the gloved hand bears the brunt of the effort. Realizing the great advantage in playing with a glove, they face the ball in such a manner that the glove acts as a receiving cushion and the ungloved hand is the lid of the trap which insures the ball being held.

When reasons are sought for a presumable decline in batting it is hardly worthwhile to go further than consideration of the glove. Many a base hit is smothered in leather and padding.

—New York *Evening Telegram*

————◇ **THURSDAY, APRIL 9** ◇————

{Quoting Chicago Cubs' pitcher Orval Overall:} I believe the rule prohibiting the pitcher from soiling a glossy ball will greatly increase the hitting department of the game. I also see trouble for umpires in enforcing it, as every pitcher will try to invent a way to get around the rule. You can't curve a glossy ball, and in my judgment there will be more pitchers knocked out of the box the coming season than ever before. Unless I am very much mistaken the hitting averages will go soaring. Supposing a pitcher has two strikes and three balls on a batsman and the next one is fouled over the stand. That means a new, slippery ball. The pitcher wouldn't dare try to curve it on account of its glossy surface, which prevents getting a good grip. He has no choice but to stick the ball over the plate with the prayer that it be knocked no farther than the back fence.

—*The Sporting News*

## ◇ FRIDAY, APRIL 10 ◇

WHEELING, W. Va., April 10—A topic of much discussion among the Giants this morning is the "dry spitter," a new pitching delivery of which Christy Mathewson claims to be the originator. Matty calls his freak the "spitless spitter," for he does not moisten the ball, yet it breaks like a spitter. He used it in Columbus yesterday, and it fooled several batters.

The "dry spitter" differs radically from the common spit ball not only because the ball is not moistened, but because it is a slow instead of a fast ball. Speed and a quick break have been the essential qualities of the spit-ball delivery, but Matty throws his deceiver without any effort.

In yesterday's game the ball floated up to the plate without any force behind it, and just as the batter would take a healthy swing the sphere would suddenly waver and drop dead into Needham's mitt. It was like a piece of paper fluttering along and encountering a puff of wind from the opposite direction.                                    —Sid Mercer, New York *Globe*


ST. LOUIS, April 10—Hans Wagner would take first, second and all the rest of the prizes offered in an off-again-up-again contest. According to the very latest, as served out by the great Honus himself while passing through here last night, he will play for Pittsburgh this season. He was cornered, and after being well pumped admitted he will "probably consent to help the team out."                          —New York *Evening Mail*


## ◇ SATURDAY, APRIL 11 ◇

New York fans whose appetites have been whetted by glowing reports of the new Giants down in Dixie will get lots of action at this afternoon's doubleheader at the Polo Grounds.

The main wing of McGraw's army rolled into Jersey City this morning at 9:15 after an all-night ride from Wheeling, posed for the snap shotters, hurried across the ferry, and hiked to Harlem. After a hasty lunch they will don uniforms for the big reception which will formally open the baseball season in the greater city.

—Sid Mercer, New York *Globe*

Half a hundred baseball players entertained 10,000 enthusiasts at the Polo Grounds yesterday afternoon, when the Giants were welcomed home. A doubleheader was the opening attraction of the season, the colts, or young recruits, playing the New York Athletic Club, and the real Giants lining up against Yale. John McGraw's men won both games, the first, a four-inning affair, 14 to 2, and the second, which went the full nine innings, 9 to 1.

Not in years has there been such a crowd at the Polo Grounds at a preliminary game. It augured well for a prosperous season.

—New York *Tribune*

{Included among the National League managers' statements at the opening of the season were the following:} John McGraw: The Giants will show New York what wonderful things can be accomplished by a few changes in personnel. We are going to be every bit as strong as we were in 1904 and 1905. This year we will have a team far ahead of last year's in every department, batting, fielding, and pitching. The Giants have just one team to beat this year, the Chicago Cubs. If we beat that outfit, and I am confident we will, New York will get another pennant.

Frank Chance: There is only one thing for the world's champions to do this year, and that is to repeat. We have taken two pennants straight with this team, and there is nothing to indicate we will not make it three in a row. We are now on top, and the others are doing the uphill fighting, so it looks all the more certain for another world's pennant in Chicago.

Fred Clarke: Without Hans Wagner I must admit I am worried. The Dutchman's decision to leave may have a very bad effect on the team, and may bring about other disappointing consequences. Pittsburgh's team, on pure dope, seems good enough to finish in the first division. As for reaching the top, I would have hopes if Wagner was with us.

—New York *Sun*

Good old Mike Donlin has been dubbed Turkey. Turkey lay down on three strikes the first time up Saturday, but maybe he didn't clout the leather after that. And who ever said Donlin has a bum leg? He appears faster now than at any time in his career. The season's layoff appears to have done Donlin a lot of good.

—New York *Evening Mail*

When fans reach the new Washington Park {Brooklyn's ball park} tomorrow they will realize what the improvements on the grounds mean. President Charles H. Ebbets of the Brooklyn baseball club states that the improvements have cost $22,000. He feels that the support accorded the Superbas {the principal nickname of the Brooklyn team} deserves recognition, and the new stand and grounds, with every convenience for patrons and players, is a model plant.

The new twenty-five-cent seats in centerfield are substantially built and will afford an excellent view of the game. They are far and away ahead of any similar seats on the circuit. With the additional seats, and with the arrangements made to handle an overflow on big days, 20,000 people can be comfortably accommodated. The boxes, of which there are 42, will provide for 252. There are over 5,200 seventy-five-cent seats and 600 more can be placed around the grandstand on the inside of the field in three raised rows. There are 8,500 fifty-cent seats and over 1,500 twenty-five-cent seats. With benches in the outfield and standing room, almost 4,000 more spectators can get in the grounds.

The "dugouts" of the new-fangled players' benches have been put into good shape. They are in their old positions but are made of cement foundations sunk into the ground about ten inches. They will not interfere in any way with the spectators' view. The roof is covered with tar paper, and a comfortable bench has been placed in each.

—Brooklyn *Eagle*

{On April 14, Opening Day, in Philadelphia, the Giants won 3 to 1. Winning pitcher, Mathewson; losing pitcher, McQuillan.}

From 16,284 throats there rose a mighty roar of blissful anticipation when a white leather sphere dropped from Mayor Reyburn's hand yesterday as he stood in the upper pavilion at the Phillies' grounds, and {manager Billy} Murray's men started the season's pennant race.

When the sun began to show a disposition to vanish and the wind began to send the faithful into overcoats, those throats were congealed with gloom, and there were few who did not sorrowfully admit that Mathewson had bunked those Phillies. The score was 3 to 1. In a nutshell, the Phillies could not connect with Mathewson. The stellar twirler, whose elusive curves have led the Giants so often to victory, was in fine form, and his mighty arm spelled disaster for Murray's men.

When the curtain was rung up on the show by the Mayor's ball-tossing stunt, grandstand and bleachers were filled by a great crowd. So rapidly did the mad ones arrive on the scene of carnage that a slice of the field on the north edge of the outfield was roped off and immediately stormed by those who came late, only to find the unwelcome "standing room only" sign to freeze their hopes.

There were the usual ceremonies before the battle began, ceremonies dear to the faithful. The peanut vendor was on hand, the waffle man did a land-office business, and the score card and the lemonade men were equally happy. They were on the job for the Summer, and they found the fans as willing as ever to part with nickels and dimes. While the early ones waited for the opening stunt they whistled, keeping time with their feet. They munched peanuts, snared waffles and speculated as to which batteries would be selected.

They were all on their feet in an instant when the blare of a brass band heralded the customary march and countermarch of contesting players on the field of battle. In their white uniforms the Phillies made a gladsome showing in the bright sunshine. McGraw's men also received a noisy salute from a delegation of crazed ones who had journeyed from Manhattan. The Gothamites bought a large piece of the upper pavilion, and from this point of vantage yelled themselves hoarse.

The game began with Mayor Reyburn facing a dozen cameras, the manipulators of which had followed him to the upper pavilion. He good-naturedly posed for the snapshot battery and then prepared to perform the customary ball-tossing stunt that invariably ushers in a new season of baseball.

The momentous time came when Umpire Klem {the only umpire for the game} stood in front of where the Mayor was seated and signaled him to toss down the ball. No sooner did the ball reach the umpire's hand than he in turn tossed it to Pitcher {George} McQuillan, the Phillies' new twirler. The latter carefully rubbed the new ball on the ground near the box, swung his arm with a mighty movement and drove the sphere over the plate, where Shannon stood waiting.

The first ball of the National League season in this city went wide of the plate. Twice did McQuillan drive the ball towards the plate, but it was not until the fourth time that Umpire Klem filled the fans with good cheer by yelling "Strike!" There was a great cheer when Shannon fanned twice again and the season began with a strikeout. As the game dragged on, it had its thrilling episodes, but usually favorable to the Giants. The Phillies simply could not touch Christy Mathewson. That's the whole story. They could not fathom him and until the last inning drew blanks with a regularity which caused the faithful to groan in anguish. Mathewson had them all buffaloed, and he fanned some Quakers with ridiculous ease.

—Philadelphia *Inquirer*

PHILADELPHIA, April 15—There is no more antitoxin in Christy Mathewson's system. The wise M.D.'s of the South squirted a lot of this dyphtheria killer into Matty's system two years ago, with the result that "Big Six" was weak around the knees last year, and everybody mistook this as a sign of Matty's decadence. {Mathewson gained his nickname when Sam Crane, principal baseball writer for the New York *Evening Journal*, likening Mathewson to New York's most famous fire engine, called him the Big Six of Baseball.} But all this medical juice has lost its effectiveness, and Matty jumped in yesterday and, defying cold winds, pitched a game of the kind that made him famous as the greatest pitcher in the land.

The game brought out the significant fact that the Giants are to be feared this year. The men, new and old, worked so well together that McGraw must be congratulated. The infield was like a stone wall. Bridwell and Tenney played the kind of ball that helps win pennants. Doyle handled himself admirably, and Devlin looks even better than last year. Most important of all was the teamwork displayed by this quartet.

—New York *Evening Mail*


Tonight the New York and Philadelphia teams will be special guests of the management of "The Merry-Go-Round" at the Lyric Theatre. Mabel Hite, Mrs. Mike Donlin in private life, is the star of the production, soon to be seen on Broadway.　　　—New York *Globe*

———◇ **FRIDAY, APRIL 17** ◇———

{On April 16, in Philadelphia, the Giants lost 6 to 3. Winning pitcher, Hoch; losing pitcher, Ames.}

PHILADELPHIA, April 17—Like the little boy, the Giants are awful good when they're good, and when they're bad a cheese factory hasn't anything on them. They certainly were bad yesterday.

Well, it was coming to them. It was the first defeat of the season, and nearly everybody contributed a foozle to the lost cause. It may have been a good thing to have crowded them all into the one session. The Giants ought to feel better with that nightmare out of their system. Every good team has these spells; they show that the players are human. The Giants made more errors than they commit in a half dozen ordinary games, but it's a waste of time to weep over these things, and the Giants are not doing it.

Out of something like 35 games this Spring it was the first decision the Giants lost, so it isn't hard to forgive them.

—Sid Mercer, New York *Globe*

## ◊ SATURDAY, APRIL 18 ◊

{On April 17, in Philadelphia, the Giants won 14 to 2. Winning pitcher, Wiltse; losing pitcher, Moren. Giants' standing: 2 wins, 1 loss, tied with Brooklyn for third place.}

PHILADELPHIA, April 17—The National League's first slug-fest of 1908 turned up this afternoon, the Giants snowing the Murrayites 14 to 2. The Giants banged to all corners of the yard the slants of {Lew} Moren, {Harry} Covaleskie, and {Charles "Buster"} Brown, ripping off fifteen safeties. {The name was actually Coveleski, but as we shall see, it was variously spelled.} George Wiltse kept the Quakers from the plate for seven rounds and then eased up, the Phillies playing against a team with four substitutes.

Outside of Wiltse, Devlin was the New York player who deserves more than superficial comment, the whole team's work being so splendid it is hard to particularize. The third-sacker got three hits and stole two bases. His licks were for one, two and three cushions.

The knuckle ball got a bad advertisement, Moren, its inventor, being knocked out in the fifth inning.

The Giants were speedy in all departments and stole seven bases.

—New York *Press*


PITTSBURGH, April 18—Hans Wagner yesterday attached his name to a Pittsburgh contract, and left for Cincinnati in personal charge of President Barney Dreyfuss, who announced that the big fellow would be in the game there today.　　　　—New York *Evening Journal*

## ◊ SUNDAY, APRIL 19 ◊

{On April 18, in Brooklyn, the Giants won 4 to 0. Winning pitcher, Mathewson; losing pitcher, Pastorius. Giants' standing: 3 wins, 1 loss, tied with Chicago for second place.}

There's gloom in Brooklyn. Yesterday before 20,000 howling fans the Giants took the Dodgers on their own lot and literally wiped it up with them. Christy Mathewson pitched for the big fellows, and he stood out like a crane on an ant hill. He was never in better form, and he sent twelve Brooklyn lads back to the bench in disgrace after they had swung their floating ribs out of shape trying to hit his benders on the snoot. The best hitters on the team fell before the magic of Matty's wonderful delivery.　　　　　　　　　　　　—Hype Igoe, New York *American*

Although enthusiasts who were present were not aware of it, Mathewson pitched the last three innings barely able to stand on one foot. In running to first base to cover a throw from Tenney he turned his ankle and McGraw was ready to take him out, but Mathewson decided he would fight the game to a finish. He limped decidedly when he left his uniform in the Brooklyn clubhouse and started his return to New York.
　　　　　　　　　　　　—New York *Herald*

CINCINNATI, April 18—"I was convinced by the management and the players that the team needed me," said Hans Wagner, "and so after considerable cogitating I made up my mind to get back into the game."

Seldom has joy appeared on Fred Clarke's face as that which showed up at the Havlin Hotel when the team arrived from St. Louis this morning. When he found Wagner tears almost came to Clarke's eyes, and Wagner seemed in about the same condition. With Wagner in the van the Pirates' strength is increased fully 25 percent.
　　　　　　　　　　　　—Pittsburgh *Dispatch*

————◇ **MONDAY, APRIL 20** ◇————

{On April 19, the Giants were not scheduled to play because professional baseball was not permitted on Sundays in the state of New York.}

| | W | L | PCT. | GB | | W | L | PCT. | GB |
|---|---|---|---|---|---|---|---|---|---|
| Chicago ..... | 4 | 1 | .800 | — | Brooklyn .... | 2 | 2 | .500 | 1½ |
| New York ... | 3 | 1 | .750 | ½ | Cincinnati ... | 1 | 3 | .250 | 2½ |
| Pittsburgh ... | 3 | 1 | .750 | ½ | Boston ...... | 1 | 3 | .250 | 2½ |
| Philadelphia . | 2 | 2 | .500 | 1½ | St. Louis ..... | 1 | 4 | .200 | 3 |

## ◇ TUESDAY, APRIL 21 ◇

{On April 20, in Brooklyn, the Giants won 4 to 1. Winning pitcher, Ames; losing pitcher, Rucker. Giants' standing: 4 wins, 1 loss, in second place.}

There may be nothing in the oft-disputed theory of the power of mind over matter as applied to baseball, but it does seem that there is always something doing when John McGraw goes on the coaching lines. He may not pull in the runs, but whenever he takes his stand at third base he seems to possess the uncanny ability of hypnotizing the pitcher and drawing base runners toward him. It was that way in Brooklyn yesterday.

Over in Philadelphia the other day Manager Billy Murray of the Quakers accused McGraw of mesmerizing one or two of his pitchers. Mac's coaching was directed toward the spot where it did the most good—or harm—and though the spectators could hear little of it, the Philly pitchers soon began to exhibit strange symptoms.

McGraw started to tell Murray's pitchers what to do, and they did it. He informed them that they were about to make wild pitches, that certain batters were going to hit, and that certain base runners would steal. He called the turn a few times and soon had the rival boxmen guessing. When you get 'em guessing the game is half won.

The Giants are weaklings before left-handers, did you say? Yes, that's so. Covaleski, Pastorius, Rucker—three southpaw victims already, and the season just a week old. {Because six of their regulars were left-handed batters, there had been some question about how well the Giants would perform against southpaw pitchers.}

Next!               —Sid Mercer, New York *Globe*

Brooklynites seem to prize highly balls which go into the bleachers. During the preliminary practice McGraw grew tired of seeing balls knocked into the stands never to return. He finally sent a policeman after them and they were thrown back. Mathewson picked out a man whom he charged with stealing a ball and the culprit was arrested.

—New York *Tribune*

Umpire {Hank} O'Day is strictly enforcing the new rule which provides for a player's expulsion from the game if he leaves his position to protest a decision. O'Day pulled a couple of bum decisions yesterday, but the Giants shouted their comments without rushing up to the umpire, who was waiting for a chance to serve some bench warrants.

—New York *Globe*

———◇ **WEDNESDAY, APRIL 22** ◇———

{On April 21, in Brooklyn, the Giants won 6 to 1. Winning pitcher, Wiltse; losing pitcher, Bell. Giants' standing: 5 wins, 1 loss, tied with Chicago for first place.}

Pie—apple, mince, custard or any other kind—have the Superbas proved to be for the fast-going Giants. "Why couldn't we have those fellows all the year round?" wailed "Muggsy" McGraw after yesterday's game. "There would never be any doubt as to the championship. We'd win in a walk."

"Yes," chimed in "Larry" Fassett, once owner of the Albany team and a thirty-third-degree Giant "rooter," "it's all over now. The championship is already won. Who ever said Chicago could play ball is crazy. As for Brooklyn, Ebbets wants to get a real baseball team! And St. Louis? Why, they have no right to be in the National League."

Suddenly Bresnahan, with feet foremost, tore into third base, ripping {Whitey} Alperman's trouserettes with his spikes, and Tenney was put out of the game for disputing {umpire} "Bob" Emslie's decision on first, whereat "Larry" got into an argument with a spectator, and to show how

strong a thirty-third-degree "rooter" he is he went off and sat in a se-
cluded spot of the grandstand.                              —New York *Herald*

It is evident that McGraw has instructed his men not to bow meekly
to the rulings of umpires. They have shown a disposition to scrap from
the start but had no occasion to break loose until yesterday. {Harry} Pattee
was declared safe by a whisker in the sixth, whereupon Tenney said
things to Umpire Emslie and Fred was banished, whereupon McGraw
uncovered a wonder in Merkle, who covered first base in great style. The
new Giant had six put-outs and appeared to feel at home. He was all to
the merry at bat and in his first trial knocked out a pretty safety between
short and third. On his next appearance he laid down a neat sacrifice.
                                                        —Brooklyn *Eagle*

Today at 3 o'clock the Philadelphia and Boston National League
teams will open the season at the South End grounds, the oldest baseball
park in the country, formally opened to professional baseball in 1873. The
South End grounds have been the home of 11 world's champion teams, a
remarkable record that will probably never be equalled.
                                                        —Boston *Globe*

——◇ **THURSDAY, APRIL 23** ◇——

{On April 22, Opening Day at the Polo Grounds, the Giants beat
Brooklyn 3 to 2. Winning pitcher, Mathewson; losing pitcher, McIntire.
Giants' standing: 6 wins, 1 loss, tied with Chicago for first place.}

As a fitting climax to a game brimful of interest, Captain Mike Don-
lin aroused 25,000 enthusiasts to a frenzy of excitement at the Polo
Grounds yesterday by driving the ball into the right-field bleachers for a
home run, which brought in two runs and gave the Giants a victory over
Brooklyn 3 to 2.
It was the opening game of the season under Coogan's Bluff, and the

biggest crowd which ever saw a game in this city filled every stand, circled the field and lined the viaduct and surrounding points of vantage. The Giants had trailed throughout the game, although mighty Matty was in super form and mowed down visiting batters like a machine gun. The Superbas scored one run, however, in the fourth inning and another in the eighth, while the Giants had one lone tally to their credit.

Brooklyn had taken its last chance at the bat. The crowd had inched onto the diamond so that the players were almost swallowed up. There was one continuous roar which drowned out even the crack of bat meeting ball. The crowd would have been satisfied with a single tally. McGraw sent in Merkle to bat for Mathewson, the first man up. Two strikes were called, and then Merkle picked one he liked and sent it sailing into the right-field crowd. It counted for two bases because of the ground rule. Shannon's sacrifice advanced him to third.

The crowd begged and implored Tenney to knock it out of the field. The former Boston captain hit hard, but the ball was fielded quickly, and Merkle was caught between third and home. Tenney went to second on the play, but with two out things looked gloomy to New York rooters.

Happy Mike Donlin then strode to the plate as nonchalant as if he were facing a "prep" school pitcher and the score was 30 to 0 in favor of the Giants. {Harry} McIntire sent the first ball straight and true. Mike never moved. The umpire bellowed "Strike, one!" The next was a ball. Then a strike was called, and gloom settled down on 25,000 rooters. Was Mike nervous? He didn't show it. "Ball, two!" roared Emslie.

Two balls, two strikes, two out, and two runs needed to win the game! It was a combination you often read about, but seldom see. Donlin grasped his bat tight, stepped close to the plate and waited for the next ball. After years of waiting, as it seemed to the anxious throng, it finally shot for the plate. There was a sharp crack, and the next instant the little sphere was sailing through the air, and finally dropped into the scrambling hands of right-field bleacherites. Tenney raced home and Donlin wended his way through the crowd, which by this time had taken complete possession of the field. The Giants had pulled out a victory with the odds almost 100 to 1 against them.

To say that the crowd went wild is putting it mildly. It went clean crazy. Hats and cushions were tossed in the air; old men slapped their companions on the back and laughed and cheered like undergraduates. It was one of the greatest sights ever seen at an athletic contest, and those present will never forget it. —New York *Tribune*

Mabel Hite up in a private box in the grandstand, with flushed face and happy glistening eyes, as her husband, Mike Donlin, made that game-winning home-run wallop yesterday, took me off my feet. It was not the cheering thousands so anxious to do Mike Donlin credit that impressed me the most.

It was the little woman with tears of joy trickling down her cheeks and so wildly clapping her gloved hands (I'll bet she has not the same gloves this morning) that got my goat.

And cheering as she did, so exultant over her husband's grand hit, still there was a shade of anxiety over her pretty countenance as she saw enthusiastic fans try to carry Mike to the clubhouse.

"Oh, I hope they don't hurt him," she said, and as Mike darted away from his too exultant admirers, pale of face and utterly exhausted, the little woman sank down in her seat with a little gurgle of delight that would have made a hit behind any footlights.

—Sam Crane, New York *Evening Journal*

The only thing at the Polo Grounds greener than the grass was a squad of almost officers doing business under the firm name and style of "Holmes Private Police."

Long before the game hundreds of rooters ranged themselves in a crescent around the front of the grandstand and gradually worked their way up toward the home plate. Secretary Knowles and Manager McGraw entreated the new policemen to force the crowd around the outfield, but when the crowd discovered that the officers were afraid to interfere or were otherwise incompetent, the crescent grew and grew, until it stretched out from the right-field bleachers clear around to the bench of the visiting players.

Thousands in the stands begged and threatened alternately, but the unruly ones refused to budge. As a result many hundreds sitting in the lower sections of the grandstand could not see more than an occasional glimpse of the game. This will never do. In the words of the statesman from Minnesota, "something must be did." {The "statesman from Minnesota" was John Johnson, the popular, colorful governor of Minnesota. The son of Swedish immigrants, Johnson was a dark horse candidate for the Democratic presidential nomination. He is mentioned again in the last May 5 entry as "Yohn Yohnson."}

—William F. Kirk, New York American

A lady with a "Merry Widow" bonnet, trimmed with several acres of foliage, perched herself on the shelf in one corner of the press stand. A few score unlucky individuals behind her, finding their view of the game cut off, amused themselves by making the hat a target for wads of newspapers and hot peanuts. So many minions found the mark that two men stood up beside the lady, withstood the bombardment, and incidentally cut off the view of several more people.

—Sid Mercer, New York Globe

## ———◇ FRIDAY, APRIL 24 ◇———

{On April 23, in New York, the Giants lost to Brooklyn 4 to 1. Winning pitcher, Wilhelm; losing pitcher, Ames. Giants' standing: 6 wins, 2 losses, in second place.}

Yesterday at the Polo Grounds was different from the day before.

> *They whopped it up for Donlin*
> *With a rooter-tooter blare;*
> *They rooted him,*
> *They tooted him,*
> *And boosted him for fair,*
> *But Donlin's bat was busted*
> *And he never did get there.*

Which means that yesterday wasn't Donlin's day. The Suburbas {the *Times* regularly referred to the Brooklyn Superbas as Suburbas} simply put it all over the Giants from start to finish, and gathered four runs as easy as falling off a log, two in the fifth and two in the ninth.

Ten thousand or more were on the grounds to see the show, and, unlike Wednesday's audience, they saw it, because the crowd didn't feel like walking out in the field and taking possession. Plenty of Merry Widow hats were along the upper front row, and one in particular had so wide a brim and a bunch of lingerie on top that a hot cigarette dropped into it would have called for four alarms and the Chief's gasoline go-cart. The weather was ideal, and brought out as many hillbillies {those who watched free of charge from atop Coogan's Bluff} as the day before. Coogan's Bluff looked like a full hand.

—W. J. Lampton, New York *Times*

New York is the only city where regular policemen are not on duty at ball parks. The lack of this protection injures the reputation of the city, for on every big baseball day there is always a riot or a near-riot. In some cities baseball clubs engage policemen who are off duty, paying them for the extra work. If no other way can be provided here it should be tried. There is no use talking. New Yorkers will not respect any uniform but that of New York policemen. —Sid Mercer, New York *Globe*

{Irwin "Kaiser"} Wilhelm's whirlers had too much dampness on them yesterday, and they were altogether too slippery for the Giants.

Spit-ball pitchers are scarce in the National League. Consequently when one does appear, he is a troublemaker. Yesterday even Mike Donlin lapsed from up-to-date baseball and forced out Tenney on three separate occasions. When Donlin is fooled, the pitcher surely has something on his ball.

Miss Mabel Hite, Mike Donlin's pretty and talented little wife, who is to star in the "Merry-Go-Round" opening on Broadway tomorrow, was at the game accompanied by a bevy of enthusiastic stage-beauties, who occupied a private box and were primed from the tops of their dainty shoes to their Merry Widow hats for another celebration such as Captain Mike provided on Wednesday, but they were doomed to bitter disappointment. —Sam Crane, New York *Evening Journal*

{On April 24, in New York, the Giants lost to Brooklyn 4 to 1. Winning pitcher, Pastorius; losing pitcher, Crandall. Giants' standing: 6 wins, 3 losses, in second place.}

As it was Thursday, even so it was Friday. The earnest ball tossers from across the Bridge came back yesterday with another 4-1 score. Really, you know, Mr. Donovan {Brooklyn's manager, "Patsy" Donovan}, it isn't quite clubby.

We never like to mask the truth, and must concede that Brooklyn played better ball and deserved to win the victory. But we are all praying for the Giants to develop their normal hitting gait, because this thing is getting on our nerves. If we cannot win the next game, we must at least lose it by some other score than 4-1.

Without any paddock information, it is safe to state that Manager McGraw will summon his athletes shortly after we go to press and deliver an able lecture on the manly art of hitting. The Giants weren't hitting yesterday, and they weren't hitting the day before, and when a team isn't hitting that team invariably presents a poor front to the hopeful rooters. Every play looks stupid, every error seems flagrant, every attempt to score is derided when the scheme goes amiss. All of these things come to pass when a team isn't hitting. Let us hit.

—William F. Kirk, New York *American*

That boy {Al} Burch made a catch off Cy Seymour that ought to go down in baseball history as the best clutch ever.

In the sixth inning, when Cy leaned up against the bulb, the Superbas had accumulated two tallies and the Giants had one lone dot on their tally sheet, so a home run would have been very "peachy." Cy evidently awoke to the interesting and important situation and swung for one of his real old-time lambasters. He connected all right on the Spalding trademark. The ball shot off his chopstick on a loop-the-loop message for the clubhouse. The ball was labeled a sure enough homer, and that boy Burch evidently thought so, too, for he turned tail and tincanned so fast for the outer bulwark his red top-knot looked like a fiery streak.

He took one despairing glance at the horsehide through one corner of his offside lamp (I wish he had been crosseyed), saw that he had no possible chance of stopping the ball as a legit, and then, as if he had been on springs, he launched himself upward and forward, stuck out his gloved hand backward, and blamed if the ball didn't stick to the mitt. The force of the ball threw Burch forward and, being off his trolley, he pitched face downward and then turned a complete somersault, his nose ploughing up the ground for a city block as if a four-tongued barrow had been his proboscis.

Pitcher {Otis} Crandall, although beaten in his first game, really pitched a winning game. Not a run the Superbas made was earned, and six hits were all the victors made during the eight innings he was in the box. Crandall showed enough to warrant McGraw putting him in to take his regular turn hereafter. In my opinion, he made good—he "showed."

—Sam Crane, New York *Evening Journal*

———◇ **SUNDAY, APRIL 26** ◇———

{On April 25, in New York, the Giants lost to Brooklyn 4 to 1. Winning pitcher, Rucker; losing pitcher, Wiltse. Giants' standing: 6 wins, 4 losses, tied with Pittsburgh for second place.}

There is something magic in that combination, 4 to 1. It will go down as a record in baseball. After losing four straight the Superbas turned around and took three by the same score. It is a remarkable coincidence not likely to be repeated for years to come.

To Nap Rucker for his superb pitching and timely hit in the eighth, and {second baseman} Harry Pattee's brilliant fielding, base running and hitting is the victory chiefly due. Rucker was touched for four hits in the first three innings, and was then invincible. Pattee accepted ten chances, and time and again cut off apparently safe hits back of first and second. He stole three bases, two thefts being the third sack. {Pattee's brilliance was momentary. His major league career would be confined to eighty games in 1908, with a batting average of .216.}

Wiltse was on the firing line, and the elongated southpaw was in trouble in every inning but the second and third. In the ninth Wiltse was replaced by McGinnity, who made his first appearance of this year. The Iron Man was given a great ovation, but the Superbas scored two runs.

—Brooklyn *Eagle*


When Messrs. Ebbets and Medicus decided last Winter to raise the price of their bleacher seats to four bits (a slang expression signifying half a bean) there were those who opined that Messrs. Ebbets and Medicus had committed a strategic blunder, not because there aren't plenty of half dollars floating around in Brooklyn, but because the Brooklyn ball club had shown little cause for a boost in their drawing qualities. If Messrs. Ebbets and Medicus could evade the Sunday law and pull off a game this afternoon they could charge, and get, a dollar per head for standing room in centerfield. To back this assertion we are laying four to one.

—William F. Kirk, New York *American*


────◇ **MONDAY, APRIL 27** ◇────

BOSTON, April 27—This city of culture and beans is mildly excited— which is as far as Bostonians allow themselves to go—over the prospect of what will happen when McGraw's team, strengthened by former Boston players, meets the revamped Boston outfit, bolstered by five ex-Giants this afternoon at the South End grounds. Though Monday is a bad baseball day, it is a safe bet that a big crowd will see the fun.

{Manager} Joe Kelley has made a hit with the fans here, and so has good old Frank Bowerman, who, like Bresnahan, has caught every game so far. And maybe George Browne, Bill Dahlen, Dan McGann, and Cecil Ferguson are not waiting to get a crack at the Giants! They feel they must show up McGraw for trading them. Did you ever see a transferred player who didn't have a grudge against a club that released him?

—Sid Mercer, New York *Globe*


──── NATIONAL LEAGUE STANDINGS ────

| | W | L | PCT. | GB | | W | L | PCT. | GB |
|---|---|---|---|---|---|---|---|---|---|
| Chicago | 7 | 2 | .778 | — | Boston | 5 | 5 | .500 | 2½ |
| New York | 6 | 4 | .600 | 1½ | Cincinnati | 5 | 5 | .500 | 2½ |

| Pittsburgh ... | 6 | 4 | .600 | 1½ | Philadelphia . | 4 | 6 | .400 | 3½ |
| Brooklyn .... | 5 | 5 | .500 | 2½ | St. Louis ..... | 2 | 9 | .182 | 6 |

CINCINNATI, April 25—President Dreyfuss, of the Pittsburgh club, and Hans Wagner are having a tough time convincing the public that financial questions did not enter the decision of Wagner to retire some time ago, nor move him to come into the fold. "For some time," Dreyfuss said, "Wagner has had the privilege to name the figures in his contract, and the same privilege was extended when he was asked to sign this Spring. However, he did not care to avail himself of this offer when we talked some months ago. He was determined to retire, and the financial end of the game cut no figure with him. And so it was when he came into the fold. Finances did not come up for discussion. He simply made up his mind that he would rather play than not, and there was no argument about the figures in his contract." It has been reported that Wagner's salary was raised from $7,500 to $10,000, but neither Mr. Dreyfuss nor Wagner would discuss this matter. "There are only four people who know what my salary is," said Wagner, "and that is quite enough. My salary is satisfactory to me, and my great aim every year is to make it satisfactory to the people who pay me. If I thought I could no longer deliver an equivalent for the coin that is given me semi-monthly, I'd have my salary cut or quit the game." —Charles H. Zuber, *Sporting Life*

## ◇ TUESDAY, APRIL 28 ◇

{On April 27, in Boston, the Giants won 2 to 0. Winning pitcher, Mathewson; losing pitcher, Young. Giants' standing: 7 wins, 4 losses, in second place.}

Sixty-five hundred fans witnessed a great game at the South End grounds yesterday between the Doves and the Giants. {Boston's team was called the Doves after its owner, George B. Dovey.} It was wonderfully well-played, lasting only an hour and 16 minutes, New York winning 2 to 0, both runs coming in the eighth inning on a lucky combination of two hits, one a scratch, a sacrifice, and an excusable fumble by {second baseman Claude} Ritchey, playing close to cut off a run at the plate.

No two teams ever displayed keener rivalry than Boston and New York did yesterday, and it was a rivalry exemplified by splendid sportsmanship. Both teams hustled for everything in sight, and both were aggressive, but a cleaner, more satisfactory game could not have been played.

Fred Tenney was given a royal reception by the fans, besides being the recipient of a handsome traveling bag. Fred was full of ginger, and that he is free from care was shown by the masterly manner in which he played the bag at which he was stationed so long in Boston.

—Boston *Globe*

BOSTON, April 28—With Joe McGinnity hardly able yet to pitch a full game, and Leon Ames ill in New York, the Giants are somewhat short of pitchers.

"If Ames was here and in shape to work," said McGraw this morning, "I am sure we would win every game. I left Leon behind under a physician's care. He has some sort of kidney trouble which started from a cold, and I fear he may be out for a while. It's tough to lose him. It seems that I can't get all my pitchers together at one time. At that, if Crandall pitches as good a game as he did against Brooklyn, he'll be a winner."

—Sid Mercer, New York *Globe*

———◇ **WEDNESDAY, APRIL 29** ◇———

{On April 28, in Boston, the Giants won 3 to 2. Winning pitcher, Malarkey; losing pitcher, Dorner. Giants' standing: 8 wins, 4 losses, in second place.}

The New York Giants made another eighth-inning finish yesterday, winning 3 to 2 in a game in which the locals did more hitting {9 hits for Boston, 4 for the Giants}, but were cut off from two runs by throws by "Cy" Seymour to the plate after base hits on which a runner tried to score from second base.

—Boston *Globe*

{On April 29, in Boston, the Giants lost 7 to 6. Winning pitcher, Young; losing pitcher, Malarkey. Giants' standing: 8 wins, 5 losses, in third place.}

BOSTON, April 29—There was a merry mix-up at the Copley Square Hotel last night shortly after midnight. Dan McGann, now of the Boston Nationals, and his old manager, McGraw, were in a clinch taker. They were pulled apart by the players before McGann could be subdued.

At the end of yesterday's game when McGann went to bat and hit into a double play, McGraw made some slurring remark about McGann being an ice wagon {a slow runner}, which got to the ears of McGann. He is stopping at the same hotel where the Giants are housed. During the evening Dan walked impatiently up and down the corridor, waiting for McGraw to return from the theater.

McGraw came in with Mathewson and went to the billiard room. McGann followed, and in spite of Mathewson's intervention, struck at McGraw. Hats were spilled and there was a hot mix-up but no damage was done except to rile McGann's Kentucky blood. The scrap broke up the billiard game after the players separated the combatants.

McGraw went upstairs and was soon followed by McGann, who made a vicious pass at the Giants' manager. McGraw got the blow on his shoulder. Players had anticipated trouble and were on hand to interfere in time before any blood was spilled. —New York *American*

BOSTON, April 30.—McGraw's noodle allowed Matty to get properly warmed up yesterday when Wiltse was pulled out. {Umpire} Emslie demanded a pitcher, and as Matty was not ready, McGraw walked out and announced himself as the twirler. He claimed the customary privilege of throwing five balls to warm up. He had just tossed up the first one when Matty came running out. McGraw should therefore figure in the tabulated scores as one of the Giant pitchers.

—Sid Mercer, New York *Globe*

## ◇ FRIDAY, MAY 1 ◇

{On April 30, in Boston, Boston beat the Giants 3 to 2. Winning pitcher, Flaherty; losing pitcher, Crandall. Giants' standing: 8 wins, 6 losses, in third place.}

BOSTON, April 30—Frank Bowerman, who has been working like a beaver to show John McGraw that a mistake was made when the Romeo {Bowerman's home town in Michigan} receiver was traded last winter, hammered an Otis Crandall offering over the left-field fence in the ninth inning, with Bill Sweeney on first base, and the rap gave Boston a victory, 3 to 2. Bowerman is the happiest man in the Hub, even though he gets credit only for a two-bagger, as Sweeney had scored before Frank reached third.

New York's pitching department is in such bad trim that McGraw had no veteran he could call on and so entrusted the job to Crandall. The Cedar Rapids recruit showed his mates how to hit by banging the ball out of the lot in the fifth inning, but unfortunately did not instruct them how to field, and the poor support he received allowed the resident athletes to win.　　　　　　　　　　　　　　　　　　　　　—New York *Press*

The Giants ought to have had yesterday's game done up and iced for Youngster Crandall. All that Crandall brought back to New York was vain regret, a sigh for useless labor, an order for a pair of shoes, and a promise of a new hat the next time he goes to Boston. {A pair of shoes and a hat were given by local merchants to National Leaguers who hit home runs in Boston.}

Crandall's homer was one of the longest and highest round-trip belts ever seen in Boston. The New York, New Haven and Hartford tracks run just outside that fence, and yesterday a work train ran up alongside the fence and the crew got on top of the cars to watch the game. Crandall's hit sailed high over the heads of the trainmen and disappeared in a pile of junk.　　　　　　　　　　　　　　　—Sid Mercer, New York *Globe*

———◇ **SATURDAY, MAY 2** ◇———

PITTSBURGH, April 29—Pittsburgh will spring a novelty this season. The Pittsburgh baseball club proposes to solve the "wet grounds" problem. A contract was signed yesterday by Dreyfuss with the Pittsburgh Waterproof Company for a tarpaulin to cover the entire playing field. The tarpaulin will contain 1,800 yards of brown parafinned duck and will cost $2,000. The center of the tarpaulin will be attached to a truck 10 x 15 feet and 3 feet high. Before and after a game in threatening weather, the truck will be run out and the playing ground covered with the tarpaulin. The tarpaulin will protect the field, and there should be no more deferred games on account of wet grounds, unless rain should fall during the progress of a game. *—Sporting Life*

———◇ **SUNDAY, MAY 3** ◇———

{On May 2, in New York, the Giants lost to Philadelphia 2 to 1. Winning pitcher, McQuillan; losing pitcher, Taylor. Giants' standing: 8 wins, 7 losses, tied with Philadelphia for third place.}

To the keen disappointment of about 10,000 fans, Philadelphia defeated the Giants yesterday 2 to 1. As the spectators went home after the game they meditated on what might have been had not Umpire Emslie reversed his decision twice in the sixth inning.

The trouble came over a decision by Emslie, who called balls and strikes, in the sixth inning. With the score 2 to 1 in favor of the visitors, Seymour made a safe hit. Bresnahan followed at the bat, and on the third ball pitched Seymour started to steal second. {Catcher Fred} Jacklitsch threw to {second baseman Otto} Knabe and caught Seymour. To the majority of spectators, as well as to Seymour, it seemed like Emslie called a foul. Rigler declared Seymour out, and pandemonium broke loose. McGraw was up in arms and engaged in a heated conversation with Emslie. The latter changed his ruling and said it was a foul ball. This brought a protest from the Quaker horde. {Philadelphia coach } Kid Gleason outargued McGraw, and Emslie, after a conference with Rigler, declared Seymour out. *—New York Times*

# ——◇ MONDAY, MAY 4 ◇——

McGraw has sent an official protest to President Pulliam of Saturday's game on the claim that Umpire Emslie shouted "Foul!" on a strike by Devlin when he should have said "Strike!" The call of "Foul!" did without doubt cause Seymour, stealing second at the time, to slow up so that he merely ran into Knabe's arms "standing up."

Umpires are not called on to officiate as a general thing until the regular season begins. They have no preliminary training or exercise. They are heavy and logy physically and mentally. The players, on the contrary, by a month or six weeks' training in the South, are full of life, snap and ginger, and I don't blame them for getting hot, sore and mad to have well-made schemes go astray by slow thinking, slow moving umps.

An umpire can outlive his usefulness just as a player can, and the sooner Presidents {Ban} Johnson and Pulliam appreciate this the better off the national game will be.

Spring has "came" and something ought to be "did."

—Sam Crane, New York *Evening Journal*

————— NATIONAL LEAGUE STANDINGS —————

|            | W  | L  | PCT. | GB  |              | W | L  | PCT. | GB |
|------------|----|----|------|-----|--------------|---|----|------|----|
| Chicago    | 11 | 3  | .786 | —   | Boston       | 8 | 8  | .500 | 4  |
| Pittsburgh | 8  | 4  | .667 | 2   | Brooklyn     | 7 | 9  | .437 | 5  |
| New York   | 8  | 7  | .533 | 3½  | Cincinnati   | 5 | 7  | .417 | 5  |
| Philadelphia | 8 | 7 | .533 | 3½  | St. Louis    | 3 | 13 | .188 | 9  |

# ——◇ TUESDAY, MAY 5 ◇——

{On May 4, in New York, the Giants beat Philadelphia 12 to 2. Winning pitcher, Mathewson; losing pitcher, Sparks. Giants' standing: 9 wins, 7 losses, in third place.}

Well, sir, you should have been at the Polo Grounds yesterday, if you were not "among those present," for there was the finest piece of vivisection ever witnessed in a ball lot when the Giants suddenly got out the

—  60  —

"big stick" and swatted the ball about with such continuity and vigor that they piled up an even dozen runs against the deuce the Murrayites scored in the last gasp of the game.

Mighty Mathewson appeared in the box for the home talent, bright-eyed and rosy as a flower of June, and his performance was of the high-grade kind which glistens with quality and comes only in five-pound boxes. He toyed with the sphere as a cat would with a ball of yarn, putting it where he pleased, and in the six innings in which he officiated he let the Quakers have three hits, but he presented these at such long intervals they were in no way associated with the two feeble runs made.

—New York *Herald*

Maybe Taft will get the Presidential nomination, and maybe Roosevelt will reconsider his rash declaration and do a little running himself. It is even possible that Yohn Yohnson, of Minnesota, will put some Scandinavian wallpaper in the East Room of the White House. But we don't care; we don't care. "Big Six" is his old grand self, and we're after the pennant. —William F. Kirk, New York *American*

## ———◇ WEDNESDAY, MAY 6 ◇———

{In New York, the Giants beat Philadelphia 4 to 0. Winning pitcher, Wiltse; losing pitcher, Richie. Giants' standing: 10 wins, 7 losses, in third place.}

For the first time this season the whitewash banner was flung to the breeze of the Polo Grounds, George Wiltse hoisting it at the expense of the Phillies. New York played a brilliant defensive game behind their left-handed flinger and Bridwell and Tenney, by spectacular plays, boosted Boston as a place to learn how to field.

There was nothing quiet or pastoral about this last battle between representatives of the Empire and Keystone States, Manager McGraw and Captain Donlin being fired from the coaching lines for violating the Pulliam code and {Phillie catcher Charles "Red"} Dooin for informing Bob Emslie he was blind. —New York *Press*

Now we will have what we have been looking for since snow flurry times, when that famous deal was made whereby the Giants were immeasurably strengthened by the accumulation of Tenney, Bridwell and Needham.

Yes, the Giants and Boston will meet this afternoon for the first time in Manhattan since the shift was made that caused that friction in the Hub between McGraw and McGann.

It goes without saying that the rivalry occasioned will make the hot series just finished with the Phillies look like a lawn tennis match with a pink tea climax. —Sam Crane, New York *Evening Journal*

———◇ **THURSDAY, MAY 7** ◇———

There was no game yesterday at the Polo Grounds because rain interfered. "Old Jupe" and the grouchy weather man combined and made an enemy of every fan in Manhattan.

The fans were dead sore, and they had a right to be. Here was a series they had talked about all Winter and gloated over, only to be side-tracked by the aerial sponge squeezer who apparently doesn't know a base hit from an error. —Sam Crane, New York *Evening Journal*

I predicted several weeks ago that the Giants would finish sixth. Now I'll say they have an excellent chance to wind up in seventh place, if not in the tail-end division! —Joe Vila, *The Sporting News*

PITTSBURGH, May 6—Making the claim that the Pittsburgh club had raised its third-base line illegally, to the detriment of visiting hitters, the Chicago team registered a vicious kick during and after the game today.

The raising of the line was so palpable that bunts toward third base could hardly remain on the diamond, and several times Chicago players were worsted by this. The Pittsburgh club admits the third-base line is higher, but says this was done for draining.

After the game Umpire O'Day asked Secretary Locke of the Pittsburgh club: "Will you fix the diamond to conform with National League rules or must I report to President Pulliam by wire?"

"We will fix the diamond," said Locke.

—New York *American*

———◇ FRIDAY, MAY 8 ◇———

The new unglossed baseball cover does not seem to bear out predictions that it would knock spit-ball pitching. All the saliva artists seem as adept with this style of delivery as usual. Chesbro has experienced no difficulty, and big Ed Walsh, of the White Sox, seems better than ever. {Walsh would have his best season in 1908, with 39 victories.}

—New York *American*

———◇ SATURDAY, MAY 9 ◇———

{On May 8, in New York, the Giants' third straight game with Boston was postponed because of rain.}

CHICAGO, May 2—An agent of the pitching machine in use at Yale and Harvard for several seasons took his brass howitzer to the park yesterday morning and fired off its repertoire for the Cubs to hit at. The thing resembles a cannon mounted on a wooden frame and does everything but chew tobacco, soil new balls and kick at the umpire. Compressed air shoots the ball at the batsman fast or slow, high or low, and applies the in and out curve, the fadeaway, and the raise curve, the gravity drop, smoke ball, grape vine sinker, and fooler. The addition of a metal gland of the breech containing a wad of loose chewing gum would enable the machine to throw the spit ball, it is said.

—*Sporting Life*

———◇ SUNDAY, MAY 10 ◇———

{On May 9, in New York, the Giants beat Boston 7 to 3. Winning pitcher, Mathewson; losing pitcher, Young. Giants standing: 11 wins, 7 losses, in third place.}

Old playmates mingled on the rain-soaked grass of the Polo Ground yesterday afternoon, and the present Giants beat the old Giants and beat them handsomely. Beat them with their pitcher, par excellence, "Young Cy" Young in the box; yes; more than that, knocked him out of the box. {"Young Cy" Young was Irving Young and should not be confused with the legendary Denton "Cy" Young, who in 1908 pitched for the Boston Red Sox in his nineteenth major league season.}

Two runs were made off the great Mathewson, the terror of the baseball world, in the first inning, and those with little faith groaned inwardly or prepared to revile the Giants outwardly because they felt they might be deprived of their mess of pottage by being present when Mathewson lost his first game in 1908. But Mathewson did not lose.

—New York *Herald*

———◊ MONDAY, MAY 11 ◊———

The Giants started West yesterday for the first long trip away from home, and will open at Pittsburgh today. The games this week mark the first clash between Eastern and Western clubs, and they are important as furnishing an opportunity to judge where the chief strength lies. This Western trip will go a long way toward settling how close the fight in the National League will be this year.　　—New York *Tribune*

——— NATIONAL LEAGUE STANDINGS ———

| | W | L | PCT. | GB | | W | L | PCT. | GB |
|---|---|---|---|---|---|---|---|---|---|
| Chicago . . . . . | 13 | 5 | .722 | — | Philadelphia . | 10 | 9 | .536 | 3½ |
| Pittsburgh . . . | 10 | 6 | .625 | 2 | Cincinnati . . . | 6 | 10 | .375 | 6 |
| New York . . . | 11 | 7 | .611 | 2 | Brooklyn . . . . | 7 | 13 | .350 | 7 |
| Boston . . . . . . | 10 | 9 | .536 | 3½ | St. Louis . . . . | 6 | 14 | .300 | 8 |

———◊ TUESDAY, MAY 12 ◊———

{On May 11, in Pittsburgh, the Giants lost 5 to 2. Winning pitcher, Leever; losing pitcher, McGinnity. Giants' standing: 11 wins, 8 losses, in third place.}

The Giants came, they saw, they clouted and were vanquished 5 to 2.

Captain Clarke and his clever cohorts outguessed the McGraw maulers and landed a close-cut victory. In order to accomplish this highly commendable and fan-pleasing result they had to play the best kind of baseball they had in stock.

While the score was officially 5 to 2 in favor of Pittsburgh, a rooter with a red face and a Seed plate in his eyeglass pretty nearly called the turn as he made his way from the grandstand at the conclusion of the contest. "It was 5 to 2 in favor of Hans Wagner," he put it, and all within hearing applauded the sentiment.

Hans Wagner was pretty much the whole works, anvil, boiler shop and all.

In the field he played perfectly, at bat he drove spikes into the fond hopes of one J. McGraw, while on the bases he cut cute and game-winning capers.

In the second inning Wagner looked so dangerous McGinnity passed him down the deadhead route. Abby {Abbaticchio, a.k.a. Battey} accidentally tapped the ball along the first-base line where it was recovered by the astute Monsieur Tenney for an out, which placed Wagner on second. {Harry} Swacina next bounded the ball to the diligent Doyle, who made a low throw to Tenney. Wagner said farewell to second, hiking for third as fast as his parenthetical pins would carry him. Noting that the ball had escaped Tenney's grasp Hans kept on toward the plate, which he reached by a great slide. It is doubtful if any other player could have scored from second on such a play; few base runners would have taken such a chance, but Wagner is ever ready to take advantage of an opening.

No more runs were made until the sixth, when, with two out, Clarke held a brief conference with himself and decreed that it was time to be up and doing, and he promptly uped and dooed.

With a swish of his sphered spanker Fred sent a triple to right. Again did McGinnity discover a devilish gleam in the Wagnerian orbs and purposely sent Hans down over the fourball highway.

And the doughty German again showed his right to be classed as the great and only. Instead of trying the time-honored double steal Wagner and Clarke sprang a new one on the Giants, standing the latter completely on their heads.

Naturally the Giants expected Hans to break for second on a pitched ball. Instead, the big Teuton waited until Bresnahan had just returned the bulb to McGinnity, when, with head down and legs spread like this ( ), he started for second. McGinnity, taken completely by surprise by the boldness and suddenness of the action, heaved the ball to second. Wagner continued his wild dash until within a few feet of Doyle, when he suddenly turned and hastened back toward first, never letting up in his speed. The ball was thrown to Tenney, who awaited the arrival of the Flying Dutchman. When within a yard of the Giant first-sacker Wagner wheeled and scudded back over the route to second. Tenney started to give chase, but seeing that Clarke had started for the plate turned and threw to Bresnahan. The latter got the ball all right, but the Pirate chieftain, by a cleverly manipulated bit of contortion, evaded the touch and slid over the plate in safety, while Wagner smiled from his perch on second.

That play alone was worth the price of admission.

—C. B. Power, Pittsburgh *Dispatch*

───◇ **WEDNESDAY, MAY 13** ◇───

{On May 12, in Pittsburgh, the Giants won 8 to 2. Winning pitcher Wiltse; losing pitcher, Maddox. Giants' standing: 12 wins, 8 losses, in third place.}

Muggsy McGraw's Giants gave the Pirates an 8 to 2 slap in the face yesterday. George Wiltse had the knack of slanting them over so that Smoketown swatters turned them into unsafe territory, while Nick Maddox could not overcome his wildness during the four innings he lasted.

Hans Wagner twisted his foot in the fourth inning of Monday's game, and the injury made it necessary for him to remain out of the contest, and the absence of the German seemed to dishearten his teammates.

—Pittsburgh *Post*

───◇ **THURSDAY, MAY 14** ◇───

{On May 13, in Pittsburgh, the Giants lost 5 to 1. Winning pitcher, Camnitz; losing pitcher, Mathewson. Giants' standing: 12 wins, 9 losses, in third place.}

Christy Mathewson was clouted from the slab in the fifth inning at Exposition Park yesterday, while Howard Camnitz held the hard-hitting New Yorkers powerless until they were hopelessly trounced. Crandall, the Cedar Rapids twirler, finished for the Giants, and was more effective than Mathewson, but it was too late. It was the fastest game here this season, played in only an hour and 25 minutes. It was Mathewson's first defeat of the year. —Pittsburgh *Post*

Business Manager Frank Bancroft and members of the Cincinnati team are apprehensive that the doors of the Boston hotel where they have been stopping for several seasons may be closed to them this year as a result of the fight in that fashionable hostelry between McGraw and McGann. The incident may lead to the eviction of well-behaved as well as rowdy players. The spirit of rowdyism with which McGraw has imbued the Giants bids fair to live as long as do the men whom he taught to bulldoze umpires and behave like Bowery roughs, on and off the diamond. For several years the New York club has done more to lower the position of professional ball players than all other major league teams put together. No matter how well other clubs comport themselves, all players are classed with the Giants.

—Cincinnati *Post*, quoted in *The Sporting News*

————◇ **SATURDAY, MAY 16** ◇————

{On May 15, in Cincinnati, the Giants won 9 to 2. Winning pitcher, Taylor; losing pitcher, Campbell. Giants' standing: 13 wins, 9 losses, in third place.}

One fearful round, in which a vast amount of bad baseball was displayed, robbed the Reds of the first game of the New York series at League Park. For seven innings our boys played sterling ball behind the accurate and skillful pitching of William Campbell. Only two hits had been peeled off by Giant sluggers, and Cy Seymour, who doubled with two down in the seventh, was the only member of the New York crew to see second base up to that time. The Reds had a run to go on, and it was simply a question of retiring six more Giants and then making a dash for the dinner table. But McGraw's men are great finishers, and a lead of one run was never known to frighten them into hysterics.

Our noble athletes were suddenly seized with an attack of the wobbles. The strain of the close contest, the eager anxiety of the multitude in the stands and the fearlessness of McGraw and his men in their continuous conversation with that dignified official, Mr. Hank O'Day, worked on the nerves of the Red youngsters. It was a fine day for a balloon ascension, and the boys put one on exhibition.

Arthur Devlin opened the eighth with a lucky bounding hit over second base, of which {Miller} Huggins made a brilliant stop but could not quite get the ball to first in time. Then Campbell, steady Bill, gave his only base on balls to Nicklin, formerly Strang. Next was a fumble of Bridwell's bunt by Billy Campbell, and before the inning ended there had been six hits, five errors, a base on balls, good for nine tallies.

—Jack Ryder, Cincinnati *Enquirer*

CINCINNATI, May 16—You can never tell, as Bernard Shaw would say, just what that John McGraw person will spring next. When the Reds were seeing pinwheels, roman candles, spit-devils and other fireworks, a la the Fourth of July, the little Celt pulled an entirely new stunt on the dazed 4,000 witnessing the ruthless treatment of their pets.

McGraw began his assault by yanking Dummy Taylor off the batting order and substituting Merkle. Naturally it was expected that if Merkle had another chance to bat in this eighth round, he would be allowed to try it again. That's where McGraw sprung his new stunt.

Instead of sending Merkle to bat a second time, he sent Herzog to bat for him, thus establishing a precedent of having a man who had batted for another man having a man bat for him, making the {box} score read "Merkle batted for Taylor in the eighth. Herzog batted for Merkle in the eighth."

—Sid Mercer, New York *Globe*

## ◇——— SUNDAY, MAY 17 ◇———

{On May 16, in Cincinnati, the Giants lost 3 to 1. Winning pitcher, Coakley; losing pitcher, Mathewson. The Giants' standing: 13 wins, 10 losses, in fourth place.}

Christopher Mathewson had plenty of time to play his favorite game of checkers yesterday. {Mathewson was probably baseball's best checkers player.} There were the long hours of the morning, the beautiful moonlit evening, and all but a very few moments of the glorious afternoon. Matty had been expecting to stay at the ball yard from lunchtime until the dinner gong sounded its raucous but pleasant tone, but he was not detained so long. The kind Reds, knowing his earnest love for the checker board, refused to keep him away from his pleasant pastime. Owing to their thoughtfulness, the great pitcher was at liberty after the second round of the Saturday show. He left the yard without saying "Thank you," and did not seem highly delighted at the hospitality of our boys. But great men are not always grateful. It did not take many hits to give Matty his freedom, for the Reds secured only two singles off the famous artist. These two, however, were peacherinos, and they were mixed with two errors and a base on balls, a combination which gave the Reds three runs right off the reel. Though our boys were not getting a very large number safe, they were feeling Matty so freely that Manager McGraw, always a quick shifter, yanked him at once, and substituted Leon Ames. The change killed off the Reds, who were unable to do anything with the auburn-topped athlete, nor with Young Crandall, who pitched the last inning, after Ames had been taken out to let Herzog bat for him. Lucky that Matty started this one. Dr. A. J. Coakley worked for the Reds with great effect. The heavy-hitting Giants just couldn't get them safe off the eminent dentist's tony pitching.

—Jack Ryder, Cincinnati Enquirer

———◊ **MONDAY, MAY 18** ◊———

{On May 17, in Cincinnati, the Giants lost 7 to 2. Winning pitcher, Weimer; losing pitcher, Wiltse. Giants' standing: 13 wins, 11 losses, in fourth place.}

Tales of great feats of old-time ball players, who were always performing marvelous stunts in the last half of the ninth inning, were blotted from the memories of several thousand enthusiasts at League Park yesterday, when big John Ganzel, with the bases clogged and the contest nearly over, leaned heavily on one of George Wiltse's offerings and laced a lovely homer to the left-field corner. The tender footsies of {Johnny} Kane, {Hans} Lobert and {Mike} Mitchell pressed the pan in rapid succession, followed by the Captain's generous hoof, hot from its fast trip around the sacks. Ganzel's great drive cinched a victory that had already been won by the nervy batting of his predecessors in the line-up, but it was no less creditable for that. A man who can crack out such a hit, with the bases full, is entitled to all the candy, cigars, booze, household goods and other paraphernalia that comes to the four-base hitter on the home lot. Mr. McGraw was so rattled he forgot to take Mr. Wiltse out of the box.                               —Jack Ryder, Cincinnati *Enquirer*

A number of thoughtful women removed their expensive millinery creations during the game, gaining the gratitude of many spectators. At a ball game you can tell whether a woman is a real lady or just a plain female by noting whether she has her hat on or not.

—Jack Ryder, Cincinnati *Enquirer*

——— NATIONAL LEAGUE STANDINGS ———

| | W | L | PCT. | GB | | W | L | PCT. | GB |
|---|---|---|---|---|---|---|---|---|---|
| Chicago | 15 | 7 | .682 | — | Boston | 13 | 13 | .500 | 4 |
| Philadelphia | 13 | 9 | .591 | 2 | Cincinnati | 11 | 12 | .478 | 4½ |
| Pittsburgh | 12 | 9 | .571 | 2½ | St. Louis | 10 | 17 | .370 | 7½ |
| New York | 13 | 11 | .542 | 3 | Brooklyn | 9 | 18 | .333 | 8½ |

———◇ **TUESDAY, MAY 19** ◇———

{On May 18, in Cincinnati, the Giants lost 9 to 5. Winning pitcher, Spade; losing pitcher, Mathewson. The Giants' standing: 13 wins, 12 losses, in fourth place.}

Oh, you Reds! Oh, you Giants! Oh, you Matty! Especially, oh, you Matty! The great Giant twirler, by many judges still ranked the ablest twirler in the business, went in against the Reds yesterday for the second time in the series, and for the second time was knocked sky-high and forced to retire before a bountiful bevy of beautiful bingles {base hits}. Matty plays a grand game of checkers. The Reds are stronger at poker, bridge, whist and baseball. If Christy could inveigle Bob Spade into a bloody combat on the checkerboard he would probably whale the everlasting tar out of the Atlanta recruit. But checkers is too rough a game to be allowed in the refined atmosphere of League Park, where baseball has the call. So Spade confined his attention to the national sport yesterday and made the great Matty look like a sucker.

—Jack Ryder, Cincinnati *Enquirer*

———◇ **WEDNESDAY, MAY 20** ◇———

ST. LOUIS, May 20—The Giants escaped from a mass of rumors in Cincinnati last night, and landed here early this morning.

Among the prominent rumors squashed was one that Mike Donlin had fallen off the water wagon with a dull thud. Donlin has lots of friends in Cincinnati {where he played in 1902–1904}, and he did not lack for invitations to dally with the flowing bowl. But he waved them all away and accepted distilled water and cigars instead. However, that did not prevent the rumormongers from circulating a story that Capt. Mike was pickled Monday night.

Cincinnati is a great town for rumors, but McGraw is harboring no boozers, the Giants are a splendidly behaved bunch, and their losing streak cannot be charged to dissipation.

—Sid Mercer, New York *Globe*

{The rumors concerning Donlin are not surprising. Consider the following quotation from an editorial in *The Sporting News* on March 22, 1902, when Donlin was a member of the Baltimore Orioles.}

"In Baltimore last Thursday {March 13} Mike Donlin assaulted an innocent, modest young lady on the street, cutting her face badly. On Saturday night he was arrested in Washington with two other thugs for assaulting a streetcar conductor. He was immediately taken to Baltimore to stand trial for the first offense. When arraigned in court for striking

Miss Minnie Fields, an actress, and Ernest Clayton, her escort, Donlin pleaded guilty and said that as he was drunk at the time he didn't know what he was doing. Miss Fields told of the assault, showed her bruised and blackened face, and said the blow felled her to the ground and rendered her unconscious. Clayton's blackened eyes were also in evidence as to the weight of the ruffian's fists. Judge Ritchie sentenced Donlin to six months in jail and a fine of $250." {Donlin served five months in the Baltimore city jail and was released on August 20, when he joined the Cincinnati club.}

———◇ **THURSDAY, MAY 21** ◇———

{On May 20, in St. Louis, the Giants lost 1 to 0. Winning pitcher, Raymond; losing pitcher, McGinnity. Giants' standing: 13 wins, 13 losses, tied with Boston for fifth place.}

When Manager John McGraw strayed out to Springfield, Ill., to pick a peach from the Three-Eye {minor league} baseball orchard, he evidently took a bridle path instead of the highway, and wound up in a lemon grove. He is reported to have paid something like $4,000 for the privilege of plucking a particular fruit named Doyle, and he thought he was just taking advantage of a "rube" management.

Since that time doubts as to the character of his purchase have arisen in his mind. Mr. Doyle has been analyzed, assayed, dissected and microscopically scrutinized to the end that the peach part of him is entirely absent.

In fact, even to the naked eye Mr. Doyle's appearance at League Park yesterday was positively citric. He contributed a bunch of fat-headed work that would drive a real manager like McGraw to the woods to think it over.

In the opening round, with one down, {Raymond "Chappy"} Charles hit to Doyle, and the latter played imaginary cup-and-ball for a time sufficient for Charles to get his base. A base on balls and a scant single threatened to bring home a tally, but McGinnity stiffened and retired the side.

In the second Doyle shone. {Bill} Ludwig smashed a two-bagger down the third-base line and was sacrificed to third by {Billy} Gilbert. {Arthur "Bugs"} Raymond then hit an easy bounder to Doyle, who promptly mutilated the play, which was the easy retirement of Ludwig at the plate. Instead, he did an act of prestidigitation, following which he tossed the runner out at first. He escaped an error, but he cost the game.

One more count before we are through with the gentleman. He not only lost the game, but lost a chance to win it. In the second inning Seymour led off with a safety to left. Needham flied and Devlin put him on second with an infield out. Seymour kept up the good work by stealing third as Doyle walked. Then a double steal was started and {catcher} Ludwig hurried the ball down to {second baseman} Gilbert, hoping to get Seymour on a quick return to the plate. This would have happened and Seymour would probably have been safe with a tally, owing to a fine lead, had not Doyle kept pounding down to second, instead of halting and forcing the second baseman to make the throw home. But he kept right on and insisted that he be put out—and he was.

　　　　　　　　　　—John E. Wray, St. Louis *Post-Dispatch*


CINCINNATI, May 21—Members of the New York team predict that checkers will be the downfall of mighty Christy Mathewson if he does not curb his passion for the game. Just before leaving for St. Louis McGraw complained to one of the Reds that Matty's limited success in recent games was due to checkers.

"Matty has been besieged by checker players ever since we came on this trip," said he. "They come from far and near at all hours of the day and night to play with him, and he accommodates them all. If he doesn't cut it out he'll go to pieces as a pitcher."　　　—New York *American*


───◇ **FRIDAY, MAY 22** ◇───

{On May 21, in St. Louis, the Giants won 8 to 4. Winning pitcher, Crandall; losing pitcher, Karger. Giants' standing: 14 wins, 13 losses, in fourth place.}

Manager John McGraw may not need his well-advertised pitcher, Christy Mathewson, as badly as he supposed if a certain Mr. Crandall continues to pitch the kind of baseball that helped the Giants beat the locals yesterday.

Beginning in the second half of the fourth inning, this youngster twirled and the Cardinals were closed up like a jack-knife. But one single was made off Crandall.

"Dummy" Taylor is evidently not at his best, like McGinnity and Mathewson. The man responsible for the most unique signal code in baseball gave up two runs in the first inning. In the third, the Cardinals scored two more runs and "Dummy" was chased in favor of Crandall.

If "Dummy" never does another thing he will be worth doing in oil and hanging in the Brush mansion. Since his advent to the team {in 1900} it has become necessary for every member of the aggregation to acquire a working knowledge of how to talk with the hands. In a game Taylor's only method of communicating with his captain or manager has been through the mute's finger language, and so all his team members have become familiar with the employment of this means of communication.

Realizing the value of this in running his team, McGraw has had the men pay special attention to it until now all plays from the bench are described in digital terms.

It was for failure to follow signals thus delivered in the first Giants–St. Louis game here that Doyle was taken off the regular team at the outset of yesterday's game and replaced by Nicklin.

—St. Louis *Post-Dispatch*

———◇ **SATURDAY, MAY 23** ◇———

Not one umpire officiating in either big league is in the touch he ought to be with the fast style of the game now being played. The game has progressed so far and fast that the umpires have been left behind.

Now, in my opinion, umpires should be out in the Spring practicing just the same as the players. They should exercise down South, or somewhere else, to get the cobwebs off their think-tanks, as well as to limber up their anatomical departments. Ball players get charley horses of the legs, but umpires can get the same charley horse in the head.

—Sam Crane, New York *Evening Journal*

President Murphy, of the Cubs, says he wouldn't protest a game, no matter what happened. Good for Murphy! There are protestors enough as it is. —*Sporting Life*

─────◇ **SUNDAY, MAY 24** ◇─────

{On May 23, in St. Louis, the Giants lost a doubleheader 6 to 2 and 2 to 0. Winning pitchers, Lush and Sallee; losing pitchers, McGinnity and Wiltse. Giants' standing: 14 wins, 15 losses, in sixth place.}

The first game evoked the pathos of fans who have seen and known "Iron Man" McGinnity when he was at his best. McGinnity has not been himself these many days and this year has not been himself at all. Yesterday he was target for Cardinal batsmen who returned his delivery to all parts of the field in two innings, getting ten hits and scoring five runs. Malarkey, who succeeded him in the sixth, was invulnerable.

In the second contest three singles and a wild pitch by Wiltse gave up two runs in the first, after which neither team scored.

—John E. Wray, St. Louis *Post-Dispatch*

─────◇ **MONDAY, MAY 25** ◇─────

{On May 24, in Chicago, the Giants won 6 to 4. Winning pitcher, Taylor; losing pitcher, Fraser. Giants' standing: 15 wins, 15 losses, in fifth place.}

There is nothing more exciting than a ninth-inning batting rally when a club is way behind—a rally that snatches victory out of the fire, or comes so near it that the multitude has an excuse for going crazy. The finish of yesterday's game, bitter as was the final disappointment, drove the populace dotty, and men who haven't yelled in years split the ether with uncouth sounds and waving arms.

The first half of the ninth was exciting enough, for Roger Bresnahan poled out a smite that went far down the lea, and Roger made four bases by terrific sprinting. This feat caused the populace to arise and prepare to go home.

The exits were jammed when {Harry} Steinfeldt drew four balls. Then {Jimmy} Slagle awaited one, and hundreds, going forth, stayed their steps and strove to return. {Johnny} Kling walked; the sacks were full.

Joe Tinker could have done great things. He hoisted a pop foul for Bresnahan. Del Howard batted for {Chick} Fraser, got a ticket, and a run was forced in. At this juncture McGraw, who seemed to be gradually getting interested in the game, yanked Taylor and sent in Joe McGinnity. The Iron Man had zinc in his curves and {Johnny} Evers hit one. It rose and came right down in Shannon's hands, but just as the ball arrived Shannon thoughtfully turned his back and fled. The sun had blinded him and he feared that the ball would fall on the vacuum that terminated his neck.

Two runs in, bases still full, one gone. {Jimmy} Sheckard worried McGinnity for a pass, and in came another run. Bases still full; a hit would tie, a long drive would win. Ah, look who's here, handsome Frank Schulte! The game will surely terminate as soon as he wallops the pill. Frank hit—and raised a little fly that Donlin grasped with a cruel leer. All up to Chance. On the Heap Big Bear depended the fortunes of the afternoon. Bing. Plunk, and the grotesque apparition in centerfield had it clinched tighter than an oil king's grip upon a dollar.

Aside from the great rally and Bresnahan's homer, the feature of the day was {right-fielder} Schulte's work in the eighth, when he performed the hitherto unheard-of feat of hurling out two men at the plate in a single session. It was a wonderful thing and not likely to happen again in twenty years.                    —W. A. Phelon, Chicago *Journal*

———— NATIONAL LEAGUE STANDINGS ————

| | W | L | PCT. | GB | | W | L | PCT. | GB |
|---|---|---|---|---|---|---|---|---|---|
| Chicago ..... | 18 | 9 | .667 | — | New York ... | 15 | 15 | .500 | 4½ |
| Philadelphia . | 15 | 13 | .536 | 3½ | Boston ...... | 15 | 16 | .484 | 5 |
| Pittsburgh ... | 13 | 12 | .520 | 4 | Brooklyn .... | 13 | 18 | .419 | 7 |
| Cincinnati ... | 15 | 14 | .517 | 4 | St. Louis .... | 13 | 20 | .394 | 8 |

# ◇ TUESDAY, MAY 26 ◇

{On May 25, in Chicago, the Giants lost, in 10 innings, 8 to 7. Winning pitcher, Brown; losing pitcher, Wiltse. Giants' standing: 15 wins, 16 losses, in fifth place.}

There have been ball games and them some, but such a game as yesterday's struggle doesn't often happen. Exciting? Beyond the limit of deliriums. Ten innings of the wildest, fiercest battling; five pitchers beaten to a lemon meringue; batting and fielding feats of every variety, and the right people winning just as darkness settled down—how could you tie that combination?

C. Mathewson, who is very handsome, assayed to pitch at the kickoff, and the Cubs warmed to him as if he were homelier than a mud fence. A young man named Malarkey, who has a swinging in-shoot as his chief stock in trade, came next and did well—for a while. Then the hits seemed to rise right out of the ground all about him, and he retreated in great confusion. Long Wiltse followed, and all was going nicely with him, when a black bat, wielded by a black-haired man, batted a black ball into the black dark, and put black scowls all over Muggsy's countenance.

{Jack} Pfiester tried to fool the Giants, but they batted him to a lamb stew in short order. Brown took up the burden, and got slammed plenty, but pulled it through just the same. The umpiring was hideous. Both teams were well soaked, umpirical errors being pretty evenly divided. To hear Chance tell it, New York was given six runs, and the Cubs had nine taken away from them. According to McGraw, the Cubs were presented with seven tallies, and New York was robbed of nineteen.

The grand razoo came in the tenth. New York had been retired runless, and Slagle came up. Wiltse wove them over, but some went askew. The ump said Slagle walked. The Giants said he fanned, but it is what the ump says that goes on the score sheet. {Pat} Moran laid down a bunt, and having done his duty, went back to the bench walking on air.

Joe Tinker had the one great chance, and took it. He stood swinging the bat, when an agonized voice piped down from the stand: "Hit it, you pigeon-toed orang-outang!" The ball was black and the sky was blacker. To use the words of a long-haired poet making pretty verses in section D, "Night cast a sable seal upon the darkling field." At this moment Joe hit it, and Cy Seymour saw something go over, past, and beyond. The ball is alleged to be going yet, but this is probably an exaggeration.

—W. A. Phelon, Chicago *Journal*

Manager McGraw watched most of yesterday's game from the club-house. He was chased by Umpire Emslie in the second inning, because, after a heated argument with Blond Robert, he turned to the crowd and begged someone to send out a hairpin to Emslie for his wig. As the umpire is given to the toupee habit, the shaft struck home and he banished McGraw instanter.
—New York *American*

When Moran was passed in the third after Slagle had fouled, McGinnity ran from the bench and claimed an out on the ground that Moran was batting in Tinker's place. Emslie pulled out his score card and showed that Pat was batting in his own place. As a matter of fact, Tinker batted in Pat's place in the first inning and Pat in Tinker's place in the second, and if the Giants had noticed it they could have prevented those three Cub runs, but the rule is not retroactive. The opposing team loses the right to claim an out when the pitcher delivers a ball to the succeeding batsman.
—I. E. Sanborn, Chicago *Tribune*

## ———◇ WEDNESDAY, MAY 27 ◇———

{On May 26, in Chicago, the Giants won 7 to 4. Winning pitcher, Crandall; losing pitcher, Reulbach. Giants' standing: 16 wins, 16 losses, in fifth place.}

You can talk till the silver moon gets a copper lining about the beauties of scientific ball and the pretty features of 2 to 1 games, but if the crowd gets a chance to express itself, it will rise up and yell for games where home runs skip down the lea and two-baggers rake their way amid sylvan lanes. There is something enchanting about the music of a long, hard drive.

Action, energy and uproar—that's what a crowd wants in every

branch of sport, and in baseball most of all. That is why the three New
York games at Cub park have been feasts of joy to the beholders, and why
the attendance yesterday was the largest any Tuesday has seen in the old
grounds for many and many a year.

It was the most joyful slugging bee anyone could want. The Cubs and
Giants walked up, shook heavy bats at the pitchers, and then jammed the
sphere athwart the muzzle. The managers refused to rescue the suffering
slabmen, and Reulbach and Crandall had to stand on the slab and take it
all. They liked it too. Liked it the way a man does when he is being
scalped. Between whiles they punctured the batsmen, just to get even.

After Reulbach had hit four of the enemy, it got so that he couldn't
throw within two feet of a batter without having the man threaten to
lick him and assert that it was a direct attempt at murder.

During the hot, tempestuous afternoon Tinker, Tenney, and Seymour
all drove home runs down the yard and circled the sacks amid delirious
approval. It was a gleeful day of mighty hitting, but the Giants hit the
harder.                               —W. A. Phelon, Chicago *Journal*

## ◇ THURSDAY, MAY 28 ◇

{On May 27, in Chicago, the Giants won 1 to 0. Winning pitcher,
Wiltse; losing pitcher, Pfiester. Giants' standing: 17 wins, 16 losses, in fifth
place.}

Neither Cubs nor Giants had much swat left in their systems after
their batting jamboree of the previous three days, and they hooked up in
an airtight game in which New York scratched a 1 to 0 victory.

Wiltse accomplished what fans beg every pitcher to do when he
comes to bat with the score against him. George won his own game literally, for he held the Cubs to three hits and batted home the only run in
the seventh round. A dizzling double between {third baseman} Steinfeldt
and his base was the instrument with which Wiltse hooked the victory.

The Cubs hammered Wiltse much harder than the Giants did Pfiester,
but the Giants performed some circus stunts behind their hurler. Little
Herzog, just out of the minor incubator, was prominent in some of the
plays which killed Chicago runs and behaved so feloniously in the way of

stealing hits that he had the rooters applauding his every turn. Bridwell was not there to see his sub perform, as he was on his way to New York to shake the malaria acquired in St. Louis. If Herzog can hold that gait for any distance, Bridwell can have all the malaria he wants and McGraw won't turn a hair about it.      —I. E. Sanborn, Chicago *Tribune*

CLEVELAND, May 28—The Giants en route to an exhibition game in Buffalo. The team has braced up wonderfully since leaving St. Louis, but the loss of Bresnahan {who was injured in Monday's game} will be a serious handicap. The big catcher had his sore finger placed under an "X" ray machine Tuesday, and it was discovered that one of the small bones was fractured. Bresnahan's physician thinks that Roger will not catch for at least two weeks.

The one mystifying feature of the trip just ended is Mathewson's loss of form. He showed nothing, and got his bumps in all four Western cities.

The series gave some youngsters a chance to make good. Charley Herzog has more than fulfilled predictions made about him this Spring. Malarkey and Crandall proved their right to be seriously considered as regular pitchers, and Larry Doyle came out of the trance that almost lost him his job.      —Sid Mercer, New York *Globe*

"It's hitting that wins," said John McGraw yesterday. "They say the White Sox won a flag {in 1906} without hitting, but I know better. Their grounds prevent anyone from hitting heavily, and as they played 77 games there, it made their averages look very small. On the road they hit as hard as anybody. {Known as the Hitless Wonders, the 1906 world's champion Chicago White Sox had a team batting average that was the lowest in its league and second lowest in the majors.}

"Have you noticed how much Mike Donlin improves our lineup? He is hitting as he always did and Mike is one of the greatest natural batsmen of the business. He can slam left- and right-handed pitchers the same way, and I don't see any deterioration in his fielding or his base running.

"Shannon is beginning to hit and Devlin is bound to come back stronger. That will give us the best batting outfit in the league, and if we can find one more pitcher how are you going to hold us?"
      —Chicago *Journal*

Poor McGraw! His lot will indeed be sad if the peerless Mathewson blows up, for Christy is the only real pitcher on his staff. McGinnity is a has-been, Ames a never-was because of inordinate wildness, Luther {Taylor} a mediocre man and Wiltse a fair southpaw. Crandall has done well, but McGraw hasn't shown real confidence in him. The Giants' other new twirlers don't amount to much.

—Ralph Davis, *The Sporting News*

The Giants? Well, I said "about the seventh" for them, didn't I? Well, how about the tail end? Drubbed by Cincinnati and St. Louis, McGraw's misfits look pretty small now. The once great Matty is a "soft mark." The supposed sluggers cannot hit a pumpkin, while McGraw has publicly pronounced Doyle a pinhead. Just as I told you, the Giants are outclassed simply because McGraw didn't get new and competent players when he had the chance. —Joe Vila, *The Sporting News*

## ◇ SATURDAY, MAY 30 ◇

{On May 29, in Brooklyn, the Giants won 1 to 0. Winning pitcher, Mathewson; losing pitcher, Rucker. Giants' standing: 18 wins, 16 losses, in fourth place.}

Guess he was just holding back for bets, this Mathewson person. He drove into Brooklyn yesterday and unloaded the choicest collection of knockout drops dealt since Amos Rusie was doing a specialty.

"And they said he'd gone back," said Charley Ebbets, with tears in his eyes as big as rain checks.

"They say that about every great man," said James Corbett, who promenaded very prettily along the upper concourse. "I remember very well, myself, one time a guy got to me on a fluke, but when I had recovered—" {The former heavyweight boxing champion (1892–97), Corbett was an avid Giant fan.}

The only run came in the fourth as the result of some very hitful endeavors by our returned wanderers. Donlin hit clean to center, advanced on Seymour's sacrifice bunt, and when Needham banged out two bases, Donlin scored.

Donlin, two innings later, retired from activities. He had hit to {third baseman Tommy} Sheehan, who whipped it to first. Donlin allowed he was safe. Umpire {Frank} Rudderham spoke up in a still, small voice, saying this impression was erroneous. Over on the grounds at Highland Park or 155th street, Donlin might have used language, but in the peaceful stretches of Washington Park, he never forgot his bringing up. "Have you, by chance," he asked, "an acquaintance with Old Doctor Georgen, the oculist?"

"Such is not my good fortune," returned Mr. Rudderham, "why do you ask?"

"I should advise you to visit him," said Mr. Donlin. "Your eyesight appears defective."

"Possibly you are right," agreed Mr. Rudderham. "I cannot see you for the rest of the game."

Which is the Brooklyn equivalent for a benching.

—W. W. Aulick, New York *Times*

———◇ **SUNDAY, MAY 31** ◇———

{On May 30, in Brooklyn, the Giants won the first of two scheduled games, played in the morning, 5 to 0. Winning pitcher, McGinnity; losing pitcher, Pastorius. The scheduled afternoon game was postponed because of rain. Giants' standing: 18 wins, 15 losses, in third place.}

Over in Brooklyn they don't bet that the home team will win—they make book on how much the opposing forces will win by. This sport furnishes the only uncertainties of the entertainment. The answer yesterday was five.

The game was very fast. It had to be, for it was a match race with the rain, and the pair ran to a head for nine innings. Sheehan flied out to Shannon just on the stroke of noon and ended the engagement. Then the floods descended, and there wasn't an afternoon game, which meant an appreciable percentage loss to McGraw's pets, to say nothing of the sorrow represented by the failure to house a paying army in the grandstand.

—W. W. Aulick, New York *Times*

BOSTON, June 1—The Giants will be entitled to unusual credit if they win two of three games here. Several players are under the care of Dr. {James} Creamer, club physician. He is trying to drive malaria germs out of Bridwell's system and is prescribing for Leon Ames, ill in New York. Roger Bresnahan is here, but is not likely to catch as his bad finger is as stiff as a board.

Sammy Strang Nicklin will play the short field today. Herzog had to quit in Saturday's game. He played the day before against the advice of his physician, and in the Decoration Day game he suddenly became nauseated and was relieved by Nicklin. Herzog went home to Baltimore Saturday night and will remain there for a few days. Bridwell did not make the trip and is not expected to play until next Thursday.

Cy Seymour is on the job, but there is no telling when he will break down. Seymour is playing with a very obstinate "charley horse." Trainer Richards and Dr. Creamer have advised him to rest, but against his better judgment, Seymour is permitting his loyalty to the club to keep him in the game.                    —Sid Mercer, New York *Globe*


Once more we beg leave to repeat the old saying that Giants cannot beat left-handers. Rucker and Pastorius failed last Friday and Saturday and Pfiester lost twice in the Chicago series. The count is almost 2 to 1 against the port-flingers who have faced McGraw's men.
                    —Sid Mercer, New York *Globe*


——— NATIONAL LEAGUE STANDINGS ———

| | W | L | PCT. | GB | | W | L | PCT. | GB |
|---|---|---|---|---|---|---|---|---|---|
| Chicago ..... | 22 | 12 | .647 | — | Cincinnati ... | 18 | 16 | .529 | 4 |
| Philadelphia . | 17 | 14 | .548 | 3½ | Boston ...... | 17 | 19 | .472 | 6 |
| New York ... | 18 | 15 | .545 | 3½ | St. Louis .... | 15 | 24 | .385 | 9½ |
| Pittsburgh ... | 17 | 15 | .531 | 4 | Brooklyn .... | 13 | 22 | .371 | 9½ |

# ———◇ TUESDAY, JUNE 2 ◇———

{On June 1, in Boston, the Giants lost 4 to 0. Winning pitcher, Dorner; losing pitcher, Wiltse. Giants' standing: 18 wins, 16 losses, in fifth place.}

Gus Dorner was wild enough in the first half of the game yesterday to lose two games, but he gained the somewhat anomalous distinction of shutting out McGraw's so-called "Giants" 4 to 0.

New York had the bases full twice, in the first inning with none out and in the fourth with two gone, but could not score. Dorner held New York to three scattered hits, and while he had something good on the ball, he never would have applied the Kalsomine brush {"Kalsomine" is an alternate spelling for "calcimine," a whitewash. In baseball vernacular, to whitewash a team is to shut it out.} had not he received great support. He was so constantly in the hole on account of wildness that he had to "put them over," and the ball in consequence was hit very hard at times.

—Boston *Herald*

CINCINNATI, June 1—President {Garry} Herrmann and Manager Ganzel, of the Cincinnati Reds, began negotiations to secure Joe McGinnity, who has been placed on the market by the New York Giants.

—New York *Evening Journal*

# ———◇ WEDNESDAY, JUNE 3 ◇———

{On June 2, in Boston, the Giants lost 4 to 3. Winning pitcher, Flaherty; losing pitcher, Crandall. Giants' standing: 19 wins, 18 losses, in fifth place.}

BOSTON, June 3—Sammy Strang Nicklin has probably played his last game as a Giant. Nicklin performed in very poor style yesterday. He may have been trying as hard as he could, but it did not look that way. Sammy's inaccurate fielding cut a large gash in whatever chance the Giants had to win the game and McGraw was disgusted with him.

It is thought that McGinnity will quit the game. He has been a high-salaried man for years, and no club in either league is willing to take him and assume his present contract, which calls for something like $4,000 a season with a bonus of $1,000. Had it not been for this obstacle McGinnity could have been used in a trade, but wartime salaries are no longer in vogue. So waivers were asked on the pitcher who would have brought a small fortune not many seasons ago.

—Sid Mercer, New York *Globe*

───◇ **THURSDAY, JUNE 4** ◇───

{On June 3, in Boston, the Giants won 3 to 0. Winning pitcher, Mathewson; losing pitcher, Young. Giants' standing: 20 wins, 18 losses, in fifth place.}

Christy Mathewson, better known as "Big Six" and the "Checker Champion" of Greater New York, pitched for the Giants, and for that reason the third game of the series did not result in a Boston victory. Matty was in great form. He allowed but three singles, fanned eleven batsmen and gave one pass. Two Boston players reached second, but not one got any farther.

—Boston *Herald*

After all the furor about Joe McGinnity, there is a large possibility that the "Iron Man" will not quit the Giants unless he does so of his own will. A shortage of effective pitchers at the Polo Grounds and McGinnity's recent work are the principal reasons why the original shift may not go through.

Incidentally there may be an inquiry into the publicity department of the Cincinnati club. That is where news of many National League deals leaks out. From Cincinnati came the announcement that New York had asked waivers on McGinnity. These things are supposed to be confidential.

Such a thing nearly always affects the work of a player, and the National Commission should provide a penalty for those who give out confidential matters.

—Sid Mercer, New York *Globe*

{On June 4, in New York, the Giants lost to St. Louis 7 to 5. Winning pitcher, Sallee; losing pitcher, Taylor. Giants' standing: 20 wins, 19 losses, in fifth place.}

There was a ball game at the Polo Grounds yesterday, the first we have seen at the old park for many days. The sun shone brightly, a large crowd assembled, and the grass never looked greener. But the Gallant Giants were trimmed by Measly Missourians.

Mr. {Harry "Slim"} Sallee, pretty nigh as tall as those windmills we read about in the farm journals, did the flinging for the foreign fleet, and won. Luther Burbank Taylor, he of the quiet mouth and nimble fingers, worked for the home talent until replaced by Crandall along at the shank end of the game. It wasn't the mute's fault that he was yanked out of the contest. Had it not been for loose work back of him in the fatal eighth, Mr. Taylor might have beaten his foe. But he didn't, so why indulge in post-mortems?

Some things make delightful reading, and other things never should be put in print. The awful eighth is one of those other things:

{Bobby} Byrne singled. {John "Red"} Murray fanned. Spike Shannon dropped {Joe} Delahanty's long fly, Byrne scoring. {Ed} Konetchy hit to Devlin, who made an unusual heave, the ball going to the right-field bleachers, Delahanty scoring. {Art} Hostetter added to the gloom by singling and scoring Konetchy. {Joseph "Patsy"} O'Rourke made a Texas league two-bagger. Gilbert hit to Doyle, who tried without success to catch Hostetter at the plate. Four runs.

—William F. Kirk, New York *American*

Conversation on yesterday's game should be conducted with a clothespin adorning the nose. This is about the 'steenth game the Giants have tossed away this season. When they were champions they allowed the other teams to do this tossing act. The Cardinals once were obliging, but it is a terrible sight to see the Giants stealing the St. Louis "stuff," and on the Polo Grounds, too!

—Sid Mercer, New York *Globe*

── ◇ **SATURDAY, JUNE 6** ◇ ──

{On June 5, in New York, the Giants lost to St. Louis 4 to 2. Winning pitcher, Karger; losing pitcher, Wiltse. Giants' standing: 20 wins, 20 losses, in fifth place.}

"Rudderham," remarked the scholarly Master Donlin at the ninth stage of yesterday's performance, "is not an umpire. It is a verb. I recall very well on one occasion of my early youth, I was witness to the apprehension of two cut-purses on the public street, and I inquired for what these folks had been taken into custody. 'They are rudderhamers, Micky,' said my father, and I asked, then, 'What is a rudderhamer?' 'One who rudderhams, to be sure,' said my parent, briskly, and I have never forgotten his words."

Mr. Donlin then added more explicitly his views of Mr. Rudderham, and Mr. Rudderham snapped his fingers real hard and said to get off his ball ground. Mr. Donlin got, but not until he had walked right up to the umpire and given him an awful hard look. It must have taken a lot of courage to do this, because Mr. Donlin can't weigh more than 180, and Mr. Rudderham is almost a hundred-pounder. That is, counting his pad and everything.

A ninth-inning decision caused the excitement. Hostetter had gone out on Bridwell's fast run and admirable throw, and then O'Rourke batted one to Devlin, who made a wonderful stop and a quick throw to Tenney. Everybody said wasn't Devlin the grand third baseman entirely, and wasn't it nice to see 'em go fast-like, and then, "Safe!" calls this courageous Rudderham, and all baseball New York declares it's time for a justifiable murder.

Such demonstrations enliven the proceedings and take the critical mind off the final score. The Giants' bats seem on the bum, and eke the Giants' reason. For you don't win games by terrorizing a featherweight umpire.                    —W. W. Aulick, New York *Times*

When the heretofore despised St. Louis Cardinals can make the over-cocky Giants look worse than thirty cents there is surely something "rotten in Denmark."

In five innings yesterday the first Giant reached first base. Was he shoved along by the next batter? Not on your life. Not a Giant tried up-to-date baseball.

The Cardinals played teamwork yesterday and the Giants did not. The Cardinals have a team of hustling youngsters that are full of "good old ambish." I noticed that Billy Gilbert {the veteran Cardinal second baseman} had something to say all the time and wouldn't let a player fall asleep on the job for want of a little verbal prodding. But did the Giants open their mouths? If they did I failed to hear them. There is nothing like players shouting to one another. "Keep talking" has always been McGraw's idea, but Tenney, who has been a good popper-up fellow here-tofore, has gone away down into his boots.

The Giants need a shaking up—there are no two ways about it. They cannot win unless they cut out their individual work and play for the team.  —Sam Crane, New York *Evening Journal*


No matter how the team slumps, Donlin keeps his hitting up to a standard. Donlin's hustling is the oasis in the desert of long deferred hopes of Polo Grounds fans. His aggressiveness and speed in running out hits is appreciated. On ground hits to infielders, Donlin is springing them out and sliding into first base. In this way he has registered hits that would have been outs had he loafed.

—Sid Mercer, New York *Globe*


The scarcity of good material for major league umpire staffs will make it necessary to change to the double-umpire system. With batting cut down to a minimum, the slightest error by an umpire often deprives a team of a victory. There is really too much for one man to watch in a ball game.  —*Sporting Life*

───◇ SUNDAY, JUNE 7 ◇───

{On June 6, in New York, the Giants defeated St. Louis 3 to 2. Win-ning pitcher, Mathewson; losing pitcher, Fromme. Giants' standing: 21 wins, 20 losses, in fifth place.}

The Giants experienced a change of heart and manner yesterday. With the inspiration of a big crowd {15,000} they played ball and won. They weren't inert as on the two preceding days. On the contrary they had partaken of pepper. The result was a snappy, well-played game. Mathewson pitched an evenly effective game, but the Cardinals gave him a stiff battle.

The eighth inning was bristling and critical. Gilbert bunted safely. Then Mathewson did something he rarely does. He passed two men in succession, {Bill} Ludwig and {Al} Shaw. Byrne flied to Seymour and Gilbert hotfooted it for the plate. Seymour's throw shot past Needham, and Gilbert scored. Had Ludwig been spry he too would have scored, but he lost time around third base. Mathewson had backed up cleverly and fielded the ball from Needham in time to catch Ludwig.

—New York *Sun*

————◇ MONDAY, JUNE 8 ◇————

Roger Bresnahan's return today ought to brace up the team, for when Roger works behind the bat there always seems to be more life and aggressiveness on the field. Tom Needham has done nobly in Bresnahan's place, and his timely hitting has helped win several games. His throwing has turned back base runners, but somehow Needham doesn't stir up the infield as Bresnahan does.

That vague thing known as baseball luck was with the Giants Saturday. Just as sure as Mr. Rudderham isn't a good umpire, the last two-bagger of Donlin's was at least a foot foul. This hit broke a tie and won the game. When Mathewson has to pitch one of his best games to get a 3–2 decision over St. Louis, and the Giants have to have all the luck to get the winning run, either the McGrawites are playing way below form or the Cardinals are a great team.

Mr. Rudderham was not so much to blame, however, as he was standing behind the pitcher's box with the sun shining in his eyes. The ball skimmered over the grass outside of third base, and Rudderham had to make a quick guess. He hesitated a moment and then took the cue from the coachers and started to follow Donlin around the bases. The umpire evened up in the eighth. Mathewson threw Shaw at least five strikes, but

Rudderham walked him and forced Gilbert around to third base, from where he scored on Byrne's sacrifice fly.

—Sid Mercer, New York *Globe*

———— NATIONAL LEAGUE STANDINGS ————

|  | W | L | PCT. | GB |  | W | L | PCT. | GB |
|---|---|---|---|---|---|---|---|---|---|
| Chicago | 25 | 15 | .625 | — | New York | 21 | 20 | .512 | 4½ |
| Cincinnati | 23 | 17 | .575 | 2 | Boston | 19 | 22 | .463 | 6½ |
| Pittsburgh | 22 | 18 | .550 | 3 | St. Louis | 19 | 27 | .413 | 9 |
| Philadelphia | 19 | 18 | .514 | 4½ | Brooklyn | 15 | 26 | .366 | 10½ |

————◇ **TUESDAY, JUNE 9** ◇————

{On June 8, in New York, the Giants defeated St. Louis 4 to 0. Winning pitcher, McGinnity; losing pitcher, Raymond. Giants' standing: 22 wins, 20 losses, in fourth place.}

The talk of Mr. McGinnity's projected release reached the ears of the Iron Man only yesterday, being somewhat delayed in transmission. "Oh, well," quoth this wondering marvel, "if they feel like that I'll give them something to release me for."

So he fanned seven scarlet socks and shut out St. Louis neat and systematic. If we don't want pitchers who practice this sort of specialty, now's our chance to make an advantageous deal. Who wants McGinnity? A neat dresser on and off, and we pay fares. Let's hear the bids.

—W. W. Aulick, New York *Times*

Manager Jawn McGraw made plenty of noise yesterday on the third-base coaching line. He yelped at {Cardinal pitcher} "Bugs" Raymond, he chided {manager John} McCloskey, he shrieked at the umpire, and he got away with it all. He got away with it because he has been reading *The Virginian* {Owen Wister's classic Western novel, published in 1902}, and every time he says anything to the umpire now he smiles. It's a good system.

—William F. Kirk, New York *American*

# ◇ WEDNESDAY, JUNE 10 ◇

{On June 9, in New York, the Giants defeated Pittsburgh 8 to 2. Winning pitcher, Crandall; losing pitcher, Camnitz. Giants' standing: 23 wins, 20 losses, in fourth place.}

A goodly crowd—10,000 or maybe more—made the pilgrimage to the ball lot at the end of the "L" {elevated train} and probably many were attracted by the one, only, and invincible Hans Wagner, whose prowess as a ballist is ringing over the nation.

But Hans suffered an eclipse practically total. He didn't knock seven or eight balls out of the premises, he didn't steal home from first base, nor did he, in fact, do anything to make Rome meow, let alone howl.

Instead, the gathering was treated to an old-time exhibition of base-ball à la Giants—as they used to play it regularly in the misty past.
                                                              —New York *Herald*

Crandall sent up a lot of puzzling twisters, and it was hard for the Pirates to meet the ball solidly. He also cinched his own game by lifting the ball into the left-field seats in the fifth, with Devlin and Bridwell on base.                                                  —New York *Sun*

Samuel Strang Nicklin, who has served as utility player for the Giants for several years, was yesterday sold to the Baltimore club of the Eastern League.                                        —New York *Times*

Some day it is to be hoped that baseball owners will enact a law placing fines on players who use profanity in public. Men in uniform have no right to insult patrons by careless language. How quickly a player would take the matter up if a spectator should heedlessly indulge in bad grammar and worse in the presence of the player's mother or sister. Chew gum and cut out the words in black letters.
                                    —John B. Foster, New York *Evening Telegram*

{On June 10, in New York, the Giants lost to Pittsburgh 1 to 0. Winning pitcher, Leever; losing pitcher, Wiltse. Giants' standing: 23 wins, 21 losses, in fourth place.}

These Pittsburgh parties didn't terrorize us yesterday—they just outspeeded us a bit in the fourth inning and scratched in a run. These are the depressing details: Clarke hits past second. Then up comes Wagner, the extensively advertised shortstop. Mr. Wagner gives our tall young pitcher Wiltse such a hard look! Poor Wiltse quivers in every fiber. Cy Seymour, our charley-horsed centerfielder, moves to the fence limit, and wonders anxiously if this will be far enough. Mike Donlin edges out to the end of the bleachers. Everybody who hasn't had his breath bated before has it done now. And Wagner strikes out.

Pirates, eh?

The Pittsburgh second baseman, a gent with a serial name, called variously Abby and Battey {Abbaticchio}, goes out on a sacrifice. First baseman {Jim} Kane then drives the ball to Bridwell, who flops it to Tenney, not quite in time to nip the runner. Tenney slams it home, but Clarke is there ahead of it by a fraction of a second. If we had been a trifle fast and Clarke a trifle slow, our cherished plate would not have been passed.

—W. W. Aulick, New York *Times*

It isn't often that Hank O'Day is caught napping, but a young player just getting his "cup of coffee" in the league put one over on Hank and Mr. Klem yesterday.

Bresnahan hit a two-bagger down the left-field line. Klem {umpire at the plate} did not follow the runner as he squared around to note whether the ball went fair or foul. There being no play at first base, O'Day wheeled and moved toward second. With the attention of both arbitrators drawn away, {Jim} Kane mussed up Roger's sprint with a very palpable interference. Bresnahan stopped and stumbled, and then merely trotted down to second, not expecting that the incident had been overlooked. The ball beat him to the base by several feet, and he was touched out.

If two umpires are not enough to see all plays, why not hire a third umpire to sit in the grandstand and decide plays not covered by the other two? O'Day had no alternative but to call Bresnahan out as his back was turned to the interference. If Klem had seen it he should have so informed O'Day and in that case a reversal of the decision would have been proper. Perhaps Klem didn't see it. Many umpires will not disagree with a co-laborer even when they know he is making a wrong decision. Such dignity is unnecessary. The Giants did the only thing they could to get even. The few runners who got on first base after that trod on the toes of Mr. Kane. {This was Jim Kane's one moment of glory, for the 55 games in which he played for Pittsburgh in 1908 constituted his entire major league career.}

—Sid Mercer, New York *Globe*

In justice to Manager McGraw, I may say that he is not to blame for the rank treatment accorded "Iron Man" McGinnity. Just as McGinnity pitched a beautiful shut-out in Brooklyn, it became known that the club had asked waivers on him. At first McGraw came in for a roast because of this, but I soon learned on excellent authority that John T. Brush, with Andy Freedman behind him, was responsible for the strange move. {Andrew Freedman had preceded John Brush as president and principal owner of the Giants, and although he had sold his controlling interest late in 1902 he was still influential in club operations.} It seems that John and Andy have been trying to find a way to cut McGinnity's $5,000 salary ever since he was hurt at Waco. McGinnity has an iron-clad contract and has refused to accept a cut. So Brush decided to unload the famous pitcher, with the result that local fans are up in arms.

—William Rankin, *The Sporting News*

———◇ **FRIDAY, JUNE 12** ◇———

{On June 11, in New York, the Giants lost to Pittsburgh 5 to 2. Winning pitcher, Willis; losing pitcher, Mathewson. Giants' standing: 23 wins, 22 losses, in fifth place.}

It wasn't Matty's fault that he lost yesterday, any more than George Wiltse should be blamed for Wednesday's defeat. Both men pitched magnificent ball, and both went down to glorious defeat.

Old Honus Wagner was very much in evidence yesterday. The wonderful Teuton was everywhere, choking off sure hits and encouraging his comrades at any and all times when encouragement was needed. His huge bow legs carried him from third base to second base, and his large paws, the fingers of which seemed like tentacles of a devil fish, raked in everything that came within a mile of them. Oh, Honus, how could you do it?

—William F. Kirk, New York *American*

———◇ **SATURDAY, JUNE 13** ◇———

{On June 12, in New York, the Giants lost to Pittsburgh 4 to 0. Winning pitcher, Maddox; losing pitcher, McGinnity. Giants' standing: 23 wins, 23 losses, tied for fourth place with Philadelphia.}

About 6,000 fans came to see the Giants win the final game of the series, and after the dust had lifted about 6,000 fans, accompanied by about 6,000 grouches, plodded wearily homeward.

To come down to cases, the Giants played like a lot of suffragettes. When the stern voice of duty called, with eager base runners on the bags, the local swatsmiths had their ears stuffed with cotton. More than once a good, clean single would have sent runs home, but the good clean single was not forthcoming.

To make a bad matter worse, Roger Bresnahan sprained an ankle in the second inning, and was carried from the grounds.

The accident to Bresnahan is a calamity indeed. Needham is a good, steady catcher, but he cannot infuse ginger into the local lads with anything like the skill shown by Bresnahan, and if there's anything we need now it is ginger. We had about as much ginger yesterday as a bowl of cold custard.

—William F. Kirk, New York *American*

───◇ **SUNDAY, JUNE 14** ◇───

{On June 12, in New York, the Giants defeated Cincinnati, in 10 innings, 3 to 2. Winning pitcher, Crandall; losing pitcher, Ewing. Giants' standing: 24 wins, 23 losses, in fourth place.}

Our boys looked like sure winners during most of the game, holding a lead of 2 to 0 up to the ninth. But as has been frequently remarked the national game is an uncertain affair, and you can never be positive of anything until the last man is out. That is why 15,000 fans remained for the finish, and this is the reward they received for their patience.

Good old Mike Donlin {whose base running was spectacular} is playing like three or four men, and doing fully half of the Giants' aggressive work. —Jack Ryder, Cincinnati *Enquirer*

───◇ **MONDAY, JUNE 15** ◇───

By the way, little old New York did itself proud in attendance figures. Whether a city is a baseball standby or not is shown by how it supports a losing team. What other city could or would have turned out 20,000 people in the face of three straight defeats of the home team, and the local players putting up bush league ball? —Sam Crane, New York *Evening Journal*

Manager McGraw has shaken up his batting order, dropping Bridwell out entirely. This will give Charley Herzog his first real chance to deliver the goods. —New York *Globe*

─── NATIONAL LEAGUE STANDINGS ───

| | W | L | PCT. | GB | | W | L | PCT. | GB |
|---|---|---|---|---|---|---|---|---|---|
| Chicago ..... | 30 | 16 | .652 | — | Philadelphia . | 21 | 22 | .488 | 7½ |
| Pittsburgh ... | 26 | 20 | .565 | 4 | Boston ...... | 22 | 26 | .458 | 9 |
| Cincinnati ... | 26 | 20 | .565 | 4 | St. Louis .... | 22 | 30 | .423 | 11 |
| New York ... | 24 | 23 | .511 | 6½ | Brooklyn .... | 16 | 30 | .348 | 14 |

{On June 15, in New York, the Giants' scheduled doubleheader with Cincinnati was stopped in the fourth inning of the first game because of rain.}

Unless President Pulliam can find a way to transfer Umpire {James} Johnstone from the Polo Grounds and from the games the Giants play abroad, a scandal is liable to arise that will be detrimental to baseball.

Umpire Johnstone's inconsistency yesterday in his attitude on the rain should be brought to the attention of the National Committee.

The game was started under doubtful possibilities. The Reds made a run in the first inning and also in the second. It was raining in torrents even then. The Giants in the second made two runs. The Reds came back in the third with one more. The Giants accumulated five runs in the third and it was still pouring down. The Reds made no tallies in their fourth stanza.

Doyle started the fourth with a single, and Seymour walked. Then Mr. Johnstone got an attack of cold feet and motioned his associate, Umpire Rigler, to come to the plate for a consultation.

"What would you do?" asked the sole boss of the situation. Rigler replied, "You ought to have called time in the second inning." Then Johnstone shouted: "Time!".

But, mind you, it was not until the Giants were four runs to the good, with a prospect of making more.

That Johnstone had the original idea of making the players take the full count was evident when at the start of the fourth inning the Reds were showing dilatory tactics and he hollered, "You might as well get up here; you will have to play out the game anyhow."

Johnstone's sudden change of front can only be explained by the fact that the Giants were in the lead.

Umpire Johnstone has thrown out statements that he blames McGraw for being assaulted a year or two ago near the Polo Grounds after a clash on the field.

Captain Donlin, during the wait, after time had been called, asked

Johnstone, "Why did you decide to call time after the Giants got the lead?"

Johnstone replied, "If it had been a clear day you wouldn't have had a show."

Now is that a nice remark for one of President Pulliam's immaculate umps? If that does not show animus, I don't know what can.

—Sam Crane, New York *Evening Journal*


While the third inning was being played, Dummy Taylor appeared on the coaching lines wearing Groundkeeper Murphy's rubber boots. Johnstone failed to see the joke that was plain to everybody else and fined Taylor $10 and sent him to the clubhouse.     —New York *World*


McGraw's suspension went into effect yesterday. It was for three games, and had yesterday's doubleheader been played two-thirds of the sentence would have been served. Pulliam's order simply keeps McGraw off the coaching lines. In Johnstone's report the umpire averred that {on the preceding Saturday} McGraw had called him a piece of cheese. "And I can prove it," said McGraw.     —New York *Globe*


After it was all over Joe McGinnity, still in uniform, was sitting on the balcony of the clubhouse, smoking a pipe and basking in the favorable smiles of the multitude as they filed out in the rain. A special officer, after the manner of his kind, was hustling some small boys in a very determined manner. Joe asked the cop why he didn't take on someone of his size, and Mr. Cop replied that he would take him on if he would come down. The Iron Man accepted the challenge, descended and was hit in the eye by the officious guardian of the law. McGinnity came back strong, and it required the united efforts of McGraw and a special policeman to separate the combatants. The cop's coat was torn off his back and he also lost his job, but McGinnity will be able to pitch the next time he is called on.     —Cincinnati *Enquirer*

──────◇ **WEDNESDAY, JUNE 17** ◇──────

{On June 16, the Giants' scheduled game with Cincinnati was postponed so that Yale and Princeton could use the Polo Grounds for their Ivy League championship game.}

──────◇ **THURSDAY, JUNE 18** ◇──────

{On June 17, in New York, the Giants defeated Cincinnati in a doubleheader, 2 to 1 and 4 to 2. Winning pitchers, Mathewson and McGinnity; losing pitchers, Coakley and Weimer. Giants' standing: 26 wins, 23 losses, in fourth place.}

Revenge is sweet, and revenge is ours. The Ganzel Gang trotted to the Polo Grounds yesterday to win a doubleheader. They were met by McGraw's merry men, and the Polo Grounders handed them a double dose of disaster.

Mathewson was in fine form, so he was. The Reds were on his stuff all through the remarkably fast first game (it lasted only an hour and a quarter) and the nearer Cincinnati base runners got to home plate the steadier became "Big Six." Christy threw out his arm in the series between the Giants and Athletics two years ago, and now the poor fellow has to depend on his fielders.

In the second game McGraw handed a new white ball to Joe McGinnity, and Ganzel sent Weimer, known as "Tornado Jake," onto the firing line for the Reds. Weimer is a classy twirler, one of the best southpaws in the business. But he was outpitched by McGinnity, who never looked better.　　　　　　　　　　—William F. Kirk, New York *American*


The Giants have been getting their bumps right along. The fans are wise to the fact that McGraw and his men have absolutely no chance to finish near the top. If the Cubs win the series this week, it will be all over.
　　　　　　　　　　—Joe Vila, *The Sporting News*

# ◇ FRIDAY, JUNE 19 ◇

{On June 11, in New York, the Giants lost to Chicago 7 to 5. Winning pitcher, Lundgren; losing pitcher, Wiltse. Giants' standing: 26 wins, 24 losses, in fourth place.}

Fourteen thousand yesterday saw the Cubs play the waiting and bunting game. They saw the champions get a man on first base at the beginning of the fourth, fifth, sixth, and eighth innings, and they saw three of the five score. They also saw a sacrifice in three of the five innings.

The fans are criticizing the Giants more and more for not playing the sacrifice game. It is the only thing in a close game. They are getting weary of seeing Devlin come to bat and bang into a double play or raise a fly. For some reason Arthur never tries to lay down the ball any more, and he is not a bad bunter. He certainly can sacrifice better than he can hit. Seymour has done the same thing when a sacrifice was in order. Perhaps it is unjust to criticize these players, for they may be under orders to bat a certain way, but there is a lot of growling among the fans. When the Cubs were "laying 'em down" yesterday the remark was passed along, "Why don't the Giants play that game?"

—Sid Mercer, New York *Globe*

In the seventh inning when Schulte threw Doyle out at the plate with what would have been the tying tally, Doyle appeared to be a bit too wagonish in cavorting from second, but that was because Steinfeldt got in some funny work that escaped the argus eye of Umpire Hank O'Day. Steinie deliberately blocked the innocent Larry at third by doing the little shoulder stunt that will always slow a runner and throw him off his stride. Now, as Larry, notwithstanding the premeditated interruption, was barely nipped by Schulte's good throw, Steinie's little trick did what was intended.          —Sam Crane, New York *Evening Journal*

Although McGraw was not supposed to be directing his club, for he is under suspension, it made no difference in the tactics used by the Giants. The coaches were permitted by Umpire Klem to incite the fans to all kinds of hooting and jeering, and the players resorted to all kinds of tricks to upset Cub pitchers. One tenth of the antics performed by McGraw's troupe yesterday would have sent half the Chicago club off the field had it resorted to them in Chicago.              —Chicago *News*

──◇ **SATURDAY, JUNE 20** ◇──

{On June 19, in New York, the Giants defeated the Cubs 6 to 3. Winning pitcher, Crandall; losing pitcher, Pfiester. Giants' standing: 27 wins, 24 losses, in fourth place.}

Manager Jawn McGraw had his suspension lifted yesterday by the Hon. Mr. {Harry} Pulliam. Jawn didn't send a message of thanks to Haberdashery Harry, because he has had suspensions lowered and lifted so often the story is old indeed. But the little manager was on the coaching lines, sending suggestions to all corners of the diamond and hurling the harpoon into Manager Chance and Southpaw Pfiester, and the magnetism of the man went a long way before the final curtain dropped.

Otis Crandall, the fine young pitcher, won the hearts of Manhattan fans. The husky youngster showed his class by refusing to blow up. More than once the Cubs had men on the bags when a hit might have spelled disaster, and great was the yelping of Chance's coachers. Crandall, however, refused to be awed in the presence of greatness. His more seasoned rival, Pfiester, might have taken a few lessons from this recruit, so far as steadiness was concerned.

Before going any further, let us dwell on a phenomenal piece of fielding. In the fifth inning, Pfiester led off with a clean single and took second on Evers' sacrifice. Artie Hofman smashed one hard and cruelly toward the centerfield ropes. It looked like a certain home run. Seymour started with the crack of the bat, hurried over the greensward like a leopard, gave a great leap skyward at the "flycological" moment, and speared the ball with his bare hand. There was a hush for a moment until Seymour lit on the grass with the ball in his possession.

Then—well, you might buy a seat for every game during the rest of the season and never hear such an outburst of applause again. Even the hardened regulars got up in their seats and yelled like Roosevelt rooters.

Fair women in the upper tier waved their M. W. {Merry Widow} lids until the hatpins fell into the necks of the fanatics beneath, but the fanatics plucked out the hatpins and kept on shrieking. It was perhaps the greatest ovation ever given a ball player for a fielding performance.

—William F. Kirk, New York *American*

───◇ SUNDAY, JUNE 21 ◇───

{On June 20, in New York, the Giants defeated Chicago 4 to 0. Winning pitcher, Mathewson; losing pitcher, Fraser. Giants' standing: 28 wins, 24 losses, in fourth place.}

The oldest baseball inhabitant remembers only one other game when more persons assembled on the Polo Grounds than yesterday, and he doesn't remember that very well. At 2 o'clock, an hour and a half before the time for play, they were selling nice, soft standing room, and nothing else.

Half an hour before post time the overflow broke through the confines and streamed out on the field. A band of special policemen had as much luck getting them off the green as Old King Canute had when he tried to boss the bounding main. So after a while the specials said the crowd could stay on the grounds, and the crowd said thank you for nothing. {This writer estimated that 25,000 were in attendance.}

Our esteemed Matty was all there. He threw 'em in fast and savage and plentiful, and every now and then Roger Bresnahan had to walk away from the plate or stoop down and pick up a little gravel, or stall in some other equally genteel way so's Matty wouldn't be so fast. But even at that, Christy was the Lightning Kid and struck out six Cubs.

Evers was a victim in the fourth. He was the first man up and had no more idea of what Matty was doing than Dummy Taylor has of that ventriloquist's turn over on the roof garden yonder. When Matty had puzzled him three times Umpire Klem made the customary decision. Mr. Evers then spoke. He spoke eloquently, pointedly, and for a long time.

"Is that all?" asked Mr. Klem.

"It is all I can think of now," admitted Mr. Evers.

"Perhaps if you had a little leisure you could think of something more," said the umpire kindly. "Suppose you go over to that nice, quiet clubhouse for the rest of the afternoon and think up some more things. You may tell them to me Monday."

—W. W. Aulick, New York *Times*

To players and faithful fans yesterday was by far the hottest of the season. The sun was scorchingly blistering and coats and some collars were peeled off in quick order. During the second inning someone in the grandstand back of the plate turned on the fire hose. The crowd in the closely packed aisles for a distance of forty feet received enough water to wet them to the skin before it was turned off.

—New York *Evening Telegram*

In New York's seventh on Saturday, Fraser tried to work Tenney on bad balls and passed him, filling the bases with two out, preferring to take a chance with Doyle. While Tenney was being passed, McGraw grasped the situation and its psychological possibilities. He sent Mathewson from the bench to murmur instructions to Doyle, waiting his turn at bat. No sooner did Doyle step to the plate than those instructions were plain. He palpably tried to get hit by the first ball pitched, but failed. Then Donlin, who was coaching, made it all the more palpable by showing Doyle how to stick out his hip. The youngster proved an apt pupil and on the next ball, which would have been a strike, he turned his back, standing almost on top of the plate, and stuck out his hip so that the ball glanced off it.. The trick was done amateurishly, was palpably intentional and did not even have the element of surprise in it. Klem was not unprepared for the trick, as Kling called his attention to Doyle's purpose the first time it was tried. Yet Klem sent Doyle to first and forced in the only run needed to win the game. Klem dared not do otherwise. He knew that if he refused to allow the trick McGraw & Co. would make a frantic demonstration and would infuriate the crowd, which already had once broken away from the helpless Pinkertons in an effort to get nearer the play. He knew that the crowd would attack him before or after the game, and he would have as much protection as the 25-cent bleachers in a cloudburst, and not half as good a chance to make a getaway. And McGraw knew that Klem knew it, and hence Doyle had only to get hit in order to win the game.

—I. E. Sanborn, *The Sporting News*

———◇ MONDAY, JUNE 22 ◇———

If Mike Donlin keeps up his present rate of gaining in the batting average race, he will finish as did the old yacht *America* which beat the British yachts so badly that the Englishmen were forced to admit "there was no second."

Donlin has a percentage of .329, leading {John} Titus of Philadelphia by 11 points. Seymour is the next Giant to Donlin, with .272, and then Tenney with .263.

—New York *Globe*

——— NATIONAL LEAGUE STANDINGS ———

| | W | L | PCT. | GB | | W | L | PCT. | GB |
|---|---|---|---|---|---|---|---|---|---|
| Chicago | 32 | 19 | .627 | — | Philadelphia | 23 | 26 | .469 | 8 |
| Pittsburgh | 33 | 22 | .600 | 1 | Boston | 24 | 30 | .444 | 9½ |
| Cincinnati | 29 | 24 | .547 | 4 | St. Louis | 23 | 34 | .404 | 12 |
| New York | 28 | 24 | .538 | 4½ | Brooklyn | 20 | 33 | .377 | 13 |

———◇ TUESDAY, JUNE 23 ◇———

{On June 22, in New York, the Giants beat Chicago 7 to 1. Winning pitcher, Wiltse; losing pitcher, Lundgren. Giants' standing: 29 wins, 24 losses, in fourth place.}

Even as in Chicago a few weeks ago, so it was at the Polo Grounds. The wonderful Champions of the World got another kick in the slats, and started for their native haunts much chastened in spirit. When twilight began to tint the edge of Coogan's Bluff, a person named Francois Chance propelled his bow legs toward the clubhouse, thinking thoughts we dare not put in type. The Chicago invaders came here with bells on, growling awful threats. They went away peaceably, pathetically, like nice, well behaved little Cubs.

The Giants outplayed the visitors in every department of the game. One of the biggest Monday crowds that ever swarmed into the yard sat back and gloated. They gloated when Frank Chance struck out, they gloated when Wiltse outpitched Mr. Carl Lundgren, they gloated when Kid Bridwell pulled off his sweet shortstop plays, and most of all they gloated when the final score was hung up on the old blackboard in left field. In fact it was the gloatingest gang you ever saw.

There are a few little boosts to be distributed.

Boost No. 1. Mr. Bresnahan was all there, lame leg or no lame leg. His throwing was beautiful and his batting timely.

Boost No. 2. Mr. Frederick Tenney was in grand form. Fred is certainly playing a sugar brand of ball for Manager Jawn, and seems to improve with age.

Boost No. 3. George Wiltse was steady at all stages, and won his game easily. George will win many more this season. Watch him.

Boost No. 4. Little Mr. Bridwell is playing splendid ball in the short field. He is fast, graceful and steady, and when it comes to a pinch, we'd just as soon see him up there as anybody.

Boost No. 5. Larry Doyle performed like a Lajoie. {A major leaguer for 20 years (1896–1916), Napoleon Lajoie is still regarded as baseball's best second baseman, and in 1908, in his fourth season as player-manager for Cleveland, he, along with Honus Wagner, was one of the sport's two greatest superstars.}

Boost No. 6. Manager Chance done his derndest.

—William F. Kirk, New York *American*


The Giants have up to date this season won as many games from the Cubs as they did all last year. The record stood at the end of last season: Chicago, 15; New York, 6. Now it stands: New York, 6; Cubs, 2.

—New York *World*


It was announced yesterday that Johnny Evers has been suspended by President Pulliam for three days. This was scarcely a surprise to Manager

Chance or any of the Cubs, but it angered them clear through. Umpire Klem has the reputation of being the most cordially disliked umpire on Pulliam's staff. Almost every player in the league would back up Chance's opinion on such a statement. Klem takes advantage of his position and the immunity given him by Pulliam to deride players to the point where they say and do things for which they are suspended and fined. But this does not reach the ears of the league president. The evidence on which players are punished is strictly ex parte, for the man sentenced is never heard in his own behalf. The umpire is judge, jury and prosecuting attorney and is well termed "the autocrat of the diamond."

—Chicago *News*

Cincinnati walloped Pittsburgh yesterday in a close game. Among the Pirates' few hits was a lone little bingle by Honus Wagner that had no effect on the result of the contest; but, at the same time, it established a record that will probably live after yesterday's game, the 1908 pennant race and even the National League are forgotten.

Wagner's unnoticed single completed a record of 2,000 hits in his 12 years of service in the big league. Two thousand hits! Just think about it for a minute! This is a record that will probably stand as long as baseball is the sport of Americans. How many youngsters are there in the game today who can set out with any confidence to equal it? The Seymours, Donlins, Stones, Cobbs, and even Lajoies come and go, but leave the crown with the "Flying Dutchman."

In his twelve years of fast company Wagner has played in 1,505 games. He has been officially at bat 5,772 times, and his 2,000 hits therefore give him a grand average of .347. {By 1980, fifteen players had gained 3,000 hits, one of whom, Ty Cobb, twenty-one years old in 1908, ended his career with more than 4,000.}

—J. W. McConaughy, New York *Evening Journal*

———◇ **WEDNESDAY, JUNE 24** ◇———

{On June 23, in New York, the Giants split a doubleheader with Boston, winning 6 to 3 and losing 9 to 7. Winning pitchers, McGinnity and Flaherty; losing pitchers, Dorner and Mathewson. Giants' standing: 30 wins, 25 losses, in fourth place.}

They played the kind of ball at the Polo Grounds yesterday that brings the crowds back.

The biggest inning was the seventh in the second game, when the Giants made five runs. It happens like this sometimes, even outside of fairy tales. With two men on base, the Giants four runs down, Merkle pinch-hits for Taylor. Strike lustily, good Merkle, and we shall be pleased with you.

Merkle smacks the ball over the top of the rail in the left-field bleachers and three runners trot home.

Everything is suspended for the minute. Some politicians in the front row voice the general sentiment when they say Merkle can have any office within the gift of a grateful electorate. They tell him about Denver {on July 7 the Democratic Party's national convention would open there} and ask him how he'd like to have Bryan as the tail of the ticket, and Roger Bresnahan almost kisses him. {In July, William Jennings Bryan would, for the third time, become the Democratic nominee for president.}

Boston finally won against Matty, but there is another day, and that day is today. Have a care, Hubsmiths.

—W. W. Aulick, New York *Times*


Shortstop Herzog has jumped the Giants. He is at his home in Ridgely, Md., and declares he will never again play with the Giants as long as McGraw is manager. The trouble came about Saturday night when the manager ordered Herzog to accompany the team to Elizabeth for a Sunday game, subsequently called off.

Herzog refused, saying his weak wrist would not permit him to play, and he didn't care to go along to view the game. McGraw is said to have applied an epithet to Herzog in the excitement of the mutiny. This wounded the sensitive youngster, who immediately packed for home when McGraw refused a personal apology.

The loss of Herzog will be keenly felt if anything happens to Bridwell. This leaves the Giants with but one utility man, Merkle.

—New York *Herald*

{On June 24, in New York, the Giants defeated Boston in a doubleheader, 4 to 0 and 7 to 1. Winning pitchers, Wiltse and Mathewson;
losing pitchers, Lindaman and Young. Giants' standing: 32 wins, 25 losses,
in third place.}

The Gingery Giants copped two more yesterday, and Josephus Kelley
led his band of braves to the Elevated train with not a sign of a smile on
his freckled map. Crushed by their double defeat, they stumbled into
their seats and cussed the guards all the way downtown.

It is well that we didn't have to do much shuddering, because the
weather was so beastly sultry the nerves needed a rest. One rooter in the
right-field bleachers was overcome, but he must have hailed from Boston,
as he shouted "Summon a physician!" before he wilted. Eighteen or
twenty needy young practitioners sprang to his relief before you could
count twenty-three, and he was brought out of his trance in time to see
the Bostonians getting their second lacing.

Wiltse pitched in the first battle and had Kelley's gang on his staff
{slang expression meaning "had everything under control"} from beginning to end. Much outspoken criticism was heard in the stands before the
game, as not a few of our brightest rooters allowed that Wiltse should not
pitch so often. McGraw refused to change his mind and put George
through his paces, showing the doubting tommies that he was crazy like a
fox. Mac is winning back ever so many old friends. All the world loves a
winner—if he can win every day.

Mr. {Vive} Lindaman started for the Kelley folks, but he didn't last. It
was too hot for him to use his spit ball, so he substituted a new one,
known in Boston as the "perspiration pellet." The formidable Mr. Lindaman, instead of forcing his salivary glands, simply rubbed the ball across
his forehead, moistening it not wisely, but too well. He lasted three
innings.                          —William F. Kirk, New York *American*


I have heard of a player backing up his own throw, but I never saw it
until Tuesday. Doyle, in an endeavor to get a slow bounder to first ahead
of the batter, tossed the ball wide to Tenney. The batter passed first and
then turned as if to dash for second, but Doyle followed the ball and got

it after it had passed Tenney and held the runner on first. So those who saw the rare play can bet that Doyle backed up his own throw—and win.

—Sam Crane, New York *Evening Journal*

───◇ **FRIDAY, JUNE 26** ◇───

{On June 25, in New York, the Giants split a doubleheader with Boston, losing 14 to 10 and winning 7 to 4. Winning pitchers Dorner and Taylor; losing pitchers, Crandall and Lindaman. Giants' standing: 33 wins, 26 losses, in third place.}

Not even in the weird imagination of the Welsh Rarebit Fiend artist has there been played a baseball game such as the first contest at the end of the "L" yesterday.

That game certainly was of the pippin variety. Even fans who did nothing but put dots alongside names of the run makers on their score cards had a busy two hours and a half. They kept dotting dots on the score card with such regularity that it looked like a contest in a polka-dot shirtwaist factory.

One fellow in the grandstand undertook the monumental task of dotting down runs, hits and errors as the game proceeded. When he had covered his score card in every available spot he used his cuffs, then his shirt front, and finally he began to tear pieces from his newspaper, putting runs, hits and errors in different pockets. —New York *Herald*

{Harry} Smith, the Boston catcher, got hit in the arm yesterday and a boy brought him a glass of water, and Roger Bresnahan, the batter, took the glass and drank it, the jolly old cutup.

—W. W. Aulick, New York *Times*

───◇ **SATURDAY, JUNE 27** ◇───

{On June 26, in New York, the Giants defeated Boston 2 to 0. Winning pitcher, McGinnity; losing pitcher, Flaherty. Giants' standing: 34 wins, 26 losses, in third place.}

Honest Joe Kelley, the man who would be king, has left our lovely city. With two games out of seven, he has gone and left us—and his loss we deeply feel. We would like to have Joe and his aggregation of ex-Giants tenting on our old camp grounds all Summer, Kelley's the "nine of least resistance."

Iron Man McGinnity went into the game with everything, including his glove and his "Old Sal" curve. Joe showed numerous marks of old age. His arm was so shaky that visiting batsmen couldn't follow its motions, and his hand quaked so quakerish-like that the ball shook its way across the plate without meeting a bat on the nose more than three times. Poor old Joe! Nothing is more pathetic than the sight of a pitcher who still imagines he can win. Poor old Joe!

The game was a pitcher's battle until the sixth inning, when Artie Devlin slapped out a lovely home run. The luck was with Artie. The ball hit the greensward about fifty feet from the right-field bleachers and bounced into the home of the proletariat. {Until 1931, a fair ball that bounced into the stands was a home run.} A fellow about sixteen years of age, with freckles on his map, stole the ball and took it home to his mother, but Devlin didn't care. Devlin wants his new shoes, that case of spirits and all the haberdashery which belongs to home-run heroes.

—William F. Kirk, New York *American*

## ———◇ SUNDAY, JUNE 28 ◇———

{On June 27, in Brooklyn, the Giants won a doubleheader, 4 to 3 and 5 to 2. Winning pitchers, Wiltse and Mathewson; losing pitchers, Rucker and Wilhelm. Giants' standing: 36 wins, 26 losses, in third place.}

Continuing their steady advance on the Cubs and Pirates, the Giants invaded Brooklyn and before the biggest crowd yet thrust into Mr. Ebbets' improved ball park, felled the Superbas twice in a long seance enjoyed by a few thousand Manhattan rooters and bitterly mourned by faithful adherents of the Brooklyn team whose slogan is "We care not how many games they lose to other teams just so they beat New York."

Mathewson was a hero to those who came across the river to cheer for their Giants. Not only did he go the full route in the second game, but he went to Wiltse's rescue in the first. The Donovanites had been touching up "Hooks" {Wiltse's nickname alluded to the shape of his nose} rather freely, and they finally established a tie in the eighth. After New York nosed ahead in the ninth, McGraw decided to take no more chances. He chased Matty to the box and before the dazed Donovanites knew they were being counted out he whiffed three in a row.

Mathewson continued to hurl the ball into Bresnahan's mitt during the short interval between games and then took up his pitching burden again. The second game was not as keenly relished by the spectators as the first, for Mathewson never lost control of the situation. He seemed to just breeze along under wraps. Whenever the foundation for a Brooklyn rally was laid, "Big Six" steamed up and made the batters miss.

—New York *Press*

————◇ **MONDAY, JUNE 29** ◇————

Are some ball players being robbed of more base hits by a ruling of President Harry Pulliam than by fancy fielding stunts? This is being asked by many scorers and fans.

Pulliam ruled that when a ball is hit to a fielder, and that fielder attempts to force another player but fails, the batsman should be given a fielder's choice instead of a hit, unless it was clear that the fielder could not have thrown him out at first.

It seems like an injustice to say a batsman reached first on a fielder's choice when his wallop panned out to be as valuable as a hit. But President Pulliam says the batsman does not get a hit, so batting averages will be computed accordingly. —Brooklyn *Eagle*

————— NATIONAL LEAGUE STANDINGS —————

| | W | L | PCT. | GB | | W | L | PCT. | GB |
|---|---|---|---|---|---|---|---|---|---|
| Chicago ..... | 37 | 21 | .638 | — | Philadelphia . | 26 | 28 | .481 | 9 |
| Pittsburgh ... | 40 | 24 | .625 | — | Boston ...... | 27 | 36 | .429 | 12½ |
| New York ... | 36 | 26 | .581 | 3 | St. Louis .... | 24 | 40 | .375 | 16 |
| Cincinnati ... | 32 | 30 | .516 | 7 | Brooklyn .... | 21 | 38 | .356 | 16½ |

———— ◇ **TUESDAY, JUNE 30** ◇ ————

{On June 29, in Brooklyn, the Giants lost 11 to 7. Winning pitcher, Holmes; losing pitcher, Crandall. Giants' standing: 36 wins, 27 losses, in third place.}

More heat prostrations were at Washington Park yesterday than in all the rest of the city combined. When the Giants' outfielders crawled to the dressing rooms after the game they feebly asked for the score, and were told that Brooklyn had won 11 to 7. "Is that all?" asked Mike Donlin, as he tried to get under two shower baths at once. The Brooklyn players hit the ball so often and so hard that Donlin, Shannon and Seymour ran around with their tongues hanging out. Crandall, McGinnity and Malarkey took turns in the box, but each was hit hard.

—New York *Tribune*

———— ◇ **WEDNESDAY, JULY 1** ◇ ————

{On June 30, in Brooklyn, the Giants won 3 to 0. Winning pitcher, Taylor; losing pitcher, Pastorius. Giants' standing: 37 wins, 27 losses, in third place.}

"Dummy" Taylor was opposed by Pastorius, and it was the Silent Man all the way. The Brooklyn twirler was not hit much harder, but he didn't have "Dummy's" control.

Taylor has not had a good season so far, and there were rumors of his being a "has been," but he fooled a few persons yesterday. He was never in better form, and the Superbas couldn't hit the ball where there wasn't a Giant fielder. Five safe drives was their total.

—New York *Tribune*

According to advice from Cincinnati, the New York National League club has just closed one of the greatest deals ever pulled off in baseball. It is authoritatively stated that Manager McGraw outbid several other major league clubs and will secure Pitcher {Richard} "Rube" Marquard of the

Indianapolis team of the American Association for $11,000, more than has ever been paid for the release of any single player.

The other player who figures in the deal is Jack Meyers of the St. Paul club. Meyers, a catcher, attracted so much attention this season he was sought by several American League managers. He is said to be a full-blooded Chippewa Indian. The price paid for Meyers is reported to be $6,000.

Information of the deal comes from Cincinnati because details of such deals must be filed with the National Commission, of which Garry Herrmann, owner of the Cincinnati club, is president. The papers were filed there yesterday.

Marquard is the twirling sensation of the year in minor league circles. His succession of victories has kept Indianapolis close to the top in the American Association, and among his victories are two no-hit games.

—New York *Globe*

------◇ **THURSDAY, JULY 2** ◇------

{On July 1, in Brooklyn, the Giants lost 4 to 0. Winning pitcher, Rucker; losing pitcher, McGinnity. Giants' standing: 37 wins, 28 losses, in third place.}

Rucker, Brooklyn's clever left-handed artisan, toppled the Giants at will and blanked them impressively. Rucker distributed eight strikeouts; he made the ball talk, hum and cut curious capers, and often hostile batters didn't know whether they were hitting at a baseball, a pea or an elusive streak.          —New York *Sun*

Mabel Hite (Mrs. Mike Donlin) and a friend lunched at Washington Park yesterday. They captured two ham sandwiches and two bottles of soda from one of Harry Stevens' minions. {For many years Harry Stevens was in charge of concessions at the Polo Grounds, and at this time he also performed the same duty in Brooklyn.} No harm resulted, though Miss Hite's understudy was ready to step in at any moment during the performance of "The Merry-Go-Round" last night.

—New York *Globe*

{On July 2, in New York, the Giants defeated Philadelphia 4 to 3. Winning pitcher, Mathewson; losing pitcher, Foxen. Giants' standing: 38 wins, 28 losses, in third place.}

Christy Mathewson wasn't at his best yesterday, and the Giants have given better exhibitions of the great national game, but Christy and his teammates were good enough to win, and the victory will look just as good toward the shank of the season as a no-hit shut-out.

The terrible heat kept down the attendance, but those present witnessed one of the tightest struggles of the season. Matty was wilder than he has been for some time. Seldom does the big fellow pass two men in a row, but he did it in the first inning. He seemed uncertain in other innings, and his support was anything but superlative. Still we won.

Umpire Rigler, unaccompanied by the genial Mr. Johnstone, had his work cut for him, and held the unruly ball gainers fairly well in hand, considering he was out there all by his dear little lonesome. Nobody seemed to know where Rigler's pal Johnstone might be, and nobody seemed to give a gosh darn.

Our manager, Gentle Jawn McGraw, he of the shrinking, retiring disposish, had a terrible run-in with Rigler in the second chapter, claiming that Foxy {Bill} Foxen had done the balk act. Jawn put it to Rigler in a calm, statesmanlike way, never forgetting his dignity.

"Did you call me a piece of cheese?" demanded Rigler.

"By no means," retorted Manager Jawn. "I said you were the hole in a piece of cheese."

Umpire Rigler shuddered. It was the first time he had been called anything so insignificant as the hole in a piece of cheese. "Go home!" hissed Umpire Rigler. "Avaunt!" And Jawn avaunted.

—William F. Kirk, New York *American*

{On July 3, in New York, the Giants defeated Philadelphia 8 to 3. Winning pitcher, Crandall; losing pitcher, Sparks. Giants' standing: 39 wins, 28 losses, in third place.}

With their ambitions centered on passing the Pesky Pirates and Chesty Cubs, the Giants kicked the wind out of the Peculiar Phillies. Otis Crandall improved after a bad start and held Murray's men in the hollow of his hand after the fourth inning.

The difference in the play of the teams shows in the box score. The hits and errors were the same, ten and three, and yet the home crew scored five more tallies than its opponents. Manager Billy Murray thought part of this discrepancy was due to the desire of his players to keep their uniforms clean. Titus did not slide to the plate in the first inning and the failure to hit the dirt cost him {a fine of} $25. Two other sluggish athletes from the banks of the Schuylkill were also massacred at the fourth bag and died in an erect attitude.          —New York *Press*

——◇ **SUNDAY, JULY 5** ◇——

{On July 4, in New York, the Giants defeated Philadelphia in a doubleheader, 1 to 0 and 9 to 3. Winning pitchers, Wiltse and McGinnity; losing pitchers, McQuillan and Corridon. Giants' standing: 41 wins, 28 losses, in third place.}

The Giants twice defeated the Phillies yesterday, and last night started on the second Western trip. The Fourth of July celebration showed a new world's record in George Wiltse's retirement of the Quakers without a hit or run in ten innings in the morning game. In the past, hurlers have gone one round beyond nine without allowing hits, but something turned up to hoodoo the performance. Wiltse came within an ace of letting down his opponents in nine rounds without a man reaching first base. Unfortunately Charles Rigler, Pulliam's fighting umpire, suffered from an attack of astigmatism on the fourth serve to George McQuillan, the 27th Phillie who strode to the plate, and called a ball when Wiltse put a third strike over. Then the left-hander hit his rival hurler in the arm, and Philadelphia got its only man on base in the game.

—New York *Press*

In recognition of their clean-up of the series with the Phillies, Presi-

dent Brush gave each member of the team an order for a new pair of
baseball shoes worth $7.50 each.               —*Sporting Life*

## ————◇ MONDAY, JULY 6 ◇————

CINCINNATI, July 6—The Giants left New York at 9 o'clock Saturday
night, and arrived here in time for supper last night, tired and thoroughly
wilted. It was a fearful ride, and it was well that the start was made early,
as a good night's rest has made the players fresh again.

          —Sid Mercer, New York *Globe*


     Ever since the Pirates paid a visit to the Polo Grounds June 19–21, the
Giants have made teamwork the most distinguishable part of their games
and have climbed consistently. I may appear egotistical, but ever since I
brought attention to the woeful lack of up-to-date baseball the Giants
were playing a month ago, their total lack of playing for one run by
banging the ball into double plays and force-outs, instead of bunting by
"suicide splash" methods, the Giants adopted the plan and have carried it
through with the most successful results. I, of course, did not originate
the idea, but I did assist in bringing to the notice of McGraw and the
players their faults. It was like an outsider looking over the shoulders of
card players and seeing mistakes they possibly could not.

          —Sam Crane, New York *Evening Journal*


     Mike Donlin and Hans Wagner are having a fight for batting honors
in the National League. Turkey leads the league with the fine percentage
of .342. The Flying Dutchman added fifteen points to his average last
week and is second, with .336.           —New York *World*


CINCINNATI, July 6—Another move on the baseball checkerboard has
landed Outfielder Harry McCormick in John McGraw's bandwagon once
more. Following a conference between Manager Murray of the Phillies
and McGraw last Saturday, title to McCormick passed to New York. He

will report here tomorrow and will be a utility outfielder and emergency batsman.

New Yorkers will remember him as one of McGraw's outfielders in 1904, the first year the Giants won the pennant under McGraw's management.                                          —Sid Mercer, New York *Globe*


Fred Merkle pulled up lame on the road from New York to Cincinnati yesterday and is nursing a badly swollen foot, the origin of which is not clear to him.                    —New York *Evening Telegram*


## ——— NATIONAL LEAGUE STANDINGS ———

| | W | L | PCT. | GB | | W | L | PCT. | GB |
|---|---|---|---|---|---|---|---|---|---|
| Pittsburgh ... | 43 | 27 | .614 | — | Philadelphia . | 27 | 34 | .443 | 11½ |
| Chicago ..... | 41 | 26 | .612 | ½ | Boston ...... | 31 | 39 | .443 | 12 |
| New York ... | 41 | 28 | .594 | 1½ | St. Louis .... | 27 | 42 | .391 | 15½ |
| Cincinnati ... | 36 | 34 | .514 | 7 | Brooklyn .... | 25 | 41 | .379 | 16 |


## ———◇ TUESDAY, JULY 7 ◇———

{On July 6, in Cincinnati, the Giants won 2 to 1. Winning pitcher, Mathewson; losing pitcher, Ewing. Giants' standing: 42 wins, 28 losses, in third place.}


CINCINNATI, July 6—Steadily climbing the ticklish pennant ladder, the Giants used Cincinnati as a stepping stone today.

Larry Doyle kept up his brilliant work by which he enthused Polo Grounds fans last week. New York made six hits and Doyle got three of them. Also, Larry capered about second base in clever style, making five pretty assists and three put-outs.

To show how futile the home players' efforts were at bat, 22 put-outs were made by the New York catcher and infield.

                                          —New York *Tribune*

## ──── ◇ WEDNESDAY, JULY 8 ◇ ────

{On July 7, in Cincinnati, the Giants lost 4 to 3. Winning pitcher, Spade; losing pitcher, Crandall. Giants' standing: 42 wins, 29 losses, in third place.}

Coming from behind with great speed, the Reds, who looked like certain losers for six rounds at League Park yesterday, nosed out the fighting Giants. Just when the pessimists were predicting a shut-out for our boys, said boys found their batting eyes, put them to the best possible use and turned a 3 to 0 defeat into a very ornate 4 to 3 win.
—Jack Ryder, Cincinnati *Enquirer*


## ──── ◇ THURSDAY, JULY 9 ◇ ────

{On July 8, in Cincinnati, the Giants lost 8 to 3. Winning pitcher, Weimer; losing pitcher, McGinnity. Giants' standing: 42 wins, 30 losses, in third place.}

With the utmost brutality, the Reds attacked the chesty Giants yesterday and blew them off the baseball map. Rapping one star pitcher after another with great freedom, our noble fourth-placers achieved a total of a dozen bingles.

Joe McGinnity lasted six rounds, and then sought a shady seat on the bench. The removal of the Iron Man brought George Wiltse on, stalking in stately fashion to the mound and modestly acknowledging the applause in recognition of his great no-hit game last Saturday. But Wiltse found the Reds a more difficult proposition than the Phillies. The southpaw remained for exactly one round.

The poor work of the Giants in the field was relieved by a wonderful catch by Mike Donlin, which saved several runs in the lucky seventh when he went back at great speed, did a few acrobatic stunts with his arms and legs, leaped seven feet into the sunshine and came down with the ball in his fin.
—Jack Ryder, Cincinnati *Enquirer*

Another surgeon was called in to treat Merkle last night. The operation yesterday left the big fellow resting easy, but he is not out of danger yet, and McGraw will take no chances. Merkle cannot be moved and will probably stay here until next week and then go to his home in Toledo. He has little chance to get back in harness this month.

—New York *Globe*

Rube Marquard is not swelled up in the least because a big bunch of money will be handed over for him. He says: "There is nothing to gloat over. If I am worth that amount of money to the New York club, I should get a good salary. I tried to break into the big company with the Cleveland club, but they could not see where I came in at all. When I start in fast baseball, I want to get a salary that will make it worthwhile." And they say he is a rube.                    —New York *Globe*

## ———◇ FRIDAY, JULY 10 ◇———

{On July 9, in Cincinnati, the Giants won 2 to 1. Winning pitcher, Mathewson; losing pitcher, Coakley. Giants' standing: 43 wins, 30 losses, in third place.}

Mr. J. J. McGraw paid the Reds a high compliment yesterday by selecting Christopher Mathewson to twirl the final game of the Giant series. This desperate move was taken to avoid a third straight defeat. Matty was called on, instead of being saved for Pittsburgh today, as had been McGraw's intention.

The Reds could not do much with the great checker player. No team can when Matty is in form. Dr. Coakley was only a shade less effective than the great Mathewson. The eminent dentist had his famous slow ball frequently on exhibition, and it was a puzzler for fair. His work would have beaten any pitcher but Matty.

—Jack Ryder, Cincinnati *Enquirer*

PITTSBURGH, July 10—Dave Brain has been transferred from Cincinnati to the Giants. McGraw closed the deal with Manager Ganzel after yesterday's game. He takes Merkle's place as utility infielder. The deal was an outright purchase, price not stated.

—Sid Mercer, New York *Globe*

———◇ **SATURDAY, JULY 11** ◇———

{On July 10, in Pittsburgh, the Giants lost 7 to 6. Winning pitcher, Leever; losing pitcher, Wiltse. Giants' standing: 43 wins, 31 losses, in third place.}

A sizzling, sweltering, nerve-racking, now-you-have-it-now-you-haven't game. That's the sort of seance the Pirates and Giants gave on Exposition Field yesterday.

First the Giants took a big lead only to be overtaken. Clarke and his men forged to the front, and again did McGraw coach his combination to the tie-it-up stage.

In the eighth the Pirates went one to the merry, but they were overtaken again in the first of the ninth. Naturally all this whipsawing got on the nerves of the panting push, and it was not to be wondered that more than one spectator fell back and gasped for breath.

With the score standing 6 to 6 the Pirates prepared to make a flying finish.

{Tommy} Leach was first up. On the way to the plate he was stopped by Clarke, who whispered a few words of encouragement to his right lieutenant.

Tommy nodded, smiled and pushed his little personality plateward.

Leach spat on his small, sun-kissed salary grabbers and faced the tall heaver, Wiltse. Two balls and two strikes had been registered when Leach crossed his toes and let fly at the next delivery.

There was a noise like the fall of a truck horse on a board sidewalk. The ball and bat kissed and parted forever. "I am going on a long journey," shrieked the blistered bulb, and the bat chuckled, "On your way, and I don't care if you never come back."

Mike Donlin and Cy Seymour hastened hence.

Around the bases sped the little Leach lad. Those short legs of his were moving like piston rods on a record-breaking electric engine.

Rounding first he hiked for second, Donlin and Seymour still in quest of the bounding bulb.

Passing second Tommy dodged under the dust and came up at third. Seymour and Donlin, still doing the sleuth act, were now near the fence in right center.

Leaving third Leach began to show signs of fatigue. His action was not quite so spirited, yet he was going some.

At this juncture the ball was retrieved and hurled with great haste in the direction of the shinguarded Mr. Bresnahan.

On came Tommy. Fans stood on the seats and yelled. Some of them may have stood on their heads. No one was seated.

When within ten feet of the plate Leach threw his frame to earth, it slid over the pan an instant before Bresnahan got his mitts on the ball.

So energetically had Leach exerted himself he was "all in" and could not have pushed a grain of sand out of his way if he had tried with both hands and feet.

Wagner, Clarke and other Pirates ran out, kissed Tommy, lifted him from the dirt, embraced him and then carried him to the bench.

After carrying the little one to the shade of the bench the Clarkesonians did an Indian dance, the spectators tried to get their nerves into working order and it was all over.

—C. B. Power, Pittsburgh *Dispatch*

CINCINNATI, July 11—Reports from the Good Samaritan Hospital, where Fred Merkle underwent two operations on his foot for blood poisoning, are to the effect that serious complications have arisen. Unless they are checked it is likely that the foot will be amputated.

The foot is about the size of a big pumpkin, and even the lower leg up to the knee is affected. —New York *Evening Journal*

{On July 11, in Pittsburgh, the Giants lost 6 to 2. Winning pitcher, Willis; losing pitcher, Taylor. Giants' standing: 43 wins, 32 losses, in third place.}

The Pirates still are the Giants' hoodoos. The victory of the Pittsburghs was their seventh of the season over the New Yorks, who thus far have taken the Corsairs {the Pirates} only twice. The issue yesterday was again decided by the men on the firing line. Willis was eight times better than Luther Taylor, the sum total of the Giant clubbing attack being a three-bagger by Mike Donlin. —New York *Press*

Game to the core and loyal to Pittsburgh is the Mighty Hans Wagner. During the past week it was noticed that Wagner was missing chances and making more errors than had been chalked up against him in many months. Yesterday an explanation of Wagner's foozles was forthcoming. He has been playing with a finger so disjointed and inflamed that when he showed it to Manager Clarke the latter asked Hans to take a rest in order to have the injured member properly cared for. Hans declined, saying he believed the team needed his services and he would continue to do his best. How's that for gameness and loyalty?
—C. B. Power, Pittsburgh *Dispatch*

Several ministers and two or three judges were spectators yesterday. Baseball appeals to all classes. It is the one real sport.
—Pittsburgh *Dispatch*

{From an interview with Mr. and Mrs. Mike Donlin at their residence in New York's Hotel Cumberland:} "I've been before the public about ten or twelve years," Mike said, "and they have read a great deal about me. Several of my public appearances I deeply regret, and I have tried to atone for my foolishness.

"My best friends will tell you I could get in trouble easier than the man who invented it. If there was a scrap at the Battery and I was in Harlem it would be my misfortune to get to the scene of trouble just as the 'pat' wagon pulled up. But I don't take any more chances. I wouldn't stop to listen to a street organ for fear I'd get in wrong."

"Fifty-fourth street is the dead line for me now," laughed Mike, "and I never run out of the base line. I'd need a guide on Broadway. I've got a reserved seat on a crystal chariot and I'm not looking for a rain check either. Croton cocktails and cow juice is my limit."

"You look a great deal thinner than a year ago. Are you on a diet?"

"Diet!" screamed Mrs. Donlin in merriment. "If you saw him pull down half a dozen portions of corned beef and cabbage you wouldn't wonder where those home drives come from. He's the original cabbage kid."

"How about it, Mike?"

"She's got me by several feet," said Mike. "I think cabbage should be the national flower."

"Has he any other dissipations?" I asked.

"My mother's strawberry shortcake," said his wife. "The way he buries that double-deck delicacy is a caution."

"There's some talk about you going into vaudeville, Mike. Is there any truth in the story?"

"He's stuck on reciting 'Curfew Shall Not Ring Tonight,' " said his wife, "but I want to make a real actor of him."

"What do you expect to do when your playing days are over?"

"I hope to manage a team," said Mike, modestly.

"And he'll get his hope if I have to pay the players myself," said his plucky wife.

"And your ambition?" I asked her.

"I'm going to buy her a theater," was Mike's gallant response.

—Joe Fitzgerald, New York World

———◇ **MONDAY, JULY 13** ◇———

PITTSBURGH, July 13—There is absolutely nothing to do in Pittsburgh on Sunday, so it was a long, weary day for the players who were here.

—Sid Mercer, New York Globe

|            | W  | L  | PCT. | GB   |              | W  | L  | PCT. | GB    |
|------------|----|----|------|------|--------------|----|----|------|-------|
| Chicago .... | 45 | 29 | .608 | —    | Philadelphia . | 32 | 37 | .464 | 10½ |
| Pittsburgh ... | 46 | 30 | .605 | —    | Boston ...... | 34 | 42 | .447 | 12 |
| New York ... | 43 | 32 | .573 | 2½ | Brooklyn .... | 29 | 43 | .403 | 15 |
| Cincinnati ... | 40 | 37 | .519 | 6½ | St. Louis .... | 28 | 47 | .373 | 17½ |

## ◇ TUESDAY, JULY 14 ◇

{On July 13, in Pittsburgh, the Giants won a doubleheader, 7 to 0 and 7 to 4. Winning pitchers, Mathewson and McGinnity; losing pitchers, Leifield and Maddox. Giants' standing: 45 wins, 32 losses, in third place.}

Pittsburgh, July 13—By winning both games from Pittsburgh, the Giants are in a fine way to crowd the Pirates out of second place and go to Chicago prepared to give the Cubs the battle of their life.

Mathewson continued his brilliant work by holding the Pirates to three hits and no runs in the first game.

Joe McGinnity and Maddox faced each other in the second duel. The Iron Man won easily.                    —New York *Tribune*

## ◇ WEDNESDAY, JULY 15 ◇

The feud between the Cubs and Giants is of ancient origin and has several causes. One of the chief ones was the temerity of the West Siders to win the National League championship in 1906. New York critics have never forgiven the Cubs for that and whenever Chicago's team gets into Gotham it is panned in proper style in nearly all newspapers. Another cause that hurt even worse was the way Chance "showed up" McGraw when the Giant manager locked Umpire Johnstone out of the Polo Grounds and gave out the statement that the police had locked him out for fear of trouble.                    —Chicago *News*

PITTSBURGH, July 14—Mike Donlin is the first player in either major league to make 100 hits this year. Mike reached the century mark yesterday, when, in the fifth inning, he made a three-bagger. Last year this honor was carried off by Wagner in the National League, and by Ty Cobb in the American League. —New York *World*

———◇ **THURSDAY, JULY 16** ◇———

{On July 15, in Chicago, the Giants won 11 to 0. Winning pitcher, Wiltse; losing pitcher, Brown. Giants' standing: 46 wins, 32 losses, in second place.}

CHICAGO, July 15—The Cubs fell from the top perch to third place after being shut out by New York, 11 to 0.

The Giants knocked the pitching heart of Mordecai Brown, slammed Jack Pfiester to every part of the lot and stung Orvie Overall so hard it looked as if the Cubs' famous score of 19 to 0 against New York two years ago would be duplicated. {The Cubs' 19 to 0 humiliation of the Giants occurred in Chicago on June 7, 1906. The losing pitcher was Mathewson, who allowed six runs in the one-third inning that he pitched.}

Wiltse pitched in wonderful form, and the result tossed the three National League leaders into a merry jumble. The Pittsburghs gained the lead and New York took second place, both passing the champions.

—New York *Herald*

———◇ **FRIDAY, JULY 17** ◇———

{On July 16, in Chicago, the Giants won 4 to 3. Winning pitcher Crandall; losing pitcher, Reulbach. Giants' standing: 47 wins, 32 losses, in second place.}

CHICAGO, July 17—How would you like to be enjoying a fine bath under a shower, with no thought of anything except a big supper right ahead, and then suddenly have nine special messengers rush in and tell you that you had just two minutes to get on the baseball diamond and save a game which you thought was won when you started the bath?

Well, that's what happened to Mathewson yesterday. He was the man enjoying the bath, and the messengers were Giant ball players carrying urgent orders from McGraw to come back and stave off the final rush of the once-champion Cubs.

It came about in the final inning of the game. Crandall held Chicago safe until the ninth, and then went up long enough to fill the bases, with only one out and three runs needed to tie the score. In the din and confusion McGraw's voice could be heard yelling for Matty.

Five minutes before Matty had been warming up in deep centerfield, but when he was wanted it transpired that he had taken to the bath.

Wet as he was he pulled on a pair of somebody's trousers and another blouse, some stockings which were footless, and did not stop to look for socks. His feet were wet and he couldn't get his baseball shoes on, so he grabbed a pair of street shoes, and, without a cap, raced out to see why his name was being yelled so persistently.

In the meantime Manager Chance was protesting the delay and McGraw, Donlin, Tenney and Devlin were working every known trick to stall. The limit of Umpire Johnstone's patience was reached before Matty appeared, and McGinnity had to go into the box, and the first thing he knew a run was over with the bases still full.

Then Matty, in his makeshift uniform, waddled across the field. A lovely finish for the third act of a melodrama, with Mathewson, the hero, ready to work and lift the mortgage from the farm. And work Mathewson did.

He was entitled to put five balls over the plate before starting to pitch, but he only shot two over and nodded that he was ready. Everybody who saw that nod knew that the stuff was off for Chicago. One more run came in while a man was being put out at first on a little love tap, and then Big Six calmly struck out the last Cub batter.

Chance tried to pull off a trick yesterday which failed. When it was announced that Crandall would pitch, Chance told McGraw that Chicago would bat first. Under the rules the home team has a right to say when it will take its first inning. {Until 1951 major league rules gave the home team the option of starting the game at bat or in the field.} Chance figured that Crandall would line out a few hits, and perhaps a run or two. The scheme didn't work. Crandall was steady as a stone wall.

—Nie, New York *Evening Mail*

Harry McCormick is an addition to the college men on the New York team. Mathewson, Devlin, Shannon, {Fred} Snodgrass, and Tenney were "rah-rah" boys. {Like Mathewson, McCormick attended Bucknell and, like all of the Giants' other college men, he played football as well as baseball.} Mike Donlin also claims distinction along that line. "I went through Harvard," says Mike. "It was during my first trip there with the St. Louis team. One morning I went out to Cambridge, entered Harvard at the front door, went through, and came out a rear door."

—New York *Globe*

———◇ **SATURDAY, JULY 18** ◇———

{On July 17, in Chicago, the Giants lost 1 to 0. Winning pitcher, Brown; losing pitcher, Mathewson. Giants' standing: 47 wins, 33 losses, in second place.}

The fans who came out yesterday grunting, disgruntled, sore, stung, and aching to vent their anger, went home pleased, flattered, satisfied and gleesome. They saw Brown pitch one of the greatest games of his career. They saw the Cubs, who had for a week played like Coshocton Gings {a Chicago juvenile baseball team} on the back lots, round into fighting trim and put up a defense that was magnificent, and they saw Joseph Tinker.

Mr. Tinker was the whole works in several innings. It was his stop and throw to the plate that started a double play killing off the Giants with the bases full and runs sprouting like alfalfa in Pasadena. It was his superb pickup and hurl to first that beat Bridwell to the base by the eightieth of a step and saved another bundle of runs, and finally Joe delivered the goods with one of the grandest wallops ever scored on any field.

That romantic biff {base hit} came in the fifth. Joe had two strikes called, and Matty was pitching a peculiar ball that came up with a high swing, then dropped suddenly and faded into the mitt of Rhino Bresnahan.

Joe aimed for the last of these, and got it. As the ball headed down deep left field, it was ticketed home run to a certainty, and the fans began to go insane.

As Joe turned third, artful Artie Devlin crossed his bows and delayed him some. He still had time and was keeping on, when H. Goat {Heinie} Zimmerman, coaching on the line, seized him and forced him back to third. Screams of rage rose from the people and the Cub bench. Joe took a look, saw that there still remained the slimmest sort of a chance, and shook H. Goat off furiously. He plunged for the plate and, Bridwell throwing with a strange slowness, beat the ball by the eighth of an inch.

The scene that followed was long to be remembered. People rose, smote one another, wailed, roared, guffawed and squalied {screamed}. Tinker steamed on to the bench; Chance rose, and called in Zimmerman. What happened in the doghouse, screened by red awnings, no one knows, but the awnings shook as if mighty whales were battling in the deep and strange sounds of lurid dialogue, mingled with the batting of heads against the woodwork, streamed forth on the people, who rubbered hard but could not see. Whatever happened, H. Goat Zimmerman came forth to coach no more.       —W. A. Phelon, Chicago *Journal*


Mr. Mathewson went into the fray with a blot upon his bright escutcheon, whatever that is. Matty sat in a checker orgy the night before with Mr. Barnes, the local sharp, and was beaten 1 to 0. These fateful statistics followed him into the arena and were painted in large letters of lime where Matty's blue eyeballs couldn't help seeing them.
                                    —Charles Dryden, Chicago *Tribune*


CHICAGO, July 18—Mike Donlin had a narrow escape from being killed in an automobile accident here last night. A big sixty-horsepower machine in which he was riding on Michigan avenue skidded on the slippery street, turned completely around, and collided with a fast-moving automobile, the property of Mayor Busse. The mayor was driving his own machine.                —Nie, New York *Evening Mail*

When Joe Tinker smashed out his home run for the Cubs on July 17, William Hudson, watching from the top of a four-story flat outside the park, was so excited he fell off the building and broke his neck.

—*Sporting Life*

PITTSBURGH, July 17—Today was celebrated as "Wagner Day" in honor of Hans Wagner. Before the Boston game, members of both teams gathered around home plate and Wagner, much embarrassed, was the center of attraction. He was presented with a gold watch and chain, valued at $700, as a token of esteem from admirers who subscribed one dollar each. Also the Carnegie Lodge of Elks, of which Wagner is a member, gave him a beautiful charm. Then a small boy came forward and, opening a box, handed him a rooster, which he said "could lick anything."

—*The Sporting News*

Mr. Rigler uses a hotel register inside his blouse instead of the wind-pad {umpire's chest protector, made of rubber and filled with air} used by most umps. The back of the book is worn outward to circumvent deadly foul tips. He stands in well with urbane hotel clerks, who supply him with all the registers he requires.      —*Sporting Life*

———◇ **SUNDAY, JULY 19** ◇———

{On July 18, in Chicago, the Giants lost 5 to 4. Winning pitcher, Overall; losing pitcher, Wiltse. Giants' standing: 47 wins, 34 losses, in third place.}

Hero Tinker is a regular little third-rail athlete. His home run Friday led to the destruction of one fan, and a two-bagger yesterday skinned the Giants in the ninth round and caused an overwrought bug {fan} to throw a fit. The rest threw cushions in a riot of joy.

Joe's triple in the sixth shook Mr. Wiltse much. That blow led to our first tally. In the eighth Wiltse gave up two more runs and in the ninth he blew up completely, his remnants scattered around the diamond in the shape of steam-heated cushions. The black pads sailed out of the stands like a shower of buzzards turned loose by dotty bugs in an effort to pay homage to the greatness of Hero Tinker. A pass to Evers laid the fuse for the explosion. Moran whaled a double over third base and the Cubs were in position for Mr. T. to apply the match. Joseph leaned his faithful pestle against the first pitch and—bingorino! Away went the ball between left and center. McCormick and Seymour approached each other, but the bounding pill passed a given point long before they reached said point. Mac and Cy wheeled about and headed for the box stalls as Evers and Moran hustled the other way and it was all over but chucking the cushions. That final swipe meant another home run had it been needed. However, Mr. Tinker will not need the extra suit, especially since he has a magazine offer of $1 per word to write a story of his home run.

—Charles Dryden, Chicago *Tribune*

McGraw, distressed by the unexpected turn in events, poked a boy in the jaw on the way to the clubhouse. Police had to escort him off the field after he had dressed                    —New York *Herald*

The boy who fell fifty feet from a stand on a roof yesterday is dead. The Building Department has condemned the stands which seat more than one thousand.                    —New York *World*

{The following appeared in "Inquisitive Fans," a column of letters to the sports editor, appearing each Sunday in the Chicago *Tribune*. The significance of this letter will come out later.}

Sports Editor of the Tribune: In the last half of the ninth, with the score tied, two men out and a runner on third, the batter hits to left and the runner scores. The batter, seeing the runner score, stops between home and first. The ball is thrown to first baseman, who touches his base before the runner reaches it. Can runner score on this? {Signed} Joseph Rupp, Chicago

Answer: No. Run cannot score when third out is made before reaching first base.                    —Chicago *Tribune*

{On July 19, in St. Louis, the Giants won, in 16 innings, 6 to 4. Winning pitcher, Crandall; losing pitcher, Karger. Giants' standing: 48 wins, 34 losses, in third place.}

New York and St. Louis fought one of the most sensational battles of the season at League Park, with the Giants finally winning in 16 innings. Not only was yesterday's game as exciting as extra-inning contests usually are, but there was added excitement on the diamond and in the grandstand. Excitement on the diamond was furnished by the fact that the umpires lost control of the game and for a good part of the time players did pretty much as they pleased.

Some of the poorest umpiring seen in a good many days might have been overlooked, as officials are liable to make mistakes. There was no excuse, however, for the way Johnstone and Rudderham allowed the players to handle them. New York had the umpires under fire from the start and the climax was reached in the fifth inning when Donlin rushed up as though he was going to do Johnstone bodily harm and followed him around making remarks. Donlin repeated the trick of following Johnstone twice more on decisions he did not like. Bresnahan handed it to both umpires and McGraw and other members of the team also took a hand. New York finally got the Cardinals started, and for a while it looked like the players were running the game. New York violated nearly every coaching rule, even yelling derisive terms loud enough to be heard in the stands.

During the game a chap in the grandstand "rooting" for New York made some personal remarks to others around him. He was requested by {team} Secretary Beckamp to be more quiet and became defiant. He made a lunge at those standing around him and it looked like he was going after Police Commissioner Bland, seated back of him. He was finally led away by two policemen.              —St. Louis *Globe-Democrat*

McGrawism, to coin a word, seems effective if objectionable.

For years the rowdyism of McGraw teams has been proverbial. McGraw has stamped his own aggressive personality on every team with which he has been identified. He remolds staid veterans to his own ways and makes a success of it.

Today by adopting tactics almost obsolete, he has browbeaten his way nearly to the front. What is the quality of baseball that is peculiarly McGraw's? None can believe that mere talk, bluff and bullying can alone make a baseball team. McGraw knows baseball; and better, he knows how to impart it quickly. Give him the physical makings and he will put brains, technical excellence and ambition into the outfit and make something of it.

One has to lift the bonnet to a man like "Muggsy."

By his works ye shall know him, and there is surely no better test that can be applied to McGraw. We don't like his methods—they beat us; we don't like his taunts and sneers and umpire baiting—but they win for him, somehow.                                    —St. Louis *Post-Dispatch*

——— NATIONAL LEAGUE STANDINGS ———

| | W | L | PCT. | GB | | W | L | PCT. | GB |
|---|---|---|---|---|---|---|---|---|---|
| Pittsburgh .. | 49 | 33 | .598 | — | Philadelphia . | 39 | 38 | .506 | 7½ |
| New York .. | 48 | 34 | .585 | 1 | Boston ...... | 37 | 45 | .451 | 12 |
| Chicago .... | 47 | 34 | .580 | 1½ | Brooklyn .... | 30 | 48 | .385 | 17 |
| Cincinnati .. | 45 | 39 | .536 | 5 | St. Louis..... | 29 | 53 | .354 | 20 |

——◇ **TUESDAY, JULY 21** ◇——

Larry Doyle got a telegram from President Pulliam telling him he had been suspended for three days for his run-in with Hank O'Day in Chicago. Doyle's suspension was brought about in the second game with the Cubs, when there was a lot of excitement over Crandall going out of the box, and McGinnity, and later Mathewson, going in. Doyle's kicking helped kill time so that Matty could dress and save the game.

—New York *Evening Mail*

Some time ago I noted that Mike Donlin was rapidly passing Hans Wagner for popularity and as a drawing card around the circuit. Today

Mike got a telegram from Chicago stating that the cup offered by a newspaper to the most popular ball player had been voted to him by a tremendous majority of Windy City fans.

—Nie, New York *Evening Mail*

Herzog is willing to return to the Giants, but McGraw resents the Baltimore boy's hasty departure and refuses to make concessions. The manager positively denies he used harsh language toward Herzog and is sore because he has been put in a bad light by the young fellow. Herzog has written and telegraphed his desire to rejoin the team, but his pleas have not been answered.     —Sid Mercer, New York *Globe*

## ——◇ WEDNESDAY, JULY 22 ◇——

{On July 21, in St. Louis, the Giants split a doubleheader, 4 to 2 (in 12 innings) and 1 to 3. Winning pitchers: Mathewson and Lush; losing pitchers, Sallee and Taylor. Giants' standing: 49 wins, 35 losses, in second place.}

St. Louis wound up one of the hardest-fought series of the season by getting an even break in a doubleheader. Three games were played, and with an even break in luck and umpiring, the Cardinals would have taken all three. That is a fine record for a team at the bottom of the league against one fighting for the lead.

—St. Louis *Globe-Democrat*

CLEVELAND, July 22—The Giants reached here this morning en route to New York for the important series with Pittsburgh which begins at the Polo Grounds Friday. By getting away from St. Louis a day earlier than the other Eastern teams finish their engagements in the West they will get a day of rest before tackling the Pirates.

Not all of the players are making this jump. Spike Shannon packed his grip and took another train last night. He said farewell to the Giants rather hurriedly, for during the second game of yesterday's doubleheader McGraw received a wire from Harry Pulliam notifying him that Pittsburgh had refused to waive claim on Shannon. Thus the player who cost the New York club $10,000 two years ago is disposed of for a paltry $1,500, the usual waiver price.

—Sid Mercer, New York *Globe*

———◇ **THURSDAY, JULY 23** ◇———

The real reason why Shannon was let go by McGraw on waivers to Pittsburgh was simply because "Spike" had shown no inclination to take care of himself and his batting and fielding fell off accordingly. His contract had what is known as a "booze clause," and it is claimed that he more than once broke that part of the agreement. Shannon is a fine ball player, and, if he takes care of himself, a great one. He is very liable to jump in and do splendid work for the Pirates, but his usefulness for the Giants was at an end.     —Nie, New York *Evening Mail*

TOLEDO, July 23—Fred Merkle, unless complications set in, will report to the Giants ready to play within a week or ten days. He was on crutches for the first time yesterday and now that he can get around his recovery is expected to be rapid.     —New York *Evening Mail*

Hans Wagner Says!!! "You can't play good ball without vim—you've got to be full of enthusiasm and energy and keep your brain going—always. You can't afford to take alcoholic stimulants or anything that has a 'let-down' effect. Coca-Cola is the only beverage I have ever drunk that had vim, vigor and go to it—that quenched the thirst and assisted my mental and physical activity."

—from an advertisement in
*The Sporting News*

With the Giants and Pirates clashing at the Polo Grounds this afternoon a series starts that may be the turning point in the National League race. The series has the big city baseball crazy. All boxes and reserved seats in the upper grandstand have been sold for today's game, and for tomorrow's contest there is a bigger demand. It would not surprise me to see all attendance records broken tomorrow, and this afternoon I look for a 20,000 crowd. That, for a common, ordinary Friday, will be going some.
—Sam Crane, New York *Evening Journal*

It is pretty well established that harmony does not exist in the ranks of the Chicago Cubs, at least not enough to call the champions a happy family. For some time rumors of dissension among the Cubs have been bandied about. Vague rumors have developed into reliable facts. The tale related here was told by two Chicago men close to the Chicago club, and verified by several players—not members of the New York club. Here are the alleged "inside" facts.

Just before the Cubs came East on their first trip it was announced that Sheckard's eyesight was nearly ruined by the explosion of a bottle of ammonia in the Chicago clubhouse. About the same time Zimmerman was sent to a hospital. Some excuse was made for his dropping out of the game so suddenly.

It has developed within the last few days that the injuries to Sheckard and Zimmerman were the result of a free-for-all fight in the Chicago clubhouse, in which Chance played a conspicuous part. According to our information, after a few hot words had been passed Zimmerman went at Sheckard. During the melee Sheckard threw something at Zimmerman.

Angered by this style of attack, Zimmerman picked up a bottle of ammonia and hurled it at Sheckard. The bottle struck Sheckard in the forehead between the eyes. The force of the throw broke the bottle and the fluid streamed down Sheckard's face.

Manager Chance, thoroughly enraged, buckled into Zimmerman, and the uproar continued. Chance is known for his fighting prowess, but it is claimed that Zimmerman stood his ground until Chance called on other players for help. Then, it is alleged, Zimmerman was borne to the floor by force of superior numbers, and while he was down he received such a beating it was necessary to cart him to the hospital for repairs. Afterward the players took sides on the matter and the affair created bad feeling all around.

Sheckard and Zimmerman were out of the game for two or three weeks. That weakened the team, and when Schulte had to quit on account of illness the Cubs could not gain ground.

—New York *Globe*

At a banquet in New York last December Johnny Evers declared that the absolute lack of friction between members of the Chicago team was responsible for its success, and that Frank Chance was like a father to the boys. Perhaps the lack of good feeling now keeps the Cubs out of first place. Perhaps Chance has become a stepfather. After a game lost this season Chance yelled at his men, "You're a fine lot of curs, you are." Not exactly the sort of talk boys expect from their father. Rumor has it that "curs" was not the word used, but it will do under the circumstances.

—New York *Evening Mail*

───◇ **SATURDAY, JULY 25** ◇───

{On July 24, in New York, the Giants defeated Pittsburgh 2 to 1. Winning pitcher, Wiltse; losing pitcher, Willis. Giants' standing: 50 wins, 35 losses, in second place.}

Nothing prodigal, sonny, about the return of our Giants eh? No sneaking in the back way and seeking for sympathy. They drove right up to the front door, unloaded their wandering bats, and demanded respectful consideration. Being entitled to the same.

For they beat the bunch Piratic in a fashion most emphatic, and they'll drive 'em from the attic, never fear.

It was fine at the Polo Grounds yesterday. A gallus band was strewn over the greensward, and the merry musicians played all they knew about "Tannhauser" when Wagner went to bat, and every time we made a good play the drums beat joyously. When we finally won there was one last triumphant blare, something on the order of those that had been given out every time Larry Doyle went to bat.

For Master Doyle was the batting hero. In the first inning Tenney opened with a single, and then Larry cracked a three-bagger to the right-field bleachers, and Tenney could hardly see to cross the plate for the noise. That was Mr. Doyle's entrance. In the third inning he cleanly singled to right, and in the sixth he doubled to the right-field bleachers. Music cue. "Conquering Hero."

—W. W. Aulick, New York *Times*

The jam at 155th street is something to be avoided on a hot day. The runway is littered with pestiferous ticket speculators who insist on pushing their wares in one's face. More inconvenience is encountered inside. The wiseacres now come on big days with a pocketful of quarters to "slip" the various officials, who always bar the way to those who are not Joseph to their elaborate system of graft but step aside as soon as they see a flash of silver.

This graft idea is strong at both New York parks and is an institution founded on the habit of New Yorkers in reaching for small change the minute they run against opposition. Yesterday a fireman in uniform was taking "handouts" at the Polo Grounds. The back of the grandstand was packed, and this fireman was stationed at the head of an aisle. Those with business down the aisle found it difficult to break through, but anyone willing to drop something into the laddie's mitt was not held up. Those personally conducted passengers were steered down the aisle by the fire fighter, who brushed aside others in his haste to earn money.

—Sid Mercer, New York *Globe*

Good old reliable Honus Wagner has turned many a clever trick when opposed to the Giants, but never before anything quite so smooth as he sprang yesterday, in the third inning, when Willis issued his only pass of the day, to Wiltse. Tenney tried to sacrifice and the little pop fly looked good when {third baseman} Leach sat down as he started for it. But Wagner raced in like a streak of lightning over half the distance to the

plate and scooping it up with his bare hand an inch from the carpet fired
to Swacina for the grandest double play ever seen in New York.
—E. J. Lanigan, New York *Press*


The veteran baseball editor of the Boston *Globe*, Mr. Tim Murnane—
in his youth a major league player of note—never said a truer word than
when he uttered his protest:

"Bar big gloves from baseball and batting averages will bob up. The
real artist can play without gloves or mitts. The old-timers worked without gloves. Take the mitts off present players and see how many great
stars are left. The big mitt has made the ball player. Men break into the
game simply because they can hit. The big mitt does the rest. Sporting
goods manufacturers are responsible for the big gloves. Outfielders should
be compelled to catch in their bare hands or use very small gloves. The
only exceptions should be the catcher and perhaps the first baseman.
Without big mitts, batting averages would jump. More action and harder
hitting would make baseball more thrilling than it is now."

We have no desire to revert to the glove-less game, but there is a wide
margin between no gloves and the present huge mitts which enable the
veriest dub to face a cannon shot. The big mitt should be confined to the
catcher; the first baseman should be restricted to a small mitt; the pitcher
and infielders should wear only small gloves; and outfielders should wear
no gloves at all.                                   —*Sporting Life*


———◇ **SUNDAY, JULY 26** ◇———


{On July 25, in New York, the Giants lost to Pittsburgh 7 to 2. Winning pitcher, Leifield; losing pitcher, Mathewson. Giants' standing: 50
wins, 36 losses, in third place.}


That baseball game at the Polo Grounds yesterday was a News Item.
Thirty thousand of our fellow-citizens were among those present.

And of course it wasn't long before the stands were too small to hold
the crowd. Then they spread over the ground, and half an hour before

play time was called they threatened to shove first base up to the pitcher's box and move third bag over to home plate. So Johnny McGraw, he gets him a bat, and he whales a lot of those fellows proper, and as fast as he drives back one bunch they're sagging out at another end, just like a bolster full of gas. And Fred Knowles, ripping off his coat and yelling "Who will stand by my right hand to hold the bridge with me?" rushes out and has as much luck as a man fishing in a bathtub.

But Joe Humphreys, the persuasive, throws himself into what he hopes to make a breach, and flitting from group to group, and pointing a terrible umbrella at each, entreatingly, "Don't crowd onto the field, fellows, or the game'll be forfeited. I ask you, please. It's up to youse." {A well-known "man about town," Joe Humphreys was perhaps the Giants' most enthusiastic and vociferous supporter.}

At which they crowd all the harder, and jump over the outstretched ropes, and from that time on there isn't any more boundary line than a rabbit, and it's two bases every time you fire into the crowd, and it's ten to one you don't catch a foul, and it must have cost the club something awful in lost balls, for giving anything back wasn't the specialty of fellows yesterday.

As for the game itself Larry Doyle won it and lost it. In the second, Wagner, first up, cracks a bad one into the crowd around left field, and that's two bases under the rules. Then he tries to steal, and Bresnahan throws to third, and everybody say it's an easy out, for Devlin doesn't have to move to catch the ball and tag the runner. But what does Hans do but jump about sixteen feet in the air, clean over the outstretched hands of Devlin, and make the base. There's something you never saw before, did you? Abby slams into the right-field crowd, and Wagner scores.

We got our runs in the fifth, when Bridwell walked, Matty hit to right and Tenney sacrificed. Then up comes Doyle, with that sheepish, sleepy look on his face that he wears whether making a record play or doing a fan, and he smashes brave and bold to left, scoring Brid and Matty, and the crowd is on the field calling for their Doyley. They do some more calling in the seventh, but it isn't the same. In that inning {Owen} Wilson singles for a starter, Swacina walks, and {George} Gibson hits into the crowd, scoring Wilson and tying the game, and then—

Leifield hits to Doyle, and lo! our Larry fumbled! What, lissome, lightning Larry? Yes, our youngster sure backslid. And what fell out when Larry missed? The grandstand and the bleachers hissed. And did that let the Pirates win? You bet your life it did. For, a minute later, Doyle makes another bad one, and Leifield scores the winning run.

—W. W. Aulick, New York *Times*

After the crowd and the importance of the game was the batting of Honus Wagner. He batted five times and five times he smote the ball safely, two of his hits being doubles. Such mighty swatting against a pitcher of Mathewson's caliber was worth the price of admission alone.

—New York *Tribune*

Each time he hit safely, after his second hit, Hans Wagner signaled to Mike Donlin in right field, "That's 3, Mike," "That's 4" and "That's 5."

—New York *World*

Fred Merkle, who had been threatened with blood poisoning, batted for Matty in the seventh. He looked pale and sick, not equal to a game yet. Herzog, the little shortstop, who had a disagreement with McGraw and quit the team, was also in uniform yesterday.

—New York *Tribune*

———◇ **MONDAY, JULY 27** ◇———

Though official figures were not announced, Saturday's crowd broke the record for the Polo Grounds. That means that considerably more than 25,000 viewed the game—not counting the thousands who stood on the 155th street viaduct and on Coogan's Bluff, nor those on the free list.

On Oct. 10, 1905, the Giants and Athletics played the second game of the world's series before an immense crowd. The National Commission, which had charge of the box office, announced that 24,992 had paid to see this game. The word of Secretary Fred Knowles after Saturday's game is accepted as fact, and Mr. Knowles declared it was the biggest crowd ever.

In neither league do club owners give out actual attendance figures.

Some profess to, but the writer knows positively that there are always some "added starters" to these statements. The New York club has never announced attendance figures, and except for the big game in 1905, estimates are mere guesswork.          —Sid Mercer, New York *Globe*

By his great hitting Friday and Saturday Hans Wagner passed Mike Donlin in the race for National League batting honors. The great Honus made seven hits in eight times at bat, while Michael Angelo failed to peel off even one safety in seven trips to the plate. Wagner's average is .340, and Donlin's is .328.                    —New York *Globe*

───── NATIONAL LEAGUE STANDINGS ─────

| | W | L | PCT. | GB | | W | L | PCT. | GB |
|---|---|---|---|---|---|---|---|---|---|
| Pittsburgh ... | 53 | 35 | .602 | — | Cincinnati . | 46 | 42 | .523 | 7 |
| Chicago ..... | 49 | 35 | .583 | 2 | Boston ..... | 38 | 47 | .447 | 13½ |
| New York ... | 50 | 36 | .581 | 2 | Brooklyn .. | 31 | 54 | .365 | 20½ |
| Philadelphia . | 42 | 38 | .525 | 7 | St. Louis ... | 30 | 54 | .357 | 21 |

───◇ TUESDAY, JULY 28 ◇───

{On July 27, in New York, the Giants lost to Pittsburgh 4 to 3. Winning pitcher, Maddox; losing pitcher, Crandall. Giants' standing: 50 wins, 37 losses, in third place.}

Before the Pittsburgh Pirates got through bumping the ball to parts of the field where New York outfielders were not they had established a lead the Giants could never overcome. As usual Hans Wagner was the chief factor in the Giant downfall. The "Flying Dutchman" hit for two bases the first and second time he came to bat. The first time he tallied on Abbaticchio's sacrifice and Wilson's double. The next time Honus scored Clarke and came through himself on a sacrifice and Wilson's triple to right.

Crandall succeeded in checking the "Flying Dutchman's" great batting streak {seven straight hits} when he made him foul out to Bridwell.

Roger Bresnahan made a season's record recently with three sacrifice hits. Yesterday he made another with four consecutive bases on balls. The last gift to Roger came in the eighth and resulted in a merry-go-round that brought the Giants within a run of the Pirates. {Nick} Maddox had been very effective until then, when he walked Bresnahan and Donlin. Cy Seymour wouldn't wait and banged a fly on which Bresnahan took third. Donlin stole second and in doing so bumped Wagner. The "Flying Dutchman" limped around as though he was crippled for life. Nearly the whole Pirate crew gathered around to sympathize. Fred Clarke and Donlin had a few words about it and Umpire Bob Emslie had to interfere. Finally Maddox tried again and almost broke Devlin's arm with a wild pitch.

When Maddox was waved out of the box and Young Cy Young appeared to take his place, it dawned on the Giants and the fans that the wily Wagner had pulled off a trick. {Irving Young, mentioned in the entry of May 10, had recently been traded from Boston to Pittsburgh.} While he was apparently in agony Young had been warming up like a house afire back of the stand. When the pitchers changed places Honus ceased to limp.                              —New York *World*


Miss Neuralgia Nearsilk, in the stand, asked her escort: "Who is that peculiar-looking person out there where I am pointing?" "That," replied the provider, "is Hans Wagner. He is the greatest ball player that ever lived."

"Mercy to goodness!" exclaimed Neuralgia, "if he can play that well with his legs all bowed up, just think what a player he would be if his legs were straight!"

A funny thing happened in the third inning. With two men out Mike Donlin smashed what looked like a sure two-bagger down the line between Wagner and Leach. Honus started after the ball like the cute little fielder he is, and actually wrapped his big paw around it some thirty feet outside the diamond. Not content with this phenomenal stop he threw to first without even looking, but Michael had just crossed the bag. Mike and Hans are in a bitter struggle for batting supremacy, so you can't blame either of them for working overtime in cutting off the other's hits.
                              —William F. Kirk, New York *American*

By disregarding the custom of letting the first pitch go by, the Pirates won yesterday. Most young pitchers try to put their first offering to a batsman over the plate. A great many times it is safe to do this, for many good hitters scorn to move at the first offering. Crandall kept sticking the first one over yesterday. Fred Clarke passed the word to waste no time. The result was that of the Pirates' five extra-base hits in the second and fourth innings four were made off the first ball pitched. From these hits came all the Pittsburgh runs.

Members of the Pittsburgh team insist Umpire Klem was handed a gold brick by allowing Doyle to take his base in the ninth. It was a good "stall," however, for McGraw and Doyle got away with it. The ball Doyle dodged seemed to have missed him by a foot, but it hit something. Spectators thought it tipped Doyle's bat. Larry stood on his head, wriggled around on one ear, came down kerflop, and then arose with an expression of great pain. He limped around in a circle embracing his own right shoulder. After a minute of this performance he faced Klem with a "dying sheep" expression. The stony-hearted arbitrator told Larry to quit kidding and come back and bat. McGraw ran over to Doyle and began to massage the supposed wound. Tommy Leach ran up and when he observed McGraw's hand under Doyle's blouse and noticed a fresh look of agony on Larry's face, he yelled: "Look out for McGraw, he's pinching him." Klem ran down to the group and when Doyle bared his shoulder the umpire saw a black and blue spot. He motioned Doyle to first, and Leach informed the umpire he had been the victim of a "skin" game, and that McGraw's thumb and forefinger, not the ball, had produced the welt.

—Sid Mercer, New York *Globe*

In fielding Wagner's second hit, McCormick was about as fast as the progress of the erection of St. John's Cathedral. And it was that way throughout the game. There may be things McCormick does well, but in this list you can't include playing left field.

—W. W. Aulick, New York *Times*

Among those present at the Herald Square Theatre last night were Mr. and Mrs. Michael Donlin. They occupied a box, and Mr. Mike's new

$350 dress suit and diamond studs attracted almost as much favorable comment as Mrs. Mike's $500 bird-of-paradise hat.

—New York *Evening Mail*

CHICAGO, July 28—It is said here that the Chicago Cubs will protest against the action of the New York Giants in not playing a scheduled game in St. Louis last Wednesday {see July 22, second entry}. The *Tribune* has the following editorial on the subject:

"That the New York Giants club is a law unto itself long has been an axiom among those who have followed that organization. The latest illustration was furnished when the New York club omitted to play Wednesday's scheduled game in St. Louis for no known reason except to have an opportunity to reach New York the day before they would begin a crucial series with Pittsburgh. Presumably it was Manager McGraw's belief that his club would stand a better chance if his players had a good night's rest before the series instead of having to sleep in hot berths and then get out and play ball.

"In order to do this the Giants had to have collusion on the part of the St. Louis club. If the latter had refused to postpone Wednesday's game, the Giants would have had to stay and play. That would have meant reaching New York on Friday morning and playing Pittsburgh that afternoon. They would then have been on even terms with Pittsburgh, which had to play Brooklyn on Thursday while the Giants were resting, then travel all night on a sleeper and meet New York on its own grounds without a solid night's sleep.

"Unless checked sharply, such practices can evolve into great injury to the game. From postponing a game to help a club it is only a short step to laying down for the same purpose."

—New York *Evening Mail*

───◇ **WEDNESDAY, JULY 29** ◇───

{On July 28, in New York, the Giants and Pittsburgh played a 16-inning game ended by darkness with the teams tied 2 to 2. Since the game ended in a tie, there were no pitchers of record. Giants' standing remained 50 wins, 37 losses, third place.}

The most sensational game of the season was called at 7 o'clock last night to allow rooters to catch their breath. When the charming Mr. Klem took off his cap and announced that nothing more was to be expected in the way of amusement, the score was 2 to 2.

Sixteen innings with two runs per side is not a usual combination, and when the sixteen innings are as full of startling situations and splendid plays as in yesterday's struggle, it's something you can tell to your grandchildren, when they come.

A statistician could have secured some very interesting dope in connection with the great battle. It would be absorbing to know, for instance, how many cold chickens, steaks and chops were left on dinner tables last evening in various sections of Manhattan; how many wives greeted their frantic husbands with, "Well, I thought you were never going to come"; how many engagements for the theater were broken.

"I know what I'll catch when I get home," said one rooter. "My wife won't do a thing but lecture me." "Tell her it was an extra-inning game," suggested a friend. "I told her that last night when there wasn't an extra-inning game," was the disconsolate reply.

—William F. Kirk, New York *American*

About 80,000 paid to see the Giant-Pirate series. The average price paid by fans is 65 cents, so altogether some $50,000 was taken in between Friday and Tuesday, or about as much as the Pittsburgh team takes in during a full month at home. —New York *Evening Mail*

———◇ **THURSDAY, JULY 30** ◇———

{On July 29, in New York, the Giants defeated St. Louis 1 to 0. Winning pitcher, Mathewson; losing pitcher, Sallee. Giants' standing: 51 wins, 37 losses, in third place.}

Fast baseball at the Polo Grounds yesterday, and praise be that Mr. Shortstop Charles took it into his hand to fumble, and that a bit later

Mr. Johnstone cautioned our Captain. "Have a care, Michael," he counseled, "or I will do you disciplinary mischief."

"As far as you like," decided Mr. Donlin, "a rebuff at your hands is equivalent to a Class A compliment."

And Mr. Johnstone said that just for that Donlin had to get out of the game. And Donlin made for the clubhouse and was in his store clothes in time that would have made the late Bysonby look like a loiterer.

You never heard of a man kicking himself out of a game because he got a base on balls, did you? You have to pay a lot of attention to the Polo Grounds these days. Things happen up there.

—W. W. Aulick, New York *Times*

──◇ **SATURDAY, AUGUST 1** ◇──

{On July 31, in New York, the Giants defeated St. Louis 9 to 2. Winning pitcher, Taylor; losing pitcher, Lush. Giants' standing: 53 wins, 37 losses, in third place.}

Now, who would suspect that Fred Tenney had a vein of humor in his Down East makeup?

But Fred Tenney did really spring a new joke yesterday, a rich one too, for it was impromptu and coming from a man who always wears a Cotton Mather visage was the surprise of the season, an epoch, as it were.

Tenney's joke, which is bound to become famous, was sprung on the unsuspecting populace in the eighth inning. Whatever it was that struck the usually mobile Frederick, it hit him hard. He started to steal second while {St. Louis pitcher} "Bugs" Raymond held the ball, and Fred made the pilfer all right. "Bugs" threw the ball to third, thinking that Luther Taylor, the runner on third, would be foolish to walk off and be "ketched." But Luther, although his hearing is not the best, has a "wiseness" that does acrobating stunts, simply stood where he was.

Then, what do you think? Fred, the funny Puritan, just ran back to first and gave "Bugs" the cracked-lip smile. "Bugs" was dumbfounded. The joke coming from Tenney was as dense to "Bugs" as a glass of beer that is all froth. So "Bugs" looked at Tenney and Tenney looked at "Bugs" and probably said "bughouse."

there was a passed ball. Otherwise Tuesday's record of 16 innings would surely have looked like an ordinary game, and we'd all have had to stay in our seats until Umpire Johnstone called the session.

Neither Mathewson nor Sallee would yield the fraction of an inch, so the fourth-inning run was a large lump of luck. Doyle went out at first because Gilbert was alert. Bresnahan bowled over to Charles, who fumbled and became immediately as popular with the spectating 5,000 as he would have been in St. Louis if he'd scored a home run on the telegraph bulletin boards. After Charles has fumbled, and Bresnahan is safe on first, there's a passed ball, and Bresnahan scores, and that's all the scoring.      —W. W. Aulick, New York *Times*

───◇ **FRIDAY, JULY 31** ◇───

{On July 30, in New York, the Giants defeated St. Louis 11 to 0. Winning pitcher, McGinnity; losing pitcher, Karger. Giants' standing: 52 wins, 37 losses, in third place.}

What a merry time it was at the Polo Grounds yesterday! The crack of bats enlivened every inning, and when the sun was setting the tired scorers announced that New York had scored eleven runs on 16 hits, including four lusty singles in four times at bat by McGinnity, which, as Muggsy McGraw remarked, is "going some" for a pitcher.
     —New York *Tribune*

It got so bad in the eighth inning that Capt. Mike Donlin, losing all interest in the game and despairing of being relieved from duty by ordinary methods, must start a doings with Umpire Johnstone.

But where is the chance for a battle when the umpire tells Mike to walk on four balls? You, nor I, gentle reader, could figure out a possibility. But Mike could and did. "It was four balls, all right," agreed Mr. Donlin, "but doggone that pitcher's ornery skin, why didn't he give 'em to me sooner? He was more than twenty seconds in giving me that last one. Why, a Manhattan Beach waiter is a section of chain lightning compared to that can of cold molasses!"

ended in a tie, there were no pitchers of record. Giants' standing remained 50 wins, 37 losses, third place.}

The most sensational game of the season was called at 7 o'clock last night to allow rooters to catch their breath. When the charming Mr. Klem took off his cap and announced that nothing more was to be expected in the way of amusement, the score was 2 to 2.

Sixteen innings with two runs per side is not a usual combination, and when the sixteen innings are as full of startling situations and splendid plays as in yesterday's struggle, it's something you can tell to your grandchildren, when they come.

A statistician could have secured some very interesting dope in connection with the great battle. It would be absorbing to know, for instance, how many cold chickens, steaks and chops were left on dinner tables last evening in various sections of Manhattan; how many wives greeted their frantic husbands with, "Well, I thought you were never going to come"; how many engagements for the theater were broken.

"I know what I'll catch when I get home," said one rooter. "My wife won't do a thing but lecture me." "Tell her it was an extra-inning game," suggested a friend. "I told her that last night when there wasn't an extra-inning game," was the disconsolate reply.

—William F. Kirk, New York *American*

About 80,000 paid to see the Giant-Pirate series. The average price paid by fans is 65 cents, so altogether some $50,000 was taken in between Friday and Tuesday, or about as much as the Pittsburgh team takes in during a full month at home. —New York *Evening Mail*

———◊ **THURSDAY, JULY 30** ◊———

{On July 29, in New York, the Giants defeated St. Louis 1 to 0. Winning pitcher, Mathewson; losing pitcher, Sallee. Giants' standing: 51 wins, 37 losses, in third place.}

Fast baseball at the Polo Grounds yesterday, and praise be that Mr. Shortstop Charles took it into his hand to fumble, and that a bit later

$350 dress suit and diamond studs attracted almost as much favorable comment as Mrs. Mike's $500 bird-of-paradise hat.

—New York *Evening Mail*


CHICAGO, July 28—It is said here that the Chicago Cubs will protest against the action of the New York Giants in not playing a scheduled game in St. Louis last Wednesday (see July 22, second entry). The *Tribune* has the following editorial on the subject:

"That the New York Giants club is a law unto itself long has been an axiom among those who have followed that organization. The latest illustration was furnished when the New York club omitted to play Wednesday's scheduled game in St. Louis for no known reason except to have an opportunity to reach New York the day before they would begin a crucial series with Pittsburgh. Presumably it was Manager McGraw's belief that his club would stand a better chance if his players had a good night's rest before the series instead of having to sleep in hot berths and then get out and play ball.

"In order to do this the Giants had to have collusion on the part of the St. Louis club. If the latter had refused to postpone Wednesday's game, the Giants would have had to stay and play. That would have meant reaching New York on Friday morning and playing Pittsburgh that afternoon. They would then have been on even terms with Pittsburgh, which had to play Brooklyn on Thursday while the Giants were resting, then travel all night on a sleeper and meet New York on its own grounds without a solid night's sleep.

"Unless checked sharply, such practices can evolve into great injury to the game. From postponing a game to help a club it is only a short step to laying down for the same purpose."

—New York *Evening Mail*


——◇ **WEDNESDAY, JULY 29** ◇——


(On July 28, in New York, the Giants and Pittsburgh played a 16-inning game ended by darkness with the teams tied 2 to 2. Since the game

{On August 1, in New York, the Giants beat St. Louis 6 to 1. Winning pitcher, Crandall; losing pitcher, Beebe. Giants' standing: 54 wins, 37 losses, in third place.}

Using {Cardinal president} Stanley Robison's St. Louis athletes as mops the Giants cleaned up on the series with the Missourians and humbled them in easy fashion. As the Cubs were beaten by the Doves, the McGrawites repose within easy striking distance of second place and not far from the top.

The doings of the fifth inning, when four runs were recorded, broke the hearts of President Robison and Manager McCloskey. Fred Beebe, the St. Louis twirler, lasted through this inning, but after he had been hit for two singles and a double in the next period was derricked. Beebe was provoked at his withdrawal and fired his glove in such fashion that Charles, the Cardinal third-sacker, received it in his face.

—New York *Press*

{From a signed article in the New York *World* by Richard "Rube" Marquard.}

When the report circulated that I had been sold to the Giants for $11,000 I was the most interested person in Indianapolis in hearing about it. But at the time you couldn't prove by me that there was $11,000 in the whole world. Funny, isn't it, that a man can be worth so much money to somebody else and maybe not have a solitary sou himself!

I was born in Cleveland, O., on Oct. 9, 1887. I hate to admit it, but you can see that I will not be old enough to vote until next October. Another thing the matter with me, besides my youth, is that I am 6 feet 3 inches tall. I weigh 182 pounds. Therefore I am a long, lank kid.

My parents, who were French, died when I was a kid and I've practically been my own boss ever since. I attended institutions of learning in Cleveland, but I got most of my education on ball fields. If a man keeps his eyes and ears open he can pick up a lot of knowledge on the diamond—knowledge that has nothing to do with playing baseball, too.

But when "Bugs" pitched the next ball Tenney darted for second again, and blamed if he didn't do the second-story act again, and all in one inning.

The funniest thing about the joke was that Tenney would have been out if a St. Louis player had thrown the ball to first and Tenney had been touched, or if the ball had been thrown to second and that base touched, but this didn't dawn on the Cardinals.

Tenney made the mistake of touching second and thus made himself liable to being put out by any opposing player who had the wisdom to tag him on the second-base bag.

A base runner cannot run backward, but it was not in Umpire Johnstone's province to put the Cardinals wise.

But Tenney springing the "gag"! Anything can make me laugh now. Fred, you little rascal!

The Cardinals were toyed with yesterday, as on Thursday, and that brings up the question of whether it is good to "show up" an opposing team as the Giants did. It appears to me as a reflection on the league itself.

—Sam Crane, New York *Evening Journal*


Mike Donlin, one of the best ball players who ever graced a New York uniform, and without doubt the most popular player the city has ever had, will make his debut as an actor with his wife in vaudeville at a local theater in October a few days after the close of the season.

Donlin and his wife, known theatrically as Mabel Hite, the cleverest funny woman on the stage today, signed contracts yesterday with a firm of managers whereby they will get $20,000 for a ten weeks' engagement. They have several offers from other managers to continue the contract on the same terms, and an offer has been made to star them together in a musical comedy.

Donlin's theatrical career will mark the end of his baseball history. He wants to quit while at the height of his popularity, and will go out of the National League in a blaze of glory. His theatrical engagements will keep him busy through the Winter and until late in the Summer, so ball playing will be out of the question. Donlin is a high-salaried man on the diamond, but would never earn as much there as in vaudeville, and he knows the value of money.     —Nie, New York *Evening Mail*

I began to grow when I was born and I've kept it up ever since. Unless I cease stretching out I guess they'll have to hoist the sky a little higher so that I can hobble along without bumping my head on it every time I step up the gutter. I'm now so tall my friends have nicknamed me the "human lighthouse" and the "animated steeple" and I have to stoop when I consult with the umpire.

I have not figured out whether my height is an advantage or a handicap. Sometimes I believe the short pitcher has the advantage because he can throw an upshoot easier than the tall pitcher, but then the tall fellow can shoot the ball downward in a straight slant that annoys batters.

I remember the first big game I ever pitched. It was in Cleveland, my home town, and a great crowd turned out. I struck out 24 men and allowed only one hit, and the next day I was famous in my town. I was heralded as a second Rube Waddell. (One of baseball's best left-handed pitchers, Rube Waddell, whose major league career began in 1897, was famed for striking out batters; his last winning season came in 1908. Marquard gained his nickname because of a supposed pitching resemblance to Waddell.)

About this time I had a big chicken farm 25 miles west of Cleveland, and when I wasn't playing ball I spent my time raising chickens for the Cleveland markets. Raising chickens paid me as well, if not a lot better, than playing baseball, but the game had a fascination for me, and I could not keep out of it.

Unlike most athletes, I have no fixed method of training. I eat anything I want, providing I think it will agree with me. My methods of living and of diet are simple in the extreme. In fact, I have always been an exponent of the simple life. Only once did I try "living high." That was after I had begun pitching professional ball. I got the idea I ought to tog myself out in gay raiment, so I took the money I got for pitching and bought a gorgeous suit of clothes. It was of a florid cast of countenance, and it made itself heard in the dark, it was so loud. To match it I had a pair of yellow shoes that sneezed like a man with hay fever when I walked. I thought I was the best dressed man in the country till my friends saw me, and then I heard so many things about my appearance that I shook the duds forever. Since then I've lived quietly.

When I report to New York, I will do my best to help McGraw win the pennant. I shall strive to show New Yorkers they were not "gold-bricked" when they got me.

—Richard "Rube" Marquard, New York *World*

───◇ **MONDAY, AUGUST 3** ◇───

Not in years has the National League had such a contest as is being waged at present. In the last two years the Cubs clinched their hold on the pennant by August 1, and it was merely a matter of speculation just how many games they would be in advance of other teams at the end of the season. The story is altogether different this season. The Pirates, Cubs and Giants are very evenly matched, and it is impossible to say which team will finish in front.　　　　　—New York *Tribune*

Donlin, Seymour, Tenney and Devlin have taken part in all Giants' games, which speaks well for their physical condition and their behavior toward umpires.　　　　　—New York *World*

CHICAGO, Aug. 3—Umpire Klem says the tendency of knights of the indicator is to call decisions too fast, before the play is really over, and thereby hangs nearly half the mistakes they make and the trouble they have with players and spectators.

"Naturally," he said, "we umpires want to make our decisions sharp, clear and decisive, so everyone may know we are not guessing. Lack of positiveness in giving close decisions is sure to bring on a heap of trouble with the players.

"Still, there is an immense amount of kicking because the umpire calls a ball or strike before the ball is actually over the plate and the 'break' is missed. That hurts the pitcher or the batter and a kick is sure to follow. The same holds true on close base decisions. A little less haste will result in a good deal more accuracy."

—New York *Evening Telegram*

|            | W  | L  | PCT. | GB  |           | W  | L  | PCT. | GB   |
|------------|----|----|------|-----|-----------|----|----|------|------|
| Pittsburgh ... | 57 | 36 | .613 | —   | Cincinnati ... | 48 | 47 | .505 | 10   |
| Chicago ..... | 55 | 37 | .598 | 1½  | Boston ...... | 41 | 52 | .441 | 16   |
| New York ... | 54 | 37 | .593 | 2   | Brooklyn .... | 33 | 57 | .367 | 22½  |
| Philadelphia . | 48 | 40 | .545 | 6½  | St. Louis .... | 31 | 61 | .337 | 25½  |

——— ◇ TUESDAY, AUGUST 4 ◇ ———

{On August 3, in New York, the Giants defeated Cincinnati 6 to 0. Winning pitcher, Wiltse; losing pitcher, Spade. Giants' standing: 55 wins, 37 losses, in third place.}

Covered with whitewash the Cincinnati Reds left the field after their first game of the series with the Giants. It was merely a fresh coat McGraw's men gave the Reds, who had been shut out 29 innings in succession before reaching town. Sharp fielding, in which Al Bridwell played the star part, kept them from home plate.

—New York *World*

Jack Barry, a good, reliable ball player, was grabbed by McGraw yesterday morning and got in the game toward the latter part of the afternoon. There are two stories as to how Barry became a Giant. The New Yorks claim to have purchased him from St. Louis, while the Cardinal management says they released him unconditionally. The latter sounds reasonable. Barry is a good player, and such men are not wanted on the St. Louis team. He knows more about the game than Manager McCloskey ever dreamed of and perhaps was trying to teach the rest of the squad how to take a game occasionally. That is the same as treason in the Cardinal camp, where last place and no work suits everyone down to the ground.

If you count Marquard and Jack Myers, who will join the team later this month, the Giants could put three full teams in the field. There are 25 men in New York uniform every day at the Polo Grounds, and

McGraw is not thinking of letting anyone go. He is not going to lose the pennant on account of accidents to his regulars.

—Nie, New York *Evening Mail*

If Bridwell keeps on stopping those seeming impossibilities and getting them over to first ten feet ahead of the runner, like he did yesterday, he'll be using the star's dressing room and getting his name featured on big type on the program. The more you watch his play the more firmly you are convinced that in order to be a proper shortstop a man doesn't have to do a kangaroo crouch and walk like a pretzel. Hello, Hans!

—W. W. Aulick, New York *Times*

It looks as if President Harry Pulliam, who never before allowed his emotions for the Giants to run away with him, realizes the advantage of having them "cop" the flag. The worthy executive is casting no stones in the runaway of McGraw. Indeed, he is even bringing pressure to further Giant interests, so it is hinted by those who know.

Evidently the umpires have caught the spirit of their boss. It must be acknowledged that umpiring will not beat the Giants out of anything in 1908. Without casting reflections on the integrity of the umpires, it is nevertheless noticeable that seldom is a visitor favored on a "hairline" decision.

—New York *American*

CHICAGO, Aug. 3—Bookmaking on baseball games in Chicago has not been profitable, and bookmakers announced they are going out of the business.

Among those who have made books and the amounts lost are: James O'Leary, $6,000; Barney Zacharias, $15,000; John Burns, $4,000; "Honey" Waixel, $2,500; Philip Wexler, $1,500; Samuel Tuckhorn, $3,500; Patrick O'Malley, $3,500; and Romey Held, $1,000.

Besides their losses, thousands of dollars have been lost by proprietors of cigar stores and saloons.

"The baseball 'fan' is too wise. He knows too much about the game," said one disgusted bookmaker.

—New York *American*

{On August 4, in New York, the Giants defeated Cincinnati in a doubleheader, 4 to 3 (in 12 innings) and 4 to 1 (8 innings, called because of darkness). Winning pitcher, Mathewson (both games); losing pitcher, Coakley (both games). Giants' standing: 57 wins, 37 losses, in second place.}

By winning both games from Cincinnati the Giants bounded into second place, coming within five points of Pittsburgh.

It took the Giants twelve innings to win the first game because McGinnity weakened in the ninth and the visitors tied the score by making two runs. Mathewson, who sat in the clubhouse waiting to work the second game, was called upon to do the lifesaving. When he entered the box one run had tallied and the second came over on a long fly off his delivery, but after that the Reds never had much of a chance.

The second game, though, was the better of the two, and J. Bentley Seymour did most of the scintillating, for on one occasion he drove the leather down to the right-field gate for a home run and on another occasion he smashed it so hard it struck the slat fence over the right-field bleachers and never came back. About 16,000 spectators roared and shouted and yelled, and women in the grandstand screamed their delight. The affair took on the complexion of a testimonial to Seymour.

—New York *Herald*

Yesterday at Washington Park in Brooklyn's game with St. Louis only one ball was in play during the entire game. The sphere started at 4 o'clock and held out for nine rounds. The Cardinals and Dodgers slapped the horsehide all over, but it always came back for more. It was fouled around in the normal way, but always came back. It was whacked to the clubhouse gate for a home run, and after the umpire looked it over to see if it was damaged it went right back to the pitcher's mound. {Brooklyn first baseman} Tim Jordan also smashed it good and hard when he fouled it against the right-field bleachers, but it was still in good shape. "It looked as if I would have to take the ball out in the eighth inning," said Umpire Klem, "but I saw the ball was game and always coming back for more. In order that it might set a record I concluded it would be wise to let the ball play until it wept down and out. Since it will hardly happen again, I would like to find who has the ball just to keep it as a souvenir."

—Mark Roth, New York *Globe*

PHILADELPHIA, Aug. 5—Frank Chance, who is a member of the joint rules committee of the major leagues, is flatfooted against the "spit ball," and is instituting a campaign to have legislation passed next Winter abolishing it. The leader of the Cubs has never been an advocate of the "spit-ball" delivery, but until his recent visit to Buffalo to watch the work of Pitcher {George} McConnell, of the Bisons, he never actively opposed it.

Several reasons were advanced by Chance for prohibiting the use of this style of delivery. It is hard on catchers, injuring their hands; it causes fielders to make wild throws; it is repulsive both in name and to the view of spectators, and its abolition would do much to increase batting.

At Buffalo, Chance found three catchers injured through the use of this form of delivery. McConnell is entirely a "spit-baller," and during the game the fielders had to lose time in handling the ball by wiping it off every time before they threw it. Although McConnell pitched a good game, winning 2 to 0, Chance refused to negotiate for him solely because he relies on the "spit ball." {McConnell would pitch for three seasons with the New York Yankees and, after Chance had departed in 1912, for two years with the Cubs, winning 17 games while losing 41.}

—New York *Evening Telegram*

CHICAGO, Aug. 5—Efforts to stamp out gambling in baseball will immediately be made by the American League. President Johnson will issue a bulletin to every American League club, calling attention to the prevalence of betting and asking each club owner to enforce to the letter the section in the league constitution prohibiting betting.

President Johnson figures that it may be necessary to arrest everyone caught making bets at ball parks. If the city police cannot be trusted to enforce the order, he will recommend that club owners assign private detectives to ferret out bettors and those receiving bets.

—New York *Evening Telegram*

{On August 5, in New York, the Giants played a 4 to 4 tie with Cincinnati, the game called at the end of 9 innings because of rain.}

There was no change yesterday in the National League standing, for stupid play and a foolish attempt by the Giants to show they could be as funny against Cincinnati as against St. Louis robbed New York of a chance to climb into first place while the Cubs and Pirates were idle. The Giants led 3 to 0 at the end of the eighth, but the Reds got to Crandall in the ninth, and, helped by some horseplay, in which the idolized Donlin figured, they scored four runs. Only good batting by McCormick and Herzog, who are so young they still take baseball seriously, saved the Giants from an absolutely needless defeat, as the run they drove in tied the game.

Tenney was badly spiked in the fourth and gave way to Merkle, who played an excellent game, making one unassisted double play that was the most brilliant play of the afternoon. In the sixth inning Kane and Huggins had walked, and Lobert drove a screaming liner to right. Merkle leaped high, speared the hit with one hand and completed the double play by beating Huggins to the bag by ten feet. He got the ball to Bridwell at second base in time for a triple play, but Bridwell dropped a perfect throw. Merkle's catch was as pretty as any piece of fielding seen in New York this season.

Crandall had beautiful support for eight innings, and he and the Giant fielders kept out of hot water until that unhappy last period.

Lobert singled to right, and Donlin, after picking up the ball, played with it, tossing it from one hand to the other. Lobert made for second base, and, naturally, beat Donlin's leisurely throw. {George "Dode"} Paskert tapped through shortstop, and Mitchell walked. Crandall was taken out and Taylor took his place. {Larry} McLean forced Mitchell and Lobert scored. {George "Admiral"} Schlei's fly to Seymour scored Paskert, and {Bob} Coulson, who ran for McLean, scored on {Mike} Mowrey's single after {Rudy} Hulswitt had made a safe hit, and the latter got home when Arthur Devlin hit him in the back in an attempt to stop him at the plate.

The Giants' trouble had been that they were too sure of the game, and no team can go against the Reds with that spirit.

—New York *Tribune*

Mr. and Mrs. Mike Donlin yesterday signed an eight weeks' contract to appear in "vodevil." They open Oct. 26 at Hammerstein's, and this booking will not take them any further than Brooklyn. After that they may roam out to Chicago and other cities.

Mrs. Donlin, one of the cleverest comediennes on the stage today, says she will not order Mike to appear for rehearsal just now. At present she is "pulling" for him to lead the National League in batting, and she hasn't missed a game at the Polo Grounds since "The Merry-Go-Round" closed two weeks ago.

"It's not true that I intend to quit baseball," says Mike. "If I divide my time between the diamond and the stage, my baseball career will help me get money in vaudeville, and I might as well get all that is coming to me.

"I also wish to correct a few statements going the rounds," continued "der Captain." "I wish it distinctly understood that I am not going to try to play Hamlet, nor do I intend to do that Salome thing, for by the time I start the weather will be too cold for such costumes. Mrs. Donlin is whipping our act into shape. She will be the real scream in it and I am content to be a piece of scenery if she hands me the part."

—New York *Globe*

President Ban Johnson of the American League might well turn his anti-gambling crusade to New York. Since the "lid" was clamped on the gambling end of metropolitan horse racing, a number of new faces, unfamiliar to "dyed-in-the-wool" fans have made their appearance. {In July a bill passed by the legislature and signed by the governor had prohibited horse-race wagering within the state of New York.} These recruit enthusiasts are noticeable for the large sums of money they carry with them.

There is more gambling on baseball about local parks now than at any time in the history of the game. It hasn't become an open proposition yet, but it is drifting that way.

New York bettors are not educated to the game yet. Over in Chicago, St. Louis and Cincinnati, the gambling element has been well schooled. But it will not take New Yorkers long to get wise if the thing is permitted. —New York *Tribune*

———◇ **FRIDAY, AUGUST 7** ◇———

{On August 6, in New York, the Giants lost to Cincinnati 5 to 0. Winning pitcher, Spade; losing pitcher, McGinnity. Giants' standing: 57 wins, 38 losses, in third place.}

There was plenty of German ginger up at the Polo Grounds yesterday. The poor old Zinzinnati boys won a game, and Manager Ganzel presented every member of the club, while said members were shower bathing, with his best regards. Manager McGraw handed his perspiring gladiators the best regards he could get out of his system, and there was enough paprika in his well-formed sentences to make a bunch of old cabbage look like a Mexican dinner.

A heavy rain came our way about 3 o'clock, and for one solid hour it came down like the first inning of the Deluge. Thousands of fans who might have attended in ordinary circumstances stayed downtown, and the gathering reminded us of an enthusiastic bunch of Highland {Yankees} rooters. Perhaps that is one reason why the Giants were not there with the old paper {refers to paper money, as used for tickets}. They have been going along at such a lively clip they are not used to small crowds, and the empty bleachers must have taken their ginger away.

Umpire Rigler was about the busiest cup of tea you ever saw. The grounds were so wet almost every ball pitched had to be taken to cover for a dry cleaning. It was up to Rigler to decide whether the ball was too wet to handle and to hit, and you can be sure he looked them over judiciously. Most umpires wouldn't know a dry ball from a highball, but Umpire Rigler never made one bad decision. Perhaps fifty balls were exchanged during the dismal affair, and he didn't miss one.

—William F. Kirk, New York *American*

Mr. John J. McGraw thought he was cutting into a fine, ripe can-
teloupe this afternoon and was much surpised to find a lemon of the
sourest variety. The Giant leader forced the Reds to play ball after a hard
rain had soaked the yard and there was every legitimate reason for a
postponement. Mr. McGraw acted in this inhospitable manner because he
thought our boys would be easy picking, and he saw a chance of landing
in first place. It never occurred to him that his pennant chasers would not
win. But the red worm, having been stepped on six straight times, was
due to turn. It not only turned; it stood up on its hind legs, reared,
bucked, and tore around in the most scandalous manner. Therefore the
long losing streak, beat by the tie game yesterday, was smashed today
when our boys, sore at having to play on a soaked field, daubed the chesty
Giants with whitewash.

—Jack Ryder, Cincinnati *Enquirer*

## ———◇ SATURDAY, AUGUST 8 ◇———

{On August 7, in New York, the Giants' scheduled game with the
Cubs was postponed because of rain.}

When the Chicago Cubs won the National League pennant, a newspaper man out in Chicago {Charles Dryden of the *Tribune*} started to call
Frank Chance the "peerless leader." Today the Cubs are battling to keep
their heads above fourth place and one does not hear much of the peerless
leader thing unless a laugh goes with it.

For the time being you've got to give the title to Johnny McGraw.
Few people, even the most rabid fans, realize what a wonderful fight
McGraw has made this season, and that the Giants are second is due far
more to his wonderful generalship than to the playing of the team.

Everywhere McGraw is feared by opposing players, and there is not a
fan in Pittsburgh or Chicago or St. Louis or Cincinnati or Boston or
Philadelphia who down in his heart would not like to see McGraw leading their team.        —Nie, New York *Evening Mail*

In my estimation, the New York club makes a big mistake in not
giving out the numbers who attend games. If they did so it would set a

record we want here in good old New York, the best baseball city on earth. Out in Chicago they say they cop the country on crowds, but in New York we know different. The money is here, anyhow. Most Chicago patrons are twenty-five-centers, but in New York baseball patrons do not think they are getting their money's worth unless they give up four bits.

In New York if 1,000 twenty-five-centers look at a game it is considered a big crowd. In Chicago the two-bit people run the game. That is the difference between New York and Chicago on everything.

—Sam Crane, New York *Evening Journal*

Baseball is only in its infancy, declare many able critics, and it looks as though ball parks now in existence would be all too small for the multitudes ten years from now. What is to be done? It is impossible to elongate present fields in most cases. On some grounds—like the Cub park, for instance—the limit has been reached in seating capacity. Mr. Murphy has double-decked his stands clear round the field, and put boxes on the grass till catchers and first basemen have little room to chase foul flies. Even then, people are turned away. The solution: Take a lesson from England. I have a photograph of the grandstand at Epsom, the great English race course. It has six decks, rising high in the air. Six decks—just think of it! A six-decked stand, running round the field, as is now the case at Cub park, would hold 60,000—and the day is not far distant when 60,000 people will be at baseball games. Yes.

—W. A. Phelon, *Sporting Life*

———◇ **SUNDAY, AUGUST 9** ◇———

{On August 8, in New York, the Giants defeated Chicago 4 to 1. Winning pitcher, Wiltse; losing pitcher, Brown. Giants' standing: 58 wins, 38 losses, in second place.}

That's how we like to win—with 30,000 folks sitting, standing, and hanging around saying "Ain't they grand!" when we make a hit or get a ball off the other pitcher. Victory is twice as sweet when witnessed. Remember when you got a stranglehold on your first cigarette and puffed proudly without getting sick as She came along? Remember the admiration, tinctured with awe, with which She regarded you? Ever so much more satisfactory than puffing back of the woodshed, eh?

That's the way it was yesterday. We beat the Chicagos, with as big a crowd as the Polo Grounds ever held on hand. And maybe the final score wasn't of the sort that you whistle as you go out! We're willing to bet none of the grand old masters of song ever put over a composition worthy of mention on the same staff as that score of yesterday.

And we all knew Chicago yesterday. We'd been getting a gradual line on Chicago since they started from the top of the chute some days ago, and we were unafraid even when they threatened us with Brown. "Brown? Brown?" we tried to remember where and how we had heard this word. Oh, yes, to be sure. Pitcher for Chicago, isn't he? Very well, Brown. Stand there on that little slab where we can see you, and we will change your color in about one consecutive inning. Hold fast, there, Brown, or you'll fade in this strong sunlight.

Even the best of teams couldn't have stopped us yesterday. We had our crowd with us.  —W. W. Aulick, New York *Times*


We have it on good authority that Mr. Francois Chance gave an interview Saturday in which he alleged that the Giants had shot their bolt. "We have their number now," said Mr. Chance, "and they are due for a cleaning. They do not class with us." Right you are, Francois. They do not.

The haughty Cubs, as they lined up yesterday against the gingery Giants, were another Falstaff's army. {See Shakespeare's *Henry IV*, *Part I*, Act IV, Scene 2.} They were so beaten up when the ninth inning was history they looked like so many Teddy bears in a second-hand store. {Named after President Theodore Roosevelt, the Teddy bear had first appeared in the summer of 1904.} Every time one of 'em got a wallop in the stomach he said "Ma-ma" just as cute. (Chicago papers please copy.)

George Wiltse pitched a splendid game and received brilliant support. This clever southpaw is working in a more masterful manner than ever in his career, and you can't hand him too many bouquets.

 —William F. Kirk, New York *American*

Who is today's greatest baseball player? Most fans would probably give the accolade to Hans Wagner, but two players have come up to challenge Wagner for the title of "the greatest ball player," Mike Donlin, of the Giants, and Ty Cobb, the sensational young player of Detroit, who has made greater strides to the front in two years of major league service than any other player ever did in the same length of time.

Mike Donlin's admirers—and no man that ever wore the uniform of the Giants was more popular in this city than Turkey Donlin—claim he is handicapped by his position in right field. Otherwise nobody would dispute that he is Wagner's equal. His batting has been the most consistent and timely of any player in the National League. Few players know the game as well as Donlin. From his position he sizes up every play at once, and as captain of the team doesn't hesitate to "call" his men when they slip up or praise them when they do good work. Donlin infuses the Giants with the spirit that wins pennants.

—G. O. Tidden, New York *World*


I see but one team with a chance to beat us, Pittsburgh. Chicago I cannot see with smoked glasses. Frank Chance's braves are not possessed of the proper spirit, in my estimation. Everything was lovely while the Windy City lads were showing a stern chase to the rest of the company. But when collared the Cubs have proved quite docile.

Chicago had some tough luck, but no more than fell the way of New York. We have outgamed them and will continue so to do. But the Pirates! Ah, there's the dig. Pittsburgh may be a one-man team, but that man is a "dilly." The Pirates are every bit as aggressive as any member of baseball's select society. Where I figure to beat them out is in teamwork and all around generalship. Then, too, we have the advantage of finishing the season at home. The Pirates will wind up on the road.

—George Wiltse, New York *American*


Chicago, in my mind, is the one team we have to beat. I figure the Cubs stronger than the Pirates because of the experience of Frank Chance's men and the confidence that the successes of two consecutive years have engendered. Chicago boasts a crackerjack pitching staff, and has a hard-hitting, fast-fielding, heady, aggressive team. I believe the Giants outgame the Cubs, and I think this will win the pennant for us.

Pittsburgh, of course, must be reckoned with. But the Pirates are more or less a one-man aggregation. Without Hans Wagner Pittsburgh would have a hard time to get into the first division.

Our greatest chance, I believe, lies in the fact that we will finish the season at home. The encouragement of a friendly big city is no small factor in a team's success.

—Christy Mathewson, New York *American*

————◇ **MONDAY, AUGUST 10** ◇————

On Saturday, August 8, the sandwich man at the Polo Grounds announced officially that he had sold 92,687,463,106 sandwiches during the afternoon. He leaves for Europe on an early boat and will endeavor to cop a German nobleman for his daughter. The peanut man will probably follow suit.                —Rube Goldberg, New York *Evening Mail*


Breezing along, Hans Wagner starts the week at the top of the National League swat artists, nine points ahead of Mike Donlin. Last week the big Dutchman added seven points to his average and now is batting .335. Donlin fell off one point to .326.

Donlin is New York's only representative in select society. Larry Doyle is batting .274, an improvement of eight points in a week, and Bresnahan and Bridwell are the next best regulars with .268 and .267.

—New York *Evening Mail*

——— NATIONAL LEAGUE STANDINGS ———

| | W | L | PCT. | GB | | W | L | PCT. | GB |
|---|---|---|---|---|---|---|---|---|---|
| Pittsburgh ... | 60 | 37 | .619 | — | Cincinnati ... | 51 | 51 | .500 | 11½ |
| New York ... | 58 | 38 | .604 | 1½ | Boston ...... | 44 | 54 | .449 | 16½ |
| Chicago ..... | 56 | 41 | .577 | 4 | Brooklyn .... | 36 | 60 | .375 | 23½ |
| Philadelphia . | 51 | 42 | .548 | 7 | St. Louis .... | 32 | 65 | .330 | 28 |

{On August 10, in New York, the Giants defeated Chicago 3 to 2. Winning pitcher, Mathewson; losing pitcher, Overall. Giants' standing: 59 wins, 38 losses, in second place.}

Das German Cubs, Sheckard, Steinfeldt, Slagle and all the rest of 'em were taken over the hurdles yesterday before the largest Monday crowd that ever saw a baseball game in the United States. At least 20,000 people were there to see McGraw's men pound the stuffing out of the world's champs, and what they didn't do in the way of cheering and chuckling might as well be left undone.

Monday, as a rule, is a poor baseball day. People who spend Sunday batting around Coney Island and Fort George do not generally possess any pepper on washday. It is a blue day, is Monday, particularly for folks who draw salaries on Saturday. John T. Brush is not exactly an optimist, and he never dreamed that yesterday's game would pack the grounds.

The game was a magnificent pitchers' battle between Christy Mathewson and Jumbo Overall, and it would be hard to say which deserves more credit. Matty was found for more hits, but inasmuch as he held the Cubs to two runs and beat them, he must be accorded a slight shade.

Our trio of runs came in the opening chapter. Tenney lined to center, and Herzog, who played second base in place of Doyle, drew a base on balls. Doyle, by the way, hurt his ankle in practice before the game, and may be out for some time. Herzog showed steadiness and class, and looks like a dandy understudy for Laughing Larry. After he had reached first base, Bresnahan doubled to left, the ball rolling to the crowd.

An obliging special policeman, one of those efficient guardians of the peace we all respect so much, stopped the ball and chucked it back toward the plate. Nobody wanted this sleuth to break into the assist column, and perhaps, being a true policeman, that is why he did it. Herzog could have scored easily, but he was sent back to third base by Umpire O'Day, who ruled it a blocked ball.

McGraw walked out to the special policeman and said something. It was too far for us to determine what Gentle Jawn got off, but a sound came wafting along on the Summer zephyrs that made a noise like "cheese." That's right, Jawn. Give 'em the dickens. It didn't make much difference, the way things turned out, as Herzog scored by a splendid slide when Donlin sent a chopper down the groove.

Then Donlin and Bresnahan tried a little double stealing, and while Captain Mike was waltzing up and down the line between first and second base Roger made a bolt for the plate. Evers threw wild and Roger scored hands down, Captain Mike going to third base. Seymour's fly to centerfield scored Mike, and that is how we got 'em.
—William F. Kirk, New York *American*

We kept our 3 to 0 lead till the eighth, and then Tinker rounded his batting work with his third hit, a beautiful drive to left center good for three bases. Pay a little attention to Tinker, you batting statisticians, and figure out what sort of a percentage three hits out of three times at bat is, eh? When Overall was thrown out at first by Herzog, Tinker squeezed home, and just to show we appreciate Chicago endeavor we gave Tinker our kind applause and cautioned him not to do it again while he's in these parts.
—W. W. Aulick, New York *Times*

INDIANAPOLIS, Aug. 10—That Pitcher Rube Marquard, of the Indianapolis team, has experienced a reversal of form cannot be denied. Rube has lost six and won only one game since the announcement of his sale to the New York Giants.
—New York *American*

———◇ **WEDNESDAY, AUGUST 12** ◇———

{On August 11, in New York, the Giants lost to Chicago 4 to 0 in a game called after 6 innings because of rain. Winning pitcher, Pfiester; losing pitcher, Wiltse. The second game of a scheduled doubleheader was postponed. Giants' standing: 59 wins, 39 losses, in second place.}

Not only every midweek but every Saturday record went by the board yesterday. Fully 10,000 disappointed fans raged around the entrances after all had been closed.

The scene inside, after it began to rain hard, was really wonderful. Chicago was four runs ahead in the sixth inning when the Giants came to bat. It was raining so hard nine umpires out of ten would have called the game, giving Chicago a 2 to 0 victory. Perhaps O'Day thought of doing so, but scarcely a fan had made a move to bolt, although only a part of the grandstand offered protection from the driving rain, and once the inning started no umpire would have dared to stop play.

The ball was so wet Pfiester could do little with it, and a score of thousand straw hats leaped up in the rain as Wiltse walked to first on four balls. Tenney followed, and the crowd went crazy as he slammed a single over second, one of two hits by the Giants all afternoon. Every man was on his feet as Herzog came to bat.

The youngster stabbed valiantly at a straight ball, but it shot toward Evers, who made a wonderful stop and threw to Tinker in time to catch Tenney at second. Tinker hurled the ball to Chance, trying for a double play, and the fury of the fans was unrestrained as Rigler called Herzog out. There was reason for the roar of disapproval, for it looked as if Herzog had beaten the ball by at least a foot. McGraw, ordered off the field by O'Day a few minutes before, rushed out from his temporary retirement protesting vigorously, as did Donlin, but the protest was of no avail.

The cross timbers supporting the roof of the grandstand afforded a good view and a seat as well, and they were in demand from the start. In climbing up to one of them a man's foot turned the wheel that controls a fire hydrant, and five seconds later water spurted out of a two-inch nozzle and drenched a hundred persons sitting in the line of fire. The crowd in the aisle at the back was so dense it was nearly ten minutes before the source of the trouble could be found.

Bar one time—and we don't place too much faith in that Ark story at that—there never has been so much rain falling in one place as descended yesterday on the Polo Grounds. At the seventh-inning point Mr. O'Day called the game. Many gentlemen then spoke their mind to him. The mildest among them said Mr. O'Day was a "robber." But most of them were quite frank, and the consensus of opinion was that Mr. O'Day is the person who struck Billy Patterson, stole the remains of A. T. Stewart, sunk the *Maine*, and did his best to press the crown of thorns on the brow of the laboring man.          —W. W. Aulick, New York *Times*

Figures on the check carried away by the Chicago club were the largest ever paid a visiting club for three days of play. It took several money bags to cart the receipts away yesterday and a detail of police was provided to see that no strong-armed persons interfered with the circulation of this wad through the streets of Harlem.

—Sid Mercer, New York *Globe*

If the lady who parted with her slipper in the mud near second base about 3:45 yesterday, while doing 440 yards across the field in record time, will leave her name and address with Groundkeeper John Murphy, the article will be returned to her. Otherwise it may be put on the bargain counter. It's as good as new but slightly water stained. Those sprints across the field in the pelting rain were highly enjoyed by those under cover. Incidentally the latest styles in hosiery were duly noted and approved of with loud acclaim. —New York *Globe*

——◇ **THURSDAY, AUGUST 13** ◇——

{On August 12, in New York, Brooklyn beat the Giants 5 to 1. Winning pitcher, Rucker; losing pitcher, Crandall. Giants' standing: 59 wins, 40 losses, in second place.}

About the time William Jennings Bryan was accepting the Presidential nomination in quaint old Lincoln, Nebraska, the New York Giants were accepting a lemon in honor of the Brooklyn club's President Ebbets.

Brooklyn hasn't got a very good baseball club, but for some strange reason the Donovan men play their heads off to beat the McGraw men. No matter how many games they may drop to second-rate clubs like St. Louis, they invariably jump in and play like fiends incarnate when they reach the Polo Grounds. There isn't much brotherly love between the Dodgers and Polo Grounders. The relations between these bands of gladiators are very much Cain and Abel.

Our Giants played a listless game, but the main reason for our humiliation was a stocky southpaw named Rucker. He had everything and didn't forget to use everything. Before his speedy cannonading the Giants looked like a tame lot of children.

—William F. Kirk, New York *American*


Mike Donlin struck out twice, and the crowd hooted the Giant captain as he fanned the second time. It's hard to be an idol at the Polo Grounds.

—Brooklyn *Eagle*

———◇ **FRIDAY, AUGUST 14** ◇———

{On August 13, in New York, the Giants defeated Brooklyn 5 to 3. Winning pitcher, Mathewson; losing pitcher, Bell. Giants' standing: 60 wins, 40 losses, in second place.}

Leon Ames, who made his debut yesterday, didn't do so well, and Brooklyn got three runs before the second inning was finished. "Big Six" went in next inning, pitching out the game in his usual gilt-edged style.

The last of the fifth had plenty of action and brought victory to the Giants. Donlin started it with a stiff three-bagger to left. {George "Whitey"} Alperman had just taken {John} Hummell's place at second base and celebrated his arrival by laying for Captain Mike as he rounded second, giving him the shoulder in such a manner that Mike whirled several times and fell heavily on his back. It was as deliberate a piece of foul work as was ever seen on a baseball diamond, and when O'Day told Mike to go to third base, the crowd cheered the umpire and hissed Alperman roundly.

Alperman deserved all the roasting he got. Baseball is usually free from football tactics, and it should be kept so. If a lot of young rah! rah! boys want to kick the bridgework out of each other's mouths in a rugby game, let 'em do it. But when a professional baseball player tries a trick that may result in broken bones and perhaps ruin a man's earning capacity, he is not thoroughbred.

—William F. Kirk, New York *American*

The Giants are becoming so speedy they get "pinched" for speeding. After they walloped Brooklyn there was little time to catch the train for St. Louis. All but Mathewson, Merkle and Devlin got away to a good start. This trio, with Secretary Fred Knowles, hopped into a taxicab and ordered the "shofar" to go as fast as he liked.

Not many of these "demon drivers" get a chance to carry the mighty Mathewson, and this one certainly pried apart the zephyrs in the race to the ferry {from Manhattan to Jersey City, from where westward-bound trains then departed}.

The pinch came when the car was within hailing distance of the boat. When Matty promised to trim Chicago and Pittsburgh the man in blue and brass decided to lock up the "shofar" and his car and send the players on their way.

The "cop's" parting remark to Matty was: "If you shoot 'em over as fast as this car was traveling you'll win the pennant."

The "shofar" was fined, but the club will pay the freight.

—New York *Evening Mail*

## ——◇ SATURDAY, AUGUST 15 ◇——

ST. LOUIS, Aug. 15—It could hardly be called a team, the aggregation which rolled into town. It was more like a caravan or an army of invaders, the party of 37 people, for, besides the players, there is an enlarged collection of war correspondents, and, to add eclat to the outfit Mrs. Michael Donlin (nee Mabel Hite), Mrs. J. Bentley Seymour, and Mrs. William Malarkey are along, and in Chicago Mrs. Arthur Devlin will join them.

Such a pretentious crowd cannot travel without a physician, so Dr. James Creamer, surgeon extraordinary to the Giants at home, is making the journey.

—Nie, New York *Globe*

ST. LOUIS, Aug. 15—The Giants arrived shortly before 10 o'clock last night, hot, tired and dusty, but on time, and this was a godsend, for the heat throughout the journey had been fierce.

It was fortunate that Secretary Knowles arranged to take the flyer

Thursday at 6:30 P.M., for the boys were assured a good night's rest before today's game.

Mike Donlin's wife, Mabel Hite, has become a pronounced fan, and is "rooting terribly hard" for Mike to beat out Wagner for batting honors. When McGraw bought a paper last night at the Union Station, Mrs. Donlin rushed up and asked "How many hits did Wagner get?" McGraw replied, "Hans won the game as usual." Mrs. Donlin said plaintively, "Oh, pshaw!" with a pucker of her pretty lips.

—Sam Crane, New York *Evening Journal*

Ball players are very much worked up over the action of the National Commission in prohibiting club owners from making presents to players, and there is a strong probability of their forming a players' protective association to combat the act and to fight against further restrictions of their rights, as regards presents, bonuses and the salary question.

One prominent player of the Cardinals told me, "We have to get together, that's all, and join a labor organization as a body. We cannot be secure in our rights unless we are banded together under some such body that we know we must stick to or show ourselves lobsters if we don't stick. We don't want a ball player at the head of our organization, but someone out of baseball altogether who is a good executive and can enforce our rights with regular labor confederation methods.

"The club owners are making enough money to give us a fair show. The next thing we know they will spring a low salary limit on us, and then where will we be? I spoke to several of the Reds and they are all for a protective association, and several Giants also told me they are with me. I am going to talk to the Eastern players and get them to work for it among the players I can't see. We will get the thing going this Winter sure as you're a foot high."

—Sam Crane, New York *Evening Journal*

———◇ **SUNDAY, AUGUST 16** ◇———

{On August 15, in St. Louis, the Giants won 5 to 1. Winning pitcher, Wiltse; losing pitcher, Sallee. Giants' standing: 61 wins, 40 losses, in second place.}

St. Louis, Aug. 15—With Wiltse the Wonderful in the box, the Gotham athletes took the first game of the series from the St. Louis Cardinals, knocking {Harry Franklin} Sallee, who twice has beaten them this season, off the rubber. Captain Mike Donlin delivered the key blow in the fifth, with Bresnahan on second, a long fly to centerfield. Shaw came in on the ball, went out on it, and finally lost it, Bresnahan walking home ahead of the galloping Mike, credited with a four-bagger.

—New York *Press*

In the last inning Roger Bresnahan drew a base on balls, and was then picked off base. But Roger's wits were with him and he didn't make a futile attempt to get back. He just quietly walked to second base, claiming a balk, and Mr. Johnstone approved of it.

Also in the ninth, with Koney {first baseman Ed Konetchy} at bat and two strikes on him, Wiltse sailed one through close to the outside corner. Mr. Klem hesitated, and again Bresnahan used his wits and threw the ball to the third baseman instead of the pitcher.

"Strike three! You're out," cried Klem.

—James Crusinberry, St. Louis *Post-Dispatch*

{From a signed article in the New York *World* by Larry Doyle.}

L. L. Doyle, that's me. That stands for Lawrence Louis Doyle, the signboard they nailed onto me at the christening font in Breese, Ill., but my friends insist on calling me "Laughing Larry."

Breese was well named. I think it was the windiest place on earth. That's how I account for my early affection for the mines. I wanted to get off the earth without being blown off, so what was more natural than to burrow?

It is not surprising that I began to play baseball at an early age. It was about the only thing for me to do. I was never imbued with the idea of setting the world afire with my superior mentality, therefore I didn't make the town schoolteacher earn his salary. And so while the other kids were pretending to assimilate problems in elementary arithmetic I was building a foundation as a ball player. And I've never regretted it.

Swinging on the ball with a bat developed my arms and shoulders, and it was not long before I was physically qualified to work in the mines. My father was a miner, and he "broke me in" as a coal digger.

Working in a mine is like going up in a balloon, only in the opposite direction. You don't think anything of it if you are used to it, but when you first go down into the earth there comes a sudden realization of what might happen to you. Nowadays the mines can be lighted by electricity, and it's comparatively simple to go through a mine. But when you get caught without a light in some deep labyrinth in the bowels of the earth it's no picnic.

Of course, I kept up my ball playing. When I had time to myself I managed to get up a game. One day I was in a game when some strangers came along and watched. I landed on one ball for a homer, and three innings later I repeated the trick. After the game one of the men said I was wasting my time playing for fun. He said I could make money playing with semi-professional teams, and once I got the idea I couldn't get rid of it. I began to sell my services, and there was a big demand for them. I quit mining, and gave all my time to ball playing.

I joined the Mattoon team, in the Three-Eye League. I remained with the team when it was taken into the K.I.T. League. I played pretty good ball with these fellows, and then was traded to Springfield. I had a fair streak with this team, batted around .325 and had a good fielding average.

I noticed that Dan Brouthers {An outstanding major league first baseman in the 1880s and '90s, Brouthers became one of baseball's first scouts, acting in this capacity for John McGraw.} trailed the team a good deal, and last year when I heard that Manager McGraw had paid $4,500 for me I began to think I could really play the national game. I have played pretty hard since joining the Giants, but I have not been very lucky.

Nearly all ball players smoke, and I'm no exception. I don't drink intoxicating liquor, though, because I don't like it. I don't believe there is a man in the big league now who diets himself. A ball player is supposed to be tough enough to eat anything that doesn't eat him first, and we're all blessed with prodigious appetites, but I am inclined to believe I've got several other men's appetites in addition to my own. I eat enough for three ordinary men. I haven't any favorite article of food. I play them all without showing any partiality, and at that I'm only five feet nine inches in height and weigh 165 pounds.

I play baseball for the fun I get out of it, and the managers are foolish enough to pay me for having fun.

—Larry Doyle, New York *World*

───◇ MONDAY, AUGUST 17 ◇───

{On August 16, in St. Louis, the Giants lost a doubleheader, 6 to 5 and 3 to 2. Winning pitchers, Lush and Karger; losing pitchers, McGinnity and Ames. Giants' standing: 61 wins, 42 losses, in second place.}

Muggsy McGraw and his Giants will have to settle into a steadier pace and exert more energy if they expect to win the pennant. By dropping a doubleheader to our lowly Cardinals the chances for the Gotham team were sadly crippled.

McGraw has not the class of the team that won the world's championship for him in 1905. He has a splendid club, with hitting and fielding strength, experienced in all tricks of the game and aggressive to the point of danger. But it is not a power like his champions of three years ago. If he sticks to second place to the end of the season he will be doing well.

Without Mathewson or Wiltse in the box, the Giants are a second-class team. Should one of these twirlers be rendered incapable, McGraw would probably fall to the second division in a hurry.

On the Polo Grounds in New York, where policemen dare not tread and visiting players and umpires are in danger of their lives, victories have been comparatively easy for the Giants. Their determination and reputations have undoubtedly struck many officials with fear.

The Giants try to carry this magnetic power over umpires on the road. But criticism parsed on the umpires Saturday seemed to have had a bracing effect yesterday. They turned about and on one or two occasions actually showed a will of their own and a power to speak out against the Giants.

McGraw, Bresnahan, Donlin and the others tried the same tactics as on Saturday and to the surprise of all Klem and Johnstone stood their ground. At one time Bresnahan tried the same trick of hurling the ball to the third baseman when a doubtful third strike came up, but little Klem called it a ball and stood his ground without apparent fear when Bresnahan whirled and faced him.

—James Crusinberry, St. Louis *Post-Dispatch*


ST. LOUIS, Aug. 17—St. Louis fans yesterday got up on their hind legs and yelled gleefully as Cardinal after Cardinal glided over the gum of home plate. New York fans cannot imagine the hunger of Mound City rooters to beat the Giants, and of all rabid fans I have to give the medal to those in St. Louis. They want everything in sight and as much more as is hidden. They are all umpires, and how they clamor in their greedy hoggishness for all the best of it. I have the idea the name "rooter" originated in St. Louis on account of the insatiable desire of St. Louis fans to "hog" everything. There was not even a strike called that the decision was not greeted with a roar of disapproval, and the most insane objections were made by spectators a mile or so away who couldn't see whether the ball cut the plate or was a yard wide of it.

St. Louis fans do not appear able to see anything beyond what their own players do, but it was always so in Kerry Patch village. Sectional pride is proper and natural, but the Giants are surely entitled to the same courteous treatment that is accorded St. Louis players in the big city.

—Sam Crane, New York *Evening Journal*


They have fallen off slightly, but the leaders in the chase for National League batting honors stand about as they did a week ago. Hans Wagner still leads by a safe margin, with Mike Donlin runner-up. Against .338 a week ago Wagner now boasts of .334, and Donlin dropped to .321.

Outside of Wagner and Donlin the National League has but two .300 athletes, Zimmerman and Evers, of the Cubs, with .313 and .300. Bridwell now is McGraw's second batter, his .281 four points better than Larry Doyle's average. Roger Bresnahan is fourth with .262.

—New York *Evening Mail*

— 173 —

Ames and Bresnahan indulged in a bit of comedy quarreling in the sixth inning that brought down wrathy words from Captain Mike Donlin. Bresnahan signaled for one kind of curve and Ames refused to throw it. {Tom} Reilly was batting. Ames persisted and started to throw what he wished and Bresnahan deliberately stood to one side, refusing to catch the ball. It happened that Reilly tried to bunt and fouled it. Donlin came on the tear and order was restored.

—St. Louis *Post-Dispatch*

──────── NATIONAL LEAGUE STANDINGS ────────

| | W | L | PCT. | GB | | W | L | PCT. | GB |
|---|---|---|---|---|---|---|---|---|---|
| Pittsburgh ... | 64 | 39 | .622 | — | Cincinnati ... | 55 | 53 | .509 | 11½ |
| New York ... | 61 | 42 | .592 | 3 | Boston ...... | 46 | 59 | .438 | 19 |
| Chicago ..... | 58 | 45 | .563 | 6 | Brooklyn .... | 38 | 64 | .372 | 25½ |
| Philadelphia . | 56 | 44 | .560 | 6½ | St. Louis .... | 36 | 68 | .346 | 28½ |

──────◇ **TUESDAY, AUGUST 18** ◇──────

{On August 17, in St. Louis, the Giants won 3 to 0, a game called after 6 innings because of rain. Winning pitcher, Mathewson; losing pitcher, Sallee. Giants' standing: 62 wins, 42 losses, in second place.}

Even the elements delight in kicking our lowly Cardinals. Yesterday a thunderstorm lingered on the outside of the park until enough innings had been played to declare a game, then the storm broke into the grounds and sent the players scampering, with the Giants the victors.

In the middle of the fifth the storm seemed to linger at the main entrance. The New Yorkers were at bat. They had to be retired and then put three Cardinals out or it would be no game. One Giant was out and one was on third base. A terrific thunder clap caused McGraw to leap from the bench. He ran to the third-base coaching line. Cy Seymour was there. "Steal home on the next play," yelled McGraw. Seymour dashed for home and ran into Catcher {John} Bliss with the ball in his hands. He was out. Jack Barry was at bat. "Strike out, Jack," yelled McGraw. Jack swung wildly and then scampered with the other New Yorkers to their fielding positions.

Three Cardinals had to be put out before a game could be completed. Again and again the storm cried its warning in thunderous calls. Bobby Byrne rolled a ground ball to Bridwell and was out. Reilly popped to Bridwell. Bliss delayed things by singling. Then Beebe hit to Herzog and was thrown out, completing enough play to allow a game.

The rain descended at once, though not heavy enough to call the game until after another inning had been played.

Christy Mathewson was on the mound for the Giants. He is the same great twirler as of old. His speed may not be so great as in the past, but his wits are greater. The team is filled with confidence as soon as he steps into the box. He is one of the greatest pitchers the game has ever seen and he seems good for several years to come.

—James Crusinberry, St. Louis *Post-Dispatch*

SPRINGFIELD, Ill., Aug. 18—The Giants left St. Louis with an even break, much less success than they anticipated. Mathewson does not play Sunday ball, although there is no clause in his contract to that effect. When he first joined the Giants {late in 1900} he expressed the wish not to work on Sundays, and his desire has been granted ever since. {Mathewson's mother wanted her son to become a minister, and she was not pleased when he entered professional baseball; to appease her, he agreed not to play on Sundays.} But if he had been on the field Sunday chances are the Giants would have won both games.

In these pinch times when every victory counts an awful lot, if Matty could be induced to throw aside his "scruples" the Giants would have a much rosier show to win the pennant. Matty is loyal to his club, but I and all of his fellow-players wish he would step into the breach and help out on Sundays. Rival clubs take advantage of Matty's refusal to play on the first day of the week and crowd in doubleheaders at every opportunity. It places McGraw at a disadvantage and also his team.

I think Matty is the only player now who does not play on Sunday. If he is thoroughly conscientious he deserves credit. But is he?

—Sam Crane, New York *Evening Journal*

CINCINNATI, Aug. 19—It was a delightful trip the Giants took to Springfield yesterday {for an exhibition game}, making a pleasant break in the hard grind. The boys were entertained with a whole-souled heartiness that, coming after the hoodlumish treatment in St. Louis, was like an oasis of pleasure in a desert of disgust.

The game was distinguished by the appearance of John J. McGraw, who took Doyle's place at second base in the last two innings. Unfortunately, the new utility man didn't have a chance, but he cavorted around like a young fellow. Mac had no opportunity to hit, as he didn't go to bat.

{One would scarcely surmise from Sam Crane's account of this "pleasant break in the hard grind" that on the day the Giants visited Springfield the city was in fact an armed camp. On the preceding weekend, seven blacks had been killed by a white mob, and so the governor declared martial law and sent National Guard troops to patrol the streets of this "oasis of pleasure."}

—Sam Crane, New York *Evening Journal*

{On August 19, in Cincinnati, the Giants won, in 10 innings, 3 to 1. Winning pitcher, Wiltse; losing pitcher, Spade. Giants' standing: 63 wins, 42 losses, in second place.}

The Giants are one notch nearer to those awful Pirates by taking a fierce ten-round battle at League Park. Fighting every inch of the way, the teams came to the ninth round with McGraw's outfit a run to the good. The Reds got their lone tally in the ninth and had a wonderful opportunity to win, but George Wiltse was too tough. The enemy closed the deal by some fancy slugging in the tenth.

The game was a delightful struggle, with Bob Spade lined up against George Wiltse, presently the league's greatest southpaw. The left-hander had much the better of the argument. The cadaverous but skillful Mr. Wiltse pitched a remarkably clever game against a team which usually drives southpaws to the tall and uncut. Mr. Wiltse allowed four singles, only one of which was a clean drive.

—Jack Ryder, Cincinnati *Enquirer*

Pittsburgh and Chicago will puncture New York's pennant prospects on the present trip and send the Giants home fighting to keep out of fourth place. The Pirates are going at so fast a gait it is doubtful if they will be displaced. —*The Sporting News*

It has leaked out that McGraw had nothing to do with the purchase of Rube Marquard. The Giants' pitching staff looked a bit wabbly a while back, and John T. Brush thought he would surprise McGraw by digging up a new box artist. Accordingly, Mr. Brush did sneak away to look over minor leaguers. Through the Indianapolis officials Mr. Brush learned that two or three teams were bidding for Marquard, and that was enough for him. He plunked down $11,000, then told McGraw what he had done. There is no record of McGraw being tremendously enthused over the purchase. —Nie, New York *Globe*

──◇ **FRIDAY, AUGUST 21** ◇──

{On August 20, in Cincinnati, New York won 2 to 0. Winning pitcher, Mathewson; losing pitcher, Coakley. Giants' standing: 64 wins, 42 losses, tied with Pittsburgh for first place.}

With a tie for first place in sight, Manager McGraw sent the great Mathewson against the Reds, and the dope worked out right, although our boys pounded Matty for eight solid bingles, while the Giants got just four off Dr. A. J. Coakley. The Reds' work on the green also was more consistent than that of McGraw's men, but the lone Red foozle cost a Giant tally, while New York erred thrice without losing anything.

Matty was hit hard enough to cause a lot of anxiety in Giant bosoms, but his own steadiness, with much-needed assistance from Doyle and Bridwell, pulled him through.

—Jack Ryder, *Cincinnati Enquirer*

In the sixth yesterday things got tangled up dangerously, and I could feel the carmine perspiration oozing from every pore. With one out, Lobert lambasted a double to right, and Paskert followed with a solid single going fast and over second. It looked a cinch that Lobert would score, but the wise Mr. Bridwell, after making a robbery stop, seeing he had no chance to nail the batter at first, whipped the ball like a shot to Devlin, and Lobert, who had overrun third, was nipped by an eyelash, and then only because Devlin had his foot between the bag and Lobert's "kangaroos."

Umpire Klem was fortunately right where the play was made and called the runner out. The crowd yelled blue thunder, but after the game Ganzel acknowledged the decision was right, but he made an awful belch at the time, possibly for effect. It was a narrow squeak, and Klem deserves all kinds of credit for following the play so closely.

It was superb headwork on Bridwell's part—quick thought and quick action. It possibly saved the game.

—Sam Crane, New York *Evening Journal*

———◇ **SATURDAY, AUGUST 22** ◇———

Washington, Aug. 21—Catcher Charley Street, of the Washington team, this morning accomplished the unparalleled feat of catching a baseball thrown from one of the small windows near the top of the Washington monument, 505 feet from the ground.

Street made the attempt at the instigation of the *Washington Post* to settle the question long under dispute as to whether the catch could be made. Before Street made the catch 12 balls had been dropped, most being deflected by the stiff breeze which made it impossible to reach them. On the thirteenth ball Street made the catch. The ball struck his mitt with terrific force and jarred him considerably.

Street caught against Detroit in the afternoon and did not display ill effects from his experience.                              —Cincinnati *Enquirer*

CINCINNATI, Aug. 22—Mathewson has cut out checker playing on this visit to Cincinnati and for the entire trip. Several noted checker players, including the champion of Ohio, have called on Matty and invited him to the checker club, but Matty refused. It is strictly business on this trip.
—Sam Crane, New York *Evening Journal*

"McGraw, Knowles & Mathewson"—that's how the sign over the door will read on the Marbridge Building at 34th street and Broadway soon after the Giants play off the world's series. The manager, star pitcher, and secretary of the New York club will have the largest billiard hall in America, and a nice little cafe will be run on the side.

Ball players, as a rule, do not make good businessmen. That was why Mr. Knowles was taken into the company. The man who beats the cash register when the Giants' secretary is counting up the house will have to go some and in addition McGraw will make his employees wear tights so that there will be no pockets in which to carry loose change.
—Nie, New York *Globe*

———◇ **SUNDAY, AUGUST 23** ◇———

{On August 22, in Cincinnati, the Giants won 5 to 1. Winning pitcher, McGinnity; losing pitcher, Ewing. Giants' standing: 65 wins, 42 losses, in second place.}

After offering old Joe McGinnity to the Cincinnati club for almost nothing yesterday morning, Manager McGraw was forced to send the veteran in against the Reds at League Park in the afternoon, and the Iron Man performed in his 1903 style. Isn't baseball a funny proposition? Here is a pitcher the Giants are trying to give away. Necessity forces his use a few hours after the gift proposition is made, and the old boy works like a Mathewson.

McGinnity would not have been used if the Red management had cared to take him at their own terms, as McGraw had requested in the morning. But the offer was spurned, and the Iron Man remained a Giant. So he was available when Ames blew up at the getaway.

Ames was wild and utterly unable to locate the plate. He passed the first two men, and McGraw, with characteristic promptness, yanked him out, and called on old Joe to show why he should not be allowed to seek salary elsewhere. The Iron Man proceeded to pitch rings around the Reds, making our boys look like a lot of bloomer girls.

McGinnity has nerve, control and a dinky curve ball, and he gets by on the first two. A Red batter steps to the plate. Old Joe slips the first one right over. According to immemorial custom, the batter never hits at the first one, so old Joe has him in the hole right off the reel. Then a little nerve, perfect control and the queer little curve, calculated to an inch, causes a pop-up or a small-sized fanning bee.

—Jack Ryder, Cincinnati *Enquirer*

CINCINNATI, Aug. 22—There was one drawback to the complete happiness of the Giants when they left town tonight—the fact that Catcher Snodgrass had his thumb so badly lacerated when hit by a foul in practice he will not be able to play again this season, and perhaps never, as amputation may be necessary. {Snodgrass would in fact be an outfielder on three Giant pennant-winning teams, 1911–13.}

—New York *World*

———◇ MONDAY, AUGUST 24 ◇———

"A doubleheader may not be played between Pittsburgh and New York this afternoon. I was not notified that two games were to be played 24 hours in advance in accordance with league rules and consequently we are not compelled to do so."

Thus spoke John McGraw, manager of the New York Giants, yesterday at 3 P.M. The team arrived in the morning from Cincinnati, having an open date.

McGraw did not say he would refuse to play two games, but pointed out his right to do so. "Pittsburgh cannot force us to play," he continued. "League rules plainly say that the president of the league or the home club shall notify the other club at least 24 hours before time for calling the first game. This the management of the Pittsburgh team did not do and so it is up to me whether the Pirates and Giants shall play two games tomorrow."                                    —E. M. Thierry, Pittsburgh *Dispatch*

PITTSBURGH, Aug. 24—Manager McGraw decided early this morning he would agree to play a doubleheader. McGraw at first thought his players would be too tired after their trip from Cincinnati to do themselves justice, but after calling roll this morning he found everyone in prime fettle and eager to play. The Giants' manager then called Barney Dreyfuss on the phone and told him two games would be played.
                                    —Sam Crane, New York *Evening Journal*

Local fans will have the opportunity of seeing the championship struggle at Pittsburgh today between the Pirates and Giants. A monster electric diamond, known as Campton's baseball bulletin, has been erected at Madison Square Garden and another at the Gotham theater on 125th street. All remaining games this season will be shown at both places.
                                    —New York *Evening Mail*

—————— NATIONAL LEAGUE STANDINGS ——————

| | W | L | PCT. | GB | | W | L | PCT. | GB |
|---|---|---|---|---|---|---|---|---|---|
| Pittsburgh ... | 66 | 42 | .611 | — | Cincinnati ... | 56 | 56 | .500 | 12 |
| New York ... | 65 | 42 | .607 | ½ | Boston ...... | 49 | 63 | .438 | 19 |
| Chicago ..... | 64 | 47 | .577 | 3½ | Brooklyn .... | 40 | 68 | .370 | 26 |
| Philadelphia . | 57 | 49 | .538 | 8 | St. Louis ..... | 40 | 70 | .364 | 27 |

————◇ TUESDAY, AUGUST 25 ◇————

{On August 24, in Pittsburgh, the Giants won a doubleheader, 4 to 1 and 5 to 1. Winning pitchers, Wiltse and Mathewson; losing pitchers, Willis and Leifield. Giants' standing: 67 wins, 42 losses, in first place.}

In the presence of 16,440 sorely depressed human megaphones the hateful New York Giants on Exposition Park field pushed our beloved Pirates out of first place in the race for the happy emblem of baseball superiority.

It was one of the largest gatherings of baseball fans and bugs in the history of Pittsburgh, and it was a representative one, composed largely of well-groomed men and fashionably dressed women.

So great was the outpouring hundreds sat on the grass, forming a human frame two-thirds of the way around the yard.

—C. B. Power, Pittsburgh *Dispatch*

PITTSBURGH, Aug. 25—Perhaps the hundreds of New York rooters did not "gloat a few" last evening. New Yorkers owned the town last night and as I fumbled around for my downy couch at 11 o'clock I could still hear Joe Humphreys's foggy voice reiterating that Mike Donlin would beat out Hans Wagner by several "gas house" (N.Y.) blocks.

For the first time this season the Giants have an undisputed hold on first place, and I don't know how they can be "ketched."

It took the Giants a while before they could get a correct and proper line on Willis in the first game, but they "sure did" at last, and my! oh my! what a stinging of the bulb there was! Wiltse started the eighth with a safe Texas-leaguer to short center. Tenney's little dump, intended for a suicide splash, went a little too fast to Willis, and Wiltse was smothered at second. Then Doyle, king slugger of the day, singled to center. Bresnahan was on pins and needles. It was up to him to do things, for in the first inning he had failed to lean against the ball when he had a chance to send in runs, and dear old Roger had his teeth set and his head up. He lined a beauty over second that {Roy} Thomas tried to make a circus catch of and pitched forward onto his face in a vain attempt to clutch the sphere. Roy plowed up the ground for yards with his nose, but the ball scooted under him and netted Roger three bases. Tenney and Doyle cavorted over the bases, while Pittsburgh fans made music with their mouths that sounded like a banshee's wail.

At this stage our old friend Mike Donlin essayed to do a Donlin stunt. His wife looked down from her private box and shouted: "Mike, dear, if you don't make a hit I will never speak to you again, and you can take back your old bracelet."

These were her exact words, for I heard them. Mike must have, too, for he certainly tickled the ball. He shot it on a dead line to left like a bullet, and Fred Clarke might as well have tried to stop a twelve-inch shell. The ball went shooting to the low fence in deep left, and another home run was down to Mike's credit, as well as smiles and return to favor of his pretty better half. That clinched the game there and then. All the pepper the Pirates had shown went up in the smoke of their brunette burg.

With the first game tucked away, and Mathewson in the box, it looked very sweet for both games. And so it resulted. After Doyle banged a safe hit in the first inning and took third on Thomas's error and scored on Donlin's sacrifice bunt, the game looked lead-pipe to a certainty. But when Doyle drove in two more in another inning by a double and Donlin shoved over a pair by a drive over second later on, it was all over for fair.

Mathewson's pitching was simply up to his class, which is the top notch of them all. He lighted up when forced to do so and showed how he is the peer of any twirler in the business. You can't beat him—that's all, and the game never saw his equal.

—Sam Crane, New York *Evening Journal*

Sam Crane, who played second base in fast company long before many present-day fans dreamed of baseball, is with the Giants. {Crane played for eight teams during seven seasons from 1880 until 1890.}

—Pittsburgh *Dispatch*

When McGraw put through his deal with Boston the big cheer of the fans was that Fred Tenney would be their first baseman. A young catcher named Needham and an infielder called Bridwell were thrown in to make weight. That was the dope.

Nobody here knew anything about Bridwell then, but now thousands of New York fans can recognize him by his shoelaces. He is the little god of the bleachers, idol of the infield, pinch-hitter of the coming champions. Three months ago fans yawned and wondered when "McGraw would brace up the short field." Now they wonder what Bridwell's contract next year will call for.

Bridwell goes after everything. Always a weak hitter, he has developed a knack of going to the plate and pasting one out when it is up to him to get runs across. From a mild, graceful player he changed into a brilliant, aggressive one. A constitutionally weak batter, he has become the prize game hitter of the team. He deserves his cheers, and every time you give one for Bridwell give one for the manager that made him find himself.  —J. W. McConaughy, New York *Evening Journal*

———◇ **WEDNESDAY, AUGUST 26** ◇———

{On August 25, in Pittsburgh, the Giants won 5 to 3. Winning pitcher, Crandall; losing pitcher, Maddox. Giants' standing: 68 wins, 42 losses, in first place.}

PITTSBURGH, Aug. 25—It was Crandall's turn to beat the Pirates, and the best new pitcher the Giants have unearthed since the discovery of Mathewson was up to his task. He pitched a cool, heady game, and although hit as hard as Maddox, the Pirate boxman, he showed better judgment and was almost always in full control of the situation with men on base.
                                                            —New York *Tribune*

PITTSBURGH, Aug. 25—Today, in murky Pittsburgh, home of the smokestack and the stogie, our Gingery Giants proved beyond all doubt they are the class of the league.

The Pirates do not look so terrible now. One week ago it was the general impression around the circuit that if the Giants were to win the pennant they would have to beat Pittsburgh. But McGraw, crafty little gent that he is, gave out an interview and said: "I do not fear Pittsburgh in the least. It is Chicago we must beat to win the flag." This surprising statement, coming just when the Pirates were soaring and the Cubs losing, astounded and unnerved the Pittsburghers. The supreme contempt shown by Manager Mac for the club on top evidently got the "goat" of Mr. Frederick Clarke. McGraw does not know a thing. He goes to the races too much.

The Pirates seem to have lost their nerve. In practice today they roamed around like tramps moving up a pace in the bread line. They didn't make many slips because they didn't go after much of anything. Their heads are down. Three weeks ago it was generally conceded that one of the three clubs would break under the terribly grueling strain of the three-cornered fight that has thrilled the baseball world. The Pirates have broken.

Thousands of dollars have been wagered in this city on the exciting race. The bets are not generally made at the park, and they are not made by real lovers of the game. The gambling element in Pittsburgh, always notorious plungers on the national game, confine their operations to cafes and poolrooms. The money certainly goes down, and tonight there is many a lantern jaw in the homes of the millionaires.

—William F. Kirk, New York *American*

PITTSBURGH, Aug. 25—A feature which gave much amusement to fans yesterday occurred in the third. Doyle had made a nice triple, but later permitted Tommy Leach to engage him in conversation, and Doyle, forgetting himself, stepped off the bag. Catcher Gibson, taking the sign from Leach, whipped the ball down and poor Doyle was caught by an inch, though he made a noble try to knock Leach to bits getting back to the bag. —New York *Herald*

PITTSBURGH, Aug. 26—The Giants have begun to spend that world's championship money. Arthur Devlin will buy Mrs. Devlin a Persian lamb coat, Roger Bresnahan will have his home in Toledo repainted. Mabel Hite will get another diamond bracelet with Donlin's share, and Larry Doyle is thinking of buying an interest in the Breese (Ill.) *Weekly Clarion* and becoming an editor.

All around the hotel this morning one could stumble over a Giant busy with paper and pencil figuring out what he wants most.

—Nie, New York *Globe*

Malarkey will be sent to Buffalo in the Eastern League. McGraw thinks he may develop into a winning pitcher with more work and experience than he can get with the Giants. Malarkey lacks confidence, as a remark he made when McGraw told him to warm up one day during a game shows: "Why, Mr. McGraw," he said, "I don't think I have got a thing." Anyone who knows McGraw can imagine what a hit that made with him. {This marked the end of Malarkey's one-season major league career, which included a single victory, gained in relief over Boston on April 28.}

—Sam Crane, New York *Evening Journal*

Every great championship team has owed much success to a great catcher. Boston {the Red Sox} had {Lou} Criger. Billy Sullivan was a mainspring of the White Sox, and Johnny Kling has been a power for the Cubs. The Giants have Bresnahan.

The Big Toledo detective is one of the small group of backstops who stands 'way out from the ordinary run of receivers. {During the off-season Bresnahan was employed as a private detective in his home town.} Bresnahan knows baseball as few men know it, and he has the build and force to put his knowledge into action.

In a hot game when things begin to go wrong he is a composite of ginger and bad language. In his clumsy shinguards and wind-pad, his head in a wire cage, through which at intervals comes a stream of reproof and comment as he fusses around the plate, he suggests a grotesque overgrown hen trying to get the family in out of the rain. And generally he succeeds.

Bresnahan does not have a delightful personality. He once made a speech to Arthur Devlin which brought in return a punch on the nose. But Bresnahan isn't there to be loved.

In the batting box he is almost as valuable as he is behind. He is a game, vicious hitter and when it takes one to bring in needed runs fans would as soon see Roger at the plate as some men who are ahead of him in percentage. But his great specialty is "waiting." He gets more bases on balls than any man in either league. {By the end of the season he would lead the league in bases on balls with 83.} His patience makes Job look like a petulant party.

—J. W. McConaughy, New York *Evening Journal*

{On August 26, in Pittsburgh, the Giants won 4 to 3. Winning pitcher, McGinnity; losing pitcher, Young. Giants' standing: 69 wins, 42 losses, in first place.}

PITTSBURGH, Aug. 26—The Gingery Giants made it four straight, doing more than their closest friends expected. The town is in mourning. Barney Dreyfuss refuses to be interviewed. Fred Clarke is confined to bed. Honus Wagner has mental "charley horse." All Pittsburgh weeps.

The game today, the best of the series, was won in the eleventh hour. In the ninth inning, with the score 3 to 2, the long-suffering fans began to perk up. But Jawn McGraw never stopped. Out near the third-base line he crouched, and you should have heard the things he told "Young Cy" Young. Even as the Giant leader spoke, it came to pass and Young was chased to the bench.

Like other games of late, it was not that we won, it was the way we came from behind. It was like 1905. Many a game was won then by pluck and strategy and, unless the writer is greatly mistaken, many another game is going to be ours. The Giants are now invincible.

Luther Taylor pitched until taken out in the eighth to allow Needham to bat. The deaf mute pitched one of his old-time games, mowing Pirates down with ease and grace. McGinnity pitched the eighth, and when the Giants assumed the lead, McGraw took no chances. Although Joe was working smoothly, Mac sent in "Big Six" to retire the last three men.                    —William F. Kirk, New York *American*


The Giants have been the surprise of the year. I admire them for their pugnacity and earnestness. McGraw has the laugh on all of us who tried to show he erred in his trade with Boston. McGraw made a fine deal, and the results prove it. Tenney never played better, while Bridwell has developed into a good hitter and a brilliant shortstop. Doyle, too, is improving all the time and is a star with the stick. Donlin, Bresnahan, Devlin, Seymour, Mathewson, and Wiltse deserve all the credit due to men who have played grand ball.                    —Joe Vila, *The Sporting News*

If there is one Giant who deserves a bigger share of glory for New York's position at the top of the ladder, it's Frederick "Cambridge" Tenney. He is like wine—he improves with age.

He is not only playing a grand game, but his coaching is making the youngsters, Bridwell and Doyle, the spiciest pair ever to cavort around the keystone corner of an infield. And his great ability to "stretch" has given Arthur Devlin the greatest fielding season he has had since joining the Giants.

With his swatstick, too, Tenney has a record to be proud of. Best of all, he is a pinch-hitter of the first water. Game after game he has won with a timely clout. In the tightest pinch he is as cool as a five-cent piece of ice to a Houston street dweller on a midsummer day.

Tenney follows the Comiskey school of fielding his position, going in fast for bunts, and being a quick and clever left-handed thrower, he often catches the runner at second on what was considered simply an out at first. His plays made in this way were a great innovation back in the '90's and resulted in the play later being made a double play.

Yes, John McGraw was as crazy as a fox when he secured Tenney.

—W. S. Farnsworth, New York *Evening Journal*

{From a signed article in the New York *American* by Christy Mathewson.}

To the casual fan there may seem very little difference in the shoots and curves that fly past the batsman. But the man at the plate knows differently. To him the various kinds of curves are numbered by the hundreds, and when he faces a first-class twirler with perfect control they all look equally hard to bat.

A pitcher's value is almost invariably measured by his ability to change his pace or mix up the style of ball he is delivering. Unless he mixes them up pretty well he is of little use against a clever team.

Of various balls used by latter-day pitchers the fast ball, which may end with an inward shoot, outward shoot or upward shoot, comes first. All pitchers must be able to use this ball with more or less success. Then comes the slow ball, which does not curve or revolve; the drop curve, one of the most popular curves; the out-curve, which is seldom used in the big leagues; the raise ball, an underhand curve, used with very little success by anyone except McGinnity; the fall-away, which I have used, if I may be pardoned for saying so, with greater effectiveness than any other pitcher (it is my favorite); and the spit ball, a style of delivery the science of which cannot be explained and one very difficult to control.

During the past few years I have relied almost entirely on the drop curve, fast ball and fall-away, and I believe they are the most useful to pitchers today.

It takes a good physical specimen to be a successful twirler. Knotted muscles, however, are not essential, as the ball is propelled mainly by a body swing and the bulk of the power is derived from the back and shoulders, the arm acting as a whipcord to snap the ball. The more a pitcher learns to get the power from his body, the more he will save his arm and the longer he will be able to do himself justice in the box.

I attribute much of my success to my ability to get most of the propelling force from the swing of the body.

When mastered there is no more successful ball than the drop curve. It can be made to break very abruptly or a gradual break can be put to it. When it breaks quickly the batter invariably hits over it and misses it entirely. It is what I usually rely on when there is a man on third base and no one out.　　　　　—Christy Mathewson, New York *American*

────◇ **FRIDAY, AUGUST 28** ◇────

{On August 27, in Chicago, the Giants lost 5 to 1. Winning pitcher, Pfiester; losing pitcher, Wiltse. Giants' standing: 69 wins, 43 losses, in first place.}

When two stellar athletic bodies, traveling through space in the same orbit and with equal velocity, meet in the middle of a baseball diamond, something will smash. There was no exception to the law of the universe when the New York Giants crashed head on into the world's champions on the West Side yesterday. The impact was terrific, both projectiles were jarred severely, but Chicago came out of the wreck an easy victor.

By a wide margin the largest crowd that has squeezed into the park this year saw the triumph and rooted themselves into a compact jam of yelping humanity. From noon until time to start the game long lines of eager patrons besieged every ticket window, and an hour before the battle was scheduled to start not another inch of space was left in the enlarged stands. Under this tremendous pressure President Murphy's resolution to keep the field clear melted like wax in a candle flame. First an effort was made to keep the overflow on foul ground. The old lady who tried to keep back the ocean with her broom would have been an odds-on favorite in comparison. Soon the dammed up stream burst its barrier and flowed around the entire field.

Groomed and tuned up for the great occasion George Wiltse was pitted against his long-time southpaw opponent, Jack Pfiester, the man with the nine-lived hoodoo, and all the glory was Pfiester's.

The Cubs' support of Pfiester was brilliant. Tinker was a chief factor and once prevented a probable tally by a dashing one-handed pinch of a hit from Seymour. Once Evers not only cut off a clean hit for which he had to dive headlong, but actually sat up in time to throw the runner out at first without getting to his feet.

For three innings it was an even break, with the issue oscillating first one way and then the other. A double play from Tinker to Evers to Chance snuffed out a budding Giant run in the first, and in the next three rounds the one hit an inning was nullified by clever defense.

In the fourth Chance's men solved Wiltse's delivery for a cluster of four hard drives. Evers led with a double into the crowd, and Steinfeldt pounded a liner into right. Cap Donlin tore in like a race horse and tried for the hit but muffed it close to the ground, and Evers scored. A foul fly put Howard down, but Tinker responded to the mad yelling with a single. When Kling followed with that wallop over Bridwell's head it seemed as if the fans would tear the plant and themselves into pieces in the delirium of their joy. Far out past the last outpost the ball traveled into a scattered line of rooters, and as Steinfeldt, Tinker, and Kling scampered across the plate the joy knew no bounds. But only one of the three tallies would stand on account of the ground rules, for an ever-curious daughter of Eve had picked up the ball, perhaps thinking it was another apple from the garden of Eden, and her act left no doubt that the hit had gone into the crowd. If she can be identified that woman will be barred from the park forever, as relentlessly as her primeval ancestress was shut out from that other paradise.          —I. E. Sanborn, Chicago *Tribune*

To McGraw and his men the disappointment of the day was Wiltse, for the Cubs are supposedly weak in front of a portwheeler.

McGraw was annoyed but not frightened. "I didn't expect Wiltse to get such a beating," he said, "and I thought we could hit more effectively against Pfiester. Still, we were pretty tired from our ride, and the strain of taking four games from Pittsburgh evidently had a reaction. Tomorrow is a rest day. We will rest and get back all our steam. On Saturday Matty will pitch, and we will win sure as fate. The flag is as good as cinched for the Polo Grounds."

Chance and his tribe are wildly exuberant and think they will stop Mathewson cold. "We are hitting," said the Chicago manager, "and that is what gets the games. If we can hit a left-hander as hard as we did Wiltse, we will hit Matty or any other right-hander."          —New York *Sun*

CHICAGO, Aug. 27—Chicago presents the spectacle of a great city positively raving over baseball. Everything else is forgotten—politics, business, home and family. At downtown bulletin boards, where the game was reproduced in miniature, crowds were estimated at 50,000.

In offices tickers bringing bulletins absorbed all the attention. Grocers' boys and telephones conveyed the news of the great game to thousands of residences, for in Chicago women understand baseball and are as deeply interested as men. Hundreds of buildings in the vicinity of the ball park were black with spectators, while telegraph and telephone poles looked as though immense swarms of giant bugs had settled at their tops.

—New York *Herald*

A girl with a white dress and immense purple hat got behind the catcher, and over 900 fans lost all sight of the game. She stuck for seven innings, amid cries of "A dollar for a foul tip into the purple lid," and then left with a contemptuous glare at the wild myriads.

—Chicago *Journal*

The tribe of speculators, which has had poor picking in Cub tickets since the plant was enlarged, started to dip its hands into pockets of local fans again. The club has used every effort to keep tickets out of speculators' hands, but it is impossible to do so altogether. Refusing to sell tickets to scalpers only compels them to send helpers in relays to buy two or three seats at a time. The public cannot be protected altogether without serious inconvenience to themselves.

—I. E. Sanborn, Chicago *Tribune*

CHICAGO, Aug. 29—The Giants' spirit was amply illustrated by Mathewson last night. It looked like it might rain today and make a doubleheader necessary on Sunday. Matty hunted up McGraw and volunteered to pitch Sunday. "Big Six," it must be recalled, has a clause in his contract saying he shall not be called on to pitch Sunday ball—and he never has pitched on the Sabbath—but so much depends on these games Christy was willing to lay aside his principles for one afternoon.

—Nie, New York *Globe*

Today's and tomorrow's games at Chicago will be reproduced at Madison Square Garden on the electric diamond commencing promptly at 4 o'clock New York time. It will be the first time in many years that New York fans will have the opportunity to witness a Sunday game.

—New York *Evening Mail*

CINCINNATI, August 24—Herewith is an announcement that may foretell a revolution in baseball. It is an assured fact that in the major leagues games will be played at night if plans of President Herrmann, of the Cincinnati club, and George P. Cahill, a Philadelphia inventor, prove feasible. Herrmann, Cahill and several Cincinnati men organized the Night Baseball Development Co., incorporated at Columbus with a capital stock of $50,000. Five steel towers, 100 feet high, will be erected at League Park at once, and powerful searchlights will be mounted on the towers. Cahill has been working on the lighting part of the scheme for more than four years and believes he has solved the problem.

President Herrmann has great faith in the practicability of the Cahill system. If it works successfully every fan who has ever been docked a half day's pay for sneaking out to the ball park will worship Mr. Herrmann. Think of it! Baseball every afternoon and evening. Great double bill. Two frolics daily. Take the children in the afternoon and come back yourself for the night show. Pitchers for today: Ewing and Mathewson at 3:30; Spade and Wiltse at 8 P.M. No tie games. Play never stopped on account of darkness. Stay and see the finish.           —*Sporting Life*

{From a signed article in the New York *American* by Christy Mathewson.}

The fall-away or fadeaway ball is the most effective style of pitching I have yet discovered.

So far as I know, I am the only pitcher that habitually uses this method. I have tried to teach it to several players, but none ever suceeded in getting it down well enough to make use of it.

I use the fadeaway in every game and it has never failed me when my control was in working order. It is the ball that has won for me all my baseball honors.

It is an exceptionally slow ball and relieves the strain on the pitcher as well as puzzling batsmen. A simple definition for the fall-away is a ball that curves out from a left-handed batter when pitched by a right-handed pitcher.

The ball sails through the air at a deceptive gait until it is about six feet from the batsman, where it begins to curve outward and downward. The rotary motion of hand just before the ball is let go imparts the outward curve to the ball. As it passes the batsman it is revolving at a great rate.

Such a ball is calculated to deceive the greatest batter. He is deceived at the start as to the speed of the ball. As it rushes toward him it looks like a fast high ball; six feet from him, when it begins to drop, it has the appearance of a slow drop ball, and then as he swings it is traveling in two directions at once.

I invariably use the ball when two men are on base, and the opposing batsmen know it. The knowledge, however, does them little good.

There would doubtless be many pitchers besides myself using the ball today but for the difficulty in acquiring the peculiar twists of the hand which are necessary when delivering the fadeaway.

{Carl Hubbell, the great left-handed pitcher who won 253 games for the Giants between 1928 and 1943, told the author of this book that his screwball pitch and Matty's fadeaway were identical. Among all the pitchers in baseball's Hall of Fame, only Mathewson and Hubbell had mastered this pitch.}

—Christy Mathewson, New York *American*

———◇ SUNDAY, AUGUST 30 ◇———

{On August 29, in Chicago, the Giants lost 3 to 2. Winning pitcher, Brown; losing pitcher, Mathewson. Giants' standing: 69 wins, 44 losses, in first place.}

Concentrating their attack into one brilliant, irresistible rush in a single wildly delirious inning, Chicago's world's champions won the second game of their epoch-making series with the New York Giants, climbed one notch higher in their uphill scramble for the pennant, and sent next to the largest mob that ever jammed the Cub plant into the seventy-seventh level of terrestrial paradise.

By that well-timed assault, Chance's men battered the great Christy Mathewson until he actually was groggy for a few minutes, and turned what started out as a Giant victory into defeat in the short space of time required for making five solid hits.

Before that sensational period rooters were dreading the possibility that their own hero of three-fingered fame, Mordecai Brown, was doomed to defeat. Starting off with a whirlwind attack McGraw's tribe tore off three rattling hits and scored a run with only one out. Chicago's army of fans was aghast. Then, with a sudden turn of the kaleidoscope, fate shifted the tide.

Brown's famous opponent began as if he was going to pitch the battle of his life. For three innings the tall, fair-haired Giant was as invincible as a stone wall, as puzzling as the whispering of a Sphinx. Then in the fourth inning came the furious Cub attack, and for ten minutes there was more joy to the square inch in Chicago than there ever were microbes in its atmosphere. Hofman started with a line soak into the left-field crowd for a ground-rule double. Sheckard's careful bunt advanced the runner a notch nearer the goal. Chance then pushed a little fly just out of Bridwell's reach. Hofman was across the plate tying the score while thousands of hats went sailing into the air. But this demonstration was a whisper by comparison with what was coming.

Evers, Steinfeldt, and Howard in quick succession socked the ball squarely on the nose and the hits were like rapid-fire shots from a magazine gun in the hands of a sharpshooter. The earth trembled with the tremendous roaring, and when Evers crossed the plate with the third and what proved to be the winning run, nothing was left in the throats of the rooters but a consistent succession of gleeful yelps.

With the lead of two runs there was little chance that Brown would fail to hold the Giants back the rest of the way.

Only once before in the history of the West Side park have as many people been accommodated within these historic precincts, at the first game of the world's series with Detroit last October.

—I. E. Sanborn, Chicago *Tribune*


The most remarkable thing about the scoreboards which the *Tribune* used to show about 10,000 enthusiasts the progress of the game was the way in which the crowd endowed the lights with personalities. The incandescent bulbs were joshed and hissed every bit as heartily as were the players miles away.

Four hours men stood on the sidewalks and sat on the curb with their feet in the gutters to have good places from which to view the reproduction of the conflict. From the top windows of the Hartford building to the lower ones where bankers sat in easy chairs and watched the flashing lights with closer interest and for a longer time than they ever watched a stock ticker, from every inch of ground at the intersection of Madison and Dearborn where a human body could be squeezed cheers and jeers arose. At the second scoreboard displayed from the Illinois Central station at Randolph street was a similar scene.

The intense interest and direct personal way in which the lights were considered was shown when at a particularly thrilling point Mr. Brown was about to pitch and a streetcar blocked the view of many on the west side of the street. Fearful that they might miss something hundreds shouted:

"Hold the ball a minute, Brownie! Hold it."

—Chicago *Tribune*

During the past week thousands of businessmen temporarily gave up business to devote themselves to baseball. From 2 o'clock until 6 each afternoon crowds besieged scoreboards, bulletins, and tickers to secure the latest results of Giants' games.

Steady processions departed from offices to hunt the nearest source of information and obtain the latest news. Department stores and factories organized relays and sent boys to get the score. In some places regular forces of messengers were established by which hungry fans could obtain information from the West. Wherever there was a ticker in a hotel or other public place a throng packed so closely around it that the nearest man to the instrument was informally chosen spokesman for the crowd and yelled the result inning after inning.

Drivers of trucks and cabs drove blocks out of their way to scan bulletin boards. Streetcars were halted in front of scoreboards, and even in hospitals the baseball tidings were carried to patients. Everything was sidetracked for the latest news from the seat of the baseball war.

—New York *Times*

The ground rules yesterday were such as perhaps were never made before. So dense was the crowd back of first and so close to the base line it was agreed to make a hit among those fans good for only one base.

—New York *Sun*

Mathewson started so splendidly it seemed for a time that "Big Six" would destroy the hoodoo that attaches itself to him every time he hooks up with Brown. Since 1905 Matty has not beaten Brown. {Mathewson had last defeated Brown on June 13, 1905, when the Giants won 1 to 0.}

—New York *Press*

───◇ **MONDAY, AUGUST 31** ◇───

{On August 30, in Chicago, the Giants lost 2 to 1. Winning pitcher, Pfiester; losing pitcher, Crandall. Giants' standing: 69 wins, 45 losses, in first place.}

Jack Pfiester came into his own yesterday by winning his third straight game from the skyrockety Giants, triumphing over Crandall in the final battle of the series, which gave Chicago's Cubs a clean sweep, a clear title to second place, and closed all but half a game of the gap that was separating them from first place only four days ago.

No longer will Chicago's fans struggle with the pretzel curves of the great southpaw's patronymic; no longer will it be mispronounced by seven out of every eight bugs and bugettes. Pfiester, the spelling of which has been the occasion of as many wagers as its mispronunciation, will be dropped as meaningless and inappropriate, and for the rest of time and part of eternity Mr. Pfiester of private life will be known to the public and the historians as Jack the Giant Killer.

Pitching brilliantly before absolutely faultless support, Jack held the Giants to a single run, which came from a pass. Five times they hit him for safeties, but two were infield scratches. Chance's warriors touched Crandall for only five hits, but every one was of the cleancut variety, and three counted in the run column, leaving only two for the waste basket.

Manager McGraw's choice of Crandall, instead of sending Wiltse back to the slab, was a confession of desperation. After the trimming the Cubs gave the Giants' willowy southpaw on Thursday the Gotham leader knew that Wiltse could not stop the Cubs yesterday. Gambler by nature, McGraw took the gambler's chance and sent a youngster against the veteran world beaters, knowing it would not cost the Giants anything and might mean a lucky break and victory.

Right well young Crandall performed. He was harder to beat than

— 197 —

either of the stars who had taken their beating in the series. But he was no match in the pinches for his rival, the Killer, and he had no such perfect team behind him.　　　　　—I. E. Sanborn, Chicago *Tribune*


CHICAGO, Aug. 30—On a warm, sunny Sunday afternoon near the end of August a close observer might have seen 17 or 18 men in automobiles rushing madly for the Union Station in Chicago. The foam of battle still lingered on their lips, à la asparagus, and the bumps of their saturnine features indicated they had been running for Sweeney {a slang expression meaning to run away from something threatening or dangerous}. They were the Giants, going away from here. They were leaving the city by Lake Michigan more in sorrow than anger, victims of a series as disastrous as some of the 1906 and 1907 campaigns.

Singularly enough, the crowd today was not nearly so large as the Thursday or Saturday gatherings. The total count today could not have been over 17,000—and on a bright Sunday afternoon. Charley Murphy stood as near the turnstile as he could get. His ear is so finely trained that when the turnstile is not clicking over .300 he knows it in a jiffy, and he began to fidget when time for the game was almost called and the gates began to look comfortably wide instead of being crammed.

"It was the newspapers that scared 'em away," declared the magnate. "They had altogether too much dope this morning about the terrible crush yesterday. Thousands of baseball fans read the statements and decided to stay at home, on the front porch. It was thoughtless of them, to say the least." With this diatribe, the friend of Big Bill Taft reached into his pocket and gave a scribe a good ten-cent cigar. {William Howard Taft had lately become the Republican Party's nominee for president.} Hard luck, Charley. The papers ought to be ashamed of themselves.

The solitary run gained by McGraw's men yesterday came in the second inning. Donlin walked and Cy Seymour singled clean to right field, Captain Mike going to third. Devlin hit into a fast double play, Evers to Tinker to Chance. Those double plays have done much damage to our boys here in Chicago. {Franklin P. Adams's poem "Tinker to Evers to Chance" would be published in the New York *Evening Mail* in July 1910.}　　　　　—William F. Kirk, New York *American*

SOUTH BEND, Ind., Aug. 30 {en route to Boston}—The Giants might have changed their luck if they hadn't lost so many runs by weird base running. The limit of foolish work on the bases was when Barry allowed himself to be forced out at second yesterday on Bridwell's single to right. It was as clean a hit as was ever made, and Barry was guilty of a most serious error of judgment in not running. He was looking right at the ball, too, and ran back to first, thinking Evers, with the ball going ten feet over his head, would catch it. As Crandall walloped a long fly to Hofman, on whose catch Barry could have easily reached third, with only one out, the seriousness of his mistake can be appreciated. It may have lost the game.           —Sam Crane, New York *Evening Journal*

After the game a cushion battle between 3,000 in the stands and 5,000 in the field raged for 15 minutes, during which many women were injured and their hats demolished. The police were powerless. In this way the crowd expressed its joy over the victory.      —New York *World*

Mike Donlin and Hans Wagner are still battling for National League batting honors. The Turkey didn't gain on the Teuton last week even if the Giants did trounce the Pirates four straight. Wagner has an average of .337 while Donlin is batting .322. Among Giant regulars, Doyle and Bridwell have the second and third highest batting averages, .296 and .281.
                                       —New York *World*

Sacrificing a runner on first or second is almost never done by the Giants, the hit-and-run play being used almost exclusively. Once in a while a Giant will attempt to catch the enemy unawares by laying down a sacrifice bunt, but the general rule of play, as stated by Manager McGraw himself, is to eliminate the sacrifice play as much as possible and stick to "hitting it out."

"What's the use of having hitters if they can't advance the base runner in that way?" queried McGraw.           —Chicago *News*

| | W | L | PCT. | GB | | W | L | PCT. | GB |
|---|---|---|---|---|---|---|---|---|---|
| New York ... | 69 | 45 | .605 | — | Cincinnati ... | 58 | 59 | .498 | 12½ |
| Chicago ..... | 70 | 47 | .599 | ½ | Boston ...... | 50 | 67 | .427 | 20½ |
| Pittsburgh ... | 69 | 47 | .595 | 1 | Brooklyn .... | 43 | 71 | .377 | 26 |
| Philadelphia . | 60 | 52 | .536 | 8 | St. Louis .... | 42 | 73 | .365 | 27½ |

─── ◇ TUESDAY, SEPTEMBER 1 ◇ ───

BOSTON, Sept. 1—By taking the Lake Shore "flyer" out of Chicago at 5:30 Sunday afternoon the Giants got here last night and obtained a good night's rest before tackling Boston in a doubleheader today. It took some tall hustling to make the train, but through Secretary Knowles' thoughtfulness auto cars were on hand outside the ball park, and the players were whirled to the Lake Shore station with time to spare.

The players spent the long day on the train playing various games of cards, McGraw even allowing the great American game of "Hanky Pank" {any of several games, popular in carnivals, usually costing five or ten cents to play} to be played for a small limit, to take the attention and minds of the boys off baseball and the strenuous pennant race.

—Sam Crane, New York *Evening Journal*

Just how hard a road the Giants still have to travel is illustrated by looking over their schedule. McGraw's men have 40 games to play in 29 playing days. This means a number of doubleheaders, a majority with strong teams. It surely is a hard schedule, but it is, in a measure, offset by the fact that two-thirds of the games will be played on the Polo Grounds.

—New York *Evening Mail*

John J. McGraw, Jekyll and Hyde.

That is how the little manager looks to folks who really know him. Outside New York so few fans know anything about J. Muggs off the field that he has come to be regarded as the incarnation of rowdyism, the personification of meanness and howling blatancy.

That's what J. Muggs is, all right, when it comes to the arena. But off the field McGraw is the kindliest, most generous and most sympathetic of men. The supporter of a herd of pensioners—a long list of poor creatures, who, if McGraw should die or be reduced to sudden poverty, would at once fall into utter destitution. The most loyal of friends, the most steadfast of good fellows.

John J. McGraw spends his big salary, it is said, in horse racing. He does—a few dollars of it. Fifty percent of John McGraw's money goes direct to the support of sick, crippled, helpless dependents, mostly people who have no claim on him but were brought to his notice by sympathetic friends. The little manager has a charity list that would make most millionaires look like pikers. He has charity toward all, malice toward none, and will go miles out of his way to help an invalid woman or crippled child.

John McGraw's great heart contracts to the dimensions of a bean when he gets on a ball field. The gentle sympathy and eager kindliness narrow down to the shape of a spike, with rust on the same. The generous giver becomes the howling wolf. The prince of nature's noblemen becomes so fierce, so vicious, so unendurable, his own men ever and anon take a punch at his chops in the dressing room.

How do you figure it all out?                                    —Chicago *Journal*

───◇  **WEDNESDAY, SEPTEMBER 2**  ◇───

{On September 1, in Boston, the Giants won a doubleheader, 4 to 1 and 8 to 0. Winning pitchers, Wiltse and Mathewson; losing pitchers, Tuckey and Flaherty. Giants' standing: 71 wins, 45 losses, in first place.}

The New York Giants made the most of their doubleheader yesterday and won both games. They needed them, for Pittsburgh put Cincinnati away twice and jumped to second place. The Cubs were surprised by the Cardinals, who downed them in a ten-inning game, and now Chicago isn't quite as sure of the pennant as it was 24 hours ago.

                                                         —New York *Sun*

BOSTON, Sept. 1—Getting back into their rapid stride which carried them to the top of the league heap, John J. McGraw's Glittering Giants, ambitious to recover ground lost in Chicago, twice feasted on Joe Kelley's Doves.

The Manhattan Marvels played wonderfully in all departments of the game, making only one error behind Wiltse and according Mathewson perfect support. The star whaler of the day was Arthur Devlin, who could not make a hit in Chicago. McGraw's classy third-sacker got in six screaming, slashing slaps, one a homer over the left-field fence and another a triple to deep center. —New York *Press*

Yesterday was Mike Donlin's birthday, not the anniversary of his birth but of his regeneration. It was just one year ago yesterday since Mike looked on wine when it was red and boarded the water wagon, and, accordingly, Mrs. Donlin and a few friends surprised him last night with a little banquet. Water, watermelon, water ices, and finger bowls formed the principal features of the affair, and miniature little sprinkling wagons were the souvenirs. A large cake graced the center of the table, and in it was stuck one lighted candle. The cake bore a card which read, "From the Retail Liquor Dealers' Association."

The whole team contributed something to the celebration, and Mike made a little speech and said he would stick to the water wagon until there were twenty candles on the cake. —Nie, New York *Globe*

When work shuts up its dusty shop, and world-worn millionaires
Trail in behind their office boys on "L" and Subway stairs,
When brain-spent boss and nerve-spent clerk and brawn-spent workingman
Fight greedily in swarming trains to get what space they can,
Some urchin on a platform seat cries out in screaming glee
Behind a page of two-foot type, "The Giants wins, b'Gee!"
And furrowed scowls are smoothed in smiles, and everything the day
Has brought of trial, defeat and grief is cast, the while, away.

"The Giants Wins!" That triumph makes our own defeats no less.
It eases not the rugged road to what we call success.

It neither lifts the load we bear, nor vanquishes a foe
Of all the eager enemies along the way we go.
And yet it wakes the same old thrill we used to know of old
Before the red, warm blood of youth ran sluggishly and cold.
And through that throng of wan-faced boys and jaded, faded men,
There runs a rumbling undertone: "We've won! We've won again!"

Who says the world is growing old; that all men used to know
Of simple, honest happiness has vanished long ago?
Who says that city graft and greed, and city craft and guile
Have robbed all city human kind of everything worth while?
When men still feel a boy's delight, and in a boy's own way
Cheer on the valiant victors in the Game they used to play.
No pessimism need appal; forgive them for their sins,
But bet on them as long as they will shout "The Giants wins!"

—James J. Montague, editorial page, New York *American*

———◇ **THURSDAY, SEPTEMBER 3** ◇———

Yesterday's game at the South End grounds was called off on account of wet grounds, and Manager John McGraw was in good humor as he sat and fanned with a few friends. He is extra sweet on Doyle.

"I hung on to Doyle," McGraw said, "when the New York fans and critics were calling for his scalp and even furnished me with a hand-painted tin can. I stuck to Doyle, and today I would not trade him for any man playing baseball. Think of it, in the last series at Pittsburgh and Chicago Doyle got in no less than 18 safe hits. Every time he went to bat he hit the ball clean and hard. There is nothing like having confidence in one's own judgment." —T. H. Murnane, Boston *Globe*

———◇ **FRIDAY, SEPTEMBER 4** ◇———

{On September 3, in Boston, the Giants won a doubleheader, 3 to 0 and 8 to 5. Winning pitchers: McGinnity and Ames; losing pitchers, Lindaman and Dorner. Giants' standing: 73 wins, 45 losses, in first place.}

The old South End battlefield saw another slaughter of innocents yesterday. After "Iron Man" McGinnity pitched a shut-out, Ames twirled a strong game until the seventh, when Boston scored three runs. Then the great Mathewson came to the rescue and held Boston hitless for one inning, and he in turn was relieved by Taylor.

The Giants were on their toes every minute while the home team went through the game as a matter of form. The crowd seemed to show a preference for the visitors, several young fellows singing between innings, "Cherries Will Soon Be Ripe." —Boston *Globe*

Most Boston fans want to see the Giants win, now that their own team is out of the race, but local pride pushes them along in the desire to witness a victory by their own. If Western fans would only forget their rabid soreness against New York and anything and everything hailing from the big city, baseball would be better off and the danger of a war between this country and Japan would be reduced to a minimum.

If an issue does arise between the two countries, just have them put two representative ball teams on the diamond and any question between them, even of the gravest nature, would be settled then and there. In my humble opinion, when baseball becomes the all national sport, as it is bound to be, the game will do more to subdue war talk than the big navies. —Sam Crane, New York *Evening Journal*

———◇ **SATURDAY, SEPTEMBER 5** ◇———

{On September 4, in Philadelphia, the Giants won 8 to 1. Winning pitcher, Wiltse; losing pitcher, Sparks. Giants' standing: 74 wins, 45 losses, in first place.}

There is no balm in Gilead or any other Pennsylvania flag station for the Phillies. From the time Frederick Tenney, the boisterous Brunonian {referring to Brown University}, hit the first ball of the game for a double, it was a long joy ride for New York.

The Giants constructed 15 safe hits, and every man who had a bat made a hit except Bresnahan. Larry Doyle made four hits and might have had five had he not been intentionally passed on his last trip to the plate.

Wiltse, the Giant boxman, got results. He curled his cross-fire around the pates of Quaker clubbers with deadly effect, holding them to four hits.                                             —Philadelphia *North American*


PHILADELPHIA, Sept. 5—Without the leadership of Manager McGraw the Giants go into battle today and twice Monday. It may be for a longer time, but let's hope it's for three days only. Mac was suspended indefinitely by President Pulliam for yelling "Fifteen minutes late" at Umpire Klem in Boston Thursday, when as a matter of fact, Klem was nearly 20 minutes behind a play at first base which caused the trouble. McGraw's suspension, however, is purely technical. He can keep out of sight of umpires here and still be where he can put his hand on any player on the Giants' bench. That and the language of Luther Taylor will do the rest. Where Mac will be missed most will be in the coaching box, and the way the Giants got caught napping at first and second yesterday because no one looked out for them was something marvelous to behold.

—Nie, New York *Globe*


CINCINNATI, Sept. 5—For the world's series games there will be hereafter four umpires, the National Commission announced today. Two shall come from the National and two from the American League staff of umpires. A recommendation to this effect, made some weeks ago by the commission, has been approved by both leagues. {Only two umpires, one from each league, had been assigned to world series games played before 1908.}

—Chicago *Journal*


ST. LOUIS, Sept. 4—Ball players of the future may form a part of the American Federation of Labor. President Samuel Gompers approves it, seeing no reason why, like other labor, it should not organize and tote union cards and work on a union schedule.

"I can see no reason why they should not organize if they wish to," he said. "Baseball playing has become a skilled profession, and many thousands who assemble to see games prove it has become a utility. As skill is required to play I see no objection to those of the craft joining for mutual advantage."

If ball players decide to form a union fans may be furnished the delightful spectacle of a "strike" different from those common to baseball parks. And there may be "walkouts" when a southpaw shows up for work without a card. The question of the future for members of major league teams may be "Do you belong to the union?" rather than "What is your batting average?"                                          —Chicago *Tribune*

# SPECIAL REPORT: CONTROVERSY IN PITTSBURGH

{While in Philadelphia the Giants were winning easily, in Pittsburgh the Pirates and Cubs played one of the most crucial games in the history of baseball. New York fans recognized that since it involved the Giants' two rivals for the pennant, the contest was important, but few of them could have comprehended the true significance of what took place at Exposition Park. With one slight exception, no New York newspaper reported anything remarkable about the game except that it had been an extraordinary pitchers' battle. One sentence in the final edition of the *Globe* reported that Chicago would protest the outcome but did not mention the grounds for the protest. Fans in Chicago and Pittsburgh, however, were not unmindful of what underlaid this action.}

PITTSBURGH, Sept. 4—In a magnificently pitched battle the Cubs received the short end of a 1 to 0 verdict in ten innings.

But there is an outside chance that the defeat will be wiped out and the Cubs and Pirates ordered to do it all over again on the strength of a protest which the Cub management will file with President Pulliam.

To get wise to the preceding remark it is necessary to acquire a few details of what happened to terminate that grand struggle between Brown and Willis. Manager Clarke opened the Pittsburgh tenth with a single. Leach sacrificed him to second. Wagner then bounded a fast one toward right field. Evers almost made a brilliant stop but could only check the force of the ball enough to hold Clarke at third. {Warren} Gill, a late recruit from the minors, was next and Brown soaked him in the slats with a curve, filling the bases with one out. Abby was then struck out.

Wilson, never a fearsome batsman, was next and what did this recent graduate from the minors do but soak the first ball Brown pitched on the nose. It went like a shot past Evers, landing safely in short center, and Clarke scored the winning run.

Everybody thought it was over and started for the clubhouse. That everybody included First Baseman Gill and O'Day, and thereby hangs the protest. Gill ran halfway to second base and as soon as he saw the hit fall safely he returned to the Pirates' bench. He did not go within 30 feet of second base at any time.

Evers, seeing Gill's break for the bench, yelled for Slagle to throw the ball. Jimmy did and Evers touched second base with it, then wheeled to claim a force out, only to see Umpire O'Day making fast tracks for an exit with his back turned completely to what had been pulled off. Evers made his claim for the out, which retired the side and consequently wiped out Clarke's run, but the veteran umpire remarked: "Clarke was over the plate, so his run counted anyway."

If O'Day had watched the finish of that base hit and had seen what really came off, he could not have decided otherwise than in Chicago's favor, ruling out Clarke's run and leaving the score tied at 0 to 0. Everyone knows no run can count if the third out is made before the batsman reaches first, or if the third man out is forced out. Gill hadn't touched second base yet, and so Clarke's run could not have scored but for the fact O'Day took it for granted the game was over when Wilson's hit landed safe.  —I. E. Sanborn, Chicago *Tribune*

President Charles W. Murphy, of Chicago, in a telegram to Harry C. Pulliam says:

"Chicago protests today's game. . . . Chicago claims Gill should have touched second base before he ran to the clubhouse, and will prove by affidavits of a number of persons that he failed to do so."

As soon as Clarke crossed the plate, Umpire Hank O'Day turned to the players' bench to get a drink of water. Evers yelled at Slagle, who threw the ball to Evers, who called, "O'Day, O'Day." Hank failed to hear him owing to the noise made by the crowd leaving the park. Tinker, however, ran to the hydrant and called the thirsty umpire's attention to what happened, but Hank merely remarked: "Clarke has crossed the plate."

"I do not expect the protest will be allowed," said Mr. Murphy, "but it is certainly just, and should prove a strong argument in favor of the double-umpire system."                                        —Pittsburgh *Post*

{At this point I call attention to the "letter to the editor" reproduced from the July 19 issue of the Chicago *Tribune*. This letter, published when the Cubs were at home, may have provided the idea for the play that brought on Charles Murphy's protest. This game against Pittsburgh marked the Cubs' first opportunity since the appearance of the letter to put into effect this play, which they had never tried before. It should be noted that after Wilson had presumably driven home the winning run, not only Evers but other members of the Chicago team, including Slagle and Tinker, did not immediately head for the clubhouse but held their ground as if they were anticipating Gill's infraction. This play, incidentally, provided a brief moment of notoriety for Warren Gill, whose major league career was confined to 27 games in 1908.}

———◇ **SUNDAY, SEPTEMBER 6** ◇———

{On September 5, in Philadelphia, the Giants won 5 to 1. Winning pitcher, Mathewson; losing pitcher, McQuillan. Giants' standing: 75 wins, 45 losses, in first place.}

The Phillies failed again to lower New York's percentage in the chase for the pennant, and the Giants, with Pittsburgh's defeat by Chicago, now top the procession by 15 points.

After the first inning McQuillan, who started for the Phillies, was easy for the Giants. McGraw's hirelings catered to anything "Big Mac" shot up to the plate, finally hitting him so hard in the sixth Foxen finished the game.

In the face of the Giants' hitting, Mathewson pitched a game hard to

beat. The efforts of the Phillies to dent the whirling horsehide were painful to behold. They got seven hits, but with men on base Mathewson held
the batters in the hollow of his hand.        —Philadelphia *Inquirer*


That final play of Friday's game between the Cubs and Pirates is one
that does not come often, but next time it happens it is safe to predict that
none who took part in the game will overlook the importance of touching the next base. Mr. Murphy's protest, backed up with a batch of affidavits, will not likely result in throwing out this game—in fact Murphy
himself does not expect it. He does hope, however, that the incident will
add emphasis to the demand for the double-umpire system. O'Day is one
of the best officials who ever umpired, but he certainly should have had
an assistant in a game in which two of the fastest teams in the major
leagues were engaged in a bitter struggle for the upper hand in one of the
hottest three-cornered fights for the pennant ever waged in the National
League.        —Pittsburgh *Post*


————◇ **MONDAY, SEPTEMBER 7** ◇————

PHILADELPHIA, Sept. 7—Can a man play ball and think at the same time?
Can a player run bases, watch opposing players, tell when to start and
when not to?

I think not. When he can he is above the ordinary and soon becomes
a manager. Of course there is an exception every now and then—occasionally the game produces a man like Wagner, but not often.

For the last two days the Giants have been left to think for themselves. McGraw has been under suspension and off the coaching lines, and
what the players have done, when they tried to figure out in their own
noodles the right plays, has been something weird.

In two days here Donlin has been caught off base four times.
Bresnahan tried twice to steal second when there was no chance in the
world to make the play, and McCormick has been nailed far off first base.
Others, too, have been put out the same way and have tried the hit and
run at the most inopportune moments.

If he never earned the title before McGraw has certainly stamped himself this year the world's greatest manager. He has plugged along with hardly more than two pitchers. He has had a long uphill fight. He has seen his team throw away game after game and yet he has pulled them through by quick thinking and by judiciously nursing along his two great box artists.

McGraw has his own systems of play which have been tremendously successful, and yet they are directly opposite to the way most players like to go after a game.

And that is what causes the trouble when the team is left to itself. The men persist in trying the moves which are directly opposite to what McGraw calls the "Giants' system," but which is in reality "McGraw's system." And when they do—well, they tried it here Friday and Saturday.

—Nie, New York *Globe*

## ———— NATIONAL LEAGUE STANDINGS ————

|  | W | L | PCT. | GB |  | W | L | PCT. | GB |
|---|---|---|---|---|---|---|---|---|---|
| New York ... | 75 | 45 | .625 | — | Cincinnati ... | 60 | 64 | .484 | 17 |
| Pittsburgh ... | 76 | 49 | .608 | 1½ | Boston ...... | 52 | 73 | .416 | 25½ |
| Chicago ..... | 76 | 50 | .603 | 2 | Brooklyn .... | 44 | 78 | .361 | 32 |
| Philadelphia . | 65 | 54 | .546 | 9½ | St. Louis .... | 44 | 79 | .358 | 32½ |

## ————◇ TUESDAY, SEPTEMBER 8 ◇————

{On September 7, in Philadelphia, the Giants split a doubleheader, winning 5 to 0 and losing 2 to 1. Winning pitchers: Wiltse and Richie; losing pitchers, Foxen and Crandall. Giants' standing: 76 wins, 46 losses, in first place.}

The Phillies secured some balm by snatching the afternoon battle yesterday right out of the hands of the New Yorks after one of the most exciting finishes made at Broad and Huntingdon streets this year.

The morning game went to New York by 5 to 0, the Phillies giving a dopey exhibition of how not to hit when men were on base, besides doing several foolish stunts. And during the first eight innings of the afternoon game it looked as if New York would get another shut-out victory. Up to the ninth the Giants had a 1 to 0 margin, and it looked a foregone conclusion what the outcome was to be.

That last inning will not be forgotten for a long time. After Titus had been retired, {Sherwood} Magee smashed a sizzling liner to right for a base, and then {Kitty} Bransfield plastered the horsehide against the fence of the left-field bleachers, scoring Magee and sending the crowd wild. {Fred} Osborne sent a wicked-looking grounder to Bridwell, who fumbled the ball, Kitty reaching third and Osborne first. Captain Mike Doolan then earned all sorts of praise by shooting one between Devlin and Bridwell sending in Bransfield with the winning run.

—Philadelphia *Inquirer*

Roger Bresnahan's the boy to get on base. Did you ever notice him when he comes to bat and see him pull his shirt out all around his waistline? Do you know why he does that? He widens his girth so that the pitcher may hit him. Roger has often got his base with a howl that makes you think his ribs are caved in, and the ball only rapped the flowing folds of that shirt.

And that's on the level.

—Gym Bagley, New York *Evening Mail*

So much had the surroundings of the Polo Grounds been changed this afternoon six score "old fans" who had occupied seats since the days of the Brotherhood in 1890 were ousted from their positions and wandered aimlessly around the grandstand and bleachers looking for available sites to preempt for another 20 years. This field was opened to the public in 1890 and has not been changed since then.

In the "Roost," as it was called, in the right corner of the field bleachers, something like 50 patrons have sat year after year, and they were turned out today simply because baseball has become so popular that the Polo Grounds could not accommodate the spectators.

To take the place of 1,000 bleacher seats which have been withdrawn, there is a new stand that will accommodate 3,000 fans.

It has been built with a sweeping curve, and when the other improvements are finished there will be a stand on the right-field side of the diamond that will practically mean a complete circuit of the diamond.

—New York *Evening Telegram*


The Pittsburgh baseball club blames the closing of the Cosmopolitan National Bank for the loss to Chicago last Saturday. Half a dozen of the club's leading players had money in this bank, and when they heard of its closure they became nervous and could not play their game, so it is said, and Chicago won 2 to 0.

—Chicago *Tribune*


─────◇ **WEDNESDAY, SEPTEMBER 9** ◇─────


{On September 8, in New York, the Giants defeated Brooklyn in 11 innings, 1 to 0. Winning pitcher, Mathewson; losing pitcher, Rucker. Giants' standing: 77 wins, 46 losses, in first place.}


In the last inning of one of the most bitterly contested pitchers' battles ever fought at the Polo Grounds, with 15,000 fans praying that the game would not be called on account of darkness, young Al Bridwell (may his tribe increase) cuffed a clean single to left and chased Cy Seymour across the plate with the winning run.

When all you fans are old, and have your grandchildren around your knees, and are talking about great baseball games, don't forget to allude to a little game played at the Polo Grounds yesterday. Seldom have two twirlers fought such a grueling fight. Young Nap Rucker kept his various offerings coming over the plate with bewildering versatility, and while he allowed many more hits than his brilliant rival, Mathewson, he pitched a masterly game and only caved in the eleventh hour because he was pitted against the greatest twirler that ever threw a ball.

With its new seating capacity, the Polo Grounds will accommodate about 25,000 before the "S.R.O." sign is flaunted. As the park stands today, it has the largest seating capacity of any ball park in the country.

—William F. Kirk, New York *American*

Larry Doyle, the phenomenal young second baseman, was badly spiked by Hummell and will not play again for at least ten days. The accident may prove to be a very serious handicap to the Giants, for Larry has been stinging the ball better than perhaps any other player on the team and was the sensation of the Western jaunt. There was never a Giant batting rally that Larry didn't figure in, and his fielding was such that he was considered the prize package kid of the season.

There was no excuse for Hummell cutting Doyle down. Hummell was out so far on a force play that he hadn't a show to make the bag. So why was Doyle spiked so high up on his leg? I don't want to accuse Hummell of deliberately spiking Doyle, but it was surely an accident that could have been avoided.

The Brooklyns are almost as well satisfied to beat the Giants as to win the pennant, and considering the old-time inter-city feeling between the two burgs, that is possibly commendable, but crippling of players should not enter into a strife, no matter how bitter.

—Sam Crane, New York *Evening Journal*

{The following item was the most detailed reference to Chicago's protest of the September 4 game in the only New York newspaper that mentioned the incident.}

President Pulliam has thrown out the Chicago club's protest of last Friday's game in Pittsburgh, and the 1 to 0 victory of Pittsburgh will stand. Pulliam had affidavits of all kinds submitted by the Chicago club, but he and Hank O'Day held that the game was fairly won, and that Chicago's kick was far-fetched. The Cubs couldn't prove their contention, so Mr. Pulliam backed up his umpire.

"I think the baseball public prefers to see games settled on the field and not in this office," said Pulliam. —New York *Globe*

The usual pell-mell rush through the press box resulted in an accident yesterday. After each game there is a helter-skelter scramble through that part of the stand. {At this time the press box in the Polo Grounds was located in the lower grandstand, close to the field.} The fans step on the necks and hands of the poor scribes who are forced to linger a few moments after the game and then take a six-foot jump into the diamond. Yesterday a big, heavy fan missed his footing and fell heavily on his side, with his leg doubled under him. He sustained a fractured knee and had to be assisted from the field by the surgeon who was called to attend him. After this rush every day the wreckage of seats is strewn all over the press box. Someday there will be a bad accident.

—Sid Mercer, New York *Globe*

———◇ **THURSDAY, SEPTEMBER 10** ◇———

{On September 9, in New York, the Giants beat Brooklyn 7 to 3. Winning pitcher, Ames; losing pitcher, Bell. Giants' standing: 78 wins, 46 losses, in first place.}

Leon Ames pitched a winning game yesterday. He had speed and control. Once upon a time Ames was very liberal with passes. Yesterday he was as stingy as a passenger agent under the Interstate Commerce law. That the big fellow once more can take his turn on the rubber brought smiles to the face of John McGraw. It means the Giants are fortified in the pitcher's box to stand off the Pirates and Cubs, who simply refuse to lose.

The Giants didn't have to work so hard for victory as on Tuesday. The absence of {catcher} Billy Bergen made a chapter in the game that could be headed "Base Running Made Easy." Billy Maloney, who is now very rusty as a backstop, caught for Brooklyn. {A major league outfielder since 1901, Maloney had not caught in a game since 1902.} To be charitable, he did his best, but that best was something awful when it came to throwing to bases. Herzog, subbing for Doyle, added four steals to his record.                                                 —New York *World*

Had it not been for an accident, one of those unlucky and unexpected gags that butt in at the wrong moment to thwart a well-laid and daring plot, the Giants would have pulled off a stunt never before even attempted in big league society.

Occasionally, very occasionally, a runner steals home while the pitcher is making love to the ball. But for two men to work this, and in succession—that's going some.

Herzog pulled it on Bell yesterday and got away with it. Donlin followed him and made it, too, even cleaner than his brother thief. But Devlin, who knew it was coming and stood pat, had his bat in the way of the ball. He fouled it off unintentionally, and Mike's joke on the pitcher didn't take.

And, outside of that, how the Giants did steal bases—only nine of them. It was a constant procession around the corners, and most of them standing. They didn't even take the trouble to hit the dirt.

—Gym Bagley, New York *Evening Mail*

The Giants will play all the rest of their games at home, except those of September 10, scheduled for Brooklyn, and of October 1, 2 and 3, in Philadelphia. This advantage is fully appreciated by those acquainted with McGraw's methods and the extreme partisanship of Polo Grounds patrons. President Pulliam's best umpires will be assigned to the metropolis, but even the assurance of a square deal on decisions will not remove the handicap visiting players are under on the Giants' grounds. Because of the great advantage McGraw's team gains by its long stretch of games at home, it may be that the best team in the National League will not represent it in the world series of 1908.     —*The Sporting News*

———◇ FRIDAY, SEPTEMBER 11 ◇———

{On September 10, in Brooklyn, the Giants won 6 to 5. Winning pitcher, Taylor; losing pitcher, Rucker. Giants' standing: 79 wins, 46 losses, in first place.}

We beat the Brooklyns yesterday, but we knew we had been to the races. Pretty close, public, pretty close. Too close for comfort. However, it was a win, and as Pittsburgh suffered a lapse {losing to Cincinnati}, you may increase your ticket on the Giants.

Twelve thousand human persons, men and women, gathered together in peace and unity, and the management of the Brooklyn club indulged in the first smile of the season. That is to say when you use the word smile in its restricted sense. And an outturning of fair femininity such as makes us look upon ourselves as the only matinee idol worth specifying. Now, all this is very grateful, and moves to a sort of permissible gratulation, until the rude native next to us blurts out: "It's like this every Thursday—this is Ladies' Day."

Ladies' Day in Brooklyn means that ladies don't pay to get in. Oh, gallant Brooklyn! Oh, wise Brooklyn! Make a few notes of that, McGraw. {Since the 1890s women had been admitted free to Thursday games in Brooklyn. Several other cities also held "Ladies' Day," but the practice had not yet been sanctioned by the Giants or Yankees.}

—W. W. Aulick, New York *Times*

For some reason that has not been explained, the Patsies who look like dog meat when arrayed against other clubs seem to give us more trouble and distress to the square inch than any aggregation in the league. When they are playing Joe Kelley's Oslers, or Ganzel's Goats, or McCloskey's Misfits, they give up the ghost without even squawking—peacefully, prayerfully, like little Nell taking the count in "The Old Curiosity Shop." When they fling their spears against our brawny demons, they are beautiful in their Battling Nelson aggressiveness and mighty hard propositions all the way. They certainly made the gooseflesh come yesterday.

Joe McGinnity did the heaving for us until the seventh, when Dummy Taylor put on the pitching spangles. Up to that time in the seventh that they began to land on Joseph {and scored three runs}, he had been pitching a clean, consistent game, but suddenly the bingles began to jingle, and McGraw acted with his usual speed, calling the Iron Man to shelter before it was too late. The deaf mute let in the tying tally with a wild pitch, but after that the Brooklynites stopped their trouble-making, and it ended well.        —William F. Kirk, New York *American*

McGraw need not worry about Doyle being out. Charley Herzog is playing a great game at second, just as he had done at short and at third when the occasion demanded and is, without doubt, the best young player of the year. Yesterday he batted .500, stole a base, scored a run, and batted in another, and did great work in the field.

Donlin, however, was the Giants' best hitting bet of the day, getting four hits in four trips to the plate, three of them bunts placed just exactly right.

Umpire Johnstone made a ruling yesterday which will establish a precedent. When it came time for {Jim} Holmes {Brooklyn's second pitcher} to bat in the seventh Patsy Donovan sent Alperman from the bench with a bat in his hand. McGraw promptly jerked McGinnity from the box and then Donovan called Alperman and trotted Holmes up. Alperman had never reached the plate, but Johnstone said he was the batter and ruled Holmes out of the game.          —Nie, New York *Globe*

It is difficult to pick out one man on McGraw's team and prove that he has done more than any other player toward lifting the team into first place. And therein lies the secret of the Giants' success. It is not a one-man team. The absence of any one star will not demoralize it. Larry Doyle, for example, has been a big factor in the victories of the last few weeks, but the Giants are winning without Doyle.

—Sid Mercer, New York *Globe*

It is high time baseball games were started at 3:30 instead of 4. There wouldn't be much chance of an extra-inning game unless an earlier start were made.                              —New York *Sun*

———◇ **SATURDAY, SEPTEMBER 12** ◇———

{On September 11, in New York, the Giants beat Brooklyn 6 to 1. Winning pitcher, Crandall; losing pitcher, Wilhelm. Giants' standing: 80 wins, 46 losses, in first place.}

If the Pittsburgh and Chicago diamond athletes could see the brand of baseball the Giants are putting up now they certainly would feel like changing their routes when they depart from their reservations a few days hence. Those Brooklyn boys suffered another deep dent yesterday.

Well, sir! you ought to have seen that young fellow Herzog and that other young fellow McCormick, and also the young fellow Crandall, working at their trade! They did some joyous jolting, you may be sure.

Truly, each succeeding day makes the Giants look more and more like pennant winners.       —New York *Herald*

Fred Tenney was full of pepper yesterday and radiated so much ginger he was almost a crab. He scolded Bresnahan, Crandall, Herzog, and the whole family. Tenney has bolstered up the infield of the Gingery Giants more than anybody except McGraw realizes.

Tenney had a repartee duel with Gentle Roger Bresnahan in the seventh inning that is worthy of more than passing mention. While {Tommy} McMillan was at bat Fred imagined there was a lack of speed in the battery work of Crandall and Bresnahan, so he shouted, "Wake up, Roger, wake up!" Roger resented this deeply. He looked at Tenney more in sorrow than anger. But there was an air of "Don't try to repeat!" about the stocky backstop that made Frederick close his trap. A moment later Tenney went after a hard, low foul ball that nobody could have captured. When he started back for the initial sack Gentle Roger shouted "What's the matter, Fred? Did you think it would bite you?" If we had two more crabs on the team like Bresnahan and Tenney we would never lose a game.     —William F. Kirk, New York *American*

———◇ **SUNDAY, SEPTEMBER 13** ◇———

{On September 12, in New York, the Giants beat Brooklyn 6 to 3. Winning pitcher, Mathewson; losing pitcher, McIntire. Giants' standing: 81 wins, 46 losses, in first place.}

There may on exceptional occasions have been more people at the Polo Grounds than yesterday, but never more noise. And at that the attendance was around 20,000, but a crowd of this size doesn't make us think in headlines any longer. We accepted the first-time filling of the new left-field bleachers just as in former times we accepted the Brooklyn Bridge, the Jersey Tunnel, the cocktail with an olive instead of a cherry, the Times Building, and other evidences of advance.

—W. W. Aulick, New York *Times*

What mightily pleased the Brooklyn end of the big crowd was the exceptional debut made by Jim Dunn, the raw recruit from Evansville of the Three-Eye League, who arrived after an all-night train ride to become Brooklyn's catcher. Things looked mighty bad for the Superbas before Dunn's arrival. Billy Bergen {the regular catcher, who had been injured} had gone home for the season. Al Farmer {second-string catcher} had sent in his resignation, and Billy Maloney {outfielder turned catcher} had been indefinitely suspended for his little argument with Johnstone the day before.

Maloney's notification came while the team was practicing. A messenger boy, in full regalia, appeared on the field, and after interviewing Manager Donovan, took the envelope to Maloney, working behind the bat. Billy signed for it in proper form and, after involuntarily digging into his pocket for the tip that wasn't there, opened the missive and read its contents. He then went on practicing, for be it known, a player is not officially in eclipse until the game starts. Then he is compelled to obliterate himself.

Dunn's advent into fast company was about as sensational as Heinie Batch {a Brooklyn infielder-outfielder} a season or two ago {actually on June 20, 1904}. On that occasion Batch made two home runs off Mathewson. Dunn, batting against the same pitcher, came up for his introduction to the vast populace in the second inning and with two men on base slammed out a double to right that hit the fence with a bang. The two runners scored and Dunn tallied himself soon after, thus being instrumental in all the runs scored by the Superbas.

The next time up, Dunn drove a clean single to left and was immediately voted a "find" by the populace. On his fourth trip to the plate, with two men on base, Dunn made good by caroming a hot one off Herzog's shoe, filling the bases.

Dunn held McIntire nicely and won respect as a thrower by nailing Tenney, the first man to attempt a steal. Only two bases were stolen on him, quite a change from the recent wholesale robbery of New York runners. {Despite this auspicious start, Dunn's major league career ended after he had competed in only 30 games in 1908 and 1909, compiling a composite batting average of .169.} —Brooklyn *Eagle*


Headed this way are the Pesky Pirates, the Chesty Cubs, the down-trodden Cardinals, and the Remarkable Reds. The third and last invasion of the East by Western clubs starts on Tuesday.

Among the games to be played by the Giants will be four doubleheaders, two with the Reds and one each with the Cubs and Pirates, making it necessary to squeeze into eight playing days 12 games. If McGraw's pitchers can stand up under this strain it looks like New York for a certainty to represent the National League in the world's series.

—New York *Press*


## ———◇ MONDAY, SEPTEMBER 14 ◇———

Mike Donlin will have to do some mighty slugging during the remainder of the season to take the batting lead away from Hans Wagner. Wagner's current average is .350, while Donlin is batting .327.

—New York *World*


## ——— NATIONAL LEAGUE STANDINGS ———

| | W | L | PCT. | GB | | W | L | PCT. | GB |
|---|---|---|---|---|---|---|---|---|---|
| New York ... | 81 | 46 | .638 | — | Cincinnati ... | 63 | 70 | .474 | 21 |
| Chicago ..... | 83 | 51 | .620 | 1½ | Boston ...... | 55 | 77 | .417 | 28½ |
| Pittsburgh ... | 82 | 51 | .617 | 2 | Brooklyn .... | 44 | 85 | .341 | 38 |
| Philadelphia . | 71 | 56 | .555 | 10 | St. Louis .... | 44 | 87 | .336 | 39 |


## ———◇ TUESDAY, SEPTEMBER 15 ◇———

{On September 14, in New York, the Giants beat Brooklyn 4 to 3. Winning pitcher, Wiltse; losing pitcher, Pastorius. Giants' standing: 82 wins, 46 losses, in first place.}

Mr. J. Bentley Seymour, master mechanic at the baseball business, while in the performance of his duty at the Polo property yesterday had five opportunities at bat. He didn't miss any of them. First time up he slapped the leather into right field for two bases. Second time up he hit it into the middle of the lot for three bases. Third time up he hit it into right for two bases. Fourth time up he drove it into the middle for a fine single, and the fifth time up he hit it for a still finer single into right.

Fair day's labor? Well, rather!　　　　　—New York *Herald*


In the ninth Bridwell was badly spiked by Jordan, but no one knew it and Brid played out the inning. When he came to the bench, McGraw saw a big rip in his pants and blood stains on the cloth.

"What's that?" asked Mac.

"Oh, I got a scratch," replied Bridwell. "That's all."

But McGraw sent for Dr. Creamer and had the wound, an ugly one, patched up, before he would let Brid go to bat.

That is an example of the grit that obtains among this bunch, a grit that will land the old rag.

See if it doesn't.　　　　　—Gym Bagley, New York *Evening Mail*


———◇　**WEDNESDAY, SEPTEMBER 16**　◇———


{On September 15, in New York, the Giants beat St. Louis, 5 to 4. Winning pitcher, Mathewson; losing pitcher, Higginbotham. Giants' standing: 83 wins, 46 losses, in first place.}


Leon Ames pitched great ball until the bingles began to collect in the eighth. He had control, and he had speed and curves thrown in. In the inning which brought on his downfall, he seemed to have as much as any twirler could expect, and yet the Miserable Missourians hit everything he had.

It was up to Matty, and "Big Six" responded nobly. Perhaps the Democratic Party can get along without McCarren {Patrick Henry McCarren, a well-known Brooklyn politician who had been a state senator since 1888} and it is a cinch that Republicans can get along without Hirsute Hughes {Governor Charles Evans Hughes of New York, who had lost out to Taft in a battle for the 1908 Republican presidential nomination} but the Giants cannot get along without Matty, and you can lay your last dime that way. Long live King Christy!

—William F. Kirk, New York *American*

─────◇ **THURSDAY, SEPTEMBER 17** ◇─────

{On September 16, in New York, the Giants beat St. Louis 6 to 2. Winning pitcher, Crandall; losing pitcher, Baldwin. Giants' standing: 84 wins, 46 losses, in first place.}

New York's pennant outlook took on additional improvement yesterday. The Poloists won from the Cardinals and the Pittsburghs broke even in a doubleheader with Philadelphia. The Chicagos beat Boston and tied Pittsburgh for second place. The first three teams have each won 84 games, but the Giants have lost six less than either of the other two.

—New York *Sun*

Yesterday's game between the Giants and Cardinals was New York's at all stages. It was not creditable baseball to either side, but the Giants were properly doing only enough playing to win, sparing their better efforts for future, more important occasions.

Donlin was ordered off the field in the seventh for disputing a decision by O'Day, in which Donlin was called out at first base, and a happy remark by McGraw, relating to Donlin's dispute, resulted in the manager being sent to the bench.          —New York *Tribune*

The great question now in local fandom is, Will Mike Donlin be sequestered for three days on account of his run-in with Umpire Hank O'Day yesterday?

I can say, officially, that Captain Donlin said nothing that will cause Sir Michael's retirement for the three days. I want to say, too, that Donlin was a wee bit lacking in good judgment by making such a holler, inasmuch as the Giants need his services at this stage of the game and the loss of his services would be a very serious handicap.

Thanks to the good sense with which Hank O'Day is blessed, he has taken a correct and proper view of the situation and instead of making a Donnybrook affair of the little "difficoolty," will handle the little clash himself, and the fiery but too irascible Michael will be on the job this afternoon.

Hank O'Day is one of the very few real umpires, and as such he should be appreciated by Mike Donlin, Roger Bresnahan and the other fiery Giants, who can be just as "crabby" and unreasonable as the worst umpire that ever lived. Umpire O'Day should be nursed, not trampled upon.

O'Day makes mistakes, of course, but when one thinks of all that an umpire must go through during a baseball season one feels like giving a medal to good old Hank O'Day. And I would be the first to "produce" for a medal for Hank. I have played ball with him and against him, and I can say that no squarer man ever lived. {O'Day had been a major league pitcher from 1884 through 1890 and won 70 games while losing 110. For part of 1889 he was a Giant, winning 9 and losing only 1. Among the other National League umpires, only Emslie, a pitcher for three years in the 1880s, had played major league baseball.}

—Sam Crane, New York *Evening Journal*


That the country at large is conceding the banner to New York was evidenced by the presence in the Brush stadium yesterday of experts from Detroit, sent here to get a line on the Giants. {In the American League, the Detroit Tigers were battling for the pennant and the right to play in the World Series.} The Michigan scouts, after witnessing the battle, reported that for ability to find weak points in an adversary there was nothing to compare with McGraw's aggregation. —New York *Press*


The conduct of McGraw recently has been most reprehensible, and has excited editorial comment from critics all over the circuit. The opinion is general among baseball writers that the sooner the National League decides that it can get along without McGraw and his hoodlumism, the sooner will the ideal state of affairs be realized. McGraw was barred from the American League, he is persona non grata at most race tracks in the country, but he has for several years found a haven in the National

League, which has boasted ever since the inauguration of the Pulliam administration of a policy of advancement. One big step needs still to be taken, and when it comes to pass, McGraw will be beyond the pale of major league balldom. {McGraw was never "barred from the American League." In July 1902, after prolonged feuding with American League President Ban Johnson, McGraw resigned as manager of Baltimore, and left the American League for good, to go to the Giants. His departure led some American Leaguers for a while to compare McGraw to Benedict Arnold.}                    —Ralph Davis, *The Sporting News*


The long-nosed rooters are crazy whenever young Herzog does anything noteworthy. Cries of "Herzog! Herzog! Goot poy, Herzog!" go up regularly, and there would be no let-up even if a million ham sandwiches suddenly fell among these believers in percentages and bargains.

                    —Joe Vila, *The Sporting News*


President Pulliam's decision on the protest filed by the Chicago club, in re its game of September 4, is in effect a dismissal for lack of proof to sustain the claim. When Wilson batted the ball that sent a runner home, the overflow crowd invaded the field and thereafter it would have been practically impossible for two umpires to have kept the four runners and the ball under supervision. The official in charge does not know that Gill proceeded to second and acquired legal right to that base, but the presumption that he did cannot be removed by the claim of members of the Chicago team. The umpire may not accept testimony of a player as a basis for a ruling. It is a baseball axiom that only that which the umpire sees occurs on a ball field. If the force-out did occur—Gill and five of his teammates say it did not—the umpire missed it and by implication officially ruled there was none by allowing the run that terminated the game. Chicago's protest was ill-advised and served only to afford the carping class of patrons an opportunity to question the integrity of the game.

                    —*The Sporting News*

It's all right!

John T. Brush says so.

"Florry" Ziegfeld's pretty show girls from the "Follies of 1908," 25 in number—count 'em—will, by permission of Mr. Brush, invade the Polo Grounds tomorrow and collect ten-cent subscriptions from the fans for the trophy to be presented by the *American* to the Giants at the end of the season. {The first of Ziegfeld's famous "Follies" had been produced in 1907.}

And some more good news!

The girls will go to the Polo Grounds from the New York Theatre in one of those rubberneck automobiles, a Knickerbocker five-seater, accommodating 25 people. The auto is contributed by Mrs. Frank B. Walker, president of the Knickerbocker Automobile Company, at 41st street and Broadway. The trophy committee {whose membership included Sam H. Harris, Florenz Ziegfeld, Victor Moore, De Wolf Hopper, George M. Cohan, and James J. Corbett} went to engage the machine from the Knickerbocker Company and stated the purpose to which it is to be put.

"Why," said Mrs. Walker, a businesswoman from head to heels, "I'm as enthusiastic a fan as any of you. You cannot pay me for the machine if it is to be used to gather money for a trophy. I'll donate its use for nothing."          —J. W. Hamer, New York *American*


─────◇  **FRIDAY, SEPTEMBER 18**  ◇─────


{On September 17, in New York, the Giants beat St. Louis 10 to 5. Winning pitcher, Taylor; losing pitcher, Raymond. Giants' standing: 85 wins, 46 losses, in first place.}


After yesterday's culmination of Missouri courtesies we are not going to take much more stock in those magazine muck-rakings aimed at St. Louis sinfulness. If you ask us, the Westerners are represented, in a baseball way of speaking, by nine as perfect gents as ever left a series behind them. They left yesterday, accompanied by our best wishes. Would that they might have remained always.

There was some hitting yesterday. Five pitchers trotted out before the crowd, and four were used. Mr. Marquard's pitching appearance was purely Pickwickian. He didn't face a St. Louis batter. You see, McGinnity had started the game and had pitched four innings, at the end of which time the score was 3 to 1 in our favor. But to get at this result McGinnity had been let out of the batting procession, Barry hitting for him.

So McGinnity is out of the game, and across the lawn lopes something about 18 feet high, or so it seems, and the aidful umpire says: "Ladiesgmn, this is Mr. Marquard come to pitch for you. Grant him a little greet." Mr. Marquard, who arrived in town a couple of days ago, comes high—if we win the pennant we won't have to buy a flagpole, that is, if we can get Marky to stand still long enough. But after Marquard has thrown a few practice balls to Bresnahan, along comes Taylor, and the skyscraper retires to the bench.

—W. W. Aulick, New York *Times*


The main feature of the afternoon was the appearance of Mr. Marquard, the $11,000 peach. History tells us that once in the dim and distant past $10,000 was paid for Mike Kelley {a first baseman, Kelley played for Louisville's National League team in 1899, his sole major league season, and batted .241.}, and such later stars as Theodore Breitenstein and Spike Shannon also came under the head of "ten-thousand-dollar beauties." {Breitenstein pitched for St. Louis and Cincinnati in the 1890s, and in one five-year stretch, 1892–1896, lost 122 games.} But Mr. Marquard raised 'em a thousand, and he seemed to know it when McGraw sent him to the box to warm up and stall while Dummy Taylor was getting his more experienced wing in trim. Mr. Marquard may or may not prove to be a big league star, but if he falls a bit short, it won't be because he is lacking in genuine nerve and boyish self-confidence. He was in the pitcher's box only long enough to give the yearning fans one peek at him, but they were impressed by his pitching manners, and so was McGraw.

—William F. Kirk, New York *American*


Bingham—you may have heard of Bingham, he's got an office in the Police Commissioner's Department at 300 Mulberry Street—has at last woke up to the fact that when 20,000 or 30,000 citizens gather in a public place they are entitled to some sort of police protection.

So the regular bulls will be scattered around the Polo Grounds when the Giants and Pirates grapple. John T. Brush handed Brother Bingham a line of conversation regarding the necessity of policing the grounds during the stay of Pirates and Cubs that Bingham fell for, and he will send a couple of hundred blue-boys to hang around and make themselves useful should they be needed.     —Gym Bagley, New York *Evening Mail*


I tell you the Giants can't lose out unless they all drop dead. That looks cinchy enough, doesn't it? The McGraw bunch is going altogether too fast to allow any team coming from behind and beating them to the nearby wire.     —Sam Crane, New York *Evening Journal*


> The old man called his son aside,
>     And kissed him on the brow.
> "Remember, my boy," the parent said,
>     "You're a full-fledged voter now.
> Look out, my son, for the country's good,
>     Let truth be your guiding star;
> Always live up to the golden rule,
>     No matter where you are.
> If you think Bill Taft is the better man,
>     Then let him be your choice;
> Or vote for William Jennings Bryan,
>     The man with the silvery voice.
> If Governor Hughes looks good to you
>     As head of this beautiful state,
> Then vote for him; if not, then vote
>     For the other candidate."
>
> But here the son broke in and said,
>     "These guys are new to me.
> I never heard of Taft or Hughes
>     Or Bryan, honestly.
> I never saw those queer old names
>     When looking through the score.
> I'd understand you better, pa,
>     If you mentioned John McGraw."
>                 —R. L. "Rube" Goldberg, New York *Evening Mail*

{On September 18, in New York, the Giants defeated Pittsburgh in a doubleheader, 7 to 0 and 12 to 7. Winning pitchers, Mathewson and Wiltse; losing pitchers, Maddox and Leever. Giants' standing: 87 wins, 46 losses, in first place.}

The greatest throng of humanity ever attracted to a baseball game saw the Giants in a vicious, terrific five hours' battle defeat the Pirates twice and drive them out of the pennant race.

The event was national. It is doubtful if during the war so many people throughout the entire nation watched bulletins so anxiously. Then they waited to hear if Chancellorsville, Gettysburg or Antietam had been lost or won, whether a father, brother or son had died on the field of battle.

Yesterday the nation quivered and shook while 18 young men, most of whom will soon be quietly farming or running a cafe, played two games of baseball.

At the scene of combat the tension was evidenced in various ways. Men talked, or rather gibbered, to themselves. Forgetting all feminine reserve, women leaped up to cry as tears dotted their cheeks: "Hit the ball! Kill it! Run, oh, for heaven's sake, run!"

When Mike Donlin lifted the white horsehide sphere into the right bleachers, clinching the first game, this heart-deadening tension in the merest fragment of time changed to a roar that sounded like the swish of a planet, the crack of doom. "Matty" was pitching. The game was safe.

When little Herzog clipped the ball, with the score tied in the second game, and brought Bridwell home, giving New York a one-tally advantage, 40,000 mortals joined in a Olympian wake. If any one of these spectators had received an unexpected legacy of $30,000,000 he might have been dazed or delighted. He could not have done what he did yesterday. Herzog had hit the ball. America was getting something off its chest.

The common, garden variety of citizens of this nation is generally cool, collected and has to be "shown." Maybe that comes from Yankee blood. Give him a fight, a real soul-stirring sensation and he'll make a "jumping Frenchman look like a cigar store Indian." What the Giants did yesterday made a man forget grocer, butcher and undertaker bills.

The Giants fought with the desperation of the Bunker Hill warriors and the precision of Dewey's men at Manila. Of mixed Irish and German descent, they seemed to mix the pugnacity and persistence of both races.

There was no cheering, no demonstration in the first game when the mighty Mathewson strode to the box. While the fans regarded him safe as the Bank of England, they were uncertain. There was the brawny Wagner, with arms like a gorilla and elliptical legs, who leads the league in hitting. Wagner's face is drawn and ascetic. He seems about as happy as the Ancient Mariner when the spigot ran dry. You could feel, hear, see nothing but an awful tension.

In the second inning Mike Donlin began the scoring. He hit clean to short left. There was no effort. He chopped the ball downward. In sharp contrast was Cy Seymour, who hit under and flied out. This may account for Donlin's excellence in hitting. He keeps the ball on terra firma.

Arthur Devlin, a quiet, well-mannered young man, who took the H. O. {home economics, notoriously easy} course at Georgetown, set his teeth and lashed the ball for two bases inside the left foul line. He also hit down. Harry McCormick, a great hulking lad, who, like an elephant, which is said to be awful fast on its pins, swashed a drive to center and Donlin galloped home.

Still the awful hush, dreadful tension.

Fred Tenney, an ancient person, who went Ponce de Leon a couple better and discovered the fountain of youth, started the third inning with a two-base clout to left field. Out on the third-base coaching corner McGraw made some deaf and dumb signals with a broken forefinger. Thanks to Dummy Taylor all the Giants understand this lingo. Maybe that's why the Dummy is kept on the salary roll.

Herzog sacrificed Tenney according to orders and Mike Donlin brought him home. Donlin was speedily becoming the whole show.

Still the awful hush, dreadful tension. What were two runs lead with that gorilla person, "The Flying Dutchman," waiting to hit the ball to Kansas City!

In the fifth Mathewson gazed hard at Pitcher Maddox, a well-formed youth with a face like a dried apple. When one pitcher gets a hit off another it makes the "one" grin. Mathewson nearly laughed when he splashed a two-bagger to left. Maddox accumulated six more stresses in his neck.

It seemed to distract him and he passed Herzog. Bresnahan, the catcher, who suggests a Crusader in his complete suit of armor, leaned against the "pill" for two bases, scoring Mathewson.

Still the awful hush, dreadful tension.

It just didn't seem possible that Pittsburgh would lose. Or was it that everybody was so fearfully anxious they hesitated to yell?

With a lead of three runs and two out, Mike Donlin came to bat. His wife, Mabel Hite, leaned from an upper box exhorting him to "Kill it; bring them home; win the game!"

Eliminating all romance it cannot be said that Mike looked aloft with the love light in his eyes. No, he merely said to that unfortunate pitcher: "Put one over."

The foolish pitcher did, and a lad from Amsterdam avenue and 145th street finally got the ball in the right-field bleachers. It sailed upward and onward. Even as it sailed the creases in Maddox's face deepened, while Fred Clarke said part of what you say when starting a telephone conversation.

And now the deluge. The scene was more spectacular, more spontaneous than any before at the Polo Grounds.

The second game was more convulsive. George Wiltse had small control and not much speed and looked like a tired man in the box. With two out in the first Tommy Leach, who is a wealthy automobile dealer in the winter, clipped a two-bagger, the "Flying Dutchman" followed with another, and Abbaticchio laced a home run into the bleachers.

Now came an entirely new set of sensations. It would be small advantage for the Giants to win one game. It must be for them to annihilate Pittsburgh and perhaps cinch the pennant with double victory. The multitude was horribly nervous, shaky, almost sick. A three-run lead!

McGraw, Donlin, Herzog and Wiltse did not seem to think the case serious. They would hang on.

"Coming from behind" is the Giants' specialty this year. The championship team of 1905 was a more perfect team. It usually started off in the first inning by scoring and dismaying its opponents. This team is more spectacular and likes to fight with the enemy ahead. Thus yesterday in the seventh inning of the second game the Giants slaughtered their rivals by scoring six runs, and after that it was no contest.

—New York *World*

One thing is sure—the fair femininity part of yesterday's layout was very much front row, and most of the gazelles had their dear little score cards, too, keeping close track of hits and errors. Truth to say, they called most of the errors hits and most of the hits errors, but that didn't detract from their charms. It was announced in the *American* that the Ziegfeld showgirls would be on assignment, and thousands craned their necks in vain to pick out "the dozen prettiest girls in town." There were so many pretty girls the fair solicitors were lost in the sugary swarm. Oh, you Betties!                    —William F. Kirk, New York *American*


The speculator pest was upon the Polo Grounds yesterday. The vendors must have reaped a harvest, for ordinary admissions were going at $1.50 each, seats in uncovered stands at $2, grandstand reserved seats from $3 to $5, and box seats from $5 up, according to the gullibility and wealth of the purchaser.

Yesterday a canvas was made before the game of regular ticket agencies in a dozen hotels along Broadway and 42nd street, but only one reply was received:

"We can't do anything for you; go to the speculators, they have all the tickets."                    —New York *Times*


Two fans were perched on an advertising sign about 45 feet above the level of the diamond. Puzzle—tell how they got there and earn a season pass to the Yankee grounds.                    —New York *Evening Mail*


CHICAGO, Sept. 12—Chicago's baseball romance ran into headwinds last Saturday when Frank Chance, manager of the world's champions, forbade the marriage of Artie Hofman and beautiful Rae Looker until after the baseball season is over. The wedding was to have taken place on September 7, the minister engaged, the invitations were about to be mailed, everything was in readiness. Mr. Hofman protested energetically when informed that a postponement of the nuptials would be necessary—"for the good of the team." But his protest went for naught. "I guess Miss

Looker and I can wait," said Mr. Hofman tonight. "She's as anxious to have the Cubs win as I am."          —Charles H. Zuber, *Sporting Life*

CINCINNATI, Sept. 15—The "spit ball" delivery has another powerful opponent in National League President Pulliam. "It's unclean; it prevents good fielding; it handicaps scientific batting; it's a freak, and so has no place in a straight sport." These are some of the arguments Pulliam advances against use of the "spit ball," which is being agitated almost as much these days as the political situation and the proper pronunciation of the word "lallapaloosa." "While I have not decided on a crusade against the 'spit ball,' " said Pulliam here, "I am strongly opposed to the use of that style of delivery. It is possible that between now and the time of the next meeting of the National League, there will be framed legislation to which both leagues will agree, and will do away with this offensive style of pitching. The 'spit ball' is no more essential to baseball than is the dog-faced boy to the three-ringed circus. Both are freaks, without which the big show would be much better off." {No restrictions were placed by the major leagues on the use of the spit-ball pitch until 1921, when seventeen men became designated spitballers, and they alone could thereafter employ the pitch. Spitballing in the big leagues ended when Burleigh Grimes retired after the 1934 season.}

                                    —Charles H. Zuber, *Sporting Life*

————◇  **SUNDAY, SEPTEMBER 20**  ◇————

{On September 19, in New York, the Giants lost to Pittsburgh 6 to 2, in 10 innings. Winning pitcher, Leifield; losing pitcher, Crandall. Giants' standing: 87 wins, 47 losses, in first place.}

Smoke beat 'em. Wagner had his shoes full of it, and their gross tonnage is some. Leach concealed it under his cap; Leifield, the pitcher, had it up his sleeve, and Abbaticchio, the son of Caesar, had a bat loaded with it.

Sometimes the thick greasy vapor lay over the arena soppy as molasses on the bread you used to eat at home. Occasionally it lifted enough to glimpse the unholy grin on the face of Fred Clarke, and he does have an unholy grin. Again it settled down so you couldn't see whether Hans

Wagner had on a sheath gown or an ulster. {The latest creation of Parisian dress designers, the sheath gown was a current sensation on both sides of the Atlantic. It was so tight-fitting a woman could not walk in one but for a slit in its side, and in August, Anthony Comstock, head of the Society for the Suppression of Vice, had threatened to arrest and prosecute any woman who publicly appeared in New York City in a sheath gown.}

A lot of people said it was smoke wafted in from Minnesota, Dakota or some other distant place where there are forest fires. But the wise fans know differently. It was smoke from the "Smoky City." The "smoke-town" players were at home, as a clam in high water. They didn't give a whoop who pitched, what McGraw said on the coaching line, or whether a fair matron keeled over with nose bleed when an excited clergyman made the figure eight with his right elbow. They can beat the Giants in smoke, and they did.

The elbow catastrophe happened in the ninth, with the score 2 to 2, three on base and Mike Donlin at bat. He was a young parson, of weak countenance and there was Jersey mud on his heels. He stood with 1,000 others back of the seats on the grandstand and hadn't uttered a word until this supreme moment.

"Bang it, Mike! Slam it, Mike! Give 'em blazes, Mike!" were some of the things he yelled. A saloonkeeper nearby said the parson made it stronger than "blazes." He told Dr. Creamer, the Giants' physician, who was hustled up from the press box, that the "guy ought to be locked up."

By the time Dr. Creamer had stopped the nose bleed Mike Donlin had fouled out to Tommy Leach and the game was lost. The tenth inning saw Pittsburgh lace Pitcher Crandall all over the farm, bump in four runs and win 6 to 2. Chicago also won against Philadelphia, so while the Giants dropped a few points their two rivals crept up, but—wait till Monday.                                                          —New York *World*


"Bet a million" John W. Gates was one of the 30,000 who saw the Giants go down to defeat yesterday. {A legendary figure on Wall Street, Gates was famed for his spectacular stock market transactions.}

John W. reached New York at noon today {Saturday} on the belated *Mauretania* from Liverpool with gloom plastered all over his countenance because he missed the doubleheader on Friday.

A week ago Saturday he boarded the *Mauretania*, believing he could reach New York in time to take in all of the Pittsburgh series. His son, Charley Gates, had made all the arrangements and had a box hired for Friday's games. All day Friday Charley was on board the revenue cutter off quarantine waiting for the big Cunarder to come up the bay.

As soon as he got back to Manhattan on Friday night he sent a wireless message to his father with the baseball scores, which made the financier more impatient than ever. When the *Mauretania* neared her pier Gates was willing to bet all kinds of the long green stuff that he would see the game that afternoon, and as soon as he set foot on solid ground he jumped into his auto and started for the Polo Grounds.

—C. B. Power, Pittsburgh *Dispatch*

DETROIT, Sept. 19—Now listen to the yell. The diamond athletes will not be handed a package of money for winning world championships after this. The National Commission has decided to put a ban on the offering of all bonus money.

Last year the Detroit owners gave their entire receipts to the champions, even after they had lost four straight in the world's series. Charley Murphy, of the Cubs, who won the games, didn't like it. He didn't want to shell out and raised a kick against such tactics.

Other league magnates had no great love for the scheme, and so the commission has forbidden the offering of special inducements or rewards. The players get 60 percent of the proceeds, anyway, and they figure this is enough.

This isn't the viewpoint of the player. He argues that he ought not to get 60 percent of the money, but all of it.      —New York *American*

———◇ **MONDAY, SEPTEMBER 21** ◇———

Don't let the dull, deadening thought sear your untutored soul that because the Pirates laid us aboard Saturday and made a sieve of First Mate Ames and Quartermaster Crandall that Capt. McGraw isn't going to nail the champion bunting to the Polo Grounds mast.

I saw him myself buy the nails Saturday after the game. They were coffin size, the size that fits Pittsburgh and Chicago.

You don't begrudge the Pirates one game, do you? And that's all they're going to get. And the same goes for the Cubs when they hit town.

On Saturday Merkle got a chance at first when Tenney went to the clubhouse to rest his bad leg. And this boy is some first baseman. He's not as brilliant as Frederick, but it isn't always the most highly polished button on the soldier's coat that stops the bullet. Sometimes the soldier ducks.

Only once did Merkle show fog in his top hamper. There was a man on the bag, and, taking plenty of room, Bresnahan shot the signal across. Crandall pitched wide, but Merkle came in just as Roger was making ready to throw the Pirate out, and the move was wasted. Then Roger sprung a few sarcastic remarks in Merkle's direction because he didn't get the sign. Merkle didn't reply. He returned meekly to the base, with, no doubt, a mental resolve not be caught dozing again.

—Gym Bagley, New York *Evening Mail*

Complaints of regular patrons of the Polo Grounds that the best reserved seats on big days are to be secured only by purchasing from speculators at exorbitant prices is responsible for a new system of ticket distribution which goes into effect today.

Hereafter no reserved or box seats will be sold until the day of the game, and reservations can then be purchased only inside the park after admission has been paid. Purchasers of grandstand tickets can buy reserved seats at the box office in the rear of the stand. It will be a case of first come, first served.

There has been a demand for tickets for this week's games that is unprecedented in the experience of New York club officials. But Secretary Knowles has remailed checks for thousands of dollars to those who wished to purchase by mail, and his office force will be busy all week returning money to persons who wish to purchase in advance. This is an inconvenience and a hardship to regular patrons, and ticket speculators are to blame. —Sid Mercer, New York *Globe*

The secret of the Giants' success lies in the strength of the reserve force. McGraw saw this some months ago and immediately imparted the idea to John T. Brush. Mr. Brush threw open the bankroll and told

McGraw to go as far as he liked. What did McGraw do? He went out and grabbed Merkle and Herzog. He already had Doyle. A little later he got McCormick and Dave Brain, and still later he took Jack Barry from St. Louis. He wanted Barry for his experience.

McGraw is prepared for any emergency. Now do you wonder why New York is up in the lead?

—Bozeman Bulger, Chicago *Journal*


More improvements are to be made at the Polo Grounds before the end of the season. John T. Brush is satisfied that the Giants will win the pennant, and is preparing for the record crowds that will attend the world's series games. Contracts have been let to add a seating capacity of about 7,000.

When the improvements are completed New York will have the largest baseball park in the country. The seating capacity will be close to 30,000, and will be second only to the athletic fields at Yale and Harvard.

—New York *Evening Mail*


———— NATIONAL LEAGUE STANDINGS ————

| | W | L | PCT. | GB | | W | L | PCT. | GB |
|---|---|---|---|---|---|---|---|---|---|
| New York ... | 87 | 47 | .649 | — | Cincinnati ... | 66 | 72 | .478 | 23 |
| Chicago ..... | 86 | 53 | .619 | 3½ | Boston ...... | 57 | 81 | .413 | 32 |
| Pittsburgh ... | 86 | 54 | .614 | 4 | Brooklyn .... | 47 | 90 | .343 | 41½ |
| Philadelphia . | 73 | 61 | .544 | 14 | St. Louis .... | 47 | 91 | .341 | 42 |


———— ◇ **TUESDAY, SEPTEMBER 22** ◇ ————

{On September 21, in New York, the Giants lost to Pittsburgh 2 to 1. Winning pitcher, Willis; losing pitcher, Mathewson. Giants' standing: 87 wins, 48 losses, in first place.}

> *Why did Pittsburgh win the game,*
> *Hank O'Day?*
> *Don't you think it was a shame,*
> *Hank O'Day?*

*When you made that rank decision,*
*When the thousands voiced derision,*
*Where in hades was your vision,*
    *Hank O'Day?*

Pittsburgh left the island with an even break for the series, but the victory yesterday should never have been posted on the old blackboard. Granting that Pittsburgh might have shoved one tally across the plate, the worst we were entitled to was a draw.

In the third inning Umpire O'Day made an inexcusably bad decision when he called Wilson safe on first base. Umpires are human, and when they miss a "close one" now and then they should not be put on the pan, but the ruling made by O'Day, which practically put the Giants out of the running for the day, was absolutely weird.

Wilson led off the third with a grounder toward right field that looked like the sweetest kind of a single. Young Mr. Herzog dug after it like lightning, made a marvelous stop well out of the diamond, wheeled like a shot and sent the ball to Tenney in time to catch Wilson by at least a full yard. Perhaps O'Day didn't dream that Herzog could stop the ball, because he waved his arm majestically before the play was quite completed. Christy Mathewson, who seldom registers a kick, rushed over to O'Day in frantic protest and nearly swooned when he saw the Czar of the day wasn't kidding.

The decision, one of the worst ever seen on the grounds, robbed Herzog of the credit due to making a phenomenal play, and, far more important, cost the Giants the game. Gibson followed with a two-base hit, sending Wilson to third, and after Willis and Thomas had popped out, Fred Clarke got in a single down the left-field line—a hit that barely grazed Devlin's paws. On this slap Wilson and Gibson scored and the harm was done.

Manager Jawn got in bad with the twin umpires in the last of the third. Mac is trying to be a good boy these days, but he had witnessed that piece of arbitration in the first half of the same act, and the iron had entered his soul. So, naturally, he just couldn't help "alludin'" to certain judges of certain plays, and Umpire Klem, flying madly to the rescue of his brother in crime, called Manager Jawn in from the coaching lines. As the little corporal hoofed it for the bench he paused the tiniest part of a second and says to Klem, says he, "Herzog threw Wilson out three feet," he says. "Get off the field," Umpire Klem says, says he. "Throughout this long September afternoon I do not wish to see your face again!"

"All right," said Manager Jawn, and with these words he ducked into the little coop behind the players' bench and was swallowed up in the darkness for the time being.

But not for long. Chancing to gaze in the direction of the coop, Umpire Klem saw a tiny chink, and behind the chink two bright black eyes were shining, like the black eyes of an alert mouse peering from a hole in the wall.

"Murphy!" bellowed Umpire Klem, "shut that gate!"

The sturdy groundkeeper looked first at the gate and then at the umpire. For a moment he wavered between love and duty, and love won. He walked away and left the door open. If a German umpire wanted that door shut, reasoned the worthy groundkeeper, the German umpire would have to shut it himself. All honor to Murphy! In years to come children of present-day fans will tell in low whispers how Groundkeeper Murphy defied the umpire and refused to shut the coop door in the face of Manager Jawn McGraw.

—William F. Kirk, New York *American*

"They've got to show us. We are in the fight for the flag until the last inning of the last game of the season," declared Manager Fred Clarke after the Pirates had won the closing game of the series. The victory filled the Pirates with fresh hopes, and the smiles floating around the lobby of the Hotel Somerset were brighter than so many electric lights in a coal mine.

And the game—whew, it was a torrid affair! The best part of it was that Matty, he of the inflated chest and enlarged dome, a tall individual who has repeatedly done things to our beloved swatters, is charged with the defeat. —C. B. Power, Pittsburgh *Dispatch*

Yesterday's game was played in hurry-up style, only an hour and nineteen minutes being consumed in running it off.

—New York *Press*

{On September 22, in New York, the Giants lost a doubleheader to Chicago 4 to 3 and 2 to 1. Winning pitchers, Overall and Brown; losing pitchers, Ames and Crandall. Giants' standing: 87 wins, 50 losses, in first place.}

In two fierce, grueling games which took the stamina out of players and spectators alike, Frank Chance's Chicago Cubs beat John McGraw's New York Giants twice yesterday. If the Giants lose today the Cubs will lead the pennant race.

The Cubs played better ball all the way, but they had some luck, and Lajoie says that luck is half the game of baseball. In addition, the Giants turned in some stupid work, made a couple of errors and failed to hit the ball at critical moments.

McGraw sent in "Red" Ames to pitch the first game. First inning Schulte got a single and that ended the attack. Second inning it was one, two, three and out. Third inning, Overall, a huge person, lifted a fly into the left-field crowd. Anything that hits the crowd in these games goes for a two-bagger. And it might be observed that a New York crowd is most complacent.

It shifted twice for Chicago's right-fielder to catch line drives in the second and materially helped Chicago to win. But when McCormick tried to get one in the left field the rooters clung to the turf. In any other city the crowd would have helped the home team, which is as it should be, for loyalty is part of the game.

McCormick could have seized Overall's drive if he had the nerve of Billy Sunday, who leaped over several rows of rooters at the moment of his conversion to evangelism. {The famous evangelist Billy Sunday had been a major league outfielder from 1883 to 1890.} The crowd didn't open for McCormick; he had no aspirations to be an evangelist, and Overall got a two-bagger. He took third on Haydon's out, on which Bridwell made a wretched mistake. He had the grounder and could have thrown Overall out. Instead he let the big pitcher lumber to third base, where Devlin was waiting for the ball. Following this, Bridwell tried to field a grounder from Schulte, booted the ball, and Overall scored.

Encouraged by this, Chicago cut loose in the next inning and won the game. Steinfeldt hit a beautiful single to center. He was nailed at second by Devlin, who captured Hofman's intended sacrifice. Tinker pasted a single past Bridwell, sending Hofman to second, and that long-legged youth then stole third. He did it cleverly with a Chicago slide, throwing his body one way, his hand toward the base.

The whole Chicago team is clever, machine-like, and game. They have Pittsburgh beaten at every point of the game, and the only way New York can win is to out-hit them.

Kling then grounded to Tenney, who fired the ball to Ames, covering first, and Ames dropped it. Overall came to bat again and whaled a long fly to centerfield. Seymour caught the ball, but he could not get it home in time to head off Tinker.

Chicago's success appeared to "rattle" the Giants. Herzog did not try to get a high fly from Haydon, which fell fair while Donlin, Seymour, Bridwell and Herzog gazed hard at the hole it made in the soft green turf. As these gentlemen bent their eyes earthward, Johnny Kling, who receives a matter of $7,000 for six months' work, cantered over the plate.

New York was baffled by Overall until the lucky seventh, when Capt. Mike Donlin jammed a two-bagger in right field. Seymour singled to right. Then Devlin doubled to right, scoring Donlin. Chance was scared now. He yanked Overall and put in "Three-Fingered" Brown. McCormick doubled to right, scoring Seymour and Devlin.

The Polo Grounds were now in bedlam. Perhaps the fans were never before so insane. "Dummy" Taylor sprained three fingers trying to say something and women unpinned their hats, chucking them into the diamond. This, at least, was novel.

For some reason McGraw ordered Bridwell to bunt, and to an outsider this seemed bad judgment. Said bunt resulted in McCormick being thrown out at third and after which Barry, who batted for Ames, flied out and likewise Tenney. The men were hitting hard and why not let Bridwell hit the ball? After that New York had no chance.

Otis Crandall pitched the second game and held the Cubs to five hits. But he gave two bases on balls in the sixth, thus enabling Chicago to score a brace of runs. Previous to this New York in the fourth inning had made one tally. Herzog, who made two marvelous stops during the day, led off with a double. Bresnahan brought him home with another double.

McGinnity relieved Ames in the eighth inning of the first game and did the same for Crandall in the eighth inning. The "Iron Man," Crandall, and Ames all pitched good ball. It was not their fault the Giants lost. The team was overcome by "Three-Fingered" Brown, who finished the first game for Overall and pitched the whole second game. The only thing for McGraw to do to beat Chicago is to dig up a pitcher with only two fingers. —New York *World*

In the second game yesterday we almost get a run several times. Read about what happened in the seventh.

Everybody up, of course {for the seventh-inning stretch}. Loud loyalty and deep rooting. If Master Donlin makes a single we will forgive the past. We will be among those present on his opening night to give him a hand. We will—Master Mike makes good. Thank you, Sir. Now, if we can persuade honest Seymour to do likewise. We cannot. Honest Seymour flies out. But look here—Devlin is walking, and Donlin is still on the diamond. Hope lives. But McCormick dies ten thousand deaths, as the horrible Haydon gathers in his high fly. Now it is Bridwell, and Bridwell waits patiently as Brown deals off the bad ones. Four of a kind fills the bases, and the roar is so loud you can touch it.

Three men on bases. Come on, Crandall, and bang your way into a million hearts. Three men on bases, and a single will tie the score. {Merkle was sent in to bat for Crandall.} Come on, Merkle, if they won't let Crandall bat. We trust in you, Merkle darlin'. You'd never let us down, would you, Merkle, with three men on base, a single to tie, and a chance to win? Step up, good man, and play baseball. Pshaw! Why did you hit at that first one? Why did you not wait? It wasn't worth your effort. Pick out a bonny one, Merkle, and then strike for the freedom of your sires, and a little bit more. Not that one, not that, Merkle. Didn't we give you waiting orders? Never mind, there is one chance left. Use it wisely. Get a firm hold on your bat, and slash away along the third-base line. If you are not in position, make it the right field, up as near the grandstand as you can get without fouling. Or, if you think you can pull it off, a Texas-leaguer will demoralize them. Or you might—Mr. Merkle has just struck out, gentlemen. Donlin, Devlin, and Bridwell, what of them? Were you ever at a reception where the lion of the hour and day came over to your corner, shook hands with the neighbor on your right, and the neighbor on your left, and then—looked coldly past you and walked on, leaving you with your dexter fork extended in the air and feeling foolish all over? That's how Messrs. Donlin, Devlin, and Bridwell felt when Mr. Merkle passed them up. Let's all go home. And they call themselves Cubs!  —W. W. Aulick, New York *Times*


There is no joy in Manhattan. Even so—it is well not to become too hilarious. A glance at the remainder of the schedule reveals some cold and chillsome facts.

While the Cubs are right at the heels of New York and in position to pull the Giants down, the rest of the tab shows that the Bears play only 11 more games, while New York plays 17. Of the 17, 8 are with Philadelphia, and it is a cinch that the Quakers will meekly heave up the sponge. With that big margin—17 games as compared to 11—the ultimate pennant chance seems more than feeble.

If the Cubs win 10 of the 11 games left—a most prodigious feat—they will finish with 100 won and 54 lost. To beat that New York would have to win 14 and lose 3. Take a more reasonable view. If the Cubs win 8 and lose 3, New York must win 12 and lose 5. It is tough going for the Cubs, but it is well to hope for the best—especially to hope that Philadelphia will play real ball.

The Pirates are not yet done for. They are only a game and a half back of the Cubs, and have 12 to go. In short, the race is still of the closest, fiercest pattern, and no prophet ever prophed who could foretell the finish.  —W. A. Phelon, Chicago *Journal*


"Muggsy" McGraw, the "Napoleon of baseball," was outgeneraled all the way yesterday, and to his bad judgment may be charged the loss of the second game.

To begin with, "Muggsy" tried to be foxy and "put something over" on Chance, with disastrous results. Before the first game he had Marquard, his $11,000 beauty, warm up as though intending to work him. He even went so far as to let Marquard walk out on the diamond just as the game was about to start, then suddenly called him back and out came Ames, who had been warming up secretly behind the grandstand. McGraw tried this trick again in the second game, Marquard and McGinnity warming up, and at the last minute Crandall showing from behind the stand. McGraw hoped to catch Chance napping and get some other pitcher than Overall and Brown. Instead he got two beatings.

—Chicago *News*

Hank O'Day won't allow "Dummy" Taylor on the coaching lines. He chased "Dummy" every time he got up. It's a pity the Giants can't use an orator when they carry him on the payroll.

—Chicago *Tribune*

Al Bridwell's batting slump hurts now, and Larry Doyle, the man the Cubs fear most, is a victim of his own carelessness. Bridwell has not made a timely hit for a long time, and his fielding is not as true as it was. Yesterday Bridwell had several chances to tie the score, but he didn't have a hit in his system. Neither did Tenney. Had Doyle been on the job yesterday one of the games might have been bagged. But Larry came up to the Polo Grounds the other day, got frisky, slipped, and fell down and now he is on the shelf again, as his fall reopened the wound in his ankle.

—Sid Mercer, New York *Globe*

## ◇ THURSDAY, SEPTEMBER 24 ◇

{On September 23, in New York, the Giants and Cubs played the most celebrated, most widely discussed, most controversial contest in the history of American sports. The game was declared a 1 to 1 tie.}

Rioting and wild disorder, in which spectators and players joined, causing a scene never witnessed in New York before, marked the conclusion at the Polo Grounds yesterday of the game between the Giants and Cubs. By cleverness in seeing an opportunity to deprive the Giants of their final and deciding run and quickness in seizing it, the Cubs had forced the umpire, Henry O'Day, to declare the game a tie, after half of the spectators had gone home in the belief that New York had won 2 to 1, and many of the New York players had left the field.

Through what appeared to be the carelessness of a single player, Merkle, in leaving first base after Bridwell's winning run had been scored and retiring from the field without touching second base and with the ball still in play, the final score as it stood last night was 1 to 1 instead of a victory for the home team.

In the fight between members of the opposing nines for the possession of the ball and the efforts of spectators, who rushed upon the field, to prevent the Chicago players from enjoying the fruits of their quick-wittedness, several players and the umpire were roughly handled and more or less severely hurt. Efforts of special policemen to clear the grounds were unavailing, and it took the regular policemen, called in from the outside, half an hour or more to quell the disturbance.

No similar situation had ever been seen in the history of baseball in New York. When the eighth inning came to a close the score was 1 to 1, and the 20,000 enthusiasts that filled the grandstand and bleachers to overflowing were "rooting" for the Giants with desperate hope. Chicago failed to score in the first half of the ninth, and in the last half Bridwell went to bat with McCormick on third base and Merkle, who had replaced Tenney, on first.

Bridwell made a clean hit over second base. McCormick raced home, making the score 2 to 1 in favor of the Giants, and there seemed nothing else to do but go home cheering. That is what most of the players did, and that, according to the decision rendered later by O'Day, is what young Mr. Merkle, the runner on first base, did. That little oversight of Merkle's gave Chicago their chance.

The runner had been forced off first by Bridwell's hit. The ball was in centerfield. Hofman, covering that position, saw Merkle leave first base and saunter toward the clubhouse. He threw the ball to Evers, on second, but it went wild and McGinnity caught it. He had seen the opening left by Merkle's mistake as quickly as the Chicagoans, and had rushed out from the coaching lines to take a hand in the proceedings. {Hofman's role in this incident has generally been underestimated, and yet because of his quickness in going after the ball instead of heading for the clubhouse, as most players would have done under similar circumstances, no one contributed more than he to the success of the play. One wonders if he would have been less alert if Frank Chance had not prevented him from marrying two weeks earlier. See the relevant entry for September 19.}

With the ball in his hand, McGinnity also started for the clubhouse.

Frank Chance got into action at this point and succeeded in holding McGinnity until other Chicago players could join in the effort to recover the ball. McGinnity, overpowered, threw the ball as far as he could into the crowd behind third base, the spectators having already begun to pile into the field. Steinfeldt and Tinker followed the ball into the crowd. Tinker seized it and threw to Evers, who stood proudly on second base holding the ball aloft, while O'Day, who had run down to second to see the play, was immediately surrounded by Chicago players.

Chance ran to O'Day, claiming the run did not count because Merkle had been forced at second. A riotous mob at once surrounded the couple, and although most did not know what it was all about everyone evidently recognized a good opportunity to get a shot at the umpire. Those within reach began pounding him on all available exposed parts not covered by the protector, while the unfortunate attackers on the outskirts began sending messages by way of cushions, newspapers, and other missiles.

A flying squadron of real police, reinforced by the special men, rushed O'Day to McGraw's coop under the grandstand and Chance was escorted off the field. Then the mob ran about the grounds throwing cushions and generally preparing for O'Day's reappearance, when it was made known that the game might not be given to the Giants. The police cleared the grounds and order was restored.

O'Day, under the press of circumstances, did not render a decision on the field, but after he had dressed he told a reporter of the *Herald* that Merkle had not gone to second and the run did not count. He said a run could not be tallied on the third out if the man was forced and put out at second.

Merkle said after the game that he had touched second en route for the clubhouse, and McGraw refused to say any more than that the game had been won fairly.

O'Day seemed very uncertain as to what he should do and was a long time coming to a decision, and when he did he seemed uncertain as to its justification. Should he report the game to President Pulliam as a tie the New York club will protest, for there was ample police protection on the grounds to clear the field and continue the contest.

The decision was really Emslie's, who was officiating on the bases, but he says he did not see the play, as he was watching first base, and O'Day had run out into the pitcher's box prepared to watch it.

The same situation arose in Pittsburgh on September 4, when Gill, on first base, ran for the clubhouse instead of going to second. As O'Day was officiating alone, he did not see the play, and the Cubs protested the Pirates' victory to President Pulliam, who upheld the umpire. O'Day saw all that happened yesterday, for he ran out, prepared for the occurrence.

Mr. Pulliam could not be seen last night up to a late hour, and he made no decision in the matter, but he gave out the following statement: "I made no decision in the matter, and I will not do so until it is presented to me in proper form."

The fact that Mr. Pulliam recognizes in his statement that there was some irregularity at the grounds intimates that he intends making a decision. Last night he was closeted at the New York Athletic Club with O'Day and Emslie, and until he renders a decision the game stands on the umpires' decision that Merkle was forced at second.

As for the game itself, Mathewson allowed the Cubs only five measly hits. Only one did any damage, and that was Tinker's home run in the fifth, and that only did about $3.50 worth to a certain shoe store.

Players to whom the Chicago club pays all sorts of fancy prices to knock the delivery of most pitchers where the fielders cannot get the ball looked like thirty cents when "Matty" got through. He struck out nine Cubs, usually with men on base. Pfiester shot up the slants from the port side for Chance's men and was effective in all but two innings.

The game was pregnant with thrilling plays and surprises. The first surprise was a revised batting order by McGraw, who placed Merkle in Tenney's place and shifted his other men around. (This was the only time during the entire season that Tenney failed to appear in the Giant starting line-up.) The youngster played like a fiend and came through with a single in the ninth that helped win the game. If he would only remember to run to second base when it is required—which reminds us of a man who had a thousand-dollar back and a ten-cent head.

Nobody made any progress toward home plate until Tinker hit for the circuit in the fifth. The ball went over second like a cannon shot and went skating through the grass in right center. Mike Donlin went over to stop it and tried to place his foot in its course, but failed, and the ball rolled to the ropes. Two or three ardent fans in a perfectly polite manner suggested to Mike that if he had stretched his anatomy on the greensward he might have stopped the ball and ended Tinker's wanderings on second base.

In the sixth the Giants came back and scored a run. Herzog reached first on a single to Steinfeldt, who threw too late to get the runner and wild as well, so the little second baseman drew up at second. Bresnahan sacrificed, and Herzog tied the score on Donlin's hit over second. Seymour scratched out a hit in front of second base when Emslie got in Evers' way and spoiled the play. Devlin flied out, however, and McCormick grounded to Evers.

Things went along until the ninth with the score a tie. Seymour, the first Giant up, burned a brown streak in the grass with a hot one down to Evers and found the ball waiting for him at first. Devlin, the only man to get two hits in the afternoon, singled but was forced at second by McCormick's grass cutter to Evers. Merkle came along with a timely single, moving McCormick to third.

Then Bridwell pinched one over second, which was followed by the main play of the afternoon—a squeeze play executed by the fans and O'Day, the latter squeezing in his coop.

The game was a baseball cocktail and "Matty" was the cherry in the ante-dinner drink. In fact, all our boys did rather well if Fred Merkle could gather the idea into his noodle that baseball custom does not permit a runner to take a shower and some light lunch in the clubhouse on the way to second.

Then again, taking it on the whole, an enormous baseball custom has had it from time immemorial that as soon as the winning run has crossed the plate everyone adjourns as hastily and yet nicely as possible to the clubhouse and exits.                    —New York *Herald*


Frank Chance tried to take from John McGraw yesterday a well-earned victory. Unless Mr. Pulliam decides against New York, the game goes to her credit, for Umpires O'Day and Emslie admitted to newspaper men that they had not seen the play. O'Day was back of the catcher when the riot started and endeavored to reach first base, where Chance was struggling in the clutch of a mob. Emslie was trying to save himself and his wig from being trampled.

The crowd, following them, jammed into the home bench, upsetting Murphy, the groundkeeper, and stepping on McGraw's bulldog. They broke through the little door McGraw uses as exit when banished and groped their way in the darkness over barrels, boxes and trap holes. The umpires finally reached their dressing room, but the riot outside continued.

Chance was the target, and though he is a pugilist the crowd would have treated him harshly but for two fat policemen. Surrounded by them and some of his players, the Chicago manager "flying wedged" himself to the clubhouse. He was still bawling that he would protest the game and calling for O'Day.

When the umpires emerged in their citizen clothes O'Day was rattled and evasive; Emslie was rattled and frank. He said: "The crowd got to me so quick that I didn't see the play. I tried to reach O'Day to find out whether he got it, but you know what happened. I don't know what to say. I didn't see the play."

O'Day shouted back over his shoulder: "Merkle didn't run to second; the last run don't count; it's a tie game."

McGraw said that never in his life had he heard of a "no game" being called. "If we forfeited the game O'Day should have said so. As a matter of fact Merkle tells me he did reach and touch second. No Chicago player was on second base with the ball, anyway. It's simply a case of squeal. We won fair and square."     —New York *World*


McGraw had some forcible comments after the game. "How can umpires decide it is no game?" asked Mac. "Umpires can't go out on the field and make rules. Either the game should be declared forfeited on account of the crowd overrunning the field and preventing further play, or it was won by us. The Chicago club can protest, of course, but they wouldn't have any grounds for a protest. The play in the ninth inning wasn't a question of interpretation of the rules, which is the only ground on which protest can be made. Emslie says he didn't see the play, and Merkle swears he touched the bag."     —New York *Sun*


Minor league brains lost the Giants a game after they had it cleanly and fairly won.

The Cubs and Hank O'Day were primed for the situation, having been through it once before, in Pittsburgh. With one voice the Cubs set up a yelp like a cage of hungry hyenas, and O'Day, working behind the plate, ran to the pitching slab to see what came off at second base. Capt. Donlin realized the danger about to overtake the Giants, so he set off after the fat-headed Merkle while McGinnity, coaching at third base, butted into the fracas at the middle station.

The facts gleaned from active participants and survivors are these: Hofman fielded Bridwell's knock and threw to Evers for a force play on the absent Merkle. But McGinnity cut in and grabbed the ball before it reached the eager Trojan {Evers, who came from Troy, New York}. Three Cubs landed on the Iron Man from as many directions at the same time and jolted the ball from his cruel grasp. It rolled among the spectators who had swarmed upon the diamond like an army of starving potato bugs.

At this thrilling juncture "Kid" Kroh, the demon southpaw, swarmed upon the human potato bugs and knocked six of them galley-west. The triumphant Kroh passed the ball to Steinfeldt after cleaning up the gang that had it. Tinker wedged in, and the ball was conveyed to Evers for the force-out of Merkle, while Capt. Donlin was still some distance off towing that brilliant young gent by the neck.

Some say Merkle eventually touched second base, but not until he had been forced out by Hofman to McGinnity to six potato bugs to "Kid" Kroh to some more Cubs, and the shrieking, triumphant Mr. Evers, the well-known Troy shoe dealer. There have been some complicated plays in baseball, but we do not recall one like this in a career of years of monkeying with the national pastime.

—Charles Dryden, Chicago *Tribune*

It seems that a new magnate has "Jimmied" his way into the game and is trying to run baseball on entirely different lines than ideal ones. Charles Murphy, president of the Chicago club, has no sentiment for baseball, only for the money there may be in it for him. In fact, the "Chubby One" is considered a joke all over the National League, and nowhere more so than in Chicago. He is out for the "dough," and nothing else about the great sport appeals to him.

But, not being satisfied with trying to run his own club in his own city to the detriment of the baseball public, he comes to New York and endeavors to dictate how the game should be run here.

He will have a good, fat chance!

Directly after the argument on the field, which was brought about by Manager Chance and his fellow players developing that old yellow streak of claiming victories they can't win on the field, Murphy saw his opportunity to make a claim for yesterday's game on a cowardly technicality. Manager Chance and his players in fact incited a riot, and but for the fortunate presence of hundreds of New York's "finest" there would have been a serious riot.

Merkle did make a run for the clubhouse to escape the onrushing fans, as is the habit with the Giants, but he turned after going only a few feet and broke for second. Hofman did return the ball, but it went far over Evers' head, hit Tinker in the back and went on to Kling. Merkle was then on second with Mathewson, and as Evers, Tinker and Pfiester all rushed toward second, Matty, according to his own story, to which he will take an affidavit if such a ridiculous act is necessary, took Merkle by the arm and said: "Come on to the clubhouse; we don't want to mix up in this," and both Matty and Merkle left the base together.

Chance was frantic; he rushed up to both Umpires O'Day and Emslie in the endeavor to make them listen to his unsportsmanlike claim, but both those officials waved him away and said, according to bystanders and players, "We didn't see anything that warrants your claim or protest that Merkle didn't run to second. He was there the last we saw." And these were the words of both umpires, as hundreds will swear to.

Chance was insistent, however, and his doubled fists came dangerously close to O'Day's face. O'Day at last had to throw the irate Cub captain aside, and he was soon lost in the crowd, but was so angry he struck several citizens and was himself somewhat roughly used, as he by all right should have been. The police broke into the surging crowd and at last got O'Day and Emslie to their dressing room in the grandstand, Chance and his players gradually making their tumultuous ways to their dressing rooms.

And here is where the great Charley Murphy (in his own mind) bursts on to the scene.

I had hurried down from the press box to get an interview with the umpires. I found their door firmly braced against intrusion, but I managed to get my head through the open space of the door and I asked H.

— 250 —

O'Day, "Is it the Giants' game?" I understood him to say "Yes," but immediately after he said, "Wait until I am dressed," and the door was shut. I waited for O'Day to appear and was soon joined by several other newspaper men who also wanted to get the "latest."

While waiting anxiously, who should appear on the scene but his "augustness" (in his own mind) the "Chubby One," gorgeous in a Tim Woodruff vest and in his own vast conceit.

"How about this?" he said. "I want to know; the game wound up one to one, and we will have to play a doubleheader tomorrow." Looking for the money all the time. That never escapes his sordid mind. What did he care about the disappointed hopes of the army of New York fans who had seen their favorites win a victory fairly and squarely? Not a thing. If he could cause the Giants to lose on a technicality he would scheme that way if he could get the few extra dollars accruing to him by an extra game unfairly arranged.

—Sam Crane, New York *Evening Journal*

"If," Christy Mathewson said, "this game goes to Chicago by any trick of argument, you can take it from me that if we lose the pennant thereby, I will never play professional baseball again.

"I had started for the clubhouse when I heard Chance call to Hofman to throw the ball to second. I remembered the trick they had tried to play on Pittsburgh and caught Merkle by the arm and told him to go to second. Merkle touched the bag. I saw him do it."

—New York *Evening Mail*

———◇ **FRIDAY, SEPTEMBER 25** ◇———

{On September 24, in New York, the Giants beat the Cubs 5 to 4. Winning pitcher, Wiltse; losing pitcher, Brown. Giants' standing: 88 wins, 50 losses, in first place.}

President Pulliam supported Umpires O'Day and Emslie and declared Wednesday's game a 1 to 1 tie. As neither club has an open date the tie contest will not be played off.

The end of the controversy, however, is not yet in sight, as President Brush has served notice that he will appeal from the ruling, while President Murphy claims the game by forfeit, 9 to 0, owing to the fact that the New York team was not at the Polo Grounds yesterday at 1:30 to play off the tie game. In announcing his verdict, Pulliam said he would stand by his umpires, regardless of the merits of the controversy. As the case stands the game will go on the records as a tie unless the Board of Directors of the National League takes action at its next meeting.

—New York *Times*

Amid the jangling of cowbells, the blowing of horns, unparalleled shouting of 25,000 "fans" in every tone of the scale, from a deep barytone to the highest soprano, almost continuous in its constancy throughout the game, on a darkened and gnat-swarmed field, the Giants came home a winner yesterday.

After the game had been apparently won in the first and fifth innings and the score stood at 5 to 0 the Cubs fell on Wiltse in the seventh session and collected three runs, with no one out. Then Mathewson, big, reliable "Matty," was rushed out to save the day, with Kling dancing on third like a performing bear after his triple. Kling scored but never again was home plate in danger from the Cub tread. "Matty" had saved the day and perhaps the pennant.

Baseball enthusiasm blew out another cylinder head yesterday. The "rooters" came armed with cowbells and horns, and from the bulging appearances of their pockets it was suspected that a few vegetables were concealed in convenient and accessible recesses. The general sentiment was that if a contingency should arise such as that of Wednesday those some distance from the umpire should not be handicapped by intervening space.

The other side, so to speak, was also reinforced, and about 100 bluecoats swung their sticks about the side lines. It was reported from the Bronx, Brooklyn and other outlying districts that many cowbells were missing and that so many cows had gone astray that the price of milk would probably go up two points in those regions in the near future.

Seldom has such partisan feeling been evidenced on a ball field as was displayed yesterday. When the Chicago team took the field they were jeered to the echo, and even the Putnam railroad engines in the distance hissed out steam at them. The names hurled at "Hank" O'Day when he took the field must have kept some "rooters" up all night thinking up the epithets, while the players constantly exchanged quips throughout the game.

"Three-Fingered" Brown was sent in to do the pitching for the Cubs. He worked so hard he almost lost another digit as he curled his fingers about the ball and sent up his best. He lasted only five innings, when Coakley {recently purchased by Chicago from Cincinnati} and Overall both tried to save the day but were powerless.

Donlin, next to "Matty," deserves credit for the victory. He made a double and triple which accounted for four of New York's runs.

In the seventh a mist settled over the field that all but obscured the outfielders from the grandstand. It was so dark "Matty" had to walk up to the plate to see Bresnahan's signals. In spite of this, Emslie, behind the bat, refused to call the game.

Every time Chance went to bat he was greeted with all sorts of names, and those greetings seemed to hang over the diamond in the humid atmosphere. As if attracted by the epithets hurled at Chance, ranging from "yellow dog" through all the various stages of head, from "in head" to "bone head," a swarm of gnats came over the diamond like one of the plagues of Egypt. One lodged in "Matty's" eye, delaying the game, while all the occupants of the right-field bleachers were fanning with handkerchiefs and newspapers, and here and there miniature campfires of newspapers were started to drive the pests away. Every time Chance was greeted with these pleasant titles his appearance reminded the "rooters" of Hank O'Day, and he would be pounced on again with renewed vigor.

—New York *Herald*


President Pulliam's now-famous decision that Wednesday's victory of the Giants over the Cubs goes as a tie game is not final, so local "bugs" and "bugesses" can keep their lingerie on.

President Charley Murphy, of the Cubs, claimed everything in sight, but, as usual with the "Chubby One," he overreached himself, and not only are the Cubs a good 13 points behind the Giants, but the disputed game he so confidently counted on is not his by a great big long shot.

And, moreover, the Giants have as good a chance to be credited with a victory as the Cubs have to have it called a tie, as poor Umpire Hank O'Day, after much weak-kneed wavering and careful consideration of National League politics, finally decided.

Formerly I thought Hank O'Day was like adament, and if he made up his mind one way he would stick to that through thick and thin, but I don't think so now—and that is letting Hank off easy.

President Brush is desirous of having the New York baseball public put right on the case. After yesterday's game he said: "There is no need of our patrons fearing that any such robbery as was attempted yesterday being carried through without our resentment and every possible measure in our power being used to prevent the Chicago club, or any other, taking our patrons' money and robbing us of fairly earned victories as well. The New York club will fight for its rights every inch of the way."

—Sam Crane, New York *Evening Journal*

Something happened at the Polo Grounds yesterday that never happened on a ball field before. The game was scheduled for 3:30. Before 2 o'clock there were 20,000 fans on the grounds. That's coming early to avoid a rush, isn't it? But it wasn't that.

Chicago had made a bluff that they would be lined up and ready to play the first game of a doubleheader at 1:30. This was in accordance with President Pulliam's ruling that Wednesday's game was a tie. A tie game has to be played out, and as yesterday was the last day the Cubs would be here, it was the only day on which the tie could be settled.

This looked even better than a bargain doubleheader. There might be trouble. Someone might take a punch at Chance. And it was in anticipation of a scrap that the crowd assembled so early.

A ball game and a free fight, all for the price of one admission, doesn't often fall to the lot of anyone.

But nothing like that. Not even an approach to it. Chance and his bunch lined up and went through the farce of making ready for a game, and that was all there was to it. All they got was the laugh.

—Gym Bagley, New York *Evening Mail*

The dispute that has arisen between two teams of the National League at the very climax of the baseball season may or may not be disheartening according to the point of view. It had not seemed possible that there could be any increase of interest in baseball, but just now it is the subject that seems to claim most of the attention the multitude of our fellow-citizens can spare from business and domestic affairs.

The decision of Umpire O'Day seems to an unprejudiced outsider fair and impartial. Merkle substituted his own judgment that the game was won after Bridwell's safe hit enabled McCormick to make a run, for obedience to the rules. He should have taken his second base. Undoubtedly if he had started for the base and fallen or even dropped dead, between the bases, McCormick's run would not have counted. Such an error of judgment could scarcely be overlooked in amateur sport. It would be foolish to expect professional players to overlook it.

The ensuing row in which a mob of spectators took part, overrunning the field, prevented the playing of another inning. We do not see how the umpire's decision can be set aside, unless the testimony of many unprejudiced eye witnesses is proved mistaken. But what a life the umpire leads!
—Editorial page, New York *Times*


Fred Tenney is playing solely on his nerve. His feet are in very bad shape, and his back is lame. Every time he stoops it is pain. But McGraw had enough of Merkle the day before and called on Tenney for his brains. A one-legged man with a noodle is better than a bonehead.
—Gym Bagley, New York *Evening Mail*


Oh, joy! oh, joy! John Ganzel and his Reds will be our guests in two games this afternoon, and Honest John will take his medicine like a sport.
—New York *American*


———◇ **SATURDAY, SEPTEMBER 26** ◇———

{On September 25, in New York, the Giants lost two games to Cincinnati, 7 to 1 and 5 to 2. Winning pitchers, Spade and Dubuc; losing pitchers, Marquard and McGinnity. Giants' standing: 88 wins, 52 losses, in first place.}

Harry C. Pulliam, president of the National League, issued this statement yesterday:

"The umpires in charge of the contest {on September 23} filed their written reports at National League headquarters on September 24, stating that the game resulted in a tie score. The report was accepted in the usual manner without prejudice to the rights of either club.

"Under the constitution of the National League either club may appeal from the decision of the umpires within five days of the date of the game. The New York club has notified this office that it will appeal from the decision of the umpires.

"In compliance with the National League constitution, the protest of the New York club will be submitted to the Chicago club, and that club has five days in which to file its answer, if it so desires. The same procedure will prevail in the event that the Chicago club protests the decision.

"When the case is made up a decision will be rendered by the president of the league, which decision is subject to appeal within five days to the Board of Directors, whose decision is final."

—New York *Tribune*


The Gingery Giants lined up in a doubleheader against the Gingery Germans from Zinzinnati, and in both games we had to rap our poor, battered knuckles on the table and say "That's good," while Messrs. {Dick} Hoblitzel, Ganzel, Lobert, Schlei, {Bob} Beecher, et al., worthy Teutons all, were raking in the chips. Ach, du lieber!

The National League race is now a lulu—the luluest kind of a lulu what is. We are sailing grandly in the van with a juicy lead of one point, closely pursued by the Cursed Cubs and Peevish Pirates. They can't beat us until they catch us, and we are still peering downward, like Freedom from her mountain height, but we don't need to use spyglasses.

Mr. Marquard had stage fright, to be perfectly candid. {In the first game "Rube" Marquard made his major league debut.} He did not know what to do with his hands, and he wasn't quite sure what to do with the ball. First he tucked it under his right armpit, then he slammed it into his glove, then he spat on it, then he made a wild pitch with it, and then he aimed it over in the groove, only to see it soaring safe into the outfield.

Gentle Roger Bresnahan tried his derndest to hold up the young pitcher, and stopped more than one apparently wild pitch, but the kid was not quite ready for the ordeal, and after he had been clouted grievously, and had shown unmistakable signs of unsteadiness, he left the mound.

The Gingery Germans got away with a flying start. Marquard curved his first ball over the plate for a strike and was wildly cheered. But then he got too much ambish and put so much on the next shoot that it lit on the ribs of little Johnny Kane. {Dick} Egan popped to Herzog, and Kane stole second base. Lobert, the vest-pocket edition of Honus Wagner, tripled terribly, Kane scoring, and Lobert scored in a walk as Herr Beecher lammed out another three-bagger.

With two out in the fifth, the Gingery Germans got busy again. Spade singled to right, and little Johnny Kane also singled, the ball caroming off Bridwell's glove. Then Mr. Egan singled to center, scoring Spade and sending Kane to third. Mr. Marquard chipped in with a wild pitch, allowing Kane to tally, and when Lobert singled through the box, Mr. Egan scored. With Beecher at bat, Bresnahan got a fingernail nearly torn off in attempting to stop one of Marquard's wild heaves, and retired in favor of Needham. After this inning Marquard also retired and was replaced by {Louis "Bull"} Durham, another rookie from Indianapolis.

McGinnity was the pitcher that went to the well once too often in the second struggle, and before he had been relieved the damage was done.               —William F. Kirk, New York *American*


Fred Tenney is quite lame, and he gave way to Merkle in the fourth inning of the second game yesterday. No plays came up in which Merkle had to think, so he got by.

—Jack Ryder, Cincinnati *Enquirer*


Fans who attended last Wednesday's game and saw or heard things which can help to establish New York's claim of a legitimate victory over the Cubs will confer a favor on the management of the New York club by giving their testimony as they enter the grounds today. The club's attorney, Mr. Sullivan, and a notary will be there to take this testimony, which will be put in the form of affidavits and used as evidence to support the New York club's protest. Many fans have stated that the umpires did not see the alleged play at second base and refused to call it. Their testimony will help greatly.        —New York *Globe*

CHICAGO, Sept. 25—During a fight over Pres. Pulliam's decision calling the disputed Giant-Cub game a tie the skull of Thomas Crocker was fractured. He is in the county hospital, probably fatally injured, and George Brooks is under arrest.

According to the police Brooks used a baseball bat to settle the argument. Brooks defended the claims of the New York team and Crocker upheld the contention of the Cubs. During the resulting fight Brooks is said to have struck Crocker with the bat, after declaring, "I'll show you how Mike Donlin makes a three-base hit."       —Boston *Globe*

───◇ **SUNDAY, SEPTEMBER 27** ◇───

{On September 26, in New York, the Giants beat Cincinnati in a doubleheader, 6 to 2 and 3 to 1. Winning pitchers, Mathewson and Ames; losing pitchers, Ewing and Dubuc. Giants' standing: 90 wins, 52 losses, in first place.}

While the sun refused to shine on the Harlem meadow yesterday, it was anything but doleful for the 30,000 fans that saw the Giants redeem themselves and take a tighter grip on the narrow lead for the pennant. Cincinnati was just plain Sin-Sin-Natty this time. The Giants won two games almost as they pleased, with Christy Mathewson and Leon Ames doing the pitching.

Those who thought, after the double drubbing the Reds gave McGraw's men on Friday, that the Giants were cooped up in the elevator with all the doors locked and going down, have another guess. Nobody expected anything but a victory when Big Six appeared in the firing line for the opener. When Ames strolled to the rubber for the nightcap it was different.

Since Amesie returned to service he has been an in and outer, good one day and bad the next. Yesterday was one of Leon's good days. He was as steady as a rock and when it looked as though a pair of Redlegs might get to the plate he gave the boys behind him such easy grounders they couldn't do otherwise but accept them.

Fred Tenney was the hero with the willow. Fred was entitled to two home runs but could only land one because his legs are bad and interfere sadly with his locomotion. —New York *World*


After Ed Reulbach, of the Chicago Cubs, had pitched the first game in Washington Park yesterday, in which Brooklyn failed to make a run, he volunteered to pitch the second, and Brooklyn did not make a run in that contest.

Reulbach's willingness to do overwork permitted Chance to give his other pitchers a much-needed rest. Instead of being compelled to use three men in Brooklyn, he got along with two, Overall and Reulbach. Brown, the three-fingered marvel, upon whom the final fight is likely to rest, will have four solid days of comfort in which to build up his strength.

No pitcher in the National League has ever been able to show such command over another team as Reulbach did yesterday. He has the record all to himself of two shut-out games in one afternoon. In the American League, Walter Johnson, of Washington, pitched three shut-out games to the Highlanders, but they were in successive afternoons. {No other major league pitcher has yet matched Reulbach's feat of pitching two shut-outs in one day. Johnson's three shut-outs, incidentally, although pitched in three consecutive games, were spread over four days, September 4, 5, and 7, 1908.} —New York *Herald*


The New York National League club is engaged in one of its familiar fourflushes in an endeavor to convince the baseball public in Gotham that the Giants were robbed of a hard-earned victory on a mere technicality.

And because Broadway, from Times Square to the Battery, is the native heath of the fourflush; because New Yorkers have become so accustomed to it they take their hats off to a good one; because the average Gotham fan's knowledge of baseball is confined to the standing of the Giants in the pennant race and the number of games Mathewson has won; because in baseball, as in everything else, anything from across the Hudson, the Harlem, or the East River is regarded as barbarian and a rank outsider to be repulsed at any cost, the officials of the New York Nationals are likely to get away with this latest New York bluff.

Outside of Manhattan island, however, where baseball is considered a national pastime and not a form of paying tribute to New York, it is a recognized fact that the Giants lost that victory over the Cubs by a blunder more stupid than the rankest of fielding errors ever perpetrated.

If New York newspapers printed baseball news pertaining to anything outside Manhattan and Brooklyn, the Gotham fans might have understood from the Pittsburgh tangle what came off before their own eyes last Wednesday. Possibly, too, Merkle might have read about that play and have remembered it long enough to avoid duplicating Gill's bush league blunder. In that case the Giants would have another victory to their credit and would not be fourflushing about technicalities to cover the ignorance of the rules displayed by one of their players.

There was only one thing to do Wednesday after Merkle had been forced out. The decision should have been made known at once, the field should have been cleared, and the game finished in extra innings. There was plenty of light to go on with the battle, and there were less than 13,000 people at the game. Consequently with any kind of management the field could have been cleared.

But there are no screens or barriers to prevent Polo Grounds fans from pouring out on to the diamond as soon as they think a game is over, or nearly over, and there has been no real police protection there all season. The danger existing in this absence of regular policemen has been pointed out repeatedly and the league warned that it was courting not only serious trouble but actual scandal in permitting such conditions to go on unchanged. Now that the scandal has arrived there is no occasion for handing out sympathy.

If it had happened at any other grounds than New York there is no question but that the umpire would have forfeited the game to the visiting club on account of the crowd's interference. Anywhere else an umpire would have been assured sufficient police protection to enable him to do his duty as prescribed by the rules without endangering the wholeness of his scalp. One hates to think what would have happened to O'Day in New York if he had remained and tried to make the Giants resume the game. New York fans have been taught by years of tolerating McGraw-ism that New York is a law unto itself in baseball.

—I. E. Sanborn, Chicago Tribune

Here are several rules which bear on last Wednesday's game:

Rule 59. One run shall be scored every time a base runner, after having legally touched the first three bases, shall legally touch the home base before three men are put out; provided, however, that if he reach home on or during a play in which the third man be forced out or be put out before reaching first base, a run shall not count. A force-out can be made only when a base runner legally loses the right to the base he occupies and is thereby obliged to advance as the result of a fair-hit ball not caught on the fly.

Rule 77. Every club shall furnish sufficient police force to preserve order upon its own grounds, and in the event of a crowd entering the field during a game, and interfering with the play in any manner, the visiting club may refuse to play until the field be cleared. If the field be not cleared within fifteen minutes thereafter, the visiting club may claim, and shall be entitled to the game by a score of nine runs to none.

This, then, brings it up to the present situation. Umpire O'Day declared Merkle out for not going to second base on Bridwell's hit. It was a force play, pure and simple, as covered by Rule 59. Immediately after the umpire rendered his decision, the umpires were spirited away by the police, who assured the crowd there would be no further play. When the umpires finally broke out of captivity it was too dark to resume play. Frank Chance and his players did not remain on the field for fifteen minutes after the crowd broke restraint. In fact, they were swept aside by the angry tumult and were lucky to escape with sound skins when the fans found out what it was all about.

President Pulliam called the game a tie, and as a result it should have been played off as a postponement. But his decision was not reached until it was practically too late for the New York management to notify its players of a doubleheader the following day, if such had been desired. Frank Chance had notified the Giants he would lay claim to a game by forfeit if a doubleheader were not played, and he made good his threat. Pulliam by instructing his umpires not to report to the park till 3:30

practically eradicated the game from the schedule, despite a resolution adopted at the last National League meeting that each club must play 22 games with every other club during the season where such may be accomplished.

In declaring the game a tie, President Pulliam established a new precedent; in not ordering it played over and seeing that such was done after he made the strange decision he countenanced a fracture of the rules and gave Frank Chance good ground for a claim to forfeiture; and in leaving the matter to the Board of Directors of the National League, he has shifted an unwelcome burden from his own shoulders to those of others.

—New York *American*

Pending the final adjudication of the disputed game of Wednesday, Sept. 23, I want you to know why I assigned umpires for but one game at the Polo Grounds on Sept. 24, and why the provisions of the National League constitution governing the playing off of postponed and tie games were not enforced.

I was present at the game which ended in a scene of great confusion. With a desire to protect the interests of both clubs and to carry out the provisions of our laws, I sent for the umpires in charge of the game that night. They informed me that the game resulted in a tie.

While in conference with the umpires I received a formal protest from the Chicago club claiming the game by a score of 9 to 0. The moment this claim of Chicago was received I was estopped from taking any steps to have the tie game played off on the next day by the provisions of section 22 of the constitution, which provides that the claim, together with the accompanying proofs, must be furnished to the other club, which club has five days in which to reply.

A second communication from the Chicago club was received at or about 11 o'clock the next morning stating it did not desire to protest the decision of the umpires. It was then too late in my judgment to give the proper notice to both clubs that the game must be played over on that day, and therefore I did not assign umpires for two games.

—Harry C. Pulliam, in the Chicago *Tribune*

Christy Mathewson said this to the writer:

"Fred Merkle did touch second base, and I was there with him when he did it. He started directly for the clubhouse when Bridwell made his hit, but when he heard the shouting and took in the situation, he turned back and threaded his way through the crowd to the second bag. He touched it, and wanted to stay, but I was at his side and said, 'Come on, now, let's beat it to the clubhouse.' Then we went to the clubhouse together."

Umpire O'Day in a report to President Pulliam states that Merkle started for second base, ran part of the distance and then streaked for the clubhouse. As a matter of fact, Umpire O'Day didn't see anything in connection with Merkle's actions. Numerous affidavits filed with the management of the Giants will prove that O'Day saw nothing that happened on the diamond after he had seen Bridwell's hit! His back was to the field and the crowd from that instant until he crawled into his coop!
—William F. Kirk, New York *American*

## ———◇ MONDAY, SEPTEMBER 28 ◇———

New York has eight more games to play with Philadelphia, and it is with the Phillies that the Giants expect to recover lost ground. The two teams have played 14 games, of which New York has won 11. For some reason the Quakers are the easiest team in the league for the Giants to beat, and it is due to this fact that followers of the Giants look to see their favorites increase their lead.

The one big advantage enjoyed by the Giants is that their hard games are apparently over.                                            —New York *Times*

CINCINNATI, Sept. 28—President Murphy of the Chicago Cubs today made the following statement:

"I am making the claim that Chicago is now in the lead in the National League race, as the tie game of Wednesday went to us when the New Yorks failed to show up to play a doubleheader on Thursday.

"Under section 45 of the National League constitution, the New York club was obliged to play a doubleheader on Thursday, as it was the last opportunity we had of meeting the New Yorks this season. The section provides that 'a tie or a drawn game, or a game prevented by rain or other causes, shall be played off on the same ground on which scheduled during the same or any subsequent series, the date to be optional with the home club.'

"In the present instance Thursday was the only date left on which the game could be played, and when the Giants failed to come out to play the game they forfeited it.

"As a member of the Board of Directors of the league, I shall vote to have the game given to the Cubs, and I believe the other directors will do likewise."                                                                —New York *Globe*

Neither the Cubs nor the Pirates can play a game after next Sunday, October 4, not even if rain should prevent every game this week. Their season ends on that day. The Giants, however, have until Wednesday, October 7, in which to complete their quota of games. On Monday, Tuesday and Wednesday of next week the Giants are scheduled to play Boston. It is possible the result of the race will not be decided until October 7, and in such a case I can see the players of the Cubs and Pirates around the tickers, and a blamed sight more nervous than if they were on the diamond fighting to win.

The Cubs have only six more games to play, and it is therefore impossible for them to win more than 99 games, and if the Pirates should win the seven games they still have to play their total of winning games would be 99. But either the Cubs or Pirates will lose next Sunday, for they face each other then.

The Giants can, if they win all of their 11 games to come, have 101 victories. They can lose two out of the 11 and still win 99 games, the limit that either the Cubs or Pirates can get.

                                          —Sam Crane, New York *Evening Journal*

Amid the wild, enthusiastic cheering of 20,000 delirious fanatics, Mike Donlin was presented the *Evening Journal*'s handsome loving cup for the most popular local player during the intermission between the first and second games between the Giants and Reds on Saturday. For fully ten minutes the applause lasted, and the outburst continued until Donlin took his position in right field at the beginning of the second encounter.

—New York *Evening Journal*

Larry Doyle is out for the season. He may be able to do a pinch-hitting stunt later in the week, but at present he is still on crutches.

—New York *Globe*

I have received many letters asking me about Charley Herzog's nationality and what Sunday school he plays. I answered one in which I replied that Herzog's forebears were his personal property and no one's business save his own.

But Herzog himself wishes it known that he is a Dutchman. So many fans wished him a happy new year Saturday it made him tired.

"They've got me wrong," said Herzy to me after the game. "I'm as Dutch as sauerkraut, but that's all."

What he meant by "that's all" is probably explained when he added: "You see, when I was a kid, I fell off a cliff and broke my nose. It was never set properly, and that's what makes it stick out so now."

Herzy's nose does stick out a bit, that's a fact. When he slides to a base he must turn on his side. Otherwise he'd be so high off the ground he might as well try to make the bag standing.

—Gym Bagley, New York *Evening Mail*

*I don't care whether the tadpole with the fish fell in love, at all;*
*Nor whether in slime they both did time, till they got the final call;*
*For that was so very long ago, that really no one knows.*
*Nor do I wot, for it matters not, that they dined at Delmonico's.*
*If a ship cuts the time of passage across the raging main,*
*Or she gets the gate, because too late to beat an aeroplane.*
*It wouldn't matter a cent's worth, you may believe me when I say,*
*If a ride on the cars from here to Mars would only take a day.*
*I wouldn't cough up a button to see an angel's face—*

*You can't get nourishment from these,*
*They're only gags for foolish gees;*
*And nothing like it, if you please—*
*When Merk touched second base.*

*The campaign doesn't bother me, I don't even read its news;*
*I wouldn't care if every hair in his whiskers votes for Hughes.*
*It's a pipe he'll be elected, he's nowhere now but there,*
*I'll put you wise, those other guys are not in it, but I don't care.*
*I wouldn't give a nickel to see Miss Liberty do a Salome dance,*
*Nor a suffragette—and it may be yet—spring Moe Levy pants.*
*I don't care whether Bingham only has his coppers for his toys,*
*Nor his bluff when he pulled that stuff about stopping the city's noise.*
*I haven't any tears to shed 'cause he beat it, our own Hal Chase.\**
          *But if you'll only tell me, Bo*
          *The thing that we already know,*
          *The thing that worries Murphy so—*
          *That Merk touched second base.*

                              —Gym Bagley, New York *Evening Mail*

## ——— NATIONAL LEAGUE STANDINGS ———

| | W | L | PCT. | GB | | W | L | PCT. | GB |
|---|---|---|---|---|---|---|---|---|---|
| New York ... | 90 | 52 | .634 | ½ | Cincinnati ... | 71 | 77 | .480 | 22½ |
| Chicago ..... | 93 | 54 | .633 | — | Boston ...... | 61 | 84 | .421 | 31 |
| Pittsburgh ... | 92 | 55 | .626 | 1 | Brooklyn .... | 48 | 96 | .333 | 43½ |
| Philadelphia . | 77 | 65 | .542 | 13½ | St. Louis .... | 49 | 98 | .333 | 44 |

## ———◇ TUESDAY, SEPTEMBER 29 ◇———

{On September 28, in New York, the Giants beat Philadelphia 7 to 6.
Winning pitcher, McGinnity; losing pitcher, Corridon. Giants' standing:
91 wins, 52 losses, in first place.}

---

*The controversial New York Yankee first baseman who had recently jumped his team.

The gallant Knight of the Wallop, "Turkey Mike" Donlin, at about 5:35 P.M. yesterday saw a mud-covered baseball coming toward him through the gathering darkness. It came from the hand of Philadelphia Pitcher Frank Corridon, and it came just where Mike wanted it. Roger Bresnahan was on third base and the Giants needed a run to tie the score. So what did "Turkey" do? He just landed on that seal-brown sphere and hit it as hard as he ever hit a ball in his life. It traveled low and fast to the right-field fence. Roger walked home and Donlin half slid and half ran to third base, with 3,000 fans making about as much noise as 10,000 could under ordinary conditions. Then Cy Seymour walked up for a crack at the battered mud ball. Cy was as good as Mike. He slapped a liner to left. Only a single was needed to score Jack Barry, who had stepped in to run for Donlin, or Cy's crack would have been good for three bases. The Giants had pulled out of as tight a hole as they had been in for several days.                                                    —New York *World*


CINCINNATI, Sept. 28—While the Cubs rested in quiet seclusion, the Giants jammed the Chicago contenders back a couple of points in the frantic scramble for the pennant.

The Peerless Leader was disappointed because the champions had to remain idle though the sun shone. Fear of the deadly technicality microbe induced the Cubs to abandon playing off a postponed game this afternoon. The original intention was to remain idle today, and double up Tuesday. But while in New York Frank Bancroft of the Reds got Chance on the phone and arranged to play an extra game on Monday. Then occurred the rumpus at the Polo Grounds.

While the Reds were at the Polo Grounds on Saturday the wily John T. Brush tipped his mitt to Bancroft by asking a number of questions about switching the game here. That set Bancroft to thinking. This morning he and Garry Herrmann looked up the rules and found that tie games "shall be played off in subsequent series."

Notice the delicate point John T. Brush is flirting with. Our present series here does not become subsequent until tomorrow. Hence if a postponed game was played today Brush might subpoena a bunch of ham-fat actors and such and have the combat thrown out as illegal on the ground it was not subsequent according to Hoyle. After talking the matter over with the Peerless Leader and others, Mr. Murphy decided not to take a chance. Today's game will be played on Friday.

—Charles Dryden, Chicago *Tribune*

When Barry, running for Donlin, danced over the rubber on Seymour's hit yesterday, the game was won. As he ambled home, Barry stopped just short of the plate and then jumped on it. But even that didn't satisfy Donlin. He ran out and took Barry back and made him stand on the pan, at the same time pointing to the act and calling Klem's attention to it.

"He is touching the base, isn't he?" asked Mike of Klem.

Klem smiled and said, "Yes."

"Just so nobody can protest it," quothe Mike.

—Gym Bagley, New York *Evening Mail*

———◇ **WEDNESDAY, SEPTEMBER 30** ◇———

{On September 29, in New York, the Giants split a doubleheader with Philadelphia, 6 to 2 and 0 to 7. Winning pitchers: Mathewson and Coveleski; losing pitchers, McQuillan and Crandall. Giants' standing: 92 wins, 53 losses, in second place.}

More in anger than in sorrow, it has to be reported that Philadelphia sprung something yesterday. It was named something unpronounceable, and spelled C-o-v-a-l-e-s-k-i {a misspelling of Coveleski's name}. It pitched, and that's why we're in second place.

Two games were scheduled at the Polo Grounds yesterday between the Giants and Quakers, and one of them was played and won, 6 to 2. In this game, Mathewson pitched, and without having to extend himself, he made the sluggards from the Schuyl-kill look their class. And none of the 15,000 crowd so much as gaped at the result. It was to be expected.

That was the way it went in the first game, with Matty pitching about as he liked, easy and graceful and not too exertful, and everybody in good humor, and the fans wondering whether Matty wasn't going to pitch another nine innings, and the grill at the back of the stand coming in for a strong play, and a lot of new celebrities in the new grandstand, and only the laziest sort of interest in the Pittsburgh and Chicago scores, for we're going right along now, fellows, and we don't have to be geographical to be happy, and something of this confident feeling gets into the cosmos of old boy McGraw, and he grows indulgent and says to that minor child Crandall—which is only 19 years old, so they say, and pitches like it exactly {Crandall would in fact celebrate his twenty-first birthday on October 8}—says McGraw, then, "Go on in, Otey, for this second game, and you can win it all right, son, for you're the strong, hefty infant, and they'll never get to that stuff of yours, and even if they did, we can hit anything they bring out, and we can always fall back on Matty to help you out, so you go on and show these Philadelphians that New York can celebrate a bit on its own account on Founders' Day."

And Otis Crandall, big and kiddish and important, and without a pitching thing in this big world to recommend him, gets into the game, and they kill him fatally.

Philadelphia put one over on us. His name was Covaleski. Crandall starts and retires the first three men and that's all right. Umpire Klem gets out in front of the grandstand and sneezes three times, and then somebody says: "Tell us the name of Philadelphia's pitcher," and then Klem says, sort of shortlike and resentful: "I done told you his name; it's —" and he sneezes some more, and a gentleman in the grandstand who is a linguist by day, says: "Why that must be Mr. Covaleski," and there isn't anybody can argue the point.

Mr. Colvaleski comes from the Warsaw team of the Plander Leaguesky, and they say that all along the Nevsky Prospekt his name has got it on the Goldbrick Twins for being a household word. Last time out in his own country he shut the Kischeneffs out, and made the flower and glory of the Moscow sluggers look anemic. Bar a couple of strikeoutskys in the course of the afternoon, this gentleman was all to the pitchovitch.

Everybody has a funny little something to say about the pitcher for Philadelphia, and the pitcher for Philadelphia has a funny little something to hand out to most of the crowd, including Giant batsmen. When the fifth inning has come around, and we have failed to score, we're beginning to believe this fellow has something. In the fifth we set out to win the game and stop our fooling and send Covaleski back to the coal mines. Devlin leads off with a two-bagger to the left-field fence, and right on top of this Merkle drives out a double to right. Now, you who did not see the game are saying: "Ah, that is where Devlin scored." You are wrong. Devlin did not score. Devlin has not scored yet. Devlin made a play that for pure asininity overlaps any of the inexcusably bad throws he has made in the last three days, and everybody knows these errors have been hard to beat. When Devlin doubled and Merkle doubled Devlin stood still as long as he could without taking root, and only got off second base when Merkle came crashing around and gave the signal to clear the track. Even at that it looked as if we couldn't possibly help scoring. Two on base, nobody out, Bridwell up. And Bridwell lines to {second baseman} Knabe, doubling Merkle off second, Crandall is thrown out by Cov. & Co., and there are no runs, and maybe Devlin is popular, eh?

And right on top of this, the sixth inning, Philadelphia gets nine men up, with the first man, Cov., & Co., making three bases as Merkle chases futilely around right field for the ball, and they score five runs. Doggone these foreigners anyway. Why don't they confine themselves to skat or ski-balling or whatever their national game is, and leave America for the Americans?

—W. W. Aulick, New York *Times*

The National League race is more of an enigma this fair September morning than it has ever been. The three leading teams are grouped in a cute little bunch, like a tangled ball of yarn. What the outcome will be, no sage can say. But the Giants are still there, and don't forget it.

The team that crawled up by inches from the second division to its present advantageous position is anything but a perfect team as it stands today. Three or four seasoned regulars are playing on their nerve, when they ought to be taking a vacation. Tenney is sticking to his position because the season is drawing to a close with the heartbreaking race still unsolved. Roger Bresnahan, who was hurt again yesterday, is in the cast of characters simply because his presence is needed. Mike Donlin, who got a little wrench of his bad ankle in Monday's struggle, wanted to play until Dr. Creamer said it was out of the question. That's the kind of boys, New York fans, who are keeping us on the baseball map.

—William F. Kirk, New York *American*

NEW YORK, Sept. 29—In yesterday's game McGraw acted like a wild man and passed several remarks to many Phillies, which has aroused their fighting spirit. It is now anything to down New York.

Also, just know, Bresnahan's injury was due to his attempt to cripple {Red} Dooin. While {shortstop Dave} Shean was tossing Seymour out in the fifth inning of the first game, Bresnahan, on third, made a dash for the plate. Bransfield relayed the ball home to head him off, and as Bresnahan slid he came feet forward right at Dooin's legs. The shock of the collision sent Bresnahan rolling away from the plate, and Dooin was spiked. But, as it afterward proved, Bresnahan got the worst of his attempt to cripple Dooin.

—Philadelphia *Inquirer*


Now here's a problem: If Bresnahan had caught the second game, would the Giants have lost, Covaleskie to the contrary, notwithstanding? Would the Bresnahan nut, if he could have stood up behind the bat on that bum gamp for nine innings, have pulled his team through?

There was one way for him to stay in, not to hit the ball and in consequence be compelled to run the bases. He could have intentionally struck out each time up. Even if he was of no use at the bat, he would still have been the directing hand and mind.

But the first time up he singled. That was his undoing. He had to hopscotch it to first. He could only put down one leg. Now it stands to reason that a guy getting to first on one leg would have to hit far away. But Bresnahan didn't. It was an infield which he beat out—on one foot.

Both Shean and {second baseman} Knabe went after the ball. They committed no error on the hit. And Roger was on the bag long before the ball was returned.

I'm no mind reader, but if the truth were told, I'd gamble a bag of Harry Stevens' gubers that when Shean and Knabe saw Bresnahan hobbling so painfully down the line they came to the conclusion that it would be a shame to throw out so game a player.

Roger had to give in for a pinch-runner, and of course that put him out of the game.

—Gym Bagley, New York *Evening Mail*

The electric light plant for playing midnight baseball will be ready for use in the Reds' park in two weeks. Mr. Herrmann is investing $4,000 in the scheme. Should the idea prove a failure the lights will enable the park to be used for political meetings. Three huge light towers have been erected in the yard. {Night baseball in the major leagues indeed began in Cincinnati, but not until May 24, 1935.}　　　　—Chicago *Tribune*

───◇ **THURSDAY, OCTOBER 1** ◇───

{On September 30, in New York, the Giants beat Philadelphia 2 to 1. Winning pitcher, Ames; losing pitcher, Moore. Giants' standing: 93 wins, 53 losses, in first place.}

The stirring, nerve-racking fight for the National League pennant took a sudden turn yesterday that makes New York's chances look bright again. The Giants won from Philadelphia, but the change in the situation came in the ninth inning of a game in Cincinnati, when the Reds batted out a startling victory over Chicago, forcing the Cubs, who started the day in the lead, into third place, Pittsburgh having won an uphill game from St. Louis. The strain on the Giants is nonetheless acute, although they can lose two more games of the seven they have to play and still tie with Chicago if the Cubs win their remaining games. If, however, Pittsburgh cleans up, the Giants must win six of their seven.

　　　　　　　　　　　　　　　　　　　—New York *Tribune*

Yesterday's Polo Grounds triumph was a game in keeping with the day. A fair game on a fair afternoon, with cool air sending a tingle through your veins, and just enough folks in the stand to make things clubby, and old boy Donlin in right field with his whip in his hand, making throws to home plate and third base that up to this time have been peculiar only to Right-Fielder Catapult of the Julius Caesar League.

Also, it's only justice to say, in a few brief but well-intended words, that Leon Ames pitched baseball yesterday, and pitched it the last time out, and looks for all the world as if he were gaited up for championship class.

As for runs, we got ours in the first, Herzog walking and going to second on Pitcher {Earl} Moore's throw and scoring when Shean threw McCormick's hit into the stand. McCormick scored on Devlin's hit to right.                    —W. W. Aulick, New York *Times*


CINCINNATI, Sept. 30—Mr. H. Lobert, the finely trained athlete, turned a cruel trick on the Cubs this pleasant afternoon. In the ninth round with the bases full he smote a single that tallied two runs and beat the champions, 6 to 5. Tonight they repose in third place, 2 points behind the Pirates, and 6 in the rear of the hated Giants.

The champions still have a chance, but it is thinner than the ham in the sandwiches at the Philadelphia ball park. Only those who have inhaled said sandwiches know how thin that is. But the game is lost, so what's the use of beefing? Moreover, the gents who did not score behind or in front of Lobert's swat went on and touched the next base.

                    —Charles Dryden, Chicago *Tribune*


CHICAGO, Sept. 27—It certainly is staggering to some of us old-timers to look back 15 or 20 years and, by comparison, force one's self to realize the vast growth of the national game. How many of us, for instance, ever saw or heard of a political campaign for the election of a President of the United States held up by greater interest in a baseball campaign?

Yet that is the situation in which the country finds itself now. There is more interest today in what clubs are going to play for the world's championship than in the outcome of the November election. It is absurd in a way when one thinks of it that the decision of a baseball pennant, which means almost nothing to the welfare of the country or its citizens, should obscure even for a minute that which affects every man, woman and child in the land.

Politicians are complaining about it, sages are writing about it in their political reviews and editorials are being penned about it, so there can be no mistake in thinking such a situation exists. One local politician told me that four out of every five times he asked someone what he thought would be the outcome of the next Presidential election the reply would be: "Oh, to —— with that. Who's going to win the pennant?"

                    —I. E. Sanborn, *The Sporting News*

{On October 1, in Philadelphia, the Giants split a doubleheader, winning 4 to 2 and losing 6 to 3. Winning pitchers, Mathewson and Coveleski; losing pitchers, Corridon and Wiltse. Giants' standing: 94 wins, 54 losses, in first place.}

Another crimp was put in the pennant aspirations of the tribe of McGraw by the Phillies yesterday.

After the first session of a doubleheader had been chucked into the maw of the hungry New Yorkers by {left-fielder} Sherwood Magee {by muffing a line drive that let in the winning run}, the Murrays copped the second chapter by whaling the horsehide while Coveleski, fresh from having dosed the Giants with whitewash over on Papa Knickerbocker's isle, again mowed them down.

It's in the dope that Coveleski, the Phillies' "Iron Man," will prove the undoing of the Giants. They are afraid of him, and as he is likely to twirl again tomorrow, the McGrawites are expected to take a tumble. All the faithful say that defeat for New York will be spelled C-o-v-a-l-e-s-k-i.

Probably not since the Athletics and Giants clinched for the world's championship has there been such an influx of dippy ones from where the white lights dangle. Everybody who could get away or had the price seemed to have beat it over from Manhattan to work their lungs for McGraw's bunch, and many a gloom-nipped Gothamite hiked it back Madison Squareway, green hats and all, with dope tucked away in their thinktanks that New York's chances of swiping the bunting are getting more emaciated every day. —Philadelphia *Inquirer*

PHILADELPHIA, Oct. 1—While the Giants still figure prominently as pennant winners, there is no question that the team is now a sadly battle-scarred lot of ball tossers. If the pets from the Polo Grounds can win tomorrow and Saturday, it will be on nerve and nothing else. Bresnahan's lameness may keep him out for the remainder of the season, though the fiery backstop wants to work if there is a chance for him to appear behind the plate.

Donlin's leg is so bad he ought to be on crutches. Seymour got a slight twist in his right leg today, which slowed him up and caused him a good deal of pain the rest of the afternoon.

About 8,000 people saw the game, not as large a crowd as the Philadelphia management had hoped to see. It seems, however, that our beauties and their rivals were playing against several competing attractions. There was a football game somewhere, a special matinee somewhere else, and besides the residents of this quaint old city are all wrought up over a coming festival to be known as "Founders Day."

Hundreds of business houses and dwellings are profusely decorated with bunting, strangers are pouring into town, and there isn't much time to talk baseball. Nobody seems to know just who the "Founders" are or why any body of men should get a "day" for founding Philadelphia.

As a result of the second struggle's sad ending the three contenders are squeezed into the funniest little corner you éver dreamed of. Never was there such a race before. The baseball public is on the verge of dementia doperina, and the players of the three leading clubs are worn to a frazzle. Chances are that this week will tell the tale.

—William F. Kirk, New York *American*

It's a funny thing when you have to spring the dope that Mike Donlin lost a game. But that's just what happened in the second session of the doubleheader here in Philadelphia yesterday. But it wasn't Donlin's fault. It was the fault of his bum ankle. At least four runs came across in that sad, sad story of the second spasm because Mike couldn't shag flies.

It was pitiful, that is pitiful for the bunch of New York bugs who journeyed to this burg to see the Giants clean up the Phillies and cinch the old rag. Rockets that ordinarily Donlin would make a pie of fell safe many feet from the crippled right-fielder. He just couldn't get to them.

But McGraw had to keep him in on the chance that his batting eye would pull over a run or two at a critical moment.

And this same thing did happen in the sixth inning. Mike packed a double which brought across a couple of runs.

—Gym Bagley, New York *Evening Mail*

The only way in which McGraw can beat that gentleman with the Russian suffix to his name, which is pronounced like an automobile with its muffler off, running on three cylinders, is to dress his team in kimonos and disguise them as Japs. Then, if the same disguised ball players make a noise like the Mikado's army, Covaleskie might dig for the tall timber.

—New York *Herald*

———◇ **SATURDAY, OCTOBER 3** ◇———

{On October 2, in Philadelphia, the Giants won 7 to 2. Winning pitcher, Ames; losing pitcher, McQuillan. Giants' standing: 95 wins, 54 losses, in second place.}

After a week of deliberation President Harry C. Pulliam last night rendered a decision on the protested New York–Chicago game of September 23. President Pulliam rules the game a tie and says the Chicago club has no claim for a forfeited game on September 24. The text of the announcement is:

"The game was played at the Polo Grounds and was declared a drawn contest by the umpires in charge.

"Against this decision the Chicago and New York clubs filed protests, as follows:

"Sept. 23, 10:00 P.M. Chicago appeals from decision declaring a draw and claims forfeiture.

"Sept. 24, 11:00 A.M. Chicago serves notice it does not protest decision.

"Sept. 25. Chicago claims a forfeiture by 9 to 0 for failure of New York club to play off on Sept. 24 the tie of previous day.

"Sept. 25. New York club gives notice of appeal from decision of umpires and at expiration of time limit files briefs, together with documentary evidence.

"Sept. 30. Chicago formally waives its right to five days in which to reply to New York, resting its case on the report of the umpires, and claiming thereby a forfeited game on Sept. 24.

"The contentions of Chicago for a forfeiture on Sept. 24 will be disposed of first. When Chicago filed its original claim it tied the hands of the president of the league in his endeavor to reach a speedy adjudication. Under the constitution the filing of the claim precluded the president from taking any step looking toward the immediate playing off of the game.

"There was nothing to do but serve notice of claim on New York and wait five days for reply. When Chicago filed its second communication, it was too late to insist on playing off of the game on a few hours' notice.

"Since the last and final claim for a forfeiture, filed by Chicago Sept. 25, cannot be entertained, the same is hereby dismissed.

"Before going into the merits of the protest filed by New York against the decision of the umpires, I shall quote the rule governing the scoring of runs:

" 'Rule 59. One run shall be scored every time a base runner, after having legally touched the first three bases, shall legally touch home base before three men are put out; provided, however, that if he reach home on or during a play in which the third man be forced out or be put out before reaching first base a run shall not count. A force out can be made only when a base runner legally loses the right to the base he occupies and is thereby obliged to advance as the result of a fair hit not caught on the fly.'

"The play: Bridwell at bat, McCormick on third, Merkle on first, and two out. Bridwell hits the ball, which results in a fair hit not caught on the fly.

"What is necessary to score this run? Bridwell must reach first safely, so must Merkle reach second, he being forced in advance on Bridwell's hit.

"Under the rules the umpire is sole judge of the play, and on this play both ruled that Merkle was forced out for failure to touch second— O'Day on his personal observation of Merkle and Emslie by information received from O'Day.

"This left the game a tie, and O'Day in his report gives the reason why the game was not continued. He says: 'The people had run out on the field. I did not ask to have the field cleared, as it was too dark to continue play.'

"New York, in support of its claim for the game, contends: First, that neither O'Day nor Emslie saw the play; second, that as proof of this claim the fact is cited of the umpires' failure to order the field cleared for the purpose of continuing the game; third, that no decision was rendered on the field to the effect that the run did not score.

"No claim is made that Merkle touched second base, it being held by inference that this requirement was a technicality. Numerous affidavits by players and spectators are submitted in support of the contentions of the New York club. Among the affidavits of players are those of Bridwell and McCormick, but none from Merkle.

"The question to be decided is: Shall the decision of the umpires be upheld, or shall it be set aside on the evidence submitted by players and spectators?

"In a similar case, covering the identical play under the same conditions, in a game played at Pittsburgh Sept. 4, with Chicago, the latter club protested the decision of the umpire, and submitted affidavits by players and newspaper correspondents. My ruling in this case was as follows:

" 'This is a case simply of fact and judgment, and the ruling of the umpire is final. The question of whether there was a force play or not cannot be substantiated by evidence of spectators. It rests solely with the umpire. The umpire, by allowing the winning run, ruled that there was no force at second, because if there had been the run could not have scored.'

"At Pittsburgh there was but one umpire. At New York there were two, and the purpose of the double-umpire system is to cover all plays. This play in question, missed by Emslie, was seen by O'Day, who, being the umpire-in-chief, ruled that the run did not count.

"Much as I deplore the unfortunate ending of a brilliantly played game as well as the subsequent controversy, I have no alternative than to be guided by the law. I believe in sportsmanship, but would it be good sportsmanship to repudiate my umpires simply to condone the undisputed blunder of a player?

"The playing rules say that the decision of an umpire on a question of fact is final. This whole controversy hinges on a simple question—Was Merkle forced out at second base? Umpire-in-chief O'Day says he was. O'Day is no novice, and there is no reason to doubt his accuracy in his decision. As an umpire he ranks second to none; his integrity has never been questioned.

"My decision in this matter is just as it was in the Pittsburgh decision and as in every other protest that has come before me—to uphold the umpire on questions of fact.

"I rule that this game ended in a tie score and that Chicago has no claim for a forfeited game on Sept. 24.

"This ruling is subject to appeal to the Board of Directors, and in that event a meeting of the board will be called for Monday, October 5."

—New York *American*

PHILADELPHIA, Oct. 2—Flying at the throats of the Phillies like nine wildcats, the Gingery Giants made enough runs in the first inning to make victory a certainty.

It was a cold, windy day, more fitted for football than baseball. McQuillan and Foxen, the first two men sent to the slab by Manager Murray, couldn't get warm enough to pitch and couldn't pitch enough to get warm, and, thanks to their lack of control and general ineffectiveness, we piled up our commanding lead.

Ames pitched for the Giants, and Leon was at his best. The powerful young redhead didn't let himself out any more than he had to, realizing that the sudden change in the weather wasn't the best thing in the world for a pitcher's salary limb, but when he had to use the old steam he certainly had it to use.

The fireworks began promptly at 3:30. Mr. McQuillan, who has sent many a Giant back hitless to the water bucket in days gone by, strolled to the mound and squared off at his foemen like a real, honest-to-goodness winner. He patted the new white ball, talked to it a moment and then tried to get it over the plate. Mr. Tenney waited, and waited, and waited, and then walked. Young Herzog, who was the candy child today, clouted an inshoot one good, sincere clout. The ball started like a flash of light for centerfield. Tenney walked home, and the estimable Mr. Herzog never stopped till he pulled up, panting, on third base. Harry McCormick singled to center without seeming to exert himself, and Herzog waddled homeward with a shining countenance. Captain Mike came mighty near ripping off a long, safe one when he pulled a hard grounder over first base, but Bransfield made a fine stop, touched first and threw out McCormick at second.

If you had been there, gentle reader, you would have leaned back at this stage of the game with the remark that two runs look pretty good for a starter. The Giants, however, were out for more plums. Cy Seymour drew a base on balls, and Knabe fumbled Devlin's hard grounder. Mr. McQuillan began to get white around the gills, and presented Roger Bresnahan with a complimentary, filling the bases. Bridwell went up with the firm intention of cleaning up, but he, too, ambled to first on four balls, forcing in Seymour. McQuillan didn't do any more flinging, Mr. Foxen taking up the burden. Foxen was no great improvement. He began by walking Ames, thus crowding Devlin into the harbor. He kept up the good work by giving Tenney his second base on balls, Bresnahan paddling homeward.

The ingenious manager of the scrapplers decided it was not Foxen's day and sent in Moren. Herzog didn't falter in the presence of the newcomer, clouting another single, scoring Ames and Bridwell. Two hits for one young fellow in one inning is a notable achievement, and Herzog was in bad with local fans for the rest of the afternoon. McCormick ended the inning by making the third out. This is how the Gingery Giants made their seven tallies, and that is how they won the game.

—William F. Kirk, New York *American*

"I am sure Mathewson will send us up the ladder a little further today," said McGraw this morning. "They can talk about him being tired or overworked, but he isn't. Once Matty gets loosened up in the pitcher's box it will be only a question of making runs behind him. The Phillies hit him the other day because he started slowly, but I will see that he is well warmed up today. The weather is a little cool, and a pitcher's arm is apt to stiffen up with a cold wind blowing. Let Matty get up a sweat and he will go through the Phillies like a rifle bullet through a cigar box."

—Sid Mercer, New York *Globe*

PHILADELPHIA, Oct. 3—So worked up was the populace that one New York fan who rooted for the Giants too exuberantly got a severe thrashing, although he put up a game battle and delivered many telling punches before he was finally knocked into dreamland. There was one Philadelphia policeman who didn't interfere until he saw the New Yorker getting the best of it, and then he held the latter's arms while the frantic Quaker fans made a punching bag out of the stranger.

Oh, I tell you, this race is a peach. But what a great big laugh we will give 'em when the Giants cop the rag.

—Sam Crane, New York *Evening Journal*

PHILADELPHIA, Oct. 3—Manager McGraw is ill in his room at the Continental Hotel and may not lead his team to battle in the final game with Philadelphia this afternoon.

"He has worried himself sick," said Secretary Knowles. "No man ever worked harder against difficulties and bad luck than McGraw has in the past month, and as game as he is the strain is breaking him down. I will be glad when it is all over."

But unless positively forbidden by the doctor, McGraw will be in uniform today. He feels that as long as cripples like Donlin and Bresnahan are hobbling around in their appointed places nothing but sheer physical incapacity should make him give up the active leadership.

—J. W. McConaughy, New York *Evening Journal*

ST. LOUIS, Oct. 2—Manager Clarke of Pittsburgh tonight declared that should Pittsburgh lose a game tomorrow or the game on Sunday in Chicago through his players being in bad shape, and if losing these games loses the pennant, he will sue the Pullman Company for heavy damages.

The Pittsburgh team reached here this morning after having been up almost all night trying to keep warm or from being burned to death by a fire a porter insisted on building in a blind stove. The team had to get out twice and help extinguish fires which were burning the car. There was no steam in the car all night and the players were badly frozen.

—Chicago *Tribune*

Fifty thousand dollars for Christy Mathewson!

That is the stupendous sum offered by Charles W. Murphy and Frank

L. Chance, of the Chicago Cubs, to the New York club for Mathewson. The New York management promptly spurned the offer and remarked that they would not sell Matty at any price.

—New York Evening Journal

A correspondent writes, "Mr. Marquard carries documentary assurance from the New York club that guarantees him a full share in the world's series money if the Giants win." He was smart enough to make that provision before leaving Indianapolis, and yet they call Mr. Marquard a Rube. He is foolish like a pawnbroker.     —Sporting Life

———◇ SUNDAY, OCTOBER 4 ◇———

{On October 3, in Philadelphia, the Giants lost 3 to 2. Winning pitcher, Coveleski; losing pitcher, Mathewson. Giants' standing: 95 wins, 55 losses, in third place.}

Great is Covelaski.

Covelaski, the gunner from the Tri-State field, who shot three holes through the Giants' armor in one week's time and has shoved McGraw and his tribe down to third place.

If New York loses the championship nobody can the Giants blame more than the same Covelaski. Three victories from New York in one week is going some, especially when the Giants were going at a pace which would have beaten the majority of pitchers in either big league.

And to make Covelaski's achievement all the greater, he easily outpitched the great Mathewson from beginning to end. The Giants would have been lucky to have scored yesterday had the outfield of the Murrays been on their toes. A fumble by Magee on Tenney's single in the opening inning greatly aided the Giants to their first run, while in the ninth a juggling act by Osborne, followed by Titus letting McCormick's single go through him, gave the New Yorks their last tally.

And to show he possesses the stuff which great pitchers are made of, he kept his nerve about him in the ninth when, with McCormick on third base and none out, he prevented the Giants getting the tying run across. Donlin hit a weak little fly to Osborne. Seymour tapped one to Knabe and McCormick was run down between third and home. Then to wind up hís brilliant performance Covelaski fanned Devlin, and the Giants fell to third place.

When Devlin whiffed on the third strike the crowd of 6,622 fans went wild with joy and swarming on the field, surrounded Covelaski and followed him to the clubhouse, patting him on the back and going through other wild demonstrations. The exhibition of joy by the fans would lead one to think the result of the game had won the championship for Philadelphia. But as long as it had put the Giants out of the running for the time being the crowd was satisfied. McGraw never was a favorite here, and whenever he is licked the victory is doubly relished by local fandom.

The "Joints" {Out-of-town writers often referred to the Giants as "Joints," mocking the way some New Yorkers pronounced the word: "Joy-ints."} were a sore lot when they left the field, and Devlin was perhaps one of the worst ones with a grouch. As he was about to go in the clubhouse a small boy hurled a remark at him and this aroused his ire and he kicked the youngster. The crowd quickly swarmed around the entrance of New York's dressing room after this and waited for the Giants to appear on the "Hump" from the Broad street door. But outside of jeering every member of the New Yorks and unmercifully "kidding" McGraw as he worked his way to the North Philadelphia Station the crowd went to their suppers peacefully.

—Philadelphia *Inquirer*


Philadelphia, Oct. 3—There is an end to human endurance. Mathewson, the grandest Roman of them all, had been called on once too often. No arm can stand the strain of constant use, and Matty had worked more than his share. For half the game Mathewson was the same cool, deliberate, unsolvable mystery as of yore. Then the great strain told. Covelaski had settled down to his arduous task after the first inning with all the novel cunning for which he is now noted.

—New York *American*

If the Pirates win today, they will win the pennant even if New York wins all three from Boston. If the Cubs win, the best the Giants can do is to tie them for first place. This is not counting on what action the Board of Directors may take in deciding the disputed New York–Chicago game. Both clubs have appealed from President Pulliam's decision, and the board will meet in Cincinnati tomorrow to make a final decision. A decision in New York's favor and three games from Boston would mean that New York could win the pennant provided the Pirates lose today. Should the Pirates win today and the decision of the board be in New York's favor, the latter could tie Pittsburgh by winning three from Boston.

—New York *Sun*

If the Giants lose the pennant, Coveleski deserves the credit for defeating them. He seems to have the Indian sign on the stickers, big and little, from Coogan's Bluff. He hails from Shamokin, Pa., in the coal field, and is a Polak. Last summer he was twirling for an amateur team in Wildwood, N.J., having graduated from a coal miners' aggregation. In the Jersey marshes Murray picked him up last Autumn, and this Spring he was very green. In the early part of the season the Giants drubbed him 14 to 2.

He spent the Summer in the Tri-State League and as an alumnus of that organization he has developed into the man who has put such a crimp in the New York pennant aspirations. {Beyond these three victories against the Giants, Harry Coveleski won only one game for Philadelphia in 1908. When he completed his nine-year major league career in 1918, he had gained 81 victories. He was an older brother of Stanley Coveleski, the American League spitball pitcher elected to the Hall of Fame in 1969.}

—New York *Herald*

———◇ **MONDAY, OCTOBER 5** ◇———

{On October 4, the Giants were not scheduled to play, but in Chicago the Cubs beat the Pirates 5 to 2, providing the Giants with the chance to tie for first place.}

CHICAGO, Oct. 4—Chicago's Cubs, world's champions, closed their dramatic struggle to retain their title with a victory over Pittsburgh. Before the greatest crowd that ever saw a baseball game, the two teams engaged in one of the most desperate and determined games in the history of baseball.

The game, climaxing the heartbreaking race of the last two months, saw two of the gamest clubs in the league locked in the death combat. Loss of the game meant hopeless defeat to either, victory meant the pennant for one and in all probability for the other. All the strain and effort, all the brains and energy and hard work, the suffering and sacrifices that the two clubs have endured, were wasted for the defeated one, and well endured by the winner. And before 30,247 maddened fans they fought it out to the finish, and Chicago won.

The finish of the battle for the championship of 1908 was perhaps the most thrilling event of all the long, strenuous season. Piled in the immense stands were nearly 20,000 persons, and banked in immense solid masses around the great field, twenty deep, stood an army. They realized the situation, and that the 18 men in uniform on the narrowed space of green were doing battle for the honor of their cities, for the championship of their league, and perhaps of the world, and that to each man the game meant $2,000 in cash.

Chance had chosen Brown to lead, and Clarke had gambled the whole season on Willis. They had met before again and again and Brown usually was victor, but this time in a strain that shook the nerves and tried the souls of men both managers were confident, and Brown won. Pitching with wonderful nerve and coolness, backed in superb style by Evers and Tinker and Chance especially, with Kling catching in grand form, Brown proved too much for the Pirates.

The game was grandly played. Chicago outplayed, outhit and outran the Pirates. They won the game on class and nerve, and demonstrated that they have the best ball team in the league.

Twice, when hits were desperately needed, Schulte, who almost got interested in baseball at last, pounded out singles that drove in runs. The Cubs were away in front and Schulte's two drives gave them two tallies before the Pirates could score. And then, in the sixth, came danger. For a few moments it looked as if the Pirates in one rally might ruin all the grand work the Cubs have done in the last month, and the crowd became scared and apprehensive. Twice men smashed out hits after two were out, and each after two strikes had been called, and the score was tied.

There the fighting spirit of the Cubs asserted itself and Brown himself won the game. It was in that inning that the season's race was decided, and Willis and Clarke made a move that brought disaster on them.

Two men were out when Tinker drove a double into the crowd to left—a hit that might have been a triple but for the crowd. Kling was next, and Willis chose to pass him and face Brown. It looked like good generalship, but it proved bad, for Brown is one of those men who get mad when others affect to despise them, and, gripping his bat tighter he drove a screaming hit to right that scored Tinker, and gave the Cubs the lead, never to be lost.

The defensive work of Chicago was grand, the stops of Evers and Tinker setting the crowd mad with applause. But for Chance was reserved the major honors, for in the eighth, by one of the most astounding plays ever made, he stopped the Pirates.

Leach hit a fierce line drive straight over first, and it looked a sure double until Chance, with a running jump, shoved out one hand, turned backwards and clung to the ball. Against that kind of defensive work Pittsburgh had no chance.

The Pirates quit while fighting, but when Wilson hit a hard bounder straight at Tinker and the ball flashed to Evers on top of second, forcing {Alan} Storke, the crowd broke. With a roar like an ocean breaking a dike the thousands poured down in the battleground in the wildest, craziest demonstration of the year. Brown, carried aloft on the shoulders of admirers, was borne around and around. For 15 minutes the players, unable to escape to the clubhouse, were carried over the field, while the air was black with cushions, hundreds of men—women, too—hurling the cushions high in the air, throwing coats, screaming and flinging hats.

But even then the demonstration was not over, and an hour after the game was done a thousand fans still waited outside the park. As Chance backed his automobile out hundreds swarmed around him, cheering wildly. Evers escaped to a cab, with a hundred men trying to unhitch the horse and pull the cab themselves, and as for Brown, who tried to slip across to Joe's and wash the dust of battle from his throat, he found about 500 there waiting, each wanting to buy him a keg.

—Hugh S. Fullerton, New York *American*

There was a decided novelty yesterday at the Polo Grounds. It was the sight of a crowd of 3,500 New York baseball fans rooting hard for the Chicago Cubs to win a game. The game was reproduced on two electric scoreboards, placed near home plate. By following the twinkling of small bulbs the fan could figure out play by play.

When Gibson, the last Pirate up, forced Storke at second the fans shook hands all around and yelled: "The Giants will get them yet."

—New York *World*

For the first time in Pittsburgh evening papers printed extras Sunday, giving an account of the final game. —New York *Times*

Fred Knowles, secretary of the Giants, is thinking of having a sign placed on the Polo Grounds reading: "Miners not allowed here." The placard will have special application to Mordecai Brown and Harry Covaleski, who wielded the pick and shovel before they entered the national game. —New York *Press*

What with accidents and the sudden lapse from his superb midseason form of George Wiltse, it is safe to say that McGraw and his Giants would have been in a sorry case in the last ten days of the desperate fighting had it not been for the splendid work of Leon Ames. He came suddenly into his best form a week ago, and has since beaten Cincinnati once and Philadelphia twice. He and Mathewson have been the only victorious New York pitchers since Wiltse, despite an awful beating, was saved from defeat in a Pittsburgh game by the terrific hitting of the Giants. —New York *Tribune*

─────── NATIONAL LEAGUE STANDINGS ───────

| | W | L | PCT. | GB | | W | L | PCT. | GB |
|---|---|---|---|---|---|---|---|---|---|
| Chicago | 98 | 55 | .641 | — | Cincinnati | 73 | 81 | .474 | 25½ |
| Pittsburgh | 98 | 56 | .638 | ½ | Boston | 63 | 88 | .417 | 34 |
| New York | 95 | 55 | .633 | 1½ | Brooklyn | 52 | 98 | .347 | 44½ |
| Philadelphia | 80 | 70 | .533 | 16½ | St. Louis | 49 | 105 | .318 | 47½ |

{On October 5, in New York, the Giants beat Boston 8 to 1. Winning pitcher, Ames; losing pitcher, Tuckey. Giants' standing: 95 wins, 55 losses, in third place.}

The Board of Directors of the National League is skating on very thin ice. Whether the decision of the league umpires shall be upheld and the president of the league sustained in his rulings, or playing rules cast aside in favor of baseball by affidavit, is the grave question before this body, and the directors are hemming, hawing, delaying and pondering on the affidavits of partisans. As a result of this shaky condition of mind on the part of the directors, the decision in the disputed game of September 23 is still in abeyance. The directors are taking a night to think it over and determine whether they shall enforce the league rules and sustain their umpires and their president or yield to extreme pressure brought on them by argument by affidavit and by shrewd legal cross-questioning, and hand a decisive game to a club which threw it away through a stupid performance on the part of one of its players. The extent of the pressure is shown by the fact that the directors refused to announce a verdict last night after a session lasting for eight hours with no intermission for dinner. They will meet again this morning and endeavor to make up their minds. Meanwhile the entire baseball world waits eagerly.

The board consists of Messrs. Herrmann, of Cincinnati; Murphy, of Chicago; Dreyfuss, of Pittsburgh; Ebbets, of Brooklyn; and Dovey, of Boston, with President Pulliam as chairman ex-officio. All were present when the meeting was called to order by President Pulliam at the Sinton Hotel at 10 o'clock yesterday morning. Mr. Pulliam's first act was to rule that Messrs. Murphy and Dreyfuss were ineligible to vote on account of being directly interested in the case. Mr. Murphy retired at once, but Mr. Dreyfuss claimed a right to vote on the ground that the case did not concern his club. Mr. Pulliam pointed out that a vote for New York might enable Pittsburgh to finish the season tied for first place and that, therefore, Mr. Dreyfuss was directly interested. The other three directors sustained the president's position, and Mr. Dreyfuss was barred. He left for home, declaring he would have voted in favor of a forfeit to Chicago if he had been allowed to do so.

President Pulliam retired from his position in the chair, stating he felt it improper to preside in a case in which protests of his own decision were being considered. Mr. Ebbets was appointed chairman of the meeting, and the board got down to hearing testimony. President Brush made his argument in favor of having the game declared a victory for his club, assisted by Attorney Thomas Cogan of this city, his legal adviser. Mr. Brush presented a large number of affidavits from persons who saw the game, some of which declared that Merkle ran down and touched second base, others claimed that O'Day never walked into the diamond, but went straight to the dressing room and never called the game a tie. These affidavits were accepted and carefully considered. Among them were several from New York players, including Fred Merkle, who swore that he started for the clubhouse, but did not go far without returning and touching second base. This last affidavit was not presented in President Brush's original protest to the league president, but was obtained in time to offer to the Board of Directors.

President Murphy advanced his claim in favor of a forfeit to his club because the New York club refused to play off the tie of September 23 on the following day.

The umpires who officiated were then called and subjected to a very rigid cross-examination, including searching questions as to what they did before and after the game and on the following day, as well as their actions at the crucial period of the disputed play. Both O'Day and Emslie testified separately to the main facts, namely, that Merkle did not touch second base until a play had been made on him there and he had been declared out by Umpire Emslie, and that O'Day called the game a tie before leaving the diamond. They could not be shaken on these important points, though every effort was made to muddle them by severe cross-questioning on unimportant details. When Umpire Emslie, the first to be examined, came out of the directors' room, he said:

"I would never have believed that men could swear to such statements as are made in some of the affidavits presented by the New York club. Several of these affidavits are absolutely false. It is a revelation to me that such documents could be obtained."

Umpire O'Day, after his ordeal of cross-questioning, simply shrugged his shoulders. He was evidently highly disgusted with some of the statements to which he had listened.

The umpires agreed on the details of the decision, declaring Merkle out at second and the score a tie. They declared that O'Day's decision of a tie score was made while he was in the center of the diamond and that his declaration on this point caused him to be hustled and jostled by the crowd as he retired to his dressing room. After the umpires had been examined the directors took a recess for dinner.

The board met again at 9 o'clock and remained in session for an hour and a half and then adjourned until this morning at 10 o'clock.

Mr. Ebbets said: "This is a very important matter, one which will establish a precedent for many years to come. We cannot be too hasty in our decision." Mr. Herrmann declared that the directors had not had sufficient time to consider all the affidavits presented by the New York club. None of the directors attempted to explain why affidavits of players and partisan spectators were entitled to be considered as evidence.

—Jack Ryder, Cincinnati *Enquirer*

The Gingery Giants, playing before one of the largest Monday crowds ever seen at the Polo Grounds, began their series with Boston in rosy fashion. The young pitching prodigy named Tuckey, who has been touted as another Covaleski, tried to outpitch Leon Ames—and a mighty swell chance he had! In the words of the immortal Milton:

> On a perfectly fine Autumn day
> Pitcher Tuckey attempted to play;
>   Perhaps we were lucky
>   With said Pitcher Tuckey,
> But we certainly tucked him away!

Everybody East and West is pulling for the Giants to win, except people that dwell in cities where they have major league baseball clubs, and people that live in cities where they have minor league baseball clubs, and people that reside in cities where they have amateur baseball clubs. Otherwise, the Giants are all right.

The gathering yesterday was surprisingly large. Monday, as we have frequently observed, is a bad day to take your girl to the ball game. If she goes to bed early Sunday night she has to run the washing machine, and if she doesn't have to run the washing machine she doesn't go to bed early

Sunday night, and in either event there isn't much doing at the old ball game. Furthermore, as campaign orators say, no true gent would feel like going to a ball game on Monday if Sunday is his day off. But the crowd was there.

Leon Ames was in rare form. Leon is a great help to the folks these days. When Ames has control—and he has it these days—there is no beating him. —William F. Kirk, New York *American*

CINCINNATI, Oct. 6—After the three voting directors of the National League reconvened today to consider the appeal from the decision of President Pulliam declaring the Giants-Cubs disputed game a tie, it became known that two of them had voted to award the game to New York.

The third of the directors, however, steadfastly refused to vote with the other two. He advanced many reasons for his attitude and up to latest accounts had not been won over.

A unanimous vote is necessary for a decision.

Garry Herrmann, who has the reputation of being the fairest man in baseball, was put down as favoring New York.

"I don't think a team should lose a game because a man did not run to second base on a clean hit when there was no chance to get him out if he did," he is reported to have said to friends last night.

President Ebbets, of Brooklyn, to the great surprise of dopesters, is put down as strongly in favor of supporting Pulliam. His opinion is not based on a study of the case so much as a feeling that the head of the league should be sustained on a question of rules.

The third member of the board, George Dovey, of Boston, is openly in favor of declaring the game a tie and wants it played over.

"In a broad sense New York has the best of it," he says. "The fair way out of it, it seems to me, is to have them play it over."

—New York *Evening Journal*

A hush fell upon 80,000,000 people. The wheels of industry had ceased their whirr, the marts of trade had stopped marting, money had forgot to change, husbands halted on their homeward way, wives let the dinner grow cold, children choked off their prattle and the dogs no longer wagged their tails.

What had happened?

Was all the campaign dope upset and Bryan elected?

Had war been declared between the United States and Japan?

Had Wall street once again played its little joke and plunged the country in a panic?

Had all of man's precious prerogatives, since Eve crabbed his laziness by making him eat an apple (it was a crab apple), been tossed into the discard and woman at last allowed to vote?

Was it come to pass that New York City had become a state and was free?

No, little one. None of these. Something of far greater importance.

All things had stopped, even the clock, in a stilled and silent wait for the decision on that tie game.

What was war or panic or the oft-recurring election of a President to this?

Peanuts.

The board is stalling for a result that will relieve it of the responsibility. The Giants might drop a game to Boston. That would end the controversy on the field and allow the board to escape from the rebuke of deciding play in a lawyer's office.

But after yesterday's game it doesn't look as if the board has a chance to escape. —Gym Bagley, New York *Evening Mail*


If the Giants are legislated out of the championship of the National League, it will make more American League fans in this city than the Yankees have ever converted. Hundreds of New York fans have sworn they will never set foot on the Polo Grounds again if this travesty is allowed. The sporting editor of the *Globe* has received scores of letters on this subject. The following is a fair sample of how the fans feel:

Dear Sir—Put me on record!

If the Giants lose the pennant through the yellow claims of Charles Murphy, Evers, Chance, et al., I will never attend another game played by National League clubs.

I am not an American League or a National League "fan," but a baseball enthusiast who insists on fair play, common sense and the elimination of politics.

There is a new major league forming!

If the National League is so enmeshed in politics that a "technicality" wins a pennant, fair play, common sense, and justice no longer prevail.

By all means endorse the withdrawal of McGraw and his game players from the National League to the new major league that is just forming so that the many fans who would never patronize a league so dishonest as the National League would be given an opportunity to still encourage and applaud McGraw and the Giants. {The "new major league," the Federal League, began operating in 1914 and lasted for two seasons.}

—New York *Globe*


In the personal column of the want ad section of the *Tribune* this morning appears the following paid advertisement:

"Personal. Wanted. Heavy rain at the Polo Grounds, New York, on the afternoon of Wednesday, Oct. 7." {Rain would eliminate the Giants' final game and prevent them from finishing in a tie with the Cubs.}

—Chicago *Tribune*


———◇ **WEDNESDAY, OCTOBER 7** ◇———

{On October 6, in New York, the Giants beat Boston 4 to 1. Winning pitcher, Wiltse; losing pitcher, Ferguson. Giants' standing: 97 wins, 55 losses, in second place.}

After two days of deliberation the National League Board of Directors reached a conclusion yesterday afternoon in the matter of the disputed game of September 23. The directors upheld the decision of the umpires and of President Harry C. Pulliam and declared the game a tie. They ordered it to be played off at the Polo Grounds tomorrow afternoon, or as soon thereafter as the weather will permit. Though the decision stretches the league constitution slightly, by extending the season beyond the date set by the regular schedule, the directors felt it was no more than fair to both clubs that this important contest be played off, and in this decision they have the baseball public with them.

A remarkable state of affairs may result from this decision, and that is the possibility that three clubs may be tied for first place by tomorrow night. This condition will arise if New York loses to Boston today and beats the Cubs tomorrow. In that case the Cubs, Giants, and Pirates will be tied for first place, and a three-cornered series will be necessary to determine the winner of the flag. There would have to be some tall hustling to get the Pirates together again to play off a triple series, which would take at least nine days, and would delay the start of the world's series until late in October.

The claim of Chicago that it was entitled to a forfeit was not allowed for reasons made perfectly clear. President Charles W. Murphy was very much disappointed over this, but after a conference with Manager Chance he issued this statement:

"We will play them Thursday and we'll lick 'em too. We'll make it so decisive that no bone-headed baserunning can cast a shadow of doubt on the contest. We want to win the championship on the playing field. Manager Chance and his players are in good condition and will have no excuse if we fail to bring the third successive National League pennant to Chicago."

The decision of the directors {in part} is as follows:

"There can be no question but that the game should have been won by New York had it not been for the reckless, careless, inexcusable blunder of one player, Merkle. In order that a run could have been scored the following rule applied {Rule 59, presented earlier, is now quoted}.

"This rule is plain, explicit and cannot be misconstrued. While it may not have been complied with in many other games, it did not deprive the Chicago club of the right to do so if it so be desired, notwithstanding that it might be termed winning or tying a game on a technicality.

"Merkle should have had only one thing on his mind, to reach second base in safety. The evidence clearly shows the following: After Bridwell hit the ball he ran to and over first base; McCormick started for home and crossed the plate; Merkle started for second and when about halfway to the base turned and ran in the direction of the clubhouse without having reached second base. Emslie was officiating back of the pitcher, O'Day back of the catcher. When the hit was made Emslie fell to the ground to escape being hit by the ball; he got up and watched the play at first base and saw the batter had run out his hit. In the meantime the ball was fielded in by Hofman and eventually fielded to second base to Evers for a put-out on Merkle. Tinker notified Emslie that Merkle did not run to second base. Emslie stated he did not see the play; and then went to his colleague, O'Day, and asked him whether he had seen the play. O'Day answered in the affirmative, and then Emslie asked whether Merkle had run to second, and being informed that he had not, Emslie declared Merkle out. It may appear as rather peculiar that Umpire O'Day should have been watching the play at second. For this reason, we quote from O'Day's testimony:

" 'Mr. Murphy: I would like to ask you, Mr. O'Day, if the matter at Pittsburgh had caused you to anticipate a play of this sort?'

" 'Mr. O'Day: Yes, sir; and I came within an ace to tell Bob {Emslie}, but I thought I had no right by actions to tell the players what to do or to give them an inkling of what I thought.'

"To set aside an umpire's decision by evidence from persons in attendance, would, in our mind, be establishing a bad and dangerous precedent. In this case, however, there is not a single line or word of testimony offered by the New York club that could even by inference be construed to mean that Merkle reached second base at any time, excepting the affidavit of the player himself, which was not made until after Mr. Pulliam had passed on the case. We can, therefore, come to no other conclusion than that the New York club lost a well-earned victory as the result of a stupid play of one of its members.

"Query was submitted as to why the umpires did not proceed with the game after they had decided that Merkle was out and the game was a tie. In answer to this query both umpires contend it was growing dark very rapidly, and that there was the utmost confusion and uproar on the grounds; that it would have been an impossibility to clear the grounds in time to proceed with the game. We believe the umpires acted wisely under the extraordinary circumstances and conditions in calling the game when they did.

"Coming to the appeal made by the Chicago club. This, to our mind, should not be given any consideration. If there was a violation of the constitution by the New York club in having failed to play off a tie game on the only available date, the Chicago club is to be blamed. On the night of the game in question the Chicago club filed a claim with Mr. Pulliam for a forfeiture. This claim on their part tied the hands of the president and prevented the playing off of the game on the following day. Also on the day after the game in question the New York club conferred with Mr. Pulliam and asked him whether they would be required to play off the tied game and were told that they would not be required to do so. By this action the New York club clearly indicated they were ready to play off the game if required to do so.

"We hold that the New York club should in all justice and fairness be given a chance to play off the game in question. For that reason we order that the game be played on the Polo Grounds on Thursday, October 8, or as soon thereafter as weather conditions will permit."

—Jack Ryder, Cincinnati *Enquirer*

Beating Boston again the Giants won the second of three games necessary to enable them to tie Chicago.

Ferguson pitched great ball against his old team for five innings, but a good mixture of luck and timely hitting gave the Giants the lead in the sixth inning, and in the seventh they made sure of the game by scoring three runs. Wiltse would have shut Boston out had it not been for Seymour's muff of a short fly in the eighth.

—New York *Tribune*

Manager Frank Chance and the nearly-champion Cubs, accompanied by President Murphy, will leave for New York this afternoon on the Twentieth Century Limited.

Chance and his teammates, who had expected nothing worse than a series of three games against the Giants in the event the latter won all three games from Boston, as now seems probable, were incensed at the action of the triumvirate compelling them to play one game on the home field of their rivals.

In the heat of his anger Chance told of alleged actions and words of President Ebbets of Brooklyn, one of the men who gave the Cincinnati decision.

"Ebbets was not qualified to pass on our case," said Chance. "He is prejudiced and would surely give us the worst of it. Before the last Chicago series against Brooklyn Ebbets called his whole team together and told them he wanted the men to play their hardest against us and that he would see that any player playing 'soft ball' was barred from baseball for the rest of his career. That was all right, but when he added he hoped the Giants would win the pennant he gave his players a hunch the point of which cannot be overlooked.

"On another occasion Mr. Ebbets went so far as to say to a friend that he was sorry he did not let the crowd kill me at the time of my trouble in Brooklyn last year when fans threw pop bottles at me and I was saved from serious injury or even death only by a police guard."

—Harvey T. Woodruff, Chicago *Tribune*

CINCINNATI, Oct. 6—President C. W. Murphy, of the Chicago club, is not satisfied with the decision of the National League directors.

"The decision makes the tangle worse than before," said he, "and throws open the pennant race to a possible victory for all three of the leading teams, when the Giants were legally out of the race last Sunday. The Giants were given as much as possible the best of it without giving them the game direct."

{If required to play the Giants, Murphy and Chance wanted a three-game series, as provided in the National League constitution for pennant playoffs. The Giant-Cub game would not, however, be a playoff game, which occurs after two or more teams have tied at the end of the season, but the replaying of a regularly scheduled contest which had ended in a tie. On two other occasions in 1908, July 28 and August 5, Giant games ended in a tie and were replayed.}            —New York *American*

There is a deep well-founded opinion among the majority of Manhattan lovers of baseball that the New York club should refuse to play off a game that has once been rightfully won by all the ethics and precedents of honest baseball.

The New York club, or rather those officials now in the city, Manager McGraw and Secretary Knowles, are personally "dead set" against giving Charley Murphy or the Cubs a chance to gather in any more New York money or giving the Cubs the unfair opportunity of having another try at the pennant they have rightfully been beaten out of, according to President Pulliam's previous decision on a like play when he decided that games should be won on the diamond.

But Manager McGraw and Secretary Knowles, putting aside personal feelings, rightfully consider that the players of the team, who have been deprived of what rightfully belongs to them, should decide what they will do in the unfortunate dilemma that has been thrown up to them.

President Brush is on the road from Cincinnati, and the whole situation is of necessity left to him to decide.

In earlier days of baseball there was a sentiment attached to the national game that made games take on the appearance of a real battle between cities and sections, but sentiment no longer figures in the sport. It is now only a battle of dollars. The business end of baseball has so superseded the real sport that used to cause legitimate and honest rivalry for sport's sake alone I personally wouldn't care if the whole foundation of the national game went to the dogs. And this bluff of Charley Murphy of beating out the Giants on a game fairly won—and getting away with it—shows conclusively that baseball is not as it used to be, when "Old Uncle Nick" Young, a man who really loved the game, was president of the grand "old" league. You see that I say "old." The "new" dispensers of rules and regulations by which the great national game is conducted I have no use for.

Charley Murphy and Barney Dreyfuss—bah and bah again. And Charley Ebbets, booh! and bah!! Mr. Ebbets is from Brooklyn, the city that has coined more money out of Manhattan fans in the last few years with a tail-end team than any Brooklyn magnate would have even dared to do. Those much-vaunted $20,000 improvements made on Washington Park last Spring have been paid for by money Manhattan fans paid by reason of the most favorable schedule that the schedule-making Mr. Ebbets could make to give the Brooklyn club the advantage of holiday dates with this same New York club he voted against.

Mr. Charley Ebbets, in my opinion, has not feathered his nest in Brooklyn a little bit by the Giants losing the game that rightfully belongs to them.

I am sore, and I acknowledge it, over that decision.

It may be that the ones who robbed the Giants out of the game may say their president must be upheld for the good of the game, and President Pulliam will, of course, uphold his umpires for the same reason, but that does not excuse the fact that Umpire O'Day made an overnight decision and sent in a report the next morning directly contrary to what he told me after the disputed game was played.

No matter what technical construction has been put on rules, the Giants fairly and honestly won the disputed game, and the mushy weak-kneed straddle the Board of Directors made on their decision showed to me conclusively that they really thought the game belonged to the Giants rightfully and were ashamed of the final conclusion they arrived at. They should be, anyhow.  —Sam Crane, New York *Evening Journal*

## ———◇ WEDNESDAY, OCTOBER 8 ◇———

{On October 7, in New York, the Giants beat Boston 7 to 2. Winning pitcher, Ames; losing pitcher, Flaherty. Giants' standing: 98 wins, 55 losses, tied for first place with Chicago.}

The Giants brought their wonderful fight for the pennant to an end, so far as the regular season goes, by winning the third straight game from Boston.

Just at the start it looked as if Boston, in a dying gasp, was to make a triple tie possible by beating the Giants, but after the first inning Ames pitched as no one imagined he would ever learn to do, and, backed by some fielding that was startling in its brilliancy, kept the visitors from getting near the plate. He helped to win the game with his batting, too, delighting the crowd by smashing out two pretty singles.

—New York *Tribune*

The most bitterly contested championship race in the National League's history will reach a climax this afternoon. When John T. Brush arrived home yesterday morning from the directors' meeting in Cincinnati it did not take him long to announce that the New York club had consented to play the game, and the momentous battle will begin at 3 o'clock.  —New York *Sun*

Mathewson was anxious yesterday to pitch against Boston as well as against the Cubs today, but McGraw had faith in Ames and saved his star. Mathewson warmed up a little yesterday and looked strong and rested. He has not pitched since Saturday, and the rest, the longest he has had for weeks, seems to have done him lots of good. At his best, Mathewson should be able to win. If he should be hit hard, however, McGraw might call on Ames to relieve him, as the latter saved himself yesterday and got through the game without undue effort. Wiltse, too, will be on the bench, and McGinnity, Taylor, Crandall, Marquard, and Durham are other New York pitchers in reserve. —New York *Tribune*

Never before have two teams been tied at the end of a season. Never before has the race been so close. Never has it been necessary to play off the tie of six months' baseball in a single gigantic battle.

That the game will be a struggle to the death is certain. The town is in the grip of the greatest excitement, fringed with nervous prostration. It is rumored that several sanitariums are constructing additions to take care of baseball "bugs" resulting from the last few weeks of the campaign.

Tonight there may be rejoicing and the blare of trumpets in the streets, the burning of colored fire and the shooting of skyrockets. There may be a display of crepe, the wearing of mourning, and the strains of a funeral dirge. There may be nine heroes or nine corpses up at the Polo Grounds. Whether the city will be gay with a rejoicing crowd or plunged in sadness depends entirely on the outcome of the game.

—New York *Herald*

While the players will not participate in the financial returns of to-day's game, members of the winning team will receive about $2,000 each as the result of the games for the world's championship which follow. The contest will therefore be for a $40,000 stake for the players, and an almost equal amount for the owner of the winning club.

The management, knowing the ardor of the enthusiasts, threw out a strong cordon of watchmen last night to prevent the bleachers from filling up overnight. About a dozen extra men were strung out about the fence on the inside of the grounds, and they spent most of the night digging small boys from under seats and the grandstand, and repelling those attempting to climb the fence under cover of darkness.

The final round-up will come with daylight. It is expected that every nook and corner will give up youngsters and perhaps older but just as enthusiastic fans. —New York *Times*

Despite the mandates of Governor Hughes and civic authorities, more money will be bet on the game than has been wagered in the old town since the lid was put on horse racing. The West is well represented, and in true Western fashion is backing the Cubs to the limit. Several large personal wagers were laid last night at even money. In all probability the Giants will be a 10 to 9 favorite, for the unlimited financial strength of an overwhelming home following is bound in time to stop the outsiders. Gotham is loyal to its team, and, though holding out for even money, is doing so in nowise through fear of the ultimate outcome. Everyone in this city has unlimited faith in McGraw, in Mathewson and in each and every individual on the Giant roster.

—W. J. McBeth, New York *American*

Manager Frank Chance and the Cubs, overflowing with confidence, are speeding toward New York on the fastest train ever taken by a baseball club. They will arrive on Manhattan island this morning shortly after their Chicago admirers have finished breakfast.

As the hopes of local fandom climbed aboard the Twentieth Century Limited at the Lake Shore Station yesterday afternoon they were given a rousing reception by several hundred fanatics who had assembled to pay homage.

Sixteen players composed the party, in addition to President Murphy, Treasurer Williams and newspaper correspondents. The distinguished guests were assigned to a special car, which significantly was placed by railroad officials just before the diner.

The expense of the trip, one way, will be about $600, an extra item of about $200 on account of taking the limited. Baseball teams making the trips on regular trains with a 28-hour schedule are given the usual tenparty rate of $18.75. Passage on the limited requires a straight rate of $20, with an extra fare of $10 per person, so the excess cost figures $11.75 each for the party of 18. Berths and meals are about the same, though Johnny Evers figured that a person ought to eat faster on such a fast train.

But the item of expense, which cuts 10 hours off the running schedule, and appears picayune in comparison with the New York money Mr. Murphy will bring home as the Cubs' share of the receipts, was the last thing Chance or any of the players were thinking of. In small groups they stood around, talking with friends or one another, and baseball was the only topic.

Jack Pfiester is chosen in advance by Manager Chance to occupy the slab in the crucial game as the New Yorkers have been found less effective against the sidewheel delivery. Left-handed Jack has been successful in his last efforts against the chesty Giants.

If the star southpaw shows signs of weakening, or if a tense situation arises where heart and nerves of iron are required, Brown, three-fingered Mordecai, who destroyed the Pirates' hopes last Sunday, stands ready and anxious to jump into the breach.

—Harvey T. Woodruff, Chicago *Tribune*

The *Tribune* will show Cubs vs. Giants game on Electrical Baseball Board at Orchestra Hall today. For the benefit Tribune Hospital Fund. Seats now on sale at box office, Orchestra Hall, and 326 Tribune Building. Admission 25 cents and 50 cents, box seats $1.

—Advertisement, Chicago *Tribune*

When the largest crowd ever gathered in the world for a sporting event—fully a quarter of a million—were surging in and around the Polo Grounds, the occasion was marred by a fatality.

Losing his balance as he hung on to a pillar of the elevated structure at Eighth avenue and 159th street, a man supposed to be Henry T. McBride, a fireman, fell and was instantly killed. The man was on the structure in order to look over the fence at the game.

Hardly had the man breathed his last when there surged forward a score or more frantic in their daring just to get a glimpse inside the grounds, who vainly endeavored to climb up on the pillar, in falling from which McBride had just died.

Only the vigorous use of clubs by the police cleared a small circle around the dead man and kept others from climbing the pillar.

In the terrible jam in the bleachers, Edward Wheeler, 34 years old, a restaurant keeper from Brooklyn, either fell or was pushed from the top seat on the grandstand and fell to the ground, about 15 feet. His right leg was broken and he was badly cut and bruised.

The estimate of 250,000 in and around the field is, if anything, below the actual figures. There were fully twice as many persons immediately outside the fence around the grounds as there were inside, and every foothold and balancing handhold on structures of every kind with even a glimpse of the grounds was fiercely held against any newcomer.

From the press box the skyline everywhere was human heads. They were located on grandstand, roofs, fences, "L" structures, electric light poles and in the distance on smokestacks, chimneys, advertising signs and copings of apartment houses.

On the viaduct, the Speedway and cliffs back of the grandstand there was practically a solid mass of people. The partially completed addition to the grandstand, converted from a section of the bleachers to the north, seated 2,500.

A four-car "L" train which stood on a siding by the grounds, affording a fine view of the whole amphitheater, and which was covered inside and on the roofs, was suddenly moved out by the railroad company, and the fans were carried rapidly downtown.

Commissioner Bingham had placed all the police arrangements in the hands of Inspector James F. Thompson. He had 300 policemen and five mounted men under him. Fifty special policemen were also hired by the baseball management.

There was something fascinating in watching the filling of the picture by the constantly growing inpour of people. Every possible vantage point, however precarious, came to have its human cluster. The unusual number of women gave relieving touches of color here and there. And in the center of it all, in the middle foreground, the empty diamond.

Half a dozen ambulances came along and were sent inside the grounds, each loaded with doctors. People besieged the ambulances, some offering as much as five dollars to be taken aboard.

At 12:45, two and a quarter hours before the game would begin, orders came out to the police in front of the Polo Grounds to close the gate as the grounds were jammed to their utmost capacity.

Meanwhile hordes kept coming in every conceivable kind of conveyance. Every surface car that crept up to 155th street had dozens hanging on whatever a hand could find an inch to grip, not to speak of many lying flat on the roofs of cars with only a few inches between their heads and the elevated structure.

As for the elevated railroad, it is safe to say that today's traffic broke all records in its enormity.

Inside the grounds trouble started early and every few minutes one of the gates would be slightly parted and another battered citizen would emerge to be conveyed to the West 153d street police station by a husky bluecoat. Many of those inside tried to get out to meet friends for whom they had bought tickets, but as the only chance of getting out was to be arrested they stayed in.

The Cubs made no demonstration in coming to the Polo Grounds. One by one they dropped off the "L" train, quietly made their way to the clubhouse of visiting players and put on their uniforms. Most of them were unnoticed by the crowd, who failed to recognize the players in street garb.

When two o'clock came and there was no sign that the gates would again open to the tens of thousands packed in Eighth avenue many small-sized riots, started by various fights, followed. Most were brought about when a gullible person would buy a ticket from a speculator down at 155th street, only to find when he had struggled half a block further north that there his journey ended.

He would then wriggle back toward the speculator and if he could get near enough to him would invariably take a swing at him. But the speculators kept right on selling—and fighting. They were getting such prices that they could afford to throw in a little fight with each ticket.

The inevitable comic side of such gatherings was not long in eventuating. Some ingenious person conceived the idea of bridging the space between the elevated structure and the Polo Grounds fence with a plank up at about 158th street, and it was not long before there was a crowd rushing to buy downtown "L" tickets only to walk up the track and "walk the plank," dropping over the fence into the grounds. Naturally, the guards inside soon lined up at the dropping place and escorted intruders rather forcibly to the nearest "chute," through which they were unceremoniously jammed back into the crowd outside. Finally an officer of the elevated railroad appeared with a club and put a stop to that traffic on the first plank, but immediately another appeared 50 feet away, which a strapping big negro had spanned from the drop pan under the "L" to the fence.　　　　　　　　　　　　　—New York *Evening Telegram*

Police Commissioner Bingham has given orders that the crowd must be kept off the field for at least three minutes after the game, giving the players time to escape to the clubhouse. This precaution has been taken on account of the riot that followed the famous game of Sept. 23.
　　　　　　　　　　　　　—Chicago *News*

Merkle's best chance to go down in baseball history is for the Giants to lose today. At least a dozen persons will then remember him for life.
　　　　　　　　　　　　　—John E. Wray, St. Louis *Post-Dispatch*

If the Cubs don't win the pennant—tragedy! Despair, insanity, suicide, coroner's inquest, and a new chapter in baseball history.
That is the prophecy of Coroner Peter M. Hoffman in speaking of some fans who go the extremity of being irrational.
"To tell the truth I shouldn't be surprised if we had a suicide or two right here in this office," the coroner added. "One of my deputies, I am sure, will commit suicide if the Cubs don't win."
　　　　　　　　　　　　　—Chicago *Tribune*

You never saw such a sore lot of losers to grace the big town these lovely autumn days. There is all sorts of silly trash to be read in the yellow newspapers about the Cubs, the Pirates, and Harry Pulliam's decision, and the long-nosed rooters who have made the Polo Grounds this summer look like the market place in Jerusalem are simply devouring the stuff like so many hungry wolves. We are told that the Cubs and Chubby Murphy are cheap sports and skinflints who are winning games on suspicion. We are also informed that Barney Dreyfuss controls the entire situation and can make Pulliam dance a jig. Furthermore we are solemnly tipped off that if the league's directors do not hand the pennant to McGraw's men, John Tooth Brush will take his club to the American League, bag and baggage.

Nobody seems to be fair enough to realize that the Giants have been lucky to stay with the leaders so long. Had it not been for Mathewson and Wiltse, the Giants would have been where Philadelphia is. As far as team play goes, the Giants never classed with the Cubs, who, despite many accidents, have risen to the top by dint of superb ball playing.

—Joe Vila, *The Sporting News*

## ———◇ THURSDAY, OCTOBER 9 ◇———

{On October 8, in New York, the Chicago Cubs won the National League championship of 1908 by beating the Giants 4 to 2. Winning pitcher, Brown; losing pitcher, Mathewson.}

One terrible inning brought the Giants the sting of final defeat after a season of glorious struggling in the face of every possible discouragement and handicap. Fighting for a pennant already won, as far as baseball on the field is concerned, it was the fate of McGraw's gallant band to lose the crucial struggle through the wavering for a moment of the great pitcher whose splendid skill and still more splendid courage have done so much to make this the most wonderful fight the game of baseball has ever known.

It lacked 15 minutes of 3 o'clock when Klem called play in the struggle on which the attention of the whole nation was centered. As warm as on a perfect August day, with a blue sky above, conditions could not have been more perfect. Fifty thousand pairs of eyes were focused on the field where the tense gray players of Chicago, fighting to lead the league for the third time, awaited the issue, and fifty times that many gazed at bulletin boards, at tickers, at electric boards that showed every play, and at other countless devices waiting all over the country to carry the instant word of the fight from the living, throbbing wires that began at the ends of nervous fingers in the press box.

Sheckard faced "Matty" for the first ball of the game, and a great sigh—the tension was too great for a cheer—went up as Klem's raised hand flashed a strike. A moment later tense tongues loosed in a mighty roar as Sheckard swung wildly at a slow, floating ball and went back to the bench. Two strikes were quickly called on Evers, and then he shot a bounding hit to Herzog, which was thrown to Tenney for the second out. Schulte was the next man, and Mathewson, exulting in his strength, struck him out.

It was a superb start, and when the first ball that Pfiester pitched hit Tenney on the arm a great roar of joy filled the air. Herzog walked on four balls, and the crowd fairly shrieked at Bresnahan for a hit. But the third strike fooled the great catcher completely, and Herzog, foolishly dancing off first base, was thrown out by the deadly arm of Kling, completing a play that may have cost the game. Donlin was next up, and when he smashed the ball down the right field foul line for two bases the crowd was lost in such transports of joy as Tenney scored that it could hardly take the time to hoot Chance for shrieking that the ball was a foul.

Then came a base on balls to Seymour, and after a long conference Chance sent for Brown, and Pfiester walked sadly to the bench. The crowd went wild with joy, but its rapture was short lived, as the three-fingered pitcher ended the inning and a great chance to break up the game by striking Devlin out.

Chance whipped a single to left to start the next inning, but a lightning throw by Matty caught the Chicago manager off first base, and the roar from Chance on the decision seemed likely for a moment to break up the game. He argued with Johnstone for five minutes, and the umpire threatened twice to put him off the field—which he would have been justified in doing. Chance came back wringing his hands, and Hofman, waiting his turn at bat, threw his bat on the ground. He had said nothing, but his act was evidently thought more serious than his manager's unless it is that Klem is made of sterner stuff than Johnstone, for the doughty umpire behind the bat ordered Chicago's centerfielder off the grounds. Then Steinfeldt and Howard, who had replaced Hofman, struck out.

Schulte helped Brown in the second inning by two fine catches in right field, the second, of a hard drive by Bridwell, being a really great play. Tinker gave more help by a fine stop of Matty's hard grounder, and all was ready for the tragedy that was to turn wild joy and rosy hopes into gloom.

Here was Tinker, swinging the mighty bat that had so often made trouble for Mathewson, and once more he swung it with fatal effect. Matty had looked around as he prepared to pitch, and waved his fielders back, but Seymour had paid no heed, and as Tinker smashed the ball far away to left center, Seymour saw his fatal error even as he raced back. He made a great leap for the ball, but just missed a catch that would have been easy had he been ten feet further back.

Tinker was safe on third when the ball came back and almost walked home when Kling singled viciously to left. Brown sacrificed, and Sheckard raised a fly that Seymour caught, being where he belonged this time. On such small things do great issues hang. Had Seymour been ten feet further back and taken Tinker's fly, the inning, and the game, would have ended with Sheckard's fly, without a score. But, as it was, there was still a man to be put out, and before he had been retired, Evers had walked and Schulte and Chance had doubled, sending in three more runs and winning the game, as it turned out.

Gloom was in the crowd everywhere, but not on the New York bench. Matty had been hit hard, but McGraw refused to take him out, and his confidence was fully justified in the four innings Matty was still to pitch.

The Giants tried too hard to come back in their third inning. Tenney began with a clean single, the first hit off Brown, and after Herzog had fouled to Kling, Bresnahan planted the ball into right field for another safety. But Donlin could only force Bresnahan at second, and Seymour sent a groan through the crowd with a fly to Sheckard.

Then it was a procession to and from the bat until the sixth inning, when both nines were active. Chance drove out his third hit—he was the only man on either side with more than one hit—but Bresnahan caught him stealing with a perfect throw to Herzog. Steinfeldt also singled, but Howard struck out again.

Agony was piled on agony when New York came up for the seventh time. With the crowd shrieking for the "lucky" seventh to work its spell, Devlin faced Brown and drove out as pretty a single as was ever made. McCormick followed with another safe drive, and when Bridwell walked, filling the bases, with none out, an explosion of dynamite would not have been heard.

Mathewson was the next man up, and the crowd groaned when

McGraw sent Doyle to bat for him. It was strange that he should do so, for Matty is a strong batter, and Doyle has not faced an opposing pitcher in a big game since he was hurt weeks ago. Doyle hit a high foul that fell into Kling's hands. Tenney sent a run home with a long sacrifice fly, but two men were left on base when Tinker threw Herzog out and New York's best chance was gone.

Wiltse finished the game, and only a great play by McCormick saved a run in the eighth. Evers had doubled with one out and gone to third when Tenney's error left Schulte safe at first base. Chance drove a fly to McCormick, and, after a great catch, McCormick made a superb throw to the plate that enabled Bresnahan to put Evers out.

New York could do nothing in the last two innings, and four pitched balls in the ninth disposed of Devlin, McCormick, and Bridwell. Chicago had won the game and the pennant.       —New York *Tribune*

NEW YORK, Oct. 8.—All honor will be given the Cubs as long as baseball is played, for what they did this afternoon in the shadow of Coogan's Bluff. They won not only decisively but cleanly and gamely, while their adversaries attempted to take cheap and tricky advantage of them in every way. The world's champions were compelled even to fight for the privilege of getting the meager practice allowed by the rules before the game.

Nor was defeat and loss of the pennant New York's only disgrace, for the crowd contained at least one man who will be remembered to Gotham's discredit as long as Merkle. That is the dastard who sneaked up behind Manager Chance as the Cubs were leaving the scene of victory and struck him a blow in the neck.

Before the Cub manager could wheel to defend himself the coward had been swallowed up in the tremendous throng. A hurried examination of the manager at the dressing room by a surgeon in attendance disclosed that the assailant probably had broken a cartilage in Chance's neck but it was not expected that the injury would keep him out of the world's series battles.

To Mordecai Brown will belong the lion's share of credit for Chicago's third pennant—to Mordecai and Joe Tinker. It was the mighty three-fingered star who pitched both of the crucial and "final" games of the year. It was the fleet-footed and scrappy shortstop who led the Cubs in that terrific unbeatable assault in the third inning which nailed the game to Chicago's flagpole and broke the back of the great Mathewson.

The game was preceded by a bit of petty trickery by the Giants which probably had much to do with prompting the cowardly slugging which was handed Manager Chance at the close.

The crowd was so great it compelled locking the gates long before time to start the game, and it was decided not to wait until 3 o'clock, as everybody who could get inside was there already.

But the 15 minutes gained in time was taken out of the Cubs' practice. The Giants took their full allotment of 20 minutes for batting practice, then when the Cubs started on their practice they were stopped at the end of five minutes. Chance objected to this after his club had traveled 1,000 miles and had no other opportunity to limber up. As McGinnity stepped to the plate under orders to begin knocking grounders to the Giants for fielding practice Chance tried to brush him away, and the "Iron Man" raised his bat threateningly.

For an instant it looked the beginning of a riot, which would forever have disgraced the game, but other players of both teams rushed in and surrounded the belligerents, smoothing out the incident quickly. When the thing was explained to Chance there was nothing for him to do but smile contemptuously at the trick and acquiesce. The Cubs proved later they didn't need the other 15 minutes of batting practice.

—I. E. Sanborn, Chicago *Tribune*

If we turn the clock back to about an hour or two before the game begins we note that some of the boxes still remain vacant. This is because the ticket holders are in the street trying vainly to get inside. But up there in her usual place leaning over the rail is little Mabel Hite, wife of Mike Donlin.

Everybody is happy and hopeful, for the game hasn't begun yet, and it is frequently stated and never disputed that this is the limit for baseball enthusiasm. It's also the greatest ever, outer sight or big casino, according to who is telling you. And if you listen to Clayton Hamilton, who writes books to which Brander Matthews, the greatest Simple Speller in captivity, writes introductions, you learn that the Polo Grounds are "really the thematic centre of the cosmic scheme," whatever that may be. {In 1908 Clayton Hamilton was the 27-year-old drama critic of the magazine *Forum*; he would become a highly regarded playwright and critic. In 1908 Matthews was professor of dramatic literature at Columbia University and was a distinguished writer of drama, fiction, and criticism.} All this time everybody and everything is getting cheered and pelted with wads of newspaper.

A fat man comes into the right-field bleachers carrying a baby who may yet grow up to be a pitcher like Matty. He is cheered frantically and he grabs the kid with one hand and waves at the crowd with the other. Pretty girls are cheered, homely girls are cheered, fat men, thin men, tall men, short men, the girl with a hat as big as three of Fred Tenney's mitts—anything and everything for a cheer.

Now a couple of players reserved from the minor leagues appear from the clubhouse and begin to throw the ball around the diamond that has only recently been uncovered. Uncovered from what? Why, from the huge canvas sheets that have been spread on it all night. They put the diamond to bed early the night before so that it would get a good night's rest for the game of all games.

Smiling Larry Doyle, who was the Giants' regular second baseman until he hurt his leg a month ago, is the first of the regulars to show. He gets many cheers.

And then from the clubhouse emerges a melancholy figure. Shall we say it is the figure of the man who lost the pennant? Well, anyhow, it's the figure of Fred Merkle, and everybody knows that if he'd run to second when Bridwell made that safe hit at the end of the now famous disputed game the pennant would be waving from the flagstaff in center field. Amid a silence that cuts, Merkle crosses the field and begins to toss a ball about. It's clear that he feels worse than anybody else about it. Nobody has the heart to jeer him. But all the same——

Suddenly several thousand persons are released from durance and allowed to scamper to standing room behind the ropes all about the field. It looks like the serpentine dance after a victory for the Blue on Yale Field. A moment ago the field was green; now it's black.

There aren't enough real cops to boss a lively Sunday school class, and how the deuce things are ever going to be straightened out doesn't appear, unless you've been there before and know that when the umpire is ready for play the field will clear itself like magic. Everybody begins to get happily restless, and one fan says to another, "Boy, you'll be able to tell your grandchildren about this day when the Cubs—or——" Fearful of the outcome he rubs his chin doubtfully and doesn't finish.

"Robber!" "Bandit!" "Quitter!" howls the crowd all at once. The row begins in the right-field bleachers and runs all over the field as Frank Chance appears from the clubhouse, loafing carelessly along on his bowed legs and looking as if he hadn't a care in the world. Roars, hoots, hisses, jeers are showered on him as he advances, but he smiles pleasantly as if the freedom of the city had been conferred on him. Just behind him comes Three-Fingered Brown. He is also called a number of things which he isn't. He doesn't seem to mind either.

But there's a greater uproar yet when John McGraw shows up, accompanied by the lean and haggard Tenney, and the New York manager has to doff his cap before the row lets up. One by one the rest of the Giants appear.

The New Yorks take batting practice methodically, one hit to each man. Then the Cubs go in for theirs. More roars, more hisses, more cat-calls, howls of contempt, shrieks of "Oh, you robbers! You brigands!" And you think if you were a Cub you'd hunt the nearest cyclone cellar. But the Cubs wallop the horsehide as cheerfully as if the stands were empty. Meanwhile the jeers keep on. Somebody in the stand catches a foul tip from a Cub's bat. A hundred voices shout: "Keep it! Keep it! Don't give it back! Murphy will cry his eyes out if you keep it."

Meantime the twirlers are warming up, Pfiester, the left-hander, for the Cubs, and the only Matty for the Giants. This doesn't take long and at a quarter of three o'clock the real trouble begins. It is time.

—New York *Sun*


Never before has the capacity of Coogan's Bluff been strained beyond the limit as it was yesterday. Never before have veteran hillbillies, who have worn the grass out in their accustomed places, been rudely shoved aside by strangers and vandals occupying their favorite spots. Every hillbillie tradition was ruthlessly ripped to shreds by the pushing thousands, and Coogan's was no longer the Coogan's of other days.

By 2 o'clock Coogan's was loaded to the gunnels and the tens of thousands stretched along the entire semi-circle from the Jumel Mansion {the celebrated, still existent manor house built in 1765 at 160th Street and Edgecombe Avenue} to Eighth avenue. For nearly a mile there was a mass of people lining stairs, viaducts, streets, Speedway, bluffs, crags, rocks, peaks, grass, plots, trees, and any other available space not previously occupied.

The view from Coogan's was gorgeous and beggared description. It was one of those perfect October days which so seldom come when you want them, and the scene was like a Turner picture {a reference to the English landscape painter J. M. W. Turner (1775-1851)}. The broad bosom of the Harlem River palpitated in the Autumn glow, the hazy blue of the Bronx draped the towering palaces along the heights overlooking the silver stream, the city to the south stretched away into limitless azure, the bargains in real estate along Edgecombe avenue littered on their sacred sites, while at the foot of the bluff the eye rested on the gleaming billboards at the far end of the Polo Grounds.

If 35,000 were inside the fence, 35,000,000 were outside—the way they covered the ground and the roofs—but probably not so many as that. Never in the history of the game have there been so many to see a game who didn't see it. The standees had the call and no mistake. There were hundreds of women on the bluff, and one woman had brought her knitting along, and calmly sat on the grass and knitted while the pennant went to Chicago. She must have been a Chicago woman. Up on the lawn of the Jumel Mansion was a group of spectators. Somebody said George Washington, Aaron Burr, and Mme. Jumel were among those present. A society reporter (lady) from Brooklyn made a note of it. The enthusiasm was immense and intense, and soon soap boxes and other coigns of vantage began to appear at the back of the firing line along the bluff. Anything over two inches rented for 25 cents, and 10 cents an inch above that. Along the road, back of the bluff, delivery wagons, cabs, and automobiles lined the curb. Persons occupying them had a fine view of the backs of the front row. It was inspiring.

A little dumpy man, who couldn't see above the hip pocket of the men in front of him, said he was going home. Immediately there were cries of "Lynch him! He's a quitter!" and other personal remarks of a similar nature. He apologized and stayed till the game was over.

After a while—two hours after a while—somebody in front announced the game had begun. A hush fell on the throng on Coogan's Bluff. Every breath was baited. Never in the history of the game had there been such a moment. It sounded like a pork packer's cheer for Upton Sinclair {whose most famous novel, *The Jungle*, an exposé of the Chicago stockyards, had appeared in 1906}.

—W. J. Lampton, New York *Times*

Manager Frank Chance of the Cubs was assaulted twice yesterday. As if the blow Joe McGinnity handed him before the game was not sufficient, a frenzied fan had to inflict even more serious injury on the belligerent, hustling leader of the Chicago team.

Immediately after the failure of the Giants to score in the ninth, and it was all over but the shouting for the Cubs, Chance, with Pitcher Pfiester and Catcher Kling, started for the clubhouse. The trio kept their eyes on the crowd piling out of the east end of the big stand and out of the right-field bleachers. The policemen on duty were also apprehensive and closed around Chance and his teammates.

A fan who was scarlet from excitement and wrath bowled over two cops and let loose a right-hand swing to Chance's chin. Chance threw up his head quickly and the blow caught him flush in the neck. He went down to his knees and gasped for breath. While policemen were fighting the crowd back, someone landed a stinger on Pfiester's right jaw, staggering him. Johnny Kling fought like a Trojan for his teammates and his own skin.

A horde of policemen closed in around the three Chicago players and dragged them through the crowd like a football team rushing the men with the ball over the line. The uniformed officers found their clubs ineffective against the press of the howling mob, and revolvers were drawn. This seemed to stop the rush, for the mob stood back.

Chance and his two fellow-players were literally catapulted over and through the surging, howling mob of fans. An attendant in the clubhouse threw wide the door of the press entrance and the Chicago players were thrown inside. A little policeman defended the door in Thermopylae fashion {referring to a Grecian mountain pass, famed for its heroic, eventually suicidal defense in 480 B.C. by 300 Spartans against the Persian army of Xerxes}. With the mob about him and his brother policemen unable to reach him, he held that door with stones, pieces of boards and water cans hurled at him.

Manager Chance was found to have been rather badly hurt. The blow had broken a cartilage in his neck. Together with President Murphy he was hustled to an automobile and hurried away before the crowd discovered the identity of the pair.

A conference resulted in the decision that it would be best for players to leave singly or in pairs and thus avoid attention. Pitcher Pfiester wasn't much hurt by the slam he got. Mordecai Brown was one of the last to leave. As he started to walk up the long chute toward the elevated railway station at 155th street, two policemen in uniform stepped up to accompany him. Brown looked at them,

"You fellows get away from me!" yelled Brown. "Those uniforms will surely tip me off." The policemen withdrew and the marvelous three-fingered one wandered unmolested in his ordinary street clothes.

A physician was summoned to the Hotel Somerset, where the Cubs put up, to examine Chance's throat. It was found that while the crushed cartilage will give the captain some pain, he will probably be all right in a day or two. Hot towels were applied to his neck and Chance said he would continue this treatment on the train en route to Detroit. Chance was sick from the blow and unable to eat dinner.

"I have no ill feeling against anyone," said Chance to a reporter at his hotel, "but I don't see why I should be picked out as a mark for folks that wish to indulge in such calisthenics. Certainly my actions today did not warrant any such treatment as I received."    —New York *American*


Two stupid plays lost the championship to the Giants. Merkle's boyish desire to be the first man in the clubhouse on Sept. 23 was the first offense. Cy Seymour's wretched fielding yesterday was in a great measure responsible for the loss of the game.

In the third inning Tinker was the first batter to face Mathewson. Tinker is a bold, bad hitter against the Giants. Seymour was playing a short field, and he stubbornly refused to budge, though Matty and Donlin both signed him to go further back.

Tinker's fly to center should have been an easy out. It would have been had Seymour played the batter properly and it would have been caught had Seymour not misjudged it so badly. Instead of sprinting back and turning around, Seymour kept taking short backward steps. Finally he lunged at the ball and missed it altogether. The fans in centerfield moaned and after the game many of them said it was a play that any schoolboy fielder would have made. Then Cyrus groped about in the crowd and fielded the ball very slowly, allowing Tinker to get to third. Had this fly been caught chances are there would have been no runs in that inning, and the opportunity for a shut-out would have been splendid.

The scene yesterday was really the most disgraceful ever pulled off around here and it is to be hoped that Mr. Brush will get proper protection for the Cubs when they come here again.

Baseball is baseball, and if the Giants couldn't win fairly there should be no win otherwise.

No one who saw the game could say that the umpires were sore at McGraw. Some decisions seemed to favor the local players and if with that and the rowdyism they couldn't win, the game should go to the better team. New York had everything in its favor.

They were playing on the home ground, they had the crowd and umpires with them, the other team had spent the night on the cars coming here. Matty, the greatest pitcher we ever had, was in the box and the whole team was right, except for a few scratched skins. What more could a fellow ask for?

McGinnity started a row the very first thing by bumping Chance off the plate while the latter was hitting out flies. That was only the first incident. Once when Kling was chasing a foul from Doyle's bat, two beer bottles, a drinking glass and a derby hat were thrown at him.

Is that baseball? Does that do New York any good?

Gee whiz! If we can't lose a pennant without dirty work let's quit altogether.                                         —Tad, New York *Evening Journal*


The Cubs will be acknowledged as champions, but their title is tainted, and New York lovers of baseball will never acknowledge them as the true winners of the pennant.

Whenever I mention the Giants from now on I shall accord them their rightful title, and I am firm in the opinion that I am right.

Yesterday they looked outclassed for the reason that they were far from being in the playing form the Cubs were. It cannot be denied that the Chicago players were far fresher and in better shape for such a crucial contest after their several days' rest than were the Giants, who were forced to play their very best up to the very day before the deciding game.

If those men on the Board of Directors had concocted a scheme to give the Giants the worst of it they couldn't have done it any more to the point. The Giants were not outgamed, but they were outplayed just from lack of condition.

The Giants did not play up-to-date baseball either. They should almost have cinched the victory in the first inning, for with men on first and second and none out, Bresnahan, instead of trying to advance the runners, tried to knock the cover off the ball and fanned. Herzog then made a play that possibly lost all chances the Giants had. When Kling dropped Bresnahan's third strike, possibly purposely, for Johnny Kling is a very foxy player, Herzog made a break for second although Bresnahan was already out whether Kling held the ball or not. Kling took advantage of Herzog's dumbness and threw to Chance and "Herzie" was pinched. As Donlin followed with a double, it can be seen how damaging Herzog's mistake was.

The minute that "Miner" Brown took Pfiester's place in the box, that strange fatality that has always followed Matty when against the great three-fingered boxman bobbed up and "Big Six" got his bumps.

—Sam Crane, New York *Evening Journal*


BUFFALO, Oct. 9—The world's champions Cubs are rushing to Detroit to meet the Tigers tomorrow and defend their title.

Frank Chance's Cubs have proven their title as the greatest aggregation ever gathered on a diamond, game, true and loyal to the core.

Chance was not seriously hurt when hit in the throat by a spectator on his way to the clubhouse. It broke a cartilage in his throat and pained him a good deal, but physicians assured him there was nothing serious about the injury, and he ate a hearty dinner last night. Steinfeldt was struck in the face at the same time Chance was hit, and Hofman was hit in the nose by a pop bottle hurled by an irate fan.

Telegrams of congratulations poured in on the club as it was rushing out of New York last night, including a message from Judge Keneshaw M. Landis {who in 1920 would become the first commissioner of professional baseball}. The one most appreciated was this message from Barney Dreyfuss: "Hearty congratulations. Clean baseball was bound to triumph over affidavits and rowdyism. Best wishes for success in world's series."

—Chicago *News*


Great are the Cubs and nearly as great are their fans.

Yesterday they massed themselves in Orchestra Hall, where the *Tribune* baseball board pictured the plays, a howling, shrieking, ball-mad crowd, wild in its enthusiasm, sometimes pleading, sometimes threatening, always "pulling."

Through it all sat a handsome young woman whose eyes shone and cheeks flushed as the cheering increased, and who, when the Giants retired at the close of the ninth, turned to the gray-haired woman by her side and said:

"This is our anniversary day, mother. He had to win. It's wonderful, isn't it?" and she laughed and cried at the same time.

If the crowd had known that the wife of the great Cub leader was in their midst, Mrs. Frank Le Roy Chance would have been given an ovation that seldom falls to the lot of a woman.

Another Cub wife was in the throng. With a party of friends Mrs. "Joe" Tinker sat only a few rows behind Mrs. Chance, madly waving a Cub banner.

Upon leaving the building she shouted over and over:

"Four to two, four to two."                    —Chicago *Tribune*


"We will beat Detroit easily," declared Mrs. Frank Chance last night, previous to boarding a train for the scene of tomorrow's battle. The wife of the Cubs' captain was excited and in a hurry to depart.

"I want to help Frank beard the Tigers in their lair," she said smiling. "I know we will win, but Frank says he always plays better ball when he can see me in the grandstand. Of course that is silly, but I want to be there just the same."

"You certainly have a chance," a friend suggested.

"Now, I think that's real mean of you," pouted the young woman. "You know everyone tells that, but as a pun I think it is awful.

"Just as soon as the season is over and we have demonstrated to Detroit that they are not in our class, Mr. Chance and I plan a fishing trip to Wisconsin. He is very fond of fishing, and so am I. Then we are going to California for the winter.

"Yes, we like Chicago, but those lake winds are fearfully chilly in the winter. California is the place for winter months. Besides, Mr. Chance has so many friends there. He formerly attended Washington College in that state and was offered a scholarship at Leland Stanford to play football. He played football but did not like it as much as baseball."

Mrs. Chance, young, pretty and with a large quantity of light brown hair, was recognized by a number of persons and several women stepped forward, introduced themselves and wished that her husband might have all sorts of luck in the championship games. —Chicago *Journal*


Manager McGraw took things philosophically.

"I do not feel badly," McGraw said. "My team merely lost something it had honestly won three weeks ago. This cannot be put too strongly. Chicagoans always will remember the fight I gave them before they could gain their third pennant in succession." —New York *Press*


Probably no member of the Giants took the defeat as keenly as did Christy Mathewson. Long after the other players had donned their street clothes and made for home Matty set down disconsolate in the dressing room.

Folks that lingered tried to cheer the peerless pitcher, but he could not speak. He seemed loath to go out and face the people. Some few of the faithful remained until toward dusk, when the great pitcher showed at the Eighth avenue gate. He got a cheer that must have gone a great way in uplifting his fallen spirits.

Matty tried to speak but couldn't. He waved at the crowd and hurried away with bowed head. "I did the best I could," he said as he left the clubhouse, "but I guess fate was against me."

—New York *American*

Bridwell was the only member of the New York team to offer the Cubs congratulations after their victory yesterday.

—Chicago *Journal*

A people who can become as excited about anything as the majority of New Yorkers can about the baseball pennant is far from being lost to hope.

Were we a wooden, lethargic populace, incapable of caring a rap whether the pennant of 1908 fluttered over the Polo Grounds or held horizontal in the breeze that sweeps over Lake Michigan, we might well account ourselves unworthy of the terrific work that must be done before the Augean stable of municipal rottenness has been cleaned. {A reference to the mythological King Augeas, whose stables contained 3,000 oxen and had not been cleaned in thirty years. One of the twelve "labors of Hercules" was the cleansing of the Augean stables.}

But we know now that we *can* become excited, energetically, masterfully excited, and as soon as we understand how properly to apply that tremendous dynamite force to the really important things of life, we will get what we ought to have, individually and collectively, and no thieving corporations, no swinish bosses, no bludgeon-bearing election thieves can stand a minute before us.

Today a multitude of men are bewailing the grewsome {sic} fact that Merkle did not run to second in that tie game. That omission cost New York the pennant. It was a common error, the slovenly heedlessness that keeps most of mankind in its rut, and exalts the men who play the game, be it business, or love, or war, to the bitter end.

Merkle's blunder cost New York the pennant. True. This does not lower the price of beef; it does not make travel on the Third avenue "L" any less hazardous; it does not save the old from toil or the poor from hunger. It affects not one jot the status of any of the hundreds of thousands who were wrought up over the victory that has been borne away to Chicago.

But it evoked excitement. No human being in New York yesterday can deny that. And excitement makes the world go round; causes the pulse to beat higher, the thrill of battle to rouse the sluggish blood, the brain to do ten times the work it can do when plodding along in emotionless tranquility.

And in that possibility of enthusiasm lies the certainty of the future.

The day will come when the people of this city will be just as excited about the struggle over the rights of the masses, just as enthusiastic over the fight between public plunderers and their protesting prey; in brief, just as interested in the things that concern them, and concern them vitally, as in the settlement of a baseball championship, involving personally a handful of men.

When that day comes there will be trouble for public despoilers, long repentant years in jail for criminal bosses, and an epidemic of public welfare such as now seems too Utopian even to dream of.

This newspaper, being loyal to New York, chronicles its sorrow that the pennant has been rudely taken from us. But it rejoices in the patent fact that the people of New York are capable of tumultuous enthusiasm, for in that it sees the hope of every betterment that it has earnestly and honestly sought to bring about.

—Editorial page, New York *American*

—— FINAL NATIONAL LEAGUE STANDINGS ——

| | W | L | PCT. | GB | | W | L | PCT. | GB |
|---|---|---|---|---|---|---|---|---|---|
| Chicago | 99 | 55 | .643 | — | Cincinnati | 73 | 81 | .474 | 26 |
| New York | 98 | 56 | .636 | 1 | Boston | 63 | 91 | .409 | 36 |
| Pittsburgh | 98 | 56 | .636 | 1 | Brooklyn | 53 | 101 | .344 | 46 |
| Philadelphia | 83 | 71 | .539 | 16 | St. Louis | 49 | 105 | .318 | 50 |

# POSTSCRIPT

In the world series of 1908, Chicago beat Detroit, four games to one. Chicago's winning pitchers: Brown (games one and four) and Overall (games two and five). The only home run in the series was hit by Joe Tinker in game two.

On July 19, 1909, in New York City, National League President Harry Pulliam committed suicide. Since the end of the 1908 season he had taken a leave of absence from his job, because of a severe state of depression, which, his doctors said, had been brought on by the turmoil that followed the Giant-Cub game of September 23.

On October 22, 1912, in New York City, Mabel Hite died of intestinal cancer at the age of 27.

# INDEX

Entries of particular significance are marked with an asterisk (\*). Parenthetical abbreviations identify the home base and position of those who were active in 1908. Thus, for example, Crandall, Otis (*NY p*), was a New York pitcher; Dryden, Charles (*CH w*), was a Chicago writer; and Cobb, Ty (*AL*), was an American League player. The following abbreviations have been used:

| | | | | | |
|---|---|---|---|---|---|
| BO | Boston | AL | American League | *of* | outfielder |
| BR | Brooklyn | NL | National League | *p* | pitcher |
| CH | Chicago | *c* | catcher | *pr* | league president |
| CI | Cincinnati | *co* | coach | *r* | retired |
| NY | New York | *d* | doctor | *s* | secretary |
| PH | Philadelphia | *g* | groundkeeper | *t* | trainer |
| PI | Pittsburgh | *if* | infielder | *u* | umpire |
| SL | St. Louis | *m* | manager | *w* | writer |
| | | *ml* | minor leaguer | | |

Abbaticchio, Ed (*PI if*), 65, 92, 140, 207, 230, 232

Adams, Franklin P., ix, 198

Alperman, Charles "Whitey" (*BR if*), 46, 167, 217

American Federation of Labor, 205\*

Ames, Leon "Red" (*NY p*), 9, 23, 28, 31–32\*, 42, 45, 50, 56, 81, 83, 167, 172, 174, 180, 203–04, 214\*, 221, 234, 239–41, 242, 258–59, 273, 279–80, 287\*, 288, 290–91, 299–300

Anti-Semitism, 224, 265, 305

Attendance figures, 38, 40, 44, 47–48\*, 49–50\*, 51, 55, 59, 68, 89, 91, 94, 95, 99, 101\*, 134, 137–38\*, 139–40\*, 144\*, 153, 158–59, 159–60, 163\*, 164, 166\*, 182, 189–90\*, 194–95\*, 198, 215, 218, 228\*, 244, 258, 268, 275, 283, 285, 290, 302–05\*, 306, 312–13\*

Aulick, W. W. (*NY w*), 82, 87, 90, 92, 102, 106, 136, 139, 142, 145, 146, 152, 160, 164, 165, 216, 219, 226, 242, 270, 273

Bagley, Gym (*NY w*), 211, 215, 221, 227, 235, 254, 255, 265, 268, 271, 275, 292

Baldwin, O. F. (*SL p*), 222

Bancroft, Frank (*CI s*), 67, 267

Barry, Jack (*SL, NY of*), 151\*, 174, 199, 226, 236, 240, 267, 268

Batch, Emil "Heinie" (*ml*), 219

Batting, general comments, 11, 80\*

Batting averages, 103, 115, 140, 162, 173, 220, 322

Beaumont, Clarence "Ginger" (*BO of*), 9

Beebe, Fred (*SL p*), 148, 175

Beecher, Bob (*CI of*), 256

Beecher, Roy (*NY p*), 32

Bell, George (*BR p*), 46, 167, 214, 215

*EVERYMAN, I will go with thee, and be thy guide,*
*In thy most need to go by thy side*

IMMANUEL KANT, son of a saddler, was born on 22 April 1724 in Königsberg, East Prussia. In 1740 he went to the university in Königsberg where he studied mathematics, theology and philosophy. In 1755 he took his doctoral degree in philosophy, after which he became a *Privat-dozent* (lecturer) at the university. It was during this time that his significance as a teacher of moral philosophy was recognized. In 1770 he was appointed to the chair of logic and metaphysics, and went on to establish his reputation as one of the greatest modern philosophers.

Kant had published several works before his appointment as professor; they included *Theory of the Heavens* (1755), which attempted to reconcile the hypotheses of Newton and Leibniz, and *Dreams of a Visionary* (1766), which was probably his first most significant work. His best known work, *Critique of Pure Reason*, was published in 1781, and formed the basis of all his subsequent writings through which his fame spread. The *Metaphysic of Ethics* (1785) and *Metaphysic of Nature* (1786) followed. The remaining critiques, *Of Practical Reason* and *Of Judgment* appeared in 1783 and 1790 respectively.

Königsberg had become a great centre of philosophic activity under Kant's influence, and his method had been adopted by nearly all the German universities. But later, in 1792, Kant's teaching was censored by the Prussian government because of the anti-Lutheran ideas in his rationalistic thesis, *On Religion within the Limits of Reason Alone*. Subsquently Kant's health began to deteriorate and he resigned his chair in 1797. He died on 12 February 1804.

A.D. LINDSAY was first Vice-Chancellor of Keele University, a former Master of Balliol College, Oxford, and author of *Kant*.

J.M.D. MEICKLEJOHN was in 1855 the first to put Kant into intelligible English.

EVERYMAN (logo) CLASSICS

# IMMANUEL KANT

## *Critique of Pure Reason*

Introduction by A.D. Lindsay

Translated by J.M.D. Meiklejohn

Dent: London and Melbourne
EVERYMAN'S LIBRARY

All rights reserved
Made in Great Britain by
Guernsey Press Co. Ltd, Guernsey, C.I. for
J.M. Dent & Sons Ltd
Aldine House, 33 Welbeck Street, London W1M 8LX

This edition was first published in
Everyman's Library in 1934
Last reprinted 1986

No 1909 Paperback ISBN 0 460 11909 5

# INTRODUCTION

THIS translation of Meiklejohn's is of the second edition of Kant's *Critique of Pure Reason*. The first edition was published in 1781. It had been the fruit of some ten years' study and meditation. Kant had gone on finding that the problem he had first envisaged in his letter to Marcus Herz in 1772 developed more and more ramifications and his projected solution unexpected complications. He had put off the date at which the book was to appear year after year. Finally he felt that something decisive must be done if this process of postponement was not to go on indefinitely and he stopped his preparatory sketching and wrote out the whole in a few months. He says in the Preface to the first edition that though he is entirely satisfied about the completeness of his critical system he is not satisfied with its exposition and in particular makes clear that he is not quite happy about the all-important section entitled 'Deduction of the Pure Conceptions of the Understanding.'

The reception of the first edition evidently confirmed Kant's misgivings. For he found that several of his critics ascribed to him a doctrine of subjective idealism with which he had no sympathy. He strove to correct this misunderstanding in a small work entitled *Prolegomena to any future Metaphysic which may pretend to be Scientific*, which he published in 1783, and in the changes of this second edition of the *Critique of Pure Reason*, which he published in 1787.

The principal changes in the second edition are a new and much longer Preface, a rather more systematic Introduction, certain not very important changes in the 'Aesthetic', an entirely new version of the Transcendental Deduction of the Categories, some changes and an important concluding section of the 'Principles of the Pure Understanding,' and a new treatment of what Kant calls the refutation of idealism, which involved changes in the 'Paralogisms of Rational Psychology.'

Kant's own view of the changes will be found at the conclusion of the Preface to this edition of 1787. It will be seen there that he affirms that there has been no alteration of the teaching of the first *Critique*. He says there that his critical examination of pure reason has necessarily, from the nature of reason, a completeness which made any substantial alteration impossible. Kant's thought undoubtedly developed. For example when he wrote the *Critique of Judgment* in 1790 he had changed his mind as to there being *a priori* principles involved in aesthetics; when he wrote the first edition of the first *Critique* he thought there were none. Nevertheless he always considered such developments to fall within the main lines of the system thought out in the seventies. But he goes on to say that 'in the exposition there is still much to be done.' With changes in what he called the exposition he concerned himself to the end of his life and with such changes the alterations in the second edition are, in his opinion, entirely concerned.

The moral of all this, then, according to Kant, ought to be that one should read the *Critique* in the second edition and not in the first, and that I think is the moral. Nevertheless there has always been controversy as to the merits of the two editions, and some critics have preferred the first. It is not necessarily perverse to prefer an author's first to his second thoughts. I should for example be sorry to be told that it was perverse to prefer the first to the final edition of Wordsworth's *Prelude*. But the relation between the two editions of the *Critique* is peculiar. Kant quite definitely held that he had been misunderstood in the first edition and he made the changes in his second edition principally to correct that misunderstanding. The second *Critique* lends itself to a realist rather than to an idealist interpretation of Kant, and it was intended to do that. Of course those who like Schopenhauer think that Kant, idealistically interpreted, wrote the truth, and, with a realist interpretation, fell into error, naturally prefer what they conceive to have been Kant's first thoughts. There are other critics who treat Kant mainly as a notorious expounder of certain idealist fallacies to which the philosophic mind is prone. Such critics naturally prefer the first edition, into which it is not difficult to read these errors, to the second where Kant is obviously, but in their view inconsistently, trying to correct them. But in face of Kant's explicit declaration about his intention in making the changes in the second edition, such attitudes are surely historically indefensible.

It will be noticed that Kant goes on to say that in order to prevent the second edition running to excessive length, he has left out certain passages of the first which are not essential to the main argument, but whose omission is to some extent a loss. This remark almost certainly refers to what have been called the psychological sections of the 'Deduction' in the first edition, and is the justification of the practice followed in some translations of printing both the first and the second edition versions of the 'Deduction.' There is clearly something to be said for this practice, but I think nevertheless Kant was right in leaving out these passages and that his meaning is better appreciated by reading the second edition as he left it, without these additions from the first.

So much for the difference between the two editions. To write an Introduction to the *Critique* itself might well seem a work of supererogation. Has it not got a long and excellent Preface and a long Introduction written by the author himself?

It is true that much the best road to the understanding of the *Critique* is a careful study of Kant's own Prefaces and Introduction. The reader should consider what Kant has to say as to how inquiries become scientific; he should try to follow Kant when he explains in the Introduction how the large questions he has raised in the Preface about the possibility of metaphysics boil down to the apparently abstract logical problem as to the possibility of *a priori* synthetic judgments: when he has done these two things, he will have the best Introduction to the *Critique*. He will do even better if he follows a direction which Kant gives in the Preface to the first edition, which most commentators of Kant seem to ignore, and considers very carefully, before he reads the Transcendental Deduction of the Categories, the preceding section. Kant left it in the second edition unchanged and it is called 'Transition to the Transcendental Deduction of the Categories.' There Kant explains why he finds it so much harder to offer a *deduction* of the *a priori* concepts than it was to do the same for space and time. If the reader follows what Kant means there, he will find the 'Deduction' itself intelligible.

Nevertheless although Kant in this edition has done a great deal to introduce what he has to say, no one has ever found the *Critique of Pure Reason* an easy book, and some introductory remarks may be of service.

Goethe once made the paradoxical remark that to read the *Critique of Pure Reason* is like the stepping into a brightly lighted room. That remark is paradoxical but not so absurd as it seems. For the *Critique*, although a very difficult work, is one of the most illuminating works ever written. Once its teaching is mastered it sheds light on all manner of puzzling problems. But that illumination is not to be gained easily. I once heard someone say that George Meredith's later novels should be read first for the fourth time. The point of that epigram applies to many great achievements of the human spirit. The reader or the listener (if a great work of music is in question) has to learn to rise to the height of the argument before he can understand what the author has to tell him; the greater the work of art, the harder that is. It is the mark of a certain kind of novel that if you have read it once, you do not want to read it again. The little there is in it is obvious at once, and the saying reveals the shallowness of such books. But a profound work of art is only first read or heard when it has been read or heard several times.

At this the reader may glance at the length of the work and exclaim: 'Am I to read five hundred odd pages four times before I begin to understand this work? If so, life is not long enough.' He may be consoled by being told that what needs re-reading badly is only the part of the *Critique* up to the end of the 'Analytic,' rather less than half. But of course some illumination and understanding of the *Critique* will come long before the alarming ideal I have propounded is achieved. What I am concerned to say is that the *Critique* has to be read by every one in faith that parts which are at first obscure will become clearer later.

At the same time a work may be profound without being, on first reading, quite so difficult as the *Critique*. The Gospels, Plato's *Dialogues*, or in quite another category, *Alice in Wonderland*, e.g., are illuminating at once, though they have the infinity in them which makes them more and more illuminating the more they are studied. The *Critique* really is much more difficult than it need be. Kant's method of composition has made it needlessly obscure.

It is not easy to believe, yet it is a fact that Kant was a popular lecturer, and from all the evidence obviously a very great teacher. Those who knew his lectures complained of the difficulty of the *Critique*. The work is undoubtedly written in an obscure way. I think myself that there is an explanation of the contrast between the lucidity of Kant's lectures and the obscurity of the *Critique*, and the explanation does help towards understanding. Kant's lecturing, like practically all lecturing in German universities in the eighteenth century, was an exposition of a text-book. His students at his lectures in metaphysics for example were presumed to have read Baumgarten's *Metaphysics*. That supplied the thread and context of Kant's remarks. He sat very loose to his text-book and used all his efforts to make his hearers understand. When he came to write the *Critique* he felt that he had to find something to correspond with the framework supplied by Baumgarten's text-book. He found it in what he describes as the guiding thread supplied by formal logic. That science had, he held, investigated the forms of pure thought and therefore he used the classifications of formal logic from which to construct the framework of the *Critique*. To this logical scheme he rigidly and almost pedantically adhered, but within the limits of this structure he wrote much more as he lectured, using often alternative arguments to make his points clear. This is the explanation of the combination, so puzzling in the *Critique*, of a rigid logical structure and a free and almost careless argumentation about details. Kant is remarkably consistent in what may be called his main plot and often inconsistent in his detailed arguments.

It follows from this that it is vitally important to grasp the plot of the *Critique* and to see how that plot is worked out in the logical structure of the book. These two things are explained in the Preface and in the Introduction respectively.

But there is one further point to be made before anything is said about the Preface. The *Critique of Pure Reason* is only part of a larger scheme of the Critical Philosophy which was completed in the *Critique of Practical Reason* and the *Critique of Judgment*. The investigation of the nature and limitation of science and of the possibilities of metaphysics ran to such a length that the other parts of the original scheme were worked out in the later *Critiques*, but the *Critique of Practical Reason* at any rate was not an afterthought. Its main lines were conceived by Kant from the beginning. In his first preliminary sketching of the *Critique* it was to deal with morals as well as with knowledge. Kant was always both scientist and moralist, always convinced of the vital importance of both these activities of the human spirit, always concerned to defend the independence, integrity, and distinctive nature of each. He had an almost equal reverence for Newton and for Rousseau. He thought that as Newton had been the first thoroughly to set forth the laws and principles of the natural sciences, so Rousseau had been the first to discover the principles of conduct.

But the progress of the natural sciences threatened the integrity of ethics, while attempts which had been made by earlier critics to save the reality of moral principles by proving the reality of freedom, of the soul and of God seemed to set impossible limits to the progress of the natural sciences. Newtonian physics seemed to assume the reality of infinite space and infinite time and further to assume that all events are rigorously and mechanically determined in space and time. Such assumptions left no room for the individuality or the freedom of the moral self, or of the reality of moral purposes in the world. The progress of the natural sciences had depended upon a repudiation of final causes and envisaged a completely mechanical account of reality. Kant had got from Rousseau a conception of moral conduct for which, as he says, the autonomy of the will is the supreme principle of morality. The reality of freedom was therefore for him as indispensable to ethics as its non-reality was to physics. This was the dilemma with which human thought was confronted. Metaphysics as Kant knew it had concerned itself principally with the reality of the self, the freedom of the will and the existence of God. Hence the conflict produced by the steady success of the natural sciences and their ever-growing prestige seemed to be a conflict between science and metaphysics. The signs all pointed to the victory of the sciences. Their progress was steady, their methods and principles were winning increasing agreement; they went on producing practical results and giving man steadily increased control over nature. Metaphysics on the other hand showed no such progress and had won no such agreement.

Kant, as we shall see, was prepared to abandon metaphysics as it had previously been understood. He had early come to hold that it was not possible to give an intellectually valid proof of the reality of the soul, of free-will and of the existence of God. But if to abandon metaphysics meant to agree that science and not metaphysics revealed to us the nature of reality, what would then happen to the assumptions of moral conduct? These can only be saved if we can show that the validity of the sciences does not imply that they reveal to us the fundamental nature of reality and that the sciences and moral conduct are equally valid, and yet not contradictory, because they represent different approaches to reality.

We shall then only understand the relations of the sciences to the principles of conduct if we investigate the metaphysical status of the sciences and the scientific status of metaphysics.

Kant makes a great point in the Preface of the contrast between those inquiries which have reached what he calls the sure path of a science and those which have not. The argument is that metaphysics has failed to do what has been achieved by logic, by mathematics, and by physics. He proposes, therefore, that we should examine the conditions which led to the revolution by which those other inquiries became sciences and consider how far such conditions are applicable to and such a revolution to be expected from metaphysics. It is important however to remember that while Kant mentions logic and mathematics as inquiries which have become scientific, he is really in the *Critique*, when he talks about science, almost always thinking of physics. He had as early as 1764 written an essay on the subject as to whether metaphysics should follow the methods of mathematics or not; had come to the conclusion that the certainty of mathematics arose from the fact that in mathematics we are concerned with the mind's own constructions. Metaphysics which is an attempt to discover the nature of reality which is independent of us, cannot attain a certainty which depends upon such a condition. But the natural or applied sciences also investigate a reality which is independent of us. An investigation of the conditions of their success is likely to give us more help in discovering the secret of metaphysics.

Now one obvious difference between mathematics and physics is that physics depends partly on observation and experiment. Its several propositions have not the intuitive certainty of mathematics, and yet for all that there is all the difference between science and a mere collection of observations. The paradoxical fact about the natural sciences appeared to Kant to be that they had acquired insight into nature just in so far as man's inquirings into nature had been informed by thought. An inquiry, he declared in the *Metaphysical First Principles of Natural Science*, has in it just so much of genuine science as it has in it mathematics. Yet the difference between mathematics and the natural sciences remains, the difference expressed in calling the latter, as is sometimes done, the applied mathematical sciences. The natural sciences must depend upon empirical observation as mathematics need not do; because of the necessary defects of empirical observations, their propositions lack the intuitive certainty of mathematics, and yet in so far as they manage to inform themselves with mathematics, they become scientific and acquire a certainty and necessity quite beyond the reach of any collection of empirical observations.

In the Preface to this edition Kant examines the way in which inquiries have become scientific and sums up the results of his examination by saying: 'Reason only perceives that which it produces after its own design. It must proceed in advance with principles of judgment according to unvarying laws and compel nature to reply to its questions. . . . It is only the principles of reason which can give to concordant phenomena the validity of laws, and it is only when experiment is directed by these rational principles that it can have any real utility. Reason must approach nature with the view, indeed, of receiving information from it, not, however, in the character of a pupil, who listens to all that his master chooses to tell him, but in that of a judge, who compels the witnesses to reply to those questions which he himself thinks fit to propose.'

But there is, Kant had observed, something paradoxical about this. Science is a free activity of the human spirit: it demands creativeness, invention, imagination; but how does the creativeness of the mind produce laws which are valid for things which the mind does not produce and over which it has no control? How does the free activity of the mind become objective? Kant put this difficulty, perhaps more clearly than he ever put it in the *Critique*, in a letter to Marcus Herz in 1772 when he first began to grapple with the Critical Philosophy. 'On what principle is based the relation between that in us which is called a representation and the object? If the representation contains nothing but the way in which the subject is affected by the object, then it is easy to see how it might correspond to this object as its effect, and how this determination of our mind could represent something, i.e. have an object. Possible or sensible representations have, therefore, a conceivable relation to objects, and the principles, which are borrowed from the nature of our soul, have a conceivable validity for all things in so far as they are objects of the senses. Similarly, if that in us which is called presentation were active in regard to the object, i.e. if the object was actually through it brought into being, as the thoughts of God are represented as the originals of things, then, too, the conformity of presentations and objects would be understandable. We can, that is, at least understand the possibility of an archetypal intellect on whose intuition things are themselves based— or of an ectypal intellect, which creates the data of its logical activity out of the sensible intuition of the things. But our understanding is neither through its representations the cause of objects (except in conduct when good purposes bring things into being), nor is the object the cause of the representations of the understanding. The pure concepts of the understanding, then, cannot be abstracted from the feelings of the senses: they cannot express the receptivity of presentations through the senses. They must have their source in the nature of the soul, but not so far as it is either affected by objects or brings objects into being.'

Kant goes on to say that it had been proposed to get over this difficulty by supposing a pre-established harmony between mind and its objects, but that such a *deus ex machina* is obviously no explanation at all.

Kant is obviously thinking of his predecessors. The English empiricists had made the passivity of the mind the test of objectivity. When Hume had found that there were certain concepts, as in especial causation, which were not produced by the action of objects on the senses and were yet indispensable to knowledge, this solution proved obviously unsatisfactory. The Continental rationalists, on the other hand, had stressed the importance of the mind's activity in knowledge, but failed to show how such activity could be valid of objects independent of the mind.

It may strike the reader that there is one obvious solution of the difficulty which Kant does not seem to have thought of. The natural sciences involve both theorizing and observation. May we not say that the mind forms freely theories of the behaviour of objects and then tries them on objects by experiment? The mind becomes fitted to objects as living creatures to their environment, by a process of trial and error.

The answer to this suggestion is that Kant recognized how much of the work of the natural sciences is of this kind. He has described it in an appendix to the 'Dialectic,' entitled 'Of the Regulative Employment of the Ideas of Pure Reason,' and he discusses the principles which inspire it at greater length in the *Critique of Judgment.* But he was convinced that this process of intellectual trial and error assumed certain principles which were not regarded as verifiable or refutable by experiment. The most obvious of these is the principle of causation. Hume had pointed out that in all our judgments about the external world we assume the principle of causation and that yet we could offer no proof of its validity. Kant proposes to generalize Hume's problem about causation, to ask how we can discover a complete list of these genuinely *a priori* principles, which we take and must take for granted in all our scientific investigations, and then to consider how they can be valid of all the objects we are going to experience.

From this position he comes to see that the large problem with which he had started—which I have described as that of determining the metaphysical status of science and the scientific status of metaphysics—boils down to a logical problem as to the validity of a certain type of judgment, synthetic *a priori* judgment. The judgment that every event has a cause is in Kant's view *a priori*. It does not depend on our experience. Rather in making it we, in his words, prescribe to experience. We say confidently that though we cannot anticipate what events we shall experience, we know that they will all be subject to the principle of causation: they will be determined in time by a rule. The judgment is also synthetic. The notion of causation is not derived by analysis from the notion of an event. The connection of these two ideas is affirmed in the judgment.

This then is Kant's problem. Science involves our assumption of the objective validity of certain principles which underlie all our theorizing and experiment. How are we to find a complete list of such principles and how are we to show their objective validity? And what light will the examination of the validity of such principles throw on the question of the possibility of reaching in metaphysics *a priori* principles which will hold of reality?

In the Preface Kant suggests what he calls his Copernican revolution. As Copernicus had explained the movements of the stars by suggesting that their apparent movements are partly due to the movement of the observer; so he proposes to explain the application of the mind's *a priori* principles to objects by suggesting that 'objects conform to the mind.'

This is Kant's 'critical idealism.' What does he mean by it? It is quite clear from his letter to Herz that he does not mean that the mind makes objects. To hold that would be to adopt one of the alternatives which he ruled out at the beginning. He clearly thinks that there is a halfway house between the realism of an *intellectus ectypus* or passive mind and the idealism of an *intellectus archetypus* or creative mind. We can see most clearly what he means by approaching the problem rather differently and asking what the natural sciences do for us. Kant's answer is that they enable us to anticipate what we shall experience. If we analyse what we mean in any scientific judgment which claims to be true, we shall find that it states that under such and such circumstances we shall have such and such experiences. Earlier thinkers had held that by thought we got from how things appear to how things are: Kant holds that we get from how things appear to how they will appear. The task of thought is not to turn the mind away from what we perceive, but to help it to transcend some of the limitations of our perceptions, or, to speak more accurately, to set somewhat further back the limits of our perception: for thought never entirely transcends these limits. Our knowledge is always conditioned by the fact that we are finite minds living in a particular place and at a particular time; but thought can extend the range of our perceptions in space and time. But in our scientific judgments we are always making statements about our possible experience. Even when we talk of what the earth was like before mind existed upon it, we can only do that by saying what would have been seen or experienced, if we had, say, in Mr. Wells's Time Machine been able to go back in time and look. Knowledge in Kant's view is not a process in which perception gives place to thought: it always involves both thought and perception, but thought enables us with a wider range to anticipate from what we actually perceive to what we will or should perceive under all sorts of conditions.

Now, if this is so, it follows that we can only know in terms of our experiencing, and we can only know things in so far as they can be objects of our experience. If thinking only enables us to know, e.g., how things would look under the conditions of a possible experience, to ask what things are in themselves apart from their appearance, is to ask how they would look if they didn't look, or what we should know them to be if we could know them apart from looking. But both these conditions are impossible.

The application of this position to space and time in the 'Aesthetic' is simple. If we reflect on the nature of our perception we can see that it involves a double formal element in space and time. All perception involves these forms, and as all thinking refers ultimately to perception, we never get outside the conditions of space and time. This does not mean that space and time are subjective in the sense of being illusions: they are elements in that apprehension of things which we call perception. But we cannot get outside the conditions of perception. If we ask what space and time are apart from perception, that is one form of asking how things would look if they didn't look. And Kant thinks that philosophical puzzles about space and time arise from our considering them in that impossible way, and treating them as things in themselves. That is what Kant means by calling them transcendentally ideal. On the other hand they are empirically real, given elements in experience. This transcendentally subjective nature makes no more difficulty in our determinations of space and time being objective than does the arbitrary and subjective nature of our standards of measurement prevent our measurement being objective. If we calculate in inches and measure in inches, the subjective reasons for our measuring in inches rather than centimetres do not enter into the question as to whether one line is longer than another. So if we think in terms of space and perceive in space, since thinking is always a reference from present experience to possible experience, space being common to all the points of reference, its real nature, whatever that be, does not enter into the rightness or wrongness of this reference. Space and time are then like entries on both sides of a balance sheet.

When Kant comes to consider the objectivity of *a priori* principles, such as causation, he is, as he explains, faced with a more difficult problem. With what right can we assume that all events we may experience will be subject to the rule of causal determination? The solution of the 'Aesthetic' seems barred. For if we think in terms of causation, we do not apparently perceive in terms of causation. Hume's point indeed had been that we perceive succession and add to that perceived succession the notion of necessary connection; and that that addition has no validity. It was a psychological habit from which we could not escape and nothing more. Kant's answer is to make a distinction between perceiving and perceiving something as an object. So far as mere perceiving is concerned, there is no difference between our successively perceiving things which exist simultaneously and our successively perceiving what has successively existed. Objective succession then is not just perceived. We only perceive it in so far as we have made a distinction between succession in apprehending and apprehension of succession, until, in Kant's phrase, we have put time into the object. We do this normally without being aware of it. It is only when we make mistakes that we realize what is always happening, as e.g. when we are on a steamer leaving a pier, and we seem 'to see the pier moving.' But if we ask what this implies, we find that we have applied to what we perceive the principles of objective determination in space, and we have made a judgment. And one of these principles is the principle of causation. If, e.g., anything could cause anything, there would be no means of determining whether the fact that the pier is seen to occupy a smaller portion of our field of vision was due to the fact that it had moved or that we had moved. So in all our perception of objects we have decided that certain changes we perceive are due to changes in us and others are due to changes in the things. Therefore, the perception of objects already implies the principles of objective determination in space and time. But causation and the other *a priori* assumptions of science which Kant has discovered in his list of categories are simply the principles of objective determination in space and time. Scientific thinking is anticipation of objective experience, and the experiment and observation which check it, imply objective perception; imply an experience in which the distinction between subjective and objective has already been made, and the principles of objective determination in space and time have already been active. Thus we get a solution of the question as to how principles like causation can be valid of all experience which is on all fours with the solution given in the 'Aesthetic' of the similar question in regard to space and time. Causation is involved in both thinking and objective perception, and therefore it can be a principle implied in objective thinking without that involving that the nature of reality is to be an order of events causally determined in time. The validity of scientific principles has no relevance to the metaphysical status of these principles.

Kant has thus found a solution of his problem which preserves the integrity and independence of science without prejudice to the integrity of the principles of conduct. He has saved the objectivity of science by a limitation of the scope of science, by insisting that all that scientific thinking can do is to anticipate experience, and that therefore its principles have no application beyond the limits of experience. This position has the further negative result, worked out at great length in the 'Dialectic,' that all metaphysical reasoning about the nature of reality, based on applying the principles of thought beyond the limitations of experience, leads only to contradictions.

This is Kant's phenomenalism. If it were all he had to say, his doctrine of the limitations of reason would have anticipated the scientific agnosticism of Comte. But though this first *Critique* is mainly concerned with denying the claims made on behalf of reason's power to apprehend the nature of reality, Kant has a more positive doctrine of reason which appears in the 'Dialectic.' It is only fully developed in the other two *Critiques*.

Kant has shown the validity of the assumptions of the sciences by showing that they are principles of the possibility of objective experience. They are implied in any judgment which claims to be true. For without them the distinction between subjective and objective has no meaning. But if we can assume the validity of principles which we can show to be implied in the distinction between truth and falsehood, we can equally assume the validity of principles which can be shown to be implied in the distinction between right and wrong. As Kant has shown in the 'Analytic'

to this *Critique* that there could be no meaning in the distinction
between true and false if we denied the validity of the categories,
so he shows in his discussion of conduct that there can be no
meaning in the distinction between right and wrong unless we
assume the freedom of the will and the transcendency of moral
purposes.  The principles implied in conduct have a metaphysical
status, for, unlike the principles of the sciences, they are assumptions about the nature of reality or they are nothing.  If Kant's
negative doctrine sets severe limits to the speculative reason, his
positive doctrine makes high claims for practical reason.  His
criticism of the metaphysical status of the principles of science
leaves room for the metaphysical status of the principles of
conduct.  As he says in the Preface to this edition: 'I must,
therefore, abolish *knowledge*, to make room for *belief*.  The
principles on which he has established the entire validity of
science in its own sphere, do themselves limit that sphere and
confirm the validity of the principles of conduct in their sphere.
So this conflict which had threatened the integrity of either
science or conduct is averted.

We have taken a long time to learn the lesson of Kant and in
many quarters this conflict now rages.  Science has, of course,
changed very much since Kant's time.  He is perhaps most out
of date in his apparent assumption of the finality of Newtonian
physics.  But we are still continually told that the success of
mechanical principles in physics proves that freewill is a delusion,
and that we can only be saved if we will mould our theory of
conduct on the lines of the sciences, as there are still those who
think that the integrity of moral conduct can only be defended
by throwing doubts on the achievements of science.  Most
people care primarily for one side or the other, look at science
with the eyes of a moralist or at morals with the eyes of a scientist.  Kant was remarkable in his determination to vindicate alike
both these activities of the human spirit.  For that reason
perhaps more than for any other his teaching will always be
of influence.

                                        A. D. LINDSAY.

# SELECT BIBLIOGRAPHY

COLLECTED WORKS. The standard edition is that sponsored by the Berlin Academy and published from 1902 onwards. Twenty-eight volumes have so far appeared. Kant's published works, his correspondence and unpublished remains, including the *Opus Postumum*, are complete in Vols I–XXIII. The remaining volumes are to contain reconstructions of Kant's lectures.

A more convenient edition of the main writings is by Ernst Cassirer, 1912–23. Individual works, together with a comprehensive selective selection from Kant's correspondence, are available in the Philosophische Bibliothek series of Meiner Verlag, Hamburg. The edition of the *Kritik der reinen Vernunft* by Raymond Schmidt is of special importance. Another convenient German edition of this work is in the Reclam series, by Ingeborg Heidemann.

INDIVIDUAL WRITINGS, with English translations where available. *Allgemeine Naturgeschichte und Theorie des Himmels*, 1755 (parts of which are trans. by W. Hastie in *Kant's Cosmogony*, 1900). *Principiorum primorum cognitionis metaphysicae nova dilucidatio*, 1755 (trans. as *A New Exposition of the First Principles of Metaphysical Knowledge* by F. E. England in *Kant's Conception of God*, 1929). *Der einzig mögliche Beweisgrund zu einer Demonstration des Daseins Gottes*, 1763 (no English trans.). *Beobachtungen über des Gefühl des Schönen und Erhabenen*, 1764 (trans. by J. Goldthwait as *Observations on the Feeling of the Beautiful and the Sublime*, 1960). *Untersuchung über die Deutlichkeit der Grundsätze der natürlichen Theologie und der Moral*, 1764 (trans. as *An Inquiry into the Distinctness of the Principles of Natural Theology and Morals* by L. W. Beck, 1949; also in *Kant's Selected Pre-critical Writings*, translated by G. B. Kerferd and D. E. Walford, 1968). *Träume eines Geistersehers, erläutert durch Träume der Metaphysik*, 1766 (English trans. by E. E. Goerwitz as *Dreams of a Spirit-Seer, illustrated by Dreams of Metaphysics*, 1900). *De mundi sensibilis atque intelligibilis forma et principiis*, 1770 (trans. as *On the Form and Principles of the Sensible and Intelligible World* in Kerferd and Walford, op. cit.). *Kritik der reinen Vernunft*, 1781; second edition with important changes, 1787. (Trans. as *Critique of Pure Reason* (1) by J. M. D. Meiklejohn, 1855; (2) by N. Kemp Smith, 1929). *Prolegomena zu einer jeden künftigen Metaphysik, die als Wissenschaft wird auftreten können*, 1783 (various translations, mostly as *Prolegomena to any Future Metaphysics*: the most modern are by L. W. Beck, 1952 and by P. G. Lucas, 1953). *Idee zu einer allgemeinen Geschichte in welbürgerliche Absicht*, 1784 (trans. as *Idea for a Universal History from a Cosmopolitan Point of View* by L. W. Beck in *Kant on History*, 1963; also by H. B. Nisbet in *Kant's Political Writings*, 1970). *Grundlegung zur Metaphysik der Sitten*, 1785 (trans. by T. K. Abbott as *Fundamental Principles of the Metaphysic of Morals*, 1873; many later versions, of which the best are by L. W. Beck, 1949 and H. J. Paton—as *The Moral Law*—1949). *Metaphysische Anfangsgründe der Naturwissenschaft*, 1786 (trans. as *Metaphysical Foundations of Natural Science* by J. Ellington, 1970). *Kritik der praktischen Vernunft*, 1788 (trans. as *Critique of Practical Reason* (1) by T. K. Abbott in *Kant's Theory of Ethics*, 1873, (2) by L. W. Beck, 1949). *Kritik der Urteilskraft*, 1790 (trans. as *Critique of Judgment* (1) by J. H. Bernard, 1892, (2) by J. C. Meredith, 1911–28). *Religion innerhalb der Grenzen der blossen Vernunft*, 1793 (trans. as *Religion within the Limits of Reason alone* by T. M. Greene and H. H. Hudson, 1934). *Zum ewigen Frieden*, 1795 (many translations as *Perpetual Peace*, among the most modern being those by L. W. Beck, 1949 and by H. B. Nisbet in op. cit.). *Metaphysik der Sitten*, 1797 (trans. of part I as *The Metaphysical Elements of Justice* by J. Ladd,

1965; of part II as *The Doctrine of Virtue* by Mary Gregor, 1964; also partial trans. in Abbott, op. cit). *Anthropologie in pragmatischer Hinsicht*, 1798 (trans. as *Anthropology from a Pragmatic Point of View* by Mary Gregor, 1974). *Uber die wirklichen Fortschritte der Metaphysik seit Leibniz und Wolff*, 1804 (incomplete essay, edited posthumously; no trans.).

GENERAL WORKS on Kant include A. D. Lindsay, *Kant*, 1934; S. Körner, *Kant*, 1955; J. Kemp, *The Philosophy of Kant*, 1968; R. Scruton, *Kant* (Past Masters), 1982. Compare also E. Caird, *The Critical Philosophy of Kant*, 1889. For a general survey of Kant's philosophical development see H. J. de Vleeschauwer, *The Evolution of Kantian Thought*, (trans. by A. R. C. Duncan, 1962), together with the chapter on Kant in L. W. Beck's *Early German Philosophy*, 1969.

COMMENTARIES on the *Critique of Pure Reason*. N. Kemp Smith, 1918 covers the whole work at length; H. J. Paton (*Kant's Metaphysic of Experience*, 1936) deals with the first half only. A. C. Ewing (1938) and T. D. Weldon (1945) are briefer. P. F. Strawson, *The Bounds of Sense*, 1966, and J. Bennett, *Kant's Analytic*, 1966 and *Kant's Dialectic*, 1974, are more modern but sit looser to the text. In German there are notable commentaries by H. Vaihinger on the early part of the work (1881) and by H. Heimsoeth on the Dialectic (1966 ff.).

STUDIES of Kant's main argument or of particular parts of it include H. A. Prichard, *Kant's Theory of Knowledge*, 1909; R. Kroner, *Kant's Weltanschauung*, 1914 (trans. by J. E. Smith, 1956); M. Heidegger, *Kant and the Problem of Metaphysics*, 1929 (trans. by J. S. Churchill, 1962); H. J. de Vleeschauwer, *La Déduction transcendentale dans l'oeuvre de Kant*, 1934-9; G. Bird, *Kant's Theory of Knowledge*, 1962; R.P. Wolff, *Kant's Theory of Mental Activity*, 1963; L. W. Beck, *Studies in the Philosophy of Kant*, 1965; D. P. Dryer, *Kant's Solution for Verification in Metaphysics*, 1967; W. A. Galston, *Kant and the Problem of History*, 1975; R. C. S. Walker, Kant, Arguments of the Philosophers S., 1978; J. N. Findlay, *Kant and the Transcendental Object; A Hermeneutic Study*, 1981. Among modern collections of articles on Kant are those edited by R. P. Wolff, *Kant*, 1967; M. S. Gram, *Kant: Disputed Questions*, 1967; T. Penelhum and J. J. MacIntosh, *The First Critique*, 1969; L. W. Beck, *Kant Studies Today*, 1969; J. N. Findlay, *Kant and the Transcendental Object: A Hermenentic Study*, 1981; R. E. Butts, *Kant and the Double Government Methodology*, 1984. See also the periodical *Kantstudien*.

LIFE AND LETTERS. There is an excellent selection of Kant's letters in *Kant's Philosophical Correspondence*, translated and edited by A. Zweig, 1967. For a short account of Kant's life see T. K. Abbott's *Kant's Theory of Ethics*, 1873. There is also a life by J. W. H. Stuckenberg, 1882. The standard biography in German is by K. Vorländer, 1924. See also *Kant und Konigsberg* by K. Stavenhagen, 1949.

# TRANSLATOR'S PREFACE TO THE ORIGINAL ENGLISH EDITION

THE following translation has been undertaken with the hope of rendering Kant's *Kritik der reinen Vernunft* intelligible to the English student.

The difficulties which meet the reader and the translator of this celebrated work arise from various causes. Kant was a man of clear, vigorous, and trenchant thought, and, after nearly twelve years' meditation, could not be in doubt as to his own system. But the Horatian rule of

> Verba praevisam rem non invita sequentur

will not apply to him. He had never studied the art of expression. He wearies by frequent repetitions, and employs a great number of words to express, in the clumsiest way, what could have been enounced more clearly and distinctly in a few. The main statement in his sentences is often overlaid with a multitude of qualifying and explanatory clauses; and the reader is lost in a maze, from which he has great difficulty in extricating himself. There are some passages which have no main verb; others, in which the author loses sight of the subject with which he set out, and concludes with a predicate regarding something else mentioned in the course of his argument. All this can be easily accounted for. Kant, as he mentions in a letter to Lambert, took nearly twelve years to excogitate his work, and only five months to write it. He was a German professor, a student of solitary habits, and had never, except on one occasion, been out of Königsberg. He had, besides, to propound a new system of philosophy, and to enounce ideas that were entirely to revolutionize European thought. On the other hand, there are many excellencies of style in this work. His expression is often as precise and forcible as his thought; and, in some of his notes especially, he sums up, in two or three apt and powerful words, thoughts which, at other times, he employs pages to develop. His terminology, which has been so violently denounced, is really of great use in clearly determining his system, and in rendering its peculiarities more easy of comprehension.

A previous translation of the *Kritik* exists, which, had it been satisfactory, would have dispensed with the present. But the translator had, evidently, no very extensive acquaintance with the German language, and still less with his subject. A translator ought to be an interpreting intellect between the author and the reader; but, in the present case, the only interpreting medium has been the dictionary.

Indeed, Kant's fate in this country has been a very hard one. Misunderstood by the ablest philosophers of the time, illustrated, explained, or translated by the most incompetent—it has been his lot to be either unappreciated, misapprehended, or entirely neglected. Dugald Stewart did not understand his system of philosophy—as he had no proper opportunity of making himself acquainted with it; Nitsch [1] and Willich [2] undertook to introduce him to the English philosophical public; Richardson and Haywood 'traduced' him. More recently, an *Analysis of the Kritik*, by Mr. Haywood, has been published, which consists almost entirely of a selection of sentences from his own translation: a mode of analysis which has not served to make the subject more intelligible. In short, it may be asserted that there is not a single English work upon Kant which deserves to be read, or which can be read with any profit, excepting Semple's translation of the *Metaphysic of Ethics*. All are written by men who either took no pains to understand Kant, or were incapable of understanding him. [3]

The following translation was begun on the basis of a MS. translation, by a scholar of some repute, placed in my hands by Mr. Bohn, with a request that I should revise it, as he had perceived it to be incorrect. After having laboured through about eighty pages, I found, from the numerous errors and inaccuracies pervading it, that hardly one-fifth of the original MS. remained. I, therefore, laid it entirely aside, and commenced *de novo*. These eighty pages I did not cancel, because the careful examination

[1] *A General and Introductory View of Professor Kant's Principles.* By F. A. Nitsch. London, 1796.

[2] Willich's *Elements of Kant's Philosophy*, 8vo, 1798.

[3] It is curious to observe, in all the English works written specially upon Kant, that not one of his commentators ever ventures, for a moment, to leave the words of Kant, and to explain the subject he may be considering, in his own words. Nitsch and Willich, who professed to write on Kant's philosophy, are merely translators; Haywood, even in his notes, merely repeats Kant; and the translator of *Beck's Principles of the Critical Philosophy*, while pretending to give, in his Translator's Preface, his own views of the Critical Philosophy, has fabricated his Preface out of selections from the works of Kant. The same is the case with the translator of Kant's *Essays and Treatises* (2 vols. 8vo, London, 1798). This person has written a preface to each of the volumes, and both are almost literal translations from different parts of Kant's works. He had the impudence to present the thoughts contained in them as his own; few being then able to detect the plagiarism.

which they had undergone made them, as I believed, not an unworthy representation of the author.

The second edition of the *Kritik*, from which all the subsequent
ones have been reprinted without alteration, is followed in the
present translation. Rosenkranz, a recent editor, maintains that
the author's first edition is far superior to the second; and Schopenhauer asserts that the alterations in the second were dictated by
unworthy motives. He thinks the second a *Verschlimmbesserung*
of the first; and that the changes made by Kant, 'in the weakness
of old age,' have rendered it a 'self-contradictory and mutilated
work.' I am not insensible to the able arguments brought forward
by Schopenhauer; while the authority of the elder Jacobi, Michelet,
and others, adds weight to his opinion. But it may be doubted
whether the motives imputed to Kant could have influenced him
in the omission of certain passages in the second edition—whether
*fear* could have induced a man of his character to retract the
statements he had advanced. The opinions he expresses in many
parts of the second edition, in pages 427–32, for example,[1] are
not those of a philosopher who would surrender what he believed
to be truth, at the outcry of prejudiced opponents. Nor are his
attacks on the 'sacred doctrines of the old dogmatic philosophy,'
as Schopenhauer maintains, less bold or vigorous in the second
than in the first edition. And, finally, Kant's own testimony
must be held to be of greater weight than that of any number of
other philosophers, however learned and profound.

No edition of the *Kritik* is very correct. Even those of Rosenkranz and Schubert, and Mödes and Baumann, contain errors
which reflect somewhat upon the care of the editors. But the
common editions, as well those printed during, as after Kant's
life-time, are exceedingly bad. One of these, the 'third edition
improved, Frankfort and Leipzig, 1791,' swarms with errors, at
once misleading and annoying. Rosenkranz has made a number
of very happy conjectural emendations, the accuracy of which
cannot be doubted.

It may be necessary to mention that it has been found requisite
to coin one or two new philosophical terms, to represent those
employed by Kant. It was, of course, almost impossible to
translate the *Kritik* with the aid of the philosophical vocabulary
at present used in England. But these new expressions have been
formed according to Horace's maxim—*parcè detorta*. Such is the
verb *intuite* for *anschauen*; the manifold in intuition has also been
employed for *das Mannigfaltige der Anschauung*, by which Kant

[1] Of the present translation.

designates the varied contents of a perception or intuition. Kant's own terminology has the merit of being precise and consistent.

Whatever may be the opinion of the reader with regard to the possibility of metaphysics—whatever his estimate of the utility of such discussions—the value of Kant's work, as an instrument of mental discipline, cannot easily be overrated. If the present translation contribute in the least to the advancement of scientific cultivation, if it aid in the formation of habits of severer and more profound thought, the translator will consider himself well compensated for his arduous and long-protracted labour.

J. M. D. MEIKLEJOHN

## BACO DE VERULAMIO

INSTAURATIO MAGNA-PRAEFATIO

DE NOBIS IPSIS SILEMUS: DE RE AUTEM, QUAE AGITUR, PETIMUS: UT HOMINES EAM NON OPINIONEM, SED OPUS ESSE COGITENT; AC PRO CERTO HABEANT, NON SECTAE NOS ALICUJUS, AUT PLACITI, SED UTILITATIS ET AMPLITUDINIS HUMANAE FUNDAMENTA MOLIRI. DEINDE UT SUIS COMMODIS AEQUI—IN COMMUNE CONSULANT—ET IPSI IN PARTEM VENIANT. PRAETEREA UT BENE SPERENT, NEQUE INSTAURATIONEM NOSTRAM UT QUIDDAM INFINITUM ET ULTRA MORTALE FINGANT, ET ANIMO CONCIPIANT: QUUM REVERA SIT INFINITI ERRORIS FINIS ET TERMINUS LEGITIMUS.

# CONTENTS

# CONTENTS

# CONTENTS

# CONTENTS

# CONTENTS

# PREFACE TO THE FIRST EDITION (1781)

HUMAN reason, in one sphere of its cognition, is called upon to consider questions, which it cannot decline, as they are presented by its own nature, but which it cannot answer, as they transcend every faculty of the mind.

It falls into this difficulty without any fault of its own. It begins with principles, which cannot be dispensed with in the field of experience, and the truth and sufficiency of which are, at the same time, insured by experience. With these principles it rises, in obedience to the laws of its own nature, to ever higher and more remote conditions. But it quickly discovers that, in this way, its labours must remain ever incomplete, because new questions never cease to present themselves; and thus it finds itself compelled to have recourse to principles which transcend the region of experience, while they are regarded by common sense without distrust. It thus falls into confusion and contradictions, from which it conjectures the presence of latent errors, which, however, it is unable to discover, because the principles it employs, transcending the limits of experience, cannot be tested by that criterion. The arena of these endless contests is called *Metaphysic*.

Time was, when she was the *queen* of all the sciences; and, if we take the will for the deed, she certainly deserves, so far as regards the high importance of her object-matter, this title of honour. Now, it is the fashion of the time to heap contempt and scorn upon her; and the matron mourns, forlorn and forsaken, like Hecuba:

> Modo maxima rerum,
> Tot generis, natisque potens . . .
> Nunc trahor exul, inops.[1]

At first, her government, under the administration of the *dogmatists*, was an absolute *despotism*. But, as the legislative continued to show traces of the ancient barbaric rule, her empire gradually broke up, and intestine wars introduced the reign of *anarchy*; while the *sceptics*, like nomadic tribes, who hate a permanent habitation and settled mode of living, attacked from time to time those who had organized themselves into civil communities. But their number was, very happily, small; and

[1] Ovid, *Metamorphoses*.

thus they could not entirely put a stop to the exertions of those who persisted in raising new edifices, although on no settled or uniform plan. In recent times the hope dawned upon us of seeing those disputes settled, and the legitimacy of her claims established by a kind of *physiology* of the human understanding—that of the celebrated Locke. But it was found that—although it was affirmed that this so-called queen could not refer her descent to any higher source than that of common experience, a circumstance which necessarily brought suspicion on her claims—as this *genealogy* was incorrect, she persisted in the advancement of her claims to sovereignty. Thus metaphysics necessarily fell back into the antiquated and rotten constitution of *dogmatism*, and again became obnoxious to the contempt from which efforts had been made to save it. At present, as all methods, according to the general persuasion, have been tried in vain, there reigns nought but weariness and complete *indifferentism*—the mother of chaos and night in the scientific world, but at the same time the source of, or at least the prelude to, the re-creation and reinstallation of a science, when it has fallen into confusion, obscurity, and disuse from ill-directed effort.

For it is in reality vain to profess *indifference* in regard to such inquiries, the object of which cannot be indifferent to humanity. Besides, these pretended *indifferentists*, however much they may try to disguise themselves by the assumption of a popular style and by changes in the language of the schools, unavoidably fall into metaphysical declarations and propositions, which they profess to regard with so much contempt. At the same time, this in-difference, which has arisen in the world of science, and which relates to that kind of knowledge which we should wish to see destroyed the last, is a phenomenon that well deserves our attention and reflection. It is plainly not the effect of the levity, but of the matured *judgment* [1] of the age, which refuses to be any longer

[1] We very often hear complaints of the shallowness of the present age, and of the decay of profound science. But I do not think that those which rest upon a secure foundation, such as Mathematics, Physical Science, etc., in the least deserve this reproach, but that they rather maintain their ancient fame, and in the latter case, indeed, far surpass it. The same would be the case with the other kinds of cognition, if their principles were but firmly established. In the absence of this security, indifference, doubt, and finally, severe criticism are rather signs of a profound habit of thought. Our age is the age of criticism, to which everything must be subjected. The sacredness of religion, and the authority of legislation, are by many regarded as grounds of exemption from the examination of this tribunal. But, if they are exempted, they become the subjects of just suspicion, and cannot lay claim to sincere respect, which reason accords only to that which has stood the test of a free and public examination.

entertained with illusory knowledge. It is, in fact, a call to reason, again to undertake the most laborious of all tasks—that of self-examination, and to establish a tribunal, which may secure it in its well-grounded claims, while it pronounces against all baseless assumptions and pretensions, not in an arbitrary manner, but according to its own eternal and unchangeable laws. This tribunal is nothing less than the *Critical Investigation of Pure Reason*.

I do not mean by this a criticism of books and systems, but a critical inquiry into the faculty of reason, with reference to the cognitions to which it strives to attain *without the aid of experience*; in other words, the solution of the question regarding the possibility or impossibility of Metaphysics, and the determination of the origin, as well as of the extent and limits of this science. All this must be done on the basis of principles.

This path—the only one now remaining—has been entered upon by me; and I flatter myself that I have, in this way, discovered the cause of—and consequently the mode of removing—all the errors which have hitherto set reason at variance with itself, in the sphere of non-empirical thought. I have not returned an evasive answer to the questions of reason, by alleging the inability and limitation of the faculties of the mind; I have, on the contrary, examined them completely in the light of principles, and, after having discovered the cause of the doubts and contradictions into which reason fell, have solved them to its perfect satisfaction. It is true, these questions have not been solved as dogmatism, in its vain fancies and desires, had expected; for it can only be satisfied by the exercise of magical arts, and of these I have no knowledge. But neither do these come within the compass of our mental powers; and it was the duty of philosophy to destroy the illusions which had their origin in misconceptions, whatever darling hopes and valued expectations may be ruined by its explanations. My chief aim in this work has been thoroughness; and I make bold to say, that there is not a single metaphysical problem that does not find its solution, or at least the key to its solution, here. Pure reason is a perfect unity; and therefore, if the principle presented by it prove to be insufficient for the solution of even a single one of those questions to which the very nature of reason gives birth, we must reject it, as we could not be perfectly certain of its sufficiency in the case of the others.

While I say this, I think I see upon the countenance of the reader signs of dissatisfaction mingle with contempt, when he hears declarations which sound so boastful and extravagant; and yet they are beyond comparison more moderate than those advanced by the commonest author of the commonest philosophical programme, in which the dogmatist professes to demonstrate the simple nature of the soul, or the necessity of a primal being. Such a dogmatist promises to extend human knowledge beyond the limits of possible experience; while I humbly confess that this is completely beyond my power. Instead of any such attempt, I confine myself to the examination of reason alone and its pure thought; and I do not need to seek far for the sum-total of its cognition, because it has its seat in my own mind. Besides, common logic presents me with a complete and systematic catalogue of all the simple operations of reason; and it is my task to answer the question how far reason can go, without the material presented and the aid furnished by experience.

So much for the completeness and thoroughness necessary in the execution of the present task. The aims set before us are not arbitrarily proposed, but are imposed upon us by the nature of cognition itself.

The above remarks relate to the *matter* of our critical inquiry. As regards the *form*, there are two indispensable conditions, which any one who undertakes so difficult a task as that of a critique of pure reason, is bound to fulfil. These conditions are *certitude* and *clearness*.

As regards *certitude*, I have fully convinced myself that, in this sphere of thought, *opinion* is perfectly inadmissible, and that everything which bears the least semblance of an hypothesis must be excluded, as of no value in such discussions. For it is a necessary condition of every cognition that is to be established upon *a priori* grounds, that it shall be held to be absolutely necessary; much more is this the case with an attempt to determine all pure *a priori* cognition, and to furnish the standard—and consequently an example—of all apodeictic (philosophical) certitude. Whether I have succeeded in what I professed to do, it is for the reader to determine; it is the author's business merely to adduce grounds and reasons, without determining what influence these ought to have on the mind of his judges. But, lest anything he may have said may become the innocent cause of doubt in their minds, or tend to weaken the effect which his arguments might otherwise produce—he may be allowed to point out those passages which may occasion mistrust or difficulty, although these do not concern the main purpose of the present work. He does this solely with the view of removing from the mind of the reader any doubts which might affect his judgment of the work as a whole, and in regard to its ultimate aim.

I know no investigations more necessary for a full insight into the nature of the faculty which we call *understanding*, and at the same time for the determination of the rules and limits of its use, than those undertaken in the second chapter of the Transcendental Analytic, under the title of *Deduction of the Pure Conceptions of the Understanding*; and they have also cost me by far the greatest labour—labour which, I hope, will not remain uncompensated. The view there taken, which goes somewhat deeply into the subject, has two sides. The one relates to the objects of the pure understanding, and is intended to demonstrate and to render comprehensible the objective validity of its *a priori* conceptions; and it forms for this reason an essential part of the *Critique*. The other considers the pure understanding itself, its possibility and its powers of cognition—that is, from a subjective point of view; and, although this exposition is of great importance, it does not belong essentially to the main purpose of the work, because the grand question is, What and how much can reason and understanding, apart from experience, cognize? and not, How is the *faculty of thought* itself possible? As the latter is an inquiry into the cause of a given effect, and has thus in it some semblance of an hypothesis (although, as I shall show on another occasion, this is really not the fact), it would seem that, in the present instance, I had allowed myself to enounce a mere *opinion*, and that the reader must therefore be at liberty to hold a different *opinion*. But I beg to remind him, that, if my subjective deduction does not produce in his mind the conviction of its certitude at which I aimed, the objective deduction, with which alone the present work is properly concerned, is in every respect satisfactory.

As regards *clearness*, the reader has a right to demand, in the first place, *discursive* or logical clearness, that is, on the basis of conceptions, and, secondly, *intuitive* or aesthetic clearness, by means of intuitions, that is, by examples or other modes of illustration *in concreto*. I have done what I could for the first kind of intelligibility. This was essential to my purpose; and it thus became the accidental cause of my inability to do complete justice to the second requirement. I have been almost always at a loss, during the progress of this work, how to settle this question. Examples and illustrations always appeared to me necessary, and, in the first sketch of the *Critique*, naturally fell into their proper places. But I very soon became aware of the magnitude of my task, and the numerous problems with which I should be engaged; and, as I perceived that this critical investigation would, even if delivered in the driest *scholastic* manner, be far from being brief,

I found it unadvisable to enlarge it still more with examples and explanations, which are necessary only from a *popular* point of view. I was induced to take this course from the consideration also, that the present work is not intended for popular use, that those devoted to science do not require such helps, although they are always acceptable, and that they would have materially interfered with my present purpose. Abbé Terrasson remarks with great justice, that if we estimate the size of a work, not from the number of its pages, but from the time which we require to make ourselves master of it, it may be said of many a book—*that it would be much shorter, if it were not so short.* On the other hand, as regards the comprehensibility of a system of speculative cognition, connected under a single principle, we may say with equal justice —many a book would have been much clearer, if it had not been intended to be so very clear. For explanations and examples, and other helps to intelligibility, aid us in the comprehension of *parts*, but they distract the attention, dissipate the mental power of the reader, and stand in the way of his forming a clear conception of the *whole*; as he cannot attain soon enough to a survey of the system, and the colouring and embellishments bestowed upon it prevent his observing its articulation or organization—which is the most important consideration with him, when he comes to judge of its unity and stability.

The reader must naturally have a strong inducement to co-operate with the present author, if he has formed the intention of erecting a complete and solid edifice of metaphysical science, according to the plan now laid before him. Metaphysics, as here represented, is the only science which admits of completion—and with little labour, if it is united, in a short time; so that nothing will be left to future generations except the task of illustrating and applying it *didactically*. For this science is nothing more than the *inventory* of all that is given us by *pure reason*, systematically arranged. Nothing can escape our notice; for what reason produces from itself cannot lie concealed, but must be brought to the light by reason itself, so soon as we have discovered the common principle of the ideas we seek. The perfect unity of this kind of cognitions, which are based upon pure conceptions, and uninfluenced by any empirical element, or any *peculiar* intuition leading to determinate experience, renders this completeness not only practicable, but also necessary.

Tecum habita, et nôris quam sit tibi curta supellex.[1]

---

[1] Persius.

Such a system of pure speculative reason I hope to be able to publish under the title of *Metaphysic of Nature*.[1] The content of this work (which will not be half so long) will be very much richer than that of the present *Critique*, which has to discover the sources of this cognition and expose the conditions of its possibility, and at the same time to clear and level a fit foundation for the scientific edifice. In the present work, I look for the patient hearing and the impartiality of a *judge*; in the other, for the goodwill and assistance of a *co-labourer*. For, however complete the list of *principles* for this system may be in the *Critique*, the correctness cf the system requires that no *deduced* conceptions should be absent. These cannot be presented *a priori*, but must be gradually discovered; and, while the *synthesis* of conceptions has been fully exhausted in the *Critique*, it is necessary that, in the proposed work, the same should be the case with their *analysis*. But this will be rather an amusement than a labour.

[1] In contradistinction to the *Metaphysic of Ethics*. This work was never published. See page 476.—*Tr.*

# PREFACE TO THE SECOND EDITION (1787)

WHETHER the treatment of that portion of our knowledge which lies within the province of pure reason, advances with that undeviating certainty which characterizes the progress of *science*, we shall be at no loss to determine. If we find those who are engaged in metaphysical pursuits unable to come to an understanding as to the method which they ought to follow; if we find them, after the most elaborate preparations, invariably brought to a stand before the goal is reached, and compelled to retrace their steps and strike into fresh paths, we may then feel quite sure that they are far from having attained to the certainty of scientific progress, and may rather be said to be merely groping about in the dark. In these circumstances we shall render an important service to reason if we succeed in simply indicating the path along which it must travel, in order to arrive at any results—even if it should be found necessary to abandon many of those aims which, without reflection, have been proposed for its attainment.

That *Logic* has advanced in this sure course, even from the earliest times, is apparent from the fact that, since Aristotle, it has been unable to advance a step, and thus to all appearance has reached its completion. For, if some of the moderns have thought to enlarge its domain by introducing *psychological* discussions on the mental faculties, such as imagination and wit, *metaphysical* discussions on the origin of knowledge and the different kinds of certitude, according to the difference of the objects (Idealism, Scepticism, and so on), or *anthropological* discussions on prejudices, their causes and remedies: this attempt, on the part of these authors, only shows their ignorance of the peculiar nature of logical science. We do not enlarge, but disfigure the sciences when we lose sight of their respective limits, and allow them to run into one another. Now logic is enclosed within limits which admit of perfectly clear definition; it is a science which has for its object nothing but the exposition and proof of the *formal* laws of all thought, whether it be *a priori* or empirical, whatever be its origin or its object, and whatever the difficulties—natural or accidental—which it encounters in the human mind.

The early success of logic must be attributed exclusively to the narrowness of its field, in which abstraction may, or rather must, be made of all the objects of cognition with their characteristic distinctions, and in which the understanding has only to deal with itself and with its own forms. It is, obviously, a much more difficult task for reason to strike into the sure path of science, where it has to deal not simply with itself, but with objects external to itself. Hence, logic is properly only a *propaedeutic*—forms, as it were, the vestibule of the sciences; and while it is necessary to enable us to form a correct judgment with regard to the various branches of knowledge, still the acquisition of real, substantive knowledge is to be sought only in the sciences properly so called, that is, in the objective sciences.

Now these sciences, if they can be termed *rational* at all, must contain elements of *a priori* cognition, and this cognition may stand in a two-fold relation to its object. Either it may have to *determine* the conception of the object—which must be supplied extraneously, or it may have to *establish its reality*. The former is *theoretical*, the latter *practical*, rational cognition. In both, the *pure* or *a priori* element must be treated first, and must be carefully distinguished from that which is supplied from other sources. Any other method can only lead to irremediable confusion.

*Mathematics* and *Physics* are the two theoretical sciences which have to determine their objects *a priori*. The former is purely *a priori*, the latter is partially so, but is also dependent on other sources of cognition.

In the earliest times of which history affords us any record, *Mathematics* had already entered on the sure course of science, among that wonderful nation, the Greeks. Still it is not to be supposed that it was as easy for this science to strike into, or rather to construct for itself, that royal road, as it was for logic, in which reason has only to deal with itself. On the contrary, I believe that it must have remained long—chiefly among the Egyptians—in the stage of blind groping after its true aims and destination, and that it was revolutionized by the happy idea of one man, who struck out and determined for all time the path which this science must follow, and which admits of an indefinite advancement. The history of this intellectual revolution—much more important in its results than the discovery of the passage round the celebrated Cape of Good Hope—and of its author, has not been preserved. But Diogenes Laertius, in naming the supposed discoverer of some of the simplest elements of geometrical demonstration—elements which, according to the ordinary opinion, do not even require to be proved—makes it apparent that the change introduced by the first indication of this new path, must have seemed of the utmost importance to the mathematicians of that age, and it has thus been secured against the chance of oblivion. A new light must have flashed on the mind of the first man (*Thales*, or whatever may have been his name) who demonstrated the properties of the *isosceles* triangle. For he found that it was not sufficient to meditate on the figure, as it lay before his eyes, or the conception of it, as it existed in his mind, and thus endeavour to get at the knowledge of its properties, but that it was necessary to produce these properties, as it were, by a positive *a priori* construction; and that, in order to arrive with certainty at *a priori* cognition, he must not attribute to the object any other properties than those which necessarily followed from that which he had himself, in accordance with his conception, placed in the object.

A much longer period elapsed before *Physics* entered on the highway of science. For it is only about a century and a half since the wise BACON gave a new direction to physical studies, or rather—as others were already on the right track—imparted fresh vigour to the pursuit of this new direction. Here, too, as in the case of mathematics, we find evidence of a rapid intellectual revolution. In the remarks which follow I shall confine myself to the *empirical* side of natural science.

When GALILEI experimented with balls of a definite weight on the inclined plane, when TORRICELLI caused the air to sustain a weight which he had calculated beforehand to be equal to that of a definite column of water, or when STAHL, at a later period, converted metals into lime, and reconverted lime into metal, by the addition and subtraction of certain elements,[1] a light broke upon all natural philosophers. They learned that reason only perceives that which it produces after its own design; that it must not be content to follow, as it were, in the leading-strings of nature, but must proceed in advance with principles of judgment according to unvarying laws, and compel nature to reply to its questions. For accidental observations, made according to no preconceived plan, cannot be united under a necessary law. But it is this that reason seeks for and requires. It is only the principles of reason which can give to concordant phenomena the validity of laws, and it is only when experiment is directed by these rational principles that it can have any real utility. Reason must approach nature with the view, indeed, of receiving information from it, not, however, in the character of a pupil, who listens to all that

---

[1] I do not here follow with exactness the history of the experimental method, of which, indeed, the first steps are involved in some obscurity.

his master chooses to tell him, but in that of a judge, who compels the witnesses to reply to those questions which he himself thinks fit to propose. To this single idea must the revolution be ascribed, by which, after groping in the dark for so many centuries, natural science was at length conducted into the path of certain progress.

We come now to *Metaphysics*, a purely speculative science, which occupies a completely isolated position, and is entirely independent of the teachings of experience. It deals with mere conceptions—not, like mathematics, with conceptions applied to intuition—and in it, reason is the pupil of itself alone. It is the oldest of the sciences, and would still survive, even if all the rest were swallowed up in the abyss of an all-destroying barbarism. But it has not yet had the good fortune to attain to the sure scientific method. This will be apparent, if we apply the tests which we proposed at the outset. We find that reason perpetually comes to a stand, when it attempts to gain *a priori* the perception even of those laws which the most common experience confirms. We find it compelled to retrace its steps in innumerable instances, and to abandon the path on which it had entered, because this does not lead to the desired result. We find, too, that those who are engaged in metaphysical pursuits are far from being able to agree among themselves, but that, on the contrary, this science appears to furnish an arena specially adapted for the display of skill or the exercise of strength in mock contests—a field in which no combatant ever yet succeeded in gaining an inch of ground, in which, at least, no victory was ever yet crowned with permanent possession.

This leads us to inquire why it is that, in metaphysics, the sure path of science has not hitherto been found. Shall we suppose that it is impossible to discover it? Why then should nature have visited our reason with restless aspirations after it, as if it were one of our weightiest concerns? Nay, more, how little cause should we have to place confidence in our reason, if it abandons us in a matter about which, most of all, we desire to know the truth—and not only so, but even allures us to the pursuit of vain phantoms, only to betray us in the end? Or, if the path has only hitherto been missed, what indications do we possess to guide us in a renewed investigation, and to enable us to hope for greater success than has fallen to the lot of our predecessors?

It appears to me that the examples of mathematics and natural philosophy, which, as we have seen, were brought into their present condition by a sudden revolution, are sufficiently remarkable to fix our attention on the essential circumstances of the change which has proved so advantageous to them, and to induce us to make the experiment of imitating them, so far as the analogy which, as rational sciences, they bear to metaphysics may permit. It has hitherto been assumed that our cognition must conform to the objects; but all attempts to ascertain anything about these objects *a priori*, by means of conceptions, and thus to extend the range of our knowledge, have been rendered abortive by this assumption. Let us then make the experiment whether we may not be more successful in metaphysics, if we assume that the objects must conform to our cognition. This appears, at all events, to accord better with the *possibility* of our gaining the end we have in view, that is to say, of arriving at the cognition of objects *a priori*, of determining something with respect to these objects, before they are given to us. We here propose to do just what COPERNICUS did in attempting to explain the celestial movements. When he found that he could make no progress by assuming that all the heavenly bodies revolved round the spectator, he reversed the process, and tried the experiment of assuming that the spectator revolved, while the stars remained at rest. We may make the same experiment with regard to the intuition of objects. If the intuition must conform to the nature of the objects, I do not see how we can know anything of them *a priori*. If, on the other hand, the object conforms to the nature of our faculty of intuition, I can then easily conceive the possibility of such an *a priori* knowledge. Now as I cannot rest in the mere intuitions, but—if they are to become cognitions—must refer them, as *representations*, to something, as *object*, and must determine the latter by means of the former, here again there are two courses open to me. *Either*, first, I may assume that the conceptions, by which I effect this determination, conform to the object—and in this case I am reduced to the same perplexity as before; *or* secondly, I may assume that the objects, or, which is the same thing, that *experience*, in which alone as given objects, they are cognized, conform to my conceptions—and then I am at no loss how to proceed. For experience itself is a mode of cognition which requires understanding. Before objects are given to me, that is, *a priori*, I must presuppose in myself laws of the understanding which are expressed in conceptions *a priori*. To these conceptions, then, all the objects of experience must necessarily conform. Now there are objects which reason *thinks*, and that necessarily, but which cannot be given in experience, or, at least, cannot be given *so* as reason thinks them. The attempt to think these objects will hereafter furnish an excellent test of the new method of thought which we have adopted, and which is based on the principle that we only cognize in things *a priori* that which we ourselves place in them.[1]

This attempt succeeds as well as we could desire, and promises to metaphysics, in its first part—that is, where it is occupied with conceptions *a priori*, of which the corresponding objects may be given in experience—the certain course of science. For by this new method we are enabled perfectly to explain the possibility of *a priori* cognition, and, what is more, to demonstrate satisfactorily the laws which lie *a priori* at the foundation of nature, as the sum of the objects of experience—neither of which was possible according to the procedure hitherto followed. But from this deduction of the faculty of *a priori* cognition in the first part of metaphysics, we derive a surprising result, and one which, to all appearance, militates against the great end of metaphysics, as treated in the second part. For we come to the conclusion that our faculty of cognition is unable to transcend the limits of possible experience; and yet this is precisely the most essential object of this science. The estimate of our rational cognition *a priori* at which we arrive is that it has only to do with phenomena, and that things in themselves, while possessing a real existence, lie beyond its sphere. Here we are enabled to put the justice of this estimate to the test. For that which of necessity impels us to transcend the limits of experience and of all phenomena, is the *unconditioned*, which reason absolutely requires in things as they are in themselves, in order to complete the series of conditions. Now, if it appears that when, on the one hand, we assume that our cognition conforms to its objects as things in themselves, *the unconditioned cannot be thought without contradiction*, and that when, on the other hand, we assume that our representation of things as they are given to us does not conform to these things as they are in themselves, but that these objects, as phenomena, conform to our mode of representation, *the contradiction disappears*: we shall then be

[1] This method, accordingly, which we have borrowed from the natural philosopher, consists in seeking for the elements of pure reason in that *which admits of confirmation or refutation by experiment*. Now the propositions of pure reason, especially when they transcend the limits of possible experience, do not admit of our making any experiment with their *objects*, as in natural science. Hence, with regard to those *conceptions* and *principles* which we assume *a priori*, our only course will be to view them from two different sides. We must regard one and the same conception, *on the one hand*, in relation to experience as an object of the senses and of the understanding, or *on the other hand*, in relation to reason, isolated and transcending the limits of experience, as an object of mere thought. Now if we find that, when we regard things from this double point of view, the result is in harmony with the principle of pure reason, but that, when we regard them from a single point of view, reason is involved in self-contradiction, then the experiment will establish the correctness of this distinction.

convinced of the truth of that which we began by assuming for
the sake of experiment; we may look upon it as established that
the unconditioned does not lie in things as we know them, or as
they are given to us, but in things as they are in themselves,
beyond the range of our cognition.[1]

But, after we have thus denied the power of speculative reason
to make any progress in the sphere of the supersensible, it still
remains for our consideration whether data do not exist in *practical*
cognition, which may enable us to determine the transcendent
conception of the unconditioned, to rise beyond the limits of all
possible experience from a *practical* point of view, and thus to
satisfy the great ends of metaphysics. Speculative reason has
thus, at least, made room for such an extension of our knowledge;
and, if it must leave this space vacant, still it does not rob us of
the liberty to fill it up, if we can, by means of practical data—nay,
it even challenges us to make the attempt.[2]

This attempt to introduce a complete revolution in the procedure
of metaphysics, after the *example* of the Geometricians and Natural
Philosophers, constitutes the aim of the *Critique of Pure Speculative
Reason*. It is a treatise on the method to be followed, not a
system of the science itself. But, at the same time, it marks out
and defines both the external boundaries and the internal structure
of this science. For pure speculative reason has this peculiarity,
that, in choosing the various objects of thought, it is able to define
the limits of its own faculties, and even to give a complete
enumeration of the possible modes of proposing problems to
itself, and thus to sketch out the entire system of metaphysics.
For, on the one hand, in cognition *a priori*, nothing must be

---

[1] This experiment of pure reason has a great similarity to that of the
*Chemists*, which they term the experiment of *reduction*, or, more usually,
the *synthetic* process. The *analysis* of the metaphysician separates pure
cognition *a priori* into two heterogeneous elements, viz. the cognition of
things as phenomena, and of things in themselves. *Dialectic* combines these
again into harmony with the necessary rational idea of the unconditioned,
and finds that this harmony never results except through the above distinction,
which is, therefore, concluded to be just.

[2] So the central laws of the movements of the heavenly bodies established
the truth of that which Copernicus, at first, assumed only as a hypothesis,
and, at the same time, brought to light that invisible force (Newtonian
attraction) which holds the universe together. The latter would have
remained for ever undiscovered, if Copernicus had not ventured on the
experiment—contrary to the senses, but still just—of looking for the observed
movements not in the heavenly bodies, but in the spectator. In this Preface
I treat the new metaphysical method as a hypothesis with the view of rendering
apparent the first attempts at such a change of method, which are always
hypothetical. But in the *Critique* itself it will be demonstrated, not hypothetically, but apodeictically, from the nature of our representations of space
and time, and from the elementary conceptions of the understanding.

attributed to the objects but what the thinking subject derives from itself; and, on the other hand, reason is, in regard to the principles of cognition, a perfectly distinct, independent unity, in which, as in an organized body, every member exists for the sake of the others, and all for the sake of each, so that no principle can be viewed, with safety, in one relationship, unless it is, at the same time, viewed in relation to the total use of pure reason. Hence, too, metaphysics has this singular advantage—an advantage which falls to the lot of no other science which has to do with *objects*—that, if once it is conducted into the sure path of science, by means of this criticism, it can then take in the whole sphere of its cognitions, and can thus complete its work, and leave it for the use of posterity, as a capital which can never receive fresh accessions. For metaphysics has to deal only with principles and with the limitations of its own employment as determined by these principles. To this perfection it is, therefore, bound, as the fundamental science, to attain, and to it the maxim may justly be applied:

> Nil actum reputans, si quid superesset agendum.

But, it will be asked, what kind of a treasure is this that we propose to bequeath to posterity? What is the real value of this system of metaphysics, purified by criticism, and thereby reduced to a permanent condition? A cursory view of the present work will lead to the supposition that its use is merely *negative*, that it only serves to warn us against venturing, with speculative reason, beyond the limits of experience. This is, in fact, its primary use. But this, at once, assumes a *positive* value, when we observe that the principles with which speculative reason endeavours to transcend its limits, lead inevitably, not to the *extension*, but to the *contraction* of the use of reason, inasmuch as they threaten to extend the limits of sensibility, which is their proper sphere, over the entire realm of thought, and thus to supplant the pure (practical) use of reason. So far, then, as this criticism is occupied in confining speculative reason within its proper bounds, it is only negative; but, inasmuch as it thereby, at the same time, removes an obstacle which impedes and even threatens to destroy the use of practical reason, it possesses a positive and very important value. In order to admit this, we have only to be convinced that there is an absolutely necessary use of pure reason—the moral use—in which it inevitably transcends the limits of sensibility, without the aid of speculation, requiring only to be insured against the effects of a speculation which would involve it in contradiction with itself. To deny the positive advantage of the service which this criticism renders us, would be as absurd as to maintain that the system of police is productive of no positive benefit, since its main business is to prevent the violence which citizen has to apprehend from citizen, that so each may pursue his vocation in peace and security. That space and time are only forms of sensible intuition, and hence are only conditions of the existence of things as phenomena; that, moreover, we have no conceptions of the understanding, and, consequently, no elements for the cognition of things, except in so far as a corresponding intuition can be given to these conceptions; that, accordingly, we can have no cognition of an object, as a thing in itself, but only as an object of sensible intuition, that is, as phenomenon—all this is proved in the Analytical part of the *Critique*; and from this the limitation of all possible speculative cognition to the mere objects of *experience*, follows as a necessary result. At the same time, it must be carefully borne in mind that, while we surrender the power of *cognizing*, we still reserve the power of *thinking* objects, as things in themselves.[1] For, otherwise, we should require to affirm the existence of an appearance, without something that appears—which would be absurd. Now let us suppose, for a moment, that we had not undertaken this criticism, and, accordingly, had not drawn the necessary distinction between things as objects of experience, and things as they are in themselves. The principle of causality, and, by consequence, the mechanism of nature as determined by causality, would then have absolute validity in relation to all things as efficient causes. I should then be unable to assert, with regard to one and the same being, e.g. the human soul, that its will is *free*, and yet, at the same time, subject to natural necessity, that is, *not free*, without falling into a palpable contradiction, for in both propositions I should take the soul in *the same signification*, as a thing in general, as a thing in itself —as, without previous criticism, I could not but take it. Suppose now, on the other hand, that we *have* undertaken this criticism, and have learnt that an object may be taken in *two senses*, first, as a phenomenon, secondly, as a thing in itself; and that, according

[1] In order to *cognize* an object, I must be able to prove its possibility, either from its reality as attested by experience, or *a priori*, by means of reason. But I can *think* what I please, provided only I do not contradict myself; that is, provided my conception is a possible thought, though I may be unable to answer for the existence of a corresponding object in the sum of possibilities. But something more is required before I can attribute to such a conception objective validity, that is real possibility—the other possibility being merely logical. We are not, however, confined to theoretical sources of cognition for the means of satisfying this additional requirements, but may derive them from practical sources.

to the deduction of the conceptions of the understanding, the principle of causality has reference only to things in the first sense. We then see how it does not involve any contradiction to assert, on the one hand, that the will, in the phenomenal sphere—in visible action, is necessarily obedient to the law of nature, and, in so far, *not free*; and, on the other hand, that, as belonging to a thing in itself, it is not subject to that law, and, accordingly, is *free*. Now, it is true that I cannot, by means of speculative reason, and still less by empirical observation, *cognize* my soul as a thing in itself, and consequently, cannot cognize liberty as the property of a being to which I ascribe effects in the world of sense. For, to do so, I must cognize this being as existing, and yet not in time, which—since I cannot support my conception by any intuition—is impossible. At the same time, while I cannot *cognize*, I can quite well *think* freedom, that is to say, my representation of it involves at least no contradiction, if we bear in mind the critical distinction of the two modes of representation (the sensible and the intellectual) and the consequent limitation of the conceptions of the pure understanding, and of the principles which flow from them. Suppose now that morality necessarily presupposed liberty, in the strictest sense, as a property of our will; suppose that reason contained certain practical, original principles *a priori*, which were absolutely impossible without this presupposition; and suppose, at the same time, that speculative reason had proved that liberty was incapable of being thought at all. It would then follow that the moral presupposition must give way to the speculative affirmation, the opposite of which involves an obvious contradiction, and that *liberty* and, with it, morality must yield to the *mechanism of nature*; for the negation of morality involves no contradiction, except on the presupposition of liberty. Now morality does not require the speculative cognition of liberty; it is enough that I can think it, that its conception involves no contradiction, that it does not interfere with the mechanism of nature. But even this requirement we could not satisfy, if we had not learnt the two-fold sense in which things may be taken; and it is only in this way that the doctrine of morality and the doctrine of nature are confined within their proper limits. For this result, then, we are indebted to a criticism which warns us of our unavoidable ignorance with regard to things in themselves, and establishes the necessary limitation of our theoretical *cognition* to mere phenomena.

The positive value of the critical principles of pure reason in relation to the conception of *God* and of the *simple nature* of the *soul*, admits of a similar exemplification; but on this point I shall not dwell. I cannot even make the assumption—as the practical interests of morality require—of God, Freedom, and Immortality, if I do not deprive speculative reason of its pretensions to transcendent insight. For to arrive at these, it must make use of principles which, in fact, extend only to the objects of possible experience, and which cannot be applied to objects beyond this sphere without converting them into phenomena, and thus rendering the *practical extension* of pure reason impossible. I must, therefore, abolish *knowledge*, to make room for *belief*. The dogmatism of metaphysics, that is, the presumption that it is possible to advance in metaphysics without previous criticism, is the true source of the unbelief (always dogmatic) which militates against morality.

Thus, while it may be no very difficult task to bequeath a legacy to posterity, in the shape of a system of metaphysics constructed in accordance with the *Critique of Pure Reason*, still the value of such a bequest is not to be depreciated. It will render an important service to reason, by substituting the certainty of scientific method for that random groping after results without the guidance of principles, which has hitherto characterized the pursuit of metaphysical studies. It will render an important service to the inquiring mind of youth, by leading the student to apply his powers to the cultivation of genuine science, instead of wasting them, as at present, on speculations which can never lead to any result, or on the idle attempt to invent new ideas and opinions. But, above all, it will confer an inestimable benefit on morality and religion, by showing that all the objections urged against them may be silenced for ever by the *Socratic* method, that is to say, by proving the ignorance of the objector. For, as the world has never been, and, no doubt, never will be, without a system of metaphysics of one kind or another, it is the highest and weightiest concern of philosophy to render it powerless for harm, by closing up the sources of error.

This important change in the field of the sciences, this loss of its fancied possessions, to which speculative reason must submit, does not prove in any way detrimental to the general interests of humanity. The advantages which the world has derived from the teachings of pure reason are not at all impaired. The loss falls, in its whole extent, on the *monopoly of the schools*, but does not in the slightest degree touch the *interests of mankind*. I appeal to the most obstinate dogmatist, whether the proof of the continued existence of the soul after death, derived from the simplicity of its substance; of the freedom of the will in opposition to the general mechanism of nature, drawn from the subtle but impotent distinction of subjective and objective practical necessity; or of the existence of God, deduced from the conception of an *ens realissimum*—the contingency of the changeable, and the necessity of a prime mover, has ever been able to pass beyond the limits of the schools, to penetrate the public mind, or to exercise the slightest influence on its convictions.  It must be admitted that this has not been the case, and that, owing to the unfitness of the common understanding for such subtle speculations, it can never be expected to take place.  On the contrary, it is plain that *the hope of a future life* arises from the feeling, which exists in the breast of every man, that the temporal is inadequate to meet and satisfy the demands of his nature.  In like manner, it cannot be doubted that the clear exhibition of duties in opposition to all the claims of inclination, gives rise to the consciousness of *freedom*, and that the glorious order, beauty, and providential care, everywhere displayed in nature, give rise to the belief in a wise and great Author of the Universe.  Such is the genesis of these general convictions of mankind, so far as they depend on rational grounds; and this public property not only remains undisturbed, but is even raised to greater importance, by the doctrine that the schools have no right to arrogate to themselves a more profound insight into a matter of general human concernment, than that to which the great mass of men, ever held by us in the highest estimation, can without difficulty attain, and that the schools should therefore confine themselves to the elaboration of these universally comprehensible, and, from a moral point of view, amply satisfactory proofs.  The change, therefore, affects only the arrogant pretensions of the schools, which would gladly retain, in their own exclusive possession, the key to the truths which they impart to the public.

> Quod mecum nescit, solus vult scire videri.

At the same time it does not deprive the speculative philosopher of his just title to be the sole depositor of a science which benefits the public without its knowledge—I mean, the *Critique of Pure Reason*.  This can never become popular, and, indeed, has no occasion to be so; for fine-spun arguments in favour of useful truths make just as little impression on the public mind as the equally subtle objections brought against these truths.  On the other hand, since both inevitably force themselves on every man who rises to the height of speculation, it becomes the manifest duty of the schools to enter upon a thorough investigation of the rights of speculative reason, and thus to prevent the scandal which metaphysical controversies are sure, sooner or later, to cause even to the masses. It is only by criticism that metaphysicians (and, as such, theologians too) can be saved from these controversies and from the consequent perversion of their doctrines. Criticism alone can strike a blow at the root of Materialism, Fatalism, Atheism, Free-thinking, Fanaticism, and Superstition, which are universally injurious—as well as of Idealism and Scepticism, which are dangerous to the schools, but can scarcely pass over to the public. If governments think proper to interfere with the affairs of the learned, it would be more consistent with a wise regard for the interests of science, as well as for those of society, to favour a criticism of this kind, by which alone the labours of reason can be established on a firm basis, than to support the ridiculous despotism of the schools, which raise a loud cry of danger to the public over the destruction of cobwebs, of which the public has never taken any notice, and the loss of which, therefore, it can never feel.

This critical science is not opposed to the *dogmatic procedure* of reason in pure cognition; for pure cognition must always be dogmatic, that is, must rest on strict demonstration from sure principles *a priori*—but to *dogmatism*, that is, to the presumption that it is possible to make any progress with a pure cognition, derived from (philosophical) conceptions, according to the principles which reason has long been in the habit of employing—without first inquiring in what way and by what right reason has come into the possession of these principles. Dogmatism is thus the dogmatic procedure of pure reason *without previous criticism of its own powers*, and in opposing this procedure, we must not be supposed to lend any countenance to that loquacious shallowness which arrogates to itself the name of popularity, nor yet to scepticism, which makes short work with the whole science of metaphysics. On the contrary, our criticism is the necessary preparation for a thoroughly scientific system of metaphysics, which must perform its task entirely *a priori*, to the complete satisfaction of speculative reason, and must, therefore, be treated, not popularly, but scholastically. In carrying out the plan which the *Critique* prescribes, that is, in the future system of metaphysics, we must have recourse to the strict method of the celebrated WOLF, the greatest of all dogmatic philosophers. He was the first to point out the necessity of establishing fixed principles, of clearly defining our conceptions, and of subjecting our demonstrations to the most severe scrutiny, instead of rashly jumping at conclusions. The example which he set, served to awaken that spirit of profound and thorough investigation which is not yet extinct in Germany. He would have been peculiarly well fitted to give a truly scientific character to metaphysical studies, had it occurred to him to prepare the field by a criticism of the *organum*, that is, of pure reason itself. That he failed to perceive the necessity of such a procedure, must be ascribed to the dogmatic mode of thought which characterized his age, and on this point the philosophers of his time, as well as of all previous times, have nothing to reproach each other with. Those who reject at once the method of WOLF, and of the *Critique of Pure Reason*, can have no other aim but to shake off the fetters of *science*, to change labour into sport, certainty into opinion, and philosophy into philodoxy.

In this *second edition*, I have endeavoured, as far as possible, to remove the difficulties and obscurity, which, without fault of mine perhaps, have given rise to many misconceptions even among acute thinkers. In the propositions themselves, and in the demonstrations by which they are supported, as well as in the form and the entire plan of the work, I have found nothing to alter; which must be attributed partly to the long examination to which I had subjected the whole before offering it to the public, and partly to the nature of the case. For pure speculative reason is an organic structure in which there is nothing isolated or independent, but every single part is essential to all the rest; and hence, the slightest imperfection, whether defect or positive error, could not fail to betray itself in use. I venture, further, to hope, that this system will maintain the same unalterable character for the future. I am led to entertain this confidence, not by vanity, but by the evidence which the equality of the result affords, when we proceed, first, from the simplest elements up to the complete whole of pure reason, and then, backwards from the whole to each individual part. We find that the attempt to make the slightest alteration, in any part, leads inevitably to contradictions, not merely in this system, but in human reason itself. At the same time, there is still much room for improvement in the *exposition* of the doctrines contained in this work. In the present edition, I have endeavoured to remove misapprehensions of the aesthetical part, especially with regard to the conception of Time; to clear away the obscurity which has been found in the deduction of the conceptions of the understanding; to supply the supposed want of sufficient evidence in the demonstration of the principles of the pure understanding; and, lastly, to obviate the misunderstanding of the paralogisms which immediately precede the Rational Psychology. Beyond this point—the end of the second Main Division of the Transcendental

Dialectic—I have not extended my alterations,[1] partly from want of time, and partly because I am not aware that any portion of the remainder has given rise to misconceptions among intelligent and impartial critics, whom I do not here mention with that praise which is their due, but who will find that their suggestions have been attended to in the work itself.

[1] The only addition, properly so called—and that only in the method of proof—which I have made in the present edition, consists of a new refutation of psychological *Idealism*, and a strict demonstration—the only one possible, as I believe—of the objective reality of external intuition. However harmless Idealism may be considered—although in reality it is not so—in regard to the essential ends of metaphysics, it must still remain a scandal to philosophy and to the general human reason to be obliged to assume, as an article of mere belief, the existence of things external to ourselves (from which, yet, we derive the whole material of cognition even for the internal sense), and not to be able to oppose a satisfactory proof to any one who may call it in question. As there is some obscurity of expression in the demonstration as it stands in the text, I propose to alter the passage in question as follows: 'But this permanent cannot be an intuition in me. For all the determining grounds of my existence which can be found in me, are representations, and, as such, do themselves require a permanent, distinct from them, which may determine my existence in relation to their changes, that is, my existence in time, wherein they change.' It may, probably, be urged in opposition to this proof, that, after all, I am only conscious immediately of that which is in me, that is, of my *representation* of external things, and that, consequently, it must always remain uncertain whether anything corresponding to this representation does or does not exist externally to me. But I am conscious, through internal *experience*, of my *existence in time* (consequently, also, of the determinability of the former in the latter), and that is more than the simple consciousness of my representation. It is, in fact, the same as the *empirical consciousness of my existence*, which can only be determined in relation to something, which, while connected with my existence, is *external to me*. This consciousness of my existence in time is, therefore, identical with the consciousness of a relation to something external to me, and it is, therefore, experience, not fiction, sense, not imagination, which inseparably connects the external with my internal sense. For the external sense is, in itself, the relation of intuition to something real, external to me; and the reality of this something, as opposed to the mere imagination of it, rests solely on its inseparable connection with internal experience as the condition of its possibility. If with the *intellectual consciousness* of my existence, in the representation: *I am*, which accompanies all my judgments, and all the operations of my understanding, I could, at the same time, connect a determination of my existence by *intellectual intuition*, then the consciousness of a relation to something external to me would not be necessary. But the internal intuition in which alone my existence can be determined, though preceded by that purely intellectual consciousness, is itself sensible and attached to the condition of time. Hence this determination of my existence, and consequently my internal experience itself, must depend on something permanent which is not in me, which can be, therefore, only in something external to me, to which I must look upon myself as being related. Thus the reality of the external sense is necessarily connected with that of the internal, in order to the possibility of experience in general; that is, I am just as certainly conscious that there are things external to me related to my sense, as I am that I myself exist, as determined in time. But in order to ascertain to what given intuitions objects, external to me, really correspond, in other words, what intuitions belong to the external sense and not to imagination, I must have recourse, in every particular case, to those rules according to which experience in general

In attempting to render the exposition of my views as intelligible as possible, I have been compelled to leave out or abridge various passages which were not essential to the completeness of the work, but which many readers might consider useful in other respects, and might be unwilling to miss. This trifling loss, which could not be avoided without swelling the book beyond due limits, may be supplied, at the pleasure of the reader, by a comparison with the first edition, and will, I hope, be more than compensated for by the greater clearness of the exposition as it now stands.

I have observed, with pleasure and thankfulness, in the pages of various reviews and treatises, that the spirit of profound and thorough investigation is not extinct in Germany, though it may have been overborne and silenced for a time by the fashionable tone of a licence in thinking, which gives itself the airs of genius— and that the difficulties which beset the paths of Criticism have not prevented energetic and acute thinkers from making themselves masters of the science of pure reason to which these paths conduct —a science which is not popular, but scholastic in its character, and which alone can hope for a lasting existence or possess an abiding value. To these deserving men, who so happily combine profundity of view with a talent for lucid exposition—a talent which I myself am not conscious of possessing—I leave the task of removing any obscurity which may still adhere to the statement of my doctrines. For, in this case, the danger is not that of being refuted, but of being misunderstood. For my own part, I must henceforward abstain from controversy, although I shall carefully attend to all suggestions, whether from friends or adversaries, which may be of use in the future elaboration of the system of this Propaedeutic. As, during these labours, I have advanced pretty far in years—this month I reach my sixty-fourth year— it will be necessary for me to economize time, if I am to carry out my plan of elaborating the Metaphysics of Nature as well as of Morals, in confirmation of the correctness of the principles

(even internal experience) is distinguished from imagination, and which are always based on the proposition that there really is an external experience. We may add the remark, that the representation of something *permanent* in existence, is not the same thing as the *permanent representation*; for a representation may be very variable and changing—as all our representations, even that of matter, are—and yet refer to something permanent, which must, therefore, be distinct from all my representations and external to me, the existence of which is necessarily included in the determination of my own existence, and with it constitutes *one* experience—an experience which would not even be possible internally, if it were not also at the same time, in part, external. To the question *How?* we are no more able to reply, than we are, in general, to think the stationary in time, the co-existence of which with the variable, produces the conception of change.

established in this *Critique of Pure Reason*, both Speculative and Practical; and I must, therefore, leave the task of clearing up the obscurities of the present work—inevitable, perhaps, at the outset —as well as the defence of the whole, to those deserving men who have made my system their own. A philosophical system cannot come forward armed at all points like a mathematical treatise, and hence it may be quite possible to take objection to particular passages, while the organic structure of the system, considered as a unity, has no danger to apprehend. But few possess the ability, and still fewer the inclination, to take a comprehensive view of a new system. By confining the view to particular passages, taking these out of their connection and comparing them with one another, it is easy to pick out apparent contradictions, especially in a work written with any freedom of style. These contradictions place the work in an unfavourable light in the eyes of those who rely on the judgment of others, but are easily reconciled by those who have mastered the idea of the whole. If a theory possesses stability in itself, the action and reaction which seemed at first to threaten its existence, serve only, in the course of time, to smooth down any superficial roughness or inequality, and—if men of insight, impartiality, and truly popular gifts, turn their attention to it—to secure to it, in a short time, the requisite elegance also.

KÖNIGSBERG, *April* 1787.

# INTRODUCTION

## I. OF THE DIFFERENCE BETWEEN PURE AND EMPIRICAL KNOWLEDGE

THAT all our knowledge begins with experience there can be no doubt. For how is it possible that the faculty of cognition should be awakened into exercise otherwise than by means of objects which affect our senses, and partly of themselves produce representations, partly rouse our powers of understanding into activity, to compare, to connect, or to separate these, and so to convert the raw material of our sensuous impressions into a knowledge of objects, which is called experience? In respect of time, therefore, no knowledge of ours is antecedent to experience, but begins with it.

But, though all our knowledge begins with experience, it by no means follows, that all arises out of experience. For, on the contrary, it is quite possible that our empirical knowledge is a compound of that which we receive through impressions, and that which the faculty of cognition supplies from itself (sensuous impressions giving merely the *occasion*), an addition which we cannot distinguish from the original element given by sense, till long practice has made us attentive to, and skilful in separating it. It is, therefore, a question which requires close investigation, and is not to be answered at first sight—whether there exists a knowledge altogether independent of experience, and even of all sensuous impressions. Knowledge of this kind is called *a priori*, in contradistinction to empirical knowledge, which has its sources *a posteriori*, that is, in experience.

But the expression, '*a priori*,' is not as yet definite enough, adequately to indicate the whole meaning of the question above started. For, in speaking of knowledge which has its sources in experience, we are wont to say, that this or that may be known *a priori*, because we do not derive this knowledge immediately from experience, but from a general rule, which, however, we have itself borrowed from experience. Thus, if a man undermined his house, we say, 'he might know *a priori* that it would have fallen;' that is, he needed not to have waited for the experience that it did actually fall. But still, *a priori*, he could not know even this much. For, that bodies are heavy, and, consequently, that they fall when their supports are taken away, must have been known to him previously, by means of experience.

By the term 'knowledge *a priori*,' therefore, we shall in the sequel understand, not such as is independent of this or that kind of experience, but such as is absolutely so of *all* experience. Opposed to this is empirical knowledge, or that which is possible only *a posteriori*, that is, through experience. Knowledge *a priori* is either pure or impure. Pure knowledge *a priori* is that with which no empirical element is mixed up. For example, the proposition, 'Every change has a cause,' is a proposition *a priori*, but impure, because change is a conception which can only be derived from experience.

## II. The human intellect, even in an unphilosophical state, is in possession of certain cognitions 'a priori'

The question now is as to a *criterion*, by which we may securely distinguish a pure from an empirical cognition. Experience no doubt teaches us that this or that object is constituted in such and such a manner, but not that it could not possibly exist otherwise. Now, in the first place, if we have a proposition which contains the idea of necessity in its very conception, it is a judgment *a priori*; if, moreover, it is not derived from any other proposition, unless from one equally involving the idea of necessity, it is absolutely *a priori*. Secondly, an empirical judgment never exhibits strict and absolute, but only assumed and comparative universality (by induction); therefore, the most we can say is—so far as we have hitherto observed, there is no exception to this or that rule. If, on the other hand, a judgment carries with it strict and absolute universality, that is, admits of no possible exception, it is not derived from experience, but is valid absolutely *a priori*.

Empirical universality is, therefore, only an arbitrary extension of validity, from that which may be predicated of a proposition valid in most cases, to that which is asserted of a proposition which holds good in all; as, for example, in the affirmation, 'All bodies are heavy.' When, on the contrary, strict universality characterizes a judgment, it necessarily indicates another peculiar source of knowledge, namely, a faculty of cognition *a priori*. Necessity and strict universality, therefore, are infallible tests for distinguishing pure from empirical knowledge, and are inseparably connected with each other. But as in the use of these criteria the empirical limitation is sometimes more easily detected than the contingency of the judgment, or the unlimited universality which we attach to a judgment is often a more convincing proof than its necessity, it may be advisable to use the criteria separately, each being by itself infallible.

Now, that in the sphere of human cognition we have judgments which are necessary, and in the strictest sense universal, consequently pure *a priori*, it will be an easy matter to show. If we desire an example from the sciences, we need only take any proposition in mathematics. If we cast our eyes upon the commonest operations of the understanding, the proposition, 'Every change must have a cause,' will amply serve our purpose. In the latter case, indeed, the conception of a cause so plainly involves the conception of a necessity of connection with an effect, and of a strict universality of the law, that the very notion of a cause would entirely disappear, were we to derive it, like Hume, from a frequent association of what happens with that which precedes, and the habit thence originating of connecting representations— the necessity inherent in the judgment being therefore merely subjective. Besides, without seeking for such examples of principles existing *a priori* in cognition, we might easily show that such principles are the indispensable basis of the possibility of experience itself, and consequently prove their existence *a priori*. For whence could our experience itself acquire certainty, if all the rules on which it depends were themselves empirical, and consequently fortuitous? No one, therefore, can admit the validity of the use of such rules as first principles. But, for the present, we may content ourselves with having established the fact, that we do possess and exercise a faculty of pure *a priori* cognition; and, secondly, with having pointed out the proper tests of such cognition, namely, universality and necessity.

Not only in judgments, however, but even in conceptions, is an *a priori* origin manifest. For example, if we take away by degrees from our conceptions of a body all that can be referred to mere sensuous experience—colour, hardness or softness, weight, even impenetrability—the body will then vanish; but the space which it occupied still remains, and this it is utterly impossible to annihilate in thought. Again, if we take away, in like manner, from our empirical conception of any object, corporeal or incorporeal, all properties which mere experience has taught us to connect with it, still we cannot think away those through which we cogitate it as substance, or adhering to substance, although our conception of substance is more determined than that of an object. Compelled, therefore, by that necessity with which the conception of substance forces itself upon us, we must confess that it has its seat in our faculty of cognition *a priori*.

III. PHILOSOPHY STANDS IN NEED OF A SCIENCE WHICH SHALL DETERMINE THE POSSIBILITY, PRINCIPLES, AND EXTENT OF HUMAN KNOWLEDGE 'A PRIORI'

Of far more importance than all that has been above said, is the consideration that certain of our cognitions rise completely above the sphere of all possible experience, and by means of conceptions, to which there exists in the whole extent of experience no corresponding object, seem to extend the range of our judgments beyond its bounds. And just in this transcendental or supersensible sphere, where experience affords us neither instruction nor guidance, lie the investigations of *Reason*, which, on account of their importance, we consider far preferable to, and as having a far more elevated aim than, all that the understanding can achieve within the sphere of sensuous phenomena. So high a value do we set upon these investigations, that even at the risk of error, we persist in following them out, and permit neither doubt nor disregard nor indifference to restrain us from the pursuit. These unavoidable problems of mere pure reason are GOD, FREEDOM (of will), and IMMORTALITY. The science which, with all its preliminaries, has for its especial object the solution of these problems is named metaphysics—a science which is at the very outset dogmatical, that is, it confidently takes upon itself the execution of this task without any previous investigation of the ability or inability of reason for such an undertaking.

Now the safe ground of experience being thus abandoned, it seems nevertheless natural that we should hesitate to erect a building with the cognitions we possess, without knowing whence they come, and on the strength of principles, the origin of which is undiscovered. Instead of thus trying to build without a foundation, it is rather to be expected that we should long ago have put the question, how can the understanding arrive at these *a priori* cognitions, and what is the extent, validity, and worth which they may possess? We say, this is natural enough, meaning by the word natural, that which is consistent with a just and reasonable way of thinking; but if we understand by the term, that which usually happens, nothing indeed could be more natural and more comprehensible than that this investigation should be left long unattempted. For one part of our pure knowledge, the science of mathematics, has been long firmly established, and thus leads us to form flattering expectations with regard to others, though these may be of quite a different nature. Besides, when we get beyond the bounds of experience, we are of course safe from opposition in that quarter; and the charm of widening the range of our knowledge is so great, that unless we are brought to a stand-still by some evident contradiction, we hurry on undoubtingly in our course. This, however, may be avoided, if we are sufficiently cautious in the construction of our fictions, which are not the less fictions on that account.

Mathematical science affords us a brilliant example, how far, independently of all experience, we may carry our *a priori* know-ledge. It is true that the mathematician occupies himself with objects and cognitions only in so far as they can be represented by means of intuition. But this circumstance is easily overlooked, because the said intuition can itself be given *a priori*, and therefore is hardly to be distinguished from a mere pure conception. Deceived by such a proof of the power of reason, we can perceive no limits to the extension of our knowledge. The light dove cleaving in free flight the thin air, whose resistance it feels, might imagine that her movements would be far more free and rapid in airless space. Just in the same way did Plato, abandoning the world of sense because of the narrow limits it sets to the under-standing, venture upon the wings of ideas beyond it, into the void space of pure intellect. He did not reflect that he made no real progress by all his efforts; for he met with no resistance which might serve him for a support, as it were, whereon to rest, and on which he might apply his powers, in order to let the intellect acquire momentum for its progress. It is, indeed, the common fate of human reason in speculation, to finish the imposing edifice of thought as rapidly as possible, and then for the first time to begin to examine whether the foundation is a solid one or no. Arrived at this point, all sorts of excuses are sought after, in order to console us for its want of stability, or rather, indeed, to enable us to dispense altogether with so late and dangerous an investigation. But what frees us during the process of building from all appre-hension or suspicion, and flatters us into the belief of its solidity, is this. A great part, perhaps the greatest part, of the business of our reason consists in the analysation of the conceptions which we already possess of objects. By this means we gain a multitude of cognitions, which although really nothing more than elucidations or explanations of that which (though in a confused manner) was already thought in our conceptions, are, at least in respect of their form, prized as new introspections; whilst, so far as regards their matter or content, we have really made no addition to our conceptions, but only disinvolved them. But as this process does furnish real *a priori* knowledge,[1] which has a sure progress and useful results, reason, deceived by this, slips in, without being itself aware of it, assertions of a quite different kind; in which, to given conceptions it adds others, *a priori* indeed, but entirely foreign to them, without our knowing how it arrives at these, and, indeed, without such a question ever suggesting itself. I shall therefore at once proceed to examine the difference between these two modes of knowledge.

### IV. Of the difference between analytical and synthetical judgments

In all judgments wherein the relation of a subject to the predicate is cogitated (I mention affirmative judgments only here; the application to negative will be very easy), this relation is possible in two different ways. Either the predicate B belongs to the subject A, as somewhat which is contained (though covertly) in the conception A; or the predicate B lies completely out of the conception A, although it stands in connection with it. In the first instance, I term the judgment analytical, in the second, synthetical. Analytical judgments (affirmative) are therefore those in which the connection of the predicate with the subject is cogitated through identity; those in which this connection is cogitated without identity, are called synthetical judgments. The former may be called *explicative*, the latter *augmentative* [2] judgments; because the former add in the predicate nothing to the conception of the subject, but only analyse it into its constituent conceptions, which were thought already in the subject, although in a confused manner; the latter add to our conceptions of the subject a predicate which was not contained in it, and which no analysis could ever have discovered therein. For example, when I say, 'All bodies are extended,' this is an analytical judgment. For I need not go beyond the conception of *body* in order to find extension connected with it, but merely analyse the conception, that is, become conscious of the manifold properties which I think in that conception, in order to discover this predicate in it: it is therefore an analytical judgment. On the other hand, when I say, 'All bodies are heavy,'

---

[1] Not synthetical.—*Tr.*

[2] That is, judgments which really add to, and do not merely analyse or explain the conceptions which make up the sum of our knowledge.—*Tr.*

the predicate is something totally different from that which I think in the mere conception of a body. By the addition of such a predicate, therefore, it becomes a synthetical judgment.

Judgments of experience, as such, are always synthetical. For it would be absurd to think of grounding an analytical judgment on experience, because in forming such a judgment I need not go out of the sphere of my conceptions, and therefore recourse to the testimony of experience is quite unnecessary. That 'bodies are extended' is not an empirical judgment, but a proposition which stands firm *a priori*. For before addressing myself to experience, I already have in my conception all the requisite conditions for the judgment, and I have only to extract the predicate from the conception, according to the principle of contradiction, and thereby at the same time become conscious of the necessity of the judgment, a necessity which I could never learn from experience. On the other hand, though at first I do not at all include the predicate of weight in my conception of body in general, that conception still indicates an object of experience, a part of the totality of experience, to which I can still add other parts; and this I do when I recognize by observation that bodies are heavy. I can cognize beforehand by analysis the conception of body through the characteristics of extension, impenetrability, shape, etc., all which are cogitated in this conception. But now I extend my knowledge, and looking back on experience from which I had derived this conception of body, I find weight at all times connected with the above characteristics, and therefore I synthetically add to my conceptions this as a predicate, and say, 'All bodies are heavy.' Thus it is experience upon which rests the possibility of the synthesis of the predicate of weight with the conception of body, because both conceptions, although the one is not contained in the other, still belong to one another (only contingently, however), as parts of a whole, namely, of experience, which is itself a synthesis of intuitions.

But to synthetical judgments *a priori*, such aid is entirely wanting. If I go out of and beyond the conception A, in order to recognize another B as connected with it, what foundation have I to rest on, whereby to render the synthesis possible? I have here no longer the advantage of looking out in the sphere of experience for what I want. Let us take, for example, the proposition, 'Everything that happens has a cause.' In the conception of *something that happens*, I indeed think an existence which a certain time antecedes, and from this I can derive analytical judgments. But the conception of a cause lies quite out of the above conception, and indicates something entirely different from 'that which happens,' and is consequently not contained in that conception. How then am I able to assert concerning the general conception—'that which happens'—something entirely different from that conception, and to recognize the conception of cause although not contained in it, yet as belonging to it, and even necessarily? What is here the unknown=X, upon which the understanding rests when it believes it has found, out of the conception A a foreign predicate B, which it nevertheless considers to be connected with it? It cannot be experience, because the principle adduced annexes the two representations, cause and effect, to the representation existence, not only with universality, which experience cannot give, but also with the expression of necessity, therefore completely *a priori* and from pure conceptions. Upon such synthetical, that is augmentative propositions, depends the whole aim of our speculative knowledge *a priori*; for although analytical judgments are indeed highly important and necessary, they are so, only to arrive at that clearness of conceptions which is requisite for a sure and extended synthesis, and this alone is a real acquisition.

### V. IN ALL THEORETICAL SCIENCES OF REASON, SYNTHETICAL JUDGMENTS 'A PRIORI' ARE CONTAINED AS PRINCIPLES

1. Mathematical judgments are always synthetical. Hitherto this fact, though incontestably true and very important in its consequences, seems to have escaped the analysts of the human mind, nay, to be in complete opposition to all their conjectures. For as it was found that mathematical conclusions all proceed according to the principle of contradiction (which the nature of every apodeictic certainty requires), people became persuaded that the fundamental principles of the science also were recognized and admitted in the same way. But the notion is fallacious; for although a synthetical proposition can certainly be discerned by means of the principle of contradiction, this is possible only when another synthetical proposition precedes, from which the latter is deduced, but never of itself.

Before all, be it observed, that proper mathematical propositions are always judgments *a priori*, and not empirical, because they carry along with them the conception of necessity, which cannot be given by experience. If this be demurred to, it matters not; I will then limit my assertion to *pure* mathematics, the very conception of which implies that it consists of knowledge altogether non-empirical and *a priori*.

We might, indeed, at first suppose that the proposition $7+5=12$ is a merely analytical proposition, following (according to the principle of contradiction) from the conception of a sum of seven and five. But if we regard it more narrowly, we find that our conception of the sum of seven and five contains nothing more than the uniting of both sums into one, whereby it cannot at all be cogitated what this single number is which embraces both. The conception of twelve is by no means obtained by merely cogitating the union of seven and five; and we may analyse our conception of such a possible sum as long as we will, still we shall never discover in it the notion of twelve. We must go beyond these conceptions, and have recourse to an intuition which corresponds to one of the two—our five fingers, for example, or like Segner in his *Arithmetic* five points, and so by degrees, add the units contained in the five given in the intuition, to the conception of seven. For I first take the number 7, and, for the conception of 5 calling in the aid of the fingers of my hand as objects of intuition, I add the units, which I before took together to make up the number 5, gradually now by means of the material image my hand, to the number 7, and by this process, I at length see the number 12 arise. That 7 should be added to 5, I have certainly cogitated in my conception of a sum=$7+5$, but not that this sum was equal to 12. Arithmetical propositions are therefore always synthetical, of which we may become more clearly convinced by trying large numbers. For it will thus become quite evident, that turn and twist our conceptions as we may, it is impossible, without having recourse to intuition, to arrive at the sum total or product by means of the mere analysis of our conceptions. Just as little is any principle of pure geometry analytical. 'A straight line between two points is the shortest,' is a synthetical proposition. For my conception of *straight* contains no notion of *quantity*, but is merely *qualitative*. The conception of the *shortest* is therefore wholly an addition, and by no analysis can it be extracted from our conception of a straight line. Intuition must therefore here lend its aid, by means of which and thus only, our synthesis is possible.

Some few principles preposited by geometricians are, indeed, really analytical, and depend on the principle of contradiction. They serve, however, like identical propositions, as links in the chain of method, not as principles—for example, $a=a$, the whole is equal to itself, or $(a+b) > a$, the whole is greater than its part.

And yet even these principles themselves, though they derive their validity from pure conceptions, are only admitted in mathematics because they can be presented in intuition. What causes us here commonly to believe that the predicate of such apodeictic judgments is already contained in our conception, and that the judgment is therefore analytical, is merely the equivocal nature of the expression. We must join in thought a certain predicate to a given conception, and this necessity cleaves already to the conception. But the question is, not what we must join in thought to the given conception, but what we really think therein, though only obscurely, and then it becomes manifest, that the predicate pertains to these conceptions, necessarily indeed, yet not as thought in the conception itself, but by virtue of an intuition, which must be added to the conception.

2. The science of Natural Philosophy (Physics) contains in itself synthetical judgments *a priori*, as principles. I shall adduce two propositions. For instance, the proposition, 'In all changes of the material world, the quantity of matter remains unchanged'; or, that, 'In all communication of motion, action and reaction must always be equal.' In both of these, not only is the necessity, and therefore their origin *a priori* clear, but also that they are synthetical propositions. For in the conception of matter, I do not cogitate its permanency, but merely its presence in space, which it fills. I therefore really go out of and beyond the conception of matter, in order to think on to it something *a priori*, which I did not think in it. The proposition is therefore not analytical, but synthetical, and nevertheless conceived *a priori*; and so it is with regard to the other propositions of the pure part of natural philosophy.

3. As to Metaphysics, even if we look upon it merely as an attempted science, yet, from the nature of human reason, an indispensable one, we find that it must contain synthetical propositions *a priori*. It is not merely the duty of metaphysics to dissect, and thereby analytically to illustrate the conceptions which we form *a priori* of things; but we seek to widen the range of our *a priori* knowledge. For this purpose, we must avail ourselves of such principles as add something to the original conception —something not identical with, nor contained in it, and by means of synthetical judgments *a priori*, leave far behind us the limits of experience; for example, in the proposition, 'the world must have a beginning,' and such like. Thus metaphysics, according to the proper aim of the science, consists merely of synthetical propositions *a priori*.

### VI. The universal problem of pure reason

It is extremely advantageous to be able to bring a number of investigations under the formula of a single problem. For in this manner, we not only facilitate our own labour, inasmuch as we define it clearly to ourselves, but also render it more easy for others to decide whether we have done justice to our undertaking. The proper problem of pure reason, then, is contained in the question: 'How are synthetical judgments *a priori* possible?'

That metaphysical science has hitherto remained in so vacillating a state of uncertainty and contradiction, is only to be attributed to the fact, that this great problem, and perhaps even the difference between analytical and synthetical judgments, did not sooner suggest itself to philosophers. Upon the solution of this problem, or upon sufficient proof of the impossibility of synthetical knowledge *a priori*, depends the existence or downfall of the science of metaphysics. Among philosophers, David Hume came the nearest of all to this problem; yet it never acquired in his mind sufficient precision, nor did he regard the question in its universality. On the contrary, he stopped short at the synthetical proposition of the connection of an effect with its cause (*principium causalitatis*), insisting that such proposition *a priori* was impossible. According to his conclusions, then, all that we term metaphysical science is a mere delusion, arising from the fancied insight of reason into that which is in truth borrowed from experience, and to which habit has given the appearance of necessity. Against this assertion, destructive to all pure philosophy, he would have been guarded, had he had our problem before his eyes in its universality. For he would then have perceived that, according to his own argument, there likewise could not be any pure mathematical science, which assuredly cannot exist without synthetical propositions *a priori*— an absurdity from which his good understanding must have saved him.

In the solution of the above problem is at the same time comprehended the possibility of the use of pure reason in the foundation and construction of all sciences which contain theoretical knowledge *a priori* of objects, that is to say, the answer to the following questions:

How is pure mathematical science possible?

How is pure natural science possible?

Respecting these sciences, as they do certainly exist, it may with propriety be asked, *how* they are possible—for that they must be possible, is shown by the fact of their really existing.[1] But as to metaphysics, the miserable progress it has hitherto made, and the fact that of no one system yet brought forward, as far as regards its true aim, can it be said that this science really exists, leaves any one at liberty to doubt with reason the very possibility of its existence.

Yet, in a certain sense, this kind of knowledge must unquestionably be looked upon as *given*; in other words, metaphysics must be considered as really existing, if not as a science, nevertheless as a natural disposition of the human mind (*metaphysica naturalis*). For human reason, without any instigations imputable to the mere vanity of great knowledge, unceasingly progresses, urged on by its own feeling of need, towards such questions as cannot be answered by any empirical application of reason, or principles derived therefrom; and so there has ever really existed in every man some system of metaphysics. It will always exist, so soon as reason awakes to the exercise of its power of speculation. And now the question arises: How is metaphysics, as a natural disposition, possible? In other words, how, from the nature of universal human reason, do those questions arise which pure reason proposes to itself, and which it is impelled by its own feeling of need to answer as well as it can?

But as in all the attempts hitherto made to answer the questions which reason is prompted by its very nature to propose to itself, for example, whether the world had a beginning, or has existed from eternity, it has always met with unavoidable contradictions, we must not rest satisfied with the mere natural disposition of the mind to metaphysics, that is, with the existence of the faculty of pure reason, whence, indeed, some sort of metaphysical system always arises; but it must be possible to arrive at certainty in regard to the question whether we know or do not know the things of which metaphysics treats. We must be able to arrive at a decision on the subjects of its questions, or on the ability or inability of reason to form any judgment respecting them; and therefore either to extend with confidence the bounds of our pure reason, or to set strictly defined and safe limits to its action. This last question, which arises out of the above universal problem, would properly run thus: How is metaphysics possible as a science?

[1] As to the existence of pure natural science, or physics, perhaps many may still express doubts. But we have only to look at the different propositions which are commonly treated of at the commencement of proper (empirical) physical science—those, for example, relating to the permanence of the same quantity of matter, the *vis inertiae*, the equality of action and reaction, etc.—to be soon convinced that they form a science of pure physics (*physica pura*, or *rationalis*), which well deserves to be separately exposed as a special science, in its whole extent, whether that be great or confined.

Thus, the critique of reason leads at last, naturally and necessarily, to science; and, on the other hand, the dogmatical use of reason without criticism leads to groundless assertions, against which others equally specious can always be set, thus ending unavoidably in scepticism.

Besides, this science cannot be of great and formidable prolixity, because it has not to do with objects of reason, the variety of which is inexhaustible, but merely with Reason herself and her problems; problems which arise out of her own bosom, and are not proposed to her by the nature of outward things, but by her own nature. And when once Reason has previously become able completely to understand her own power in regard to objects which she meets with in experience, it will be easy to determine securely the extent and limits of her attempted application to objects beyond the confines of experience.

We may and must, therefore, regard the attempts hitherto made to establish metaphysical science dogmatically as non-existent. For what of analysis, that is, mere dissection of conceptions, is contained in one or other, is not the aim of, but only a preparation for metaphysics proper, which has for its object the extension, by means of synthesis, of our *a priori* knowledge. And for this purpose, mere analysis is of course useless, because it only shows what is contained in these conceptions, but not how we arrive, *a priori*, at them; and this it is her duty to show, in order to be able afterwards to determine their valid use in regard to all objects of experience, to all knowledge in general. But little self-denial, indeed, is needed to give up these pretensions, seeing the undeniable, and in the dogmatic mode of procedure, inevitable contradictions of Reason with herself, have long since ruined the reputation of every system of metaphysics that has appeared up to this time. It will require more firmness to remain undeterred by difficulty from within, and opposition from without, from endeavouring, by a method quite opposed to all those hitherto followed, to further the growth and fruitfulness of a science indispensable to human reason—a science from which every branch it has borne may be cut away, but whose roots remain indestructible.

## VII. Idea and division of a particular science, under the name of a Critique of Pure Reason

From all that has been said, there results the idea of a particular science, which may be called the *Critique of Pure Reason*. For reason is the faculty which furnishes us with the principles of knowledge *a priori*. Hence, pure reason is the faculty which contains the principles of cognizing anything absolutely *a priori*. An Organon of pure reason would be a compendium of those principles according to which alone all pure cognitions *a priori* can be obtained. The completely extended application of such an organon would afford us a system of pure reason. As this, however, is demanding a great deal, and it is yet doubtful whether any extension of our knowledge be here possible, or if so, in what cases; we can regard a science of the mere criticism of pure reason, its sources and limits, as the *propaedeutic* to a system of pure reason. Such a science must not be called a Doctrine, but only a Critique of Pure Reason; and its use, in regard to speculation, would be only negative, not to enlarge the bounds of, but to purify our reason, and to shield it against error—which alone is no little gain. I apply the term *transcendental* to all knowledge which is not so much occupied with objects as with the mode of our cognition of these objects, so far as this mode of cognition is possible *a priori*. A system of such conceptions would be called *Transcendental Philosophy*. But this, again, is still beyond the bounds of our present essay. For as such a science must contain a complete exposition not only of our synthetical *a priori*, but of our analytical *a priori* knowledge, it is of too wide a range for our present purpose, because we do not require to carry our analysis any farther than is necessary to understand, in their full extent, the principles of synthesis *a priori*, with which alone we have to do. This investigation, which we cannot properly call a doctrine, but only a transcendental critique, because it aims not at the enlargement, but at the correction and guidance of our knowledge, and is to serve as a touchstone of the worth or worthlessness of all knowledge *a priori*, is the sole object of our present essay. Such a critique is consequently, as far as possible, a preparation for an organon; and if this new organon should be found to fail, at least for a canon of pure reason, according to which the complete system of the philosophy of pure reason, whether it extend or limit the bounds of that reason, might one day be set forth both analytically and synthetically. For that this is possible, nay, that such a system is not of so great extent as to preclude the hope of its ever being completed, is evident. For we have not here to do with the nature of outward objects, which is infinite, but solely with the mind, which judges of the nature of objects, and, again, with the mind only in respect of its cognition *a priori*. And the object of our investigations, as it is not to be sought without, but altogether within ourselves, cannot remain concealed, and in all probability is limited enough to be completely surveyed and fairly estimated, according to its worth or worthlessness. Still less let the reader here expect a critique of books and systems of pure reason; our present object is exclusively a critique of the faculty of pure reason itself. Only when we make this critique our foundation, do we possess a pure touchstone for estimating the philosophical value of ancient and modern writings on this subject; and without this criterion, the incompetent historian or judge decides upon and corrects the groundless assertions of others with his own, which have themselves just as little foundation.

Transcendental philosophy is the idea of a science, for which the *Critique of Pure Reason* must sketch the whole plan architectonically, that is, from principles, with a full guarantee for the validity and stability of all the parts which enter into the building. It is the system of all the principles of pure reason. If this *Critique* itself does not assume the title of transcendental philosophy, it is only because, to be a complete system, it ought to contain a full analysis of all human knowledge *a priori*. Our critique must, indeed, lay before us a complete enumeration of all the radical conceptions which constitute the said pure knowledge. But from the complete analysis of these conceptions themselves, as also from a complete investigation of those derived from them, it abstains with reason; partly because it would be deviating from the end in view to occupy itself with this analysis, since this process is not attended with the difficulty and insecurity to be found in the synthesis, to which our critique is entirely devoted, and partly because it would be inconsistent with the unity of our plan to burden this essay with the vindication of the completeness of such an analysis and deduction, with which, after all, we have at present nothing to do. This completeness of the analysis of these radical conceptions, as well as of the deduction from the conceptions *a priori* which may be given by the analysis, we can, however, easily attain, provided only that we are in possession of all these radical conceptions, which are to serve as principles of the synthesis, and that in respect of this main purpose nothing is wanting.

To the *Critique of Pure Reason*, therefore, belongs all that constitutes transcendental philosophy; and it is the complete idea of transcendental philosophy, but still not the science itself; because it only proceeds so far with the analysis as is necessary to the power of judging completely of our synthetical knowledge *a priori*.

The principal thing we must attend to, in the division of the parts of a science like this, is: that no conceptions must enter it which contain aught empirical; in other words, that the knowledge *a priori* must be completely pure. Hence, although the highest principles and fundamental conceptions of morality are certainly cognitions *a priori*, yet they do not belong to transcendental philosophy; because, though they certainly do not lay the conceptions of pain, pleasure, desires, inclinations, etc. (which are all of empirical origin), at the foundation of its precepts, yet still into the conception of duty—as an obstacle to be overcome, or as an incite ment which should not be made into a motive—these empirical conceptions must necessarily enter, in the construction of a system of pure morality. Transcendental philosophy is consequently a philosophy of the pure and merely speculative reason. For all that is practical, so far as it contains motives, relates to feelings, and these belong to empirical sources of cognition.

If we wish to divide this science from the universal point of view of a science in general, it ought to comprehend, first, a *Doctrine of the Elements*, and, secondly, a *Doctrine of the Method* of pure reason. Each of these main divisions will have its subdivisions, the separate reasons for which we cannot here particularize. Only so much seems necessary, by way of introduction or pre-monition, that there are two sources of human knowledge (which probably spring from a common, but to us unknown root), namely, sense and understanding. By the former, objects are *given* to us; by the latter, *thought*. So far as the faculty of sense may contain representations *a priori*, which form the conditions under which objects are given, in so far it belongs to transcendental philosophy. The transcendental doctrine of sense must form the first part of our science of elements, because the conditions under which alone the objects of human knowledge are given, must precede those under which they are thought.

# TRANSCENDENTAL DOCTRINE OF ELEMENTS

## PART I

### TRANSCENDENTAL AESTHETIC

#### § 1. *Introductory*

IN whatsoever mode, or by whatsoever means, our knowledge may relate to objects, it is at least quite clear, that the only manner in which it immediately relates to them, is by means of an intuition. To this as the indispensable groundwork, all thought points. But an intuition can take place only in so far as the object is given to us. This, again, is only possible, to man at least, on condition that the object affect the mind in a certain manner. The capacity for receiving representations (receptivity) through the mode in which we are affected by objects, is called *sensibility*. By means of sensibility, therefore, objects are given to us, and it alone furnishes us with intuitions; by the understanding they are *thought*, and from it arise conceptions. But all thought must directly, or indirectly, by means of certain signs, relate ultimately to intuitions; consequently, with us, to sensibility, because in no other way can an object be given to us.

The effect of an object upon the faculty of representation, so far as we are affected by the said object, is sensation. That sort of intuition which relates to an object by means of sensation, is called an empirical intuition. The undetermined object of an empirical intuition, is called *phenomenon*. That which in the phenomenon corresponds to the sensation, I term its *matter*; but that which effects that the content of the phenomenon can be arranged under certain relations, I call its *form*. But that in which our sensations are merely arranged, and by which they are susceptible of assuming a certain form, cannot be itself sensation. It is, then, the matter of all phenomena that is given to us *a posteriori*; the form must lie ready *a priori* for them in the mind, and consequently can be regarded separately from all sensation.

I call all representations *pure*, in the transcendental meaning of

41

the word, wherein nothing is met with that belongs to sensation. And accordingly we find existing in the mind *a priori*, the pure form of sensuous intuitions in general, in which all the manifold content of the phenomenal world is arranged and viewed under certain relations. This pure form of sensibility I shall call pure intuition. Thus, if I take away from our representation of a body, all that the understanding thinks as belonging to it, as substance, force, divisibility, etc., and also whatever belongs to sensation, as impenetrability, hardness, colour, etc.; yet there is still something left us from this empirical intuition, namely, extension and shape. These belong to pure intuition, which exists *a priori* in the mind, as a mere form of sensibility, and without any real object of the senses or any sensation.

The science of all the principles of sensibility *a priori*, I call Transcendental Aesthetic.[1] There must, then, be such a science forming the first part of the transcendental doctrine of elements, in contradistinction to that part which contains the principles of pure thought, and which is called transcendental logic.

In the science of transcendental aesthetic accordingly, we shall first isolate sensibility or the sensuous faculty, by separating from it all that is annexed to its perceptions by the conceptions of understanding, so that nothing be left but empirical intuition. In the next place we shall take away from this intuition all that belongs to sensation, so that nothing may remain but pure intuition, and the mere form of phenomena, which is all that the sensibility can afford *a priori*. From this investigation it will be found that there are two pure forms of sensuous intuition, as principles of knowledge *a priori*, namely, space and time. To the consideration of these we shall now proceed.

---

[1] The Germans are the only people who at present use this word to indicate what others call the critique of taste. At the foundation of this term lies the disappointed hope, which the eminent analyst, Baumgarten, conceived, of subjecting the criticism of the beautiful to principles of reason, and so of elevating its rules into a science. But his endeavours were vain. For the said rules or criteria are, in respect to their chief sources, merely empirical, consequently never can serve as determinate laws *a priori*, by which our judgment in matters of taste is to be directed. It is rather our judgment which forms the proper test as to the correctness of the principles. On this account it is advisable to give up the use of the term as designating the critique of taste, and to apply it solely to that doctrine, which is true science—the science of the laws of sensibility—and thus come nearer to the language and the sense of the ancients in their well-known division of the objects of cognition into αισθητα και νοητα, or to share it with speculative philosophy, and employ it partly in a transcendental, partly in a psychological signification.

## SECTION I

### OF SPACE

### § 2. *Metaphysical Exposition of this Conception*

By means of the external sense (a property of the mind), we represent to ourselves objects as without us, and these all in space. Therein alone are their shape, dimensions, and relations to each other determined or determinable. The internal sense, by means of which the mind contemplates itself or its internal state, gives, indeed, no intuition of the soul as an object; yet there is nevertheless a determinate form, under which alone the contemplation of our internal state is possible, so that all which relates to the inward determinations of the mind is represented in relations of time. Of time we cannot have any external intuition, any more than we can have an internal intuition of space. What then are time and space? Are they real existences? Or, are they merely relations or determinations of things, such, however, as would equally belong to these things in themselves, though they should never become objects of intuition; or, are they such as belong only to the form of intuition, and consequently to the subjective constitution of the mind, without which these predicates of time and space could not be attached to any object? In order to become informed on these points, we shall first give an exposition of the conception of space. By exposition, I mean the clear, though not detailed, representation of that which belongs to a conception; and an exposition is metaphysical, when it contains that which represents the conception as given *a priori*.

1. Space is not a conception which has been derived from outward experiences. For, in order that certain sensations may relate to something without me (that is, to something which occupies a different part of space from that in which I am); in like manner, in order that I may represent them not merely as without of and near to each other, but also in separate places, the representation of space must already exist as a foundation. Consequently, the representation of space cannot be borrowed from the relations of external phenomena through experience; but, on the contrary, this external experience is itself only possible through the said antecedent representation.

2. Space then is a necessary representation *a priori*, which serves for the foundation of all external intuitions. We never

can imagine or make a representation to ourselves of the non-existence of space, though we may easily enough think that no objects are found in it. It must, therefore, be considered as the condition of the possibility of phenomena, and by no means as a determination dependent on them, and is a representation *a priori*, which necessarily supplies the basis for external phenomena.

3. Space is no discursive, or as we say, general conception of the relations of things, but a pure intuition. For in the first place, we can only represent to ourselves one space, and when we talk of divers spaces, we mean only parts of one and the same space. Moreover, these parts cannot antecede this one all-embracing space, as the component parts from which the aggregate can be made up, but can be cogitated only as existing in it. Space is essentially one, and multiplicity in it, consequently the general notion of spaces, of this or that space, depends solely upon limitations. Hence it follows that an *a priori* intuition (which is not empirical) lies at the root of all our conceptions of space. Thus, moreover, the principles of geometry—for example, that 'in a triangle, two sides together are greater than the third,' are never deduced from general conceptions of line and triangle, but from intuition, and this *a priori*, with apodeictic certainty.

4. Space is represented as an infinite given quantity. Now every conception must indeed be considered as a representation which is contained in an infinite multitude of different possible representations, which, therefore, comprises these under itself; but no conception, as such, can be so conceived, as if it contained within itself an infinite multitude of representations. Nevertheless, space is so conceived of, for all parts of space are equally capable of being produced to infinity. Consequently, the original representation of space is an intuition *a priori*, and not a conception.

## § 3. *Transcendental Exposition of the Conception of Space*

By a transcendental exposition, I mean the explanation of a conception, as a principle, whence can be discerned the possibility of other synthetical *a priori* cognitions. For this purpose, it is requisite, firstly, that such cognitions do really flow from the given conception; and, secondly, that the said cognitions are only possible under the presupposition of a given mode of explaining this conception.

Geometry is a science which determines the properties of space synthetically, and yet *a priori*. What, then, must be our representation of space, in order that such a cognition of it may be possible? It must be originally intuition, for from a mere conception, no propositions can be deduced which go out beyond the conception,[1] and yet this happens in geometry. (Introd. V.) But this intuition must be found in the mind *a priori*, that is, before any perception of objects, consequently must be pure, not empirical, intuition. For geometrical principles are always apodeictic, that is, united with the consciousness of their necessity, as: 'Space has only three dimensions.' But propositions of this kind cannot be empirical judgments, nor conclusions from them. (Introd. II.) Now, how can an external intuition anterior to objects themselves, and in which our conception of objects can be determined *a priori*, exist in the human mind? Obviously not otherwise than in so far as it has its seat in the subject only, as the *formal* capacity of the subject's being affected by objects, and thereby of obtaining immediate representation, that is, intuition; consequently, only as the *form of the external sense* in general.

Thus it is only by means of our explanation that the possibility of geometry, as a synthetical science *a priori*, becomes comprehensible. Every mode of explanation which does not show us this possibility, although in appearance it may be similar to ours, can with the utmost certainty be distinguished from it by these marks.

## § 4. *Conclusions from the foregoing Conceptions*

(*a*) Space does not represent any property of objects as things in themselves, nor does it represent them in their relations to each other; in other words, space does not represent to us any determination of objects such as attaches to the objects themselves, and would remain, even though all subjective conditions of the intuition were abstracted. For neither absolute nor relative determinations of objects can be intuited prior to the existence of the things to which they belong, and therefore not *a priori*.

(*b*) Space is nothing else than the form of all phenomena of the external sense, that is, the subjective condition of the sensibility, under which alone external intuition is possible. Now, because the receptivity or capacity of the subject to be affected by objects necessarily antecedes all intuitions of these objects, it is easily understood how the form of all phenomena can be given in the mind previous to all actual perceptions, therefore *a priori*, and how it, as a pure intuition, in which all objects must be determined,

---

[1] That is, the analysis of a conception only gives you what is contained in it, and does not add to your knowledge of the object of which you have a conception, but merely evolves it.—*Tr.*

can contain principles of the relations of these objects prior to all experience.

It is therefore from the human point of view only that we can speak of space, extended objects, etc. If we depart from the subjective condition, under which alone we can obtain external intuition, or, in other words, by means of which we are affected by objects, the representation of space has no meaning whatsoever. This predicate [of space] is only applicable to things in so far as they appear to us, that is, are objects of sensibility. The constant form of this receptivity, which we call sensibility, is a necessary condition of all relations in which objects can be intuited as existing without us, and when abstraction of these objects is made, is a pure intuition, to which we give the name of space. It is clear that we cannot make the special conditions of sensibility into conditions of the possibility of things, but only of the possibility of their existence as far as they are phenomena. And so we may correctly say that space contains all which can appear to us externally, but not all things considered as things in themselves, be they intuited or not, or by whatsoever subject one will. As to the intuitions of other thinking beings, we cannot judge whether they are or are not bound by the same conditions which limit our own intuition, and which for us are universally valid. If we join the limitation of a judgment to the conception of the subject, then the judgment will possess unconditioned validity. For example, the proposition, 'All objects are beside each other in space,' is valid only under the limitation that these things are taken as objects of our sensuous intuition. But if I join the condition to the conception, and say, 'All things, as external phenomena, are beside each other in space,' then the rule is valid universally, and without any limitation. Our expositions, consequently, teach the *reality* (i.e. the objective validity) of space in regard of all which can be presented to us externally as object, and at the same time also the *ideality* of space in regard to objects when they are considered by means of reason as things in themselves, that is, without reference to the constitution of our sensibility. We maintain, therefore, the *empirical reality* of space in regard to all possible external experience, although we must admit its *transcendental ideality*; in other words, that it is nothing, so soon as we withdraw the condition upon which the possibility of all experience depends, and look upon space as something that belongs to things in themselves.

But, with the exception of space, there is no representation, subjective and referring to something external to us, which could be called objective *a priori*. For there are no other subjective representations from which we can deduce synthetical propositions *a priori*, as we can from the intuition of space. (See § 3.) Therefore, to speak accurately, no ideality whatever belongs to these, although they agree in this respect with the representation of space, that they belong merely to the subjective nature of the mode of sensuous perception; such a mode, for example, as that of sight, of hearing, and of feeling, by means of the sensations of colour, sound, and heat, but which, because they are only sensations, and not intuitions, do not of themselves give us the cognition of any object, least of all, an *a priori* cognition. My purpose, in the above remark, is merely this: to guard any one against illustrating the asserted ideality of space by examples quite insufficient, for example, by colour, taste, etc.; for these must be contemplated not as properties of things, but only as changes in the subject, changes which may be different in different men. For, in such a case, that which is originally a mere phenomenon, a rose, for example, is taken by the empirical understanding for a thing in itself, though to every different eye, in respect of its colour, it may appear different. On the contrary, the transcendental conception of phenomena in space is a critical admonition, that, in general, nothing which is intuited in space is a thing in itself, and that space is not a form which belongs as a property to things; but that objects are quite unknown to us in themselves, and what we call outward objects, are nothing else but mere representations of our sensibility, whose form is space, but whose real correlate, the thing in itself, is not known by means of these representations, nor ever can be, but respecting which, in experience, no inquiry is ever made.

## SECTION II

### OF TIME

### § 5. *Metaphysical Exposition of this Conception*

1. TIME is not an empirical conception. For neither co-existence nor succession would be perceived by us, if the representation of time did not exist as a foundation *a priori*. Without this presupposition we could not represent to ourselves that things exist together at one and the same time, or at different times, that is, contemporaneously, or in succession.

2. Time is a necessary representation, lying at the foundation

of all our intuitions. With regard to phenomena in general, we cannot think away time from them, and represent them to ourselves as out of and unconnected with time, but we can quite well represent to ourselves time void of phenomena. Time is therefore given *a priori*. In it alone is all reality of phenomena possible. These may all be annihilated in thought, but time itself, as the universal condition of their possibility, cannot be so annulled.

3. On this necessity *a priori* is also founded the possibility of apodeictic principles of the relations of time, or axioms of time in general, such as: 'Time has only one dimension,' 'Different times are not co-existent but successive' (as different spaces are not successive but co-existent). These principles cannot be derived from experience, for it would give neither strict universality, nor apodeictic certainty. We should only be able to say, 'so common experience teaches us,' but not it must be so. They are valid as rules, through which, in general, experience is possible; and they instruct us respecting experience, and not by means of it.

4. Time is not a discursive, or as it is called, general conception, but a pure form of the sensuous intuition. Different times are merely parts of one and the same time. But the representation which can only be given by a single object is an intuition. Besides, the proposition that different times cannot be co-existent, could not be derived from a general conception. For this proposition is synthetical, and therefore cannot spring out of conceptions alone. It is therefore contained immediately in the intuition and representation of time.

5. The infinity of time signifies nothing more than that every determined quantity of time is possible only through limitations of one time lying at the foundation. Consequently, the original representation, time, must be given as unlimited. But as the determinate representation of the parts of time and of every quantity of an object can only be obtained by limitation, the *complete* representation of time must not be furnished by means of conceptions, for these contain only partial representations. Conceptions, on the contrary, must have immediate intuition for their basis.

## § 6. *Transcendental Exposition of the Conception of Time*

I may here refer to what is said above (§5, 3), where, for the sake of brevity, I have placed under the head of metaphysical exposition, that which is properly transcendental. Here I shall add that the conception of change, and with it the conception of motion, as change of place, is possible only through and in the representation of time; that if this representation were not an intuition (internal) *a priori*, no conception, of whatever kind, could render comprehensible the possibility of change, in other words, of a conjunction of contradictorily opposed predicates in one and the same object, for example, the presence of a thing in a place and the non-presence of the same thing in the same place. It is only in time that it is possible to meet with two contradictorily opposed determinations in one thing, that is, after each other.[1] Thus our conception of time explains the possibility of so much synthetical knowledge *a priori*, as is exhibited in the general doctrine of motion, which is not a little fruitful.

## § 7. *Conclusions from the above Conceptions*

(*a*) Time is not something which subsists of itself, or which inheres in things as an objective determination, and therefore remains, when abstraction is made of the subjective conditions of the intuition of things. For in the former case, it would be something real, yet without presenting to any power of perception any real object. In the latter case, as an order or determination inherent in things themselves, it could not be antecedent to things, as their condition, nor discerned or intuited by means of synthetical propositions *a priori*. But all this is quite possible when we regard time as merely the subjective condition under which all our intuitions take place. For in that case, this form of the inward intuition can be represented prior to the objects, and consequently *a priori*.

(*b*) Time is nothing else than the form of the internal sense, that is, of the intuitions of self and of our internal state. For time cannot be any determination of outward phenomena. It has to do neither with shape nor position; on the contrary, it determines the relation of representations in our internal state. And precisely because this internal intuition presents to us no shape or form, we endeavour to supply this want by analogies, and represent the course of time by a line progressing to infinity, the content of which constitutes a series which is only of one dimension; and we conclude from the properties of this line as to all the properties of time, with this single exception, that the parts of the line are co-existent, whilst those of time are successive. From this it is

[1] Kant's meaning is: You cannot affirm and deny the same thing of a subject, except by means of the representation, time. No other idea, intuition, or conception, or whatever other form of thought there be, can mediate the connection of such predicates.—*Tr*.

clear also that the representation of time is itself an intuition,
because all its relations can be expressed in an external intuition.

(c) Time is the formal condition *a priori* of all phenomena
whatsoever. Space, as the pure form of external intuition, is
limited as a condition *a priori* to external phenomena alone. On
the other hand, because all representations, whether they have or
have not external things for their objects, still in themselves, as
determinations of the mind, belong to our internal state; and
because this internal state is subject to the formal condition of
the internal intuition, that is, to time—time is a condition *a priori*
of all phenomena whatsoever—the *immediate* condition of all
internal, and thereby the *mediate* condition of all external phenomena. If I can say *a priori*, 'All outward phenomena are in space,
and determined *a priori* according to the relations of space,' I can
also, from the principle of the internal sense, affirm universally,
'All phenomena in general, that is, all objects of the senses, are in
time, and stand necessarily in relations of time.'

If we abstract our internal intuition of ourselves, and all external
intuitions, possible only by virtue of this internal intuition, and
presented to us by our faculty of representation, and consequently
take objects as they are in themselves, then time is nothing. It
is only of objective validity in regard to phenomena, because these
are things which we regard as objects of our senses. It is no
longer objective, if we make abstraction of the sensuousness of
our intuition, in other words, of that mode of representation which
is peculiar to us, and speak of things in general. Time is therefore
merely a subjective condition of our (human) intuition (which is
always sensuous, that is, so far as we are affected by objects), and
in itself, independently of the mind or subject, is nothing. Nevertheless, in respect of all phenomena, consequently of all things
which come within the sphere of our experience, it is necessarily
objective. We cannot say, 'All things are in time,' because in this
conception of things in general, we abstract and make no mention
of any sort of intuition of things. But this is the proper condition
under which time belongs to our representation of objects. If we
add the condition to the conception, and say, 'All things, as
phenomena, that is, objects of sensuous intuition, are in time,'
then the proposition has its sound objective validity and universality
*a priori*.

What we have now set forth teaches, therefore, the empirical
reality of time; that is, its objective validity in reference to all
objects which can ever be presented to our senses. And as our
intuition is always sensuous, no object ever can be presented to

us in experience, which does not come under the conditions of time. On the other hand, we deny to time all claim to absolute reality; that is, we deny that it, without having regard to the form of our sensuous intuition, absolutely inheres in things as a condition or property. Such properties as belong to objects as things in themselves, never can be presented to us through the medium of the senses. Herein consists, therefore, the transcendental ideality of time, according to which, if we abstract the subjective conditions of sensuous intuition, it is nothing, and cannot be reckoned as subsisting or inhering in objects as things in themselves, independently of its relation to our intuition. This ideality, like that of space, is not to be proved or illustrated by fallacious analogies with sensations, for this reason—that in such arguments or illustrations, we make the presupposition that the phenomenon, in which such and such predicates inhere, has objective reality, while in this case we can only find such an objective reality as is itself empirical, that is, regards the object as a mere phenomenon. In reference to this subject, see the remark in Section I (pages 46–7).

## § 8. *Elucidation*

Against this theory, which grants empirical reality to time, but denies to it absolute and transcendental reality, I have heard from intelligent men an objection so unanimously urged, that I conclude that it must naturally present itself to every reader to whom these considerations are novel. It runs thus: 'Changes are real (this the continual change in our own representations demonstrates, even though the existence of all external phenomena, together with their changes, is denied). Now, changes are only possible in time, and therefore time must be something real.' But there is no difficulty in answering this. I grant the whole argument. Time, no doubt, is something real, that is, it is the real form of our internal intuition. It therefore has subjective reality, in reference to our internal experience, that is, I have really the representation of time, and of my determinations therein. Time, therefore, is not to be regarded as an object, but as the mode of representation of myself as an object. But if I could intuite myself, or be intuited by another being, without this condition of sensibility, then those very determinations which we now represent to ourselves as changes, would present to us a knowledge in which the representation of time, and consequently of change, would not appear. The empirical reality of time, therefore, remains, as the condition of all our experience. But absolute reality, according to what has been said above, cannot be granted it. Time is nothing but the form of our internal intuition.[1] If we take away from it the special condition of our sensibility, the conception of time also vanishes; and it inheres not in the objects themselves, but solely in the subject (or mind) which intuites them.

But the reason why this objection is so unanimously brought against our doctrine of time, and that too by disputants who cannot start any intelligible arguments against the doctrine of the ideality of space, is this—they have no hope of demonstrating apodeictically the absolute reality of space, because the doctrine of idealism is against them, according to which the reality of external objects is not capable of any strict proof. On the other hand, the reality of the object of our internal sense (that is, myself and my internal state) is clear immediately through consciousness. The former—external objects in space—might be a mere delusion, but the latter—the object of my internal perception—is undeniably real. They do not, however, reflect that both, without question of their reality as representations, belong only to the genus phenomenon, which has always two aspects, the one, the object considered as a thing in itself, without regard to the mode of intuiting it, and the nature of which remains for this very reason problematical, the other, the form of our intuition of the object, which must be sought not in the object as a thing in itself, but in the subject to which it appears—which form of intuition nevertheless belongs really and necessarily to the phenomenal object.

Time and space are, therefore, two sources of knowledge, from which, *a priori*, various synthetical cognitions can be drawn. Of this we find a striking example in the cognitions of space and its relations, which form the foundation of pure mathematics. They are the two pure forms of all intuitions, and thereby make synthetical propositions *a priori* possible. But these sources of knowledge being merely conditions of our sensibility, do therefore, and as such, strictly determine their own range and purpose, in that they do not and cannot present objects as things in themselves, but are applicable to them solely in so far as they are considered as sensuous phenomena. The sphere of phenomena is the only sphere of their validity, and if we venture out of this, no further objective use can be made of them. For the rest, this formal

[1] I can indeed say 'my representations follow one another, or are successive;' but this means only that we are conscious of them as in a succession, that is, according to the form of the internal sense. Time, therefore, is not a thing in itself, nor is it any objective determination pertaining to, or inherent in things.

# OF SPACE AND TIME—ELUCIDATORY REMARKS 53

reality of time and space leaves the validity of our empirical knowledge unshaken; for our certainty in that respect is equally firm, whether these forms necessarily inhere in the things themselves, or only in our intuitions of them. On the other hand, those who maintain the absolute reality of time and space, whether as essentially subsisting, or only inhering, as modifications, in things, must find themselves at utter variance with the principles of experience itself. For, if they decide for the first view, and make space and time into substances, this being the side taken by mathematical natural philosophers, they must admit two self-subsisting nonentities, infinite and eternal, which exist (yet without there being anything real) for the purpose of containing in themselves everything that is real. If they adopt the second view of inherence, which is preferred by some metaphysical natural philosophers, and regard space and time as relations (contiguity in space or succession in time), abstracted from experience, though represented confusedly in this state of separation, they find themselves in that case necessitated to deny the validity of mathematical doctrines *a priori* in reference to real things (for example, in space)—at all events their apodeictic certainty. For such certainty cannot be found in an *a posteriori* proposition; and the conceptions *a priori* of space and time are, according to this opinion, mere creations of the imagination,[1] having their source really in experience, inasmuch as, out of relations abstracted from experience, imagination has made up something which contains, indeed, general statements of these relations, yet of which no application can be made without the restrictions attached thereto by nature. The former of these parties gains this advantage, that they keep the sphere of phenomena free for mathematical science. On the other hand, these very conditions (space and time) embarrass them greatly, when the understanding endeavours to pass the limits of that sphere. The latter has, indeed, this advantage, that the representations of space and time do not come in their way when they wish to judge of objects, not as phenomena, but merely in their relation to the understanding. Devoid, however, of a true and objectively valid *a priori* intuition, they can neither furnish any basis for the possibility of mathematical cognitions *a priori*, nor bring the propositions of experience into necessary accordance with those of mathematics. In our theory of the true nature of these two original forms of the sensibility, both difficulties are surmounted.

[1] This word is here used, and will be hereafter always used, in its primitive sense. That meaning of it which denotes a poetical inventive power, is a secondary one.—*Tr.*

In conclusion, that Transcendental Aesthetic cannot contain any more than these two elements (space and time) is sufficiently obvious from the fact that all other conceptions appertaining to sensibility, even that of motion, which unites in itself both elements, presuppose something empirical. Motion, for example, presupposes the perception of something movable. But space considered in itself contains nothing movable, consequently motion must be something which is found in space only through experience—in other words, is an empirical datum. In like manner, Transcendental Aesthetic cannot number the conception of change among its data *a priori*; for time itself does not change, but only something which is in time. To acquire the conception of change, therefore, the perception of some existing object and of the succession of its determinations, in one word, experience, is necessary.

## § 9. *General Remarks on Transcendental Aesthetic*

I. In order to prevent any misunderstanding, it will be requisite, in the first place, to recapitulate, as clearly as possible, what our opinion is with respect to the fundamental nature of our sensuous cognition in general. We have intended, then, to say, that all our intuition is nothing but the representation of phenomena; that the things which we intuite, are not in themselves the same as our representations of them in intuition, nor are their relations in themselves so constituted as they appear to us; and that if we take away the subject, or even only the subjective constitution of our senses in general, then not only the nature and relations of objects in space and time, but even space and time themselves disappear; and that these, as phenomena, cannot exist in themselves, but only in us. What may be the nature of objects considered as things in themselves and without reference to the receptivity of our sensibility is quite unknown to us. We know nothing more than our own mode of perceiving them, which is peculiar to us, and which, though not of necessity pertaining to every animated being, is so to the whole human race. With this alone we have to do. Space and time are the pure forms thereof; sensation the matter. The former alone can we cognize *a priori*, that is, antecedent to all actual perception; and for this reason such cognition is called pure intuition. The latter is that in our cognition which is called cognition *a posteriori*, that is, empirical intuition. The former appertain absolutely and necessarily to our sensibility, of whatsoever kind our sensations may be; the latter may be of very diversified character. Supposing that we should carry our empirical intuition even to the very highest degree of clearness, we should not thereby advance one step nearer to a knowledge of the constitution of objects as things in themselves. For we could only, at best, arrive at a complete cognition of our own mode of intuition, that is, of our sensibility, and this always under the conditions originally attaching to the subject, namely, the conditions of space and time; while the question—'What are objects considered as things in themselves?' remains unanswerable even after the most thorough examination of the phenomenal world.

To say, then, that all our sensibility is nothing but the confused representation of things containing exclusively that which belongs to them as things in themselves, and this under an accumulation of characteristic marks and partial representations which we cannot distinguish in consciousness, is a falsification of the conception of sensibility and phenomenization, which renders our whole doctrine thereof empty and useless. The difference between a confused and a clear representation is merely logical and has nothing to do with content. No doubt the conception of *right*, as employed by a sound understanding, contains all that the most subtle investigation could unfold from it, although, in the ordinary practical use of the word, we are not conscious of the manifold representations comprised in the conception. But we cannot for this reason assert that the ordinary conception is a sensuous one, containing a mere phenomenon, for *right* cannot appear as a phenomenon; but the conception of it lies in the understanding, and represents a property (the moral property) of actions, which belongs to them in themselves. On the other hand, the representation in intuition of a body contains nothing which could belong to an object considered as a thing in itself, but merely the phenomenon or appearance of something, and the mode in which we are affected by that appearance; and this receptivity of our faculty of cognition is called sensibility, and remains *toto caelo* different from the cognition of an object in itself, even though we should examine the content of the phenomenon to the very bottom.

It must be admitted that the Leibnitz-Wolfian philosophy has assigned an entirely erroneous point of view to all investigations into the nature and origin of our cognitions, inasmuch as it regards the distinction between the sensuous and the intellectual as merely logical, whereas it is plainly transcendental, and concerns not merely the clearness or obscurity, but the content and origin of both. For the faculty of sensibility not only does not present us with an indistinct and confused cognition of objects as things in themselves, but, in fact, gives us no knowledge of these at all. On the contrary, so soon as we abstract in thought our own subjective nature, the object represented, with the properties ascribed to it by sensuous intuition, entirely disappears, because it was only this subjective nature that determined the form of the object as a phenomenon.

In phenomena, we commonly, indeed, distinguish that which essentially belongs to the intuition of them, and is valid for the sensuous faculty of every human being, from that which belongs to the same intuition accidentally, as valid not for the sensuous faculty in general, but for a particular state or organization of this or that sense. Accordingly, we are accustomed to say that the former is a cognition which represents the object itself, whilst the latter presents only a particular appearance or phenomenon thereof. This distinction, however, is only empirical. If we stop here (as is usual), and do not regard the empirical intuition as itself a mere phenomenon (as we ought to do), in which nothing that can appertain to a thing in itself is to be found, our transcendental distinction is lost, and we believe that we cognize objects as things in themselves, although in the whole range of the sensuous world, investigate the nature of its objects as profoundly as we may, we have to do with nothing but phenomena. Thus, we call the rainbow a mere appearance of phenomenon in a sunny shower, and the rain, the reality or thing in itself; and this is right enough, if we understand the latter conception in a merely physical sense, that is, as that which in universal experience, and under whatever conditions of sensuous perception, is known in intuition to be so and so determined, and not otherwise. But if we consider this empirical datum generally, and inquire, without reference to its accordance with all our senses, whether there can be discovered in it aught which represents an object as a thing in itself (the raindrops of course are not such, for they are, as phenomena, empirical objects), the question of the relation of the representation to the object is transcendental; and not only are the raindrops mere phenomena, but even their circular form, nay, the space itself through which they fall, is nothing in itself, but both are mere modifications or fundamental dispositions of our sensuous intuition, whilst the transcendental object remains for us utterly unknown.

The second important concern of our Aesthetic is, that it do not obtain favour merely as a plausible hypothesis, but possess as undoubted a character of certainty as can be demanded of any theory which is to serve for an organon. In order fully to convince the reader of this certainty, we shall select a case which will serve to make its validity apparent, and also to illustrate what has been said in § 3.

Suppose, then, that space and time are in themselves objective, and conditions of the possibility of objects as things in themselves. In the first place, it is evident that both present us with very many apodeictic and synthetic propositions *a priori*, but especially space—and for this reason we shall prefer it for investigation at present. As the propositions of geometry are cognized synthetically *a priori*, and with apodeictic certainty, I inquire—whence do you obtain propositions of this kind, and on what basis does the understanding rest, in order to arrive at such absolutely necessary and universally valid truths?

There is no other way than through intuitions or conceptions, as such; and these are given either *a priori* or *a posteriori*. The latter, namely, empirical conceptions, together with the empirical intuition on which they are founded, cannot afford any synthetical proposition, except such as is itself also empirical, that is, a proposition of experience. But an empirical proposition cannot possess the qualities of necessity and absolute universality, which, nevertheless, are the characteristics of all geometrical propositions. As to the first and only means to arrive at such cognitions, namely, through mere conceptions or intuitions *a priori*, it is quite clear that from mere conceptions no synthetical cognitions, but only analytical ones, can be obtained. Take, for example, the proposition: 'Two straight lines cannot enclose a space, and with these alone no figure is possible,' and try to deduce it from the conception of a straight line and the number two; or take the proposition: 'It is possible to construct a figure with three straight lines,' and endeavour, in like manner, to deduce it from the mere conception of a straight line and the number three. All your endeavours are in vain, and you find yourself forced to have recourse to intuition, as, in fact, geometry always does. You therefore give yourself an object in intuition. But of what kind is this intuition? Is it a pure *a priori*, or is it an empirical intuition? If the latter, then neither an universally valid, much less an apodeictic proposition can arise from it, for experience never can give us any such proposition. You must therefore give yourself an object *a priori* in intuition, and upon that ground your synthetical proposition. Now if there did not exist within you a faculty of intuition *a priori*; if this subjective condition were not in respect to its form also the universal condition *a priori* under which alone the object of this external intuition is itself possible; if the object (that is, the triangle) were something in itself, without relation to you the subject; how could you affirm that that which lies necessarily in your subjective conditions in order to construct a triangle, must also necessarily belong to the triangle in itself? For to your conceptions of three lines, you could not add anything new (that is, the figure); which, therefore, must necessarily be found in the object, because the object is given before your cognition, and not by means of it. If, therefore, space (and time also) were not a mere form of your intuition, which contains conditions *a priori*, under which alone things can become external objects for you, and without which subjective conditions the objects are in themselves nothing, you could not construct any synthetical proposition whatsoever regarding external objects. It is therefore not merely possible or probable, but indubitably certain, that space and time, as the necessary conditions of all our external and internal experience, are merely subjective conditions of all our intuitions, in relation to which all objects are therefore mere phenomena, and not things in themselves, presented to us in this particular manner. And for this reason, in respect to the form of phenomena, much may be said *a priori*, whilst of the thing in itself, which may lie at the foundation of these phenomena, it is impossible to say anything.

II. In confirmation of this theory of the ideality of the external as well as internal sense, consequently of all objects of sense, as mere phenomena, we may especially remark, that all in our cognition that belongs to intuition contains nothing more than mere relations—the feelings of pain and pleasure, and the will, which are not cognitions, are excepted—the relations, to wit, of place in an intuition (extension), change of place (motion), and laws according to which this change is determined (moving forces). That, however, which is present in this or that place, or any operation going on, or result taking place in the things themselves, with the exception of change of place, is not given to us by intuition. Now by means of mere relations, a thing cannot be known in itself; and it may therefore be fairly concluded, that, as through the external sense nothing but mere representations of relations are given us, the said external sense in its representation can contain only the relation of the object to the subject, but not the essential nature of the object as a thing in itself.

The same is the case with the internal intuition, not only because, in the internal intuition, the representation of the external senses constitutes the material with which the mind is occupied; but because time, in which we place, and which itself antecedes the consciousness of, these representations in experience, and which, as the formal condition of the mode according to which objects are placed in the mind, lies at the foundation of them, contains relations of the successive, the co-existent, and of that which always must be co-existent with succession, the permanent. Now that which, as representation, can antecede every exercise of thought (of an object), is intuition; and when it contains nothing but relations, it is the form of the intuition, which, as it presents us with no representation, except in so far as something is placed in the mind, can be nothing else than the mode in which the mind is affected by its own activity, to wit—its presenting to itself representations, consequently the mode in which the mind is affected by itself; that is, it can be nothing but an internal sense in respect to its form. Everything that is represented through the medium of sense is so far phenomenal; consequently, we must either refuse altogether to admit an internal sense, or the subject, which is the object of that sense, could only be represented by it as phenomenon, and not as it would judge of itself, if its intuition were pure spontaneous activity, that is, were intellectual. The difficulty here lies wholly in the question—How can the subject have an internal intuition of itself?—but this difficulty is common to every theory. The consciousness of self (apperception) is the simple representation of the 'Ego;' and if by means of that representation alone, all the manifold representations in the subject were spontaneously given, then our internal intuition would be intellectual. This consciousness in man requires an internal perception of the manifold representations which are previously given in the subject; and the manner in which these representations are given in the mind without spontaneity, must, on account of this difference (the want of spontaneity), be called sensibility. If the faculty of self-consciousness is to apprehend what lies in the mind, it must affect that, and can in this way alone produce an intuition of self. But the form of this intuition, which lies in the original constitution of the mind, determines, in the representation of time, the manner in which the manifold representations are to combine themselves in the mind; since the subject intuites itself, not as it would represent itself immediately and spontaneously, but according to the manner in which the mind is internally affected, consequently, as it appears, and not as it is.

III. When we say that the intuition of external objects, and also the self-intuition of the subject, represent both, objects and subject, in space and time, as they affect our senses, that is, as they appear—this is by no means equivalent to asserting that these objects are mere illusory appearances. For when we speak of things as phenomena, the objects, nay, even the properties which we ascribe to them, are looked upon as really given; only that, in so far as this or that property depends upon the mode of intuition of the subject, in the relation of the given object to the subject, the object as phenomenon is to be distinguished from the object as a thing in itself. Thus I do not say that bodies seem or appear to be external to me, or that my soul seems merely to be given in my self-consciousness, although I maintain that the properties of space and time, in conformity to which I set both, as the condition of their existence, abide in my mode of intuition, and not in the objects in themselves. It would be my own fault, if out of that which I should reckon as phenomenon, I made mere illusory appearance.[1] But this will not happen, because of our principle of the ideality of all sensuous intuitions. On the contrary, if we ascribe objective reality to these forms of representation, it becomes impossible to avoid changing everything into mere appearance. For if we regard space and time as properties, which must be found in objects as things in themselves, as *sine quibus non* of the possibility of their existence, and reflect on the absurdities in which we then find ourselves involved, inasmuch as we are compelled to admit the existence of two infinite things, which are nevertheless not substances, nor anything really inhering in substances, nay, to admit that they are the necessary conditions of the existence of all things, and moreover, that they must continue to exist, although all existing things were annihilated—we cannot blame the good Berkeley for degrading bodies to mere illusory appearances. Nay, even our own existence, which would in this case depend upon the self-existent reality of such a mere nonentity as time, would necessarily be changed with it into mere appearance—an absurdity which no one has as yet been guilty of.

IV. In natural theology, where we think of an object—God —which never can be an object of intuition to us, and even to Himself can never be an object of sensuous intuition, we carefully avoid attributing to His intuition the conditions of space and

[1] The predicates of the phenomenon can be affixed to the object itself in relation to our sensuous faculty; for example, the red colour or the perfume to the rose. But (illusory) appearance never can be attributed as a predicate to an object, for this very reason, that it attributes to this object in itself that which belongs to it only in relation to our sensuous faculty, or to the subject in general, e.g. the two handles which were formerly ascribed to Saturn. That which is never to be found in the object itself, but always in the relation of the object to the subject, and which moreover is inseparable from our representation of the object, we denominate phenomenon. Thus the predicates of space and time are rightly attributed to objects of the senses as such, and in this there is no illusion. On the contrary, if I ascribe redness to the rose as a thing in itself, or to Saturn his handles, or extension to all external objects, considered as things in themselves, without regarding the determinate relation of these objects to the subject, and without limiting my judgment to that relation—then, and then only, arises illusion.

time—and intuition all His cognition must be, and not thought, which always includes limitation. But with what right can we do this if we make them forms of objects as things in themselves, and such, moreover, as would continue to exist as *a priori* conditions of the existence of things, even though the things themselves were annihilated? For as conditions of all existence in general, space and time must be conditions of the existence of the Supreme Being also. But if we do not thus make them objective forms of all things, there is no other way left than to make them subjective forms of our mode of intuition—external and internal; which is called sensuous, because it is not primitive, that is, is not such as gives in itself the existence of the object of the intuition (a mode of intuition which, so far as we can judge, can belong only to the Creator), but is dependent on the existence of the object, is possible, therefore, only on condition that the representative faculty of the subject is affected by the object.

It is, moreover, not necessary that we should limit the mode of intuition in space and time to the sensuous faculty of man. It may well be, that all finite thinking beings must necessarily in this respect agree with man (though as to this we cannot decide), but sensibility does not on account of this universality cease to be sensibility, for this very reason, that it is a deduced (*intuitus derivativus*), and not an original (*intuitus originalis*), consequently not an intellectual intuition, and this intuition, as such, for reasons above mentioned, seems to belong solely to the Supreme Being, but never to a being dependent, *quoad* its existence, as well as its intuition (which its existence determines and limits relatively to given objects). This latter remark, however, must be taken only as an illustration, and not as any proof of the truth of our aesthetical theory.

## § 10. *Conclusion of the Transcendental Aesthetic*

We have now completely before us one part of the solution of the grand general problem of transcendental philosophy, namely, the question—How are synthetical propositions *a priori* possible? That is to say, we have shown that we are in possession of pure *a priori* intuitions, namely, space and time, in which we find, when in a judgment *a priori* we pass out beyond the given conception, something which is not discoverable in that conception, but is certainly found *a priori* in the intuition which corresponds to the conception, and can be united synthetically with it. But the judgments which these pure intuitions enable us to make, never reach farther than to objects of the senses, and are valid only for objects of possible experience.

# TRANSCENDENTAL DOCTRINE OF ELEMENTS

## PART II

### TRANSCENDENTAL LOGIC

#### INTRODUCTION

##### IDEA OF A TRANSCENDENTAL LOGIC

### I

#### *Of Logic in general*

OUR knowledge springs from two main sources in the mind, the first of which is the faculty or power of receiving representations (receptivity for impressions); the second is the power of cognizing by means of these representations (spontaneity in the production of conceptions). Through the first an object is given to us; through the second, it is, in relation to the representation (which is a mere determination of the mind), thought. Intuition and conceptions constitute, therefore, the elements of all our knowledge, so that neither conceptions without an intuition in some way corresponding to them, nor intuition without conceptions, can afford us a cognition. Both are either pure or empirical. They are empirical, when sensation (which presupposes the actual presence of the object) is contained in them; and pure, when no sensation is mixed with the representation. Sensations we may call the matter of sensuous cognition. Pure intuition consequently contains merely the form under which something is intuited, and pure conception only the form of the thought of an object. Only pure intuitions and pure conceptions are possible *a priori*; the empirical only *a posteriori*.

We apply the term *sensibility* to the receptivity of the mind for impressions, in so far as it is in some way affected; and, on the other hand, we call the faculty of spontaneously producing representations, or the spontaneity of cognition, *understanding*. Our nature is so constituted, that intuition with us never can be other than sensuous, that is, it contains only the mode in which we are affected by objects. On the other hand, the faculty of thinking the object of sensuous intuition, is the understanding. Neither of these faculties has a preference over the other. Without the sensuous faculty no object would be given to us, and without the understanding no object would be thought. Thoughts without content are void; intuitions without conceptions, blind. Hence it is as necessary for the mind to make its conceptions sensuous (that is, to join to them the object in intuition), as to make its intuitions intelligible (that is, to bring them under conceptions). Neither of these faculties can exchange its proper function. Understanding cannot intuite, and the sensuous faculty cannot think. In no other way than from the united operation of both, can knowledge arise. But no one ought, on this account, to overlook the difference of the elements contributed by each; we have rather great reason carefully to separate and distinguish them. We therefore distinguish the science of the laws of sensibility, that is, Aesthetic, from the science of the laws of the understanding, that is, Logic.

Now, logic in its turn may be considered as twofold—namely, as logic of the general [universal],[1] or of the particular use of the understanding. The first contains the absolutely necessary laws

---

[1] Logic is nothing but *the science of the laws of thought, as thought*. It concerns itself only with the *form* of thought, and takes no cognizance of the *matter*—that is, of the infinitude of the objects to which thought is applied.

Now Kant is wrong, when he divides logic into logic of the general and of the particular use of the understanding.

He says the logic of the particular use of the understanding contains the laws of right thinking upon any particular set of objects. This sort of logic he calls the organon of this or that science. It is difficult to discover what he means by his logic of the particular use of the understanding. From his description, we are left in doubt whether he means by this logic *induction*, that is, the organon of science in general, or the laws which regulate the objects, a science of which he seeks to establish. In either case, the application of the term logic is inadmissible. To regard logic as the organon of science, is absurd, as indeed Kant himself afterwards shows (p. 67). It knows nothing of this or that object. The *matter* employed in syllogisms is used for the sake of example only; all forms of syllogisms might be expressed in signs. Logicians have never been able clearly to see this. They have never been able clearly to define the extent of their science, to know, in fact, what their science really treated of. They have never seen that it has to do only with the *formal*, and never with the *material* in thought. The science has broken down its proper barriers to let in contributions from metaphysics, psychology, etc. It is common enough, for example, to say that Bacon's *Novum Organum* entirely superseded the *Organon* of Aristotle. But the one states the laws under which a knowledge of objects is possible; the other the subjective laws of thought. The spheres of the two are utterly distinct.

Kant very properly states that pure logic is alone properly science. Strictly speaking, applied logic cannot be a division of general logic. It is more correctly applied psychology—psychology treating in a practical manner of the conditions under which thought is employed.

It may be noted here, that what Kant calls Transcendental Logic is properly not logic at all, but a division of metaphysics. For his Categories contain matter—as regards thought at least. Take, for example, the category of *Existence*. These categories, no doubt, are the forms of the matter given to us by experience. They are, according to Kant, not derived from experience, but purely *a priori*. But logic is concerned exclusively about the form of thought, and has nothing to do with this or that conception, whether *a priori* or *a posteriori*.

See Sir William Hamilton's Edition of Reid's *Works, passim*. It is to Sir William Hamilton, that the Translator is indebted for the above view of the subject of logic.—*Tr*.

of thought, without which no use whatever of the understanding
is possible, and gives laws therefore to the understanding, without
regard to the difference of objects on which it may be employed.
The logic of the particular use of the understanding contains the
laws of correct thinking upon a particular class of objects. The
former may be called elemental logic—the latter, the organon of
this or that particular science. The latter is for the most part
employed in the schools, as a propaedeutic to the sciences, although,
indeed, according to the course of human reason, it is the last thing
we arrive at, when the science has been already matured, and needs
only the finishing touches towards its correction and completion;
for our knowledge of the objects of our attempted science must be
tolerably extensive and complete before we can indicate the laws
by which a science of these objects can be established.

General logic is again either pure or applied. In the former, we
abstract all the empirical conditions under which the understanding
is exercised; for example, the influence of the senses, the play of
the fantasy or imagination, the laws of the memory, the force of
habit, of inclination, etc., consequently also, the sources of prejudice—in a word, we abstract all causes from which particular
cognitions arise, because these causes regard the understanding
under certain circumstances of its application, and, to the knowledge of them experience is required. Pure general logic has to do,
therefore, merely with pure *a priori* principles, and is a canon of
understanding and reason, but only in respect of the formal part
of their use, be the content what it may, empirical or transcendental.
General logic is called applied, when it is directed to the laws of
the use of the understanding, under the subjective empirical
conditions which psychology teaches us. It has therefore empirical
principles, although, at the same time, it is in so far general, that
it applies to the exercise of the understanding, without regard to
the difference of objects. On this account, moreover, it is neither
a canon of the understanding in general, nor an organon of a particular science, but merely a cathartic of the human understanding.

In general logic, therefore, that part which constitutes pure logic
must be carefully distinguished from that which constitutes applied
(though still general) logic. The former alone is properly science,
although short and dry, as the methodical exposition of an elemental
doctrine of the understanding ought to be. In this, therefore,
logicians must always bear in mind two rules:

1. As general logic, it makes abstraction of all content of the
cognition of the understanding, and of the difference of objects,
and has to do with nothing but the mere form of thought.

2. As pure logic, it has no empirical principles, and consequently draws nothing (contrary to the common persuasion) from psychology, which therefore has no influence on the canon of the understanding. It is a demonstrated doctrine, and everything in it must be certain, completely a *priori*.

What I call applied logic (contrary to the common acceptation of this term, according to which it should contain certain exercises for the scholar, for which pure logic gives the rules), is a representation of the understanding, and of the rules of its necessary employment *in concreto*, that is to say, under the accidental conditions of the subject, which may either hinder or promote this employment, and which are all given only empirically. Thus applied logic treats of attention, its impediments and consequences, of the origin of error, of the state of doubt, hesitation, conviction, etc., and to it is related pure general logic in the same way that pure morality, which contains only the necessary moral laws of a free will, is related to practical ethics, which considers these laws under all the impediments of feelings, inclinations, and passions to which men are more or less subjected, and which never can furnish us with a true and demonstrated science, because it, as well as applied logic, requires empirical and psychological principles.

## II
### Of Transcendental Logic

General logic, as we have seen, makes abstraction of all content of cognition, that is, of all relation of cognition to its object, and regards only the logical form in the relation of cognitions to each other, that is, the form of thought in general. But as we have both pure and empirical intuitions (as Transcendental Aesthetic proves), in like manner a distinction might be drawn between pure and empirical thought (of objects). In this case, there would exist a kind of logic, in which we should not make abstraction of all content of cognition; for that logic which should comprise merely the laws of pure thought (of an object), would of course exclude all those cognitions which were of empirical content. This kind of logic would also examine the origin of our cognitions of objects, so far as that origin cannot be ascribed to the objects themselves; while, on the contrary, general logic has nothing to do with the origin of our cognitions, but contemplates our representations, be they given primitively a *priori* in ourselves, or be they only of empirical origin, solely according to the laws which the understanding observes in employing them in the process of thought, in relation to each other. Consequently, general logic treats of the form of the understanding only, which can be applied to representations, from whatever source they may have arisen.

And here I shall make a remark, which the reader must bear well in mind in the course of the following considerations, to wit, that not every cognition *a priori*, but only those through which we cognize that and how certain representations (intuitions or conceptions) are applied or are possible only *a priori*; that is to say, the *a priori* possibility of cognition and the *a priori* use of it are transcendental. Therefore neither is space, nor any *a priori* geometrical determination of space, a transcendental representation, but only the knowledge that such a representation is not of empirical origin, and the possibility of its relating to objects of experience, although itself *a priori*, can be called transcendental. So also, the application of space to objects in general, would be transcendental; but if it be limited to objects of sense, it is empirical. Thus, the distinction of the transcendental and empirical belongs only to the critique of cognitions, and does not concern the relation of these to their object.

Accordingly, in the expectation that there may perhaps be conceptions which relate *a priori* to objects, not as pure or sensuous intuitions, but merely as acts of pure thought (which are therefore conceptions, but neither of empirical nor aesthetical origin)—in this expectation, I say, we form to ourselves, by anticipation, the idea of a science of pure understanding and rational [1] cognition, by means of which we may cogitate objects entirely *a priori*. A science of this kind, which should determine the origin, the extent, and the objective validity of such cognitions, must be called *Transcendental Logic*, because it has not, like general logic, to do with the laws of understanding and reason in relation to empirical as well as pure rational cognitions without distinction, but concerns itself with these only in an *a priori* relation to objects.

## III

### *Of the Division of General Logic into Analytic and Dialectic*

The old question with which people sought to push logicians into a corner, so that they must either have recourse to pitiful sophisms or confess their ignorance, and consequently the vanity of their whole art, is this—'What is truth?' The definition of the

---

[1] *Vernunfterkenntniss.* The words *reason, rational* will always be confined in this translation to the rendering of *Vernunft* and its derivatives.—*Tr.*

word *truth*, to wit, 'the accordance of the cognition with its object,' is presupposed in the question; but we desire to be told, in the answer to it, what is the universal and secure criterion of the truth of every cognition.

To know what questions we may reasonably propose, is in itself a strong evidence of sagacity and intelligence. For if a question be in itself absurd and unsusceptible of a rational answer, it is attended with the danger—not to mention the shame that falls upon the person who proposes it—of seducing the unguarded listener into making absurd answers, and we are presented with the ridiculous spectacle of one (as the ancients said) 'milking the he-goat, and the other holding a sieve.'

If truth consists in the accordance of a cognition with its object, this object must be, *ipso facto*, distinguished from all others; for a cognition is false if it does not accord with the object to which it relates, although it contains something which may be affirmed of other objects. Now an universal criterion of truth would be that which is valid for all cognitions, without distinction of their objects. But it is evident that since, in the case of such a criterion, we make abstraction of all the content of a cognition (that is, of all relation to its object), and truth relates precisely to this content, it must be utterly absurd to ask for a mark of the truth of this content of cognition; and that, accordingly, a sufficient, and at the same time universal, test of truth cannot possibly be found. As we have already termed the content of a cognition its *matter*, we shall say: 'Of the truth of our cognitions in respect of their matter, no universal test can be demanded, because such a demand is self-contradictory.'

On the other hand, with regard to our cognition in respect of its mere form (excluding all content), it is equally manifest that logic, in so far as it exhibits the universal and necessary laws of the understanding, must in these very laws present us with criteria of truth. Whatever contradicts these rules is false, because thereby the understanding is made to contradict its own universal laws of thought; that is, to contradict itself. These criteria, however, apply solely to the form of truth, that is, of thought in general, and in so far they are perfectly accurate, yet not sufficient. For although a cognition may be perfectly accurate as to logical form, that is, not self-contradictory, it is notwithstanding quite possible that it may not stand in agreement with its object. Consequently, the merely logical criterion of truth, namely, the accordance of a cognition with the universal and formal laws of understanding and reason, is nothing more than the *conditio sine qua non*, or negative condition of all truth. Further than this logic cannot go, and the error which depends not on the form, but on the content of the cognition, it has no test to discover.

General logic, then, resolves the whole formal business of understanding and reason into its elements, and exhibits them as principles of all logical judging of our cognitions. This part of logic may, therefore, be called *Analytic*, and is at least the negative test of truth, because all cognitions must first of all be estimated and tried according to these laws before we proceed to investigate them in respect of their content, in order to discover whether they contain positive truth in regard to their object. Because, however, the mere form of a cognition, accurately as it may accord with logical laws, is insufficient to supply us with material (objective) truth, no one, by means of logic alone, can venture to predicate anything of or decide concerning objects, unless he has obtained, independently of logic, well-grounded information about them, in order afterwards to examine, according to logical laws, into the use and connection, in a cohering whole, of that information, or, what is still better, merely to test it by them. Notwithstanding, there lies so seductive a charm in the possession of a specious art like this—an art which gives to all our cognitions the form of the understanding, although with respect to the content thereof we may be sadly deficient—that general logic, which is merely a canon of judgment, has been employed as an organon for the actual production, or rather for the semblance of production of objective assertions, and has thus been grossly misapplied. Now general logic, in its assumed character of organon, is called *Dialectic*.

Different as are the significations in which the ancients used this term for a science or an art, we may safely infer, from their actual employment of it, that with them it was nothing else than a logic of illusion—a sophistical art for giving ignorance, nay, even intentional sophistries, the colouring of truth, in which the thoroughness of procedure which logic requires was imitated, and their topic [1] employed to cloak the empty pretensions. Now it may be taken as a safe and useful warning, that general logic, considered as an organon, must always be a logic of illusion, that is, be dialectical, for, as it teaches us nothing whatever respecting the content of our cognitions, but merely the formal conditions of their accordance

[1] The Topic (*Topica*) of the ancients was a division of the intellectual instruction then prevalent, with the design of setting forth the proper method of reasoning on any given proposition—according to certain distinctions of the genus, the species, etc., of the subject and predicate; of words, analogies, and the like. It, of course, contained also a code of laws for syllogistical disputation. It was not necessarily an aid to sophistry.—*Tr.*

with the understanding, which do not relate to and are quite indifferent in respect of objects, any attempt to employ it as an instrument (organon) in order to extend and enlarge the range of our knowledge must end in mere prating; any one being able to maintain or oppose, with some appearance of truth, any single assertion whatever.

Such instruction is quite unbecoming the dignity of philosophy. For these reasons we have chosen to denominate this part of logic *Dialectic*, in the sense of a critique of dialectical illusion, and we wish the term to be so understood in this place.

## IV

### *Of the Division of Transcendental Logic into Transcendental Analytic and Dialectic*

In transcendental logic we isolate the understanding (as in transcendental aesthetic the sensibility) and select from our cognition merely that part of thought which has its origin in the understanding alone. The exercise of this pure cognition, however, depends upon this as its condition, that objects to which it may be applied be given to us in intuition, for without intuition the whole of our cognition is without objects, and is therefore quite void. That part of transcendental logic, then, which treats of the elements of pure cognition of the understanding, and of the principles without which no object at all can be thought, is transcendental analytic, and at the same time a logic of truth. For no cognition can contradict it, without losing at the same time all content, that is, losing all reference to an object, and therefore all truth. But because we are very easily seduced into employing these pure cognitions and principles of the understanding by themselves, and that even beyond the boundaries of experience, which yet is the only source whence we can obtain matter (objects) on which those pure conceptions may be employed—understanding runs the risk of making, by means of empty sophisms, a material and objective use of the mere formal principles of the pure understanding, and of passing judgments on objects without distinction —objects which are not given to us, nay, perhaps cannot be given to us in any way. Now, as it ought properly to be only a canon for judging of the empirical use of the understanding, this kind of logic is misused when we seek to employ it as an organon of the universal and unlimited exercise of the understanding, and attempt with the pure understanding alone to judge synthetically, affirm, and determine respecting objects in general. In this case the exercise of the pure understanding becomes dialectical. The second part of our transcendental logic must therefore be a critique of dialectical illusion, and this critique we shall term Transcendental Dialectic—not meaning it as an art of producing dogmatically such illusion (an art which is unfortunately too current among the practitioners of metaphysical juggling), but as a critique of understanding and reason in regard to their hyperphysical use. This critique will expose the groundless nature of the pretensions of these two faculties, and invalidate their claims to the discovery and enlargement of our cognitions merely by means of transcendental principles, and show that the proper employment of these faculties is to test the judgments made by the pure understanding, and to guard it from sophistical delusion.

# TRANSCENDENTAL LOGIC

## FIRST DIVISION

### TRANSCENDENTAL ANALYTIC

§ 1

TRANSCENDENTAL analytic is the dissection of the whole of our *a priori* knowledge into the elements of the pure cognition of the understanding. In order to effect our purpose, it is necessary: (1) That the conceptions be pure and not empirical; (2) That they belong not to intuition and sensibility, but to thought and understanding; (3) That they be elementary conceptions, and as such, quite different from deduced or compound conceptions; (4) That our table of these elementary conceptions be complete, and fill up the whole sphere of the pure understanding. Now this completeness of a science cannot be accepted with confidence on the guarantee of a mere estimate of its existence in an aggregate formed only by means of repeated experiments and attempts. The completeness which we require is possible only by means of an idea of the totality of the *a priori* cognition of the understanding, and through the thereby determined division of the conceptions which form the said whole; consequently, only by means of their connection in a system. Pure understanding distinguishes itself not merely from everything empirical, but also completely from all sensibility. It is a unity self-subsistent, self-sufficient, and not to be enlarged by any additions from without. Hence the sum of its cognition constitutes a system to be determined by and comprised under an idea; and the completeness and articulation of this system can at the same time serve as a test of the correctness and genuineness of all the parts of cognition that belong to it. The whole of this part of transcendental logic consists of two books, of which the one contains the conceptions, and the other the principles of pure understanding.

## TRANSCENDENTAL ANALYTIC

## BOOK I

### ANALYTIC OF CONCEPTIONS

#### § 2

By the term 'Analytic of Conceptions,' I do not understand the analysis of these, or the usual process in philosophical investigations of dissecting the conceptions which present themselves, according to their content, and so making them clear; but I mean the hitherto little attempted dissection of the faculty of understanding itself, in order to investigate the possibility of conceptions *a priori*, by looking for them in the understanding alone, as their birthplace, and analysing the pure use of this faculty. For this is the proper duty of a transcendental philosophy; what remains is the logical treatment of the conceptions in philosophy in general. We shall therefore follow up the pure conceptions even to their germs and beginnings in the human understanding, in which they lie, until they are developed on occasions presented by experience, and, freed by the same understanding from the empirical conditions attaching to them, are set forth in their unalloyed purity.

### ANALYTIC OF CONCEPTIONS

### CHAPTER I

#### OF THE TRANSCENDENTAL CLUE TO THE DISCOVERY OF ALL PURE CONCEPTIONS OF THE UNDERSTANDING

#### *Introductory*

#### § 3

WHEN we call into play a faculty of cognition, different conceptions manifest themselves according to the different circumstances, and make known this faculty, and assemble themselves into a more or less extensive collection, according to the time or penetration that has been applied to the consideration of them. Where this process, conducted as it is mechanically, so to speak, will end, cannot be determined with certainty. Besides, the conceptions which we discover in this haphazard manner present themselves by no means in order and systematic unity, but are at last coupled together only according to resemblances to each other, and arranged in series, according to the quantity of their content, from the simpler to the more complex—series which are anything but systematic, though not altogether without a certain kind of method in their construction.

Transcendental philosophy has the advantage, and moreover the duty, of searching for its conceptions according to a principle; because these conceptions spring pure and unmixed out of the understanding as an absolute unity, and therefore must be connected with each other according to one conception or idea. A connection of this kind, however, furnishes us with a ready prepared rule, by which its proper place may be assigned to every pure conception of the understanding, and the completeness of the system of all be determined *a priori*—both of which would otherwise have been dependent on mere choice or chance.

TRANSCENDENTAL CLUE TO THE DISCOVERY OF ALL PURE
CONCEPTIONS OF THE UNDERSTANDING

SECTION I. *Of the Logical Use of the Understanding in general*

§ 4

The understanding was defined above only negatively, as a non-sensuous faculty of cognition. Now, independently of sensibility, we cannot possibly have any intuition; consequently, the understanding is no faculty of intuition. But besides intuition there is no other mode of cognition, except through conceptions; consequently, the cognition of every, at least of every human, understanding is a cognition through conceptions—not intuitive, but discursive. All intuitions, as sensuous, depend on affections; conceptions, therefore, upon functions. By the word function I understand the unity of the act of arranging diverse representations under one common representation. Conceptions, then, are based on the spontaneity of thought, as sensuous intuitions are on the receptivity of impressions. Now, the understanding cannot make any other use of these conceptions than to judge by means of

them.  As no representation, except an intuition, relates immediately to its object, a conception never relates immediately
to an object, but only to some other representation thereof, be
that an intuition or itself a conception.  A judgment, therefore, is
the mediate cognition of an object, consequently the representation
of a representation of it.  In every judgment there is a conception
which applies to, and is valid for many other conceptions, and
which among these comprehends also a given representation, this
last being immediately connected with an object.  For example,
in the judgment—'All bodies are divisible,' our conception of
*divisible* applies to various other conceptions; among these, however,
it is here particularly applied to the conception of body, and this
conception of body relates to certain phenomena which occur to
us.  These objects, therefore, are mediately represented by the
conception of divisibility.  All judgments, accordingly, are functions of unity in our representations, inasmuch as, instead of an
immediate, a higher representation, which comprises this and
various others, is used for our cognition of the object, and thereby
many possible cognitions are collected into one.  But we can
reduce all acts of the understanding to judgments, so that *understanding* may be represented as the *faculty of judging*.  For it is,
according to what has been said above, a faculty of thought.  Now
thought is cognition by means of conceptions.  But conceptions,
as predicates of possible judgments, relate to some representation
of a yet undetermined object.  Thus the conception of *body*
indicates something—for example, metal—which can be cognized
by means of that conception.  It is therefore a conception, for the
reason alone that other representations are contained under it,
by means of which it can relate to objects.  It is therefore the
predicate to a possible judgment; for example: 'Every metal is a
body.'  All the functions of the understanding therefore can be
discovered, when we can completely exhibit the functions of unity
in judgments.  And that this may be effected very easily, the
following section will show.

Section II. *Of the Logical Function of the Understanding in
Judgments*

§ 5

If we abstract all the content of a judgment, and consider only
the intellectual form thereof, we find that the function of thought
in a judgment can be brought under four heads, of which each

contains three momenta. These may be conveniently represented in the following table:

I

*Quantity of judgments*

Universal
Particular
Singular

2                      3

*Quality*              *Relation*

Affirmative          Categorical
Negative             Hypothetical
Infinite               Disjunctive

4

*Modality*

Problematical
Assertorical
Apodeictical

As this division appears to differ in some, though not essential points, from the usual technique of logicians, the following observations, for the prevention of otherwise possible misunderstanding, will not be without their use.

1. Logicians say, with justice, that in the use of judgments in syllogisms, singular judgments may be treated like universal ones. For, precisely because a singular judgment has no extent at all, its predicate cannot refer to a part of that which is contained in the conception of the subject and be excluded from the rest. The predicate is valid for the whole conception just as if it were a general conception, and had extent, to the whole of which the predicate applied. On the other hand, let us compare a singular with a general judgment, merely as a cognition, in regard to quantity. The singular judgment relates to the general one, as unity to infinity, and is therefore in itself essentially different. Thus, if we estimate a singular judgment (*judicium singulare*) not merely according to its intrinsic validity as a judgment, but also as a cognition generally, according to its quantity in comparison with that of other cognitions, it is then entirely different from a general judgment (*judicium commune*), and in a complete table of the momenta of thought deserves a separate place—though, indeed, this would not be necessary in a logic limited merely to the consideration of the use of judgments in reference to each other.

2. In like manner, in transcendental logic, infinite must be distinguished from affirmative judgments, although in general logic they are rightly enough classed under affirmative. General logic abstracts all content of the predicate (though it be negative), and only considers whether the said predicate be affirmed or denied of the subject. But transcendental logic considers also the worth or content of this logical affirmation—an affirmation by means of a merely negative predicate, and inquires how much the sum total of our cognition gains by this affirmation. For example, if I say of the soul, 'It is not mortal'—by this negative judgment I should at least ward off error. Now, by the proposition, 'The soul is not mortal,' I have, in respect of the logical form, really affirmed, inasmuch as I thereby place the soul in the unlimited sphere of immortal beings. Now, because of the whole sphere of possible existences, the mortal occupies one part, and the immortal the other, neither more nor less is affirmed by the proposition, than that the soul is one among the infinite multitude of things which remain over, when I take away the whole mortal part. But by this proceeding we accomplish only this much, that the infinite sphere of all possible existences is in so far limited, that the mortal is excluded from it, and the soul is placed in the remaining part of the extent of this sphere. But this part remains, notwithstanding this exception, infinite, and more and more parts may be taken away from the whole sphere, without in the slightest degree thereby augmenting or affirmatively determining our conception of the soul. These judgments, therefore, infinite in respect of their logical extent, are, in respect of the content of their cognition, merely limitative; and are consequently entitled to a place in our transcendental table of all the momenta of thought in judgments, because the function of the understanding exercised by them may perhaps be of importance in the field of its pure *a priori* cognition.

3. All relations of thought in judgments are those (*a*) of the predicate to the subject; (*b*) of the principle to its consequence; (*c*) of the divided cognition and all the members of the division to each other. In the first of these three classes, we consider only two conceptions; in the second, two judgments; in the third, several judgments in relation to each other. The hypothetical proposition, 'If perfect justice exists, the obstinately wicked are punished,' contains properly the relation to each other of two propositions, namely, 'Perfect justice exists,' and 'The obstinately wicked are punished.' Whether these propositions are in themselves true, is a question not here decided. Nothing is cogitated by means of this judgment except a certain consequence. Finally,

the disjunctive judgment contains a relation of two or more propositions to each other—a relation not of consequence, but of logical opposition, in so far as the sphere of the one proposition excludes that of the other. But it contains at the same time a relation of community, in so far as all the propositions taken together fill up the sphere of the cognition. The disjunctive judgment contains, therefore, the relation of the parts of the whole sphere of a cognition, since the sphere of each part is a complemental part of the sphere of the other, each contributing to form the sum total of the divided cognition. Take, for example, the proposition, 'The world exists either through blind chance, or through internal necessity, or through an external cause.' Each of these propositions embraces a part of the sphere of our possible cognition as to the existence of a world; all of them taken together, the whole sphere. To take the cognition out of one of these spheres, is equivalent to placing it in one of the others; and, on the other hand, to place it in one sphere is equivalent to taking it out of the rest. There is, therefore, in a disjunctive judgment a certain community of cognitions, which consists in this, that they mutually exclude each other, yet thereby determine, as a whole, the true cognition, inasmuch as, taken together, they make up the complete content of a particular given cognition. And this is all that I find necessary, for the sake of what follows, to remark in this place.

4. The modality of judgments is a quite peculiar function, with this distinguishing characteristic, that it contributes nothing to the content of a judgment (for besides quantity, quality, and relation, there is nothing more that constitutes the content of a judgment), but concerns itself only with the value of the copula in relation to thought in general. Problematical judgments are those in which the affirmation or negation is accepted as merely possible (*ad libitum*). In the assertorical, we regard the proposition as real (true); in the apodeictical, we look on it as *necessary*.[1] Thus the two judgments (*antecedens et consequens*), the relation of which constitutes a hypothetical judgment, likewise those (the members of the division) in whose reciprocity the disjunctive consists, are only problematical. In the example above given, the proposition, 'There exists perfect justice,' is not stated assertorically, but as an *ad libitum* judgment, which someone may choose to adopt, and the consequence alone is assertorical. Hence such judgments may be obviously false, and yet, taken problematically, be con-

---

[1] Just as if thought were in the first instance a function of the *understanding*; in the second, of *judgment*; in the third, of *reason*. *Reason*, a remark which will be explained in the sequel.

ditions of our cognition of the truth. Thus the proposition, 'The world exists only by blind chance,' is in the disjunctive judgment of problematical import only: that is to say, one may accept it for the moment, and it helps us (like the indication of the wrong road among all the roads that one can take) to find out the true proposition. The problematical proposition is, therefore, that which expresses only logical possibility (which is not objective); that is, it expresses a free choice to admit the validity of such a proposition—a merely arbitrary reception of it into the understanding. The assertorical speaks of logical reality or truth; as, for example, in a hypothetical syllogism, the *antecedens* presents itself in a problematical form in the *major*, in an assertorical form in the *minor*, and it shows that the proposition is in harmony with the laws of the understanding. The apodeictical proposition cogitates the assertorical as determined by these very laws of the understanding, consequently as affirming *a priori*, and in this manner it expresses logical necessity. Now because all is here gradually incorporated with the understanding—inasmuch as in the first place we judge problematically; then accept assertorically our judgment as true; lastly, affirm it as inseparably united with the understanding, that is, as necessary and apodeictical—we may safely reckon these three functions of modality as so many momenta of thought.

SECT. III. *Of the Pure Conceptions of the Understanding, or Categories*

§ 6

General logic, as has been repeatedly said, makes abstraction of all content of cognition, and expects to receive representations from some other quarter, in order, by means of analysis, to convert them into conceptions. On the contrary, transcendental logic has lying before it the manifold content of *a priori* sensibility, which transcendental aesthetic presents to it in order to give matter to the pure conceptions of the understanding, without which transcendental logic would have no content, and be therefore utterly void.[1] Now space and time contain an infinite diversity of determinations[1] of pure *a priori* intuition, but are nevertheless the condition of the mind's receptivity, under which alone it can obtain representations of objects, and which, consequently, must always affect the conception of these objects. But the spontaneity of thought requires that this diversity be examined after a certain manner, received

[1] Kant employs the words *Mannigfaltiges*, *Mannigfaltigkeit*, indifferently, for the infinitude of the possible determination of matter, of an intuition (such as that of space), etc.—*Tr*.

into the mind, and connected, in order afterwards to form a cognition out of it. This process I call synthesis.

By the word *synthesis*, in its most general signification, I understand the process of joining different representations to each other, and of comprehending their diversity in one cognition. This synthesis is pure when the diversity is not given empirically but *a priori* (as that in space and time). Our representations must be given previously to any analysis of them; and no conceptions can arise, *quoad* their content, analytically. But the synthesis of a diversity (be it given *a priori* or empirically) is the first requisite for the production of a cognition, which in its beginning, indeed, may be crude and confused, and therefore in need of analysis— still, synthesis is that by which alone the elements of our cognitions are collected and united into a certain content, consequently it is the first thing on which we must fix our attention, if we wish to investigate the origin of our knowledge.

Synthesis, generally speaking, is, as we shall afterwards see, the mere operation of the imagination—a blind but indispensable function of the soul, without which we should have no cognition whatever, but of the working of which we are seldom even conscious. But to reduce this synthesis to conceptions, is a function of the understanding, by means of which we attain to cognition, in the proper meaning of the term.

Pure synthesis, represented generally, gives us the pure conception of the understanding. But by this pure synthesis, I mean that which rests upon a basis of *a priori* synthetical unity. Thus, our numeration (and this is more observable in large numbers) is a synthesis according to conceptions, because it takes place according to a common basis of unity (for example, the decade). By means of this conception, therefore, the unity in the synthesis of the manifold becomes necessary.

By means of analysis different representations are brought under one conception—an operation of which general logic treats. On the other hand, the duty of transcendental logic is to reduce to conceptions, not representations, but the pure synthesis of representations. The first thing which must be given to us in order to the *a priori* cognition of all objects, is the diversity of the pure intuition; the synthesis of this diversity by means of the imagination is the second; but this gives, as yet, no cognition. The conceptions which give unity to this pure synthesis, and which consist solely in the representation of this necessary synthetical unity, furnish the third requisite for the cognition of an object, and these conceptions are given by the understanding.

The same function which gives unity to the different representations in a judgment, gives also unity to the mere synthesis of different representations in an intuition; and this unity we call the pure conception of the understanding. Thus, the same understanding, and by the same operations, whereby in conceptions, by means of analytical unity, it produced the logical form of a judgment, introduces, by means of the synthetical unity of the manifold in intuition, a transcendental content into its representations, on which account they are called pure conceptions of the understanding, and they apply *a priori* to objects, a result not within the power of general logic.[1]

In this manner, there arise exactly so many pure conceptions of the understanding, applying *a priori* to objects of intuition in general, as there are logical functions in all possible judgments. For there is no other function or faculty existing in the understanding besides those enumerated in that table. These conceptions we shall, with Aristotle, call categories, our purpose being originally identical with his, notwithstanding the great difference in the execution.

### TABLE OF THE CATEGORIES

| 1 | 2 |
|---|---|
| *Of Quantity* | *Of Quality* |
| Unity | Reality |
| Plurality | Negation |
| Totality | Limitation |

#### 3
#### *Of Relation*

Of Inherence and Subsistence (substantia et accidens)
Of Causality and Dependence (cause and effect)
Of Community (reciprocity between the agent and the patient)

#### 4
#### *Of Modality*

Possibility—Impossibility
Existence—Non-existence
Necessity—Contingence

This, then, is a catalogue of all the originally pure conceptions of the synthesis which the understanding contains *a priori*, and these conceptions alone entitle it to be called a pure understanding;

---

[1] Only because this is beyond the sphere of logic proper. Kant's remark is unnecessary.—*Tr.*

inasmuch as only by them it can render the manifold of intuition conceivable, in other words, think an object of intuition. This division is made systematically from a common principle, namely, the faculty of judgment (which is just the same as the power of thought), and has not arisen rhapsodically from a search at haphazard after pure conceptions, respecting the full number of which we never could be certain, inasmuch as we employ induction alone in our search, without considering that in this way we can never understand wherefore precisely these conceptions, and none others, abide in the pure understanding. It was a design worthy of an acute thinker like Aristotle, to search for these fundamental conceptions.[1] Destitute, however, of any guiding principle, he picked them up just as they occurred to him, and at first hunted out ten, which he called *categories* (*predicaments*). Afterwards he believed that he had discovered five others, which were added under the name of *post predicaments*. But his catalogue still remained defective. Besides, there are to be found among them some of the modes of pure sensibility (*quando, ubi, situs*, also *prius, simul*), and likewise an empirical conception (*motus*)—which can by no means belong to this genealogical register of the pure understanding. Moreover, there are deduced conceptions (*actio, passio*) enumerated among the original conceptions, and of the latter, some are entirely wanting.

With regard to these, it is to be remarked, that the categories, as the true primitive conceptions of the pure understanding, have also their pure deduced conceptions, which, in a complete system of transcendental philosophy, must by no means be passed over;

---

[1] 'It is a serious error to imagine that, in his Categories, Aristotle proposed, like Kant, "an analysis of the elements of human reason." The ends proposed by the two philosophers were different, even opposed. In their several Categories, Aristotle attempted a synthesis of things in their multiplicity—a classification of objects real, but in relation to thought; Kant, an analysis of mind in its unity—a dissection of thought, pure, but in relation to its objects. The predicaments of Aristotle are thus objective, of things as understood; those of Kant subjective, of the mind as understanding. The former are results *a posteriori*—the creations of abstraction and generalization; the latter, anticipations *a priori*—the conditions of those acts themselves. It is true, that as the one scheme exhibits the unity of thought diverging into plurality, in appliance to its objects, and as the other exhibits the multiplicity of these objects converging towards unity by the collective determination of thought; while, at the same time, language usually confounds the subjective and objective under a common term;—it is certainly true, that some elements in the one table coincide in name with some elements in the other. This coincidence is, however, only equivocal. In reality, the whole Kantian categories must be excluded from the Aristotelic list, as *entia rationis*, as *notiones secundae*—in short, as determinations of thought, and not genera of real things; while the several elements would be specially excluded, as *partial, privative, transcendent,*' etc.—Hamilton's (Sir W.) *Essays and Discussions*.

though in a merely critical essay we must be contented with the simple mention of the fact.

Let it be allowed me to call these pure, but deduced conceptions of the understanding, the *predicables* [1] of the pure understanding, in contradistinction to predicaments. If we are in possession of the original and primitive, the deduced and subsidiary conceptions can easily be added, and the genealogical tree of the understanding completely delineated. As my present aim is not to set forth a complete system, but merely the principles of one, I reserve this task for another time. It may be easily executed by any one who will refer to the ontological manuals, and subordinate to the category of causality, for example, the predicables of force, action, passion; to that of community, those of presence and resistance; to the categories of modality, those of origination, extinction, change; and so with the rest. The categories combined with the modes of pure sensibility, or with one another, afford a great number of deduced *a priori* conceptions; a complete enumeration of which would be a useful and not unpleasant, but in this place a perfectly dispensable occupation.

I purposely omit the definitions of the categories in this treatise. I shall analyse these conceptions only so far as is necessary for the doctrine of method, which is to form a part of this critique. In a system of pure reason, definitions of them would be with justice demanded of me, but to give them here would only hide from our view the main aim of our investigation, at the same time raising doubts and objections, the consideration of which, without injustice to our main purpose, may be very well postponed till another opportunity. Meanwhile, it ought to be sufficiently clear, from the little we have already said on this subject, that the formation of a complete vocabulary of pure conceptions, accompanied by all the requisite explanations, is not only a possible, but an easy undertaking. The compartments already exist; it is only necessary to fill them up; and a systematic topic like the present, indicates with perfect precision the proper place to which each conception belongs, while it readily points out any that have not yet been filled up.

### § 7

Our table of the categories suggests considerations of some importance, which may perhaps have significant results in regard

[1] The predicables of Kant are quite different from those of Aristotle and ancient and modern logicians. The five predicables are of a logical, and not, like those of Kant, of a metaphysico-ontological import. They were enounced as a complete enumeration of all the possible modes of predication. Kant's predicables, on the contrary, do not possess this merely formal and logical character, but have a real or metaphysical content.—*Tr.*

to the scientific form of all rational cognitions. For, that this table is useful in the theoretical part of philosophy, nay, indispensable for the sketching of the complete plan of a science, so far as that science rests upon conceptions *a priori*, and for dividing it mathematically, according to fixed principles, is most manifest from the fact that it contains all the elementary conceptions of the understanding, nay, even the form of a system of these in the understanding itself, and consequently indicates all the momenta, and also the internal arrangement of a projected speculative science, as I have elsewhere shown.[1] Here follow some of these observations.

I. This table, which contains four classes of conceptions of the understanding, may, in the first instance, be divided into two classes, the first of which relates to objects of intuition—pure as well as empirical; the second, to the existence of these objects, either in relation to one another, or to the understanding.

The former of these classes of categories I would entitle the *mathematical*, and the latter the *dynamical* categories. The former, as we see, has no correlates; these are only to be found in the second class. This difference must have a ground in the nature of the human understanding.

II. The number of the categories in each class is always the same, namely, three—a fact which also demands some consideration, because in all other cases division *a priori* through conceptions is necessarily dichotomy. It is to be added, that the third category in each triad always arises from the combination of the second with the first.

Thus Totality is nothing else but Plurality contemplated as Unity; Limitation is merely Reality conjoined with Negation; Community is the Causality of a Substance, reciprocally determining, and determined by other substances; and finally, Necessity is nothing but Existence, which is given through the Possibility itself.[2] Let it not be supposed, however, that the third category is merely a deduced, and not a primitive conception of the pure understanding. For the conjunction of the first and the second, in order to produce the third conception, requires a particular function of the understanding, which is by no means identical with those which are exercised in the first and the second. Thus, the conception of a number (which belongs to the category of Totality) is not always possible, where the conceptions of multitude and unity exist (for example, in the representation of the infinite).

[1] In the *Metaphysical Principles of Natural Science*.
[2] Kant's meaning is: A necessary existence is an existence whose existence is given in the very possibility of its existence.—*Tr*.

Or, if I conjoin the conception of a cause with that of a substance, it does not follow that the conception of *influence*, that is, how one substance can be the cause of something in another substance, will be understood from that. Thus it is evident, that a particular act of the understanding is here necessary; and so in the other instances.

III. With respect to one category, namely, that of community, which is found in the third class, it is not so easy as with the others to detect its accordance with the form of the disjunctive judgment which corresponds to it in the table of the logical functions.

In order to assure ourselves of this accordance, we must observe: that in every disjunctive judgment, the sphere of the judgment (that is, the complex of all that is contained in it) is represented as a whole divided into parts; and, since one part cannot be contained in the other, they are cogitated as co-ordinated with, not subordinated to each other, so that they do not determine each other unilaterally, as in a linear series, but reciprocally, as in an aggregate—(if one member of the division is posited, all the rest are excluded; and conversely).

Now a like connection is cogitated in a whole of things; for one thing is not subordinated, as effect, to another as cause of its existence, but, on the contrary, is co-ordinated contemporaneously and reciprocally, as a cause in relation to the determination of the others (for example, in a body—the parts of which mutually attract and repel each other). And this is an entirely different kind of connection from that which we find in the mere relation of the cause to the effect (the principle to the consequence), for in such a connection the consequence does not in its turn determine the principle, and therefore does not constitute, with the latter, a whole—just as the Creator does not with the world make up a whole. The process of understanding by which it represents to itself the sphere of a divided conception, is employed also when we think of a thing as divisible; and, in the same manner as the members of the division in the former exclude one another, and yet are connected in one sphere, so the understanding represents to itself the parts of the latter, as having—each of them—an existence (as substances), independently of the others, and yet as united in one whole.

## § 8

In the transcendental philosophy of the ancients there exists one more leading division, which contains pure conceptions of the understanding, and which, although not numbered among the categories, ought, according to them, as conceptions *a priori*, to be valid of objects. But in this case they would augment the number of the categories; which cannot be. These are set forth in the proposition, so renowned among the schoolmen—'*Quodlibet ens est* UNUM, VERUM, BONUM.' Now, though the inferences from this principle were mere tautological propositions, and though it is allowed only by courtesy to retain a place in modern metaphysics, yet a thought which maintained itself for such a length of time, however empty it seems to be, deserves an investigation of its origin, and justifies the conjecture that it must be grounded in some law of the understanding, which, as is often the case, has only been erroneously interpreted. These pretended transcendental predicates are, in fact, nothing but logical requisites and criteria of all cognition of objects, and they employ, as the basis for this cognition, the categories of Quantity, namely, Unity, Plurality, and Totality. But these, which must be taken as material conditions, that is, as belonging to the possibility of things themselves, they employed merely in a formal signification, as belonging to the logical requisites of all cognition, and yet most unguardedly changed these criteria of thought into properties of objects, as things in themselves. Now, in every cognition of an object, there is *unity* of conception, which may be called *qualitative unity*, so far as by this term we understand only the unity in our connection of the manifold; for example, unity of the theme in a play, an oration, or a story. Secondly, there is *truth* in respect of the deductions from it. The more true deductions we have from a given conception, the more criteria of its objective reality. This we might call the *qualitative plurality* of characteristic marks, which belong to a conception as to a common foundation, but are not cogitated as a quantity in it. Thirdly, there is *perfection*— which consists in this, that the plurality falls back upon the unity of the conception, and accords completely with that conception, and with no other. This we may denominate *qualitative completeness*. Hence it is evident that these logical criteria of the possibility of cognition are merely the three categories of Quantity modified and transformed to suit an unauthorized manner of applying them. That is to say, the three categories, in which the unity in the production of the quantum must be homogeneous throughout, are transformed solely with a view to the connection of heterogeneous parts of cognition in one act of consciousness, by means of the quality of the cognition, which is the principle of that connection. Thus the criterion of the possibility of a conception (not of its object) is the definition of it, in which the unity of the conception, the truth of all that may be immediately deduced from it, and finally, the completeness of what has been thus deduced, constitute the requisites for the reproduction of the whole conception. Thus also, the criterion or test of an hypothesis is the intelligibility of the received principle of explanation, or its unity (without help from any subsidiary hypothesis)—the truth of our deductions from it (consistency with each other and with experience)—and lastly, the completeness of the principle of the explanation of these deductions, which refer to neither more nor less than what was admitted in the hypothesis, restoring analytically and *a posteriori*, what was cogitated synthetically and *a priori*. By the conceptions, therefore, of Unity, Truth, and Perfection, we have made no addition to the transcendental table of the categories, which is complete without them. We have, on the contrary, merely employed the three categories of quantity, setting aside their application to objects of experience, as general logical laws of the consistency of cognition with itself.[1]

## ANALYTIC OF CONCEPTIONS

### CHAPTER II

#### OF THE DEDUCTION OF THE PURE CONCEPTIONS OF THE UNDERSTANDING

SECT. I. *Of the Principles of a Transcendental Deduction in general*

#### § 9

TEACHERS of jurisprudence, when speaking of rights and claims, distinguish in a cause the question of right (*quid juris*) from the question of fact (*quid facti*), and while they demand proof of both, they give to the proof of the former, which goes to establish right or claim in law, the name of *Deduction*. Now we make use of a

---

[1] Kant's meaning in the foregoing chapter is this: These three conceptions of *unity*, *truth*, and *goodness*, applied as predicates to things, are the three categories of quantity under a different form. These three categories have an immediate relation to things, as phenomena; without them we could form no conceptions of external objects. But in the above-mentioned proposition they are changed into logical conditions of thought, and then unwittingly transformed into properties of things in themselves. These conceptions are properly logical or formal, and not metaphysical or material. The three categories are quantitative; these conceptions, qualitative. They are logical conditions employed as metaphysical conceptions—one of the very commonest errors in the sphere of mental science.—*Tr.*

great number of empirical conceptions, without opposition from any one; and consider ourselves, even without any attempt at deduction, justified in attaching to them a sense, and a supposititious signification, because we have always experience at hand to demonstrate their objective reality. There exist also, however, usurped conceptions, such as *fortune, fate*, which circulate with almost universal indulgence, and yet are occasionally challenged by the question, *quid juris ?* In such cases, we have great difficulty in discovering any deduction for these terms, inasmuch as we cannot produce any manifest ground of right, either from experience or from reason, on which the claim to employ them can be founded.

Among the many conceptions, which make up the very variegated web of human cognition, some are destined for pure use *a priori*, independent of all experience; and their title to be so employed always requires a deduction, inasmuch as, to justify such use of them, proofs from experience are not sufficient; but it is necessary to know how these conceptions can apply to objects without being derived from experience. I term, therefore, an explanation of the manner in which conceptions can apply *a priori* to objects, the *transcendental deduction* of conceptions, and I distinguish it from the *empirical* deduction, which indicates the mode in which a conception is obtained through experience and reflection thereon; consequently, does not concern itself with the right, but only with the fact of our obtaining conceptions in such and such a manner. We have already seen that we are in possession of two perfectly different kinds of conceptions, which nevertheless agree with each other in this, that they both apply to objects completely *a priori*. These are the conceptions of space and time as forms of sensibility, and the categories as pure conceptions of the understanding. To attempt an empirical deduction of either of these classes would be labour in vain, because the distinguishing characteristic of their nature consists in this, that they apply to their objects, without having borrowed anything from experience towards the representation of them. Consequently, if a deduction of these conceptions is necessary, it must always be transcendental.

Meanwhile, with respect to these conceptions, as with respect to all our cognition, we certainly may discover in experience, if not the principle of their possibility, yet the occasioning causes [1] of their production. It will be found that the impressions of sense give the first occasion for bringing into action the whole faculty of cognition, and for the production of experience, which contains two very dissimilar elements, namely, a matter for cognition,

[1] Gelegenheitsursachen.

given by the senses, and a certain form for the arrangement of this
matter, arising out of the inner fountain of pure intuition and
thought; and these, on occasion given by sensuous impressions,
are called into exercise and produce conceptions.  Such an investigation into the first efforts of our faculty of cognition to mount
from particular perceptions to general conceptions, is undoubtedly
of great utility; and we have to thank the celebrated Locke, for
having first opened the way for this inquiry.  But a deduction of
the pure *a priori* conceptions of course never can be made in this
way, seeing that, in regard to their future employment, which
must be entirely independent of experience, they must have a
far different certificate of birth to show from that of a descent
from experience.  This attempted physiological derivation, which
cannot properly be called deduction, because it relates merely to
a *quaestio facti*, I shall entitle an explanation of the *possession* of a
pure cognition.  It is therefore manifest that there can only be a
transcendental deduction of these conceptions, and by no means
an empirical one; also, that all attempts at an empirical deduction,
in regard to pure *a priori* conceptions, are vain, and can only be
made by one who does not understand the altogether peculiar
nature of these cognitions.

But although it is admitted that the only possible deduction of
pure *a priori* cognition is a transcendental deduction, it is not, for
that reason, perfectly manifest that such a deduction is absolutely
necessary.  We have already traced to their sources the conceptions of space and time, by means of a transcendental deduction,
and we have explained and determined their objective validity
*a priori*.  Geometry, nevertheless, advances steadily and securely
in the province of pure *a priori* cognitions, without needing to ask
from Philosophy any certificate as to the pure and legitimate origin
of its fundamental conception of space.  But the use of the conception in this science extends only to the external world of sense,
the pure form of the intuition of which is space; and in *this* world,
therefore, all geometrical cognition, because it is founded upon
*a priori* intuition, possesses immediate evidence, and the objects
of this cognition are given *a priori* (as regards their form) in intuition
by and through the cognition itself.[1]  With the pure conceptions
of Understanding, on the contrary, commences the absolute
necessity of seeking a transcendental deduction, not only of these

[1] Kant's meaning is: The objects of cognition in Geometry—angles, lines,
figures, and the like—are not different from the act of cognition which produces
them, except in thought.  The object does not exist but while we think it—
does not exist apart from our thinking it.  The act of thinking and the object
of thinking, are but one thing regarded from two different points of view.—*Tr.*

conceptions themselves, but likewise of space, because, inasmuch as they make affirmations [1] concerning objects not by means of the predicates of intuition and sensibility, but of pure thought *a priori*, they apply to objects without any of the conditions of sensibility. Besides, not being founded on experience, they are not presented with any object in *a priori* intuition upon which, antecedently to experience, they might base their synthesis. Hence results, not only doubt as to the objective validity and proper limits of their use, but that even our conception of space is rendered equivocal; inasmuch as we are very ready with the aid of the categories, to carry the use of this conception beyond the conditions of sensuous intuition—and for this reason, we have already found a transcendental deduction of it needful. The reader, then, must be quite convinced of the absolute necessity of a transcendental deduction, before taking a single step in the field of pure reason; because otherwise he goes to work blindly, and after he has wandered about in all directions, returns to the state of utter ignorance from which he started. He ought, moreover, clearly to recognize beforehand, the unavoidable difficulties in his undertaking, so that he may not afterwards complain of the obscurity in which the subject itself is deeply involved, or become too soon impatient of the obstacles in his path; because we have a choice of only two things—either at once to give up all pretensions to knowledge beyond the limits of possible experience, or to bring this critical investigation to completion.

We have been able, with very little trouble, to make it com-

---

[1] I have been compelled to adopt a conjectural reading here. All the editions of the *Critik der reinen Vernunft*, both those published during Kant's lifetime, and those published by various editors after his death, have *sie . . . von Gegenständen . . . redet.* But it is quite plain that the *sie* is the pronoun for *die reine Verstandesbegriffe*; and we ought, therefore, to read *reden*. In the same sentence, all the editions (except Hartenstein's) insert *die* after the first *und*, which makes nonsense. In page 89 also, sentence beginning '*For that objects,*' I have altered '*synthetischen Einsicht des Denkens*' into '*synthetischen Einheit.*' And in page 91, sentence beginning, '*But it is evident,*' we find '*die erste Bedingung liegen.*' Some such word as *muss* is plainly to be understood.

Indeed, I have not found a single edition of the *Critique* trustworthy. Kant must not have been very careful in his correction of the press. Those published by editors after Kant's death seem in most cases to follow Kant's own editions closely. That by Rosenkranz is perhaps the best; and he has corrected a number of Kant's errors. But although I have adopted several uncommon and also conjectural readings, I have not done so hastily or lightly. It is only after diligent comparison of all the editions I could gain access to, that I have altered the common reading; while a conjectural reading has been adopted only when it was quite clear that the reading of every edition was a misprint.

Other errors, occurring previously to those mentioned above, have been, and others after them will be, corrected in silence.—*Tr.*

prehensible how the conceptions of space and time, although *a priori* cognitions, must necessarily apply to external objects, and render a synthetical cognition of these possible, independently of all experience. For inasmuch as only by means of such pure form of sensibility an object can appear to us, that is, be an object of empirical intuition, space and time are pure intuitions, which contain *a priori* the condition of the possibility of objects as phenomena, and an *a priori* synthesis in these intuitions possesses objective validity.

On the other hand, the categories of the understanding do not represent the conditions under which objects are given to us in intuition; objects can consequently appear to us without necessarily connecting themselves with these, and consequently without any necessity binding on the understanding to contain *a priori* the conditions of these objects. Thus we find ourselves involved in a difficulty which did not present itself in the sphere of sensibility, that is to say, we cannot discover *how the subjective conditions of thought can have objective validity*, in other words, can become conditions of the possibility of all cognition of objects; for phenomena may certainly be given to us in intuition without any help from the functions of the understanding. Let us take, for example, the conception of *cause*, which indicates a peculiar kind of synthesis, namely, that with something, A, something entirely different, B, is connected according to a law. It is not *a priori* manifest why phenomena should contain anything of this kind (we are of course debarred from appealing for proof to experience, for the objective validity of this conception must be demonstrated *a priori*), and it hence remains doubtful *a priori*, whether such a conception be not quite void, and without any corresponding object among phenomena. For that objects of sensuous intuition must correspond to the formal conditions of sensibility existing *a priori* in the mind, is quite evident, from the fact that without these they could not be objects for us; but that they must also correspond to the conditions which understanding requires for the synthetical unity of thought, is an assertion, the grounds for which are not so easily to be discovered. For phenomena might be so constituted as not to correspond to the conditions of the unity of thought; and all things might lie in such confusion that, for example, nothing could be met with in the sphere of phenomena to suggest a law of synthesis, and so correspond to the conception of cause and effect; so that this conception would be quite void, null, and without significance. Phenomena would nevertheless continue to present objects to our intuition; for mere intuition does not in any respect stand in need of the functions of thought.

If we thought to free ourselves from the labour of these investigations by saying: 'Experience is constantly offering us examples of the relation of cause and effect in phenomena, and presents us with abundant opportunity of abstracting the conception of cause, and so at the same time of corroborating the objective validity of this conception;' we should in this case be overlooking the fact, that the conception of cause cannot arise in this way at all; that, on the contrary, it must either have an *a priori* basis in the understanding, or be rejected as a mere chimera. For this conception demands that something, A, should be of such a nature, that something else, B, should follow from it necessarily, and according to an absolutely universal law. We may certainly collect from phenomena a law, according to which this or that *usually* happens, but the element of necessity is not to be found in it. Hence it is evident that to the synthesis of cause and effect belongs a dignity, which is utterly wanting in any empirical synthesis; for it is no mere mechanical synthesis, by means of addition, but a dynamical one, that is to say, the effect is not to be cogitated as merely annexed to the cause, but as posited by and through the cause, and resulting from it. The strict universality of this law never can be a characteristic of empirical laws, which obtain through induction only a comparative universality, that is, an extended range of practical application. But the pure conceptions of the understanding would entirely lose all their peculiar character, if we treated them merely as the productions of experience.

TRANSITION TO THE TRANSCENDENTAL DEDUCTION OF THE
CATEGORIES

§ 10

There are only two possible ways in which synthetical representation and its objects can coincide with and relate necessarily to each other, and, as it were, meet together. Either the object alone makes the representation possible, or the representation alone makes the object possible. In the former case, the relation between them is only empirical, and an *a priori* representation is impossible. And this is the case with phenomena, as regards that in them which is referable to mere sensation. In the latter case—although representation alone (for of its causality, by means of the will, we do not here speak) does not produce the object as to its existence, it must nevertheless be *a priori* determinative in regard to the object, if it is only by means of the representation that we can cognize anything as an object. Now there are only two conditions of the possibility of a cognition of objects; firstly, *Intuition*, by means of which the object, though only as phenomenon, is given; secondly, *Conception*, by means of which the object which corresponds to this intuition is thought. But it is evident from what has been said on aesthetic, that the first condition, under which alone objects can be intuited, must in fact exist, as a formal basis for them, *a priori* in the mind. With this formal condition of sensibility, therefore, all phenomena necessarily correspond, because it is only through it that they can be phenomena at all; that is, can be empirically intuited and given. Now the question is, whether there do not exist *a priori* in the mind, conceptions of understanding also, as conditions under which alone something, if not intuited, is yet thought as object. If this question be answered in the affirmative, it follows that all empirical cognition of objects is necessarily conformable to such conceptions, since, if they are not presupposed, it is impossible that anything can be an object of experience. Now all experience contains, besides the intuition of the senses through which an object is given, a *conception* also of an object that is given in intuition. Accordingly, conceptions of objects in general must lie as *a priori* conditions at the foundation of all empirical cognition; and consequently, the objective validity of the categories, as *a priori* conceptions, will rest upon *this*, that experience (as far as regards the form of thought) is possible only by their means. For in that case they apply necessarily and *a priori* to objects of experience, because only through them can an object of experience be thought.

The whole aim of the transcendental deduction of all *a priori* conceptions is to show that these conceptions are *a priori* conditions of the possibility of all experience. Conceptions which afford us the objective foundation of the possibility of experience, are for that very reason necessary. But the analysis of the experiences in which they are met with is not deduction, but only an illustration of them, because from experience they could never derive the attribute of necessity. Without their original applicability and relation to all possible experience, in which all objects of cognition present themselves, the relation of the categories to objects, of whatever nature, would be quite incomprehensible.

The celebrated Locke, for want of due reflection on these points, and because he met with pure conceptions of the understanding in experience, sought also to deduce them from experience, and yet proceeded so inconsequently as to attempt, with their aid, to arrive at cognitions which lie far beyond the limits of all experience.

David Hume perceived that, to render this possible, it was necessary that the conceptions should have an *a priori* origin. But as he could not explain how it was possible that conceptions which are not connected with each other in the understanding, must nevertheless be thought as necessarily connected in the object—and it never occurred to him that the understanding itself might, perhaps, by means of these conceptions, be the author of the experience in which its objects were presented to it—he was forced to derive these conceptions from experience, that is, from a subjective necessity arising from repeated association of experiences erroneously considered to be objective—in one word, from '*habit*.' But he proceeded with perfect consequence, and declared it to be impossible with such conceptions and the principles arising from them, to overstep the limits of experience. The empirical derivation, however, which both of these philosophers attributed to these conceptions, cannot possibly be reconciled with the fact that we do possess scientific *a priori* cognitions, namely, those of pure mathematics and general physics.

The former of these two celebrated men opened a wide door to extravagance—(for if reason has once undoubted right on its side, it will not allow itself to be confined to set limits, by vague recommendations of moderation); the latter gave himself up entirely to scepticism—a natural consequence, after having discovered, as he thought, that the faculty of cognition was not trustworthy. We now intend to make a trial whether it be not possible safely to conduct reason between these two rocks, to assign her determinate limits, and yet leave open for her the entire sphere of her legitimate activity.

I shall merely premise an explanation of what the categories are. They are conceptions of an object in general, by means of which its intuition is contemplated as determined in relation to one of the logical functions of judgment. The following will make this plain. The function of the categorical judgment is that of the relation of subject to predicate; for example, in the proposition: 'All bodies are divisible.' But in regard to the merely logical use of the understanding, it still remains undetermined to which of these two conceptions belongs the function of subject, and to which that of predicate. For we could also say: 'Some divisible is a body.' But the category of substance, when the conception of a body is brought under it, determines that; and its empirical intuition in experience must be contemplated always as subject, and never as mere predicate. And so with all the other categories.

DEDUCTION OF THE PURE CONCEPTIONS OF THE UNDERSTANDING

SECTION II

TRANSCENDENTAL DEDUCTION OF THE PURE CONCEPTIONS OF THE
UNDERSTANDING

§ 11

*Of the Possibility of a Conjunction of the manifold representations
given by Sense*

THE manifold content in our representations can be given in an
intuition which is merely sensuous—in other words, is nothing but
susceptibility; and the form of this intuition can exist *a priori*
in our faculty of representation, without being anything else but
the mode in which the subject is affected. But the conjunction
(*conjunctio*) of a manifold in intuition never can be given us by the
senses; it cannot therefore be contained in the pure form of sensuous
intuition, for it is a spontaneous act of the faculty of representation.
And as we must, to distinguish it from sensibility, entitle this
faculty *understanding*; so all conjunction—whether conscious or
unconscious, be it of the manifold in intuition, sensuous or non-
sensuous, or of several conceptions—is an act of the understanding.
To this act we shall give the general appellation of *synthesis*, thereby to indicate, at the same time, that we cannot represent anything
as conjoined in the object without having previously conjoined it
ourselves. Of all mental notions, that of conjunction is the only
one which cannot be given through objects, but can be originated
only by the subject itself, because it is an act of its purely spontaneous activity. The reader will easily enough perceive that the
possibility of conjunction must be grounded in the very nature of
this act, and that it must be equally valid for all conjunction; and
that analysis, which appears to be its contrary, must, nevertheless,
always presuppose it; for where the understanding has not previously conjoined, it cannot dissect or analyse, because only as
conjoined by it, must that which is to be analysed have been given
to our faculty of representation.

But the conception of conjunction includes, besides the conception of the manifold and of the synthesis of it, that of the unity of it
also. Conjunction is the representation of the synthetical unity
of the manifold.[1] This idea of unity, therefore, cannot arise out

---

[1] Whether the representations are in themselves identical, and consequently
whether one can be thought analytically by means of and through the other,
is a question which we need not at present consider. Our *consciousness* of the

of that of conjunction; much rather does that idea, by combining itself with the representation of the manifold, render the conception of conjunction possible. This unity, which *a priori* precedes all conceptions of conjunction, is not the category of unity (§ 6); for all the categories are based upon logical functions of judgment, and in these functions we already have conjunction, and consequently unity of given conceptions. It is therefore evident that the category of unity presupposes conjunction. We must therefore look still higher for this unity (as qualitative, § 8), in that, namely, which contains the ground of the unity of diverse conceptions in judgments, the ground, consequently, of the possibility of the existence of the understanding, even in regard to its logical use.

### § 12

### *Of the Originally Synthetical Unity of Apperception* [1]

The *I think* must accompany all my representations, for otherwise something would be represented in me which could not be thought; in other words, the representation would either be impossible, or at least be, in relation to me, nothing. That representation which can be given previously to all thought, is called intuition. All the diversity or manifold content of intuition, has, therefore, a necessary relation to the *I think*, in the subject in which this diversity is found. But this representation, *I think*, is an act of *spontaneity*; that is to say, it cannot be regarded as belonging to mere sensibility. I call it pure apperception, in order to distinguish it from empirical; or primitive apperception, because it is a self-consciousness which, whilst it gives birth to the representation *I think*, must necessarily be capable of accompanying all our representations. It is in all acts of consciousness one and the same, and unaccompanied by it, no representation can exist *for me*. The unity of this apperception I call the transcendental unity of self-consciousness, in order to indicate the possibility of *a priori* cognition arising from it. For the manifold representations which are given in an intuition would not all of them be my representations, if they did not all belong to one self-consciousness,

one, when we speak of the manifold, is always distinguishable from our consciousness of the other; and it is only respecting the synthesis of this (possible) consciousness that we here treat.

[1] *Apperception* simply means consciousness. But it has been considered better to employ this term, not only because Kant saw fit to have another word besides *Bewusstseyn*, but because the term *consciousness* denotes a *state*, *apperception* an *act* of the *ego*; and from this alone the superiority of the latter is apparent.—*Tr.*

that is, as my representations (even although I am not conscious of them as such), they must conform to the condition under which, alone they can exist together in a common self-consciousness, because otherwise they would not all without exception belong to me. From this primitive conjunction follow many important results.

For example, this universal identity of the apperception of the manifold given in intuition, contains a synthesis of representations, and is possible only by means of the consciousness of this synthesis. For the empirical consciousness which accompanies different representations is in itself fragmentary and disunited, and without relation to the identity of the subject. This relation, then, does not exist because I accompany every representation with consciousness, but because I join one representation to another, and am conscious of the synthesis of them. Consequently, only because I can connect a variety of given representations in one consciousness, is it possible that I can represent to myself the identity of consciousness in these representations; in other words, the analytical unity of apperception is possible only under the presupposition of a synthetical unity.[1] The thought, 'These representations given in intuition, belong all of them to me,' is accordingly just the same as, 'I unite them in one self-consciousness, or can at least so unite them;' and although this thought is not itself the consciousness of the synthesis of representations, it presupposes the possibility of it; that is to say, for the reason alone, that I can comprehend the variety of my representations in one consciousness, do I call them my representations, for otherwise I must have as many-coloured and various a self as are the representations of which I am conscious. Synthetical unity of the manifold in intuitions, as given *a priori*, is therefore the foundation of the identity of apperception itself, which antecedes *a priori* all determinate thought. But the conjunction of representations into a conception is not to be found in

[1] All general conceptions—as such—depend, for their existence, on the analytical unity of consciousness. For example, when I think of *red* in general, I thereby think to myself a property which (as a characteristic mark) can be discovered somewhere, or can be united with other representations; consequently, it is only by means of a forethought possible synthetical unity that I can think to myself the analytical. A representation which is cogitated as common to *different* representations, is regarded as belonging to such as, besides this common representation, contain something *different*; consequently it must be previously thought in synthetical unity with other although only possible representations, before I can think in it the analytical unity of consciousness which makes it a *conceptus communis*. And thus the synthetical unity of apperception is the highest point with which we must connect every operation of the understanding, even the whole of logic, and after it our transcendental philosophy; indeed, this faculty is the understanding itself.

objects themselves, nor can it be, as it were, borrowed from them and taken up into the understanding by perception, but it is on the contrary an operation of the understanding itself, which is nothing more than the faculty of conjoining *a priori*, and of bringing the variety of given representations under the unity of apperception. This principle is the highest in all human cognition.

This fundamental principle of the necessary unity of apperception is indeed an identical, and therefore analytical proposition; but it nevertheless explains the necessity for a synthesis of the manifold given in an intuition, without which the identity of self-consciousness would be incogitable. For the Ego, as a simple representation, presents us with no manifold content; only in intuition, which is quite different from the representation Ego, can it be given us, and by means of conjunction, it is cogitated in one self-consciousness. An understanding, in which all the manifold should be given by means of consciousness itself, would be intuitive; our understanding can only think, and must look for its intuition to sense. I am, therefore, conscious of my identical self, in relation to all the variety of representations given to me in an intuition, because I call all of them my representations. In other words, I am conscious myself of a necessary *a priori* synthesis of my representations, which is called the original synthetical unity of apperception, under which rank all the representations presented to me, but that only by means of a synthesis.

## § 13

*The Principle of the Synthetical Unity of Apperception is the highest Principle of all exercise of the Understanding*

The supreme principle of the possibility of all intuition in relation to sensibility was, according to our transcendental aesthetic, that all the manifold in intuition be subject to the formal conditions of space and time. The supreme principle of the possibility of it in relation to the Understanding is: that all the manifold in it be subject to conditions of the originally synthetical Unity of Apperception.[1] To the former of these two principles are subject

[1] Space and time, and all portions thereof, are *Intuitions*; consequently are, with a manifold for their content, single representations. (See the *Transcendental Aesthetic*.) Consequently, they are not pure conceptions, by means of which the same consciousness is found in a great number of representations; but, on the contrary, they are many representations contained in one, the consciousness of which is, so to speak, compounded. The unity of consciousness is nevertheless *synthetical*, and therefore primitive. From this peculiar character of consciousness follow many important consequences. (See § 21.)

all the various representations of Intuition, in so far as they are given to us; to the latter, in so far as they must be capable of conjunction in one consciousness; for without this nothing can be thought or cognized, because the given representations would not have in common the act of the apperception *I think*; and therefore could not be connected in one self-consciousness.

*Understanding* is, to speak generally, *the faculty of Cognitions*. These consist in the determined relation of given representations to an object. But an object is that, in the conception of which the manifold in a given intuition is united. Now all union of representations requires unity of consciousness in the synthesis of them. Consequently, it is the unity of consciousness alone that constitutes the possibility of representations relating to an object, and therefore of their objective validity, and of their becoming cognitions, and consequently, the possibility of the existence of the understanding itself.

The first pure cognition of understanding, then, upon which is founded all its other exercise, and which is at the same time perfectly independent of all conditions of mere sensuous intuition, is the principle of the original synthetical unity of apperception. Thus the mere form of external sensuous intuition, namely, space, affords us, *per se*, no cognition; it merely contributes the manifold in *a priori* intuition to a possible cognition. But, in order to cognize something in space (for example, a line), I must draw it, and thus produce synthetically a determined conjunction of the given manifold, so that the unity of this act is at the same time the unity of consciousness (in the conception of a line), and by this means alone is an object (a determinate space) cognized. The synthetical unity of consciousness is, therefore, an objective condition of all cognition, which I do not merely require in order to cognize an object, but to which every intuition must necessarily be subject, in order to become an object for me; because in any other way, and without this synthesis, the manifold in intuition could not be united in one consciousness.

This proposition is, as already said, itself analytical, although it constitutes the synthetical unity, the condition of all thought; for it states nothing more than that all my representations in any given intuition must be subject to the condition which alone enables me to connect them, as my representation with the identical self, and so to unite them synthetically in one apperception, by means of the general expression, *I think*.

But this principle is not to be regarded as a principle for every possible understanding, but only for that understanding by means of whose pure apperception in the thought *I am*, no manifold content is given. The understanding or mind which contained the manifold in intuition, in and through the act itself of its own self-consciousness, in other words, an understanding by and in the representation of which the objects of the representation should at the same time exist, would not require a special act of synthesis of the manifold as the condition of the unity of its consciousness, an act of which the human understanding, which thinks only and cannot intuite, has absolute need. But this principle is the first *principle* of all the operations of our understanding, so that we cannot form the least conception of any other possible understanding, either of one such as should be itself intuition, or possess a sensuous intuition, but with forms different from those of space and time.

§ 14

### *What Objective Unity of Self-consciousness is*

It is by means of the transcendental unity of apperception that all the manifold given in an intuition is united into a conception of the object. On this account it is called objective, and must be distinguished from the *subjective unity* of consciousness, which is a *determination of the internal sense*, by means of which the said manifold in intuition is given empirically to be so united. Whether I can be *empirically* conscious of the manifold as co-existent or as successive, depends upon circumstances, or empirical conditions. Hence the empirical unity of consciousness by means of association of representations, itself relates to a phenomenal world, and is wholly contingent. On the contrary, the pure form of intuition in time, merely as an intuition, which contains a given manifold, is subject to the original unity of consciousness, and that solely by means of the necessary relation of the manifold in intuition to the *I think*, consequently by means of the pure synthesis of the understanding, which lies *a priori* at the foundation of all empirical synthesis. The transcendental unity of apperception is alone objectively valid; the empirical which we do not consider in this essay, and which is merely a unity deduced from the former under given conditions *in concreto*, possesses only subjective validity. One person connects the notion conveyed in a word with one thing, another with another thing; and the unity of consciousness in that which is empirical, is, in relation to that which is given by experience, not necessarily and universally valid.

## § 15

*The Logical Form of all Judgments consists in the Objective Unity of Apperception of the Conceptions contained therein*

I could never satisfy myself with the definition which logicians give of a judgment. It is, according to them, the representation of a relation between two conceptions. I shall not dwell here on the faultiness of this definition, in that it suits only for categorical and not for hypothetical or disjunctive judgments, these latter containing a relation not of conceptions but of judgments themselves—a blunder from which many evil results have followed.[1] It is more important for our present purpose to observe, that this definition does not determine in what the said relation consists.

But if I investigate more closely the relation of given cognitions in every judgment, and distinguish it, as belonging to the understanding, from the relation which is produced according to laws of the reproductive imagination (which has only subjective validity), I find that a judgment is nothing but the mode of bringing given cognitions under the objective unity of apperception. This is plain from our use of the term of relation *is* in judgments, in order to distinguish the objective unity of given representations from the subjective unity. For this term indicates the relation of these representations to the original apperception, and also their *necessary unity*, even although the judgment is empirical, therefore contingent, as in the judgment: 'All bodies are heavy.' I do not mean by this, that these representations do *necessarily* belong to each other in empirical intuition, but that by means of the *necessary unity* of apperception they belong to each other in the synthesis of intuitions, that is to say, they belong to each other according to principles of the objective determination of all our representations, in so far as cognition can arise from them, these principles being all deduced from the main principle of the transcendental unity of apperception. In this way alone can there arise from this relation a *judgment*, that is, a relation which has objective validity, and is perfectly distinct from that relation of the very same representations which has only subjective validity—a relation, to wit, which is produced according to laws of association. According

[1] The tedious doctrine of the four syllogistic figures concerns only categorical syllogisms; and although it is nothing more than an artifice by surreptitiously introducing immediate conclusions (*consequentiae immediatae*) among the premises of a pure syllogism, to give rise to an appearance of more modes of drawing a conclusion than that in the first figure, the artifice would not have had much success, had not its authors succeeded in bringing categorical judgments into exclusive respect, as those to which all others must be referred—a doctrine, however, which, according to § 5, is utterly false.

to these laws, I could only say: 'When I hold in my hand or carry a body, I feel an impression of weight;' but I could not say: 'It, the body, is heavy;' for this is tantamount to saying both these representations are conjoined in the object, that is, without distinction as to the condition of the subject, and do not merely stand together in my perception, however frequently the perceptive act may be repeated.

## § 16

*All Sensuous Intuitions are subject to the Categories, as Conditions under which alone the manifold Content of them can be united in one Consciousness*

The manifold content given in a sensuous intuition comes necessarily under the original synthetical unity of apperception, because thereby alone is the *unity* of intuition possible (§ 13). But that act of the understanding, by which the manifold content of given representations (whether intuitions or conceptions) is brought under one apperception, is the logical function of judgments (§ 15). All the manifold, therefore, in so far as it is given in one empirical intuition, is *determined* in relation to one of the logical functions of judgment, by means of which it is brought into union in one consciousness. Now the categories are nothing else than these functions of judgment, so far as the manifold in a given intuition is determined in relation to them (§ 9). Consequently, the manifold in a given intuition is necessarily subject to the categories of the understanding.

## § 17

### *Observation*

The manifold in an intuition, which I call mine, is represented by means of the synthesis of the understanding, as belonging to the necessary unity of self-consciousness, and this takes place by means of the category.[1] The category indicates accordingly, that the empirical consciousness of a given manifold in an intuition is subject to a pure self-consciousness *a priori*, in the same manner as an empirical intuition is subject to a pure sensuous intuition, which is also *a priori*. In the above proposition, then, lies the beginning of a deduction of the pure conceptions of the understanding. Now, as the categories have their origin in the under-

[1] The proof of this rests on the represented *unity of intuition*, by means of which an object is given, and which always includes in itself a synthesis of the manifold to be intuited, and also the relation of this latter to unity of apperception.

standing alone, independently of sensibility, I must in my deduction make abstraction of the mode in which the manifold of an empirical intuition is given, in order to fix my attention exclusively on the unity which is brought by the understanding into the intuition by means of the category. In what follows (§ 22), it will be shown from the mode in which the empirical intuition is given in the faculty of sensibility, that the unity which belongs to it is no other than that which the category (according to § 16) imposes on the manifold in a given intuition, and thus its *a priori* validity in regard to all objects of sense being established, the purpose of our deduction will be fully attained.

But there is one thing in the above demonstration, of which I could not make abstraction, namely, that the manifold to be intuited must be given previously to the synthesis of the understanding, and independently of it. How this takes place remains here undetermined. For if I cogitate an understanding which was itself intuitive (as, for example, a divine understanding which should not represent given objects, but by whose representation the objects themselves should be given or produced), the categories would possess no signification in relation to such a faculty of cognition. They are merely rules for an understanding, whose whole power consists in thought, that is, in the act of submitting the synthesis of the manifold which is presented to it in intuition from a very different quarter, to the unity of apperception; a faculty, therefore, which cognizes nothing *per se*, but only connects and arranges the material of cognition, the intuition, namely, which must be presented to it by means of the object. But to show reasons for this peculiar character of our understandings, that it produces unity of apperception *a priori* only by means of categories, and a certain kind and number thereof, is as impossible as to explain why we are endowed with precisely so many functions of judgment and no more, or why time and space are the only forms of our intuition.

## § 18

### *In Cognition, its Application to Objects of Experience is the only legitimate use of the Category*

To think an object and to cognize an object are by no means the same thing. In cognition there are two elements: firstly, the conception, whereby an object is cogitated (the category); and, secondly, the intuition, whereby the object is given. For supposing that to the conception a corresponding intuition could not be given, it would still be a thought as regards its form, but without any object, and no cognition of anything would be possible by means of it, inasmuch as, so far as I knew, there existed and could exist nothing to which my thought could be applied. Now all intuition possible to us is sensuous; consequently, our thought of an object by means of a pure conception of the understanding, can become cognition for us only in so far as this conception is applied to objects of the senses. Sensuous intuition is either pure intuition (space and time) or empirical intuition—of that which is immediately represented in space and time by means of sensation as real. Through the determination of pure intuition we obtain *a priori* cognitions of objects, as in mathematics, but only as regards their form as phenomena; whether there can exist things which must be intuited in this form is not thereby established. All mathematical conceptions, therefore, are not *per se* cognition, except in so far as we presuppose that there exist things which can only be represented conformably to the form of our pure sensuous intuition. But things in space and time are given only in so far as they are perceptions (representations accompanied with sensation), therefore only by empirical representation. Consequently the pure conceptions of the understanding, even when they are applied to intuitions *a priori* (as in mathematics), produce cognition only in so far as these (and therefore the conceptions of the understanding by means of them) can be applied to empirical intuitions. Consequently the categories do not, even by means of pure intuition, afford us any cognition of things; they can only do so in so far as they can be applied to empirical intuition. That is to say, the categories serve only to render empirical cognition possible. But this is what we call experience. Consequently, in cognition, their application to objects of experience is the only legitimate use of the categories.

§ 19

The foregoing proposition is of the utmost importance, for it determines the limits of the exercise of the pure conceptions of the understanding in regard to objects, just as transcendental aesthetic determined the limits of the exercise of the pure form of our sensuous intuition. Space and time, as conditions of the possibility of the presentation of objects to us, are valid no further than for objects of sense, consequently, only for experience. Beyond these limits they represent to us nothing, for they belong only to sense, and have no reality apart from it. The pure conceptions of the understanding are free from this limitation, and extend to objects of intuition in general, be the intuition like or unlike to ours, provided only it be sensuous, and not intellectual. But this extension of conceptions beyond the range of our intuition is of no advantage; for they are then mere empty conceptions of objects, as to the possibility or impossibility of the existence of which they furnish us with no means of discovery. They are mere forms of thought, without objective reality, because we have no intuition to which the synthetical unity of apperception, which alone the categories contain, could be applied, for the purpose of determining an object. Our sensuous and empirical intuition can alone give them significance and meaning.

If, then, we suppose an object of a non-sensuous intuition to be given, we can in that case represent it by all those predicates which are implied in the presupposition that nothing *appertaining to sensuous intuition belongs to it*; for example, that it is not extended, or in space; that its duration is not time; that in it no change (the effect of the determinations in time) is to be met with, and so on. But it is no proper knowledge if I merely indicate what the intuition of the object *is not*, without being able to say what is contained in it, for I have not shown the possibility of an object to which my pure conception of understanding could be applicable, because I have not been able to furnish any intuition corresponding to it, but am only able to say that our intuition is not valid for it. But the most important point is this, that to a *something* of this kind not one category can be found applicable. Take, for example, the conception of substance, that is, something that can exist as subject, but never as mere predicate; in regard to this conception I am quite ignorant whether there can really be anything to correspond to such a determination of thought, if empirical intuition did not afford me the occasion for its application. But of this more in the sequel.

### § 20

*Of the Application of the Categories to Objects of the Senses in general*

The pure conceptions of the understanding apply to objects of intuition in general, through the understanding alone, whether the intuition be our own or some other, provided only it be sensuous, but are, for this very reason, mere forms of thought, by means of which alone no determined object can be cognized. The synthesis or conjunction of the manifold in these conceptions relates, we have said, only to the unity of apperception, and is for this reason the ground of the possibility of *a priori* cognition, in so far as this cognition is dependent on the understanding. This synthesis is, therefore, not merely transcendental, but also purely intellectual. But because a certain form of sensuous intuition exists in the mind *a priori* which rests on the receptivity of the representative faculty (sensibility), the understanding, as a spontaneity, is able to determine the internal sense by means of the diversity of given representations, conformably to the synthetical unity of apperception, and thus to cogitate the synthetical unity of the apperception of the manifold of sensuous intuition *a priori*, as the condition to which must necessarily be submitted all objects of human intuition. And in this manner the categories as mere forms of thought receive objective reality, that is, application to objects which are given to us in intuition, but that only as phenomena, for it is only of phenomena that we are capable of *a priori* intuition.

This synthesis of the manifold of sensuous intuition, which is possible, and necessarily *a priori*, may be called figurative (*synthesis speciosa*), in contradistinction to that which is cogitated in the mere category in regard to the manifold of an intuition in general, and is called connection or conjunction of the understanding (*synthesis intellectualis*). Both are transcendental, not merely because they themselves precede *a priori* all experience, but also because they form the basis for the possibility of other cognition *a priori*.

But the figurative synthesis, when it has relation only to the originally synthetical unity of apperception, that is to the transcendental unity cogitated in the categories, must, to be distinguished from the purely intellectual conjunction, be entitled the *transcendental synthesis of imagination*.[1] *Imagination* is the faculty of representing an object even without its presence in intuition. Now, as all our intuition is sensuous, imagination, by reason of the subjective condition under which alone it can give a corresponding intuition to the conceptions of the understanding, belongs to sensibility. But in so far as the synthesis of the imagination is an act of spontaneity, which is determinative, and not, like sense, merely determinable, and which is consequently able to determine sense *a priori*, according to its form, conformably to the unity of apperception, in so far is the imagination a faculty of determining sensibility *a priori*, and its synthesis of intuitions according to the categories must be the transcendental synthesis of the imagination. It is an operation of the understanding on sensibility, and the first application of the understanding to objects of possible intuition, and at the same time the basis for the exercise of the other functions of that faculty. As figurative, it is distinguished from the merely intellectual synthesis, which is produced by the understanding alone, without the aid of imagination. Now, in so far as imagination is spontaneity, I sometimes call it also the *productive* imagination, and distinguish it from the *reproductive*, the synthesis of which is subject entirely to empirical laws, those of association, namely, and which, therefore, contributes nothing to the explanation of the possibility of *a priori* cognition, and for this reason belongs not to transcendental philosophy, but to psychology.

.     .     .     .     .

We have now arrived at the proper place for explaining the paradox, which must have struck every one in our exposition of the internal sense (§ 6), namely—how this sense represents us to our own consciousness, only as we appear to ourselves, not as we are in ourselves, because, to wit, we intuite ourselves only as we are inwardly affected. Now this appears to be contradictory, inasmuch as we thus stand in a passive relation to ourselves; and therefore in the systems of psychology, the internal sense is commonly held to be one with the faculty of apperception, while we, on the contrary, carefully distinguish them.

That which determines the internal sense is the understanding, and its original power of conjoining the manifold of intuition, that is, of bringing this under an apperception (upon which rests the possibility of the understanding itself). Now, as the human understanding is not in itself a faculty of intuition, and is unable to exercise such a power, in order to conjoin, as it were, the manifold of its own intuition, the synthesis of understanding is, considered *per se*, nothing but the unity of action, of which, as such, it is self-conscious, even apart from sensibility, by which, moreover, it is able to determine our internal sense in respect of the manifold which may be presented to it according to the form of sensuous intuition. Thus, under the name of a transcendental synthesis of imagination, the understanding exercises an activity upon the passive subject, whose faculty it is; and so we are right in saying that the internal sense is affected thereby. Apperception and its synthetical unity are by no means one and the same with the internal sense. The former, as the source of all our synthetical conjunction, applies, under the name of the categories, to the manifold of intuition in general, prior to all sensuous intuition of objects. The internal sense, on the contrary, contains merely the form of intuition, but without any synthetical conjunction of the manifold therein, and consequently does not contain any determined intuition, which is possible only through consciousness of the determination of the manifold by the transcendental act of the imagination (synthetical influence of the understanding on the internal sense), which I have named figurative synthesis.

This we can indeed always perceive in ourselves. We cannot cogitate a geometrical line without *drawing* it in thought, nor a circle without *describing* it, nor represent the three dimensions [1] of space without drawing three lines from the same point [2] perpendicular to one another. We cannot even cogitate time, unless, in drawing a straight line (which is to serve as the external figurative representation of time), we fix our attention on the act of the synthesis of the manifold, whereby we determine successively the internal sense, and thus attend also to the succession of this determination. Motion as an act of the subject (not as a determination of an object),[3] consequently the synthesis of the manifold in space, if we make abstraction of space and attend merely to the act by which we determine the internal sense according to its form, is that which produces the conception of succession. The understanding, therefore, does by no means *find* in the internal sense any such synthesis of the manifold, but *produces* it, in that it affects this sense. At the same time, how [the] *I* who think is distinct from the *I* which intuites itself (other modes of intuition being cogitable as at least possible), and yet one and the same with this latter as the same subject; how, therefore, I am able to say: 'I, as an intelligence and *thinking* subject, cognize myself as an object *thought*, so far as I am, moreover, given to myself in intuition—only, like other phenomena, not as I am in myself, and as considered by the understanding, but merely as I appear'—is a question that has in it neither more nor less difficulty than the question—'How can I be an object to myself?' or this—'How I can be an object of my own intuition and internal perceptions.' But that such must be the fact, if we admit that space is merely a pure form of the phenomena of external sense, can be clearly proved by the consideration that we cannot represent time, which is not an object of external intuition, in any other way than under the image of a line, which we draw in thought, a mode of representation without which we could not cognize the unity of its dimension, and also that we are necessitated to take our determination of periods of time,

---

[1] Length, breadth, and thickness.—*Tr.*     [2] In different planes.—*Tr.*

[3] Motion of an *object* in space does not belong to a pure science, consequently not to geometry; because that a thing is movable cannot be known *a priori*, but only from experience. But motion, considered as the *description* of a space, is a pure act of the successive synthesis of the manifold in external intuition by means of productive imagination, and belongs not only to geometry, but even to transcendental philosophy.

or of points of time, for all our internal perceptions from the changes which we perceive in outward things. It follows that we must arrange the determinations of the internal sense, as phenomena in time, exactly in the same manner as we arrange those of the external senses in space. And consequently, if we grant respecting this latter, that by means of them we know objects only in so far as we are affected externally, we must also confess, with regard to the internal sense, that by means of it we intuite ourselves only as we are internally affected by ourselves; in other words, as regards internal intuition, we cognize our own subject only as phenomenon, and not as it is in itself.[1]

## § 21

On the other hand, in the transcendental synthesis of the manifold content of representations, consequently in the synthetical unity of apperception, I am conscious of myself, not as I appear to myself, nor as I am in myself, but only that *I am*. This representation is a *Thought*, not an *Intuition*. Now, as in order to cognize ourselves, in addition to the act of thinking, which subjects the manifold of every possible intuition to the unity of apperception, there is necessary a determinate mode of intuition, whereby this manifold is given; although my own existence is certainly not mere phenomenon (much less mere illusion), the determination of my existence [2] can only take place conformably to the form of the internal sense, according to the particular mode in which the manifold which I conjoin is given in internal intuition,

[1] I do not see why so much difficulty should be found in admitting that our internal sense is affected by ourselves. Every act of attention exemplifies it. In such an act the understanding determines the internal sense by the synthetical conjunction which it cogitates, conformably to the internal intuition which corresponds to the manifold in the synthesis of the understanding. How much the mind is usually affected thereby every one will be able to perceive in himself.

[2] The *I think* expresses the act of determining my own existence. My existence is thus already given by the act of consciousness; but the mode in which I must determine my existence, that is, the mode in which I must place the manifold belonging to my existence, is not thereby given. For this purpose intuition of self is required, and this intuition possesses a form given *a priori*, namely, time, which is sensuous, and belongs to our receptivity of the determinable. Now, as I do not possess another intuition of self which gives the *determining* in me (of the spontaneity of which I am conscious), prior to the act of *determination*, in the same manner as time gives the determinable, it is clear that I am unable to determine my own existence as that of a spontaneous being, but I am only able to represent to myself the spontaneity of my thought, that is, of my determination, and my existence remains ever determinable in a purely sensuous manner, that is to say, like the existence of a phenomenon. But it is because of this spontaneity that I call myself an *intelligence*.

and I have therefore no knowledge of myself as I am, but merely as I appear to myself. The consciousness of self is thus very far from a knowledge of self, in which I do not use the categories, whereby I cogitate an object, by means of the conjunction of the manifold in one apperception. In the same way as I require, in order to the cognition of an object distinct from myself, not only the thought of an object in general (in the category), but also an intuition by which to determine that general conception, in the same way do I require, in order to the cognition of myself, not only the consciousness of myself or the thought that I think myself, but in addition an intuition of the manifold in myself, by which to determine this thought. It is true that I exist as an intelligence which is conscious only of its faculty of conjunction or synthesis, but subjected in relation to the manifold which this intelligence has to conjoin to a limitative conjunction called the internal sense. My intelligence (that is, I) can render that conjunction or synthesis perceptible only according to the relations of time, which are quite beyond the proper sphere of the conceptions of the understanding, and consequently cognize itself in respect to an intuition (which cannot possibly be intellectual, nor given by the understanding), only as it appears to itself, and not as it would cognize itself, if its intuition were intellectual.

### § 22

*Transcendental Deduction of the universally possible employment in experience of the Pure Conceptions of the Understanding*

In the metaphysical deduction, the *a priori* origin of the categories was proved by their complete accordance with the general logical functions of thought; in the transcendental deduction was exhibited the possibility of the categories as *a priori* cognitions of objects of an intuition in general (§§ 16 and 17). At present we are about to explain the possibility of cognizing, *a priori*, by means of the categories, all objects which can possibly be presented to our senses, not, indeed, according to the form of their intuition, but according to the laws of their conjunction or synthesis, and thus, as it were, of prescribing laws to nature, and even of rendering nature possible. For if the categories were adequate to this task, it would not be evident to us why everything that is presented to our senses must be subject to those laws which have an *a priori* origin in the understanding itself.

I premise, that by the term *synthesis of apprehension* I understand the combination of the manifold in an empirical intuition, whereby perception, that is, empirical consciousness of the intuition (as phenomenon), is possible.

We have *a priori* forms of the external and internal sensuous intuition in the representations of space and time, and to these must the synthesis of apprehension of the manifold in a phenomenon be always conformable, because the synthesis itself can only take place according to these forms. But space and time are not merely forms of sensuous intuition, but *intuitions* themselves (which contain a manifold), and therefore contain *a priori* the determination of the *unity* of this manifold.[1] (See the *Trans. Aesthetic.*) Therefore is *unity of the synthesis* of the manifold without or within us, consequently also a conjunction to which all that is to be represented as determined in space or time must correspond, given *a priori* along with (not in) these intuitions, as the condition of the synthesis of all apprehension of them. But this synthetical unity can be no other than that of the conjunction of the manifold of a given intuition in general, in a primitive act of consciousness, according to the categories, but applied to our sensuous intuition. Consequently all synthesis, whereby alone is even perception possible, is subject to the categories. And, as experience is cognition by means of conjoined perceptions, the categories are conditions of the possibility of experience, and are therefore valid *a priori* for all objects of experience.

·     ·     ·     ·     ·

When, then, for example, I make the empirical intuition of a house by apprehension of the manifold contained therein into a perception, the *necessary unity* of space and of my external sensuous intuition lies at the foundation of this act, and I, as it were, draw the form of the house conformably to this synthetical unity of the manifold in space. But this very synthetical unity remains, even when I abstract the form of space, and has its seat in the understanding, and is in fact the category of the synthesis of the homogeneous in an intuition; that is to say, the category of *quantity*,

[1] Space represented as an *object* (as geometry really requires it to be) contains more than the mere form of the intuition; namely, a combination of the manifold given according to the form of sensibility into a representation that can be intuited; so that the *form of the intuition* gives us merely the manifold, but the *formal intuition* gives unity of representation. In the Aesthetic I regarded this unity as belonging entirely to sensibility, for the purpose of indicating that it antecedes all conceptions, although it presupposes a synthesis which does not belong to sense, through which alone, however, all our conceptions of space and time are possible. For as by means of this unity alone (the understanding determining the sensibility) space and time are given as intuitions, it follows that the unity of this intuition *a priori* belongs to space and time, and not to the conception of the understanding (§ 20).

to which the aforesaid synthesis of apprehension, that is, the perception, must be completely conformable.[1]

To take another example, when I perceive the freezing of water, I apprehend two states (fluidity and solidity), which, as such, stand toward each other mutually in a relation of time. But in the time, which I place as an internal intuition, at the foundation of this phenomenon, I represent to myself synthetical *unity* of the manifold, without which the aforesaid relation could not be given in an intuition as *determined* (in regard to the succession of time). Now this synthetical unity, as the *a priori* condition under which I conjoin the manifold of an intuition, is, if I make abstraction of the permanent form of my internal intuition (that is to say, of time), the category of *cause*, by means of which, when applied to my sensibility, *I determine everything that occurs according to relations of time*. Consequently apprehension in such an event, and the event itself, as far as regards the possibility of its perception, stand under the conception of the relation of cause and effect: and so in all other cases.

· · · · ·

Categories are conceptions which prescribe laws *a priori* to phenomena, consequently to nature as the complex of all phenomena (*natura materialiter spectata*). And now the question arises —inasmuch as these categories are not derived from nature, and do not regulate themselves according to her as their model (for in that case they would be empirical)—how it is conceivable that nature must regulate herself according to them, in other words, how the categories can determine *a priori* the synthesis of the manifold of nature, and yet not derive their origin from her. The following is the solution of this enigma.

It is not in the least more difficult to conceive how the laws of the phenomena of nature must harmonize with the understanding and with its *a priori* form—that is, its faculty of conjoining the manifold—than it is to understand how the phenomena themselves must correspond with the *a priori* form of our sensuous intuition. For laws do not exist in the phenomena any more than the phenomena exist as things in themselves. Laws do not exist except by relation to the subject in which the phenomena inhere, in so far as it possesses understanding, just as phenomena have no

---

[1] In this manner it is proved, that the synthesis of apprehension, which is empirical, must necessarily be conformable to the synthesis of apperception, which is intellectual, and contained *a priori* in the category. It is one and the same spontaneity which at one time, under the name of imagination, at another under that of understanding, produces conjunction in the manifold of intuition.

existence except by relation to the same existing subject in so far as it has senses. To things as things in themselves, conformability to law must necessarily belong independently of an understanding to cognize them. But phenomena are only representations of things which are utterly unknown in respect to what they are in themselves. But as mere representations, they stand under no law of conjunction except that which the conjoining faculty prescribes. Now that which conjoins the manifold of sensuous intuition is imagination, a mental act to which understanding contributes unity of intellectual synthesis, and sensibility, manifoldness of apprehension. Now as all possible perception depends on the synthesis of apprehension, and this empirical synthesis itself on the transcendental, consequently on the categories, it is evident that all possible perceptions, and therefore everything that can attain to empirical consciousness, that is, all phenomena of nature, must, as regards their conjunction, be subject to the categories. And nature (considered merely as nature in general) is dependent on them as the original ground of her necessary conformability to law (as *natura formaliter spectata*). But the pure faculty (of the understanding) of prescribing laws *a priori* to phenomena by means of mere categories, is not competent to enounce other or more laws than those on which a *nature* in general, as a conformability to law of phenomena of space and time, depends. Particular laws, inasmuch as they concern empirically determined phenomena, cannot be entirely deduced from pure laws, although they all stand under them. Experience must be superadded in order to know these particular laws; but in regard to experience in general, and everything that can be cognized as an object thereof, these *a priori* laws are our only rule and guide.

## § 23

*Result of this Deduction of the Conceptions of the Understanding*

We cannot think any object except by means of the categories; we cannot cognize any thought except by means of intuitions corresponding to these conceptions. Now all our intuitions are sensuous, and our cognition, in so far as the object of it is given, is empirical. But empirical cognition is experience; consequently no *a priori cognition* is possible for us, except of objects of possible *experience*.[1]

[1] Lest my readers should stumble at this assertion, and the conclusions that may be too rashly drawn from it, I must remind them that the categories in the *act of thought* are by no means limited by the conditions of our sensuous intuition, but have an unbounded sphere of action. It is only the cognition

But this cognition, which is limited to objects of experience, is not for that reason derived entirely from experience, but—and this is asserted of the pure intuitions and the pure conceptions of the understanding—there are, unquestionably, elements of cognition, which exist in the mind *a priori*. Now there are only two ways in which a necessary harmony of experience with the conceptions of its objects can be cogitated. Either experience makes these conceptions possible, or the conceptions make experience possible. The former of these statements will not hold good with respect to the categories (nor in regard to pure sensuous intuition), for they are *a priori* conceptions, and therefore independent of experience. The assertion of an empirical origin would attribute to them a sort of *generatio aequivoca*. Consequently, nothing remains but to adopt the second alternative (which presents us with a system, as it were, of the *Epigenesis* of pure reason), namely, that on the part of the understanding the categories do contain the grounds of the possibility of all experience. But with respect to the questions how they make experience possible, and what are the principles of the possibility thereof with which they present us in their application to phenomena, the following section on the transcendental exercise of the faculty of judgment will inform the reader.

It is quite possible that someone may propose a species of *preformation-system* of pure reason—a middle way between the two—to wit, that the categories are neither innate and first *a priori* principles of cognition, nor derived from experience, but are merely subjective aptitudes for thought implanted in us contemporaneously with our existence, which were so ordered and disposed by our Creator, that their exercise perfectly harmonizes with the laws of nature which regulate experience. Now, not to mention that with such an hypothesis it is impossible to say at what point we must stop in the employment of predetermined aptitudes, the fact that the categories would in this case entirely lose that character of *necessity* which is essentially involved in the very conception of them, is a conclusive objection to it. The conception of cause, for example, which expresses the necessity of an effect under a presupposed condition, would be false, if it rested only upon such an arbitrary subjective necessity of uniting

of the object of thought, the determining of the object, which requires intuition. In the absence of intuition, our thought of an object may still have true and useful consequences in regard to the exercise of reason by the subject. But as this exercise of reason is not always directed on the determination of the object, in other words, on cognition thereof, but also on the determination of the subject and its volition, I do not intend to treat of it in this place.

certain empirical representations according to such a rule of relation. I could not then say—'The effect is connected with its cause in the object (that is, necessarily),' but only, 'I am so constituted that I can think this representation as so connected, and not otherwise.' Now this is just what the sceptic wants. For in this case, all our knowledge, depending on the supposed objective validity of our judgment, is nothing but mere illusion; nor would there be wanting people who would deny any such subjective necessity in respect to themselves, though they must feel it. At all events, we could not dispute with any one on that which merely depends on the manner in which his subject is organized.

### Short view of the above Deduction

The foregoing deduction is an exposition of the pure conceptions of the understanding (and with them of all theoretical *a priori* cognition), as principles of the possibility of experience, but of experience as the *determination* of all phenomena in space and time *in general*—of experience, finally, from the principle of the *original* synthetical unity of apperception, as the form of the understanding in relation to time and space as original forms of sensibility.

.        .        .        .        .

I consider the division by paragraphs to be necessary only up to this point, because we had to treat of the elementary conceptions. As we now proceed to the exposition of the employment of these, I shall not designate the chapters in this manner any further.

## TRANSCENDENTAL ANALYTIC

### BOOK II

#### ANALYTIC OF PRINCIPLES

GENERAL logic is constructed upon a plan which coincides exactly with the division of the higher faculties of cognition. These are, *Understanding, Judgment,* and *Reason.* This science, accordingly, treats in its analytic of *Conceptions, Judgments,* and *Conclusions* in exact correspondence with the functions and order of those mental powers which we include generally under the generic denomination of understanding.

As this merely formal logic makes abstraction of all content of cognition, whether pure or empirical, and occupies itself with the mere form of thought (discursive cognition), it must contain in its analytic a canon for reason. For the form of reason has its law, which, without taking into consideration the particular nature of the cognition about which it is employed, can be discovered *a priori*, by the simple analysis of the action of reason into its momenta.

Transcendental logic, limited as it is to a determinate content, that of pure *a priori* cognitions, to wit, cannot imitate general logic in this division. For it is evident that the *transcendental employment of reason* is not objectively valid, and therefore does not belong to the *logic of truth* (that is, to analytic), but as a *logic of illusion*, occupies a particular department in the scholastic system under the name of transcendental *Dialectic*.

Understanding and judgment accordingly possess in transcendental logic a canon of objectively valid, and therefore true exercise, and are comprehended in the analytical department of that logic. But reason, in her endeavours to arrive by *a priori* means at some true statement concerning objects, and to extend cognition beyond the bounds of possible experience, is altogether dialectic, and her illusory assertions cannot be constructed into a canon such as an analytic ought to contain.

Accordingly, the analytic of principles will be merely a canon for the *faculty of judgment*, for the instruction of this faculty in its application to phenomena of the pure conceptions of the understanding, which contain the necessary condition for the establishment of *a priori* laws. On this account, although the subject of the following chapters is the especial principles of *understanding*, I shall make use of the term '*Doctrine of the faculty of judgment*,' in order to define more particularly my present purpose.

## INTRODUCTION

### OF THE TRANSCENDENTAL FACULTY OF JUDGMENT IN GENERAL

If understanding in general be defined as the faculty of laws or rules, the faculty of judgment may be termed the faculty of *subsumption* under these rules; that is, of distinguishing whether this or that does or does not stand under a given rule (*casus datae legis*). General logic contains no directions or precepts for the faculty of judgment, nor can it contain any such. For as *it makes abstraction of all content of cognition*, no duty is left for it, except that of exposing analytically the mere form of cognition in conceptions, judgments, and conclusions, and of thereby establishing formal rules for all exercise of the understanding. Now if this logic wished to give some general direction how we should subsume under these rules, that is, how we should distinguish whether this or that did or did not stand under them, this again could not be done otherwise than by means of a rule. But this rule, precisely because it is a rule, requires for itself direction from the faculty of judgment. Thus, it is evident that the understanding is capable of being instructed by rules, but that the judgment is a peculiar talent, which does not, and cannot require tuition, but only exercise. This faculty is therefore the specific quality of the so-called mother wit, the want of which no scholastic discipline can compensate. For although education may furnish, and, as it were, engraft upon a limited understanding rules borrowed from other minds, yet the power of employing these rules correctly must belong to the pupil himself; and no rule which we can prescribe to him with this purpose is, in the absence or deficiency of this gift of nature, secure from misuse.[1] A physician therefore, a judge or a statesman, may have in his head many admirable pathological, juridical, or political rules, in a degree that may enable him to be a profound teacher in his particular science, and yet in the application of these rules he may very possibly blunder —either because he is wanting in natural judgment (though not in understanding), and whilst he can comprehend the general *in abstracto*, cannot distinguish whether a particular case *in concreto* ought to rank under the former; or because his faculty of judgment has not been sufficiently exercised by examples and real practice. Indeed, the grand and only use of examples, is to sharpen the judgment. For as regards the correctness and precision of the insight of the understanding, examples are commonly injurious rather than otherwise, because, as *casus in terminis*, they seldom adequately fulfil the conditions of the rule. Besides, they often weaken the power of our understanding to apprehend rules or laws in their universality, independently of particular circumstances of experience; and hence, accustom us to employ them more as formulae than as principles. Examples are thus the go-cart of the judgment, which he who is naturally deficient in that faculty, cannot afford to dispense with.

But although general logic cannot give directions to the faculty of judgment, the case is very different as regards transcendental

[1] Deficiency in judgment is properly that which is called stupidity; and for such a failing we know no remedy. A dull or narrow-minded person, to whom nothing is wanting but a proper degree of understanding, may be improved by tuition, even so far as to deserve the epithet of *learned*. But as such persons frequently labour under a deficiency in the faculty of judgment, it is not uncommon to find men extremely learned who in the application of their science betray to a lamentable degree this irremediable want.

logic, insomuch that it appears to be the especial duty of the latter to secure and direct, by means of determinate rules, the faculty of judgment in the employment of the pure understanding. For, as a doctrine, that is, as an endeavour to enlarge the sphere of the understanding in regard to pure *a priori* cognitions, philosophy is worse than useless, since from all the attempts hitherto made, little or no ground has been gained. But, as a critique, in order to guard against the mistakes of the faculty of judgment (*lapsus judicii*) in the employment of the few pure conceptions of the understanding which we possess, although its use is in this case purely negative, philosophy is called upon to apply all its acuteness and penetration.

But transcendental philosophy has this peculiarity, that besides indicating the rule, or rather the general condition for rules, which is given in the pure conception of the understanding, it can, at the same time, indicate *a priori* the case to which the rule must be applied. The cause of the superiority which, in this respect, transcendental philosophy possesses above all other sciences except mathematics, lies in this: it treats of conceptions which must relate *a priori* to their objects, whose objective validity consequently cannot be demonstrated *a posteriori*, and is, at the same time, under the obligation of presenting in general but sufficient tests, the conditions under which objects can be given in harmony with those conceptions; otherwise they would be mere logical forms, without content, and not pure conceptions of the understanding.

Our transcendental doctrine of the faculty of judgment will contain two chapters. The first will treat of the sensuous condition under which alone pure conceptions of the understanding can be employed—that is, of the *schematism* of the pure understanding. The second will treat of those synthetical judgments which are derived *a priori* from pure conceptions of the understanding under those conditions, and which lie *a priori* at the foundation of all other cognitions, that is to say, it will treat of the principles of the pure understanding.

# TRANSCENDENTAL DOCTRINE OF THE FACULTY OF JUDGMENT

## Or, Analytic of Principles

### CHAPTER I

*Of the Schematism of the Pure Conceptions of the Understanding*

In all subsumptions of an object under a conception, the representation of the object must be homogeneous with the conception; in other words, the conception must contain that which is represented in the object to be subsumed under it. For this is the meaning of the expression: An object is contained under a conception. Thus the empirical conception of a *plate* is homogeneous with the pure geometrical conception of a *circle*, inasmuch as the roundness which is cogitated in the former is intuited in the latter.

But pure conceptions of the understanding, when compared with empirical intuitions, or even with sensuous intuitions in general, are quite heterogeneous, and never can be discovered in any intuition. How then is the *subsumption* of the latter under the former, and consequently the application of the categories to phenomena, possible?—For it is impossible to say, for example: Causality can be intuited through the senses, and is contained in the phenomenon.—This natural and important question forms the real cause of the necessity of a transcendental doctrine of the faculty of judgment, with the purpose, to wit, of showing how pure conceptions of the understanding can be applied to phenomena. In all other sciences, where the conceptions by which the object is thought in the general are not so different and heterogeneous from those which represent the object *in concreto*—as it is given, it is quite unnecessary to institute any special inquiries concerning the application of the former to the latter.

Now it is quite clear that there must be some third thing, which on the one side is homogeneous with the category, and with the phenomenon on the other, and so makes the application of the former to the latter possible. This mediating representation must be pure (without any empirical content), and yet must on the one side be *intellectual*, on the other *sensuous*. Such a representation is the *transcendental schema*.

The conception of the understanding contains pure synthetical unity of the manifold in general. Time, as the formal condition

of the manifold of the internal sense, consequently of the conjunction of all representations, contains *a priori* a manifold in the
pure intuition.  Now a transcendental determination of time is
so far homogeneous with the *category*, which constitutes the unity
thereof, that it is universal, and rests upon a rule *a priori*.  On
the other hand, it is so far homogeneous with the *phenomenon*,
inasmuch as time is contained in every empirical representation
of the manifold.  Thus an application of the category to phenomena
becomes possible, by means of the transcendental determination
of time, which, as the schema of the conceptions of the understanding, mediates the subsumption of the latter under the former.

After what has been proved in our deduction of the categories,
no one, it is to be hoped, can hesitate as to the proper decision of
the question, whether the employment of these pure conceptions
of the understanding ought to be merely empirical or also transcendental; in other words, whether the categories, as conditions of a
possible experience, relate *a priori* solely to phenomena, or whether,
as conditions of the possibility of things in general, their application
can be extended to objects as things in themselves.  For we have
there seen that conceptions are quite impossible, and utterly without
signification, unless either to them, or at least to the elements of
which they consist, an object be given; and that, consequently,
they cannot possibly apply to objects as things in themselves
without regard to the question whether and how these may be
given to us; and further, that the only manner in which objects
can be given to us, is by means of the modification of our sensibility;
and finally, that pure *a priori* conceptions, in addition to the function of the understanding in the category, must contain *a priori*
formal conditions of sensibility (of the internal sense, namely),
which again contain the general condition under which alone the
category can be applied to any object.  This formal and pure
condition of sensibility, to which the conception of the understanding is restricted in its employment, we shall name the *schema*
of the conception of the understanding, and the procedure of the
understanding with these schemata we shall call the *Schematism*
of the pure understanding.

The Schema is, in itself, always a mere product of the imagination.[1]  But as the synthesis of imagination has for its aim no
single intuition, but merely unity in the determination of sensibility,
the schema is clearly distinguishable from the image.  Thus, if I
place five points one after another . . . . . this is an image of the
number five.  On the other hand, if I only think a number in

general, which may be either five or a hundred, this thought is rather the representation of a method of representing in an image a sum (e.g. a thousand) in conformity with a conception, than the image itself, an image which I should find some little difficulty in reviewing, and comparing with the conception. Now this representation of a general procedure of the imagination to present its image to a conception, I call the schema of this conception.

In truth, it is not images of objects, but schemata, which lie at the foundation of our pure sensuous conceptions. No image could ever be adequate to our conception of a triangle in general. For the generalness of the conception it never could attain to, as this includes under itself all triangles, whether right-angled, acute-angled, etc., whilst the image would always be limited to a single part of this sphere. The schema of the triangle can exist nowhere else than in thought, and it indicates a rule of the synthesis of the imagination in regard to pure figures in space. Still less is an object of experience, or an image of the object, ever adequate to the empirical conception. On the contrary, the conception always relates immediately to the schema of the imagination, as a rule for the determination of our intuition, in conformity with a certain general conception. The conception of a dog indicates a rule, according to which my imagination can delineate the figure of a four-footed animal in general, without being limited to any particular individual form which experience presents to me, or indeed to any possible image that I can represent to myself *in concreto*. This schematism of our understanding in regard to phenomena and their mere form, is an art, hidden in the depths of the human soul, whose true modes of action we shall only with difficulty discover and unveil. Thus much only can we say: The *image* is a product of the empirical faculty of the productive imagination—the *schema* of sensuous conceptions (of figures in space, for example) is a product, and, as it were, a monogram of the pure imagination *a priori*, whereby and according to which images first become possible, which, however, can be connected with the conception only mediately by means of the schema which they indicate, and are in themselves never fully adequate to it. On the other hand, the schema of a pure conception of the understanding is something that cannot be reduced into any image—it is nothing else than the pure synthesis expressed by the category, conformably to a rule of unity according to conceptions. It is a transcendental product of the imagination, a product which concerns the determination of the internal sense, according to conditions of its form (time) in respect to all representations, in so far as these representations must be conjoined *a priori* in one conception, conformably to the unity of apperception.

Without entering upon a dry and tedious analysis of the essential requisites of transcendental schemata of the pure conceptions of the understanding, we shall rather proceed at once to give an explanation of them according to the order of the categories, and in connection therewith.

For the external sense the pure image of all quantities (*quantorum*) is space; the pure image of all objects of sense in general, is time. But the pure *schema* of *quantity* (*quantitatis*) as a conception of the understanding, is *number*, a representation which comprehends the successive addition of one to one (homogeneous quantities). Thus, number is nothing else than the unity of the synthesis of the manifold in a homogeneous intuition, by means of my generating time [1] itself in my apprehension of the intuition.

Reality, in the pure conception of the understanding, is that which corresponds to a sensation in general; that, consequently, the conception of which indicates a being (in time). Negation is that the conception of which represents a not-being (in time). The opposition of these two consists therefore in the difference of one and the same time, as a time filled or a time empty. Now as time is only the form of intuition, consequently of objects as phenomena, that which in objects corresponds to sensation is the transcendental matter of all objects as things in themselves (*Sachheit*, reality). Now every sensation has a degree or quantity by which it can fill time, that is to say, the internal sense in respect of the representation of an object, more or less, until it vanishes into nothing (=o=*negatio*). Thus there is a relation and connection between reality and negation, or rather a transition from the former to the latter, which makes every reality representable to us as a quantum; and the schema of a reality as the quantity of something in so far as it fills time, is exactly this continuous and uniform generation of the reality in time, as we descend in time from the sensation which has a certain degree, down to the vanishing thereof, or gradually ascend from negation to the quantity thereof.

The schema of substance is the permanence of the real in time; that is, the representation of it as a substratum of the empirical determination of time; a substratum which therefore remains, whilst all else changes. (Time passes not, but in it passes the existence of the changeable. To time, therefore, which is itself unchangeable and permanent, corresponds that which in the

---

[1] I generate time because I generate succession, namely, in the successive addition of one to one.—*Tr.*

phenomenon is unchangeable in existence, that is, substance, and it is only by it that the succession and co-existence of phenomena can be determined in regard to time.)

The schema of cause and of the causality of a thing is the real which, when posited, is always followed by something else. It consists, therefore, in the succession of the manifold, in so far as that succession is subjected to a rule.

The schema of community (reciprocity of action and reaction), or the reciprocal causality of substances in respect of their accidents, is the co-existence of the determinations of the one with those of the other, according to a general rule.

The schema of possibility is the accordance of the synthesis of different representations with the conditions of time in general (as, for example, opposites cannot exist together at the same time in the same thing, but only after each other), and is therefore the determination of the representation of a thing at *any* time.

The schema of reality [1] is existence in a determined time.

The schema of necessity is the existence of an object in all time.

It is clear, from all this, that the schema of the category of quantity contains and represents the generation (synthesis) of time itself, in the successive apprehension of an object; the schema of quality the synthesis of sensation with the representation of time, or the filling up of time; the schema of relation the relation of perceptions to each other in all time (that is, according to a rule of the determination of time): and finally, the schema of modality and its categories, time itself, as the correlative of the determination of an object—whether it does belong to time, and how. The schemata, therefore, are nothing but *a priori determinations of time* according to rules, and these, in regard to all possible objects, following the arrangement of the categories, relate to *the series in time, the content in time, the order in time*, and finally, *to the complex or totality in time*.

Hence it is apparent that the schematism of the understanding, by means of the transcendental synthesis of the imagination, amounts to nothing else than the unity of the manifold of intuition in the internal sense, and thus indirectly to the unity of apperception, as a function corresponding to the internal sense (a receptivity). Thus, the schemata of the pure conceptions of the understanding are the true and only conditions whereby our understanding receives an application to objects, and consequently *significance*. Finally, therefore, the categories are only capable of empirical use, inasmuch as they serve merely to subject phenomena to the

---

[1] *Wirklichkeit.* In the table of categories it is called Existence (Daseyn).—*Tr.*

universal rules of synthesis, by means of an *a priori* necessary unity (on account of the necessary union of all consciousness in one original apperception); and so to render them susceptible of a complete connection in one experience. But within this whole of possible experience lie all our cognitions, and in the universal relation to this experience consists transcendental truth, which antecedes all empirical truth, and renders the latter possible.

It is, however, evident at first sight, that although the schemata of sensibility are the sole agents in realizing the categories, they do, nevertheless, also restrict them, that is, they limit the categories by conditions which lie beyond the sphere of understanding—namely, in sensibility. Hence the schema is properly only the phenomenon, or the sensuous conception of an object in harmony with the category. (*Numerus* est quantitas phaenomenon [1]—*sensatio* realitas phaenomenon; *constans* et perdurabile rerum substantia phaenomenon—*aeternitas, necessitas,* phaenomena, etc.) Now, if we remove a restrictive condition, we thereby amplify, it appears, the formerly limited conception. In this way, the categories in their pure signification, free from all conditions of sensibility, ought to be valid of things *as they are*, and not, as the schemata represent them, merely as they appear, and consequently the categories must have a significance far more extended, and wholly independent of all schemata. In truth, there does always remain to the pure conceptions of the understanding, after abstracting every sensuous condition, a value and significance, which is, however, merely logical. But in this case, no object is given them, and therefore they have no meaning sufficient to afford us a conception of an object. The notion of substance, for example, if we leave out the sensuous determination of permanence, would mean nothing more than a something which can be cogitated as subject, without the possibility of becoming a predicate to anything else. Of this representation I can make nothing, inasmuch as it does not indicate to me what determinations the thing possesses which must thus be valid as *premier* subject. Consequently, the categories, without schemata, are merely functions of the understanding for the production of conceptions, but do not represent any object. This significance they derive from sensibility, which at the same time realizes the understanding and restricts it.

---

[1] *Phaenomenon* is here an adjective.—*Tr.*

## TRANSCENDENTAL DOCTRINE OF THE FACULTY OF JUDGMENT

### Or, Analytic of Principles

### CHAPTER II

#### System of all Principles of the Pure Understanding

In the foregoing chapter we have merely considered the general conditions under which alone the transcendental faculty of judgment is justified in using the pure conceptions of the understanding for synthetical judgments. Our duty at present is to exhibit in systematic connection those judgments which the understanding really produces *a priori*. For this purpose, our table of the categories will certainly afford us the natural and safe guidance. For it is precisely the categories whose application to possible experience must constitute all pure *a priori* cognition of the understanding; and the relation of which to sensibility will, on that very account, present us with a complete and systematic catalogue of all the transcendental principles of the use of the understanding.

Principles *a priori* are so called, not merely because they contain in themselves the grounds of other judgments, but also because they themselves are not grounded in higher and more general cognitions. This peculiarity, however, does not raise them altogether above the need of a proof. For although there could be found no higher cognition, and therefore no objective proof, and although such a principle rather serves as the foundation for all cognition of the object, this by no means hinders us from drawing a proof from the subjective sources of the possibility of the cognition of an object. Such a proof is necessary, moreover, because without it the principle might be liable to the imputation of being a mere gratuitous assertion.

In the second place, we shall limit our investigations to those principles which relate to the categories. For as to the principles of transcendental aesthetic, according to which space and time are the conditions of the possibility of things as phenomena, as also the restriction of these principles, namely, that they cannot be applied to objects as things in themselves—these, of course, do not fall within the scope of our present inquiry. In like manner, the principles of mathematical science form no part of this system, because they are all drawn from intuition, and not from the pure conception of the understanding. The possibility of these principles, however, will necessarily be considered here, inasmuch as they are synthetical judgments *a priori*, not indeed for the purpose of proving their accuracy and apodeictic certainty, which is unnecessary, but merely to render conceivable and deduce the possibility of such evident *a priori* cognitions.

But we shall have also to speak of the principle of analytical judgments, in opposition to synthetical judgments, which is the proper subject of our inquiries, because this very opposition will free the theory of the latter from all ambiguity, and place it clearly before our eyes in its true nature.

## SYSTEM OF THE PRINCIPLES OF THE PURE UNDERSTANDING

### SECTION I

#### Of the Supreme Principle of all Analytical Judgments

Whatever may be the content of our cognition, and in whatever manner our cognition may be related to its object, the universal, although only negative condition of all our judgments is that they do not contradict themselves; otherwise these judgments are in themselves (even without respect to the object) nothing. But although there may exist no contradiction in our judgment, it may nevertheless connect conceptions in such a manner, that they do not correspond to the object, or without any grounds either *a priori* or *a posteriori* for arriving at such a judgment, and thus, without being self-contradictory, a judgment may nevertheless be either false or groundless.

Now, the proposition: 'No subject can have a predicate that contradicts it,' is called the principle of contradiction, and is a universal but purely negative criterion of all truth. But it belongs to logic alone, because it is valid of cognitions, merely as cognitions, and without respect to their content, and declares that the contradiction entirely nullifies them. We can also, however, make a positive use of this principle, that is, not merely to banish falsehood and error (in so far as it rests upon contradiction), but also for the cognition of truth. For *if the judgment is analytical*, be it affirmative or negative, its truth must always be recognizable by means of the principle of contradiction. For the contrary of that which lies and is cogitated as conception in the cognition of the object will be always properly negatived, but the conception itself must always be affirmed of the object, inasmuch as the contrary thereof would be in contradiction to the object.

We must therefore hold the *principle of contradiction* to be the universal and fully sufficient *principle of all analytical cognition.*

But as a sufficient criterion of truth, it has no further utility or authority. For the fact that no cognition can be at variance with this principle without nullifying itself, constitutes this principle the *sine qua non*, but not the determining ground of the truth of our cognition. As our business at present is properly with the synthetical part of our knowledge only, we shall always be on our guard not to transgress this inviolable principle; but at the same time not to expect from it any direct assistance in the establishment of the truth of any synthetical proposition.

There exists, however, a formula of this celebrated principle—a principle merely formal and entirely without content—which contains a synthesis that has been inadvertently and quite unnecessarily mixed up with it. It is this: 'It is impossible for a thing to be and not to be at the same time.' Not to mention the superfluousness of the addition of the word *impossible* to indicate the apodeictic certainty, which ought to be self-evident from the proposition itself, the proposition is affected by the condition of time, and as it were says: 'A thing$=A$, which is something$=B$, cannot at the same time be *non-B*.' But both, $B$ as well as *non-B*, may quite well exist in succession. For example, a man who is young cannot at the same time be old; but the same man can very well be at one time young, and at another not young, that is, old. Now the principle of contradiction as a merely logical proposition must not by any means limit its application merely to relations of time, and consequently a formula like the preceding is quite foreign to its true purpose. The misunderstanding arises in this way. We first of all separate a predicate of a thing from the conception of the thing, and afterwards connect with this predicate its opposite, and hence do not establish any contradiction with the subject, but only with its predicate, which has been conjoined with the subject synthetically—a contradiction, moreover, which obtains only when the first and second predicate are affirmed in the same time. If I say: 'A man who is ignorant is not learned,' the condition 'at the same time' must be added, for he who is at one time ignorant, may at another be learned. But if I say: 'No ignorant man is a learned man,' the proposition is analytical, because the characteristic *ignorance* is now a constituent part of the conception of the subject; and in this case the negative proposition is evident immediately from the proposition of contradiction, without the necessity of adding the condition 'at the same time.' This is the reason why I have altered the formula of this principle—an alteration which shows very clearly the nature of an analytical proposition.

## SECTION II

*Of the Supreme Principle of all Synthetical Judgments*

The explanation of the possibility of synthetical judgments is a task with which general Logic has nothing to do; indeed she needs not even be acquainted with its name. But in transcendental Logic it is the most important matter to be dealt with—indeed the only one, if the question is of the possibility of synthetical judgments *a priori*, the conditions and extent of their validity. For when this question is fully decided, it can reach its aim with perfect ease, the determination, to wit, of the extent and limits of the pure understanding.

In an analytical judgment I do not go beyond the given conception, in order to arrive at some decision respecting it. If the judgment is affirmative, I predicate of the conception only that which was already cogitated in it; if negative, I merely exclude from the conception its contrary. But in synthetical judgments, I must go beyond the given conception, in order to cogitate, in relation with it, something quite different from that which was cogitated in it, a relation which is consequently never one either of identity or contradiction, and by means of which the truth or error of the judgment cannot be discerned merely from the judgment itself.

Granted, then, that we must go out beyond a given conception, in order to compare it synthetically with another, a third thing is necessary, in which alone the synthesis of two conceptions can originate. Now what is this *tertium quid*, that is to be the medium of all synthetical judgments? It is only a complex,[1] in which all our representations are contained, the internal sense to wit, and its form *a priori*, Time.

The synthesis of our representations rests upon the imagination; their synthetical unity (which is requisite to a judgment), upon the unity of apperception. In this, therefore, is to be sought the possibility of synthetical judgments, and as all three contain the sources of *a priori* representations, the possibility of pure synthetical judgments also; nay, they are necessary upon these grounds, if we are to possess a knowledge of objects, which rests solely upon the synthesis of representations.

If a cognition is to have objective reality, that is, to relate to

[1] *Inbegriff.*

an object, and possess sense and meaning in respect to it, it is
necessary that the object be given in some way or another. Without this, our conceptions are empty, and we may indeed have
thought by means of them, but by such thinking we have not,
in fact, cognized anything, we have merely played with representation. To give an object, if this expression be understood
in the sense of to present the object, not mediately but immediately
in intuition, means nothing else than to apply the representation
of it to experience, be that experience real or only possible. Space
and time themselves, pure as these conceptions are from all that
is empirical, and certain as it is that they are represented fully
*a priori* in the mind, would be completely without objective
validity, and without sense and significance, if their necessary use
in the objects of experience were not shown. Nay, the representation of them is a mere schema, that always relates to the reproductive imagination, which calls up the objects of experience,
without which they have no meaning. And so is it with all
conceptions without distinction.

The *possibility of experience* is, then, that which gives objective
reality to all our *a priori* cognitions. Now experience depends
upon the synthetical unity of phenomena, that is, upon a synthesis
according to conceptions of the object of phenomena in general,
a synthesis without which experience never could become knowledge, but would be merely a rhapsody of perceptions, never fitting
together into any connected text, according to rules of a thoroughly
united (possible) consciousness, and therefore never subjected to
the transcendental and necessary unity of apperception. Experience
has therefore for a foundation, *a priori* principles of its form, that
is to say, general rules of unity in the synthesis of phenomena,
the objective reality of which rules, as necessary conditions—even
of the possibility of experience—can always be shown in experience.
But apart from this relation, *a priori* synthetical propositions are
absolutely impossible, because they have no third term, that is,
no pure object, in which the synthetical unity can exhibit the
objective reality of its conceptions.

Although, then, respecting space, or the forms which productive
imagination describes therein, we do cognize much *a priori* in
synthetical judgments, and are really in no need of experience
for this purpose, such knowledge would nevertheless amount to
nothing but a busy trifling with a mere chimera, were not space
to be considered as the condition of the phenomena which constitute
the material of external experience. Hence those pure synthetical
judgments do relate, though but mediately, to possible experience,

or rather to the possibility of experience, and upon that alone is founded the objective validity of their synthesis.

While then, on the one hand, experience, as empirical synthesis, is the only possible mode of cognition which gives reality to all other synthesis;[1] on the other hand, this latter synthesis, as cognition *a priori*, possesses truth, that is, accordance with its object, only in so far as it contains nothing more than what is necessary to the synthetical unity of experience.

Accordingly, the supreme principle of all synthetical judgments is: Every object is subject to the necessary conditions of the synthetical unity of the manifold of intuition in a possible experience.

*A priori* synthetical judgments are possible, when we apply the formal conditions of the *a priori* intuition, the synthesis of the imagination, and the necessary unity of that synthesis in a transcendental apperception, to a possible cognition of experience, and say: The conditions of the *possibility of experience* in general are at the same time conditions of the *possibility* of the *objects* of *experience*, and have, for that reason, objective validity in an *a priori* synthetical judgment.

### System of the Principles of the Pure Understanding

### SECTION III

*Systematic Representation of all Synthetical Principles of the Pure Understanding*

That principles exist at all is to be ascribed solely to the pure understanding, which is not only the faculty of rules in regard to that which happens, but is even the source of principles according to which everything that can be presented to us as an object is necessarily subject to rules, because without such rules we never could attain to cognition of an object. Even the laws of nature, if they are contemplated as principles of the empirical use of the understanding, possess also a characteristic of necessity, and we may therefore at least expect them to be determined upon grounds which are valid *a priori* and antecedent to all experience. But all laws of nature, without distinction, are subject to higher principles of the understanding, inasmuch as the former are merely applications of the latter to particular cases of experience. These higher principles alone therefore give the conception, which contains the necessary condition, and, as it were, the exponent of a rule;

[1] Mental synthesis.—*Tr.*

experience, on the other hand, gives the case which comes under the rule.

There is no danger of our mistaking merely empirical principles for principles of the pure understanding, or conversely; for the character of necessity, according to conceptions which distinguish the latter, and the absence of this in every empirical proposition, how extensively valid soever it may be, is a perfect safeguard against confounding them. There are, however, pure principles *a priori*, which nevertheless I should not ascribe to the pure understanding—for this reason, that they are not derived from pure conceptions, but (although by the mediation of the understanding) from pure intuitions. But understanding is the faculty of conceptions. Such principles mathematical science possesses, but their application to experience, consequently their objective validity, nay the possibility of such *a priori* synthetical cognitions (the deduction thereof) rests entirely upon the pure understanding.

On this account, I shall not reckon among my principles those of mathematics; though I shall include those upon the possibility and objective validity *a priori*, of principles of the mathematical science, which, consequently, are to be looked upon as the principle of these, and which proceed from conceptions to intuition, and not from intuition to conceptions.

In the application of the pure conceptions of the understanding to possible experience, the employment of their synthesis is either *mathematical* or *dynamical*, for it is directed partly on the *intuition* alone, partly on the *existence* of a phenomenon. But the *a priori* conditions of intuition are in relation to a possible experience absolutely necessary, those of the existence of objects of a possible empirical intuition are in themselves contingent. Hence the principles of the mathematical use of the categories will possess a character of absolute necessity, that is, will be apodeictic; those, on the other hand, of the dynamical use, the character of an *a priori* necessity indeed, but only under the condition of empirical thought in an experience, therefore only mediately and indirectly. Consequently they will not possess that immediate evidence which is peculiar to the former, although their application to experience does not, for that reason, lose its truth and certitude. But of this point we shall be better able to judge at the conclusion of this system of principles.

The table of the categories is naturally our guide to the table of principles, because these are nothing else than rules for the objective employment of the former. Accordingly, all principles of the pure understanding are:

1

AXIOMS of
Intuition

2

ANTICIPATIONS
of
Perception

3

ANALOGIES
of
Experience

4

POSTULATES of
Empirical Thought
in general

These appellations I have chosen advisedly, in order that we might not lose sight of the distinctions in respect of the evidence and the employment of these principles. It will, however, soon appear that—a fact which concerns both the evidence of these principles, and the *a priori* determination of phenomena—according to the categories of *Quantity* and *Quality* (if we attend merely to the form of these), the principles of these categories are distinguishable from those of the two others, inasmuch as the former are possessed of an intuitive, but the latter of a merely discursive, though in both instances a complete certitude. I shall therefore call the former *mathematical*,[1] and the latter *dynamical* principles.[2] It must be observed, however, that by these terms I mean, just as little in the one case the principles of mathematics, as those of general (physical) dynamics in the other. I have here in view merely the principles of the pure understanding, in their application to the internal sense (without distinction of the representations given therein), by means of which the sciences of mathematics and dynamics become possible. Accordingly, I have named these

---

[1] *Mathematically*, in the Kantian sense.—*Tr.*

[2] All *combination* (*conjunctio*) is either *composition* (*compositio*) or *connection* (*nexus*). The former is the synthesis of a manifold, the parts of which do not necessarily belong to each other. For example, the two triangles into which a square is divided by a diagonal, do not necessarily belong to each other, and of this kind is the synthesis of the *homogeneous* in everything that can be *mathematically* considered. This synthesis can be divided into those of *aggregation* and *coalition*, the former of which is applied to *extensive*, the latter to *intensive* quantities. The second sort of combination (*nexus*) is the synthesis of a manifold, in so far as its parts do belong necessarily to each other; for example, the accident to a substance, or the effect to the cause. Consequently it is a synthesis of that which though *heterogeneous*, is represented as connected *a priori*. This combination—not an arbitrary one—I entitle *dynamical*, because it concerns the connection of the *existence* of the manifold. This, again, may be divided into the *physical* synthesis of the phenomena among each other, and the *metaphysical* synthesis, or the connection of phenomena *a priori* in the faculty of cognition.

principles rather with reference to their application, than their content; and I shall now proceed to consider them in the order in which they stand in the table.

I

## AXIOMS OF INTUITION

The principle of these is: *All Intuitions are Extensive Quantities.*

### PROOF

All phenomena contain, as regards their form, an intuition in space and time, which lies *a priori* at the foundation of all without exception. Phenomena, therefore, cannot be apprehended, that is, received into empirical consciousness otherwise than through the synthesis of a manifold, through which the representations of a determinate space or time are generated; that is to say, through the composition of the homogeneous, and the consciousness of the synthetical unity of this manifold (homogeneous). Now the consciousness of a homogeneous manifold in intuition, in so far as thereby the representation of an object is rendered possible, is the conception of a quantity (*quanti*). Consequently, even the perception of an object as phenomenon is possible only through the same synthetical unity of the manifold of the given sensuous intuition, through which the unity of the composition of the homogeneous manifold in the conception of a *quantity* is cogitated; that is to say, all phenomena are quantities, and *extensive* quantities, because as intuitions in space or time they must be represented by means of the same synthesis, through which space and time themselves are determined.

An extensive quantity I call that wherein the representation of the parts renders possible (and therefore necessarily antecedes) the representation of the whole. I cannot represent to myself any line, however small, without drawing it in thought, that is, without generating from a point all its parts one after another, and in this way alone producing this intuition. Precisely the same is the case with every, even the smallest portion of time. I cogitate therein only the successive progress from one moment to another, and hence, by means of the different portions of time and the addition of them, a determinate quantity of time is produced. As the pure intuition in all phenomena is either time or space, so is every phenomenon in its character of intuition an extensive quantity, inasmuch as it can only be cognized in our apprehension by successive synthesis (from part to part). All phenomena are, accordingly, to be considered as aggregates, that is, as a collection of previously given parts; which is not the case with every sort of quantities, but only with those which are represented and apprehended by us as extensive.

On this successive synthesis of the productive imagination, in the generation of figures, is founded the mathematics of extension, or geometry, with its axioms, which express the conditions of sensuous intuition *a priori*, under which alone the schema of a pure conception of external intuition can exist; for example, 'between two points only one straight line is possible,' 'two straight lines cannot enclose a space,' etc. These are the axioms which properly relate only to quantities (*quanta*) as such.

But, as regards the quantity of a thing (*quantitas*), that is to say, the answer to the question: How large is this or that object? although, in respect to this question, we have various propositions synthetical and immediately certain (*indemonstrabilia*); we have, in the proper sense of the term, no axioms. For example, the propositions: 'If equals be added to equals, the wholes are equals;' 'If equals be taken from equals, the remainders are equals;' are analytical, because I am immediately conscious of the identity of the production of the one quantity with the production of the other; whereas axioms must be *a priori* synthetical propositions. On the other hand, the self-evident propositions as to the relation of numbers, are certainly synthetical but not universal, like those of geometry, and for this reason cannot be called axioms, but numerical formulae. That $7+5=12$ is not an analytical proposition. For neither in the representation of seven, nor of five, nor of the composition of the two numbers, do I cogitate the number twelve. (Whether I cogitate the number in the *addition* of both, is not at present the question; for in the case of an analytical proposition, the only point is, whether I really cogitate the predicate in the representation of the subject.) But although the proposition is synthetical, it is nevertheless only a singular proposition. In so far as regard is here had merely to the synthesis of the homogeneous (the units), it cannot take place except in one manner, although our *use* of these numbers is afterwards general. If I say: 'A triangle can be constructed with three lines, any two of which taken together are greater than the third,' I exercise merely the pure function of the productive imagination, which may draw the lines longer or shorter, and construct the angles at its pleasure. On the contrary, the number seven is possible only in one manner, and so is likewise the number twelve, which results from the synthesis of seven and five. Such propositions, then, cannot be termed axioms (for in that case we should have an infinity of these), but numerical formulae.

This transcendental principle of the mathematics of phenomena greatly enlarges our *a priori* cognition. For it is by this principle alone that pure mathematics is rendered applicable in all its precision to objects of experience, and without it the validity of this application would not be so self-evident; on the contrary, contradictions and confusions have often arisen on this very point. Phenomena are not things in themselves. Empirical intuition is possible only through pure intuition (of space and time); consequently, what geometry affirms of the latter, is indisputably valid of the former. All evasions, such as the statement that objects of sense do not conform to the rules of construction in space (for example, to the rule of the infinite divisibility of lines or angles), must fall to the ground. For, if these objections hold good, we deny to space, and with it to all mathematics, objective validity, and no longer know wherefore, and how far, mathematics can be applied to phenomena. The synthesis of spaces and times as the essential form of all intuition, is that which renders possible the apprehension of a phenomenon, and therefore every external experience, consequently all cognition of the objects of experience; and whatever mathematics in its pure use proves of the former, must necessarily hold good of the latter. All objections are but the chicaneries of an ill-instructed reason, which erroneously thinks to liberate the objects of sense from the formal conditions of our sensibility, and represents these, although mere phenomena, as things in themselves, presented as such to our understanding. But in this case, no *a priori* synthetical cognition of them could be possible, consequently not through pure conceptions of space, and the science which determines these conceptions, that is to say, geometry, would itself be impossible.

**2**

## ANTICIPATIONS OF PERCEPTION

The principle of these is: *In all phenomena the Real, that which is an object of sensation, has Intensive Quantity, that is, has a Degree.*

### PROOF

Perception is empirical consciousness, that is to say, a consciousness which contains an element of sensation. Phenomena as objects of perception are not pure, that is, merely formal intuitions,

like space and time, for they cannot be perceived in themselves.[1]
They contain, then, over and above the intuition, the materials
for an object (through which is represented something existing in
space or time), that is to say, they contain the real of sensation, as
a representation merely subjective, which gives us merely the
consciousness that the subject is affected, and which we refer to
some external object. Now, a gradual transition from empirical
consciousness to pure consciousness is possible, inasmuch as the
real in this consciousness entirely evanishes, and there remains a
merely formal consciousness (*a priori*) of the manifold in time and
space; consequently there is possible a synthesis also of the production of the quantity of a sensation from its commencement,
that is, from the pure intuition=o onwards, up to a certain quantity
of the sensation. Now as sensation in itself is not an objective
representation, and in it is to be found neither the intuition of
space nor of time, it cannot possess any extensive quantity, and
yet there does belong to it a quantity (and that by means of its
apprehension, in which empirical consciousness can within a certain
time rise from nothing=o up to its given amount), consequently
an *intensive quantity*. And thus we must ascribe intensive quantity,
that is, a degree of influence on sense to all objects of perception,
in so far as this perception contains sensation.

All cognition, by means of which I am enabled to cognize and
determine *a priori* what belongs to empirical cognition, may be
called an Anticipation; and without doubt this is the sense in
which Epicurus employed his expression προληψις. But as there is
in phenomena something which is never cognized *a priori*, which on
this account constitutes the proper difference between pure and
empirical cognition, that is to say, sensation (as the matter of
perception), it follows, that sensation is just that element in cognition which cannot be at all anticipated. On the other hand, we
might very well term the pure determinations in space and time,
as well in regard to figure as to Quantity, anticipations of phenomena, because they represent *a priori* that which may always be
given *a posteriori* in experience. But suppose that in every
sensation, as sensation in general, without any particular sensation
being thought of, there existed something which could be cognized
*a priori*, this would deserve to be called anticipation in a special
sense—special, because it may seem surprising to forestall experience, in that which concerns the matter of experience, and which

---

[1] They can be perceived only as phenomena, and some part of them must
always belong to the *non-ego*; whereas pure intuitions are entirely the products
of the mind itself, and as such are cognized *in themselves.*—*Tr.*

we can only derive from itself. Yet such really is the case here.

Apprehension,[1] by means of sensation alone, fills only one moment, that is, if I do not take into consideration a succession of many sensations. As that in the phenomenon, the apprehension of which is not a successive synthesis advancing from parts to an entire representation, sensation has therefore no extensive quantity; the want of sensation in a moment of time would represent it as empty, consequently=0. That which in the empirical intuition corresponds to sensation is reality (*realitas phaenomenon*); that which corresponds to the absence of it, negation=0. Now every sensation is capable of a diminution, so that it can decrease, and thus gradually disappear. Therefore, between reality in a phenomenon and negation, there exists a continuous concatenation of many possible intermediate sensations, the difference of which from each other is always smaller than that between the given sensation and zero, or complete negation. That is to say, the real in a phenomenon has always a quantity, which however is not discoverable in Apprehension, inasmuch as Apprehension takes place by means of mere sensation in one instant, and not by the successive synthesis of many sensations, and therefore does not progress from parts to the whole. Consequently, it has a quantity, but not an extensive quantity.

Now that quantity which is apprehended only as unity, and in which plurality can be represented only by approximation to negation=0, I term *intensive quantity*. Consequently, reality in a phenomenon has intensive quantity, that is, a degree. If we consider this reality as cause (be it of sensation or of another reality in the phenomenon, for example, a change), we call the degree of reality in its character of cause a momentum, for example, the momentum of weight; and for this reason, that the degree only indicates that quantity the apprehension of which is not successive, but instantaneous. This, however, I touch upon only in passing, for with Causality I have at present nothing to do.

Accordingly, every sensation, consequently every reality in phenomena, however small it may be, has a degree, that is, an intensive quantity, which may always be lessened, and between reality and negation there exists a continuous connection of possible realities, and possible smaller perceptions. Every colour—for example, red—has a degree, which, be it ever so small, is never

[1] Apprehension is the Kantian word for perception, in the largest sense in which we employ that term. It is the genus which includes under it as species, perception proper and sensation proper.—*Tr.*

the smallest, and so is it always with heat, the momentum of weight, etc.

This property of quantities, according to which no part of them is the smallest possible (no part simple [1]), is called their continuity. Space and time are *quanta continua*, because no part of them can be given, without enclosing it within boundaries (points and moments), consequently, this given part is itself a space or a time. Space, therefore, consists only of spaces, and time of times. Points and moments are only boundaries, that is, the mere places or positions of their limitation. But places always presuppose intuitions which are to limit or determine them; and we cannot conceive either space or time composed of constituent parts which are given before space or time. Such quantities may also be called *flowing*, because the synthesis (of the productive imagination) in the production of these Quantities is a progression in time, the continuity of which we are accustomed to indicate by the expression *flowing*.

All phenomena, then, are continuous quantities, in respect both to intuition and mere perception (sensation, and with it reality). In the former case they are extensive quantities; in the latter, intensive. When the synthesis of the manifold of a phenomenon is interrupted, there results merely an aggregate of several phenomena, and not properly a phenomenon as a quantity, which is not produced by the mere continuation of the productive synthesis of a certain kind, but by the repetition of a synthesis always ceasing. For example, if I call thirteen dollars a sum or quantity of money, I employ the term quite correctly, inasmuch as I understand by thirteen dollars the value of a mark in standard silver, which is, to be sure, a continuous quantity, in which no part is the smallest, but every part might constitute a piece of money, which would contain material for still smaller pieces. If, however, by the words thirteen dollars I understand so many coins (be their value in silver what it may), it would be quite erroneous to use the expression a quantity of dollars; on the contrary, I must call them aggregate, that is, a number of coins. And as in every number we must have unity as the foundation, so a phenomenon taken as unity is a quantity, and as such always a continuous quantity (*quantum continuum*).

Now, seeing all phenomena, whether considered as extensive or intensive, are continuous quantities, the proposition: 'All change (transition of a thing from one state into another) is continuous,' might be proved here easily, and with mathematical evidence,

[1] Simplex.—*Tr.*

were it not that the causality of a change lies entirely beyond the bounds of a transcendental philosophy, and presupposes empirical principles. For of the possibility of a cause which changes the condition of things, that is, which determines them to the contrary of a certain given state, the understanding gives us *a priori* no knowledge; not merely because it has no insight into the possibility of it (for such insight is absent in several *a priori* cognitions), but because the notion of change concerns only certain determinations of phenomena, which experience alone can acquaint us with, while their cause lies in the unchangeable. But seeing that we have nothing which we could here employ but the pure fundamental conceptions of all possible experience, among which of course nothing empirical can be admitted, we dare not, without injuring the unity of our system, anticipate general physical science, which is built upon certain fundamental experiences.

Nevertheless, we are in no want of proofs of the great influence which the principle above developed exercises in the anticipation of perceptions, and even in supplying the want of them, so far as to shield us against the false conclusions which otherwise we might rashly draw.

If all reality in perception has a degree, between which and negation there is an endless sequence of ever smaller degrees, and if nevertheless every sense must have a determinate degree of receptivity for sensations; no perception, and consequently no experience is possible, which can prove, either immediately or mediately, an entire absence of all reality in a phenomenon; in other words, it is impossible ever to draw from experience a proof of the existence of empty space or of empty time. For in the first place, an entire absence of reality in a sensuous intuition cannot of course be an object of perception; secondly, such absence cannot be deduced from the contemplation of any single phenomenon, and the difference of the degrees in its reality; nor ought it ever to be admitted in explanation of any phenomenon. For if even the complete intuition of a determinate space or time is thoroughly real, that is, if no part thereof is empty, yet because every reality has its degree, which, with the extensive quantity of the phenomenon unchanged, can diminish through endless gradations down to nothing (the void), there must be infinitely graduated degrees, with which space or time is filled, and the intensive quantity in different phenomena may be smaller or greater, although the extensive quantity of the intuition remains equal and unaltered.

We shall give an example of this. Almost all natural philosophers, remarking a great difference in the quantity of the matter [1] of different kinds in bodies with the same volume (partly on account of the momentum of gravity or weight, partly on account of the momentum of resistance to other bodies in motion), conclude unanimously, that this volume (extensive quantity of the phenomenon) must be void in all bodies, although in different proportion. But who would suspect that these for the most part mathematical and mechanical inquirers into nature should ground this conclusion solely on a metaphysical hypothesis—a sort of hypothesis which they profess to disparage and avoid? Yet this they do, in assuming that the real in space (I must not here call it impenetrability or weight, because these are empirical conceptions) is always identical, and can only be distinguished according to its extensive quantity, that is, multiplicity. Now to this presupposition, for which they can have no ground in experience, and which consequently is merely metaphysical, I oppose a transcendental demonstration, which it is true will not explain the difference in the filling up of spaces, but which nevertheless completely does away with the supposed necessity of the above-mentioned presupposition that we cannot explain the said difference otherwise than by the hypothesis of empty spaces. This demonstration, moreover, has the merit of setting the understanding at liberty to conceive this distinction in a different manner, if the explanation of the fact requires any such hypothesis. For we perceive that although two equal spaces may be completely filled by matters altogether different, so that in neither of them is there left a single point wherein matter is not present, nevertheless, every reality has its degree (of resistance or of weight), which, without diminution of the extensive quantity, can become less and less *ad infinitum*, before it passes into nothingness and disappears. Thus an expansion which fills a space—for example, caloric, or any other reality in the phenomenal world—can decrease in its degrees to infinity, yet without leaving the smallest part of the space empty; on the contrary, filling it with those lesser degrees, as completely as another phenomenon could with greater. My intention here is by no means to maintain that this is really the case with the difference of matters, in regard to their specific gravity; I wish only to prove, from a principle of the pure understanding, that the nature of our perceptions makes such a mode of explanation possible, and that it is erroneous to regard the real in a phenomenon as equal *quoad* its degree, and different only *quoad* its aggregation and extensive quantity, and

[1] It should be remembered that Kant means by matter, that which in the object corresponds to sensation in the subject—the real in a phenomenon.—*Tr.*

this, too, on the pretended authority of an *a priori* principle of the understanding.

Nevertheless, this principle of the anticipation of perception must somewhat startle an inquirer whom initiation into transcendental philosophy has rendered cautious. We may naturally entertain some doubt whether or not the understanding can enounce any such synthetical proposition as that respecting the degree of all reality in phenomena, and consequently the possibility of the internal difference of sensation itself—abstraction being made of its empirical quality. Thus it is a question not unworthy of solution: how the understanding can pronounce synthetically and *a priori* respecting phenomena, and thus anticipate these, even in that which is peculiarly and merely empirical, that, namely, which concerns sensation itself.

The quality of sensation is in all cases merely empirical, and cannot be represented *a priori* (for example, colours, taste, etc.). But the real—that which corresponds to sensation—in opposition to negation=o, only represents something the conception of which in itself contains a being (*ein seyn*), and signifies nothing but the synthesis in an empirical consciousness. That is to say, the empirical consciousness in the internal sense can be raised from o to every higher degree, so that the very same extensive quantity of intuition, an illuminated surface, for example, excites as great a sensation as an aggregate of many other surfaces less illuminated. We can therefore make complete abstraction of the extensive quantity of a phenomenon, and represent to ourselves in the mere sensation in a certain momentum,[1] a synthesis of homogeneous ascension from o up to the given empirical consciousness. All sensations therefore as such are given only *a posteriori*, but this property thereof, namely, that they have a degree, can be known *a priori*. It is worthy of remark, that in respect to quantities in general, we can cognize *a priori* only a single quality, namely, continuity; but in respect to all quality (the real in phenomena), we cannot cognize *a priori* anything more than the intensive quantity thereof, namely, that they have a degree. All else is left to experience.

[1] The particular degree of 'reality,' that is, the particular power or intensive quantity in the cause of a sensation, for example, redness, weight, etc., is called in the Kantian terminology, *its moment*. The term *momentum* which we employ, must not be confounded with the word commonly employed in natural science.—*Tr.*

### 3

#### ANALOGIES OF EXPERIENCE

The principle of these is: *Experience is possible only through the representation of a necessary connection of perceptions.*

#### PROOF

Experience is an empirical cognition; that is to say, a cognition which determines an object by means of perceptions. It is therefore a synthesis of perceptions, a synthesis which is not itself contained in perception, but which contains the synthetical unity of the manifold of perception in a consciousness; and this unity constitutes the essential of our cognition of *objects* of the senses, that is, of experience (not merely of intuition or sensation). Now in experience our perceptions come together contingently, so that no character of necessity in their connection appears, or can appear from the perceptions themselves, because apprehension is only a placing together of the manifold of empirical intuition, and no representation of a necessity in the connected existence of the phenomena which apprehension brings together, is to be discovered therein. But as experience is a cognition of objects by means of perceptions, it follows that the relation of the existence of the manifold must be represented in experience not as it is put together in time, but as it is objectively in time. And as time itself cannot be perceived, the determination of the existence of objects in time can only take place by means of their connection in time in general, consequently only by means of *a priori* connecting conceptions. Now as these conceptions always possess the character of necessity, experience is possible only by means of a representation of the necessary connection of perception.

The three *modi* of time are *permanence, succession,* and *coexistence.* Accordingly, there are three rules of all relations of time in phenomena, according to which the existence of every phenomenon is determined in respect of the unity of all time, and these antecede all experience, and render it possible.

The general principle of all three analogies rests on the necessary *unity* of apperception in relation to all possible empirical consciousness (perception) *at every time,* consequently, as this unity lies *a priori* at the foundation of all mental operations, the principle rests on the synthetical unity of all phenomena according to their relation in time. For the original apperception relates to our internal sense (the complex of all representations), and indeed relates *a priori* to its form, that is to say, the relation of the manifold empirical consciousness in time. Now this manifold must be combined in original apperception according to relations of time— a necessity imposed by the *a priori* transcendental unity of apperception, to which is subjected all that can belong to my (i.e. my own) cognition, and therefore all that can become an object for me. This synthetical and *a priori* determined unity in relation of perceptions in time is therefore the rule: 'All empirical determinations of time must be subject to rules of the general determination of time;' and the analogies of experience, of which we are now about to treat, must be rules of this nature.

These principles have this peculiarity, that they do not concern phenomena, and the synthesis of the empirical intuition thereof, but merely the *existence* of phenomena and their *relation* to each other in regard to this existence. Now the mode in which we apprehend a thing in a phenomenon can be determined *a priori* in such a manner, that the rule of its synthesis can give, that is to say, can produce this *a priori* intuition in every empirical example. But the existence of phenomena cannot be known *a priori*, and although we could arrive by this path at a conclusion of the fact of some existence, we could not cognize that existence determinately, that is to say, we should be incapable of anticipating in what respect the empirical intuition of it would be distinguishable from that of others.

The two principles above mentioned, which I called mathematical, in consideration of the fact of their authorizing the application of mathematic to phenomena, relate to these phenomena only in regard to their possibility, and instruct us how phenomena, as far as regards their intuition or the real in their perception, can be generated according to the rules of a mathematical synthesis. Consequently, numerical quantities, and with them the determination of a phenomenon as a quantity, can be employed in the one case as well as in the other. Thus, for example, out of 200,000 illuminations by the moon, I might compose, and give *a priori*, that is construct, the degree of our sensations of the sunlight.[1] We may therefore entitle these two principles constitutive.

[1] Kant's meaning is: The two principles enunciated under the heads of 'Axioms of Intuition,' and 'Anticipations of Perception,' authorize the application to phenomena of determinations of size and number, that is, of mathematic. For example, I may compute the light of the sun, and say, that its quantity is a certain number of times greater than that of the moon. In the same way, heat is measured by the comparison of its different effects on water, etc., and on mercury in a thermometer.—*Tr.*

The case is very different with those principles whose province
it is to subject the existence of phenomena to rules *a priori*.  For
as existence does not admit of being constructed, it is clear that
they must only concern the relations of existence, and be merely
*regulative* principles.  In this case, therefore, neither axioms nor
anticipations are to be thought of.  Thus, if a perception is given
us, in a certain relation of time to other (although undetermined)
perceptions, we cannot then say *a priori*, *what* and *how great* (in
quantity) the other perception necessarily connected with the
former is, but only *how* it is connected, *quoad* its existence, in this
given modus of time.  Analogies in philosophy mean something
very different from that which they represent in mathematics.
In the latter they are formulae, which enounce the equality of
two relations of quantity,[1] and are always *constitutive*, so that if
two terms of the proportion are given, the third is also given, that
is, can be constructed by the aid of these formulae.  But in
philosophy, analogy is not the equality of two *quantitative* but of
two *qualitative* relations.  In this case, from three given terms, I
can give *a priori* and cognize the *relation* to a fourth member,[2] but
not this fourth term itself, although I certainly possess a rule to
guide me in the search for this fourth term in experience, and a
mark to assist me in discovering it.  An analogy of experience is
therefore only a rule according to which unity of experience must
arise out of perceptions in respect to objects (phenomena) not as a
*constitutive*, but merely as a *regulative* principle.  The same holds
good also of the postulates of empirical thought in general, which
relate to the synthesis of mere intuition (which concerns the form
of phenomena), the synthesis of perception (which concerns the
matter of phenomena), and the synthesis of experience (which
concerns the relation of these perceptions).  For they are only
regulative principles, and clearly distinguishable from the mathematical, which are constitutive, not indeed in regard to the certainty
which both possess *a priori*, but in the mode of evidence thereof,
consequently also in the manner of demonstration.

But what has been observed of all synthetical propositions, and
must be particularly remarked in this place, is this, that these

---

[1] Known the two terms 3 and 6, and the relation of 3 to 6, not only the
relation of 6 to some other number is given, but that number itself, 12, is
given, that is, it is constructed.  Therefore 3 : 6 = 6 : 12.—*Tr*.

[2] Given a known effect, a known cause, and another known effect, we
reason, by analogy, to an unknown cause, which we do not cognize, but
whose *relation* to the known effect we know from the comparison of the three
given terms.  Thus, our own known actions : our own known motives = the
known actions of others : x, that is, the motives of others which we cannot
immediately cognize. —*Tr*.

analogies possess significance and validity, not as principles of the transcendental, but only as principles of the empirical use of the understanding, and their truth can therefore be proved only as such, and that consequently the phenomena must not be subjoined directly under the categories, but only under their schemata. For if the objects to which those principles must be applied were things in themselves, it would be quite impossible to cognize aught concerning them synthetically *a priori*. But they are nothing but phenomena; a complete knowledge of which—a knowledge to which all principles *a priori* must at last relate—is the only possible experience. It follows that those principles can have nothing else for their aim, than the conditions of the unity of empirical cognition in the synthesis of phenomena. But this synthesis is cogitated only in the schema of the pure conception of the understanding, of whose unity, as that of a synthesis in general, the category contains the function unrestricted by any sensuous condition. Those principles will therefore authorize us to connect phenomena according to an analogy, with the logical and universal unity of conceptions, and consequently to employ the categories in the principles themselves; but in the application of them to experience, we shall use only their schemata, as the key to their proper application, instead of the categories, or rather the latter as restricting conditions, under the title of formulae of the former.

## A

### FIRST ANALOGY

#### PRINCIPLE OF THE PERMANENCE OF SUBSTANCE

*In all changes of phenomena, substance is permanent, and the quantum thereof in nature is neither increased nor diminished.*

#### PROOF

All phenomena exist in time, wherein alone as substratum, that is, as the permanent form of the internal intuition, co-existence and succession can be represented. Consequently time, in which all changes of phenomena must be cogitated, remains and changes not, because it is that in which succession and co-existence can be represented only as determinations thereof. Now, time in itself cannot be an object of perception. It follows that in objects of perception, that is, in phenomena, there must be found a substratum which represents time in general, and in which all change or co-existence can be perceived by means of the relation of phenomena to it. But the substratum of all reality, that is, of all that pertains to the existence of things, is substance; all that pertains to existence can be cogitated only as a determination of substance. Conse-quently, the permanent, in relation to which alone can all relations of time in phenomena be determined, is substance in the world of phenomena, that is, the real in phenomena, that which, as the substratum of all change, remains ever the same. Accordingly, as this cannot change in existence, its quantity in nature can neither be increased nor diminished.

Our *apprehension* of the manifold in a phenomenon is always successive, is consequently always changing. By it alone we could, therefore, never determine whether this manifold, as an object of experience, is co-existent or successive, unless it had for a foundation something that exists *always*, that is, something *fixed* and *permanent*, of the existence of which all succession and co-existence are nothing but so many modes (*modi* of time). Only in the permanent, then, are relations of time possible (for simul-taneity and succession are the only relations in time); that is to say, the permanent is the *substratum* of our empirical representation of time itself, in which alone all determination of time is possible. Permanence is, in fact, just another expression for time, as the abiding correlate of all existence of phenomena, and of all change, and of all co-existence. For change does not affect time itself, but only the phenomena in time (just as co-existence cannot be regarded as a *modus* of time itself, seeing that in time no parts are co-existent, but all successive).[1] If we were to attribute succession to time itself, we should be obliged to cogitate another time, in which this succession would be possible. It is only by means of the permanent that existence in different parts of the successive series of time receives a *quantity*, which we entitle *duration*. For in mere succession, existence is perpetually vanishing and recom-mencing, and therefore never has even the least quantity. Without the permanent, then, no relation in time is possible. Now, time in itself is not an object of perception; consequently the permanent in phenomena must be regarded as the substratum of all deter-mination of time, and consequently also as the condition of the possibility of all synthetical unity of perceptions, that is, of experience; and all existence and all change in time can only be regarded as a mode in the existence of that which abides un-

---

[1] The latter part of this sentence seems to contradict the former. The sequel will explain.—*Tr.*

changeably. Therefore, in all phenomena, the permanent is the object *in itself*, that is, the substance (phenomenon);[1] but all that changes or can change belongs only to the mode of the existence of this substance or substances, consequently to its determinations.

I find that in all ages not only the philosopher, but even the common understanding, has preposited this permanence as a substratum of all change in phenomena; indeed, I am compelled to believe that they will always accept this as an indubitable fact. Only the philosopher expresses himself in a more precise and definite manner, when he says: 'In all changes in the world, the *substance* remains, and the *accidents* alone are changeable.' But of this decidedly synthetical proposition, I nowhere meet with even an attempt at proof; nay, it very rarely has the good fortune to stand, as it deserves to do, at the head of the pure and entirely *a priori* laws of nature. In truth, the statement that substance is permanent, is tautological. For this very permanence is the ground on which we apply the category of substance to the phenomenon; and we should have been obliged to prove that in all phenomena there is something permanent, of the existence of which the changeable is nothing but a determination. But because a proof of this nature cannot be dogmatical, that is, cannot be drawn from conceptions, inasmuch as it concerns a synthetical proposition *a priori*, and as philosophers never reflected that such propositions are valid only in relation to possible experience, and therefore cannot be proved except by means of a deduction of the possibility of experience, it is no wonder that while it has served as the foundation of all experience (for we feel the need of it in empirical cognition), it has never been supported by proof.

A philosopher was asked: 'What is the weight of smoke?' He answered: 'Subtract from the weight of the burnt wood the weight of the remaining ashes, and you will have the weight of the smoke.' Thus he presumed it to be incontrovertible that even in fire the matter (substance) does not perish, but that only the form of it undergoes a change. In like manner was the saying: 'From nothing comes nothing,' only another inference from the principle of permanence, or rather of the ever-abiding existence of the true subject in phenomena. For if that in the phenomenon which we call substance is to be the proper substratum of all determination of time, it follows that all existence in past as well as in future time, must be determinable by means of it alone. Hence we are entitled to apply the term substance to a phenomenon, only because we suppose its existence in all time, a notion which

---

[1] Not *substantia noumenon.*—*Tr.*

the word permanence does not fully express, as it seems rather to be referable to future time. However, the internal necessity perpetually to be, is inseparably connected with the necessity always to have been, and so the expression may stand as it is. '*Gigni de nihilo nihil*'—'*in nihilum nil posse reverti*,' are two propositions which the ancients never parted, and which people nowadays sometimes mistakenly disjoin, because they imagine that the propositions apply to objects as things in themselves, and that the former might be inimical to the dependence (even in respect of its substance also) of the world upon a supreme cause. But this apprehension is entirely needless, for the question in this case is only of phenomena in the sphere of experience, the unity of which never could be possible, if we admitted the possibility that new things (in respect of their substance) should arise. For in that case, we should lose altogether that which alone can represent the unity of time, to wit, the identity of the substratum, as that through which alone all change possesses complete and thorough unity. This permanence is, however, nothing but the manner in which we represent to ourselves the existence of things in the phenomenal world.

The determinations of a substance, which are only particular modes of its existence, are called *accidents*. They are always real, because they concern the existence of substance (negations are only determinations, which express the non-existence of something in the substance). Now, if to this real in the substance we ascribe a particular existence (for example, to motion as an accident of matter), this existence is called inherence, in contradistinction to the existence of substance, which we call subsistence. But hence arise many misconceptions, and it would be a more accurate and just mode of expression to designate the accident only as the mode in which the existence of a substance is positively determined. Meanwhile, by reason of the conditions of the logical exercise of our understanding, it is impossible to avoid separating, as it were, that which in the existence of a substance is subject to change, whilst the substance remains, and regarding it in relation to that which is properly permanent and radical. On this account, this category of substance stands under the title of relation, rather because it is the condition thereof, than because it contains in itself any relation.

Now, upon this notion of permanence rests the proper notion of the conception *change*. Origin and extinction are not changes of that which originates or becomes extinct. Change is but a mode of existence, which follows on another mode of existence of the same object; hence all that changes is permanent, and only the condition thereof changes. Now since this mutation affects only determinations, which can have a beginning or an end, we may say, employing an expression which seems somewhat paradoxical: 'Only the *permanent* (substance) is subject to change; the mutable suffers no change, but rather *alternation*, that is, when certain determinations cease, others begin.'

Change, then, cannot be perceived by us except in substances, and origin or extinction in an absolute sense, that does not concern merely a determination of the permanent, cannot be a possible perception, for it is this very notion of the permanent which renders possible the representation of a transition from one state into another, and from non-being to being, which, consequently, can be empirically cognized only as alternating determinations of that which is permanent. Grant that a thing absolutely begins to be; we must then have a point of time in which it was not. But how and by what can we fix and determine this point of time, unless by that which already exists? For a void time—preceding —is not an object of perception; but if we connect this beginning with objects which existed previously, and which continue to exist till the object in question begins to be, then the latter can only be a determination of the former as the permanent. The same holds good of the notion of extinction, for this presupposes the empirical representation of a time, in which a phenomenon no longer exists.

Substances (in the world of phenomena) are the substratum of all determinations of time. The beginning of some, and the ceasing to be of other substances, would utterly do away with the only condition of the empirical unity of time; and in that case phenomena would relate to two different times, in which, side by side, existence would pass; which is absurd. For there is only *one* time in which all different times must be placed, not as co-existent, but as successive.

Accordingly, permanence is a necessary condition under which alone phenomena, as things or objects, are determinable in a possible experience. But as regards the empirical criterion of this necessary permanence, and with it of the substantiality of phenomena, we shall find sufficient opportunity to speak in the sequel.

## B

### SECOND ANALOGY

PRINCIPLE OF THE SUCCESSION OF TIME ACCORDING TO THE LAW
OF CAUSALITY

*All changes take place according to the law of the connection of
Cause and Effect.*

#### PROOF

(That all phenomena in the succession of time are only changes,
that is, a successive being and non-being of the determinations
of substance, which is permanent; consequently that a being of
substance itself which follows on the non-being thereof, or a non-
being of substance which follows on the being thereof, in other
words, that the origin or extinction of substance itself, is impossible
—all this has been fully established in treating of the foregoing
principle. This principle might have been expressed as follows:
'*All alteration (succession) of phenomena is merely change;*' for the
changes of substance are not origin or extinction, because the
conception of change presupposes the same subject as existing
with two opposite determinations, and consequently as permanent.
After this premonition, we shall proceed to the proof.)

I perceive that phenomena succeed one another, that is to say,
a state of things exists at one time, the opposite of which existed
in a former state. In this case, then, I really connect together
two perceptions in time. Now connection is not an operation of
mere sense and intuition, but is the product of a synthetical faculty
of imagination, which determines the internal sense in respect of
a relation of time. But imagination can connect these two states
in two ways, so that either the one or the other may antecede in
time; for time in itself cannot be an object of perception, and what
in an object precedes and what follows cannot be empirically
determined in relation to it. I am only conscious, then, that my
imagination places one state before, and the other after; not that
the one state antecedes the other in the object. In other words,
the objective relation of the successive phenomena remains quite
undetermined by means of mere perception. Now in order that
this relation may be cognized as determined, the relation between
the two states must be so cogitated that it is thereby determined
as necessary, which of them must be placed before and which
after, and not conversely. But the conception which carries with
it a necessity of synthetical unity, can be none other than a pure

conception of the understanding which does not lie in mere perception; and in this case it is the conception of the *relation of cause and effect*, the former of which determines the latter in time, as its necessary consequence, and not as something which might possibly antecede (or which might in some cases not be perceived to follow). It follows that it is only because we subject the sequence of phenomena, and consequently all change, to the law of causality, that experience itself, that is, empirical cognition of phenomena, becomes possible; and consequently, that phenomena themselves, as objects of experience, are possible only by virtue of this law.

Our apprehension of the manifold of phenomena is always successive. The representations of parts succeed one another. Whether they succeed one another in the object also, is a second point for reflection, which was not contained in the former. Now we may certainly give the name of object to everything, even to every representation, so far as we are conscious thereof; but what this word may mean in the case of phenomena, not merely in so far as they (as representations) are objects, but only in so far as they indicate an object, is a question requiring deeper consideration. In so far as they, regarded merely as representations, are at the same time objects of consciousness, they are not to be distinguished from apprehension, that is, reception into the synthesis of imagination, and we must therefore say: 'The manifold of phenomena is always produced successively in the mind.' If phenomena were things in themselves, no man would be able to conjecture from the succession of our representations how this manifold is connected in the object; for we have to do only with our representations. How things may be in themselves, without regard to the representations through which they affect us, is utterly beyond the sphere of our cognition. Now although phenomena are not things in themselves, and are nevertheless the only thing given to us to be cognized, it is my duty to show what sort of connection in time belongs to the manifold in phenomena themselves, while the representation of this manifold in apprehension is always successive. For example, the apprehension of the manifold in the phenomenon of a house which stands before me, is successive. Now comes the question, whether the manifold of this house is in itself also successive—which no one will be at all willing to grant. But, so soon as I raise my conception of an object to the transcendental signification thereof, I find that the house is not a thing in itself, but only a phenomenon, that is, a representation, the transcendental object of which remains utterly unknown. What then am I to understand by the question: How can the manifold be connected in the phenomenon itself—not considered as a thing in itself, but merely as a phenomenon? Here that which lies in my successive apprehension is regarded as representation, whilst the phenomenon which is given me, notwithstanding that it is nothing more than a complex of these representations, is regarded as the object thereof, with which my conception, drawn from the representations of apprehension, must harmonize. It is very soon seen that, as accordance of the cognition with its object constitutes truth, the question now before us can only relate to the formal conditions of empirical truth; and that the phenomenon, in opposition to the representations of apprehension, can only be distinguished therefrom as the object of them, if it is subject to a rule which distinguishes it from every other apprehension, and which renders necessary a mode of connection of the manifold. That in the phenomenon which contains the condition of this necessary rule of apprehension, is the object.

Let us now proceed to our task. That something happens, that is to say, that something or some state exists which before was not, cannot be empirically perceived, unless a phenomenon precedes, which does not contain in itself this state. For a reality which should follow upon a void time, in other words, a beginning, which no state of things precedes, can just as little be apprehended as the void time itself. Every apprehension of an event is therefore a perception which follows upon another perception. But as this is the case with all synthesis of apprehension, as I have shown above in the example of a house, my apprehension of an event is not yet sufficiently distinguished from other apprehensions. But I remark also, that if in a phenomenon which contains an occurrence, I call the antecedent state of my perception, A, and the following state, B, the perception B can only follow A in apprehension, and the perception A cannot follow B, but only precede it. For example, I see a ship float down the stream of a river. My perception of its place lower down follows upon my perception of its place higher up the course of the river, and it is impossible that in the apprehension of this phenomenon, the vessel should be perceived first below and afterwards higher up the stream. Here, therefore, the order in the sequence of perceptions in apprehension is determined; and by this order apprehension is regulated. In the former example, my perceptions in the apprehension of a house might begin at the roof and end at the foundation, or vice versa; or I might apprehend the manifold in this empirical intuition, by going from left to right, and from right to left. Accordingly, in the series of these perceptions, there was no determined order, which necessitated my beginning at a certain point, in order empirically to connect the manifold. But this rule is always to be met with in the perception of that which happens, and it makes the order of the successive perceptions in the apprehension of such a phenomenon *necessary*.

I must, therefore, in the present case, deduce the *subjective sequence* of apprehension from the *objective sequence* of phenomena, for otherwise the former is quite undetermined, and one phenomenon is not distinguishable from another. The former alone proves nothing as to the connection of the manifold in an object, for it is quite arbitrary. The latter must consist in the order of the manifold in a phenomenon, according to which order the apprehension of one thing (that which happens) follows that of another thing (that which precedes), in conformity with a rule. In this way alone can I be authorized to say of the phenomenon itself, and not merely of my own apprehension, that a certain order or sequence is to be found therein. That is, in other words, I cannot arrange my apprehension otherwise than in this order.

In conformity with this rule, then, it is necessary that in that which antecedes an event there be found the condition of a rule, according to which this event follows always and necessarily; but I cannot reverse this and go back from the event, and determine (by apprehension) that which antecedes it. For no phenomenon goes back from the succeeding point of time to the preceding point, although it does certainly relate to a preceding point of time; from a given time, on the other hand, there is always a necessary progression to the determined succeeding time. Therefore, because there certainly is something that follows, I must of necessity connect it with something else, which antecedes, and upon which it follows, in conformity with a rule, that is necessarily, so that the event, as conditioned, affords certain indication of a condition, and this condition determines the event.

Let us suppose that nothing precedes an event, upon which this event must follow in conformity with a rule. All sequence of perception would then exist only in apprehension, that is to say, would be merely subjective, and it could not thereby be objectively determined what thing ought to precede, and what ought to follow in perception. In such a case, we should have nothing but a play of representations, which would possess no application to any object. That is to say, it would not be possible through perception to distinguish one phenomenon from another, as regards relations of time; because the succession in the act of apprehension would always be of the same sort, and therefore there would be nothing in the phenomenon to determine the succession, and to render a certain sequence objectively necessary. And, in this case, I cannot say that two states in a phenomenon follow one upon the other, but only that one apprehension follows upon another. But this is merely subjective, and does not determine an object, and consequently cannot be held to be cognition of an object—not even in the phenomenal world.

Accordingly, when we know in experience that something happens, we always presuppose that something precedes, whereupon it follows in conformity with a rule. For otherwise I could not say of the object, that it follows; because the mere succession in my apprehension, if it be not determined by a rule in relation to something preceding, does not authorize succession in the object. Only, therefore, in reference to a rule, according to which phenomena are determined in their sequence, that is, as they happen, by the preceding state, can I make my subjective synthesis (of apprehension) objective, and it is only under this presupposition that even the experience of an event is possible.

No doubt it appears as if this were in thorough contradiction to all the notions which people have hitherto entertained in regard to the procedure of the human understanding. According to these opinions, it is by means of the perception and comparison of similar consequences following upon certain antecedent phenomena, that the understanding is led to the discovery of a rule, according to which certain events always follow certain phenomena, and it is only by this process that we attain to the conception of cause. Upon such a basis, it is clear that this conception must be merely empirical, and the rule which it furnishes us with—'Everything that happens must have a cause'—would be just as contingent as experience itself. The universality and necessity of the rule or law would be perfectly spurious attributes of it. Indeed, it could not possess universal validity, inasmuch as it would not in this case be *a priori*, but founded on deduction. But the same is the case with this law as with other pure *a priori* representations (e.g. space and time), which we can draw in perfect clearness and completeness from experience, only because we had already placed them therein, and by that means, and by that alone, had rendered experience possible. Indeed, the logical clearness of this representation of a rule, determining the series of events, is possible only when we have made use thereof in experience. Nevertheless, the recognition of this rule, as a condition of the synthetical unity of phenomena in time, was the ground of experience itself, and consequently preceded it *a priori*.

It is now our duty to show by an example, that we never, even in experience, attribute to an object the notion of succession or effect (of an event—that is, the happening of something that did not exist before), and distinguish it from the subjective succession of apprehension, unless when a rule lies at the foundation, which compels us to observe this order of perception in preference to any other, and that, indeed, it is this necessity which first renders possible the representation of a succession in the object.

We have representations within us, of which also we can be conscious. But, however widely extended, however accurate and thorough-going this consciousness may be, these representations are still nothing more than representations, that is, internal determinations of the mind in this or that relation of time. Now how happens it, that to these representations we should set an object, or that, in addition to their subjective reality, as modifications, we should still further attribute to them a certain unknown objective reality? It is clear that objective significancy cannot consist in a relation to another representation (of that which we desire to term object), for in that case the question again arises: 'How does this other representation go out of itself, and obtain objective significancy over and above the subjective, which is proper to it, as a determination of a state of mind?' If we try to discover what sort of new property the *relation to an object* gives to our subjective representations, and what new importance they thereby receive, we shall find that this relation has no other effect than that of rendering necessary the connection of our representations in a certain manner, and of subjecting them to a rule; and that conversely, it is only because a certain order is necessary in the relations of time of our representations, that objective significancy is ascribed to them.

In the synthesis of phenomena, the manifold of our representations is always successive. Now hereby is not represented an object, for by means of this succession, which is common to all apprehension, no one thing is distinguished from another. But so soon as I perceive or assume, that in this succession there is a relation to a state antecedent, from which the representation follows in accordance with a rule, so soon do I represent something as an event, or as a thing that happens; in other words, I cognize an object to which I must assign a certain determinate position in time, which cannot be altered, because of the preceding state in the object. When, therefore, I perceive that something happens, there is contained in this representation, in the first place, the fact, that something antecedes; because it is only in relation to this, that the phenomenon obtains its proper relation of time, in other words, exists after an antecedent time, in which it did not exist. But it can receive its determined place in time, only by the presupposition that something existed in the foregoing state, upon which it follows inevitably and always, that is, in conformity with a rule. From all this it is evident that, in the first place, I cannot reverse the order of succession, and make that which happens precede that upon which it follows; and that, in the second place, if the antecedent state be posited, a certain determinate event inevitably and necessarily follows. Hence it follows that there exists a certain order in our representations, whereby the present gives a sure indication of some previously existing state, as a correlate, though still undetermined, of the existing event which is given—a correlate which itself relates to the event as its consequence, conditions it, and connects it necessarily with itself in the series of time.

If then it be admitted as a necessary law of sensibility, and consequently a formal condition of all perception, that the preceding necessarily determines the succeeding time (inasmuch as I cannot arrive at the succeeding except through the preceding), it must likewise be an indispensable law of empirical representation of the series of time, that the phenomena of the past determine all phenomena in the succeeding time, and that the latter, as events, cannot take place, except in so far as the former determine their existence in time, that is to say, establish it according to a rule. For it is of course only in phenomena that we can empirically cognize this continuity in the connection of times.

For all experience and for the possibility of experience, understanding is indispensable, and the first step which it takes in this sphere is not to render the representation of objects clear,[1] but to render the representation of an object in general, possible. It does this by applying the order of time to phenomena, and their existence. In other words, it assigns to each phenomenon, as a consequence, a place in relation to preceding phenomena, determined *a priori* in time, without which it could not harmonize with time itself, which determines a place *a priori* to all its parts. This determination of place cannot be derived from the relation of phenomena to absolute time (for it is not an object of perception); but, on the contrary, phenomena must reciprocally determine the places in time of one another, and render these necessary in the order of time. In other words, whatever follows or happens, must follow in conformity with a universal rule upon that which was contained in the foregoing state. Hence arises a series of

[1] This was the opinion of Wolf and Leibnitz.—*Tr.*

phenomena, which, by means of the understanding, produces and renders necessary exactly the same order and continuous connection in the series of our possible perceptions, as is found *a priori* in the form of internal intuition (time), in which all our perceptions must have place.

That something happens, then, is a perception which belongs to a possible experience, which becomes real only because I look upon the phenomenon as determined in regard to its place in time, consequently as an object, which can always be found by means of a rule in the connected series of my perceptions. But this rule of the determination of a thing according to succession in time is as follows: 'In what precedes may be found the condition, under which an event always (that is, necessarily) follows.' From all this it is obvious that the principle of cause and effect is the principle of possible experience, that is, of objective cognition of phenomena, in regard to their relations in the succession of time.

The proof of this fundamental proposition rests entirely on the following momenta of argument. To all empirical cognition belongs the synthesis of the manifold by the imagination, a synthesis which is always successive, that is, in which the representations therein always follow one another. But the order of succession in imagination is not determined, and the series of successive representations may be taken retrogressively as well as progressively. But if this synthesis is a synthesis of apprehension (of the manifold of a given phenomenon), then the order is determined in the object, or, to speak more accurately, there is therein an order of successive synthesis which determines an object, and according to which something necessarily precedes, and when this is posited, something else necessarily follows. If, then, my perception is to contain the cognition of an event, that is, of something which really happens, it must be an empirical judgment, wherein we think that the succession is determined; that is, it presupposes another phenomenon, upon which this event follows necessarily, or in conformity with a rule. If, on the contrary, when I posited the antecedent, the event did not necessarily follow, I should be obliged to consider it merely as a subjective play of my imagination, and if in this I represented to myself anything as objective, I must look upon it as a mere dream. Thus, the relation of phenomena (as possible perceptions), according to which that which happens is, as to its existence, necessarily determined in time by something which antecedes, in conformity with a rule—in other words, the relation of cause and effect—is the condition of the objective validity of our empirical judgments in regard to the sequence of perceptions, consequently of their empirical truth, and therefore of experience. The principle of the relation of causality in the succession of phenomena is therefore valid for all objects of experience, because it is itself the ground of the possibility of experience.

Here, however, a difficulty arises, which must be resolved. The principle of the connection of causality among phenomena is limited in our formula to the succession thereof, although in practice we find that the principle applies also when the phenomena exist together in the same time, and that cause and effect may be simultaneous. For example, there is heat in a room, which does not exist in the open air. I look about for the cause, and find it to be the fire. Now the fire as the cause, is simultaneous with its effect, the heat of the room. In this case, then, there is no succession as regards time, between cause and effect, but they are simultaneous; and still the law holds good. The greater part of operating causes in nature are simultaneous with their effects, and the succession in time of the latter is produced only because the cause cannot achieve the total of its effect in one moment. But at the moment when the effect *first* arises, it is always simultaneous with the causality of its cause, because if the cause had but a moment before ceased to be, the effect could not have arisen. Here it must be specially remembered, that we must consider the *order* of time, and not the *lapse* thereof. The relation remains, even though no time has elapsed. The time between the causality of the cause and its immediate effect may entirely vanish, and the cause and effect be thus simultaneous, but the relation of the one to the other remains always determinable according to time. If, for example, I consider a leaden ball, which lies upon a cushion and makes a hollow in it, as a cause, then it is simultaneous with the effect. But I distinguish the two through the relation of time of the dynamical connection of both. For if I lay the ball upon the cushion, then the hollow follows upon the before smooth surface; but supposing the cushion has, from some cause or another, a hollow, there does not thereupon follow a leaden ball.

Thus, the law of succession of time is in all instances the only empirical criterion of effect in relation to the causality of the antecedent cause. The glass is the cause of the rising of the water above its horizontal surface, although the two phenomena are contemporaneous. For, as soon as I draw some water with the glass from a larger vessel, an effect follows thereupon, namely, the change of the horizontal state which the water had in the large vessel into a concave, which it assumes in the glass.

This conception of causality leads us to the conception of action; that of action, to the conception of force; and through it, to the conception of substance. As I do not wish this critical essay, the sole purpose of which is to treat of the sources of our synthetical cognition *a priori*, to be crowded with analyses which merely explain, but do not enlarge the sphere of our conceptions, I reserve the detailed explanation of the above conceptions for a future system of pure reason. Such an analysis, indeed, executed with great particularity, may already be found in well-known works on this subject. But I cannot at present refrain from making a few remarks on the empirical criterion of a substance, in so far as it seems to be more evident and more easily recognized through the conception of action, than through that of the permanence of a phenomenon.

Where action (consequently activity and force) exists, substance also must exist, and in it alone must be sought the seat of that fruitful source of phenomena. Very well. But if we are called upon to explain what we mean by substance, and wish to avoid the vice of reasoning in a circle, the answer is by no means so easy. How shall we conclude immediately from the action to the *permanence* of that which acts, this being nevertheless an essential and peculiar criterion of substance (phenomenon)? But after what has been said above, the solution of this question becomes easy enough, although by the common mode of procedure—merely analysing our conceptions—it would be quite impossible. The conception of action indicates the relation of the subject of causality to the effect. Now because all effect consists in that which happens, therefore in the changeable, the last subject thereof is the *permanent*, as the substratum of all that changes, that is, substance. For according to the principle of causality, actions are always the first ground of all change in phenomena, and consequently cannot be a property of a subject which itself changes, because if this were the case, other actions and another subject would be necessary to determine this change. From all this it results that action alone, as an empirical criterion, is a sufficient proof of the presence of substantiality, without any necessity on my part of endeavouring to discover the permanence of substance by a comparison. Besides, by this mode of induction we could not attain to the completeness which the magnitude and strict universality of the conception requires. For that the primary subject of the causality of all arising and passing away, all origin and extinction, cannot itself (in the sphere of phenomena) arise and pass away, is a sound and safe conclusion, a conclusion which leads us to the conception of empirical necessity and permanence in existence, and consequently to the conception of a substance as phenomenon.

When something happens, the mere fact of the occurrence, without regard to that which occurs, is an object requiring investigation. The transition from the non-being of a state into the existence of it, supposing that this state contains no quality which previously existed in the phenomenon, is a fact of itself demanding inquiry. Such an event, as has been shown in No. A, does not concern substance (for substance does not thus originate), but its condition or state. It is therefore only change, and not origin from nothing. If this origin be regarded as the effect of a foreign cause, it is termed creation, which cannot be admitted as an event among phenomena, because the very possibility of it would annihilate the unity of experience. If, however, I regard all things not as phenomena, but as things in themselves, and objects of understanding alone, they, although substances, may be considered as dependent, in respect of their existence, on a foreign cause. But this would require a very different meaning in the words, a meaning which could not apply to phenomena as objects of possible experience.

How a thing can be changed, how it is possible that upon one state existing in one point of time, an opposite state should follow in another point of time—of this we have not the smallest conception *a priori*. There is requisite for this the knowledge of real powers, which can only be given empirically; for example, knowledge of moving forces, or, in other words, of certain successive phenomena (as movements) which indicate the presence of such forces. But the form of every change, the condition under which alone it can take place as the coming into existence of another state (be the content of the change, that is, the state which is changed, what it may), and consequently the succession of the states themselves, can very well be considered *a priori*, in relation to the law of causality and the conditions of time.[1]

When a substance passes from one state, $a$, into another state, $b$, the point of time in which the latter exists is different from, and subsequent to that in which the former existed. In like manner, the second state, as reality (in the phenomenon), differs from the first, in which the reality of the second did not exist, as $b$ from zero. That is to say, if the state, $b$, differs from the state, $a$, only in respect to quantity, the change is a coming into

[1] It must be remarked, that I do not speak of the change of certain relations, but of the change of the state. Thus, when a body moves in a uniform manner, it does not change its state (of motion); but only when its motion increases or decreases.

existence of $b-a$, which in the former state did not exist, and in relation to which that state is$=$o.

Now the question arises, how a thing passes from one state$=a$, into another state$=b$. Between two moments there is always a certain time, and between two states existing in these moments there is always a difference having a certain quantity (for all parts of phenomena are in their turn quantities). Consequently, every transition from one state into another is always effected in a time contained between two moments, of which the first determines the state which the thing leaves, and the second determines the state into which the thing passes. Both moments, then, are limitations of the time of a change, consequently of the intermediate state between both, and as such they belong to the total of the change. Now every change has a cause, which evidences its causality in the whole time during which the change takes place. The cause, therefore, does not produce the change all at once or in one moment, but in a time, so that, as the time gradually increases from the commencing instant, $a$, to its completion at $b$, in like manner also, the quantity of the reality $(b-a)$ is generated through the lesser degrees which are contained between the first and last. All change is therefore possible only through a continuous action of the causality, which, in so far as it is uniform, we call a momentum. The change does not consist of these momenta, but is generated or produced by them as their effect.

Such is the law of the continuity of all change, the ground of which is, that neither time itself nor any phenomenon in time consists of parts which are the smallest possible, but that, notwithstanding, the state of a thing passes in the process of a change through all these parts, as elements, to its second state. There is no smallest degree of reality in a phenomenon, just as there is no smallest degree in the quantity of time; and so the new state of the reality grows up out of the former state, through all the infinite degrees thereof, the differences of which one from another, taken all together, are less than the difference between o and $a$.

It is not our business to inquire here into the utility of this principle in the investigation of nature. But how such a proposition, which appears so greatly to extend our knowledge of nature, is possible completely *a priori*, is indeed a question which deserves investigation, although the first view seems to demonstrate the truth and reality of the principle, and the question, how it is possible, may be considered superfluous. For there are so many groundless pretensions to the enlargement of our knowledge by pure reason, that we must take it as a general rule to be mistrustful of all such, and without a thoroughgoing and radical deduction, to believe nothing of the sort even on the clearest dogmatical evidence.

Every addition to our empirical knowledge, and every advance made in the exercise of our perception, is nothing more than an extension of the determination of the internal sense, that is to say, a progression in time, be objects themselves what they may, phenomena, or pure intuitions. This progression in time determines everything, and is itself determined by nothing else. That is to say, the parts of the progression exist only in time, and by means of the synthesis thereof, and are not given antecedently to it. For this reason, every transition in perception to anything which follows upon another in time, is a determination of time by means of the production of this perception. And as this determination of time is, always and in all its parts, a quantity, the perception produced is to be considered as a quantity which proceeds through all its degrees—no one of which is the smallest possible—from zero up to its determined degree. From this we perceive the possibility of cognizing *a priori* a law of changes—a law, however, which concerns their form merely. We merely anticipate our own apprehension, the formal condition of which, inasmuch as it is itself to be found in the mind antecedently to all given phenomena, must certainly be capable of being cognized *a priori*.

Thus, as time contains the sensuous condition *a priori* of the possibility of a continuous progression of that which exists to that which follows it, the understanding, by virtue of the unity of apperception, contains the condition *a priori* of the possibility of a continuous determination of the position in time of all phenomena, and this by means of the series of causes and effects, the former of which necessitate the sequence of the latter, and thereby render universally and for all time, and by consequence, objectively, valid the empirical cognition of the relations of time.

# C

## THIRD ANALOGY

### PRINCIPLE OF CO-EXISTENCE, ACCORDING TO THE LAW OF RECIPROCITY OR COMMUNITY

*All substances, in so far as they can be perceived in space at the same time, exist in a state of complete reciprocity of action.*

### PROOF

Things are co-existent, when in empirical intuition the perception of the one can follow upon the perception of the other, and vice versa—which cannot occur in the succession of phenomena, as we have shown in the explanation of the second principle. Thus I can perceive the moon and then the earth, or conversely, first the earth and then the moon; and for the reason that my perception of these objects can reciprocally follow each other, I say, they exist contemporaneously. Now co-existence is the existence of the manifold in the same time. But time itself is not an object of perception; and therefore we cannot conclude from the fact that things are placed in the same time, the other fact, that the perceptions of these things can follow each other reciprocally. The synthesis of the imagination in apprehension would only present to us each of these perceptions as present in the subject when the other is not present, and contrariwise; but would not show that the objects are co-existent, that is to say, that, if the one exists, the other also exists in the same time, and that this is necessarily so, in order that the perceptions may be capable of following each other reciprocally. It follows that a conception of the understanding or category of the reciprocal sequence of the determinations of phenomena (existing, as they do, apart from each other, and yet contemporaneously), is requisite to justify us in saying that the reciprocal succession of perceptions has its foundation in the object, and to enable us to represent co-existence as objective. But that relation of substances in which the one contains determinations the ground of which is in the other substance, is the relation of influence. And, when this influence is reciprocal, it is the relation of community or reciprocity. Consequently the co-existence of substances in space cannot be cognized in experience otherwise than under the precondition of their reciprocal action. This is therefore the condition of the possibility of things themselves as objects of experience.

Things are co-existent, in so far as they exist in one and the same time. But how can we know that they exist in one and the same time? Only by observing that the order in the synthesis of apprehension of the manifold is arbitrary and a matter of indifference, that is to say, that it can proceed from A, through B, C, D, to E, or contrariwise from E to A. For if they were successive in time (and in the order, let us suppose, which begins with A), it is quite impossible for the apprehension in perception to begin with E and go backwards to A, inasmuch as A belongs to past time, and therefore cannot be an object of apprehension.

Let us assume that in a number of substances considered as phenomena each is completely isolated, that is, that no one acts upon another. Then I say that the *co-existence* of these cannot be an object of possible perception, and that the existence of one cannot, by any mode of empirical synthesis, lead us to the existence of another. For we imagine them in this case to be separated by a completely void space, and thus perception, which proceeds from the one to the other in time, would indeed determine their existence by means of a following perception, but would be quite unable to distinguish whether the one phenomenon follows objectively upon the first, or is co-existent with it.

Besides the mere fact of existence, then, there must be something by means of which A determines the position of B in time, and conversely, B the position of A; because only under this condition can substances be empirically represented as existing contemporaneously. Now that alone determines the position of another thing in time which is the cause of it or of its determinations. Consequently every substance (inasmuch as it can have succession predicated of it only in respect of its determinations) must contain the causality of certain determinations in another substance, and at the same time the effects of the causality of the other in itself. That is to say, substances must stand (mediately or immediately) in dynamical community with each other, if co-existence is to be cognized in any possible experience. But, in regard to objects of experience, that is absolutely necessary without which the experience of these objects would itself be impossible. Consequently it is absolutely necessary that all substances in the world of phenomena, in so far as they are co-existent, stand in a relation of complete community of reciprocal action to each other.

The word community has in our language [1] two meanings, and contains the two notions conveyed in the Latin *communio* and *commercium*. We employ it in this place in the latter sense—that

[1] German.

of a dynamical community, without which even the community of place (*communio spatii*) could not be empirically cognized. In our experiences it is easy to observe, that it is only the continuous influences in all parts of space that can conduct our senses from one object to another; that the light which plays between our eyes and the heavenly bodies produces a mediating community between them and us, and thereby evidences their co-existence with us; that we cannot empirically change our position (perceive this change), unless the existence of matter throughout the whole of space rendered possible the perception of the positions we occupy; and that this perception can prove the contemporaneous existence of these places only through their reciprocal influence, and thereby also the co-existence of even the most remote objects—although in this case the proof is only mediate. Without community, every perception (of a phenomenon in space) is separated from every other and isolated, and the chain of empirical representations, that is, of experience, must, with the appearance of a new object, begin entirely *de novo*, without the least connection with preceding representations, and without standing towards these even in the relation of time. My intention here is by no means to combat the notion of empty space; for it may exist where our perceptions cannot exist, inasmuch as they cannot reach thereto, and where, therefore, no empirical perception of co-existence takes place. But in this case it is not an object of possible experience.

The following remarks may be useful in the way of explanation. In the mind, all phenomena, as contents of a possible experience, must exist in community (*communio*) of apperception or consciousness, and in so far as it is requisite that objects be represented as co-existent and connected, in so far must they reciprocally determine the position in time of each other, and thereby constitute a whole. If this subjective community is to rest upon an objective basis, or to be applied to substances as phenomena, the perception of one substance must render possible the perception of another, and conversely. For otherwise succession, which is always found in perceptions as apprehensions, would be predicated of external objects, and their representation of their co-existence be thus impossible. But this is a reciprocal influence, that is to say, a real community (*commercium*) of substances, without which therefore the empirical relation of co-existence would be a notion beyond the reach of our minds. By virtue of this *commercium*, phenomena, in so far as they are apart from, and nevertheless in connection with each other, constitute a *compositum reale*. Such *composita* are possible in many different ways. The three dynamical relations then, from which all others spring, are those of Inherence, Consequence, and Composition.

.        .        .        .        .

These, then, are the three analogies of experience. They are nothing more than principles of the determination of the existence of phenomena in time, according to the three *modi* of this determination; to wit, the relation to time itself as a quantity (the quantity of existence, that is, duration), the relation in time as a series or succession, finally, the relation in time as the complex of all existence (simultaneity). This unity of determination in regard to time is thoroughly dynamical; that is to say, time is not considered as that in which experience determines immediately to every existence its position; for this is impossible, inasmuch as absolute time is not an object of perception, by means of which phenomena can be connected with each other. On the contrary, the rule of the understanding, through which alone the existence of phenomena can receive synthetical unity as regards relations of time, determines for every phenomenon its position in time, and consequently *a priori*, and with validity for all and every time.

By nature, in the empirical sense of the word, we understand the totality of phenomena connected, in respect of their existence, according to necessary rules, that is, laws. There are therefore certain laws (which are moreover *a priori*) which make nature possible; and all empirical laws can exist only by means of experience, and by virtue of those primitive laws through which experience itself becomes possible. The purpose of the analogies is therefore to represent to us the unity of nature in the connection of all phenomena under certain exponents, the only business of which is to express the relation of time (in so far as it contains all existence in itself) to the unity of apperception, which can exist in synthesis only according to rules. The combined expression of all is this: All phenomena exist in one nature, and must so exist, inasmuch as without this *a priori* unity, no unity of experience, and consequently no determination of objects in experience, is possible.

As regards the mode of proof which we have employed in treating of these transcendental laws of nature, and the peculiar character of it, we must make one remark, which will at the same time be important as a guide in every other attempt to demonstrate the truth of intellectual and likewise synthetical propositions *a priori*. Had we endeavoured to prove these analogies dogmatically, that is, from conceptions; that is to say, had we employed this method in attempting to show that everything which exists, exists only in that which is permanent—that every thing or event presupposes the existence of something in a preceding state, upon which it follows in conformity with a rule—lastly, that in the manifold, which is co-existent, the states co-exist in connection with each other according to a rule—all our labour would have been utterly in vain.   For mere conceptions of things, analyse them as we may, cannot enable us to conclude from the existence of one object to the existence of another.   What other course was left for us to pursue?   This only, to demonstrate the possibility of experience as a cognition in which at last all objects must be capable of being presented to us, if the representation of them is to possess any objective reality.   Now in this third, this mediating term, the essential form of which consists in the synthetical unity of the apperception of all phenomena, we found *a priori* conditions of the universal and necessary determination as to time of all existences in the world of phenomena, without which the empirical determination thereof as to time would itself be impossible, and we also discovered rules of synthetical unity *a priori*, by means of which we could anticipate experience.   For want of this method, and from the fancy that it was possible to discover a dogmatical proof of the synthetical propositions which are requisite in the empirical employment of the understanding, has it happened, that a proof of the principle of sufficient reason has been so often attempted, and always in vain.   The other two analogies nobody has ever thought of, although they have always been silently employed by the mind,[1] because the guiding thread furnished by the categories was wanting, the guide which alone can enable us to discover every hiatus, both in the system of conceptions and of principles.

### 4

#### The Postulates of Empirical Thought

1. That which agrees with the formal conditions (intuition and conception) of experience, is *possible*.

[1] The unity of the universe, in which all phenomena must be connected, is evidently a mere consequence of the tacitly admitted principle of the community of all substances which are co-existent.   For were substances isolated, they could not as parts constitute a whole, and were their connection (reciprocal action of the manifold) not necessary from the very fact of co-existence, we could not conclude from the fact of the latter as a merely ideal relation to the former as a real one.   We have, however, shown in its place, that community is the proper ground of the possibility of an empirical cognition of co-existence, and that we may therefore properly reason from the latter to the former as its condition.

2. That which coheres with the material conditions of experience (sensation), is *real*.

3. That whose coherence with the real is determined according to universal conditions of experience is (exists) necessary.

### Explanation

The categories of modality possess this peculiarity, that they do not in the least determine the object, or enlarge the conception to which they are annexed as predicates, but only express its relation to the faculty of cognition. Though my conception of a thing is in itself complete, I am still entitled to ask whether the object of it is merely possible, or whether it is also real, or, if the latter, whether it is also necessary. But hereby the object itself is not more definitely determined in thought, but the question is only in what relation it, including all its determinations, stands to the understanding and its employment in experience, to the empirical faculty of judgment, and to the reason in its application to experience.

For this very reason, too, the categories of modality are nothing more than explanations of the conceptions of possibility, reality, and necessity, as employed in experience, and at the same time, restrictions of all the categories to empirical use alone, not authorizing the transcendental employment of them. For if they are to have something more than a merely logical significance, and to be something more than a mere analytical expression of the form of *thought*, and to have a relation to *things* and their possibility, reality, or necessity, they must concern possible experience and its synthetical unity, in which alone objects of cognition can be given.

The postulate of the possibility of things requires also, that the conception of the things agree with the formal conditions of our experience in general. But this, that is to say, the objective form of experience, contains all the kinds of synthesis which are requisite for the cognition of objects. A conception which contains a synthesis must be regarded as empty and without reference to an object, if its synthesis does not belong to experience—either as borrowed from it, and in this case it is called an *empirical conception*, or such as is the ground and *a priori* condition of experience (its form), and in this case it is a *pure conception*, a conception which nevertheless belongs to experience, inasmuch as its object can be found in this alone. For where shall we find the criterion or character of the possibility of an object which is cogitated by means of an *a priori* synthetical conception, if not in the synthesis which constitutes the form of empirical cognition of objects? That in such a conception no contradiction exists is indeed a necessary logical condition, but very far from being sufficient to establish the objective reality of the conception, that is, the possibility of such an object as is thought in the conception. Thus, in the conception of a figure which is contained within two straight lines, there is no contradiction, for the conceptions of two straight lines and of their junction contain no negation of a figure. The impossibility in such a case does not rest upon the conception in itself, but upon the construction of it in space, that is to say, upon the conditions of space and its determinations. But these have themselves objective reality, that is, they apply to possible things, because they contain a priori the form of experience in general.

And now we shall proceed to point out the extensive utility and influence of this postulate of possibility. When I represent to myself a thing that is permanent, so that everything in it which changes belongs merely to its state or condition, from such a conception alone I never can cognize that such a thing is possible. Or, if I represent to myself something which is so constituted that, when it is posited, something else follows always and infallibly, my thought contains no self-contradiction; but whether such a property as causality is to be found in any possible thing, my thought alone affords no means of judging. Finally, I can represent to myself different things (substances) which are so constituted that the state or condition of one causes a change in the state of the other, and reciprocally; but whether such a relation is a property of things cannot be perceived from these conceptions, which contain a merely arbitrary synthesis. Only from the fact, therefore, that these conceptions express a priori the relations of perceptions in every experience, do we know that they possess objective reality, that is, transcendental truth; and that independent of experience, though not independent of all relation to the form of an experience in general and its synthetical unity, in which alone objects can be empirically cognized.

But when we fashion to ourselves new conceptions of substances, forces, action, and reaction, from the material presented to us by perception, without following the example of experience in their connection, we create mere chimeras, of the possibility of which we cannot discover any criterion, because we have not taken experience for our instructress, though we have borrowed the conceptions from her. Such fictitious conceptions derive their character of possibility not, like the categories, a priori, as conceptions on which all experience depends, but only, a posteriori, as conceptions given by means of experience itself, and their possibility must either be cognized a posteriori and empirically, or it cannot be cognized at all. A substance which is permanently present in space, yet without filling it (like that *tertium quid* between matter and the thinking subject which some have tried to introduce into metaphysics), or a peculiar fundamental power of the mind of intuiting the future by anticipation (instead of merely inferring from past and present events), or, finally, a power of the mind to place itself in community of thought with other men, however distant they may be—these are conceptions the possibility of which has no ground to rest upon. For they are not based upon experience and its known laws; and without experience, they are a merely arbitrary conjunction of thoughts, which, though containing no internal contradiction, has no claim to objective reality, neither, consequently, to the possibility of such an object as is thought in these conceptions. As far as concerns reality, it is self-evident that we cannot cogitate such a possibility *in concreto* without the aid of experience; because reality is concerned only with sensation, as the matter of experience, and not with the form of thought, with which we can no doubt indulge in shaping fancies.

But I pass by everything which derives its possibility from reality in experience, and I purpose treating here merely of the possibility of things by means of *a priori* conceptions. I maintain, then, that the possibility of things is not derived from such conceptions *per se*, but only when considered as formal and objective conditions of an experience in general.

It seems, indeed, as if the possibility of a triangle could be cognized from the conception of it alone (which is certainly independent of experience); for we can certainly give to the conception a corresponding object completely *a priori*, that is to say, we can construct it. But as a triangle is only the form of an object, it must remain a mere product of the imagination, and the possibility of the existence of an object corresponding to it must remain doubtful, unless we can discover some other ground, unless we know that the figure can be cogitated under the conditions upon which all objects of experience rest. Now, the facts that space is a formal condition *a priori* of external experience, that the formative synthesis, by which we construct a triangle in imagination, is the very same as that we employ in the apprehension of a phenomenon for the purpose of making an empirical conception of it, are what alone connect the notion of the possibility of such a thing with the conception of it. In the same manner, the possibility of continuous quantities, indeed of quantities in general, for the conceptions of them are without exception synthetical, is never evident from the conceptions in themselves, but only when they are considered as the formal conditions of the determination of objects in experience. And where, indeed, should we look for objects to correspond to our conceptions, if not in experience, by which alone objects are presented to us? It is, however, true that without antecedent experience we can cognize and characterize the possibility of things, relatively to the formal conditions, under which something is determined in experience as an object, consequently, completely *a priori*. But still this is possible only in relation to experience and within its limits.

The postulate concerning the cognition of the *reality* of things requires *perception*, consequently conscious sensation, not indeed immediately, that is, of the object itself, whose existence is to be cognized, but still that the object have some connection with a real perception, in accordance with the analogies of experience, which exhibit all kinds of real connection in experience.

From the *mere conception* of a thing it is impossible to conclude its existence. For, let the conception be ever so complete, and containing a statement of all the determinations of the thing, the existence of it has nothing to do with all this, but only with the question—whether such a thing is given, so that the perception of it can in every case precede the conception. For the fact that the conception of it precedes the perception, merely indicates the possibility of its existence; it is perception which presents matter to the conception, that is the sole criterion of reality. Prior to the perception of the thing, however, and therefore comparatively *a priori*, we are able to cognize its existence, provided it stands in connection with some perceptions according to the principles of the empirical conjunction of these, that is, in conformity with the analogies of perception. For, in this case, the existence of the supposed thing is connected with our perceptions in a possible experience, and we are able, with the guidance of these analogies, to reason in the series of possible perceptions from a thing which we do really perceive to the thing we do not perceive. Thus, we cognize the existence of a magnetic matter penetrating all bodies from the perception of the attraction of the steel-filings by the magnet, although the constitution of our organs renders an immediate perception of this matter impossible for us. For, according to the laws of sensibility and the connected context of our perceptions, we should in an experience come also on an immediate empirical intuition of this matter, if our senses were more acute—but this obtuseness has no influence upon and cannot alter the *form* of possible experience in general. Our knowledge of the existence of things reaches as far as our perceptions, and what may be inferred from them according to empirical laws, extend. If we do not set out from experience, or do not proceed according to the laws of the empirical connection of phenomena, our pretensions to discover the existence of a thing which we do not immediately perceive are vain. *Idealism*, however, brings forward powerful objections to these rules for proving existence mediately. This is, therefore, the proper place for its refutation.

### REFUTATION OF IDEALISM

Idealism—I mean *material*[1] idealism—is the theory which declares the existence of objects in space without us to be either (1) doubtful and indemonstrable, or (2) false and impossible. The first is the *problematical* idealism of Descartes, who admits the undoubted certainty of only one empirical assertion (*assertio*), to wit, *I am*. The second is the *dogmatical* idealism of Berkeley, who maintains that space, together with all the objects of which it is the inseparable condition, is a thing which is in itself impossible, and that consequently the objects in space are mere products of the imagination. The dogmatical theory of idealism is unavoidable, if we regard space as a property of things in themselves; for in that case it is, with all to which it serves as condition, a nonentity. But the foundation for this kind of idealism we have already destroyed in the transcendental aesthetic. Problematical idealism, which makes no such assertion, but only alleges our incapacity to prove the existence of anything besides ourselves by means of immediate experience, is a theory rational and evidencing a thorough and philosophical mode of thinking, for it observes the rule, not to form a decisive judgment before sufficient proof be shown. The desired proof must therefore demonstrate that we have *experience* of external things, and not mere *fancies*. For this purpose, we must prove, that our internal and, to Descartes, indubitable experience is itself possible only under the previous assumption of external experience.

### THEOREM

*The simple but empirically determined consciousness of my own existence proves the existence of external objects in space.*

### PROOF

I am conscious of my own existence as determined in time. All determination in regard to time presupposes the existence of

---

[1] In opposition to *formal* or *critical* idealism—the theory of Kant—which denies to us a knowledge of things as things in themselves, and maintains that we can know only phenomena.—*Tr.*

*something permanent* in perception. But this permanent something cannot be something in me, for the very reason that my existence in time is itself determined by this permanent something. It follows that the perception of this permanent existence is possible only through a *thing* without me, and not through the mere *representation* of a thing without me. Consequently, the determination of my existence in time is possible only through the existence of real things external to me. Now, consciousness in time is necessarily connected with the consciousness of the possibility of this determination in time. Hence it follows, that consciousness in time is necessarily connected also with the existence of things without me, inasmuch as the existence of these things is the condition of determination in time. That is to say, the consciousness of my own existence is at the same time an immediate consciousness of the existence of other things without me.

*Remark I.* The reader will observe, that in the foregoing proof the game which idealism plays is retorted upon itself, and with more justice. It assumed, that the only immediate experience is internal, and that from this we can only *infer* the existence of external things. But, as always happens, when we reason from given effects to *determined* causes, idealism has reasoned with too much haste and uncertainty, for it is quite possible that the cause of our representations may lie in ourselves, and that we ascribe it falsely to external things. But our proof shows that external experience is properly immediate,[1] that only by virtue of it—not, indeed, the consciousness of our own existence, but certainly the determination of our existence in time, that is, internal experience —is possible. It is true, that the representation *I am*, which is the expression of the consciousness which can accompany all my thoughts, is that which immediately includes the existence of a subject. But in this representation we cannot find any knowledge of the subject, and therefore also no empirical knowledge, that is, experience. For experience contains, in addition to the thought of something existing, intuition, and in this case it must be internal

---

[1] The *immediate* consciousness of the existence of external things is, in the preceding theorem, not presupposed, but proved, be the possibility of this consciousness understood by us or not. The question as to the possibility of it would stand thus: Have we an internal sense, but no external sense, and is our belief in external perception a mere delusion? But it is evident that, in order merely to fancy to ourselves anything *as* external, that is, to present it to the sense in intuition, we must already possess an external sense, and must thereby distinguish immediately the mere receptivity of an external intuition from the spontaneity which characterizes every act of imagination. For merely to imagine also an external sense, would annihilate the faculty of intuition itself which is to be determined by the imagination.

intuition, that is, time, in relation to which the subject must be determined. But the existence of external things is absolutely requisite for this purpose, so that it follows that internal experience is itself possible only mediately and through external experience.

*Remark II.* Now with this view all empirical use of our faculty of cognition in the determination of time is in perfect accordance. Its truth is supported by the fact, that it is possible to perceive a determination of time only by means of a change in external relations (motion) to the permanent in space (for example, we become aware of the sun's motion, by observing the changes of his relation to the objects of this earth). But this is not all. We find that we possess nothing permanent that can correspond and be submitted to the conception of a substance as intuition, except *matter*. This idea of permanence is not itself derived from external experience, but is an *a priori* necessary condition of all determination of time, consequently also of the internal sense in reference to our own existence, and that through the existence of external things. In the representation *I*, the consciousness of myself is not an intuition, but a merely intellectual representation produced by the spontaneous activity of a thinking subject. It follows, that this *I* has not any predicate of intuition, which, in its character of permanence, could serve as correlate to the determination of time in the internal sense—in the same way as impenetrability is the correlate of matter as an empirical intuition.

*Remark III.* From the fact that the existence of external things is a necessary condition of the possibility of a determined consciousness of ourselves, it does not follow that every intuitive representation of external things involves the existence of these things, for their representations may very well be the mere products of the imagination (in dreams as well as in madness); though, indeed, these are themselves created by the reproduction of previous external perceptions, which, as has been shown, are possible only through the reality of external objects. The sole aim of our remarks has, however, been to prove that internal experience in general is possible only through external experience in general. Whether this or that supposed experience be purely imaginary, must be discovered from its particular determinations, and by comparing these with the criteria of all real experience.

---

Finally, as regards the third postulate, it applies to material necessity in existence, and not to merely formal and logical necessity in the connection of conceptions. Now as we cannot cognize completely *a priori* the existence of any object of sense, though we can do so comparatively *a priori*, that is, relatively to some other previously given existence—a cognition, however, which can only be of such an existence as must be contained in the complex of experience, of which the previously given perception is a part— the necessity of existence can never be cognized from conceptions, but always, on the contrary, from its connection with that which is an object of perception. But the only existence cognized, under the condition of other given phenomena, as necessary, is the existence of effects from given causes in conformity with the laws of causality. It is consequently not the necessity of the existence of things (as substances), but the necessity of the state of things that we cognize, and that not immediately, but by means of the existence of other states given in perception, according to empirical laws of causality. Hence it follows, that the criterion of necessity is to be found only in the law of a possible experience—that everything which happens is determined *a priori* in the phenomenon by its cause. Thus we cognize only the necessity of *effects* in nature, the causes of which are given us. Moreover, the criterion of necessity in existence possesses no application beyond the field of possible experience, and even in this it is not valid of the existence of things as substances, because these can never be considered as empirical effects, or as something that happens and has a beginning. Necessity, therefore, regards only the relations of phenomena according to the dynamical law of causality, and the possibility grounded thereon, of reasoning from some given existence (of a cause) *a priori* to another existence (of an effect). *Everything that happens is hypothetically necessary*, is a principle which subjects the changes that take place in the world to a law, that is, to a rule of necessary existence, without which nature herself could not possibly exist. Hence the proposition, *Nothing happens by blind chance* (*in mundo non datur casus*), is an *a priori* law of nature. The case is the same with the proposition, *Necessity in nature is not blind*, that is, it is conditioned, consequently intelligible necessity (*non datur fatum*). Both laws subject the play of change to *a nature of things* (as phenomena), or, which is the same thing, to the unity of the understanding, and through the understanding alone can changes belong to an experience, as the synthetical unity of phenomena. Both belong to the class of dynamical principles. The former is properly a consequence of the principle of causality— one of the analogies of experience. The latter belongs to the principles of modality, which to the determination of causality adds the conception of necessity, which is itself, however, subject to a rule of the understanding. The principle of continuity forbids any *leap* in the series of phenomena regarded as changes (*in mundo non datur saltus*); and likewise, in the complex of all empirical intuitions in space, any break or hiatus between two phenomena (*non datur hiatus*)—for we can so express the principle, that experience can admit nothing which proves the existence of a vacuum, or which even admits it as a part of an empirical synthesis. For, as regards a vacuum or void, which we may cogitate as out and beyond the field of possible experience (the world), such a question cannot come before the tribunal of mere understanding, which decides only upon questions that concern the employment of given phenomena for the construction of empirical cognition. It is rather a problem for ideal reason, which passes beyond the sphere of a possible experience, and aims at forming a judgment of that which surrounds and circumscribes it, and the proper place for the consideration of it is the transcendental dialectic. These four propositions, *In mundo non datur hiatus, non datur saltus, non datur casus, non datur fatum*, as well as all principles of transcendental origin, we could very easily exhibit in their proper order, that is, in conformity with the order of the categories, and assign to each its proper place. But the already practised reader will do this for himself, or discover the clue to such an arrangement. But the combined result of all is simply this, to admit into the empirical synthesis nothing which might cause a break in or be foreign to the understanding and the continuous connection of all phenomena, that is, the unity of the conceptions of the understanding. For in the understanding alone is the unity of experience, in which all perceptions must have their assigned place, possible.

Whether the field of possibility be greater than that of reality, and whether the field of the latter be itself greater than that of necessity, are interesting enough questions, and quite capable of synthetical solution, questions, however, which come under the jurisdiction of reason alone. For they are tantamount to asking, whether all things as phenomena do without exception belong to the complex and connected whole of a single experience, of which every given perception is a part which therefore cannot be conjoined with any other phenomena—or, whether my perceptions can belong to more than one possible experience? The understanding gives to experience, according to the subjective and formal conditions, of sensibility as well as of apperception, the rules which alone make this experience possible. Other forms of intuition besides those of space and time, other forms of understanding besides the discursive forms of thought, or of cognition by means of conceptions, we can neither imagine nor make intelligible to ourselves; and even if we could, they would still not belong to experience, which is the only mode of cognition by which objects are presented to us. Whether other perceptions besides those which belong to the total of our possible experience, and consequently whether some other sphere of matter exists, the understanding has no power to decide, its proper occupation being with the synthesis of that which is given. Moreover, the poverty of the usual arguments which go to prove the existence of a vast sphere of possibility, of which all that is real (every object of experience) is but a small part, is very remarkable. 'All real is possible;' from this follows naturally, according to the logical laws of conversion, the particular proposition: 'Some possible is real.' Now this seems to be equivalent to: 'Much is possible that is not real.' No doubt it does seem as if we ought to consider the sum of the possible to be greater than that of the real, from the fact that something must be added to the former to constitute the latter. But this notion of adding to the possible is absurd. For that which is not in the sum of the possible, and consequently requires to be added to it, is manifestly impossible. In addition to accordance with the formal conditions of experience, the understanding requires a connection with some perception; but that which is connected with this perception is real, even although it is not immediately perceived. But that another series of phenomena, in complete coherence with that which is given in perception, consequently more than one all-embracing experience is possible, is an inference which cannot be concluded from the data given us by experience, and still less without any data at all. That which is possible only under conditions which are themselves merely possible, is not possible *in any respect*. And yet we can find no more certain ground on which to base the discussion of the question whether the sphere of possibility is wider than that of experience.

I have merely mentioned these questions, that in treating of the conception of the understanding, there might be no omission of anything that, in the common opinion, belongs to them. In reality, however, the notion of absolute possibility (possibility which is valid in every respect) is not a mere conception of the understanding, which can be employed empirically, but belongs to reason alone, which passes the bounds of all empirical use of the understanding. We have, therefore, contented ourselves with a merely critical remark, leaving the subject to be explained in the sequel.

Before concluding this fourth section, and at the same time the system of all principles of the pure understanding, it seems proper to mention the reasons which induced me to term the principles of modality postulates. This expression I do not here use in the sense which some more recent philosophers, contrary to its meaning with mathematicians, to whom the word properly belongs, attach to it—that of a proposition, namely, immediately certain, requiring neither deduction nor proof. For if, in the case of synthetical propositions, however evident they may be, we accord to them without deduction, and merely on the strength of their own pretensions, unqualified belief, all critique of the understanding is entirely lost; and, as there is no want of bold pretensions, which the common belief (though for the philosopher this is no credential) does not reject, the understanding lies exposed to every delusion and conceit, without the power of refusing its assent to those assertions, which, though illegitimate, demand acceptance as veritable axioms. When, therefore, to the conception of a thing an *a priori* determination is synthetically added, such a proposition must obtain, if not a proof, at least a deduction of the legitimacy of its assertion.

The principles of modality are, however, not objectively synthetical, for the predicates of possibility, reality, and necessity do not in the least augment the conception of that of which they are affirmed, inasmuch as they contribute nothing to the representation of the object. But as they are, nevertheless, always synthetical, they are so merely subjectively. That is to say, they have a reflective power, and apply to the conception of a thing, of which, in other respects, they affirm nothing, the faculty of cognition in which the conception originates and has its seat. So that if the conception merely agree with the formal conditions of experience, its object is called possible; if it is in connection with perception, and determined thereby, the object is real; if it is determined according to conceptions by means of the connection of perceptions, the object is called necessary. The principles of modality therefore predicate of a conception nothing more than the procedure of the faculty of cognition which generated it. Now a postulate in mathematics is a practical proposition which contains nothing but the synthesis by which we present an object to ourselves, and produce the conception of it, for example—'With a given line, to describe a circle upon a plane, from a given point;' and such a proposition does not admit of proof, because the procedure, which it requires, is exactly that by which alone it is possible to generate the conception of such a figure. With the same right, accordingly, can we postulate the principles of modality, because they do not augment [1] the conception of a thing, but merely indicate the manner in which it is connected with the faculty of cognition.

### GENERAL REMARK ON THE SYSTEM OF PRINCIPLES

It is very remarkable that we cannot perceive the possibility of a thing from the category alone, but must always have an intuition, by which to make evident the objective reality of the pure conception of the understanding. Take, for example, the categories of relation. How (1) a thing can exist only as a *subject*, and not as a mere determination of other things, that is, can be *substance*; or how (2), because something exists, some other thing must exist, consequently how a thing can be a cause; or how (3), when several things exist, from the fact that one of these things exists, some consequence to the others follows, and reciprocally, and in this way a community of substances can be possible—are questions whose solution cannot be obtained from mere conceptions. The very same is the case with the other categories; for example, how a thing can be of the same sort with many others, that is, can be a quantity, and so on. So long as we have not intuition we cannot know, whether we do really think an object by the categories, and where an object can anywhere be found to cohere with them, and thus the truth is established, that the categories are not in themselves *cognitions*, but mere *forms of thought* for the construction of cognitions from given intuitions. For the same reason is it true that from categories alone no synthetical proposition can be made. For example: 'In every existence there is substance,' that is, something that can exist only as a subject and not as mere predicate; or, 'Everything is a quantity'—to construct propositions such as these, we require something to enable us to go out beyond the given conception and connect another with it. For the same reason the attempt to prove a synthetical proposition by means of mere conceptions, for example: 'Everything that exists contingently has a cause,' has never succeeded. We could never get further than proving that, without this relation to conceptions, we could *not conceive* the existence of the contingent, that is, could not *a priori* through the understanding cognize the existence of such a thing; but it does not hence follow that this is also the condition

[1] When I think the *reality* of a thing, I do really think more than the possibility, but not *in the thing*; for that can never contain more in reality than was contained in its complete possibility. But while the notion of possibility is merely the notion of a position of a thing in relation to the understanding (its empirical use), reality is the conjunction of the thing with perception.

of the possibility of the thing itself that is said to be contingent. If, accordingly, we look back to our proof of the principle of causality, we shall find that we were able to prove it as valid only of objects of possible experience, and, indeed, only as itself the principle of the possibility of experience, consequently of the *cognition* of an object given in *empirical intuition*, and not from mere conceptions. That, however, the proposition: 'Everything that is contingent must have a cause,' is evident to everyone merely from conceptions, is not to be denied. But in this case the conception of the contingent is cogitated as involving not the category of modality (as that the non-existence of which can be *conceived*), but that of relation (as that which can exist only as the consequence of something else), and so it is really an identical proposition: 'That which can exist only as a consequence, has a cause.' In fact, when we have to give examples of contingent existence, we always refer to *changes*, and not merely to the possibility of *conceiving the opposite*.[1] But change is an event, which, as such, is possible only through a cause, and considered *per se* its non-existence is therefore possible, and we become cognizant of its contingency from the fact that it can exist only as the effect of a cause. Hence, if a thing is assumed to be contingent, it is an analytical proposition to say, it has a cause.

But it is still more remarkable that, to understand the possibility of things according to the categories, and thus to demonstrate the *objective reality* of the latter, we require not merely intuitions, but *external intuitions*. If, for example, we take the pure conceptions of relation, we find that (1) for the purpose of presenting to the conception of *substance* something *permanent* in intuition corresponding thereto, and thus of demonstrating the objective reality of this conception, we require an intuition (of matter) in *space*, because space alone is permanent and determines things as such, while time, and with it all that is in the internal sense, is in a state of continual flow; (2) in order to represent *change* as the intuition corresponding to the conception of causality, we require the

[1] We can easily conceive the non-existence of matter; but the ancients did not thence infer its contingency. But even the alternation of the existence and non-existence of a given state in a thing, in which all change consists, by no means proves the contingency of that state—the ground of proof being the reality of its opposite. For example, a body is in a state of rest after motion, but we cannot infer the contingency of the motion from the fact that the former is the opposite of the latter. For this opposite is merely a logical and not a real opposite to the other. If we wish to demonstrate the contingency of the motion, what we ought to prove is, that, *instead* of the motion which took place in the preceding point of time, it was possible for the body to have been *then* in rest, not, that it is *afterwards* in rest; for, in this case, both opposites are perfectly consistent with each other.

representation of motion as change in space; in fact, it is through it alone that changes, the possibility of which no pure understanding can perceive, are capable of being intuited. Change is the connection of determinations contradictorily opposed to each other in the existence of one and the same thing. Now, how it is possible that out of a given state one quite opposite to it in the same thing should follow, reason without an example can not only not conceive, but cannot even make intelligible without intuition; and this intuition is the motion of a point in space; the existence of which in different spaces (as a consequence of opposite determinations) alone makes the intuition of change possible. For, in order to make even internal change cogitable, we require to represent time, as the form of the internal sense, figuratively by a line, and the internal change by the drawing of that line (motion), and consequently are obliged to employ external intuition to be able to represent the successive existence of ourselves in different states. The proper ground of this fact is, that all change to be perceived as change presupposes something permanent in intuition, while in the internal sense no permanent intuition is to be found. Lastly, the objective possibility of the category of *community* cannot be conceived by mere reason, and consequently its objective reality cannot be demonstrated without an intuition, and that external in space. For how can we conceive the possibility of community, that is, when several substances exist, that some effect on the existence of the one follows from the existence of the other, and reciprocally, and therefore that, because something exists in the latter, something else must exist in the former, which could not be understood from its own existence alone? For this is the very essence of community—which is inconceivable as a property of things which are perfectly isolated. Hence, Leibnitz, in attributing to the substances of the world—as cogitated by the understanding alone—a community, required the mediating aid of a divinity; for, from their existence, such a property seemed to him with justice inconceivable. But we can very easily conceive the possibility of community (of substances as phenomena) if we represent them to ourselves as in space, consequently in external intuition. For external intuition contains in itself *a priori* formal external relations, as the conditions of the possibility of the real relations of action and reaction, and therefore of the possibility of community. With the same ease can it be demonstrated, that the possibility of things as *quantities*, and consequently the objective reality of the category of *quantity*, can be grounded only in external intuition, and that by its means alone is the notion of quantity appropriated by the internal sense. But I must avoid prolixity, and leave the task of illustrating this by examples to the reader's own reflection.

The above remarks are of the greatest importance, not only for the confirmation of our previous confutation of idealism, but still more when the subject of *self-cognition* by mere internal consciousness and the determination of our own nature without the aid of external empirical intuitions is under discussion, for the indication of the grounds of the possibility of such a cognition.

The result of the whole of this part of the Analytic of Principles is, therefore—All principles of the pure understanding are nothing more than *a priori* principles of the possibility of experience, and to experience alone do all *a priori* synthetical propositions apply and relate—indeed, their possibility itself rests entirely on this relation.

## CHAPTER III

### OF THE GROUND OF THE DIVISION OF ALL OBJECTS INTO PHENOMENA AND NOUMENA

WE have now not only traversed the region of the pure understanding, and carefully surveyed every part of it, but we have also measured it, and assigned to everything therein its proper place. But this land is an island, and enclosed by nature herself within unchangeable limits. It is the land of truth (an attractive word), surrounded by a wide and stormy ocean, the region of illusion, where many a fog-bank, many an iceberg, seems to the mariner, on his voyage of discovery, a new country, and while constantly deluding him with vain hopes, engages him in dangerous adventures, from which he never can desist, and which yet he never can bring to a termination. But before venturing upon this sea, in order to explore it in its whole extent, and to arrive at a certainty whether anything is to be discovered there, it will not be without advantage if we cast our eyes upon the chart of the land that we are about to leave, and to ask ourselves, firstly, whether we cannot rest perfectly contented with what it contains, or whether we must not of necessity be contented with it, if we can find nowhere else a solid foundation to build upon; and, secondly, by what title we possess this land itself, and how we hold it secure against all hostile claims. Although, in the course of our analytic, we have already given sufficient answers to these questions, yet a summary recapitulation of these solutions may be useful in strengthening our conviction, by uniting in one point the momenta of the arguments.

We have seen that everything which the understanding draws from itself, without borrowing from experience, it nevertheless possesses only for the behoof and use of experience. The principles of the pure understanding, whether constitutive *a priori* (as the mathematical principles), or merely regulative (as the dynamical), contain nothing but the pure schema, as it were, of possible experience. For experience possesses its unity from the synthetical unity which the understanding, originally and from itself, imparts to the synthesis of the imagination in relation to apperception, and in *a priori* relation to and agreement with which phenomena, as data for a possible cognition, must stand. But although these rules of the understanding are not only *a priori* true, but the very source of all truth, that is, of the accordance of our cognition with objects, and on this ground, that they contain the basis of the possibility of experience, as the *ensemble*[1] of all cognition, it seems to us not enough to propound what is true—we desire also to be told what we want to know. If, then, we learn nothing more by this critical examination, than what we should have practised in the merely empirical use of the understanding, without any such subtle inquiry, the presumption is, that the advantage we reap from it is not worth the labour bestowed upon it. It may certainly be answered, that no rash curiosity is more prejudicial to the enlargement of our knowledge than that which must know beforehand the utility of this or that piece of information which we seek, before we have entered on the needful investigations, and before one could form the least conception of its utility, even though it were placed before our eyes. But there is one advantage in such transcendental inquiries which can be made comprehensible to the dullest and most reluctant learner—this, namely, that the understanding which is occupied merely with empirical exercise, and does not reflect on the sources of its own cognition, may exercise its functions very well and very successfully, but is quite unable to do one thing, and that of very great importance, to determine, namely, the bounds that limit its employment, and to

---

[1] *Inbegriff.* The word *continent*, in the sense of that which contains the content (*inhalt*), if I might be allowed to use an old word in a new sense, would exactly hit the meaning.—*Tr.*

know what lies within or without its own sphere. This purpose can be obtained only by such profound investigations as we have instituted. But if it cannot distinguish whether certain questions lie within its horizon or not, it can never be sure either as to its claims or possessions, but must lay its account with many humiliating corrections, when it transgresses, as it unavoidably will, the limits of its own territory, and loses itself in fanciful opinions and blinding illusions.

That the understanding, therefore, cannot make of its *a priori* principles, or even of its conceptions, other than an empirical use, is a proposition which leads to the most important results. A transcendental use is made of a conception in a fundamental proposition or principle, when it is referred to things *in general* and considered as things *in themselves*; an empirical use, when it is referred merely to *phenomena*, that is, to objects of a possible *experience*. That the latter use of a conception is the only admissible one, is evident from the reasons following. For every conception are requisite, firstly, the logical form of a conception (of thought) in general; and, secondly, the possibility of presenting to this an object to which it may apply. Failing this latter, it has no sense, and is utterly void of content, although it may contain the logical function for constructing a conception from certain data. Now object cannot be given to a conception otherwise than by intuition, and, even if a pure intuition antecedent to the object is *a priori* possible, this pure intuition can itself obtain objective validity only from empirical intuition, of which it is itself but the form. All conceptions, therefore, and with them all principles, however high the degree of their *a priori* possibility, relate to empirical intuitions, that is, to data towards a possible experience. Without this they possess no objective validity, but are mere play of imagination or of understanding with images or notions. Let us take, for example, the conceptions of mathematics, and first in its pure intuitions. 'Space has three dimensions' —'Between two points there can be only one straight line,' etc. Although all these principles, and the representation of the object with which this science occupies itself, are generated in the mind entirely *a priori*, they would nevertheless have no significance if we were not always able to exhibit their significance in and by means of phenomena (empirical objects). Hence it is requisite that an abstract conception be *made sensuous*, that is, that an object corresponding to it in intuition be forthcoming, otherwise the conception remains, as we say, without *sense*, that is, without meaning. Mathematics fulfils this requirement by the construction of the figure, which is a phenomenon evident to the senses. The same science finds support and significance in number; this in its turn finds it in the fingers, or in counters, or in lines and points. The conception itself is always produced *a priori*, together with the synthetical principles or formulas from such conceptions; but the proper employment of them, and their application to objects, can exist nowhere but in experience, the possibility of which, as regards its form, they contain *a priori*.

That this is also the case with all of the categories and the principles based upon them, is evident from the fact, that we cannot render intelligible the possibility of an object corresponding to them without having recourse to the conditions of sensibility, consequently, to the form of phenomena, to which, as their only proper objects, their use must therefore be confined, inasmuch as, if this condition is removed, all significance, that is, all relation to an object, disappears, and no example can be found to make it comprehensible what sort of things we ought to think under such conceptions.

The conception of quantity cannot be explained except by saying that it is the determination of a thing whereby it can be cogitated how many times one is placed in it.[1] But this 'how many times' is based upon successive repetition, consequently upon time and the synthesis of the homogeneous therein. Reality, in contradistinction to negation, can be explained only by cogitating a time which is either filled therewith or is void. If I leave out the notion of permanence (which is existence in all time), there remains in the conception of substance nothing but the logical notion of subject, a notion of which I endeavour to realize by representing to myself something that can exist only as a subject. But not only am I perfectly ignorant of any conditions under which this logical prerogative can belong to a thing, I can make nothing out of the notion, and draw no inference from it, because no object to which to apply the conception is determined, and we consequently do not know whether it has any meaning at all. In like manner, if I leave out the notion of time, in which something follows upon some other thing in conformity with a rule, I can find nothing in the pure category, except that there is a something of such a sort that from it a conclusion may be drawn as to the existence of some other thing. But in this case it would not only be impossible to distinguish between a cause and an effect, but, as this power to

[1] Kant's meaning is, that we cannot have any conception of the size, quantity, etc., of a thing, without cogitating or constructing arbitrarily a unit which shall be the standard of measurement. This is observable in weights, measures, etc. Number is the schema of quantity.—*Tr.*

draw conclusions requires conditions of which I am quite ignorant, the conception is not determined as to the mode in which it ought to apply to an object. The so-called principle: Everything that is contingent has a cause, comes with a gravity and self-assumed authority that seems to require no support from without. But, I ask, what is meant by contingent? The answer is, that the non-existence of which is possible. But I should like very well to know by what means this possibility of non-existence is to be cognized, if we do not represent to ourselves a succession in the series of phenomena, and in this succession an existence which follows a non-existence, or conversely, consequently, change. For to say, that the non-existence of a thing is not self-contradictory, is a lame appeal to a logical condition, which is no doubt a necessary condition of the existence of the conception, but is far from being sufficient for the real objective possibility of non-existence. I can annihilate in thought every existing substance without self-contradiction, but I cannot infer from this their objective contingency in existence, that is to say, the possibility of their non-existence in itself. As regards the category of community, it may easily be inferred that, as the pure categories of substance and causality are incapable of a definition and explanation sufficient to determine their object without the aid of intuition, the category of reciprocal causality in the relation of substances to each other (*commercium*) is just as little susceptible thereof. Possibility, Existence, and Necessity nobody has ever yet been able to explain without being guilty of manifest tautology, when the definition has been drawn entirely from the pure understanding. For the substitution of the logical possibility of the *conception*—the condition of which is that it be not self-contradictory, for the transcendental possibility of *things*—the condition of which is, that there be an object corresponding to the conception, is a trick which can only deceive the inexperienced.[1]

It follows incontestably, that the pure conceptions of the understanding are incapable of *transcendental*, and must always be of *empirical* use alone, and that the principles of the pure understanding relate only to the general conditions of a possible experience, to objects of the senses, and never to things in general, apart from the mode in which we intuite them.

[1] In one word, to none of these conceptions belongs a corresponding object, and consequently their real possibility cannot be demonstrated, if we take away sensuous intuition—the only intuition which we possess, and there then remains nothing but the *logical* possibility, that is, the fact that the conception or thought is possible—which, however, is not the question; what we want to know being, whether it relates to an object and thus possesses any meaning.

Transcendental Analytic has accordingly this important result, to wit, that the understanding is competent to effect nothing *a priori*, except the anticipation of the form of a possible experience in general, and, that, as that which is not phenomenon cannot be an object of experience, it can never overstep the limits of sensibility, within which alone objects are presented to us. Its principles are merely principles of the exposition of phenomena, and the proud name of an Ontology, which professes to present synthetical cognitions *a priori* of things in general in a systematic doctrine, must give place to the modest title of analytic of the pure understanding.

Thought is the act of referring a given intuition to an object. If the mode of this intuition is unknown to us, the object is merely transcendental, and the conception of the understanding is employed only transcendentally, that is, to produce unity in the thought of a manifold in general. Now a pure category, in which all conditions of sensuous intuition—as the only intuition we possess—are abstracted, does not determine an object, but merely expresses the thought of an object in general, according to different modes. Now, to employ a conception, the function of judgment is required, by which an object is subsumed under the conception, consequently the at least formal condition, under which something can be given in intuition. Failing this condition of judgment (schema), subsumption is impossible; for there is in such a case nothing given, which may be subsumed under the conception. The merely transcendental use of the categories is therefore, in fact, no use at all, and has no determined, or even, as regards its form, determinable object. Hence it follows, that the pure category is incompetent to establish a synthetical *a priori* principle, and that the principles of the pure understanding are only of empirical and never of transcendental use, and that beyond the sphere of possible experience no synthetical *a priori* principles are possible.

It may be advisable, therefore, to express ourselves thus. The pure categories, apart from the formal conditions of sensibility, have a merely transcendental *meaning*, but are nevertheless not of transcendental *use*, because this is in itself impossible, inasmuch as all the conditions of any employment or use of them (in judgments) are absent, to wit, the formal conditions of the subsumption of an object under these conceptions. As, therefore, in the character of pure categories, they must be employed empirically, and cannot be employed transcendentally, they are of no use at all, when separated from sensibility, that is, they cannot be applied to an object. They are merely the pure form of the employment of the understanding in respect of objects in general and of thought, without its being at the same time possible to think or to determine any object by their means.

But there lurks at the foundation of this subject an illusion which it is very difficult to avoid. The categories are not based, as regards their origin, upon sensibility, like the *forms of intuition*, space, and time; they seem, therefore, to be capable of an application beyond the sphere of sensuous objects. But this is not the case. They are nothing but mere *forms of thought*, which contain only the logical faculty of uniting *a priori* in consciousness the manifold given in intuition. Apart, then, from the only intuition possible for us, they have still less meaning than the pure sensuous forms, space and time, for through them an object is at least given, while a mode of connection of the manifold, when the intuition which alone gives the manifold is wanting, has no meaning at all. At the same time, when we designate certain objects as phenomena or sensuous existences, thus distinguishing our mode of intuiting them from their own nature as things in themselves, it is evident that by this very distinction we as it were place the latter, considered in this their own nature, although we do not so intuite them, in opposition to the former, or, on the other hand, we do so place other possible things, which are not objects of our senses, but are cogitated by the understanding alone, and call them intelligible existences (noumena). Now the question arises, whether the pure conceptions of our understanding do possess significance in respect of these latter, and may possibly be a mode of cognizing them.

But we are met at the very commencement with an ambiguity, which may easily occasion great misapprehension. The understanding, when it terms an object in a certain relation phenomenon, at the same time forms out of this relation a representation or notion of an *object in itself*, and hence believes that it can form also *conceptions* of such objects. Now as the understanding possesses no other fundamental conceptions besides the categories, it takes for granted that an object considered as a thing in itself must be capable of being thought by means of these pure conceptions, and is thereby led to hold the perfectly undetermined conception of an intelligible existence, a something out of the sphere of our sensibility, for a *determinate* conception of an existence which we can cognize in some way or other by means of the understanding.

If, by the term noumenon, we understand a thing so far as it is *not an object of our sensuous intuition*, thus making abstraction of our mode of intuiting it, this is a noumenon in the *negative* sense of the word.    But if we understand by it an *object of a non-sensuous intuition*, we in this case assume a peculiar mode of intuition, an intellectual intuition, to wit, which does not, however, belong to us, of the very possibility of which we have no notion—and this is a noumenon in the *positive* sense.

The doctrine of sensibility is also the doctrine of noumena in the negative sense, that is, of things which the understanding is obliged to cogitate apart from any relation to our mode of intuition, consequently not as mere phenomena, but as things in themselves.    But the understanding at the same time comprehends that it cannot employ its categories for the consideration of things in themselves, because these possess significance only in relation to the unity of intuitions in space and time, and that they are competent to determine this unity by means of general *a priori* connecting conceptions only on account of the pure ideality of space and time. Where this unity of time is not to be met with, as is the case with noumena, the whole use, indeed the whole meaning of the categories is entirely lost, for even the possibility of things to correspond to the categories is in this case incomprehensible.    On this point, I need only refer the reader to what I have said at the commencement of the General Remark appended to the foregoing chapter. Now, the possibility of a thing can never be proved from the fact that the conception of it is not self-contradictory, but only by means of an intuition corresponding to the conception.    If, therefore, we wish to apply the categories to objects which cannot be regarded as phenomena, we must have an intuition different from the sensuous, and in this case the objects would be noumena *in the positive sense* of the word.    Now, as such an intuition, that is, an intellectual intuition, is no part of our faculty of cognition, it is absolutely impossible for the categories to possess any application beyond the limits of experience.    It may be true that there are intelligible existences to which our faculty of sensuous intuition has no relation, and cannot be applied, but our conceptions of the understanding, as mere forms of thought for our sensuous intuition, do not extend to these.    What, therefore, we call noumenon, must be understood by us as such in a *negative* sense.

If I take away from an empirical intuition all thought (by means of the categories), there remains no cognition of any object; for by means of mere intuition nothing is cogitated, and from the existence of such or such an affection of sensibility in me, it does not follow that this affection or representation has any relation to an object without me.    But if I take away all intuition, there still remains the form of thought, that is, the mode of determining an object for the manifold of a possible intuition. Thus the categories do in some measure really extend further than sensuous intuition, inasmuch as they think objects in general, without regard to the mode (of sensibility) in which these objects are given. But they do not for this reason apply to and determine a wider sphere of objects, because we cannot assume that such can be given, without presupposing the possibility of another than the sensuous mode of intuition, a supposition we are not justified in making.

I call a conception problematical which contains in itself no contradiction, and which is connected with other cognitions as a limitation of given conceptions, but whose objective reality cannot be cognized in any manner. The conception of a *noumenon*, that is, of a thing which must be cogitated not as an object of sense, but as a thing in itself (solely through the pure understanding), is not self-contradictory, for we are not entitled to maintain that sensibility is the only possible mode of intuition. Nay, further, this conception is necessary to restrain sensuous intuition within the bounds of phenomena, and thus to limit the objective validity of sensuous cognition; for things in themselves, which lie beyond its province, are called noumena for the very purpose of indicating that this cognition does not extend its application to all that the understanding thinks. But, after all, the possibility of such noumena is quite incomprehensible, and beyond the sphere of phenomena, all is for us a mere void; that is to say, we possess an understanding whose province does *problematically* extend beyond this sphere, but we do not possess an intuition, indeed, not even the conception of a possible intuition, by means of which objects beyond the region of sensibility could be given us, and in reference to which the understanding might be employed *assertorically*. The conception of a noumenon is therefore merely a *limitative conception*, and therefore only of negative use. But it is not an arbitrary or fictitious notion, but is connected with the limitation of sensibility, without, however, being capable of presenting us with any positive datum beyond this sphere.

The division of objects into phenomena and noumena, and of the world into a *mundus sensibilis* and *intelligibilis* is therefore quite inadmissible in a *positive sense*, although conceptions do certainly admit of such a division; for the class of noumena have no determinate object corresponding to them, and cannot therefore possess objective validity. If we abandon the senses, how can it be made conceivable that the categories (which are the only conceptions that could serve as conceptions for noumena) have

# OF PHENOMENA AND NOUMENA 189

any sense or meaning at all, inasmuch as something more than the mere unity of thought, namely, a possible intuition, is requisite for their application to an object? The conception of a noumenon, considered as merely problematical, is, however, not only admissible, but, as a limitative conception of sensibility, absolutely necessary. But, in this case, a noumenon is not a particular *intelligible object* for our understanding; on the contrary, the kind of understanding to which it could belong is itself a problem, for we cannot form the most distant conception of the possibility of an understanding which should cognize an object, not discursively by means of categories, but intuitively in a non-sensuous intuition. Our understanding attains in this way a sort of negative extension. That is to say, it is not limited by, but rather limits, sensibility, by giving the name of noumena to things, not considered as phenomena, but as things in themselves. But it at the same time prescribes limits to itself, for it confesses itself unable to cognize these by means of the categories, and hence is compelled to cogitate them merely as an unknown something.

I find, however, in the writings of modern authors, an entirely different use of the expressions, *mundus sensibilis* and *intelligibilis*,[1] which quite departs from the meaning of the ancients—an acceptation in which, indeed, there is to be found no difficulty, but which at the same time depends on mere verbal quibbling. According to this meaning, some have chosen to call the complex of phenomena, in so far as it is intuited, *mundus sensibilis*, but in so far as the connection thereof is cogitated according to general laws of thought, *mundus intelligibilis*. Astronomy, in so far as we mean by the word the mere observation of the starry heaven, may represent the former; a system of astronomy, such as the Copernican or Newtonian, the latter. But such twisting of words is a mere sophistical subterfuge, to avoid a difficult question, by modifying its meaning to suit our own convenience. To be sure, understanding and reason are employed in the cognition of phenomena; but the question is, whether these can be applied when the object is not a phenomenon—and in this sense we regard it if it is cogitated as given to the understanding alone, and not to the senses. The question therefore is, whether over and above the empirical use of the understanding, a transcendental use is possible, which applies to the noumenon as an object. This question we have answered in the negative.

[1] We must not translate this expression by *intellectual*, as is commonly done in German works; for it is *cognitions* alone that are intellectual or sensuous. Objects of the one or the other mode of intuition ought to be called, however harshly it may sound, *intelligible* or *sensible*.—*Tr.*

When therefore we say, the senses represent objects *as they appear*, the understanding *as they are*, the latter statement must not be understood in a transcendental, but only in an empirical signification, that is, as they must be represented in the complete connection of phenomena, and not according to what they may be, apart from their relation to possible experience, consequently not as objects of the pure understanding. For this must ever remain unknown to us. Nay, it is also quite unknown to us, whether any such transcendental or extraordinary cognition is possible under any circumstances, at least, whether it is possible by means of our categories. *Understanding* and *sensibility*, with us, can determine objects only *in conjunction*. If we separate them, we have intuitions without conceptions, or conceptions without intuitions; in both cases, representations, which we cannot apply to any determinate object.

If, after all our inquiries and explanations, any one still hesitates to abandon the mere transcendental use of the categories, let him attempt to construct with them a synthetical proposition. It would, of course, be unnecessary for this purpose to construct an analytical proposition, for that does not extend the sphere of the understanding, but, being concerned only about what is cogitated in the conception itself, it leaves it quite undecided whether the conception has any relation to objects, or merely indicates the unity of thought—complete abstraction being made of the modi in which an object may be given: in such a proposition, it is sufficient for the understanding to know what lies in the conception —to what it applies, is to it indifferent. The attempt must therefore be made with a synthetical and so-called transcendental principle, for example: Everything that exists, exists as substance, or, Everything that is contingent exists as an effect of some other thing, viz. of its cause. Now I ask, whence can the understanding draw these synthetical propositions, when the conceptions contained therein do not relate to possible experience but to things in themselves (noumena)? Where is to be found the *third term*, which is always requisite in a synthetical proposition, which may connect in the same proposition conceptions which have no logical (analytical) connection with each other? The proposition never will be demonstrated, nay, more, the possibility of any such pure assertion never can be shown, without making reference to the empirical use of the understanding, and thus, *ipso facto*, completely renouncing pure and non-sensuous judgment. Thus the conception of pure and merely intelligible objects is completely void of all principles of its application, because we cannot imagine any mode in which they might be given, and the problematical thought which leaves a place open for them serves only, like a void space, to limit the use of empirical principles, without containing at the same time any other object of cognition beyond their sphere.


# APPENDIX

## OF THE EQUIVOCAL NATURE OR AMPHIBOLY OF THE CONCEPTIONS OF REFLECTION FROM THE CONFUSION OF THE TRANSCENDENTAL WITH THE EMPIRICAL USE OF THE UNDERSTANDING

REFLECTION (*reflexio*) is not occupied about objects themselves, for the purpose of directly obtaining conceptions of them, but is that state of the mind in which we set ourselves to discover the subjective conditions under which we obtain conceptions. It is the consciousness of the relation of given representations to the different sources or faculties of cognition, by which alone their relation to each other can be rightly determined. The first question which occurs in considering our representations is, to what faculty of cognition do they belong? To the understanding or to the senses? Many judgments are admitted to be true from mere habit or inclination; but, because reflection neither precedes nor follows, it is held to be a judgment that has its origin in the understanding. All judgments do not require *examination*, that is, investigation into the grounds of their truth. For, when they are immediately certain (for example: Between two points there can be only one straight line), no better or less mediate test of their truth can be found than that which they themselves contain and express. But all judgment, nay, all comparisons require *reflection*, that is, a distinction of the faculty of cognition to which the given conceptions belong. The act whereby I compare my representations with the faculty of cognition which originates them, and whereby I distinguish whether they are compared with each other as belonging to the pure understanding or to sensuous intuition, I term *transcendental reflection*. Now, the relations in which conceptions can stand to each other are those of *identity* and *difference*, *agreement* and *opposition*, of the *internal* and *external*, finally, of the *determinable* and the *determining* (matter and form). The proper determination of these relations rests on the question, to what faculty of cognition they *subjectively* belong, whether to sensibility or understanding. For, on the manner in which we solve this question depends the manner in which we must cogitate these relations.

Before constructing any objective judgment, we compare the conceptions that are to be placed in the judgment, and observe whether there exists *identity* (of many representations in one conception), if a *general* judgment is to be constructed, or *difference*, if a *particular*; whether there is *agreement* when *affirmative*, and *opposition* when *negative* judgments are to be constructed, and so on. For this reason we ought to call these conceptions, conceptions of comparison (*conceptus comparationis*). But as, when the question is not as to the logical form, but as to the content of conceptions, that is to say, whether the things themselves are identical or different, in agreement or opposition, and so on, the things can have a twofold relation to our faculty of cognition, to wit, a relation either to sensibility or to the understanding, and as on this relation depends their relation to each other, transcendental reflection, that is, the relation of given representations to one or the other faculty of cognition, can alone determine this latter relation. Thus we shall not be able to discover whether the things are identical or different, in agreement or opposition, etc., from the mere conception of the things by means of comparison (*comparatio*), but only by distinguishing the mode of cognition to which they belong, in other words, by means of transcendental reflection. We may, therefore, with justice say, that *logical reflection* is mere comparison, for in it no account is taken of the faculty of cognition to which the given conceptions belong, and they are consequently, as far as regards their origin, to be treated as homogeneous; while *transcendental reflection* (which applies to the objects themselves) contains the ground of the possibility of objective comparison of representations with each other, and is therefore very different from the former, because the faculties of cognition to which they belong are not even the same. Transcendental reflection is a duty which no one can neglect who wishes to establish an *a priori* judgment upon things. We shall now proceed to fulfil this duty, and thereby throw not a little light on the question as to the determination of the proper business of the understanding.

1. *Identity and Difference.* When an object is presented to us several times, but always with the same internal determinations (*qualitas et quantitas*), it, if an object of pure understanding, is always the same, not several things, but only one thing (*numerica identitas*); but if a phenomenon, we do not concern ourselves with comparing the conception of the thing with the conception of some other, but, although they may be in this respect perfectly the same, the difference of place at the same time is a sufficient ground for asserting the *numerical difference* of these objects (of

sense). Thus, in the case of two drops of water, we may make complete abstraction of all internal difference (quality and quantity), and, the fact that they are intuited at the same time in different places, is sufficient to justify us in holding them to be numerically different. Leibnitz regarded phenomena as things in themselves, consequently as *intelligibilia*, that is, objects of pure understanding (although, on account of the confused nature of their representations, he gave them the name of phenomena), and in this case his principle of the indiscernible (*principium identitatis indiscernibilium*) is not to be impugned. But, as phenomena are objects of sensibility, and, as the understanding, in respect of them, must be employed empirically and not purely or transcendentally, plurality and numerical difference are given by space itself as the condition of external phenomena. For one part of space, although it may be perfectly similar and equal to another part, is still without it, and for this reason alone is different from the latter, which is added to it in order to make up a greater space. It follows that this must hold good of all things that are in the different parts of space at the same time, however similar and equal one may be to another.

2. *Agreement and Opposition.* When reality is represented by the pure understanding (*realitas noumenon*), opposition between realities is incogitable—such a relation, that is, that when these realities are connected in one subject, they annihilate the effects of each other, and may be represented in the formula $3 - 3 = 0$. On the other hand, the real in a phenomenon (*realitas phaenomenon*) may very well be in mutual opposition, and, when united in the same subject, the one may completely or in part annihilate the effect or *consequence of the other*; as in the case of two moving forces in the same straight line drawing or impelling a point in opposite directions, or in the case of a pleasure counterbalancing a certain amount of pain.

3. *The Internal and External.* In an object of the pure understanding, only that is internal which has no relation (as regards its existence) to anything different from itself. On the other hand, the internal determinations of a *substantia phaenomenon* in space are nothing but relations, and it is itself nothing more than a complex of mere relations. Substance in space we are cognisant of only through forces operative in it, either drawing others towards itself (attraction), or preventing others from forcing into itself (repulsion and impenetrability). We know no other properties that make up the conception of substance phenomenal in space, and which we term matter. On the other hand, as an object of

the pure understanding, every substance must have internal determination and forces. But what other internal attributes of such an object can I think than those which my internal sense presents to me? That, to wit, which is either itself *thought*, or something analogous to it. Hence Leibnitz, who looked upon things as noumena, after denying them everything like external relation, and therefore also *composition* or combination, declared that all substances, even the component parts of matter, were simple substances with powers of representation, in one word, *monads*.

4. *Matter and Form.* These two conceptions lie at the foundation of all other reflection, so inseparably are they connected with every mode of exercising the understanding. The former denotes the determinable in general, the second its determination, both in a transcendental sense, abstraction being made of every difference in that which is given, and of the mode in which it is determined. Logicians formerly termed the universal, matter, the specific difference of this or that part of the universal, form. In a judgment one may call the given conceptions logical matter (for the judgment), the relation of these to each other (by means of the copula), the form of the judgment. In an object, the composite parts thereof (*essentialia*) are the matter; the mode in which they are connected in the object, the form. In respect to things in general, unlimited reality was regarded as the matter of all possibility, the limitation thereof (negation) as the form, by which one thing is distinguished from another according to transcendental conceptions. The understanding demands that something be given (at least in the conception), in order to be able to determine it in a certain manner. Hence, in a conception of the pure understanding, the matter precedes the form, and for this reason Leibnitz first assumed the existence of things (monads) and of an internal power of representation in them, in order to found upon this their external relation and the community of their state (that is, of their representations). Hence, with him, space and time were possible—the former through the relation of substances, the latter through the connection of their determinations with each other, as causes and effects. And so would it really be, if the pure understanding were capable of an immediate application to objects, and if space and time were determinations of things in themselves. But being merely sensuous intuitions, in which we determine all objects solely as phenomena, the form of intuition (as a subjective property of sensibility) must antecede all matter (sensations), consequently space and time must antecede all phenomena and all data of experience, and

rather make experience itself possible. But the intellectual philosopher could not endure that the form should precede the things themselves, and determine their possibility; an objection perfectly correct, if we assume that we intuite things as they are, although with confused representation. But as sensuous intuition is a peculiar subjective condition, which is *a priori* at the foundation of all perception, and the form of which is primitive, the form must be given *per se*, and so far from matter (or the things themselves which appear) lying at the foundation of experience (as we must conclude, if we judge by mere conceptions), the very possibility of itself presupposes, on the contrary, a given formal intuition (space and time).

### REMARK ON THE AMPHIBOLY OF THE CONCEPTIONS OF REFLECTION

Let me be allowed to term the position which we assign to a conception either in the sensibility or in the pure understanding, the *transcendental place*. In this manner, the appointment of the position which must be taken by each conception according to the difference in its use, and the directions for determining this place to all conceptions according to rules, would be a *transcendental topic*, a doctrine which would thoroughly shield us from the surreptitious devices of the pure understanding and the delusions which thence arise, as it would always distinguish to what faculty of cognition each conception properly belonged. Every conception, every title, under which many cognitions rank together, may be called a *logical place*. Upon this is based the *logical topic* of Aristotle, of which teachers and rhetoricians could avail themselves, in order, under certain titles of thought, to observe what would best suit the matter they had to treat, and thus enable themselves to quibble and talk with fluency and an appearance of profundity.

Transcendental topic, on the contrary, contains nothing more than the above-mentioned four titles of all comparison and distinction, which differ from categories in this respect, that they do not represent the object according to that which constitutes its conception (quantity, reality), but set forth merely the comparison of representations, which precedes our conceptions of things. But this comparison requires a previous reflection, that is, a determination of the place to which the representations of the things which are compared belong, whether, to wit, they are cogitated by the pure understanding, or given by sensibility.

Conceptions may be logically compared without the trouble of inquiring to what faculty their objects belong, whether as noumena, to the understanding, or as phenomena, to sensibility. If, however, we wish to employ these conceptions in respect of objects, previous transcendental reflection is necessary. Without this reflection I should make a very unsafe use of these conceptions, and construct pretended synthetical propositions which critical reason cannot acknowledge, and which are based solely upon a transcendental amphiboly, that is, upon a substitution of an object of pure understanding for a phenomenon.

For want of this doctrine of transcendental topic, and consequently deceived by the amphiboly of the conceptions of reflection, the celebrated Leibnitz constructed an *intellectual system of the world*, or rather, believed himself competent to cognize the internal nature of things, by comparing all objects merely with the understanding and the abstract formal conceptions of thought. Our table of the conceptions of reflection gives us the unexpected advantage of being able to exhibit the distinctive peculiarities of his system in all its parts, and at the same time of exposing the fundamental principle of this peculiar mode of thought, which rested upon naught but a misconception. He compared all things with each other merely by means of conceptions, and naturally found no other differences than those by which the understanding distinguishes its pure conceptions one from another. The conditions of sensuous intuition, which contain in themselves their own means of distinction, he did not look upon as primitive, because sensibility was to him but a confused mode of representation, and not any particular source of representations. A phenomenon was for him the representation of the thing in itself, although distinguished from cognition by the understanding only in respect of the logical form—the former with its usual want of analysis containing, according to him, a certain mixture of collateral representations in its conception of a thing, which it is the duty of the understanding to separate and distinguish. In one word, Leibnitz *intellectualized* phenomena, just as Locke, in his system of *noogony* (if I may be allowed to make use of such expressions), *sensualized* the conceptions of the understanding, that is to say, declared them to be nothing more than empirical or abstract conceptions of reflection. Instead of seeking in the understanding and sensibility two different sources of representations, which, however, can present us with objective judgments of things only in *conjunction*, each of these great men recognized but one of these faculties, which, in their opinion, applied immediately to things in themselves, the other having no duty but that of confusing or arranging the representations of the former.

Accordingly, the objects of sense were compared by Leibnitz as things in general merely in the understanding.

1st. He compares them in regard to their identity or difference —as judged by the understanding. As, therefore, he considered merely the conceptions of objects, and not their position in intuition, in which alone objects can be given, and left quite out of sight the transcendental *locale* of these conceptions—whether, that is, their object ought to be classed among phenomena, or among things in themselves, it was to be expected that he should extend the application of the principle of indiscernibles, which is valid solely of conceptions of things in general, to objects of sense (*mundus phaenomenon*), and that he should believe that he had thereby contributed in no small degree to extend our knowledge of nature. In truth, if I cognize in all its inner determinations a drop of water as a thing in itself, I cannot look upon one drop as different from another, if the conception of the one is completely identical with that of the other. But if it is a phenomenon in space, it has a place not merely in the understanding (among conceptions), but also in sensuous external intuition (in space), and in this case, the physical *locale* is a matter of indifference in regard to the internal determinations of things, and one place, B, may contain a thing which is perfectly similar and equal to another in a place, A, just as well as if the two things were in every respect different from each other. Difference of place without any other conditions, makes the plurality and distinction of objects as phenomena, not only possible in itself, but even necessary. Consequently, the above so-called law is not a law of nature. It is merely an analytical rule for the comparison of things by means of mere conceptions.

2nd. The principle: 'Realities (as simple affirmations) never logically contradict each other,' is a proposition perfectly true respecting the relation of conceptions, but, whether as regards nature, or things in themselves (of which we have not the slightest conception), is without any the least meaning. For real opposition, in which A—B is=o, exists everywhere, an opposition, that is, in which one reality united with another in the same subject annihilates the effects of the other—a fact which is constantly brought before our eyes by the different antagonistic actions and operations in nature, which, nevertheless, as depending on real forces, must be called *realitates phaenomena*. General mechanics can even present us with the empirical condition of this opposition in an *a priori* rule, as it directs its attention to the opposition in the direction of forces—a condition of which the transcendental conception of reality can tell us nothing. Although M. Leibnitz did not announce this proposition with precisely the pomp of a new principle, he yet employed it for the establishment of new propositions, and his followers introduced it into their Leibnitzio-Wolfian system of philosophy. According to this principle, for example, all evils are but consequences of the limited nature of created beings, that is, negations, because these are the only opposite of reality. (In the mere conception of a thing in general this is really the case, but not in things as phenomena.) In like manner, the upholders of this system deem it not only possible, but natural also, to connect and unite all reality in one being, because they acknowledge no other sort of opposition than that of contradiction (by which the conception itself of a thing is annihilated), and find themselves unable to conceive an opposition of reciprocal destruction, so to speak, in which one real cause destroys the effect of another, and the conditions of whose representation we meet with only in sensibility.

3rd. The Leibnitzian Monadology has really no better foundation than on this philosopher's mode of falsely representing the difference of the internal and external solely in relation to the understanding. Substances, in general, must have something *inward*, which is therefore free from external relations, consequently from that of composition also. The *simple*—that which can be represented by a unit—is therefore the foundation of that which is internal in things in themselves. The internal state of substances cannot therefore consist in place, shape, contact, or motion, determinations which are all external relations, and we can ascribe to them no other than that whereby we internally determine our faculty of sense itself, that is to say, the state of representation. Thus, then, were constructed the monads, which were to form the elements of the universe, the active force of which consists in representation, the effects of this force being thus entirely confined to themselves.

For the same reason, his view of the possible community of substances could not represent it but as a *predetermined harmony*, and by no means as a physical influence. For inasmuch as everything is occupied only internally, that is, with its own representations, the state of the representations of one substance could not stand in active and living connection with that of another, but some third cause operating on all without exception was necessary to make the different states correspond with one another. And this did not happen by means of assistance applied in each particular case (*systema assistentiae*), but through the unity of the idea of a cause occupied and connected with all substances, in which they necessarily receive, according to the Leibnitzian school, their existence and permanence, consequently also reciprocal correspondence, according to universal laws.

4th. This philosopher's celebrated *doctrine of space and time*, in which he intellectualized these forms of sensibility, originated in the same delusion of transcendental reflection. If I attempt to represent by the mere understanding, the external relations of things, I can do so only by employing the conception of their reciprocal action, and if I wish to connect one state of the same thing with another state, I must avail myself of the notion of the order of cause and effect. And thus Leibnitz regarded space as a certain order in the community of substances, and time as the dynamical sequence of their states. That which space and time possess proper to themselves and independent of things, he ascribed to a necessary *confusion* in our conceptions of them, whereby that which is a mere form of dynamical relations is held to be a self-existent intuition, antecedent even to things themselves. Thus space and time were the intelligible form of the connection of things (substances and their states) in themselves. But things were intelligible substances (*substantiae noumena*). At the same time, he made these conceptions valid of phenomena, because he did not allow to sensibility a peculiar mode of intuition, but sought all, even the empirical representation of objects, in the understanding, and left to sense naught but the despicable task of confusing and disarranging the representations of the former.

But even if we could frame any synthetical proposition concerning things in themselves by means of the pure understanding (which is impossible), it could not apply to phenomena, which do not represent things in themselves. In such a case I should be obliged in transcendental reflection to compare my conceptions only under the conditions of sensibility, and so space and time would not be determinations of things in themselves, but of phenomena. What things may be in themselves, I know not, and need not know, because a thing is never presented to me otherwise than as a phenomenon.

I must adopt the same mode of procedure with the other conceptions of reflection. Matter is *substantia phaenomenon*. That in it which is internal I seek to discover in all parts of space which it occupies, and in all the functions and operations it performs, and which are indeed never anything but phenomena of the external sense. I cannot therefore find anything that is absolutely, but only what is comparatively internal, and which itself consists of external relations. The absolutely internal in matter, and as it should be according to the pure understanding, is a mere chimera, for matter is not an object for the pure understanding. But the transcendental object, which is the foundation of the phenomenon which we call matter, is a mere *nescio quid*, the nature of which we could not understand, even though someone were found able to tell us. For we can understand nothing that does not bring with it something in intuition corresponding to the expressions employed. If by the complaint of being *unable to perceive the internal nature of things*, it is meant that we do not comprehend by the pure understanding what the things which appear to us may be in themselves, it is a silly and unreasonable complaint; for those who talk thus, really desire that we should be able to cognize, consequently to intuite things without senses, and therefore wish that we possessed a faculty of cognition perfectly different from the human faculty, not merely in degree, but even as regards intuition and the mode thereof, so that thus we should not be men, but belong to a class of beings, the possibility of whose existence, much less their nature and constitution, we have no means of cognizing. By observation and analysis of phenomena we penetrate into the interior of nature, and no one can say what progress this knowledge may make in time. But those transcendental questions which pass beyond the limits of nature, we could never answer, even although all nature were laid open to us, because we have not the power of observing our own mind with any other intuition than that of our internal sense. For herein lies the mystery of the origin and source of our faculty of sensibility. Its application to an object, and the transcendental ground of this unity of subjective and objective, lie too deeply concealed for us, who cognize ourselves only through the internal sense, consequently as phenomena, to be able to discover in our existence anything but phenomena, the non-sensuous cause of which we at the same time earnestly desire to penetrate to.

The great utility of this critique of conclusions arrived at by the processes of mere reflection, consists in its clear demonstration of the nullity of all conclusions respecting objects which are compared with each other in the understanding alone, while it at the same time confirms what we particularly insisted on, namely, that, although phenomena are not included as things in themselves among the objects of the pure understanding, they are nevertheless the only things by which our cognition can possess objective reality, that is to say, which give us intuitions to correspond with our conceptions.

When we reflect in a purely logical manner, we do nothing more than compare conceptions in our understanding, to discover whether both have the same content, whether they are self-contradictory or not, whether anything is contained in either conception, which of the two is given, and which is merely a mode of thinking that given.   But if I apply these conceptions to an object in general (in the transcendental sense), without first determining whether it is an object of sensuous or intellectual intuition, certain limitations present themselves, which forbid us to pass beyond the conceptions, and render all empirical use of them impossible.   And thus these limitations prove, that the representation of an object as a thing in general is not only *insufficient*, but, without sensuous determination and independently of empirical conditions, *self-contradictory*; that we must therefore make abstraction of all objects, as in logic, or, admitting them, must think them under conditions of sensuous intuition; that, consequently, the intelligible requires an altogether peculiar intuition, which we do not possess, and in the absence of which it is for us nothing; while, on the other hand, phenomena cannot be objects in themselves.   For, when I merely think things in general, the difference in their external relations cannot constitute a difference in the things themselves; on the contrary, the former presupposes the latter, and if the conception of one of two things is not internally different from that of the other, I am merely thinking the same thing in different relations. Further, by the addition of one affirmation (reality) to the other, the positive therein is really augmented, and nothing is abstracted or withdrawn from it; hence the real in things cannot be in contradiction with or opposition to itself—and so on.

The true use of the conceptions of reflection in the employment of the understanding has, as we have shown, been so misconceived by Leibnitz, one of the most acute philosophers of either ancient or modern times, that he has been misled into the construction of a baseless system of intellectual cognition, which professes to determine its objects without the intervention of the senses.   For this reason, the exposition of the cause of the amphiboly of these conceptions, as the origin of these false principles, is of great utility in determining with certainty the proper limits of the understanding.

It is right to say, whatever is affirmed or denied of the whole of a conception can be affirmed or denied of any part of it (*dictum de omni et nullo*); but it would be absurd so to alter this logical proposition, as to say, whatever is not contained in a general conception, is likewise not contained in the particular conceptions which rank under it; for the latter are particular conceptions, for the very reason that their content is greater than that which is cogitated in the general conception. And yet the whole intellectual system of Leibnitz is based upon this false principle, and with it must necessarily fall to the ground, together with all the ambiguous principles in reference to the employment of the understanding which have thence originated.

Leibnitz's principle of the identity of indiscernibles or indistinguishables is really based on the presupposition, that, if in the conception of a thing a certain distinction is not to be found, it is also not to be met with in things themselves; that, consequently, all things are completely identical (*numero eadem*) which are not distinguishable from each other (as to quality or quantity) in our conceptions of them. But, as in the mere conception of anything abstraction has been made of many necessary conditions of intuition, that of which abstraction has been made is rashly held to be non-existent, and nothing is attributed to the thing but what is contained in its conception.

The conception of a cubic foot of space, however I may think it, is in itself completely identical. But two cubic feet in space are nevertheless distinct from each other from the sole fact of their being in different places (they are *numero diversa*); and these places are conditions of intuition, wherein the object of this conception is given, and which do not belong to the conception, but to the faculty of sensibility. In like manner, there is in the conception of a thing no contradiction when a negative is not connected with an affirmative; and merely affirmative conceptions cannot, in conjunction, produce any negation. But in sensuous intuition, wherein reality (take for example, motion) is given, we find conditions (opposite directions)—of which abstraction has been made in the conception of motion in general—which render possible a contradiction or opposition (not indeed of a logical kind)—and which from pure positives produce zero$=$o. We are therefore not justified in saying, that all reality is in perfect agreement and harmony, because no contradiction is discoverable among its conceptions.[1] According to mere conceptions, that which is internal is the substratum of all relations or external determinations.

[1] If any one wishes here to have recourse to the usual subterfuge, and to say, that at least *realitates noumena* cannot be in opposition to each other, it will be requisite for him to adduce an example of this pure and non-sensuous reality, that it may be understood whether the notion represents something or nothing. But an example cannot be found except in experience, which never presents to us anything more than *phenomena*; and thus the proposition means nothing more than that the conception which contains only affirmatives, does not contain anything negative—a proposition nobody ever doubted.

When, therefore, I abstract all conditions of intuition, and confine myself solely to the conception of a thing in general, I can make abstraction of all external relations, and there must nevertheless remain a conception of that which indicates no relation, but merely internal determinations. Now it seems to follow, that in every thing (substance) there is something which is absolutely internal, and which antecedes all external determinations, inasmuch as it renders them possible; and that therefore this substratum is something which does not contain any external relations, and is consequently simple (for corporeal things are never anything but relations, at least of their parts external to each other); and inasmuch as we know of no other absolutely internal determinations than those of the internal sense, this substratum is not only simple, but also, analogously with our internal sense, determined through *representations*, that is to say, all things are properly *monads*, or simple beings endowed with the power of representation. Now all this would be perfectly correct, if the conception of a thing were the only necessary condition of the presentation of objects of external intuition. It is, on the contrary, manifest that a permanent phenomenon in space (impenetrable extension) can contain mere relations, and nothing that is absolutely internal, and yet be the primary substratum of all external perception. By mere conceptions I cannot think anything external, without, at the same time, thinking something internal, for the reason that conceptions of relations presuppose given things, and without these are impossible. But, as in intuition there is something (that is, space, which, with all it contains, consists of purely formal, or, indeed, real relations) which is not found in the mere conception of a thing in general, and this presents to us the substratum which could not be cognized through conceptions alone, I cannot say: because a thing cannot be represented *by mere conceptions* without something absolutely internal, there is also, in the things themselves which are contained under these conceptions, and in *their intuition* nothing external to which something absolutely internal does not serve as the foundation. For, when we have made abstraction of all the conditions of intuition, there certainly remains in the mere conception nothing but the internal in general, through which alone the external is possible. But this necessity, which is grounded upon abstraction alone, does not obtain in the case of things themselves, in so far as they are given in intuition with such determinations as express mere relations, without having anything internal as their foundation; for they are not things in themselves, but only phenomena. What we cognize in matter is nothing but relations (what we call its internal determinations are but comparatively internal). But there are some self-subsistent and permanent, through which a determined object is given. That I, when abstraction is made of these relations, have nothing more to think, does not destroy the conception of a thing as phenomenon, nor the conception of an object *in abstracto*, but it does away with the possibility of an object that is determinable according to mere conceptions, that is, of a noumenon. It is certainly startling to hear that a thing consists solely of relations; but this thing is simply a phenomenon, and cannot be cogitated by means of the mere categories: it does itself consist in the mere relation of something in general to the senses. In the same way, we cannot cogitate relations of things *in abstracto*, if we commence with conceptions alone, in any other manner than that one is the cause of determinations in the other; for that is itself the conception of the understanding or category of relation. But, as in this case we make abstraction of all intuition, we lose altogether the mode in which the manifold determines to each of its parts its place, that is, the form of sensibility (space); and yet this mode antecedes all empirical causality.

If by intelligible objects we understand things which can be thought by means of the pure categories, without the need of the schemata of sensibility, such objects are impossible. For the condition of the objective use of all our conceptions of understanding is the mode of our sensuous intuition, whereby objects are given; and, if we make abstraction of the latter, the former can have no relation to an object. And even if we should suppose a different kind of intuition from our own, still our functions of thought would have no use or signification in respect thereof. But if we understand by the term, objects of a non-sensuous intuition, in respect of which our categories are not valid, and of which we can accordingly have no knowledge (neither intuition nor conception), in this merely negative sense noumena must be admitted. For this is no more than saying that our mode of intuition is not applicable to all things, but only to objects of our senses, that consequently its objective validity is limited, and that room is therefore left for another kind of intuition, and thus also for things that may be objects of it. But in this sense the conception of a noumenon is problematical, that is to say, it is the notion of a thing of which we can neither say that it is possible, nor that it is impossible, inasmuch as we do not know of any mode of intuition besides the sensuous, or of any other sort of conceptions than the categories—a mode of intuition and a kind of conception neither of which is applicable to a non-sensuous object. We are on this account incompetent to extend the sphere of our objects of thought beyond the conditions of our sensibility, and to assume the existence of objects of pure thought, that is, of noumena, inasmuch as these have no true positive signification. For it must be confessed of the categories, that they are not of themselves sufficient for the cognition of things in themselves, and without the data of sensibility are mere subjective forms of the unity of the understanding. Thought is certainly not a product of the senses, and in so far is not limited by them, but it does not therefore follow that it may be employed purely and without the intervention of sensibility, for it would then be without reference to an object. And we cannot call a noumenon an object of pure thought; for the representation thereof is but the problematical conception of an object for a perfectly different intuition and a perfectly different understanding from ours, both of which are consequently themselves problematical. The conception of a noumenon is therefore not the conception of an object, but merely a problematical conception inseparably connected with the limitation of our sensibility. That is to say, this conception contains the answer to the question— Are there objects quite unconnected with, and independent of, our intuition?—a question to which only an indeterminate answer can be given. That answer is: Inasmuch as sensuous intuition does not apply to all things without distinction, there remains room for other and different objects. The existence of these problematical objects is therefore not absolutely denied, in the absence of a determinate conception of them, but, as no category is valid in respect of them, neither must they be admitted as objects for our understanding.

Understanding accordingly limits sensibility, without at the same time enlarging its own field. While, moreover, it forbids sensibility to apply its forms and modes to things in themselves and restricts it to the sphere of phenomena, it cogitates an object in itself, only, however, as a transcendental object, which is the cause of a phenomenon (consequently not itself a phenomenon), and which cannot be thought either as a quantity or as reality, or as substance (because these conceptions always require sensuous forms in which to determine an object)—an object, therefore, of which we are quite unable to say whether it can be met with in ourselves or out of us, whether it would be annihilated together with sensibility, or, if this were taken away, would continue to exist. If we wish to call this object a noumenon, because the representation of it is non-sensuous, we are at liberty to do so.

But as we can apply to it none of the conceptions of our understanding, the representation is for us quite void, and is available only for the indication of the limits of our sensuous intuition, thereby leaving at the same time an empty space, which we are competent to fill by the aid neither of possible experience, nor of the pure understanding.

The Critique of the pure understanding, accordingly, does not permit us to create for ourselves a new field of objects beyond those which are presented to us as phenomena, and to stray into intelligible worlds; nay, it does not even allow us to endeavour to form so much as a conception of them. The specious error which leads to this—and which is a perfectly excusable one—lies in the fact that the employment of the understanding, contrary to its proper purpose and destination, is made transcendental, and objects, that is, possible intuitions, are made to regulate themselves according to conceptions, instead of the conceptions arranging themselves according to the intuitions, on which alone their own objective validity rests. Now the reason of this again is, that apperception, and with it, thought, antecedes all possible determinate arrangement of representations. Accordingly we think something in general, and determine it on the one hand sensuously, but, on the other, distinguish the general and *in abstracto* represented object from this particular mode of intuiting it. In this case there remains a mode of determining the object by mere thought, which is really but a logical form without content, which, however, seems to us to be a mode of the existence of the object in itself (noumenon), without regard to intuition which is limited to our senses.

Before ending this transcendental analytic, we must make an addition, which, although in itself of no particular importance, seems to be necessary to the completeness of the system. The highest conception, with which a transcendental philosophy commonly begins, is the division into possible and impossible. But as all division presupposes a divided conception, a still higher one must exist, and this is the conception of an object in general—problematically understood, and without its being decided whether it is something or nothing. As the categories are the only conceptions, which apply to objects in general, the distinguishing of an object, whether it is something or nothing, must proceed according to the order and direction of the categories.

1. To the categories of quantity, that is, the conceptions of all, many, and one, the conception which annihilates all, that is, the conception of *none*, is opposed. And thus the object of a conception,

to which no intuition can be found to correspond, is=nothing. That is, it is a conception without an object (*ens rationis*), like noumena, which cannot be considered possible in the sphere of reality, though they must not therefore be held to be impossible —or like certain new fundamental forces in matter, the existence of which is cogitable without contradiction, though, as examples from experience are not forthcoming, they must not be regarded as possible.

2. Reality is *something*; negation is *nothing*, that is, a conception of the absence of an object, as cold, a shadow (*nihil privativum*).

3. The mere form of intuition, without substance, is in itself no object, but the merely formal condition of an object (as phenomenon), as pure space and pure time. These are certainly something, as forms of intuition, but are not themselves objects which are intuited (*ens imaginarium*).

4. The object of a conception which is self-contradictory, is nothing, because the conception is nothing—is impossible, as a figure composed of two straight lines (*nihil negativum*).

The table of this division of the conception of *nothing* (the corresponding division of the conception of *something* does not require special description) must therefore be arranged as follows:

NOTHING

As

1
Empty conception without object,
*ens rationis*

2                                      3
Empty object of a conception,    Empty intuition without object,
*nihil privativum*                    *ens imaginarium*

4
Empty object without conception,
*nihil negativum*

We see that the *ens rationis* is distinguished from the *nihil negativum* or pure nothing by the consideration, that the former must not be reckoned among possibilities, because it is a mere fiction—though not self-contradictory, while the latter is completely opposed to all possibility, inasmuch as the conception annihilates itself. Both, however, are empty conceptions. On the other hand, the *nihil privativum* and *ens imaginarium* are empty *data* for conceptions. If light be not given to the senses, we cannot represent to ourselves darkness, and if extended objects are not perceived, we cannot represent space. Neither the negation, nor the mere form of intuition can, without something real, be an object.

# TRANSCENDENTAL LOGIC

## SECOND DIVISION

### TRANSCENDENTAL DIALECTIC

#### INTRODUCTION

##### I

*Of Transcendental Illusory Appearance*

WE termed Dialectic in general a logic of appearance.[1] This does not signify a doctrine of *probability*;[2] for probability is truth, only cognized upon insufficient grounds, and though the information it gives us is imperfect, it is not therefore deceitful. Hence it must not be separated from the analytical part of logic. Still less must *phenomenon*[3] and *appearance* be held to be identical. For truth or illusory appearance does not reside in the object, in so far as it is intuited, but in the judgment upon the object, in so far as it is thought. It is therefore quite correct to say that the senses do not err, not because they always judge correctly, but because *they do not* judge at all. Hence truth and error, consequently also, illusory appearance as the cause of error, are only to be found in a judgment, that is, in the relation of an object to our understanding. In a cognition, which completely harmonizes with the laws of the understanding, no error can exist. In a representation of the senses—as not containing any judgment—there is also no error. But no power of nature can of itself deviate from its own laws. Hence neither the understanding *per se* (without the influence of another cause), nor the senses *per se*, would fall into error; the former could not, because, if it acts only according to its own laws, the effect (the judgment) must necessarily accord with these laws. But in accordance with the laws of the understanding consists the formal element in all truth. In the senses there is no judgment — neither a true nor a false one. But, as we have no source of cognition besides these two, it follows that error is caused solely by the unobserved influence of the sensibility

[1] Schein.    [2] Wahrscheinlichkeit.    [3] Erscheinung.

upon the understanding. And thus it happens that the subjective grounds of a judgment blend and are confounded with the objective, and cause them to deviate from their proper determination,[1] just as a body in motion would always of itself proceed in a straight line, but if another impetus gives to it a different direction, it will then start off into a curvilinear line of motion. To distinguish the peculiar action of the understanding from the power which mingles with it, it is necessary to consider an erroneous judgment as the diagonal between two forces, that determine the judgment in two different directions, which, as it were, form an angle, and to resolve this composite operation into the simple ones of the understanding and the sensibility. In pure *a priori* judgments this must be done by means of transcendental reflection, whereby, as has been already shown, each representation has its place appointed in the corresponding faculty of cognition, and consequently the influence of the one faculty upon the other is made apparent.

It is not at present our business to treat of empirical illusory appearance (for example, optical illusion), which occurs in the empirical application of otherwise correct rules of the understanding, and in which the judgment is misled by the influence of imagination. Our purpose is to speak of *transcendental illusory appearance*, which influences principles—that are not even applied to experience, for in this case we should possess a sure test of their correctness—but which leads us, in disregard of all the warnings of criticism, completely beyond the empirical employment of the categories, and deludes us with the chimera of an extension of the sphere of the *pure understanding*. We shall term those principles, the application of which is confined entirely within the limits of possible experience, *immanent*; those, on the other hand, which transgress these limits, we shall call *transcendent* principles. But by these latter I do not understand principles of the *transcendental* use or misuse of the categories, which is in reality a mere fault of the judgment when not under due restraint from criticism, and therefore not paying sufficient attention to the limits of the sphere in which the pure understanding is allowed to exercise its functions; but real principles which exhort us to break down all those barriers, and to lay claim to a perfectly new field of cognition, which recognizes no line of demarcation. Thus *transcendental* and *transcendent* are not identical terms. The principles of the pure understanding, which we have already propounded, ought to be

[1] Sensibility, subjected to the understanding, as the object upon which the understanding employs its functions, is the source of real cognitions. But, in so far as it exercises an influence upon the action of the understanding, and determines it to judgment, sensibility is itself the cause of error.

of empirical and not of transcendental use, that is, they are not applicable to any object beyond the sphere of experience. A principle which removes these limits, nay, which authorizes us to overstep them, is called *transcendent*. If our criticism can succeed in exposing the illusion in these pretended principles, those which are limited in their employment to the sphere of experience, may be called, in opposition to the others, *immanent* principles of the pure understanding.

Logical illusion, which consists merely in the imitation of the form of reason (the illusion in sophistical syllogisms), arises entirely from a want of due attention to logical rules. So soon as the attention is awakened to the case before us, this illusion totally disappears. Transcendental illusion, on the contrary, does not cease to exist, even after it has been exposed, and its nothingness clearly perceived by means of transcendental criticism. Take, for example, the illusion in the proposition: 'The world must have a beginning in time.' The cause of this is as follows. In our reason, subjectively considered as a faculty of human cognition, there exist fundamental rules and maxims of its exercise, which have completely the appearance of objective principles. Now from this cause it happens, that the subjective necessity of a certain connection of our conceptions, is regarded as an objective necessity of the determination of things in themselves. This illusion it is impossible to avoid, just as we cannot avoid perceiving that the sea appears to be higher at a distance than it is near the shore, because we see the former by means of higher rays than the latter, or, which is a still stronger case, as even the astronomer cannot prevent himself from seeing the moon larger at its rising than some time afterwards, although he is not deceived by this illusion.

Transcendental dialectic will therefore content itself with exposing the illusory appearance in transcendental judgments, and guarding us against it; but to make it, as in the case of logical illusion, entirely disappear and cease to be illusion, is utterly beyond its power. For we have here to do with a *natural* and unavoidable illusion, which rests upon subjective principles, and imposes these upon us as objective, while logical dialectic, in the detection of sophisms, has to do merely with an error in the logical consequence of the propositions, or with an artificially constructed illusion, in imitation of the natural error. There is, therefore, a natural and unavoidable dialectic of pure reason—not that in which the bungler, from want of the requisite knowledge, involves himself, nor that which the sophist devises for the purpose of misleading, but that which is an inseparable adjunct of human reason, and which, even after its illusions have been exposed, does not cease to deceive, and continually to lead reason into momentary errors, which it becomes necessary continually to remove.

## II

### *Of Pure Reason as the Seat of the Transcendental Illusory Appearance*

#### A

##### OF REASON IN GENERAL

All our knowledge begins with sense, proceeds thence to understanding, and ends with reason, beyond which nothing higher can be discovered in the human mind for elaborating the matter of intuition and subjecting it to the highest unity of thought. At this stage of our inquiry it is my duty to give an explanation of this, the highest faculty of cognition, and I confess I find myself here in some difficulty. Of reason, as of the understanding, there is a merely formal, that is, logical use, in which it makes abstraction of all content of cognition; but there is also a real use, inasmuch as it contains in itself the source of certain conceptions and principles, which it does not borrow either from the senses or the understanding. The former faculty has been long defined by logicians as the faculty of mediate conclusion in contradistinction to immediate conclusions (*consequentiae immediatae*); but the nature of the latter, which itself generates conceptions, is not to be understood from this definition. Now as a division of reason into a logical and a transcendental faculty presents itself here, it becomes necessary to seek for a higher conception of this source of cognition which shall comprehend both conceptions. In this we may expect, according to the analogy of the conceptions of the understanding, that the logical conception will give us the key to the transcendental, and that the table of the functions of the former will present us with the clue to the conceptions of reason.

In the former part of our transcendental logic, we defined the understanding to be the faculty of rules; reason may be distinguished from understanding as the *faculty of principles*.

The term *principle* is ambiguous, and commonly signifies merely a cognition that may be employed as a principle, although it is not in itself, and as regards its proper origin, entitled to the distinction. Every general proposition, even if derived from experience by the process of induction, may serve as the major in a syllogism; but it is not for that reason a principle. Mathematical axioms (for example, there can be only one straight line between two points) are general *a priori* cognitions, and are therefore rightly denominated principles, relatively to the cases which can be subsumed under them. But I cannot for this reason say that I cognize this property of a straight line from principles—I cognize it only in pure intuition.

Cognition from principles, then, is that cognition in which I cognize the particular in the general by means of conceptions. Thus every syllogism is a form of the deduction of a cognition from a principle. For the major always gives a conception, through which everything that is subsumed under the condition thereof, is cognized according to a principle. Now as every general cognition may serve as the major in a syllogism, and the understanding presents us with such general *a priori* propositions, they may be termed principles, in respect of their possible use.

But if we consider these principles of the pure understanding in relation to their origin, we shall find them to be anything rather than cognitions from conceptions. For they would not even be possible *a priori*, if we could not rely on the assistance of pure intuition (in mathematics), or on that of the conditions of a possible experience. That everything that happens has a cause, cannot be concluded from the general conception of that which happens; on the contrary the principle of causality instructs us as to the mode of obtaining from that which happens a determinate empirical conception.

Synthetical cognitions from conceptions the understanding cannot supply, and they alone are entitled to be called principles. At the same time, all general propositions may be termed comparative principles.

It has been a long-cherished wish—that (who knows how late) may one day be happily accomplished—that the principles of the endless variety of civil laws should be investigated and exposed; for in this way alone can we find the secret of simplifying legislation. But in this case, laws are nothing more than limitations of our freedom upon conditions under which it subsists in perfect harmony with itself; they consequently have for their object that which is completely our own work, and of which we ourselves may be the cause by means of these conceptions. But how objects as things in themselves—how the nature of things is subordinated to principles and is to be determined according to conceptions, is a question which it seems well nigh impossible to answer. Be this, however, as it may—for on this point our investigation is yet to be made— it is at least manifest from what we have said, that cognition from principles is something very different from cognition by means of the understanding, which may indeed precede other cognitions in the form of a principle, but in itself—in so far as it is synthetical —is neither based upon mere thought, nor contains a general proposition drawn from conceptions alone.

The understanding may be a faculty for the production of unity of phenomena by virtue of rules; the reason is a faculty for the production of unity of rules (of the understanding) under principles. Reason, therefore, never applies directly to experience, or to any sensuous object; its object is, on the contrary, the understanding, to the manifold cognition of which it gives a unity *a priori* by means of conceptions—a unity which may be called rational unity, and which is of a nature very different from that of the unity produced by the understanding.

The above is the general conception of the faculty of reason, in so far as it has been possible to make it comprehensible in the absence of examples. These will be given in the sequel.

## B

### OF THE LOGICAL USE OF REASON

A distinction is commonly made between that which is immediately cognized and that which is inferred or concluded. That in a figure which is bounded by three straight lines there are three angles, is an immediate cognition; but that these angles are together equal to two right angles, is an inference or conclusion. Now, as we are constantly employing this mode of thought, and have thus become quite accustomed to it, we no longer remark the above distinction, and, as in the case of the so-called deceptions of sense, consider as immediately perceived, what has really been inferred. In every reasoning or syllogism, there is a fundamental proposition, afterwards a second drawn from it, and finally the conclusion, which connects the truth in the first with the truth in the second— and that infallibly. If the judgment concluded is so contained in the first proposition, that it can be deduced from it without the mediation of a third notion, the conclusion is called immediate (*consequentia immediata*);[1] I prefer the term conclusion of the under- standing. But if, in addition to the fundamental cognition, a second judgment is necessary for the production of the conclusion, it is called a conclusion of the reason. In the proposition: *All men*

[1] A *consequentia immediata*—if there really be such a thing, and if it be not a contradiction in terms—evidently does not belong to the sphere of logic proper, the object-matter of which is the syllogism, which always consists of three propositions, either in thought or expressed. This indeed is tantamount to declaring that there is no such mode of reasoning.—*Tr.*

*are mortal*, are contained the propositions: *Some men are mortal, Nothing that is not mortal is a man*, and these are therefore immediate conclusions from the first. On the other hand, the proposition: *All the learned are mortal*, is not contained in the main proposition (for the conception of a learned man does not occur in it), and it can be deduced from the main proposition only by means of a mediating judgment.

In every syllogism I first cogitate a *rule* (*the major*) by means of the *understanding*. In the next place I *subsume* a cognition under the condition of the rule (and this is the *minor*) by means of the *judgment*. And finally I *determine* my cognition by means of the predicate of the rule (this is the *conclusio*), consequently, I determine it *a priori* by means of the *reason*. The relations, therefore, which the major proposition, as the rule, represents between a cognition and its condition, constitute the different kinds of syllogisms. These are just threefold—analogously with all judgments, in so far as they differ in the mode of expressing the relation of a cognition in the understanding—namely, *categorical, hypothetical, and disjunctive*.

When, as often happens, the conclusion is a judgment which may follow from other given judgments, through which a perfectly different object is cogitated, I endeavour to discover in the understanding whether the assertion in this conclusion does not stand under certain conditions according to a general rule. If I find such a condition, and if the object mentioned in the conclusion can be subsumed under the given condition, then this conclusion follows from a rule which is also valid for other objects of cognition. From this we see that reason endeavours to subject the great variety of the cognitions of the understanding to the smallest possible number of principles (general conditions), and thus to produce in it the highest unity.

## C

### OF THE PURE USE OF REASON

Can we isolate reason, and, if so, is it in this case a peculiar source of conceptions and judgments which spring from it alone, and through which it can be applied to objects; or is it merely a subordinate faculty, whose duty it is to give a certain form to given cognitions—a form which is called logical, and through which the cognitions of the understanding are subordinated to each other, and lower rules to higher (those, to wit, whose condition comprises in its sphere the condition of the others), in so far as this can be done by comparison? This is the question which we have at present to answer. Manifold variety of rules and unity of principles is a requirement of reason, for the purpose of bringing the understanding into complete accordance with itself, just as understanding subjects the manifold content of intuition to conceptions, and thereby introduces connection into it. But this principle prescribes no law to objects, and does not contain any ground of the possibility of cognizing, or of determining them as such, but is merely a subjective law for the proper arrangement of the content of the understanding. The purpose of this law is, by a comparison of the conceptions of the understanding, to reduce them to the smallest possible number, although, at the same time, it does not justify us in demanding from objects themselves such a uniformity as might contribute to the convenience and the enlargement of the sphere of the understanding, or in expecting that it will itself thus receive from them objective validity. In one word, the question is, does reason in itself, that is, does pure reason contain *a priori* synthetical principles and rules, and what are those principles?

The formal and logical procedure of reason in syllogisms gives us sufficient information in regard to the ground on which the transcendental principle of reason in its pure synthetical cognition will rest.

1. Reason, as observed in the syllogistic process, is not applicable to intuitions, for the purpose of subjecting them to rules—for this is the province of the understanding with its categories—but to conceptions and judgments. If pure reason does apply to objects and the intuition of them, it does so not immediately, but mediately —through the understanding and its judgments, which have a direct relation to the senses and their intuition, for the purpose of determining their objects. The unity of reason is therefore not the unity of a possible experience, but is essentially different from this unity, which is that of the understanding. That everything which happens has a cause, is not a principle cognized and prescribed by reason. This principle makes the unity of experience possible and borrows nothing from reason, which, without a reference to possible experience, could never have produced by means of mere conceptions any such synthetical unity.

2. Reason, in its logical use, endeavours to discover the general condition of its judgment (the conclusion), and a syllogism is itself nothing but a judgment by means of the subsumption of its condition under a general rule (the major). Now as this rule may itself be subjected to the same process of reason, and thus the

condition of the condition be sought (by means of a prosyllogism) as long as the process can be continued, it is very manifest that the peculiar principle of reason in its logical use is—to find for the conditioned cognition of the understanding the unconditioned whereby the unity of the former is completed.

But this logical maxim cannot be a principle of *pure reason*, unless we admit that, if the conditioned is given, the whole series of conditions subordinated to one another—a series which is consequently itself unconditioned—is also given, that is, contained in the object and its connection.

But this principle of pure reason is evidently *synthetical*; for analytically, the conditioned certainly relates to some condition, but not to the unconditioned. From this principle also there must originate different synthetical propositions, of which the pure understanding is perfectly ignorant, for it has to do only with objects of a possible experience, the cognition and synthesis of which are always conditioned. The unconditioned, if it does really exist, must be especially considered in regard to the determinations which distinguish it from whatever is conditioned, and will thus afford us material for many *a priori* synthetical propositions.

The principles resulting from this highest principle of pure reason will, however, be *transcendent* in relation to phenomena, that is to say, it will be impossible to make any adequate empirical use of this principle. It is therefore completely different from all principles of the understanding, the use made of which is entirely *immanent*, their object and purpose being merely the possibility of experience. Now our duty in the transcendental dialectic is as follows. To discover whether the principle, that the series of conditions (in the synthesis of phenomena, or of thought in general) extends to the unconditioned, is objectively true, or not; what consequences result therefrom affecting the empirical use of the understanding, or rather whether there exists any such objectively valid proposition of reason, and whether it is not, on the contrary, a merely logical precept which directs us to ascend perpetually to still higher conditions, to approach completeness in the series of them, and thus to introduce into our cognition the highest possible unity of reason. We must ascertain, I say, whether this requirement of reason has not been regarded, by a misunderstanding, as a transcendental principle of pure reason, which postulates a thorough completeness in the series of conditions in objects themselves. We must show, moreover, the misconceptions and illusions that intrude into syllogisms, the major proposition of which pure reason has supplied—a proposition which has perhaps more of the character of a *petitio* than of a *postulatum*—and that proceed from experience upwards to its conditions. The solution of these problems is our task in transcendental dialectic, which we are about to expose even at its source, that lies deep in human reason. We shall divide it into two parts, the first of which will treat of the *transcendent conceptions* of pure reason, the second of transcendent and *dialectical syllogisms*.

## TRANSCENDENTAL DIALECTIC

### BOOK I

#### OF THE CONCEPTIONS OF PURE REASON

THE conceptions of pure reason—we do not here speak of the possibility of them—are not obtained by reflection, but by inference or conclusion. The conceptions of understanding are also cogitated *a priori* antecedently to experience, and render it possible; but they contain nothing but the unity of reflection upon phenomena, in so far as these must necessarily belong to a possible empirical consciousness. Through them alone are cognition and the determination of an object possible. It is from them, accordingly, that we receive material for reasoning, and antecedently to them we possess no *a priori* conceptions of objects from which they might be deduced. On the other hand, the sole basis of their objective reality consists in the necessity imposed on them, as containing the intellectual form of all experience, of restricting their application and influence to the sphere of experience.

But the term, *conception of reason* or rational conception, itself indicates that it does not confine itself within the limits of experience, because its object-matter is a cognition, of which every empirical cognition is but a part—nay, the whole of possible experience may be itself but a part of it—a cognition to which no actual experience ever fully attains, although it does always pertain to it. The aim of rational conceptions is the *comprehension*, as that of the conceptions of understanding is the *understanding* of perceptions. If they contain the unconditioned, they relate to that to which all experience is subordinate, but which is never itself an object of experience—that towards which reason tends in all its conclusions from experience, and by the standard of which it estimates the degree of their empirical use, but which is never itself an element in an empirical synthesis. If, notwithstanding, such conceptions possess objective validity, they may be called *conceptus ratiocinati* (conceptions legitimately concluded); in cases where they do not, they have been admitted on account of having the appearance of being correctly concluded, and may be called *conceptus ratiocinantes* (sophistical conceptions). But as this can only be sufficiently demonstrated in that part of our treatise which relates to the dialectical conclusions of reason, we shall omit any consideration of it in this place. As we called the pure conceptions of the understanding categories, we shall also distinguish those of pure reason by a new name, and call them transcendental ideas. These terms, however, we must in the first place explain and justify.

## TRANSCENDENTAL DIALECTIC

### SECTION I—*Of Ideas in General*

SPITE of the great wealth of words which European languages possess, the thinker finds himself often at a loss for an expression exactly suited to his conception, for want of which he is unable to make himself intelligible either to others or to himself. To coin new words is a pretension to legislation in language which is seldom successful; and, before recourse is taken to so desperate an expedient, it is advisable to examine the dead and learned languages, with the hope and the probability that we may there meet with some adequate expression of the notion we have in our minds. In this case, even if the original meaning of the word has become somewhat uncertain, from carelessness or want of caution on the part of the authors of it, it is always better to adhere to and confirm its proper meaning—even although it may be doubtful whether it was formerly used in exactly this sense—than to make our labour vain by want of sufficient care to render ourselves intelligible.

For this reason, when it happens that there exists only a single word to express a certain conception, and this word, in its usual acceptation, is thoroughly adequate to the conception, the accurate distinction of which from related conceptions is of great importance, we ought not to employ the expression improvidently, or, for the sake of variety and elegance of style, use it as a synonym for other cognate words. It is our duty, on the contrary, carefully to preserve its peculiar signification, as otherwise it easily happens that when the attention of the reader is no longer particularly attracted to the expression, and it is lost amid the multitude of other words of very different import, the thought which it conveyed, and which it alone conveyed, is lost with it.

Plato employed the expression *Idea* in a way that plainly showed he meant by it something which is never derived from the senses, but which far transcends even the conceptions of the understanding (with which Aristotle occupied himself), inasmuch as in experience nothing perfectly corresponding to them could be found. Ideas are, according to him, archetypes of things themselves, and not merely keys to possible experiences, like the categories. In his view they flow from the highest reason, by which they have been imparted to human reason, which, however, exists no longer in its original state, but is obliged with great labour to recall by reminiscence—which is called philosophy—the old but now sadly obscured ideas. I will not here enter upon any literary investigation of the sense which this sublime philosopher attached to this expression. I shall content myself with remarking that it is nothing unusual, in common conversation as well as in written works, by comparing the thoughts which an author has delivered upon a subject, to understand him better than he understood himself—inasmuch as he may not have sufficiently determined his conception, and thus have sometimes spoken, nay even thought, in opposition to his own opinions.

Plato perceived very clearly that our faculty of cognition has the feeling of a much higher vocation than that of merely spelling out phenomena according to synthetical unity, for the purpose of being able to read them as experience, and that our reason naturally raises itself to cognitions far too elevated to admit of the possibility of an object given by experience corresponding to them—cognitions which are nevertheless real, and are not mere phantoms of the brain.

This philosopher found his ideas especially in all that is practical,[1] that is, which rests upon freedom, which in its turn ranks under cognitions that are the peculiar product of reason. He who would derive from experience the conceptions of virtue, who would make (as many have really done) that, which at best can but serve as an imperfectly illustrative example, a model for the formation of a perfectly adequate idea on the subject, would in fact transform

[1] He certainly extended the application of his conception to speculative cognitions also, provided they were given pure and completely *a priori*, nay, even to mathematics, although this science cannot possess an object otherwhere than in *possible* experience. I cannot follow him in this, and as little can I follow him in his mystical deduction of these ideas, or in his hypostatization of them: although, in truth, the elevated and exaggerated language which he employed in describing them is quite capable of an interpretation more subdued and more in accordance with fact and the nature of things.

virtue into a nonentity changeable according to time and circumstance, and utterly incapable of being employed as a rule.   On
the contrary, every one is conscious that, when any one is held
up to him as a model of virtue, he compares this so-called model
with the true original which he possesses in his own mind, and
values him according to this standard.   But this standard is the
idea of virtue, in relation to which all possible objects of experience
are indeed serviceable as examples—proofs of the practicability
in a certain degree of that which the conception of virtue demands
—but certainly not as archetypes.   That the actions of man will
never be in perfect accordance with all the requirements of the
pure ideas of reason, does not prove the thought to be chimerical.
For only through this idea are all judgments as to moral merit or
demerit possible; it consequently lies at the foundation of every
approach to moral perfection, however far removed from it the
obstacles in human nature—indeterminable as to degree—may
keep us.

The Platonic Republic has become proverbial as an example
—and a striking one—of imaginary perfection, such as can exist
only in the brain of the idle thinker; and Brucker ridicules the
philosopher for maintaining that a prince can never govern well,
unless he is participant in *the ideas*.   But we should do better to
follow up this thought, and, where this admirable thinker leaves
us without assistance, employ new efforts to place it in clearer
light, rather than carelessly fling it aside as useless, under the very
miserable and pernicious pretext of impracticability.   A constitution of *the greatest possible human freedom* according to laws, by
which *the liberty of every individual can consist with the liberty of
every other* (not of the greatest possible happiness, for this follows
necessarily from the former), is, to say the least, a necessary idea,
which must be placed at the foundation not only of the first plan
of the constitution of a state, but of all its laws.   And in this, it
is not necessary at the outset to take account of the obstacles which
lie in our way—obstacles which perhaps do not necessarily arise
from the character of human nature, but rather from the
previous neglect of true ideas in legislation.   For there is nothing
more pernicious and more unworthy of a philosopher, than the
vulgar appeal to a so-called adverse experience, which indeed would
not have existed, if those institutions had been established at the
proper time and in accordance with ideas; while instead of this,
conceptions, crude for the very reason that they have been drawn
from experience, have marred and frustrated all our better views
and intentions.   The more legislation and government are in

harmony with this idea, the more rare do punishments become, and thus it is quite reasonable to maintain, as Plato did, that in a perfect state no punishments at all would be necessary. Now although a perfect state may never exist, the idea is not on that account the less just, which holds up this *maximum* as the archetype or standard of a constitution, in order to bring legislative government always nearer and nearer to the greatest possible perfection. For at what precise degree human nature must stop in its progress, and how wide must be the chasm which must necessarily exist between the idea and its realization, are problems which no one can or ought to determine—and for this reason, that it is the destination of freedom to overstep all assigned limits between itself and the idea.

But not only in that wherein human reason is a real causal agent and where ideas are operative causes (of actions and their objects), that is to say, in the region of ethics, but also in regard to nature herself, Plato saw clear proofs of an origin from ideas. A plant, an animal, the regular order of nature—probably also the disposition of the whole universe—give manifest evidence that they are possible only by means of and according to ideas; that, indeed, no one creature, under the individual conditions of its existence, perfectly harmonizes with the idea of the most perfect of its kind—just as little as man with the idea of humanity, which nevertheless he bears in his soul as the archetypal standard of his actions; that, notwithstanding, these ideas are in the highest sense individually, unchangeably, and completely determined, and are the original causes of things; and that the totality of connected objects in the universe is alone fully adequate to that idea. Setting aside the exaggerations of expression in the writings of this philosopher, the mental power exhibited in this ascent from the ectypal mode of regarding the physical world to the architectonic connection thereof according to ends, that is, ideas, is an effort which deserves imitation and claims respect. But as regards the principles of ethics, of legislation, and of religion, spheres in which ideas alone render experience possible, although they never attain to full expression therein, he has vindicated for himself a position of peculiar merit, which is not appreciated only because it is judged by the very empirical rules, the validity of which as principles is destroyed by ideas. For as regards nature, experience presents us with rules and is the source of truth, but in relation to ethical laws experience is the parent of illusion, and it is in the highest degree reprehensible to limit or to deduce the laws which dictate what I *ought to do*, from what *is done*.

We must, however, omit the consideration of these important subjects, the development of which is in reality the peculiar duty and dignity of philosophy, and confine ourselves for the present to the more humble but not less useful task of preparing a firm foundation for those majestic edifices of moral science. For this foundation has been hitherto insecure from the many subterranean passages which reason in its confident but vain search for treasures has made in all directions. Our present duty is to make ourselves perfectly acquainted with the transcendental use made of pure reason, its principles and ideas, that we may be able properly to determine and value its influence and real worth. But before bringing these introductory remarks to a close, I beg those who really have philosophy at heart—and their number is but small—if they shall find themselves convinced by the considerations following as well as by those above, to exert themselves to preserve to the expression *idea* its original signification, and to take care that it be not lost among those other expressions by which all sorts of representations are loosely designated—that the interests of science may not thereby suffer. We are in no want of words to denominate adequately every mode of representation, without the necessity of encroaching upon terms which are proper to others. The following is a graduated list of them. The genus is *representatio* in general (*representatio*). Under it stands representation with consciousness (*perceptio*). A *perception* which relates solely to the subject as a modification of its state, is a *sensation* (*sensatio*), an objective perception is a *cognition* (*cognitio*). A cognition is either an *intuition* or a *conception* (*intuitus vel conceptus*). The former has an immediate relation to the object and is singular and individual; the latter has but a mediate relation, by means of a characteristic mark which may be common to several things. A conception is either *empirical* or *pure*. A pure conception, in so far as it has its origin in the understanding alone, and is not the conception of a pure sensuous image,[1] is called *notio*. A conception formed from notions, which transcends the possibility of experience, is an *idea*, or a conception of reason. To one who has accustomed himself to these distinctions, it must be quite intolerable to hear the representation of the colour red called an idea. It ought not even to be called a notion or conception of understanding.

---

[1] All mathematical figures, for example.—*Tr.*

### Section II—*Of Transcendental Ideas*

Transcendental analytic showed us how the mere logical form of our cognition can contain the origin of pure conceptions *a priori*, conceptions which represent objects antecedently to all experience, or rather, indicate the synthetical unity which alone renders possible an empirical cognition of objects. The form of judgments—converted into a conception of the synthesis of intuitions—produced the categories, which direct the employment of the understanding in experience. This consideration warrants us to expect that the form of syllogisms, when applied to synthetical unity of intuitions, following the rule of the categories, will contain the origin of particular *a priori* conceptions, which we may call pure conceptions of reason or transcendental ideas, and which will determine the use of the understanding in the totality of experience according to principles.

The function of reason in arguments consists in the universality of a cognition according to conceptions, and the syllogism itself is a judgment which is determined *a priori* in the whole extent of its condition. The proposition: 'Caius is mortal,' is one which may be obtained from experience by the aid of the understanding alone; but my wish is to find a conception which contains the condition under which the predicate of this judgment is given—in this case, the conception of *man*—and after subsuming under this condition, taken in its whole extent (all men are mortal), I determine according to it the cognition of the object thought, and say: 'Caius is mortal.'

Hence, in the conclusion of a syllogism we restrict a predicate to a certain object, after having thought it in the major in its whole extent under a certain condition. This complete quantity of the extent in relation to such a condition is called *universality* (*universalitas*). To this corresponds *totality* (*universitas*) of conditions in the synthesis of intuitions. The transcendental conception of reason is therefore nothing else than the conception of the *totality of the conditions* of a given conditioned. Now as the *unconditioned* alone renders possible totality of conditions, and, conversely, the totality of conditions is itself always unconditioned; a pure rational conception in general can be defined and explained by means of the conception of the unconditioned, in so far as it contains a basis for the synthesis of the conditioned.

To the number of modes of relation which the understanding cogitates by means of the categories, the number of pure rational conceptions will correspond. We must therefore seek for, first, an *unconditioned* of the *categorical* synthesis in a *subject*; secondly, of the *hypothetical* synthesis of the members of a *series*; thirdly, of the *disjunctive* synthesis of parts in a *system*.

There are exactly the same number of modes of syllogisms, each of which proceeds through prosyllogisms to the unconditioned —one to the subject which cannot be employed as predicate, another to the presupposition which supposes nothing higher than itself, and the third to an aggregate of the members of the complete division of a conception. Hence the pure rational conceptions of totality in the synthesis of conditions have a necessary foundation in the nature of human reason—at least as modes of elevating the unity of the understanding to the unconditioned. They may have no valid application, corresponding to their transcendental employment, *in concreto*, and be thus of no greater utility than to direct the understanding how, while extending them as widely as possible, to maintain its exercise and application in perfect consistence and harmony.

But, while speaking here of the totality of conditions and of the unconditioned as the common title of all conceptions of reason, we again light upon an expression which we find it impossible to dispense with, and which nevertheless, owing to the ambiguity attaching to it from long abuse, we cannot employ with safety. The word *absolute* is one of the few words which, in its original signification, was perfectly adequate to the conception it was intended to convey—a conception which no other word in the same language exactly suits, and the loss—or, which is the same thing, the incautious and loose employment—of which must be followed by the loss of the conception itself. And, as it is a conception which occupies much of the attention of reason, its loss would be greatly to the detriment of all transcendental philosophy. The word *absolute* is at present frequently used to denote that something can be predicated of a thing considered *in itself* and intrinsically. In this sense *absolutely possible* would signify that which is possible in itself (*interne*)—which is, in fact, the *least* that one can predicate of an object. On the other hand, it is sometimes employed to indicate that a thing is valid in all respects—for example, absolute sovereignty. *Absolutely possible* would in this sense signify that which is *possible in all relations* and in every respect; and this is the most that can be predicated of the possibility of a thing. Now these significations do in truth frequently coincide. Thus, for example, that which is intrinsically impossible, is also impossible in all relations, that is, absolutely impossible. But in most cases they differ from each other *toto caelo*, and I can by no means conclude that, because a thing is in itself possible, it is also possible in all relations, and therefore absolutely. Nay, more, I shall in the sequel show, that absolute necessity does not by any means depend on internal necessity, and that therefore it must not be considered as synonymous with it. Of an opposite which is intrinsically impossible, we may affirm that it is in all respects impossible, and that consequently the thing itself, of which this is the opposite, is absolutely necessary; but I cannot reason conversely and say, the opposite of that which is absolutely necessary is intrinsically impossible, that is, that the *absolute* necessity of things is an *internal* necessity. For this internal necessity is in certain cases a mere empty word with which the least conception cannot be connected, while the conception of the necessity of a thing in all relations possesses very peculiar determinations. Now as the loss of a conception of great utility in speculative science cannot be a matter of indifference to the philosopher, I trust that the proper determination and careful preservation of the expression on which the conception depends will likewise be not indifferent to him.

In this enlarged signification then shall I employ the word *absolute*, in opposition to that which is valid only in some particular respect; for the latter is restricted by conditions, the former is valid without any restriction whatever.

Now the transcendental conception of reason has for its object nothing else than absolute totality in the synthesis of conditions, and does not rest satisfied till it has attained to the absolutely, that is, in all respects and relations, unconditioned. For pure reason leaves to the understanding everything that immediately relates to the object of intuition or rather to their synthesis in imagination. The former restricts itself to the absolute totality in the employment of the conceptions of the understanding, and aims at carrying out the synthetical unity which is cogitated in the category, even to the unconditioned. This unity may hence be called the *rational unity* [1] of phenomena, as the other, which the category expresses, may be termed the *unity of the understanding*.[1] Reason, therefore, has an immediate relation to the use of the understanding, not indeed in so far as the latter contains the ground

[1] Vernunfteinheit, Verstandeseinheit.

of possible experience (for the conception of the absolute totality of conditions is not a conception that can be employed in experience, because no experience is unconditioned), but solely for the purpose of directing it to a certain unity, of which the understanding has no conception, and the aim of which is to collect into an *absolute whole* all acts of the understanding. Hence the objective employment of the pure conceptions of reason is always *transcendent*, while that of the pure conceptions of the understanding must, according to their nature, be always *immanent*, inasmuch as they are limited to possible experience.

I understand by idea a necessary conception of reason, to which no corresponding object can be discovered in the world of sense. Accordingly, the pure conceptions of reason at present under consideration are *transcendental ideas*. They are conceptions of pure reason, for they regard all empirical cognition as determined by means of an absolute totality of conditions. They are not mere fictions, but natural and necessary products of reason, and have hence a necessary relation to the whole sphere of the exercise of the understanding. And finally, they are transcendent, and overstep the limits of all experience, in which, consequently, no object can ever be presented that would be perfectly adequate to a transcendental idea. When we use the word *idea*, we say, as regards its object (an object of the pure understanding), a great deal, but as regards its subject (that is, in respect of its reality under conditions of experience), exceedingly little, because the idea, as the conception of a maximum, can never be completely and adequately presented *in concreto*. Now, as in the merely speculative employment of reason the latter is properly the sole aim, and as in this case the approximation to a conception, which is never attained in practice, is the same thing as if the conception were non-existent —it is commonly said of the conception of this kind, *it is only an idea*. So we might very well say, the absolute totality of all phenomena is only an idea, for as we never can present an adequate representation of it, it remains for us a *problem* incapable of solution. On the other hand, as in the practical use of the understanding we have only to do with action and practice according to rules, an idea of pure reason can always be given really *in concreto*, although only partially, nay, it is the indispensable condition of all practical employment of reason. The practice or execution of the idea is always limited and defective, but nevertheless within indeterminable boundaries, consequently always under the influence of the conception of an absolute perfection. And thus the practical idea is always in the highest degree fruitful, and in relation to real actions indispensably necessary. In the idea, pure reason possesses even causality and the power of producing that which its conception contains. Hence we cannot say of wisdom, in a disparaging way, *it is only an idea*. For, for the very reason that it is the idea of the necessary unity of all possible aims, it must be for all practical exertions and endeavours the primitive condition and rule—a rule which, if not constitutive, is at least limitative.

Now, although we must say of the transcendental conceptions of reason, *they are only ideas*, we must not, on this account, look upon them as superfluous and nugatory. For, although no object can be determined by them, they can be of great utility, unobserved and at the basis of the edifice of the understanding, as the canon for its extended and self-consistent exercise—a canon which, indeed, does not enable it to cognize more in an object than it would cognize by the help of its own conceptions, but which guides it more securely in its cognition. Not to mention that they perhaps render possible a transition from our conceptions of nature and the non-ego to the practical conceptions, and thus produce for even ethical ideas keeping, so to speak, and connection with the speculative cognitions of reason. The explication of all this must be looked for in the sequel.

But setting aside, in conformity with our original purpose, the consideration of the practical ideas, we proceed to contemplate reason in its speculative use alone, nay, in a still more restricted sphere, to wit, in the transcendental use; and here must strike into the same path which we followed in our deduction of the categories. That is to say, we shall consider the logical form of the cognition of reason, that we may see whether reason may not be thereby a source of conceptions which enables us to regard objects in themselves as determined synthetically *a priori*, in relation to one or other of the functions of reason.

Reason, considered as the faculty of a certain logical form of cognition, is the faculty of conclusion, that is, of mediate judgment—by means of the subsumption of the condition of a possible judgment under the condition of a given judgment. The given judgment is the general rule (major). The subsumption of the condition of another possible judgment under the condition of the rule is the minor. The actual judgment, which enounces the assertion of the rule in the subsumed case, is the conclusion (*conclusio*). The rule predicates something generally under a certain condition. The condition of the rule is satisfied in some particular case. It follows, that what was valid in general under that condition must also be considered as valid in the particular case which satisfies this condition. It is very plain that reason attains to a cognition, by means of acts of the understanding which constitute a series of conditions. When I arrive at the proposition, 'All bodies are changeable,' by beginning with the more remote cognition (in which the conception of body does not appear, but which nevertheless contains the condition of that conception), 'All [that is] compound is changeable,' by proceeding from this to a less remote cognition, which stands under the condition of the former, 'Bodies are compound,' and hence to a third, which at length connects for me the remote cognition (changeable) with the one before me, 'Consequently, bodies are changeable'—I have arrived at a cognition (conclusion) through a series of conditions (premisses). Now every series, whose exponent (of the categorical or hypothetical judgment) is given, can be continued; consequently the same procedure of reason conducts us to the *ratiocinatio polysyllogistica*, which is a series of syllogisms, that can be continued either on the side of the conditions (*per prosyllogismos*) or of the conditioned (*per episyllogismos*) to an indefinite extent.

But we very soon perceive that the chain or series of prosyllogisms, that is, of deduced cognitions on the side of the grounds or conditions of a given cognition, in other words, the *ascending series* of syllogisms must have a very different relation to the faculty of reason from that of the *descending series*, that is, the progressive procedure of reason on the side of the conditioned by means of episyllogisms. For, as in the former case the cognition (*conclusio*) is given only as conditioned, reason can attain to this cognition only under the presupposition that all the members of the series on the side of the conditions are given (totality in the series of premisses), because only under this supposition is the judgment we may be considering possible *a priori*; while on the side of the conditioned or the inferences, only an incomplete and *becoming*, and not a presupposed or given series, consequently only a potential progression, is cogitated. Hence, when a cognition is contemplated as conditioned, reason is compelled to consider the series of conditions in an ascending line as completed and given in their totality. But if the very same cognition is considered at the same time as the condition of other cognitions, which together constitute a series of inferences or consequences in a descending line, reason may preserve a perfect indifference, as to how far this progression may extend *a parte posteriori*, and whether the totality of this series is possible, because it stands in no need of such a series for the purpose of arriving at the conclusion before it, inasmuch as this conclusion is sufficiently guaranteed and determined on grounds *a parte priori*. It may be the case, that upon the side of the conditions the series of premisses has a *first* or highest condition, or it may not possess this, and so be *a parte priori* unlimited; but it must nevertheless contain totality of conditions, even admitting that we never could succeed in completely apprehending it; and the whole series must be unconditionally true, if the conditioned, which is considered as an inference resulting from it, is to be held as true. This is a requirement of reason, which announces its cognition as determined *a priori* and as necessary, either in itself—and in this case it needs no grounds to rest upon—or, if it is deduced, as a member of a series of grounds, which is itself unconditionally true.

### Section III—*System of Transcendental Ideas*

WE are not at present engaged with a logical dialectic which makes complete abstraction of the content of cognition, and aims only at unveiling the illusory appearance in the form of syllogisms. Our subject is transcendental dialectic, which must contain, completely *a priori*, the origin of certain cognitions drawn from pure reason, and the origin of certain deduced conceptions, the object of which cannot be given empirically, and which therefore lie beyond the sphere of the faculty of understanding. We have observed, from the natural relation which the transcendental use of our cognition, in syllogisms as well as in judgments, must have to the logical, that there are three kinds of dialectical arguments, corresponding to the three modes of conclusion, by which reason attains to cognitions on principles; and that in all it is the business of reason to ascend from the conditioned synthesis, beyond which the understanding never proceeds, to the unconditioned which the understanding never can reach.

Now the most general relations which can exist in our representations are: 1st, the relation to the subject; 2nd, the relation to objects, either as phenomena, or as objects of thought in general. If we connect this subdivision with the main division, all the relations of our representations, of which we can form either a conception or an idea, are threefold: 1. The relation to the subject; 2. The relation to the manifold of the object as a phenomenon; 3. The relation to all things in general.

Now all pure conceptions have to do in general with the synthetical unity of representations; conceptions of pure reason (transcendental ideas), on the other hand, with the unconditional synthetical unity of all conditions. It follows that all transcendental ideas arrange themselves in three classes, the *first* of which contains the absolute (unconditioned) *unity of the thinking subject*, the *second* the absolute *unity of the series of the conditions* of a phenomenon, the *third* the absolute *unity of the condition of all objects of thought* in general.

The thinking subject is the object-matter of *Psychology*; the sum total of all phenomena (the world) is the object-matter of *Cosmology*; and the thing which contains the highest condition of the possibility of all that is cogitable (the being of all beings) is the object-matter of all *Theology*. Thus pure reason presents us with the idea of a transcendental doctrine of the soul (*psychologia rationalis*), of a transcendental science of the world (*cosmologia rationalis*), and finally of a transcendental doctrine of God (*theologia transcendentalis*). Understanding cannot originate even the outline of any of these sciences, even when connected with the highest logical use of reason, that is, all cogitable syllogisms—for the purpose of proceeding from one object (phenomenon) to all others, even to the utmost limits of the empirical synthesis. They are, on the contrary, pure and genuine products, or problems, of pure reason.

What modi of the pure conceptions of reason these transcendental ideas are, will be fully exposed in the following chapter. They follow the guiding thread of the categories. For pure reason never relates immediately to objects, but to the conceptions of these contained in the understanding. In like manner, it will be made manifest in the detailed explanation of these ideas—how reason, merely through the synthetical use of the same function which it employs in a categorical syllogism, necessarily attains to the conception of the absolute unity of the *thinking subject*—how the logical procedure in hypothetical ideas necessarily produces the idea of the absolutely unconditioned *in a series* of given conditions, and finally — how the mere form of the disjunctive syllogism involves the highest conception of a *being of all beings*: a thought which at first sight seems in the highest degree paradoxical.

An *objective deduction*, such as we were able to present in the case of the categories, is impossible as regards these transcendental ideas. For they have, in truth, no relation to any object, in experience, for the very reason that they are only ideas. But a subjective deduction of them from the nature of our reason is possible, and has been given in the present chapter.

It is easy to perceive that the sole aim of pure reason is the absolute totality of the synthesis *on the side of the conditions*, and that it does not concern itself with the absolute completeness *on the part of the conditioned*. For of the former alone does she stand in need, in order to preposit the whole series of conditions, and thus present them to the understanding *a priori*. But if we once have a completely (and unconditionally) given condition, there is no further necessity, in proceeding with the series, for a conception of reason; for the understanding takes of itself every step downward, from the condition to the conditioned. Thus the transcendental ideas are available only for *ascending* in the series of conditions, till we reach the unconditioned, that is, principles. As regards *descending* to the conditioned, on the other hand, we find that there is a widely extensive logical use which reason makes of the laws of the understanding, but that a transcendental use thereof is impossible; and, that when we form an idea of the absolute totality of such a synthesis, for example, of the whole series of all *future* changes in the world, this idea is a mere *ens rationis*, an arbitrary fiction of thought, and not a necessary presupposition of reason. For the possibility of the conditioned presupposes the totality of its conditions, but not of its consequences. Consequently, this conception is not a transcendental idea—and it is with these alone that we are at present occupied.

Finally, it is obvious, that there exists among the transcendental ideas a certain connection and unity, and that pure reason, by means of them, collects all its cognitions into one system. From the cognition of self to the cognition of the world, and through these to the supreme being, the progression is so natural, that it seems to resemble the logical march of reason from the premisses to the conclusion.[1] Now whether there lies unobserved at the

[1] The science of Metaphysics has for the proper object of its inquiries only three grand ideas: GOD, FREEDOM, and IMMORTALITY, and it aims at showing, that the second conception, conjoined with the first, must lead to the third, as a necessary conclusion. All the other subjects with which it occupies itself, are merely means for the attainment and realization of these ideas. It does not require these ideas for the construction of a science of nature, but, on the contrary, for the purpose of passing beyond the sphere of nature. A complete insight into and comprehension of them would render *Theology, Ethics*, and, through the conjunction of both, *Religion*, solely dependent on the speculative faculty of reason. In a systematic representation of these ideas the above-mentioned arrangement—the *synthetical* one—would be the most suitable; but in the investigation which must necessarily precede it, the *analytical*, which reverses this arrangement, would be better adapted to our purpose, as in it we should proceed from that which experience immediately presents to us—psychology, to cosmology, and thence to theology.

foundation of these ideas an analogy of the same kind as exists
between the logical and transcendental procedure of reason, is
another of those questions, the answer to which we must not
expect till we arrive at a more advanced stage in our inquiries.
In this cursory and preliminary view, we have, meanwhile, reached
our aim. For we have dispelled the ambiguity which attached to
the transcendental conceptions of reason, from their being commonly mixed up with other conceptions in the systems of philosophers, and not properly distinguished from the conceptions of
the understanding; we have exposed their origin, and thereby at
the same time their determinate number, and presented them in
a systematic connection, and have thus marked out and enclosed a
definite sphere for pure reason.

## TRANSCENDENTAL DIALECTIC

### BOOK II

#### OF THE DIALECTICAL PROCEDURE OF PURE REASON

It may be said that the object of a merely transcendental idea is
something of which we have no conception, although the idea may
be a necessary product of reason according to its original laws.
For, in fact, a conception of an object that is adequate to the idea
given by reason, is impossible. For such an object must be
capable of being presented and intuited in a possible experience.
But we should express our meaning better, and with less risk of
being misunderstood, if we said that we can have no knowledge
of an object, which perfectly corresponds to an idea, although we
may possess a problematical conception thereof.

Now the transcendental (subjective) reality at least of the pure
conceptions of reason rests upon the fact that we are led to such
ideas by a necessary procedure of reason. There must therefore
be syllogisms which contain no empirical premisses, and by means
of which we conclude from something that we do know, to something of which we do not even possess a conception, to which we,
nevertheless, by an unavoidable illusion, ascribe objective reality.
Such arguments are, as regards their result, rather to be termed
sophisms than syllogisms, although indeed, as regards their origin,
they are very well entitled to the latter name, inasmuch as they
are not fictions or accidental products of reason, but are necessitated by its very nature. They are sophisms, not of men, but
of pure reason herself, from which the wisest cannot free himself.
After long labour he may be able to guard against the error, but

he can never be thoroughly rid of the illusion which continually mocks and misleads him.

Of these dialectical arguments there are three kinds, corresponding to the number of the ideas which their conclusions present. In the argument or syllogism of the *first class*, I conclude, from the transcendental conception of the subject which contains no manifold, the absolute unity of the subject itself, of which I cannot in this manner attain to a conception. This dialectical argument I shall call the Transcendental *Paralogism*. The *second class* of sophistical arguments is occupied with the transcendental conception of the absolute totality of the series of conditions for a given phenomenon, and I conclude, from the fact that I have always a self-contradictory conception of the unconditioned synthetical unity of the series upon one side, the truth of the opposite unity, of which I have nevertheless no conception. The condition of reason in these dialectical arguments, I shall term the *Antinomy* of pure reason. Finally, according to the *third* kind of sophistical argument, I conclude, from the totality of the conditions of thinking objects in general, in so far as they can be given, the absolute synthetical unity of all conditions of the possibility of things in general; that is, from things which I do not know in their mere transcendental conception, I conclude a being of all beings which I know still less by means of a transcendental conception, and of whose unconditioned necessity I can form no conception whatever. This dialectical argument I shall call the *Ideal* of pure reason.

CHAPTER I—*Of the Paralogisms of Pure Reason*

THE logical paralogism consists in the falsity of an argument in respect of its form, be the content what it may. But a transcendental paralogism has a transcendental foundation, and concludes falsely, while the form is correct and unexceptionable. In this manner the paralogism has its foundation in the nature of human reason, and is the parent of an unavoidable, though not insoluble, mental illusion.

We now come to a conception which was not inserted in the general list of transcendental conceptions, and yet must be reckoned with them, but at the same time without in the least altering, or indicating a deficiency in that table. This is the conception, or, if the term is preferred, the judgment, *I think*. But it is readily perceived that this thought is as it were the vehicle of all conceptions in general, and consequently of transcendental conceptions also, and that it is therefore regarded as a transcendental conception, although it can have no peculiar claim to be so ranked, inasmuch as its only use is to indicate that all thought is accompanied by consciousness. At the same time, pure as this conception is from all empirical content (impressions of the senses), it enables us to distinguish two different kinds of objects. *I*, as thinking, am an object of the internal sense, and am called soul. That which is an object of the external senses is called body. Thus the expression, I, as a thinking being, designates the object-matter of psychology, which may be called the rational doctrine of the soul, inasmuch as in this science I desire to know nothing of the soul but what, independently of all experience (which determines me *in concreto*), may be concluded from this conception *I*, in so far as it appears in all thought.

Now, the *rational* doctrine of the soul is really an undertaking of this kind. For if the smallest empirical element of thought, if any particular perception of my internal state, were to be introduced among the grounds of cognition of this science, it would not be a rational, but an *empirical* doctrine of the soul. We have thus before us a pretended science, raised upon the single proposition, *I think*, whose foundation or want of foundation we may very properly, and agreeably with the nature of a transcendental philosophy, here examine. It ought not to be objected that in this proposition, which expresses the perception of one's self, an internal experience is asserted, and that consequently the rational doctrine of the soul which is founded upon it, is not pure, but partly founded upon an empirical principle. For this internal perception is nothing more than the mere apperception, *I think*, which in fact renders all transcendental conceptions possible, in which we say, I think substance, cause, etc. For internal experience in general and its possibility, or perception in general, and its relation to other perceptions, unless some particular distinction or determination thereof is empirically given, cannot be regarded as empirical cognition, but as cognition of the empirical, and belongs to the investigation of the possibility of every experience, which is certainly transcendental. The smallest object of experience (for example, only pleasure or pain), that should be included in the general representation of self-consciousness, would immediately change the rational into an empirical psychology.

*I think* is therefore the only text of rational psychology, from which it must develop its whole system. It is manifest that this thought, when applied to an object (myself), can contain nothing but transcendental predicates thereof; because the least empirical predicate would destroy the purity of the science and its independence of all experience.

But we shall have to follow here the guidance of the categories —only, as in the present case a thing, I, as thinking being, is at first given, we shall—not indeed change the order of the categories as it stands in the table—but begin at the category of substance, by which a thing in itself is represented, and proceed backwards through the series. The topic of the rational doctrine of the soul, from which everything else it may contain must be deduced, is accordingly as follows:

I

*The soul is* SUBSTANCE

| 2 | 3 |
|---|---|
| As regards its quality, it is SIMPLE | As regards the different times in which it exists, it is numerically identical, that is UNITY, not Plurality |

4

It is in relation to *possible* objects in space [1]

From these elements originate all the conceptions of pure psychology, by combination alone, without the aid of any other principle. This substance, merely as an object of the internal sense, gives the conception of *Immateriality*; as simple substance, that of *Incorruptibility*; its identity, as intellectual substance, gives the conception of *Personality*; all these three together, *Spirituality*. Its relation to objects in space gives us the conception of connection (*commercium*) with bodies. Thus it represents thinking substance as the principle of life in matter, that is, as a soul (*anima*), and as the ground of *Animality*; and this, limited and determined by the conception of spirituality, gives us that of *Immortality*.

Now to these conceptions relate four paralogisms of a transcendental psychology, which is falsely held to be a science of pure

[1] The reader, who may not so easily perceive the psychological sense of these expressions—taken here in their transcendental abstraction, and cannot guess why the latter attribute of the soul belongs to the category of *existence*, will find the expressions sufficiently explained and justified in the sequel. I have, moreover, to apologize for the Latin terms which have been employed, instead of their German synonyms, contrary to the rules of correct writing. But I judged it better to sacrifice elegance to perspicuity.

reason, touching the nature of our thinking being. We can, however, lay at the foundation of this science nothing but the simple and in itself perfectly contentless representation *I*, which cannot even be called a conception, but merely a consciousness which accompanies all conceptions. By this I, or He, or It, who or which thinks, nothing more is represented than a transcendental subject of thought=x, which is cognized only by means of the thoughts that are its predicates, and of which, apart from these, we cannot form the least conception. Hence we are obliged to go round this representation in a perpetual circle, inasmuch as we must always employ it, in order to frame any judgment respecting it. And this inconvenience we find it impossible to rid ourselves of, because consciousness in itself is not so much a representation distinguishing a particular object, as a form of representation in general, in so far as it may be termed cognition; for in and by cognition alone do I think anything.

It must, however, appear extraordinary at first sight that the condition under which I think, and which is consequently a property of my subject, should be held to be likewise valid for every existence which thinks, and that we can presume to base upon a seemingly empirical proposition a judgment which is apodeictic and universal, to wit, that everything which thinks is constituted as the voice of my consciousness declares it to be, that is, as a self-conscious being. The cause of this belief is to be found in the fact, that we necessarily attribute to things *a priori* all the properties which constitute conditions under which alone we can cogitate them. Now I cannot obtain the least representation of a thinking being by means of external experience, but solely through self-consciousness. Such objects are consequently nothing more than the transference of this consciousness of mine to other things which can only thus be represented as thinking beings. The proposition, *I think*, is, in the present case, understood in a problematical sense, not in so far as it contains a perception of an existence (like the Cartesian *Cogito, ergo sum*), but in regard to its mere possibility—for the purpose of discovering what properties may be inferred from so simple a proposition and predicated of the subject of it.

If at the foundation of our pure rational cognition of thinking beings there lay more than the mere *Cogito*—if we could likewise call in aid observations on the play of our thoughts, and the thence derived natural laws of the thinking self, there would arise an empirical psychology which would be a kind of physiology of the internal sense, and might possibly be capable of explaining the phenomena of that sense. But it could never be available for discovering those properties which do not belong to possible experience (such as the quality of simplicity), nor could it make any apodeictic enunciation on the nature of thinking beings: it would therefore not be a rational psychology.

Now, as the proposition *I think* (in the problematical sense) contains the form of every judgment in general, and is the constant accompaniment of all the categories; it is manifest, that conclusions are drawn from it only by a transcendental employment of the understanding. This use of the understanding excludes all empirical elements; and we cannot, as has been shown above, have any favourable conception beforehand of its procedure. We shall therefore follow with a critical eye this proposition through all the predicaments of pure psychology; but we shall, for brevity's sake, allow this examination to proceed in an uninterrupted connection.

Before entering on this task, however, the following general remark may help to quicken our attention to this mode of argument. It is not merely through my thinking that I cognize an object, but only through my determining a given intuition in relation to the unity of consciousness in which all thinking consists. It follows that I cognize myself, not through my being conscious of myself as thinking, but only when I am conscious of the intuition of myself as determined in relation to the function of thought. All the modi of self-consciousness in thought are hence not conceptions of objects (conceptions of the understanding—categories); they are mere logical functions, which do not present to thought an object to be cognized, and cannot therefore present my Self as an object. Not the consciousness of the *determining*, but only that of the *determinable* self, that is, of my internal intuition (in so far as the manifold contained in it can be connected conformably with the general condition of the unity of apperception in thought), is the object.

1. In all judgments I am the *determining* subject of that relation which constitutes a judgment. But that the I which thinks, must be considered as in thought always a *subject*, and as a thing which cannot be a predicate to thought, is an apodeictic and *identical* proposition. But this proposition does not signify that I, as an object, am, for myself, a *self-subsistent being* or *substance*. This latter statement—an ambitious one—requires to be supported by data which are not to be discovered in thought; and are perhaps (in so far as I consider the thinking self merely *as such*) not to be discovered in the thinking self at all.

2. That the *I* or *Ego* of apperception, and consequently in all

thought, is *singular* or simple, and cannot be resolved into a plurality of subjects, and therefore indicates a logically simple subject—this is self-evident from the very conception of an Ego, and is consequently an analytical proposition. But this is not tantamount to declaring that the thinking Ego is a simple *substance* —for this would be a synthetical proposition. The conception of substance always relates to intuitions, which with me cannot be other than sensuous, and which consequently lie completely out of the sphere of the understanding and its thought: but to this sphere belongs the affirmation that the Ego is simple in thought. It would indeed be surprising, if the conception of substance, which in other cases requires so much labour to distinguish from the other elements presented by intuition—so much trouble, too, to discover whether it can be simple (as in the case of the parts of matter), should be presented immediately to me, as if by revelation, in the poorest mental representation of all.

3. The proposition of the identity of my Self amidst all the manifold representations of which I am conscious, is likewise a proposition lying in the conceptions themselves, and is consequently analytical. But this identity of the subject, of which I am conscious in all its representations, does not relate to or concern the intuition of the subject, by which it is given as an object. This proposition cannot therefore enounce the identity of the person, by which is understood the consciousness of the identity of its own substance as a thinking being in all change and variation of circumstances. To prove this, we should require not a mere analysis of the proposition, but synthetical judgments based upon a given intuition.

4. I distinguish my own existence, as that of a thinking being, from that of other things external to me—among which my body also is reckoned. This is also an analytical proposition, for *other* things are exactly those which I think as different or *distinguished* from myself. But whether this consciousness of myself is possible *without* things external to me; and whether therefore I can exist merely as a thinking being (without being man)—cannot be known or inferred from this proposition.

Thus we have gained nothing as regards the cognition of myself as object, by the analysis of the consciousness of my Self in thought. The logical exposition of thought in general is mistaken for a metaphysical determination of the object.

Our *Critique* would be an investigation utterly superfluous, if there existed a possibility of proving *a priori*, that all thinking beings are in themselves simple substances, as such, therefore, possess the inseparable attribute of personality, and are conscious

of their existence apart from and unconnected with matter. For
we should thus have taken a step beyond the world of sense, and
have penetrated into the sphere of *noumena*; and in this case the
right could not be denied us of extending our knowledge in this
sphere, of establishing ourselves, and, under a favouring star,
appropriating to ourselves possessions in it. For the proposition:
'Every thinking being, as such, is simple substance,' is an *a priori*
synthetical proposition; because in the first place it goes beyond
the conception which is the subject of it, and adds to the mere
notion of a thinking being the *mode of its existence*, and in the
second place annexes a predicate (that of simplicity) to the latter
conception—a predicate which it could not have discovered in
the sphere of experience. It would follow that *a priori* synthetical
propositions are possible and legitimate, not only, as we have
maintained, in relation to objects of possible experience, and as
principles of the possibility of this experience itself, but are
applicable to things as things in themselves—an inference which
makes an end of the whole of this *Critique*, and obliges us to fall
back on the old mode of metaphysical procedure. But indeed the
danger is not so great, if we look a little closer into the question.

There lurks in the procedure of rational psychology a paralogism,
which is represented in the following syllogism:

*That which cannot be cogitated otherwise than as subject, does
not exist otherwise than as subject, and is therefore substance.*

*A thinking being, considered merely as such, cannot be cogitated
otherwise than as subject.*

*Therefore it exists also as such, that is, as substance.*

In the major we speak of a being that can be cogitated generally
and in every relation, consequently as it may be given in intuition.
But in the minor we speak of the same being only in so far as it
regards itself as subject, relatively to thought and the unity of
consciousness, but not in relation to intuition, by which it is
presented as an object to thought. Thus the conclusion is here
arrived at by a *Sophisma figurae dictionis*.[1]

---

[1] *Thought* is taken in the two premisses in two totally different senses.
In the major it is considered as relating and applying to objects in general,
consequently to objects of intuition also. In the minor, we understand it
as relating merely to self-consciousness. In this sense, we do not cogitate
an object, but merely the relation to the self-consciousness of the subject,
as the form of thought. In the former premiss we speak of things which
cannot be cogitated otherwise than as subjects. In the second, we do not
speak of *things*, but of *thought* (all objects being abstracted), in which the Ego
is always the subject of consciousness. Hence the conclusion cannot be,
'I cannot exist otherwise than as subject;' but only 'I can, in cogitating my
existence, employ my Ego only as the subject of the judgment.' But this is
an identical proposition, and throws no light on the mode of my existence.

That this famous argument is a mere paralogism, will be plain to any one who will consider the general remark which precedes our exposition of the principles of the pure understanding, and the section on noumena.   For it was there proved that the conception of a thing, which can exist *per se*—only as a subject and never as a predicate, possesses no objective reality; that is to say, we can never know whether there exists any object to correspond to the conception; consequently, the conception is nothing more than a conception, and from it we derive no proper knowledge. If this conception is to indicate by the term *substance*, an object that can be given, if it is to become a cognition, we must have at the foundation of the cognition a permanent intuition, as the indispensable condition of its objective reality.   For through intuition alone can an object be given.   But in internal intuition there is nothing permanent, for the Ego is but the consciousness of my thought.   If, then, we appeal merely to thought, we cannot discover the necessary condition of the application of the conception of substance—that is, of a subject existing *per se*—to the subject as a thinking being.   And thus the conception of the simple nature of substance, which is connected with the objective reality of this conception, is shown to be also invalid, and to be, in fact, nothing more than the logical qualitative unity of self-consciousness in thought; whilst we remain perfectly ignorant whether the subject is composite or not.

*Refutation of the Argument of Mendelssohn for the Substantiality or Permanence [1] of the Soul*

This acute philosopher easily perceived the insufficiency of the common argument which attempts to prove that the soul—it being granted that it is a simple being—cannot perish by *dissolution* or *decomposition*; he saw it is not impossible for it to cease to be by *extinction*, or *disappearance*.[2]   He endeavoured to prove in his *Phaedo*, that the soul cannot be annihilated, by showing that a simple being cannot cease to exist.   Inasmuch as, he said, a simple existence cannot diminish, nor gradually lose portions of its being, and thus be by degrees reduced to nothing (for it possesses no parts, and therefore no multiplicity), between the moment in which it is, and the moment in which it is not, no time can be discovered—which is impossible.   But this philosopher did not consider, that,

[1] There is no philosophical term in our language which can express, without saying too much or too little, the meaning of *Beharrlichkeit*.   *Permanence* will be sufficient, if taken in an absolute, instead of the commonly received relative sense.—*Tr*.
[2] Verschwinden.

granting the soul to possess this simple nature, which contains no parts external to each other, and consequently no extensive quantity, we cannot refuse to it any less than to any other being, intensive quantity, that is, a degree of reality in regard to all its faculties, nay, to all that constitutes its existence. But this degree of reality can become less and less through an infinite series of smaller degrees. It follows, therefore, that this supposed substance —this thing, the permanence of which is not assured in any other way, may, if not by decomposition, by gradual loss (*remissio*) of its powers (consequently by elanguescence, if I may employ this expression), be changed into nothing. For consciousness itself has always a degree, which may be lessened.[1] Consequently the faculty of being conscious may be diminished; and so with all other faculties. The permanence of the soul, therefore, as an object of the internal sense, remains undemonstrated, nay, even indemonstrable. Its permanence in life is evident, *per se*, inasmuch as the thinking being (as man) is to itself, at the same time, an object of the external senses. But this does not authorize the rational psychologist to affirm, from mere conceptions, its permanence beyond life.[2]

[1] Clearness is not, as logicians maintain, the consciousness of a representation. For a certain degree of consciousness, which may not, however, be sufficient for recollection, is to be met with in many dim representations. For without any consciousness at all, we should not be able to recognize any difference in the obscure representations we connect; as we really can do with many conceptions, such as those of right and justice, and those of the musician, who strikes at once several notes in improvising a piece of music. But a representation is clear, in which our consciousness is sufficient for the *consciousness of the difference* of this representation from others. If we are only conscious that there is a difference, but are not conscious of the difference—that is, what the difference is—the representation must be termed obscure. There is, consequently, an infinite series of degrees of consciousness down to its entire disappearance.

[2] There are some who think they have done enough to establish a new possibility in the mode of the existence of souls, when they have shown that there is no contradiction in their hypotheses on this subject. Such are those who affirm the possibility of thought—of which they have no other knowledge than what they derive from its use in connecting empirical intuitions presented in this our human life—after this life has ceased. But it is very easy to embarrass them by the introduction of counter-possibilities, which rest upon quite as good a foundation. Such, for example, is the possibility of the division of a *simple substance* into several substances; and conversely, of the coalition of several into one simple substance. For, although divisibility presupposes composition, it does not necessarily require a composition of substances, but only of the degrees (of the several faculties) of one and the same substance. Now we can cogitate all the powers and faculties of the soul—even that of consciousness—as diminished by one half, the substance still remaining. In the same way we can represent to ourselves without contradiction, this obliterated half as preserved, not in the soul, but without it; and we can believe that, as in this case everything that is real in the soul, and has a degree—consequently its entire existence—has been halved, a

If, now, we take the above propositions—as they must be accepted as valid for all thinking beings in the system of rational psychology—in synthetical connection, and proceed, from the category of relation, with the proposition: 'All thinking beings are, as such, substances,' backwards through the series, till the circle is completed; we come at last to their existence, of which, in this system of rational psychology, substances are held to be conscious, independently of external things; nay, it is asserted that, in relation to the permanence which is a necessary characteristic of substance, they can of themselves determine external things. It follows that *Idealism*—at least problematical Idealism, is perfectly unavoidable in this rationalistic system. And, if the existence of outward things is not held to be requisite to the determination of the existence of a substance in time, the existence of these outward things at all, is a gratuitous assumption which remains without the possibility of a proof.

But if we proceed *analytically*—the 'I think' as a proposition containing in itself an existence as given, consequently modality being the principle—and dissect this proposition, in order to ascertain its content, and discover whether and how this *Ego* determines its existence in time and space without the aid of anything external; the propositions of rationalistic psychology would not begin with the conception of a thinking being, but with a reality, and the properties of a thinking being in general would

particular substance would arise out of the soul. For the multiplicity, which has been divided, formerly existed, but not as a multiplicity of substances, but of every reality as the quantum of existence in it; and the unity of substance was merely a mode of existence, which by this division alone has been transformed into a plurality of subsistence. In the same manner several simple substances might coalesce into one, without anything being lost except the plurality of subsistence, inasmuch as the one substance would contain the degree of reality of all the former substances. Perhaps, indeed, the simple substances, which appear under the form of matter, might (not indeed by a mechanical or chemical influence upon each other, but by an unknown influence, of which the former would be but the phenomenal appearance), by means of such a *dynamical* division of the parent-souls, as *intensive quantities*, produce other souls, while the former repaired the loss thus sustained with new matter of the same sort. I am far from allowing any value to such chimeras; and the principles of our analytic have clearly proved that no other than an empirical use of the categories—that of substance, for example—is possible. But if the rationalist is bold enough to construct, on the mere authority of the faculty of thought—without any intuition, whereby an object is given—a self-subsistent being, merely because the unity of apperception in thought cannot allow him to believe it a composite being, instead of declaring, as he ought to do, that he is unable to explain the possibility of a thinking nature; what ought to hinder the *materialist*, with as complete an independence of experience, to employ the principle of the rationalist in a directly opposite manner—still preserving the formal unity required by his opponent?

be deduced from the mode in which this reality is cogitated, after everything empirical had been abstracted; as is shown in the following table:

1
*I think,*

2                                                        3
*as Subject,*                              *as simple Subject,*

4
*as identical Subject,*
in every state of my thought.

Now, inasmuch as it is not determined in this second proposition, whether I can exist and be cogitated only as subject, and not also as a predicate of another being, the conception of a subject is here taken in a merely logical sense; and it remains undetermined, whether substance is to be cogitated under the conception or not. But in the third proposition, the absolute unity of apperception —the simple *Ego* in the representation to which all connection and separation, which constitute thought, relate, is of itself important; even although it presents us with no information about the constitution or subsistence of the subject.   Apperception is something real, and the simplicity of its nature is given in the very fact of its possibility.   Now in space there is nothing real that is at the same time simple; for points, which are the only simple things in space, are merely limits, but not constituent parts of space.   From this follows the impossibility of a definition on the basis of materialism of the constitution of my *Ego* as a merely thinking subject. But, because my existence is considered in the first proposition as given, for it does not mean, 'Every thinking being exists' (for this would be predicating of them absolute necessity), but only, '*I exist* thinking;' the proposition is quite empirical, and contains the determinability of my existence merely in relation to my representations in time.   But as I require for this purpose something that is permanent, such as is not given in internal intuition; the mode of my existence, whether as substance or as accident, cannot be determined by means of this simple self-consciousness.   Thus, if materialism is inadequate to explain the mode in which I exist, spiritualism is likewise as insufficient; and the conclusion is, that we are utterly unable to attain to any knowledge of the constitution of the soul, in so far as relates to the possibility of its existence apart from external objects.

And, indeed, how should it be possible, merely by the aid of the unity of consciousness—which we cognize only for the reason that it is indispensable to the possibility of experience—to pass the bounds of experience (our existence in this life); and to extend our cognition to the nature of all thinking beings by means of the empirical—but in relation to every sort of intuition, perfectly undetermined—proposition, 'I think'?

There does not then exist any rational psychology as a *doctrine* furnishing any addition to our knowledge of ourselves. It is nothing more than a *discipline*, which sets impassable limits to speculative reason in this region of thought, to prevent it, on the one hand, from throwing itself into the arms of a soulless material· ism, and, on the other, from losing itself in the mazes of a baseless spiritualism. It teaches us to consider this refusal of our reason to give any satisfactory answer to questions which reach beyond the limits of this our human life, as a hint to abandon fruitless speculation; and to direct, to a practical use, our knowledge of ourselves—which, although applicable only to objects of ex perience, receives its principles from a higher source, and regulates its procedure as if our destiny reached far beyond the boundaries of experience and life.

From all this it is evident that rational psychology has its origin in a mere misunderstanding. The unity of consciousness, which lies at the basis of the categories, is considered to be an intuition of the subject as an object; and the category of substance is applied to the intuition. But this unity is nothing more than the unity in *thought*, by which no object is given; to which therefore the category of substance—which always presupposes a given in tuition—cannot be applied. Consequently, the subject cannot be cognized. The subject of the categories cannot, therefore, for the very reason that it cogitates these, frame any conception of itself as an object of the categories; for, to cogitate these, it must lay at the foundation its own pure self-consciousness—the very thing that it wishes to explain and describe. In like manner, the sub ject, in which the representation of time has its basis, cannot determine, for this very reason, its own existence in time. Now, if the latter is impossible, the former, as an attempt to determine itself by means of the categories as a thinking being in general, is no less so.[1]

---

[1] The 'I think' is, as has been already stated, an empirical proposition, and contains the proposition, 'I exist.' But I cannot say, 'Everything, which thinks, exists;' for in this case the property of thought would constitute all beings possessing it, necessary beings. Hence my existence cannot be con sidered as an inference from the proposition, 'I think,' as Descartes maintained —because in this case the major premiss, 'Everything, which thinks, exists,'

Thus, then, appears the vanity of the hope of establishing a cognition which is to extend its rule beyond the limits of experience —a cognition which is one of the highest interests of humanity; and thus is proved the futility of the attempt of speculative philosophy in this region of thought. But, in this interest of thought, the severity of criticism has rendered to reason a not unimportant service, by the demonstration of the impossibility of making any dogmatical affirmation concerning an object of experience beyond the boundaries of experience. She has thus fortified reason against all affirmations of the contrary. Now, this can be accomplished in only two ways. Either our proposition must be proved apodeictically; or, if this is unsuccessful, the sources of this inability must be sought for, and if these are discovered to exist in the natural and necessary limitation of our reason, our opponents must submit to the same law of renunciation, and refrain from advancing claims to dogmatic assertion.

But the right, say rather the necessity to admit a future life, upon principles of the practical conjoined with the speculative use of reason, has lost nothing by this renunciation; for the merely speculative proof has never had any influence upon the common reason of men. It stands upon the point of a hair, so that even the schools have been able to preserve it from falling only by incessantly discussing it and spinning it like a top; and even in their eyes it has never been able to present any safe foundation for the erection of a theory. The proofs which have been current among men, preserve their value undiminished; nay, rather gain in clearness and unsophisticated power, by the rejection of the dogmatical

must precede—but the two propositions are identical. The proposition, 'I think,' expresses an undetermined empirical intuition, that is, perception [1] (proving consequently that sensation, which must belong to sensibility, lies at the foundation of this proposition); but it precedes experience, whose province it is to determine an object of perception by means of the categories in relation to time; and existence in this proposition is not a category, as it does not apply to an undetermined given object, but only to one of which we have a conception, and about which we wish to know whether it does or does not exist, out of, and apart from this conception. An undetermined perception signifies here merely something real that has been given, only, however, to thought in general—but not as a phenomenon, nor as a thing in itself (noumenon), but only as something that really exists, and is designated as such in the proposition, 'I think.' For it must be remarked that, when I call the proposition, 'I think,' an empirical proposition, I do not thereby mean that the *Ego* in the proposition is an empirical representation; on the contrary, it is purely intellectual, because it belongs to thought in general. But without some empirical representation, which presents to the mind material for thought, the mental act, 'I think,' would not take place; and the empirical is only the condition of the application or employment of the pure intellectual faculty.

[1] See page 222.—*Tr.*

assumptions of speculative reason.  For reason is thus confined within her own peculiar province—the arrangement of ends or aims, which is at the same time the arrangement of nature; and, as a practical faculty, without limiting itself to the latter, it is justified in extending the former, and with it our own existence, beyond the boundaries of experience and life.  If we turn our attention to the *analogy of the nature* of living beings in this world, in the consideration of which reason is obliged to accept as a principle, that no organ, no faculty, no appetite is useless, and that nothing is superfluous, nothing disproportionate to its use, nothing unsuited to its end; but that, on the contrary, everything is perfectly conformed to its destination in life—we shall find that man, who alone is the final end and aim of this order, is still the only animal that seems to be excepted from it.  For his natural gifts, not merely as regards the talents and motives that may incite him to employ them—but especially the moral law in him, stretch so far beyond all mere earthly utility and advantage, that he feels himself bound to prize the mere consciousness of probity, apart from all advantageous consequences—even the shadowy gift of posthumous fame—above everything; and he is conscious of an inward call to constitute himself, by his conduct in this world—without regard to mere sublunary interests—the citizen of a better.  This mighty, irresistible proof—accompanied by an ever-increasing knowledge of the conformability to a purpose in everything we see around us, by the conviction of the boundless immensity of creation, by the consciousness of a certain illimitableness in the possible extension of our knowledge, and by a desire commensurate therewith—remains to humanity, even after the theoretical cognition of ourselves has failed to establish the necessity of an existence after death.

## Conclusion of the Solution of the Psychological Paralogism

The dialectical illusion in rational psychology arises from our confounding an idea of reason (of a pure intelligence) with the conception—in every respect undetermined—of a thinking being in general.  I cogitate myself in behalf of a possible experience, at the same time making abstraction of all actual experience; and infer therefrom that I can be conscious of myself apart from experience and its empirical conditions.  I consequently confound the possible *abstraction* of my empirically determined existence with the supposed consciousness of a possible *separate* existence of my thinking self; and I believe that I cognize what is substantial in myself as a transcendental subject, when I have nothing more in thought than the unity of consciousness, which lies at the basis of all determination of cognition.

The task of explaining the community of the soul with the body does not properly belong to the psychology of which we are here speaking; because it proposes to prove the personality of the soul apart from this communion (after death), and is therefore *transcendent* in the proper sense of the word, although occupying itself with an object of experience—only in so far, however, as it ceases to be an object of experience. But a sufficient answer may be found to the question in our system. The difficulty which lies in the execution of this task consists, as is well known, in the presupposed heterogeneity of the object of the internal sense (the soul) and the objects of the external senses; inasmuch as the formal condition of the intuition of the one is time, and of that of the other space also. But if we consider that both kinds of objects do not differ internally, but only in so far as the one *appears* externally to the other—consequently, that what lies at the basis of phenomena, as a thing in itself, may not be heterogeneous; this difficulty disappears. There then remains no other difficulty than is to be found in the question—how a community of substances is possible; a question which lies out of the region of psychology, and which the reader, after what in our Analytic has been said of primitive forces and faculties, will easily judge to be also beyond the region of human cognition.

### General Remark on the Transition from Rational Psychology to Cosmology

The proposition, 'I think,' or, 'I exist thinking,' is an empirical proposition. But such a proposition must be based on empirical intuition, and the object cogitated as a phenomenon; and thus our theory appears to maintain that the soul, even in thought, is merely a phenomenon; and in this way our consciousness itself, in fact, abuts upon nothing.

Thought, *per se*, is merely the purely spontaneous logical function which operates to connect the manifold of a possible intuition; and it does not represent the subject of consciousness as a phenomenon —for this reason alone, that it pays no attention to the question whether the mode of intuiting it is sensuous or intellectual. I therefore do not represent myself in thought either as I am, or as I appear to myself; I merely cogitate myself as an object in general, of the mode of intuiting which I make abstraction. When I represent myself as the *subject* of thought, or as the *ground* of thought, these modes of representation are not related to the categories of substance or of cause; for these are functions of thought applicable only to our sensuous intuition. The application of these categories to the *Ego* would, however, be necessary, if I wished to make myself an object of knowledge. But I wish to be conscious of myself only as thinking; in what mode my Self is given in intuition, I do not consider, and it may be that I, who think, am a phenomenon—although not in so far as I am a thinking being; but in the consciousness of myself in mere thought I am a being, though this consciousness does not present to me any property of this being as material for thought.

But the proposition, 'I think,' in so far as it declares, '*I exist* thinking,' is not the mere representation of a logical function. It determines the subject (which is in this case an object also) in relation to existence; and it cannot be given without the aid of the internal sense, whose intuition presents to us an object, not as a thing in itself, but always as a phenomenon. In this proposition there is therefore something more to be found than the mere spontaneity of thought; there is also the receptivity of intuition, that is, my thought of myself applied to the empirical intuition of myself. Now, in this intuition the thinking self must seek the conditions of the employment of its logical functions as categories of substance, cause, and so forth; not merely for the purpose of distinguishing itself as an object in itself by means of the representation *I*, but also for the purpose of determining the mode of its existence, that is, of cognizing itself as noumenon. But this is impossible, for the internal empirical intuition is sensuous, and presents us with nothing but phenomenal data, which do not assist the object of pure consciousness in its attempt to cognize itself as a separate existence, but are useful only as contributions to experience.

But, let it be granted that we could discover, not in experience, but in certain firmly-established *a priori* laws of the use of pure reason—laws relating to our existence, authority to consider ourselves as legislating *a priori* in relation to our own existence and as determining this existence; we should, on this supposition, find ourselves possessed of a spontaneity, by which our actual existence would be determinable, without the aid of the conditions of empirical intuition. We should also become aware, that in the consciousness of our existence there was an *a priori* content, which would serve to determine our own existence—an existence only sensuously determinable—relatively, however, to a certain internal faculty in relation to an intelligible world.

But this would not give the least help to the attempts of rational psychology. For this wonderful faculty, which the consciousness of the moral law in me reveals, would present me with a principle of the determination of my own existence which is purely intellectual—but by what predicates? By none other than those which are given in sensuous intuition. Thus I should find myself in the same position in rational psychology which I formerly occupied, that is to say, I should find myself still in need of sensuous intuitions, in order to give significance to my conceptions of substance and cause, by means of which alone I can possess a knowledge of myself: but these intuitions can never raise me above the sphere of experience. I should be justified, however, in applying these conceptions, in regard to their practical use, which is always directed to objects of experience—in conformity with their analogical significance when employed theoretically—to freedom and its subject.[1] At the same time, I should understand by them merely the logical functions of subject and predicate, of principle and consequence, in conformity with which all actions are so determined, that they are capable of being explained along with the laws of nature, conformably to the categories of substance and cause, although they originate from a very different principle. We have made these observations for the purpose of guarding against misunderstanding, to which the doctrine of our intuition of self as a phenomenon is exposed. We shall have occasion to perceive their utility in the sequel.

CHAPTER II—*The Antinomy of Pure Reason*

WE showed in the introduction to this part of our work, that all transcendental illusion of pure reason arose from dialectical arguments, the schema of which logic gives us in its three formal species of syllogisms—just as the categories find their logical schema in the four functions of all judgments. The first kind of these sophistical arguments related to the unconditioned unity of the *subjective* conditions of all representations in general (of the subject or soul), in correspondence with the *categorical* syllogisms, the major of which, as the principle, enounces the relation of a predicate to a subject. The second kind of dialectical argument will therefore be concerned, following the analogy with *hypothetical*

[1] The Ego.—*Tr.*

syllogisms, with the unconditioned unity of the objective conditions in the phenomenon; and, in this way, the theme of the third kind to be treated of in the following chapter, will be the unconditioned unity of the objective conditions of the possibility of objects in general.

But it is worthy of remark, that the transcendental paralogism produced in the mind only a one-sided illusion, in regard to the idea of the subject of our thought; and the conceptions of reason gave no ground to maintain the contrary proposition. The advantage is completely on the side of Pneumatism; although this theory itself passes into naught, in the crucible of pure reason.

Very different is the case when we apply reason to the *objective synthesis* of phenomena. Here, certainly, reason establishes, with much plausibility, its principle of unconditioned unity; but it very soon falls into such contradictions, that it is compelled, in relation to cosmology, to renounce its pretensions.

For here a new phenomenon of human reason meets us—a perfectly natural antithetic, which does not require to be sought for by subtle sophistry, but into which reason of itself unavoidably falls. It is thereby preserved, to be sure, from the slumber of a fancied conviction—which a merely one-sided illusion produces; but it is at the same time compelled, either, on the one hand, to abandon itself to a despairing scepticism, or, on the other, to assume a dogmatical confidence and obstinate persistence in certain assertions, without granting a fair hearing to the other side of the question. Either is the death of a sound philosophy, although the former might perhaps deserve the title of the Euthanasia of pure reason.

Before entering this region of discord and confusion, which the conflict of the laws of pure reason (antinomy) produces, we shall present the reader with some considerations, in explanation and justification of the method we intend to follow in our treatment of this subject. I term all transcendental ideas, in so far as they relate to the absolute totality in the synthesis of phenomena, *cosmical conceptions*; partly on account of this unconditioned totality, on which the conception of the world-whole is based—a conception which is itself an idea—partly because they relate solely to the synthesis of phenomena—the empirical synthesis; while, on the other hand, the absolute totality in the synthesis of the conditions of all possible things gives rise to an ideal of pure reason, which is quite distinct from the cosmical conception, although it stands in relation with it. Hence, as the paralogisms of pure reason laid the foundation for a dialectical psychology, the antinomy of pure reason will present us with the transcendental principles of a pretended pure (rational) cosmology—not, however, to declare it valid and to appropriate it, but—as the very term of a conflict of reason sufficiently indicates, to present it as an idea which cannot be reconciled with phenomena and experience.

## Section I

### System of Cosmological Ideas

THAT we may be able to enumerate with systematic precision these ideas according to a principle, we must remark, *in the first place*, that it is from the understanding alone that pure and transcendental conceptions take their origin; that the reason does not properly give birth to any conception, but only frees the conception of the understanding from the unavoidable limitation of a possible experience, and thus endeavours to raise it above the empirical, though it must still be in connection with it. This happens from the fact, that for a given conditioned, reason demands absolute totality on the side of the conditions (to which the understanding submits all phenomena), and thus makes of the category a transcendental idea. This it does that it may be able to give absolute completeness to the empirical synthesis, by continuing it to the unconditioned (which is not to be found in experience, but only in the idea). Reason requires this according to the principle: *If the conditioned is given, the whole of the conditions, and consequently the absolutely unconditioned, is also given,* whereby alone the former was possible. *First,* then, the transcendental ideas are properly nothing but categories elevated to the unconditioned; and they may be arranged in a table according to the titles of the latter. But, *secondly,* all the categories are not available for this purpose, but only those in which the synthesis constitutes a series—of conditions subordinated to, not co-ordinated with, each other. Absolute totality is required of reason only in so far as concerns the ascending series of the conditions of a conditioned; not, consequently, when the question relates to the descending series of consequences, or to the aggregate of the co-ordinated conditions of these consequences. For, in relation to a given conditioned, conditions are presupposed and considered to be given along with it. On the other hand, as the consequences do not render possible their conditions, but rather presuppose them—in the consideration of the procession of consequences (or in the descent from the given condition to the conditioned), we may be quite unconcerned whether the series ceases or not; and their totality is not a necessary demand of reason.

Thus we cogitate—and necessarily—a given time completely elapsed up to a given moment, although that time is not determinable by us. But as regards time future, which is not the condition of arriving at the present, in order to conceive it; it is quite indifferent whether we consider future time as ceasing at some point, or as prolonging itself to infinity. Take, for example, the series *m, n, o,* in which *n* is given as conditioned in relation to *m,* but at the same time as the condition of *o,* and let the series proceed upwards from the conditioned *n* to *m* (*l, k, i,* etc.), and also downwards from the condition *n* to the conditioned *o* (*p, q, r,* etc.)—I must presuppose the former series, to be able to consider *n* as given, and *n* is according to reason (the totality of conditions) possible only by means of that series. But its possibility does not rest on the following series *o, p, q, r,* which for this reason cannot be regarded as given, but only as capable of being given (*dabilis*).

I shall term the synthesis of the series on the side of the conditions —from that nearest to the given phenomenon up to the more remote—*regressive*; that which proceeds on the side of the conditioned, from the immediate consequence to the more remote, I shall call the *progressive* synthesis. The former proceeds *in antecedentia,* the latter *in consequentia.* The cosmological ideas are therefore occupied with the totality of the regressive synthesis, and proceed *in antecedentia,* not *in consequentia.* When the latter takes place, it is an arbitrary and not a necessary problem of pure reason; for we require, for the complete understanding of what is given in a phenomenon, not the consequences which succeed, but the grounds or principles which precede.

In order to construct the table of ideas in correspondence with the table of categories, we take first the two primitive *quanta* of all our intuitions, time and space. Time is in itself a series (and the formal condition of all series), and hence, in relation to a given present, we must distinguish *a priori* in it the *antecedentia* as conditions (time past) from the *consequentia* (time future). Consequently, the transcendental idea of the absolute totality of the series of the conditions of a given conditioned, relates merely to all past time. According to the idea of reason, the whole past time, as the condition of the given moment, is necessarily cogitated as given. But as regards space, there exists in it no distinction between *progressus* and *regressus*; for it is an *aggregate* and not a series—its parts existing together at the same time.

I can consider a given point of time in relation to past time only as conditioned, because this given moment comes into existence only through the past time—or rather through the passing of the preceding time. But as the parts of space are not subordinated, but co-ordinated to each other, one part cannot be the condition of the possibility of the other; and space is not in itself, like time, a series. But the synthesis of the manifold parts of space—(the syntheses whereby we apprehend space)—is nevertheless successive; it takes place, therefore, in time, and contains a series. And as in this series of aggregated spaces (for example, the feet in a rood), beginning with a given portion of space, those which continue to be annexed form the *condition of the limits* of the former—the measurement of a space must also be regarded as a synthesis of the series of the conditions of a given conditioned. It differs, however, in this respect from that of time, that the side of the conditioned is not in itself distinguishable from the side of the condition; and, consequently, *regressus* and *progressus* in space seem to be identical. But, inasmuch as one part of space is not given, but only limited, by and through another, we must also consider every limited space as conditioned, in so far as it pre supposes some other space as the condition of its limitation, and so on. As regards limitation, therefore, our procedure in space is also a *regressus*, and the transcendental idea of the absolute totality of the synthesis in a series of conditions applies to space also; and I am entitled to demand the absolute totality of the phenomenal synthesis in space as well as in time. Whether my demand can be satisfied, is a question to be answered in the sequel.

*Secondly*, the real in space—that is, matter, is conditioned. Its internal conditions are its parts, and the parts of parts its remote conditions; so that in this case we find a regressive synthesis, the absolute totality of which is a demand of reason. But this cannot be obtained otherwise than by a complete division of parts, whereby the real in matter becomes either nothing or that which is not matter, that is to say, the simple.[1] Consequently we find here also a series of conditions and a progress to the unconditioned.

*Thirdly*, as regards the categories of a real relation between phenomena, the category *of substance* and its accidents is not suitable for the formation of a transcendental idea; that is to say, reason has no ground, in regard to it, to proceed regressively with conditions. For accidents (in so far as they inhere in a substance) are co-ordinated with each other, and do not constitute a series. And, in relation to substance, they are not properly

[1] Das Einfache.

subordinated to it, but are the mode of existence of the substance itself. The conception of the *substantial* might nevertheless seem to be an idea of the transcendental reason. But, as this signifies nothing more than the conception of an object in general, which subsists in so far as we cogitate in it merely a transcendental subject without any predicates; and as the question here is of an unconditioned in the series of phenomena—it is clear that the substantial can form no member thereof. The same holds good of substances in community, which are mere aggregates, and do not form a series. For they are not subordinated to each other as conditions of the possibility of each other; which, however, may be affirmed of spaces, the limits of which are never determined in themselves, but always by some other space. It is, therefore, only in the category of *causality* that we can find a series of causes to a given effect, and in which we ascend from the latter, as the conditioned, to the former as the conditions, and thus answer the question of reason.

*Fourthly*, the conceptions of the *possible*, the *actual*, and the *necessary* do not conduct us to any series—excepting only in so far as the contingent in existence must always be regarded as conditioned, and as indicating, according to a law of the understanding, a condition, under which it is necessary to rise to a higher, till in the totality of the series, reason arrives at unconditioned *necessity*.

There are, accordingly, only four cosmological ideas, corresponding with the four titles of the categories. For we can select only such as necessarily furnish us with a series in the synthesis of the manifold.

### I
*The absolute Completeness*
*of the*
COMPOSITION
*of the given totality of all phenomena*

### 2
*The absolute Completeness*
*of the*
DIVISION
*of a given totality*
*in a phenomenon*

### 3
*The absolute Completeness*
*of the*
ORIGINATION
*of a phenomenon*

### 4
*The absolute Completeness*
*of the* DEPENDENCE *of the* EXISTENCE
*of what is changeable in a phenomenon*

We must here remark, in the first place, that the idea of absolute totality relates to nothing but the exposition of *phenomena*, and therefore not to the pure conception of a totality of things. Phenomena are here, therefore, regarded as given, and reason requires the absolute completeness of the conditions of their possibility, in so far as these conditions constitute a series—consequently an absolutely (that is, in every respect) complete synthesis, whereby a phenomenon can be explained according to the laws of the understanding.

Secondly, it is properly the unconditioned alone, that reason seeks in this serially and regressively conducted synthesis of conditions. It wishes, to speak in another way, to attain to completeness in the series of premises, so as to render it unnecessary to presuppose others. This *unconditioned* is always contained in the *absolute totality of the series*, when we endeavour to form a representation of it in thought. But this absolutely complete synthesis is itself but an idea; for it is impossible, at least beforehand, to know whether any such synthesis is possible in the case of phenomena. When we represent all existence in thought by means of pure conceptions of the understanding, without any conditions of sensuous intuition, we may say with justice that for a given conditioned the whole series of conditions subordinated to each other is also given; for the former is only given through the latter. But we find in the case of phenomena a particular limitation of the mode in which conditions are given, that is, through the successive synthesis of the manifold of intuition, which must be complete in the regress. Now whether this completeness is sensuously possible, is a problem. But the idea of it lies in the reason—be it possible or impossible to connect with the idea adequate empirical conceptions. Therefore, as in the absolute totality of the regressive synthesis of the manifold in a phenomenon (following the guidance of the categories, which represent it as a series of conditions to a given conditioned) the unconditioned is necessarily contained—it being still left unascertained whether and how this totality exists; reason sets out from the idea of totality, although its proper and final aim is the *unconditioned*—of the whole series, or of a part thereof.

This unconditioned may be cogitated—either as existing only in the entire series, all the members of which therefore would be without exception conditioned and only the totality absolutely unconditioned—and in this case the *regressus* is called infinite, or the absolutely unconditioned is only a part of the series, to which the other members are subordinated, but which is not itself submitted to any other condition.[1] In the former case the series is *a parte priori* unlimited (without beginning), that is, infinite, and nevertheless completely given. But the regress in it is never completed, and can only be called *potentially* infinite. In the second case there exists a first in the series. This first is called, in relation to past time, the *beginning of the world*; in relation to space, the *limit of the world*; in relation to the parts of a given limited whole, the *simple*; in relation to causes, absolute *spontaneity* (liberty); and in relation to the existence of changeable things, absolute *physical necessity*.

We possess two expressions, *world* and *nature*, which are generally interchanged. The first denotes the mathematical total of all phenomena and the totality of their synthesis—in its progress by means of composition, as well as by division. And the world is termed nature,[2] when it is regarded as a dynamical whole—when our attention is not directed to the aggregation in space and time, for the purpose of cogitating it as a quantity, but to the unity in the *existence* of phenomena. In this case the condition of that which happens is called a cause; the unconditioned causality of the cause in a phenomenon is termed liberty; the conditioned cause is called in a more limited sense a natural cause. The conditioned in existence is termed contingent, and the unconditioned necessary. The unconditioned necessity of phenomena may be called *natural necessity*.

The ideas which we are at present engaged in discussing I have called cosmological ideas; partly because by the term *world* is understood the entire content of all phenomena, and our ideas are directed solely to the unconditioned among phenomena; partly also, because *world*, in the transcendental sense, signifies the absolute totality of the content of existing things, and we are directing our attention only to the completeness of the synthesis—although, properly, only in regression. In regard to

[1] The absolute totality of the series of conditions to a given conditioned is always unconditioned: because beyond it there exist no other conditions, on which it might depend. But the absolute totality of such a series is only an idea, or rather a problematical conception, the possibility of which must be investigated—particularly in relation to the mode in which the unconditioned, as the transcendental idea which is the real subject of inquiry, may be contained therein.

[2] Nature, understood *adjectivé* (*formaliter*), signifies the complex of the determinations of a thing, connected according to an internal principle of causality. On the other hand, we understand by nature, *substantive* (*materialiter*), the sum total of phenomena, in so far as they, by virtue of an internal principle of causality, are connected with each other throughout. In the former sense we speak of the nature of liquid matter, of fire, etc., and employ the word only *adjectivé*; while, if speaking of the objects of nature, we have in our minds the idea of a subsisting whole.

the fact that these ideas are all transcendent, and, although they
do not transcend phenomena as regards their mode, but are concerned solely with the world of sense (and not with noumena),
nevertheless carry their synthesis to a degree far above all possible
experience—it still seems to me that we can, with perfect propriety,
designate them *cosmical conceptions*. As regards the distinction
between the mathematically and the dynamically unconditioned
which is the aim of the regression of the synthesis, I should call
the two former, in a more limited signification, cosmical conceptions, the remaining two *transcendent physical conceptions*. This
distinction does not at present seem to be of particular importance,
but we shall afterwards find it to be of some value.

## Section II

### *Antithetic of Pure Reason*

Thetic is the term applied to every collection of dogmatical
propositions. By antithetic I do not understand dogmatical
assertions of the opposite, but the self-contradiction of seemingly
dogmatical cognitions (*thesis cum antithesi*), in none of which we
can discover any decided superiority. Antithetic is not therefore
occupied with one-sided statements, but is engaged in considering
the contradictory nature of the general cognitions of reason, and
its causes. Transcendental antithetic is an investigation into the
antinomy of pure reason, its causes and result. If we employ
our reason not merely in the application of the principles of the
understanding to objects of experience, but venture with it beyond
these boundaries, there arise certain sophistical propositions or
theorems. These assertions have the following peculiarities: They
can find neither confirmation nor confutation in experience; and
each is in itself not only self-consistent, but possesses conditions
of its necessity in the very nature of reason—only that, unluckily,
there exist just as valid and necessary grounds for maintaining the
contrary proposition.

The questions which naturally arise in the consideration of this
dialectic of pure reason, are therefore: 1st. In what propositions
is pure reason unavoidably subject to an antinomy? 2nd. What
are the causes of this antinomy? 3rd. Whether and in what way
can reason free itself from this self-contradiction?

A dialectical proposition or theorem of pure reason must,
according to what has been said, be distinguishable from all

sophistical propositions, by the fact that it is not an answer to an arbitrary question, which may be raised at the mere pleasure of any person, but to one which human reason must necessarily encounter in its progress. In the second place, a dialectical proposition, with its opposite, does not carry the appearance of a merely artificial illusion, which disappears as soon as it is investigated, but a natural and unavoidable illusion, which, even when we are no longer deceived by it, continues to mock us, and, although rendered harmless, can never be completely removed.

This dialectical doctrine will not relate to the unity of understanding in empirical conceptions, but to the unity of reason in pure ideas. The conditions of this doctrine are—inasmuch as it must, as a synthesis according to rules, be conformable to the understanding, and at the same time as the absolute unity of the synthesis, to the reason—that, if it is adequate to the unity of reason, it is too great for the understanding, if according with the understanding, it is too small for the reason. Hence arises a mutual opposition, which cannot be avoided, do what we will.

These sophistical assertions of dialectic open, as it were, a battle-field, where that side obtains the victory which has been permitted to make the attack, and he is compelled to yield who has been unfortunately obliged to stand on the defensive. And hence, champions of ability, whether on the right or on the wrong side, are certain to carry away the crown of victory, if they only take care to have the right to make the last attack, and are not obliged to sustain another onset from their opponent. We can easily believe that this arena has been often trampled by the feet of combatants, that many victories have been obtained on both sides, but that the last victory, decisive of the affair between the contending parties, was won by him who fought for the right, only if his adversary was forbidden to continue the tourney. As impartial umpires, we must lay aside entirely the consideration whether the combatants are fighting for the right or for the wrong side, for the true or for the false, and allow the combat to be first decided. Perhaps, after they have wearied more than injured each other, they will discover the nothingness of their cause of quarrel, and part good friends.

This method of watching, or rather of originating, a conflict of assertions, not for the purpose of finally deciding in favour of either side, but to discover whether the object of the struggle is not a mere illusion, which each strives in vain to reach, but which would be no gain even when reached—this procedure, I say, may be termed the *sceptical method*. It is thoroughly distinct from *scepticism*—the principle of a technical and scientific ignorance, which undermines the foundations of all knowledge, in order, if possible, to destroy our belief and confidence therein. For the sceptical method aims at certainty, by endeavouring to discover in a conflict of this kind, conducted honestly and intelligently on both sides, the point of misunderstanding; just as wise legislators derive, from the embarrassment of judges in lawsuits, information in regard to the defective and ill-defined parts of their statutes. The antinomy which reveals itself in the application of laws, is for our limited wisdom the best criterion of legislation. For the attention of reason, which in abstract speculation does not easily become conscious of its errors, is thus roused to the momenta in the determination of its principles.

But this sceptical method is essentially peculiar to transcendental philosophy, and can perhaps be dispensed with in every other field of investigation. In mathematics its use would be absurd; because in it no false assertions can long remain hidden, inasmuch as its demonstrations must always proceed under the guidance of pure intuition, and by means of an always evident synthesis. In experimental philosophy doubt and delay may be very useful; but no misunderstanding is possible, which cannot be easily removed; and in experience means of solving the difficulty and putting an end to the dissension must at last be found, whether sooner or later. Moral philosophy can always exhibit its principles, with their practical consequences, *in concreto*—at least in possible experiences, and thus escape the mistakes and ambiguities of abstraction. But transcendental propositions, which lay claim to insight beyond the region of possible experience, cannot, on the one hand, exhibit their abstract synthesis in any *a priori* intuition, nor, on the other, expose a lurking error by the help of experience. Transcendental reason, therefore, presents us with no other criterion, than that of an attempt to reconcile such assertions, and for this purpose to permit a free and unrestrained conflict between them. And this we now proceed to arrange.[1]

[1] The antinomies stand in the order of the four transcendental ideas above detailed.

## FIRST ANTINOMY

### *Thesis*

The world has a beginning in time, and is also limited in regard to space.

#### PROOF

Granted, that the world has no beginning in time; up to every given moment of time, an eternity must have elapsed, and therewith passed away an infinite series of successive conditions or states of things in the world. Now the infinity of a series consists in the fact, that it never can be completed by means of a successive synthesis. It follows that an infinite series already elapsed is impossible, and that consequently a beginning of the world is a necessary condition of its existence. And this was the first thing to be proved.

As regards the second, let us take the opposite for granted. In this case, the world must be an infinite given total of coexistent things. Now we cannot cogitate the dimensions of a quantity, which is not given within certain limits of an intuition,[1] in any other way

[1] We may consider an undetermined quantity as a whole, when it is enclosed within limits, although we cannot construct or ascertain its totality by measurement, that is, by the successive synthesis of its parts. For its limits of themselves determine its completeness as a whole.

### *Antithesis*

The world has no beginning, and no limits in space, but is, in relation both to time and space, infinite.

#### PROOF

For let it be granted, that it has a beginning. A beginning is an existence which is preceded by a time in which the thing does not exist. On the above supposition, it follows that there must have been a time in which the world did not exist, that is, a void time. But in a void time the origination of a thing is impossible; because no part of any such time contains a distinctive condition of being, in preference to that of non-being (whether the supposed thing originate of itself, or by means of some other cause). Consequently, many series of things may have a beginning in the world, but the world itself cannot have a beginning, and is, therefore, in relation to past time, infinite.

As regards the second statement, let us first take the opposite for granted—that the world is finite and limited in space; it follows that it must exist in a void space, which is not limited. We should therefore meet not only with a relation of things *in space*, but also a relation of things *to space*. Now,

*Thesis*

than by means of the synthesis [1] of its parts, and the total of such a quantity only by means of a completed synthesis, or the repeated addition of unity to itself. Accordingly, to cogitate the world, which fills all spaces, as a whole, the successive synthesis of the parts of an infinite world must be looked upon as completed, that is to say, an infinite time must be regarded as having elapsed in the enumeration of all co-existing things; which is impossible. For this reason an infinite aggregate of actual things cannot be considered as a given whole, consequently, not as a contemporaneously given whole. The world is consequently, as regards extension in space, *not infinite*, but enclosed in limits. And this was the second thing to be proved.

[1] What is meant by *successive synthesis* must be tolerably plain. If I am required to form some notion of a piece of land, I may assume an arbitrary standard—a mile, or an acre—and by the successive addition of mile to mile or acre to acre till the proper number is reached, *construct* for myself a notion of the size of the land.—*Tr.*

*Antithesis*

as the world is an absolute whole, out of and beyond which no object of intuition, and consequently no correlate to which can be discovered, this relation of the world to a void space is merely a relation to *no object*. But such a relation, and consequently the limitation of the world by void space, is nothing. Consequently, the world, as regards space, is not limited, that is, it is infinite in regard to extension.[1]

[1] Space is merely the form of external intuition (formal intuition), and not a real object which can be externally perceived. Space, prior to all things which determine it (fill or limit it), or, rather, which present an *empirical intuition* conformable to it, is, under the title of absolute space, nothing but the mere possibility of external phenomena, in so far as they either exist in themselves, or can annex themselves to given intuitions. Empirical intuition is therefore not a composition of phenomena and space (of perception and empty intuition). The one is not the correlate of the other in a synthesis, but they are vitally connected in the same empirical intuition, as matter and form. If we wish to set one of these two apart from the other—space from phenomena—there arise all sorts of empty determinations of external intuition, which are very far from being possible perceptions. For example, motion or rest of the world in an infinite empty space, or a determination of the mutual relation of both, cannot possibly be perceived, and is therefore merely the predicate of a notional entity.

## OBSERVATIONS ON THE FIRST ANTINOMY

*On the Thesis*

In bringing forward these conflicting arguments, I have not

*On the Antithesis*

The proof in favour of the infinity of the cosmical succession

*Thesis*

been on the search for sophisms, for the purpose of availing myself of special pleading, which takes advantage of the carelessness of the opposite party, appeals to a misunderstood statute, and erects its unrighteous claims upon an unfair interpretation. Both proofs originate fairly from the nature of the case, and the advantage presented by the mistakes of the dogmatists of both parties has been completely set aside.

The thesis might also have been unfairly demonstrated, by the introduction of an erroneous conception of the infinity of a given quantity. A quantity is infinite, if a greater than itself cannot possibly exist. The quantity is measured by the number of given units—which are taken as a standard—contained in it. Now no number can be the greatest, because one or more units can always be added. It follows that an infinite given quantity, consequently an infinite world (both as regards time and extension) is impossible. It is, therefore, limited in both respects. In this manner I might have conducted my proof; but the conception given in it does not agree with the true conception of an infinite whole. In this there is no representation of its quantity, it is not said how large it is; consequently its conception is not the conception

*Antithesis*

and the cosmical content is based upon the consideration, that, in the opposite case, a void time and a void space must constitute the limits of the world. Now I am not unaware, that there are some ways of escaping this conclusion. It may, for example, be alleged, that a limit to the world, as regards both space and time, is quite possible, without at the same time holding the existence of an absolute time before the beginning of the world, or an absolute space extending beyond the actual world—which is impossible. I am quite well satisfied with the latter part of this opinion of the philosophers of the Leibnitzian school. Space is merely the form of external intuition, but not a real object which can itself be externally intuited; it is not a correlate of phenomena, it is the form of phenomena itself. Space, therefore, cannot be regarded as absolutely and in itself something determinative of the existence of things, because it is not itself an object, but only the form of possible objects. Consequently, things, as phenomena, determine space; that is to say, they render it possible that, of all the possible predicates of space (size and relation), certain may belong to reality. But we cannot affirm the converse, that space, as something self-subsistent, can determine real things

*Thesis*

of a *maximum*. We cogitate in it merely its relation to an arbitrarily assumed unit, in relation to which it is greater than any number. Now, just as the unit which is taken is greater or smaller, the infinite will be greater or smaller; but the infinity, which consists merely in the relation to this given unit, must remain always the same, although the absolute quantity of the whole is not thereby cognized.

The true (transcendental) conception of infinity is: that the successive synthesis of unity in the measurement of a given quantum can never be completed.[1] Hence it follows, without possibility of mistake, that an eternity of actual successive states up to a given (the present) moment cannot have elapsed, and that the world must therefore have a beginning.

In regard to the second part of the thesis, the difficulty as to an infinite and yet elapsed series disappears; for the manifold of a world infinite in extension is contemporaneously given. But, in order to cogitate the total of this manifold, as we cannot have the aid of limits constituting by themselves this total in intuition, we are obliged to give some account of our

[1] The quantum in this sense contains a congeries of given units, which is greater than any number—and this is the mathematical conception of the infinite.

*Antithesis*

in regard to size or shape, for it is in itself not a real thing. Space (filled or void)[1] may therefore be limited by phenomena, but phenomena cannot be limited by an empty space without them. This is true of time also. All this being granted, it is nevertheless indisputable, that we must assume these two nonentities, void space without and void time before the world, if we assume the existence of cosmical limits, relatively to space or time.

For, as regards the subterfuge adopted by those who endeavour to evade the consequence—that, if the world is limited as to space and time, the infinite void must determine the existence of actual things in regard to their dimensions—it arises solely from the fact that, instead of a *sensuous world*, an *intelligible world*—of which nothing is known—is cogitated; instead of a real beginning (an existence, which is preceded by a period in which nothing exists), an existence which presupposes *no other condition* than that of time; and, instead of limits of extension, boundaries of the universe. But the question relates to the

[1] It is evident that what is meant here is, that empty space, in so far as it is limited by phenomena—space, that is, *within* the world—does not at least contradict transcendental principles, and may therefore, as regards them, be admitted, although its possibility cannot on that account be affirmed.

*Thesis*

conception, which in this case cannot proceed from the whole to the determined quantity of the parts, but must demonstrate the possibility of a whole by means of a successive synthesis of the parts. But as this synthesis must constitute a series that cannot be completed, it is impossible for us to cogitate prior to it, and consequently not by means of it, a totality. For the conception of totality itself is in the present case the representation of a completed synthesis of the parts; and this completion, and consequently its conception, is impossible.

*Antithesis*

*mundus phaenomenon*, and its quantity; and in this case we cannot make abstraction of the conditions of sensibility, without doing away with the essential reality of this world itself. The world of sense, if it is limited, must necessarily lie in the infinite void. If this, and with it space as the *a priori* condition of the possibility of phenomena, is left out of view, the whole world of sense disappears. In our problem is this alone considered as given. The *mundus intelligibilis* is nothing but the general conception of a world, in which abstraction has been made of all conditions of intuition, and in relation to which no synthetical proposition — either affirmative or negative—is possible.

## SECOND ANTINOMY

*Thesis*

Every composite substance in the world consists of simple parts; and there exists nothing that is not either itself simple, or composed of simple parts.

*Antithesis*

No composite thing in the world consists of simple parts; and there does not exist in the world any simple substance.

PROOF

For, grant that composite substances do not consist of simple parts; in this case, if all combination or composition were annihilated in thought, no composite part, and (as, by the supposition, there do not exist

PROOF

Let it be supposed that a composite thing (as substance) consists of simple parts. Inasmuch as all external relation, consequently all composition of substances, is possible only in space; the space, occupied by that which is composite, must

*Thesis*

simple parts) no simple part would exist. Consequently, no substance; consequently, nothing would exist. Either, then, it is impossible to annihilate composition in thought; or, after such annihilation, there must remain something that subsists without composition, that is, something that is simple. But in the former case the composite could not itself consist of substances, because with substances composition is merely a contingent relation, apart from which they must still exist as self-subsistent beings. Now, as this case contradicts the supposition, the second must contain the truth—that the substantial composite in the world consists of simple parts.

It follows as an immediate inference, that the things in the world are all, without exception, simple beings—that composition is merely an external condition pertaining to them—and that, although we never can separate and isolate the elementary substances from the state of composition, reason must cogitate these as the primary subjects of all composition, and consequently, as prior thereto—and as simple substances.

*Antithesis*

consist of the same number of parts as is contained in the composite. But space does not consist of simple parts, but of spaces. Therefore, every part of the composite must occupy a space. But the absolutely primary parts of what is composite are simple. It follows that what is simple occupies a space. Now, as everything real that occupies a space, contains a manifold the parts of which are external to each other, and is consequently composite—and a real composite, not of accidents (for these cannot exist external to each other apart from substance), but of substances—it follows that the simple must be a substantial composite, which is self-contradictory.

The second proposition of the antithesis—that there exists in the world nothing that is simple —is here equivalent to the following: The existence of the absolutely simple cannot be demonstrated from any experience or perception either external or internal; and the absolutely simple is a mere idea, the objective reality of which cannot be demonstrated in any possible experience; it is consequently, in the exposition of phenomena, without application and object. For, let us take for granted that an object may be found in experience for this transcendental idea; the empirical intuition of such an object must then be

*Thesis*                          *Antithesis*

recognized to contain absolutely no manifold with its parts external to each other, and connected into unity. Now, as we cannot reason from the non-consciousness of such a manifold to the impossibility of its existence in the intuition of an object, and as the proof of this impossibility is necessary for the establishment and proof of absolute simplicity; it follows, that this simplicity cannot be inferred from any perception whatever. As, therefore, an absolutely simple object cannot be given in any experience, and the world of sense must be considered as the sum total of all possible experiences: nothing simple exists in the world.

This second proposition in the antithesis has a more extended aim than the first. The first merely banishes the simple from the intuition of the composite; while the second drives it entirely out of nature. Hence we were unable to demonstrate it from the conception of a given object of external intuition (of the composite), but we were obliged to prove it from the relation of a given object to a possible experience in general.

## OBSERVATIONS ON THE SECOND ANTINOMY

*On the Thesis*

When I speak of a *whole*, which necessarily consists of simple

*On the Antithesis*

Against the assertion of the infinite subdivisibility of matter,

*Thesis*

parts, I understand thereby only a substantial whole, as the true composite; that is to say, I understand that contingent unity of the manifold which is given as perfectly isolated (at least in thought), placed in reciprocal connection, and thus constituted a unity. Space ought not to be called a *compositum* but a *totum*, for its parts are possible in the whole, and not the whole by means of the parts. It might perhaps be called a *compositum ideale*, but not a *compositum reale*. But this is of no importance. As space is not a composite of substances (and not even of real accidents), if I abstract all composition therein —nothing, not even a point, remains; for a point is possible only as the limit of a space— consequently of a composite. Space and time, therefore, do not consist of simple parts. That which belongs only to the condition or state of a substance, even although it possesses a quantity (motion or change, for example), likewise does not consist of simple parts. That is to say, a certain degree of change does not originate from the addition of many simple changes. Our inference of the simple from the composite is valid only of self-subsisting things. But the accidents of a state are not self-subsistent. The proof, then, for the necessity of the simple, as the component part of all that

*Antithesis*

whose ground of proof is purely mathematical, objections have been alleged by the Monadists. These objections lay themselves open, at first sight, to suspicion, from the fact that they do not recognize the clearest mathematical proofs as propositions relating to the constitution of space, in so far as it is really the formal condition of the possibility of all matter, but regard them merely as inferences from abstract but arbitrary conceptions, which cannot have any application to real things. Just as if it were possible to imagine another mode of intuition than that given in the primitive intuition of space; and just as if its *a priori* determinations did not apply to everything, the existence of which is possible, from the fact alone of its filling space. If we listen to them, we shall find ourselves required to cogitate, in addition to the mathematical point, which is simple—not, however, a part, but a mere limit of space— physical points, which are indeed likewise simple, but possess the peculiar property, as parts of space, of filling it merely by their aggregation. I shall not repeat here the common and clear refutations of this absurdity, which are to be found everywhere in numbers: every one knows that it is impossible to undermine the evidence of mathematics by mere discursive

*Thesis*

is substantial and composite, may prove a failure, and the whole case of this thesis be lost, if we carry the proposition too far, and wish to make it valid of everything that is composite without distinction—as indeed has really now and then happened. Besides, I am here speaking only of the simple, in so far as it is necessarily given in the composite—the latter being capable of solution into the former as its component parts. The proper signification of the word *monas* (as employed by Leibnitz) ought to relate to the simple, given *immediately* as simple substance (for example, in consciousness), and not as an element of the composite. As an element, the term *atomus*[1] would be more appropriate. And as I wish to prove the existence of simple substances, only in relation to, and as the elements of, the composite, I might term the antithesis of the second Antinomy, transcendental *Atomistic*. But as this word has long been employed to designate a particular theory of corporeal phenomena (*moleculae*), and thus presupposes a basis of empirical

[1] A masculine formed by Kant, instead of the common neuter *atomon*, which is generally translated in the scholastic philosophy by the terms *inseparabile, indiscernibile, simplex.* Kant wished to have a term opposed to *monas*, and so hit upon this ἅπαξ λεγόμενον. With Democritus ἄτομος, and with Cicero *atomus* is feminine.— *Note by Rosenkranz.*

*Antithesis*

conceptions; I shall only remark, that, if in this case philosophy endeavours to gain an advantage over mathematics by sophistical artifices, it is because it forgets that the discussion relates solely to *phenomena* and their conditions. It is not sufficient to find the conception of the simple for the pure *conception* of the composite, but we must discover for the *intuition* of the composite (matter), the intuition of the simple. Now this, according to the laws of sensibility, and consequently in the case of objects of sense, is utterly impossible. In the case of a whole composed of substances, which is cogitated solely by the pure understanding, it may be necessary to be in possession of the simple before composition is possible. But this does not hold good of the *Totum substantiale phaenomenon*, which, as an empirical intuition in space, possesses the necessary property of containing no simple part, for the very reason, that no part of space is simple. Meanwhile, the Monadists have been subtle enough to escape from this difficulty, by presupposing intuition and the dynamical relation of substances as the condition of the possibility of space, instead of regarding space as the condition of the possibility of the objects of external intuition, that is, of bodies. Now we have a conception of bodies only as phe-

*Thesis*

conceptions, I prefer calling it the dialectical principle of *Monadology*.

*Antithesis*

nomena, and, as such, they necessarily presuppose space as the condition of all external phenomena. The evasion is therefore in vain; as, indeed, we have sufficiently shown in our Aesthetic. If bodies were *things in themselves*, the proof of the Monadists would be unexceptionable.

The second dialectical assertion possesses the peculiarity of having opposed to it a dogmatical proposition, which, among all such sophistical statements, is the only one that undertakes to prove in the case of an object of experience, that which is properly a transcendental idea —the absolute simplicity of substance. The proposition is, that the object of the internal sense, the thinking Ego, is an absolute simple substance. Without at present entering upon this subject—as it has been considered at length in a former chapter— I shall merely remark, that, if something is cogitated merely as an object, without the addition of any synthetical determination of its intuition—as happens in the case of the bare representation, *I*—it is certain that no manifold and no composition can be perceived in such a representation. As, moreover, the predicates whereby I cogitate this object are merely intuitions of the internal sense, there cannot be discovered in them anything to prove the

*Thesis*

*Antithesis*

existence of a manifold whose parts are external to each other, and consequently, nothing to prove the existence of real composition. Consciousness, therefore, is so constituted, that, inasmuch as the thinking subject is at the same time its own object, it cannot divide itself—although it can divide its inhering determinations. For every object in relation to itself is absolute unity. Nevertheless, if the subject is regarded *externally*, as an object of intuition, it must, in its character of phenomenon, possess the property of composition. And it must always be regarded in this manner, if we wish to know whether there is or is not contained in it a manifold whose parts are external to each other.

## THIRD ANTINOMY

*Thesis*

Causality according to the laws of nature, is not the only causality operating to originate the phenomena of the world. A causality of freedom is also necessary to account fully for these phenomena.

#### Proof

Let it be supposed, that there is no other kind of causality than that according to the laws of nature. Consequently, every-

*Antithesis*

There is no such thing as freedom, but everything in the world happens solely according to the laws of nature.

#### Proof

Granted, that there does exist *freedom* in the transcendental sense, as a peculiar kind of causality, operating to produce events in the world—a faculty, that is to say, of originating a state, and consequently a series

*Thesis*

thing that happens presupposes a previous condition, which it follows with absolute certainty, in conformity with a rule. But this previous condition must itself be something that has happened (that has arisen in time, as it did not exist before), for, if it has always been in existence, its consequence or effect would not thus originate for the first time, but would likewise have always existed. The causality, therefore, of a cause, whereby something happens, is itself a thing that has *happened*. Now this again presupposes, in conformity with the law of nature, a previous condition and its causality, and this another anterior to the former, and so on. If, then, everything happens solely in accordance with the laws of nature, there cannot be any real first beginning of things, but only a subaltern or comparative beginning. There cannot, therefore, be a completeness of series on the side of the causes which originate the one from the other. But the law of nature is, that nothing can happen without a sufficient *a priori* determined cause. The proposition, therefore—if all causality is possible only in accordance with the laws of nature—is, when stated in this unlimited and general manner, self-contradictory. It follows that this cannot be the only kind of causality.

*Antithesis*

of consequences from that state. In this case, not only the series originated by this spontaneity, but the determination of this spontaneity itself to the production of the series, that is to say, the causality itself must have an absolute commencement, such, that nothing can precede to determine this action according to unvarying laws. But every beginning of action presupposes in the acting cause a state of inaction; and a dynamically primal beginning of action presupposes a state, which has no connection—as regards causality — with the preceding state of the cause—which does not, that is, in any wise result from it. Transcendental freedom is therefore opposed to the natural law of cause and effect, and such a conjunction of successive states in effective causes is destructive of the possibility of unity in experience, and for that reason not to be found in experience—is consequently a mere fiction of thought.

We have, therefore, nothing but nature to which we must look for connection and order in cosmical events. Freedom—independence of the laws of nature—is certainly a deliverance from restraint, but it is also a relinquishing of the guidance of law and rule. For it cannot be alleged, that, instead of the laws of nature, laws of freedom may be introduced into

*Thesis*

From what has been said, it follows that a causality must be admitted, by means of which something happens, without its cause being determined according to necessary laws by some other cause preceding. That is to say, there must exist an *absolute spontaneity* of cause, which of itself originates a series of phenomena which proceeds according to natural laws—consequently transcendental freedom, without which even in the course of nature the succession of phenomena on the side of causes is never complete.

*Antithesis*

the causality of the course of nature. For, if freedom were determined according to laws, it would be no longer freedom, but merely nature. Nature, therefore, and transcendental freedom are distinguishable as conformity to law and lawlessness. The former imposes upon understanding the difficulty of seeking the origin of events ever higher and higher in the series of causes, inasmuch as causality is always conditioned thereby; while it compensates this labour by the guarantee of a unity complete and in conformity with law. The latter, on the contrary, holds out to the understanding the promise of a point of rest in the chain of causes, by conducting it to an unconditioned causality, which professes to have the power of spontaneous origination, but which, in its own utter blindness, deprives it of the guidance of rules, by which alone a completely connected experience is possible.

## OBSERVATIONS ON THE THIRD ANTINOMY

*On the Thesis*

The transcendental idea of freedom is far from constituting the entire content of the psychological conception so termed, which is for the most part empirical. It merely presents us with the conception of spontaneity of action, as the proper

*On the Antithesis*

The assertor of the all-sufficiency of nature in regard to causality (transcendental *Physiocracy*), in opposition to the doctrine of freedom, would defend his view of the question somewhat in the following manner. He would say, in answer

*Thesis*

ground for imputing freedom to the cause of a certain class of objects. It is, however, the true stumbling-stone to philosophy, which meets with unconquerable difficulties in the way of its admitting this kind of unconditioned causality. That element in the question of the freedom of the will, which has for so long a time placed speculative reason in such perplexity, is properly only transcendental, and concerns the question, whether there must be held to exist a faculty of *spontaneous* origination of a series of successive things or states. How such a faculty is possible, is not a necessary inquiry; for in the case of natural causality itself, we are obliged to content ourselves with the *a priori* knowledge that such a causality must be presupposed, although we are quite incapable of comprehending how the being of one thing is possible through the being of another, but must for this information look entirely to experience. Now we have demonstrated this necessity of a free first beginning of a series of phenomena, only in so far as it is required for the comprehension of an origin of the world, all following states being regarded as a succession according to laws of nature alone. But, as there has thus been proved the existence of a faculty which can of itself originate a

*Antithesis*

to the sophistical arguments of the opposite party: *If you do not accept a mathematical first, in relation to time, you have no need to seek a dynamical first, in regard to causality* Who compelled you to imagine an absolutely primal condition of the world, and therewith an absolute beginning of the gradually progressing successions of phenomena—and, as some foundation for this fancy of yours, to set bounds to unlimited nature? Inasmuch as the substances in the world have always existed—at least the unity of experience renders such a supposition quite necessary—there is no difficulty in believing also, that the changes in the conditions of these substances have always existed; and, consequently, that a first beginning, mathematical or dynamical, is by no means required. The possibility of such an infinite derivation, without any initial member from which all the others result, is certainly quite incomprehensible. But if you are rash enough to deny the enigmatical secrets of nature for this reason, you will find yourselves obliged to deny also the existence of many fundamental properties of natural objects (such as fundamental forces), which you can just as little comprehend; and even the possibility of so simple a conception as that of change must present

*Thesis*

series in time—although we are unable to explain how it can exist—we feel ourselves authorized to admit, even in the midst of the natural course of events, a beginning, as regards causality, of different successions of phenomena, and at the same time to attribute to all substances a faculty of free action. But we ought in this case not to allow ourselves to fall into a common misunderstanding, and to suppose that, because a successive series in the world can only have a comparatively first beginning —another state or condition of things always preceding — an absolutely first beginning of a series in the course of nature is impossible. For we are not speaking here of an absolutely first beginning in relation to time, but as regards causality alone. When, for example, I, completely of my own free will, and independently of the necessarily determinative influence of natural causes, rise from my chair, there commences with this event, including its material consequences *in infinitum*, an absolutely new series; although, in relation to time, this event is merely the continuation of a preceding series. For this resolution and act of mine do not form part of the succession of effects in nature, and are not mere continuations of it; on the contrary, the determining causes of nature cease to operate

*Antithesis*

to you insuperable difficulties. For if experience did not teach you that it was real, you never could conceive *a priori* the possibility of this ceaseless sequence of being and non-being.

But if the existence of a transcendental faculty of freedom is granted—a faculty of originating changes in the world —this faculty must at least exist out of and apart from the world; although it is certainly a bold assumption, that, over and above the complete content of all possible intuitions, there still exists an object which cannot be presented in any possible perception. But, to attribute to substances in the world itself such a faculty, is quite inadmissible; for, in this case, the connection of phenomena reciprocally determining and determined according to general laws, which is termed nature, and along with it the criteria of empirical truth, which enable us to distinguish experience from mere visionary dreaming, would almost entirely disappear. In proximity with such a lawless faculty of freedom, a system of nature is hardly cogitable; for the laws of the latter would be continually subject to the intrusive influences of the former, and the course of phenomena, which would otherwise proceed regularly and uniformly, would become thereby confused and disconnected.

*Thesis*

in reference to this event, which certainly *succeeds* the acts of nature, but does not *proceed* from them. For these reasons, the action of a free agent must be termed, in regard to causality, if not in relation to time, an absolutely primal beginning of a series of phenomena.

The justification of this need of reason to rest upon a free act as the first beginning of the series of natural causes, is evident from the fact, that all philosophers of antiquity (with the exception of the Epicurean school) felt themselves obliged, when constructing a theory of the motions of the universe, to accept a *prime mover*, that is, a freely acting cause, which spontaneously and prior to all other causes evolved this series of states. They always felt the need of going beyond mere nature, for the purpose of making a first beginning comprehensible.

*Antithesis*

## FOURTH ANTINOMY

*Thesis*

There exists either in, or in connection with the world—either as a part of it, or as the cause of it—an absolutely necessary being.

### PROOF

The world of sense, as the sum total of all phenomena, contains a series of changes.

*Antithesis*

An absolutely necessary being does not exist, either in the world, or out of it—as its cause.

### PROOF

Grant that either the world itself is necessary, or that there is contained in it a necessary existence. Two cases are possible. *First*, there must either

*Thesis*

For, without such a series, the mental representation of the series of time itself, as the condition of the possibility of the sensuous world, could not be presented to us.[1] But every change stands under its condition, which precedes it in time and renders it necessary. Now the existence of a given condition presupposes a complete series of conditions up to the absolutely unconditioned, which alone is absolutely necessary. It follows that something that is absolutely necessary must exist, if change exists as its consequence. But this necessary thing itself belongs to the sensuous world. For suppose it to exist out of and apart from it, the series of cosmical changes would receive from it a beginning, and yet this necessary cause would not itself belong to the world of sense. But this is impossible. For, as the beginning of a series in time is determined only by that which precedes it in time, the supreme condition of the beginning of a series of changes must exist in the time in which this series itself did not exist; for a beginning supposes a time preceding, in which the thing that begins to be was not in existence. The causality of the

---

[1] *Objectively*, time, as the formal condition of the possibility of change, precedes all changes; but *subjectively*, and in consciousness, the representation of time, like every other, is given solely by *occasion* of perception.

*Antithesis*

be in the series of cosmical changes a beginning, which is unconditionally necessary, and therefore uncaused — which is at variance with the dynamical law of the determination of all phenomena in time; or *secondly*, the series itself is without beginning, and, although contingent and conditioned in all its parts, is nevertheless absolutely necessary and unconditioned as a whole — which is self-contradictory. For the existence of an aggregate cannot be necessary, if no single part of it possesses necessary existence.

Grant, on the other hand, that an absolutely necessary cause exists out of and apart from the world. This cause, as the highest member in the series of the causes of cosmical changes, must originate or begin[1] the existence of the latter and their series. In this case it must also begin to act, and its causality would therefore belong to time, and consequently to the sum total of phenomena, that is, to the world. It follows

---

[1] The word *begin* is taken in two senses. The first is active—the cause being regarded as beginning a series of conditions as its effect (*infit*).[2] The second is passive—the causality in the cause itself beginning to operate (*fit*). I reason here from the first to the second.

[2] It may be doubted whether there is any passage to be found in the Latin Classics where *infit* is employed in any other than a neuter sense, as in Plautus, '*Infit me percontarier.*' The second signification of *begin* (*anfangen*) we should rather term neuter.—*Tr.*

*Thesis*

necessary cause of changes, and consequently the cause itself, must for these reasons belong to time—and to phenomena, time being possible only as the form of phenomena. Consequently, it cannot be cogitated as separated from the world of sense—the sum total of all phenomena. There is, therefore, contained in the world, something that is absolutely necessary—whether it be the whole cosmical series itself, or only a part of it.

*Antithesis*

that the cause cannot be out of the world; which is contradictory to the hypothesis. Therefore, neither in the world, nor out of it (but in causal connection with it), does there exist any absolutely necessary being.

## OBSERVATIONS ON THE FOURTH ANTINOMY

*On the Thesis*

To demonstrate the existence of a necessary being, I cannot be permitted in this place to employ any other than the *cosmological* argument, which ascends from the conditioned in phenomena to the unconditioned in conception—the unconditioned being considered the necessary condition of the absolute totality of the series. The proof, from the mere idea of a supreme being, belongs to another principle of reason, and requires separate discussion.

The pure cosmological proof demonstrates the existence of a necessary being, but at the same time leaves it quite unsettled, whether this being is the world itself, or quite distinct from it. To establish the truth of the

*On the Antithesis*

The difficulties which meet us, in our attempt to rise through the series of phenomena to the existence of an absolutely necessary supreme cause, must not originate from our inability to establish the truth of our mere conceptions of the necessary existence of a thing. That is to say, our objections must not be ontological, but must be directed against the causal connection with a series of phenomena of a condition which is itself unconditioned. In one word, they must be cosmological, and relate to empirical laws. We must show that the regress in the series of causes (in the world of sense) cannot conclude with an empirically unconditioned condition, and that the

*Thesis*

latter view, principles are requisite, which are not cosmological, and do not proceed in the series of phenomena. We should require to introduce into our proof conceptions of contingent beings—regarded merely as objects of the understanding, and also a principle which enables us to connect these, by means of mere conceptions, with a necessary being. But the proper place for all such arguments is a *transcendent* philosophy, which has unhappily not yet been established.

But, if we begin our proof cosmologically, by laying at the foundation of it the series of phenomena, and the regress in it according to empirical laws of causality, we are not at liberty to break off from this mode of demonstration and to pass over to something which is not itself a member of the series. The condition must be taken in exactly the same signification as the relation of the conditioned to its condition in the series has been taken, for the series must conduct us in an unbroken regress to this supreme condition. But if this relation is sensuous, and belongs to the possible empirical employment of the understanding, the supreme condition or cause must close the regressive series according to the laws of sensibility, and consequently must belong to the series of time. It follows

*Antithesis*

cosmological argument from the contingency of the cosmical state—a contingency alleged to arise from change—does not justify us in accepting a first cause, that is, a prime originator of the cosmical series.

The reader will observe in this antinomy a very remarkable contrast. The very same grounds of proof which established in the thesis tne existence of a supreme being, demonstrated in the antithesis—and with equal strictness—the non-existence of such a being. We found, first, that *a necessary being exists*, because the whole time past contains the series of all conditions, and with it, therefore, the unconditioned (the necessary); secondly, that *there does not exist any necessary being*, for the same reason, that the whole time past contains the series of all conditions—which are themselves therefore, in the aggregate, conditioned. The cause of this seeming incongruity is as follows. We attend, in the first argument, solely to the *absolute totality* of the series of conditions, the one of which determines the other in time, and thus arrive at a necessary unconditioned. In the second, we consider, on the contrary, the *contingency* of everything that is determined in the *series of time*—for every event is preceded by a time, in which the condition itself must be

*Thesis*

that this necessary existence must be regarded as the highest member of the cosmical series.

Certain philosophers have, nevertheless, allowed themselves the liberty of making such a *saltus* (μετάβασις εἰς ἄλλο γόνος). From the changes in the world they have concluded their empirical contingency, that is, their dependence on empirically-determined causes, and they thus admitted an ascending series of empirical conditions: and in this they are quite right. But as they could not find in this series any primal beginning or any highest member, they passed suddenly from the empirical conception of contingency to the pure category, which presents us with a series—not sensuous, but intellectual—whose completeness does certainly rest upon the existence of an absolutely necessary cause. Nay, more, this intellectual series is not tied to any sensuous conditions; and is therefore free from the condition of time, which requires it spontaneously to begin its causality in time. But such a procedure is perfectly inadmissible, as will be made plain from what follows.

In the pure sense of the categories, that is contingent the contradictory opposite of which is possible. Now we cannot reason from empirical contingency to intellectual. The opposite of that which is changed

*Antithesis*

determined as conditioned — and thus everything that is unconditioned or absolutely necessary disappears. In both, the mode of proof is quite in accordance with the common procedure of human reason, which often falls into discord with itself, from considering an object from two different points of view. Herr von Mairan regarded the controversy between two celebrated astronomers, which arose from a similar difficulty as to the choice of a proper standpoint, as a phenomenon of sufficient importance to warrant a separate treatise on the subject. The one concluded: *the moon revolves on its own axis*, because it constantly presents the same side to the earth; the other declared that *the moon does not revolve on its own axis*, for the same reason. Both conclusions were perfectly correct, according to the point of view from which the motions of the moon were considered.

*Thesis*

—the opposite of its state—is actual at another time, and is therefore possible. Consequently, it is not the contradictory opposite of the former state. To be *that*, it is necessary that in the same time in which the preceding state existed, its opposite could have existed in its place; but such a cognition is not given us in the mere phenomenon of change. A body that was in motion=$A$, comes into a state of rest=*non-A*. Now it cannot be concluded from the fact that a state opposite to the state $A$ follows it, that the contradictory opposite of $A$ is possible; and that $A$ is therefore contingent. To prove this, we should require to know that the state of rest could have existed in the very same time in which the motion took place. Now we know nothing more than that the state of rest was actual in the time that followed the state of motion; consequently, that it was also possible. But motion at one time, and rest at another time, are not contradictorily opposed to each other. It follows from what has been said, that the succession of opposite determinations, that is, change, does not demonstrate the fact of contingency as represented in the conceptions of the pure understanding; and that it cannot, therefore, conduct us to the fact of the existence of a necessary being. Change proves

*Antithesis*

| *Thesis* | *Antithesis* |
|---|---|
| merely empirical contingency, that is to say, that the new state could not have existed without a cause, which belongs to the preceding time. This cause — even although it is regarded as absolutely necessary —must be presented to us in time, and must belong to the series of phenomena. | |

## Section III

### *Of the Interest of Reason in these Self-contradictions*

WE have thus completely before us the dialectical procedure of the cosmological ideas. No possible experience can present us with an object adequate to them in extent. Nay, more, reason itself cannot cogitate them as according with the general laws of experience. And yet they are not arbitrary fictions of thought. On the contrary, reason, in its uninterrupted progress in the empirical synthesis, is necessarily conducted to them, when it endeavours to free from all conditions and to comprehend in its unconditioned totality, that which can only be determined conditionally in accordance with the laws of experience. These dialectical propositions are so many attempts to solve four natural and unavoidable problems of reason. There are neither more, nor can there be less, than this number, because there are no other series of synthetical hypotheses, limiting *a priori* the empirical synthesis.

The brilliant claims of reason striving to extend its dominion beyond the limits of experience, have been represented above only in dry formulae, which contain merely the grounds of its pretensions. They have, besides, in conformity with the character of a transcendental philosophy, been freed from every empirical element; although the full splendours of the promises they hold out, and of the anticipations they excite, manifest themselves only when in connection with empirical cognitions. In the application of them, however, and in the advancing enlargement of the employment of reason, while struggling to rise from the region of experience and to soar to those sublime ideas, philosophy discovers a value and a dignity, which, if it could but make good its assertions, would raise it far above all other departments of human knowledge—professing, as it does, to present a sure foundation for our highest hopes and the ultimate aims of all the exertions of reason. The questions: whether the world has a beginning and a limit to its extension in space; whether there exists anywhere, or perhaps, in my own thinking Self, an indivisible and indestructible unity —or whether nothing but what is divisible and transitory exists; whether I am a free agent, or, like other beings, am bound in the chains of nature and fate; whether, finally, there is a supreme cause of the world, or all our thought and speculation must end with nature and the order of external things—are questions for the solution of which the mathematician would willingly exchange his whole science; for in it there is no satisfaction for the highest aspirations and most ardent desires of humanity. Nay, it may even be said that the true value of mathematics—that pride of human reason—consists in this: that she guides reason to the knowledge of nature—in her greater, as well as in her lesser manifestations—in her beautiful order and regularity—guides her, moreover, to an insight into the wonderful unity of the moving forces in the operations of nature, far beyond the expectations of a philosophy building only on experience; and that she thus encourages philosophy to extend the province of reason beyond all experience, and at the same time provides it with the most excellent materials for supporting its investigations, in so far as their nature admits, by adequate and accordant intuitions.

Unfortunately for speculation—but perhaps fortunately for the practical interests of humanity—reason, in the midst of her highest anticipations, finds herself hemmed in by a press of opposite and contradictory conclusions, from which neither her honour nor her safety will permit her to draw back. Nor can she regard these conflicting trains of reasoning with indifference as mere passages at arms, still less can she command peace; for in the subject of the conflict she has a deep interest. There is no other course left open to her, than to reflect with herself upon the origin of this disunion in reason—whether it may not arise from a mere misunderstanding. After such an inquiry, arrogant claims would have to be given up on both sides; but the sovereignty of reason over understanding and sense would be based upon a sure foundation.

We shall at present defer this radical inquiry, and in the meantime consider for a little—what side in the controversy we should most willingly take, if we were obliged to become partisans at all. As, in this case, we leave out of sight altogether the logical criterion of truth, and merely consult our own interest in reference to the question, these considerations, although inadequate to settle the question of right in either party, will enable us to comprehend how those who have taken part in the struggle, adopt the one view rather than the other—no special insight into the subject, however, having influenced their choice. They will, at the same time, explain to us many other things by the way—for example, the fiery zeal on the one side and the cold maintenance of their cause on the other; why the one party has met with the warmest approbations, and the other has always been repulsed by irreconcilable prejudices.

There is one thing, however, that determines the proper point of view, from which alone this preliminary inquiry can be instituted and carried on with the proper completeness—and that is the comparison of the principles from which both sides, thesis and antithesis, proceed. My readers would remark in the propositions of the antithesis a complete uniformity in the mode of thought and a perfect unity of principle. Its principle was that of pure empiricism, not only in the explication of the phenomena in the world, but also in the solution of the transcendental ideas, even of that of the universe itself. The affirmations of the thesis, on the contrary, were based, in addition to the empirical mode of explanation employed in the series of phenomena, on intellectual propositions; and its principles were in so far not simple. I shall term the thesis, in view of its essential characteristic, the *dogmatism* of pure reason.

On the side of *Dogmatism*, or of the Thesis, therefore, in the determination of the cosmological ideas, we find:

1. A *practical interest*, which must be very dear to every right-thinking man. That the world has a beginning—that the nature of my thinking self is simple, and therefore indestructible—that I am a free agent, and raised above the compulsion of nature and her laws—and, finally, that the entire order of things, which form the world, is dependent upon a Supreme Being, from whom the whole receives unity and connection—these are so many foundation-stones of morality and religion. The antithesis deprives us of all these supports—or, at least, seems so to deprive us.

2. A *speculative interest* of reason manifests itself on this side. For, if we take the transcendental ideas and employ them in the manner which the thesis directs, we can exhibit completely *a priori* the entire chain of conditions, and understand the derivation of the conditioned—beginning from the unconditioned. This the antithesis does not do; and for this reason does not meet with so

welcome a reception. For it can give no answer to our question respecting the conditions of its synthesis—except such as must be supplemented by another question, and so on to infinity. According to it, we must rise from a given beginning to one still higher; every part conducts us to a still smaller one; every event is preceded by another event which is its cause; and the conditions of existence rest always upon other and still higher conditions, and find neither end nor basis in some self-subsistent thing as the primal being.

3. This side has also the advantage of *popularity*; and this constitutes no small part of its claim to favour. The common understanding does not find the least difficulty in the idea of the unconditioned beginning of all synthesis—accustomed, as it is, rather to follow our consequences, than to seek for a proper basis for cognition. In the conception of an absolute first, moreover—the possibility of which it does not inquire into—it is highly gratified to find a firmly-established point of departure for its attempts at theory; while in the restless and continuous ascent from the conditioned to the condition, always with one foot in the air, it can find no satisfaction.

On the side of the Antithesis, or *Empiricism*, in the determination of the cosmological ideas:

1. We cannot discover any such practical interest arising from pure principles of reason, as morality and religion present. On the contrary, pure empiricism seems to empty them of all their power and influence. If there does not exist a Supreme Being distinct from the world—if the world is without beginning, consequently without a Creator—if our wills are not free, and the soul is divisible and subject to corruption just like matter —the ideas and principles of morality lose all validity, and fall with the transcendental ideas which constituted their theoretical support.

2. But empiricism, in compensation, holds out to reason, in its speculative interests, certain important advantages, far exceeding any that the dogmatist can promise us. For, when employed by the empiricist, understanding is always upon its proper ground of investigation—the field of possible experience, the laws of which it can explore, and thus extend its cognition securely and with clear intelligence without being stopped by limits in any direction. Here can it and ought it to find and present to intuition its proper object—not only in itself, but in all its relations; or, if it employ conceptions, upon this ground it can always present the corresponding images in clear and unmistakable intuitions. It is quite

unnecessary for it to renounce the guidance of nature, to attach itself to ideas, the objects of which it cannot know; because, as mere intellectual entities, they cannot be presented in any intuition. On the contrary, it is not even permitted to abandon its proper occupation, under the pretence that it has been brought to a conclusion (for it never can be), and to pass into the region of idealizing reason and transcendent conceptions, where it is not required to observe and explore the laws of nature, but merely to *think* and to *imagine*—secure from being contradicted by facts, because they have not been called as witnesses, but passed by, or perhaps subordinated to the so-called higher interests and considerations of pure reason.

Hence the empiricist will never allow himself to accept any epoch of nature for the first—the absolutely primal state; he will not believe that there can be limits to his outlook into her wide domains, nor pass from the objects of nature, which he can satisfactorily explain by means of observation and mathematical thought—which he can determine synthetically in intuition, to those which neither sense nor imagination can ever present *in concreto*; he will not concede the existence of a faculty in nature, operating independently of the laws of nature—a concession which would introduce uncertainty into the procedure of the understanding, which is guided by necessary laws to the observation of phenomena; nor, finally, will he permit himself to seek a cause beyond nature, inasmuch as we know nothing but it, and from it alone receive an objective basis for all our conceptions and instruction in the unvarying laws of things.

In truth, if the empirical philosopher had no other purpose in the establishment of his antithesis, than to check the presumption of a reason which mistakes its true destination, which boasts of its insight and its knowledge, just where all insight and knowledge cease to exist, and regards that which is valid only in relation to a practical interest, as an advancement of the speculative interests of the mind (in order, when it is convenient for itself, to break the thread of our physical investigations, and, under pretence of extending our cognition, connect them with transcendental ideas, by means of which we really know only that we know nothing)— if, I say, the empiricist rested satisfied with this benefit, the principle advanced by him would be a maxim recommending moderation in the pretensions of reason and modesty in its affirmations, and at the same time would direct us to the right mode of extending the province of the understanding, by the help of the only true teacher, experience. In obedience to this advice, intellectual *hypotheses* and *faith* would not be called in aid of our practical interests; nor should we introduce them under the pompous titles of science and insight. For speculative *cognition* cannot find an objective basis any other where than in experience; and, when we overstep its limits, our synthesis, which requires ever new cognitions independent of experience, has no substratum of intuition upon which to build.

But if—as often happens—empiricism, in relation to ideas, becomes itself dogmatic, and boldly denies that which is above the sphere of its phenomenal cognition, it falls itself into the error of intemperance—an error which is here all the more reprehensible, as thereby the practical interest of reason receives an irreparable injury.

And this constitutes the opposition between Epicureanism [1] and Platonism.

Both Epicurus and Plato assert more in their systems than they know. The former encourages and advances science—although to the prejudice of the practical; the latter presents us with excellent principles for the investigation of the practical, but, in relation to everything regarding which we can attain to speculative cognition, permits reason to append idealistic explanations of natural phenomena, to the great injury of physical investigation.

3. In regard to the third motive for the preliminary choice of a party in this war of assertions, it seems very extraordinary that empiricism should be utterly unpopular. We should be inclined to believe, that the common understanding would receive it with pleasure—promising as it does to satisfy it without passing the bounds of experience and its connected order; while transcendental dogmatism obliges it to rise to conceptions which far surpass the

[1] It is, however, still a matter of doubt whether Epicurus ever propounded these principles as directions for the objective employment of the understanding. If, indeed, they were nothing more than maxims for the speculative exercise of reason, he gives evidence therein of a more genuine philosophic spirit than any of the philosophers of antiquity. That, in the explanation of phenomena, we must proceed as if the field of inquiry had neither limits in space nor commencement in time; that we must be satisfied with the teaching of experience in reference to the material of which the world is composed; that we must not look for any other mode of the origination of events than that which is determined by the unalterable laws of nature; and finally, that we must not employ the hypothesis of a cause distinct from the world to account for a phenomenon or for the world itself—are principles for the extension of speculative philosophy, and the discovery of the true sources of the principles of morals, which, however little conformed to in the present day, are undoubtedly correct. At the same time, any one desirous of *ignoring*, in mere speculation, these dogmatical propositions, need not for that reason be accused of *denying* them.

intelligence and ability of the most practised thinkers. But in this, in truth, is to be found its real motive. For the common understanding thus finds itself in a situation where not even the most learned can have the advantage of it. If it understands little or nothing about these transcendental conceptions, no one can boast of understanding any more; and although it may not express itself in so scholastically correct a manner as others, it can busy itself with reasoning and arguments without end, wandering among mere ideas, about which one can always be very eloquent, because we know nothing about them; while, in the observation and investigation of nature, it would be forced to remain dumb and to confess its utter ignorance. Thus indolence and vanity form of themselves strong recommendations of these principles Besides, although it is a hard thing for a philosopher to assume a principle, of which he can give to himself no reasonable account, and still more to employ conceptions, the objective reality of which cannot be established, nothing is more usual with the common understanding. It wants something which will allow it to go to work with confidence. The difficulty of even comprehending a supposition does not disquiet it, because—not knowing what comprehending means—it never even thinks of the supposition it may be adopting as a principle; and regards as known, that with which it has become familiar from constant use. And, at last, all speculative interests disappear before the practical interests which it holds dear; and it fancies that it understands and knows what its necessities and hopes incite it to assume or to believe. Thus the empiricism of transcendentally idealizing reason is robbed of all popularity; and, however prejudicial it may be to the highest practical principles, there is no fear that it will ever pass the limits of the schools, or acquire any favour or influence in society or with the multitude.

Human reason is by nature architectonic. That is to say, it regards all cognitions as parts of a possible system, and hence accepts only such principles as at least do not incapacitate a cognition to which we may have attained from being placed along with others in a general system. But the propositions of the antithesis are of a character which renders the completion of an edifice of cognitions impossible. According to these, beyond one state or epoch of the world there is always to be found one more ancient; in every part always other parts themselves divisible; preceding every event another, the origin of which must itself be sought still higher; and everything in existence is conditioned, and still not dependent on an unconditioned and primal existence.

As, therefore, the antithesis will not concede the existence of a
first beginning which might be available as a foundation, a complete edifice of cognition, in the presence of such hypotheses, is
utterly impossible. Thus the architectonic interest of reason,
which requires a unity—not empirical, but *a priori* and rational,
forms a natural recommendation for the assertions of the thesis
in our antinomy.

But if any one could free himself entirely from all considerations
of interest, and weigh without partiality the assertions of reason,
attending only to their content, irrespective of the consequences
which follow from them; such a person, on the supposition that he
knew no other way out of the confusion than to settle the truth
of one or other of the conflicting doctrines, would live in a state
of continual hesitation.   To-day, he would feel convinced that the
human will is free; to-morrow, considering the indissoluble chain
of nature, he would look on freedom as a mere illusion and declare
*nature* to be all-in-all.   But, if he were called to action, the play
of the merely speculative reason would disappear like the shapes
of a dream, and practical interest would dictate his choice of
principles.   But, as it well befits a reflective and inquiring being
to devote certain periods of time to the examination of its own
reason—to divest itself of all partiality, and frankly to communi-
cate its observations for the judgment and opinion of others; so
no one can be blamed for, much less prevented from placing both
parties on their trial, with permission to defend themselves, free
from intimidation, before a sworn jury of equal condition with
themselves—the condition of weak and fallible men.


SECTION IV

*Of the Necessity Imposed upon Pure Reason of presenting a Solution
of its Transcendental Problem*

To avow an ability to solve all problems and to answer all questions,
would be a profession certain to convict any philosopher of extravagant boasting and self-conceit, and at once to destroy the confidence
that might otherwise have been reposed in him.   There are, however, sciences so constituted, that every question arising within
their sphere must necessarily be capable of receiving an answer
from the knowledge already possessed, for the answer must be
received from the same sources whence the question arose.   In
such sciences it is not allowable to excuse ourselves on the plea
of necessary and unavoidable ignorance; a solution is absolutely

requisite.  The rule of *right* and *wrong* must help us to the knowledge of what is right or wrong in all possible cases; otherwise, the
idea of obligation or duty would be utterly null, for we cannot have
any obligation to that *which we cannot know*.  On the other hand,
in our investigations of the phenomena of nature, much must
remain uncertain, and many questions continue insoluble; because
what we know of nature is far from being sufficient to explain all
the phenomena that are presented to our observation.  Now the
question is: Whether there is in transcendental philosophy any
question, relating to an object presented to pure reason, which is
unanswerable by this reason; and whether we must regard the
subject of the question as quite uncertain—so far as our knowledge extends, and must give it a place among those subjects, of
which we have just so much conception as is sufficient to enable
us to raise a question—faculty or materials failing us, however,
when we attempt an answer.

Now I maintain, that among all speculative cognition, the
peculiarity of transcendental philosophy is, that there is no
question, relating to an object presented to pure reason, which
is insoluble by this reason; and that the profession of unavoidable
ignorance—the problem being alleged to be beyond the reach of
our faculties—cannot free us from the obligation to present a
complete and satisfactory answer.  For the very conception, which
enables us to raise the question, must give us the power of answering
it; inasmuch as the object, as in the case of right and wrong, is
not to be discovered out of the conception.

But, in transcendental philosophy, it is only the cosmological
questions to which we can demand a satisfactory answer in relation
to the constitution of their object; and the philosopher is not
permitted to avail himself of the pretext of necessary ignorance
and impenetrable obscurity.  These questions relate solely to the
cosmological ideas.  For the object must be given in experience,
and the question relates to the adequateness of the object to an
idea.  If the object is transcendental, and therefore itself unknown; if the question, for example, is whether the object—the
something, the phenomenon of which (internal—in ourselves) is
thought—that is to say, the soul, is in itself a simple being; or
whether there is a cause of all things, which is absolutely necessary
—in such cases we are seeking for our idea an object, of which we
may confess that it is unknown to us, though we must not on
that account assert that it is impossible.[1]  The cosmological ideas

[1] The question, what is the constitution of a transcendental object? is
unanswerable—we are unable to say *what it is*; but we can perceive that the

alone possess the peculiarity, that we can presuppose the object of them and the empirical synthesis requisite for the conception of that object to be given; and the question, which arises from these ideas, relates merely to the progress of this synthesis, in so far as it must contain absolute totality—which, however, is not empirical, as it cannot be given in any experience. Now, as the question here is solely in regard to a thing as the object of a possible experience, and not as a thing in itself, the answer to the transcendental cosmological question need not be sought out of the idea, for the question does not regard an object in itself. The question in relation to a possible experience, is not, what can be given in an experience *in concreto*—but what is contained in the idea, to which the empirical synthesis must approximate. The question must therefore be capable of solution from the idea alone. For the idea is a creation of reason itself, which therefore cannot disclaim the obligation to answer or refer us to the unknown object.

It is not so extraordinary as it at first sight appears, that a science should demand and expect satisfactory answers to all the questions that may arise within its own sphere (*questiones domesticae*), although, up to a certain time, these answers may not have been discovered. There are, in addition to transcendental philosophy, only two pure sciences of reason; the one with a speculative, the other with a practical content—*pure mathematics* and *pure ethics*. Has any one ever heard it alleged that, from our complete and necessary ignorance of the conditions, it is *uncertain* what exact relation the diameter of a circle bears to the circle in rational or irrational numbers? By the former the sum cannot be given exactly, by the latter only approximately; and therefore we decide that the impossibility of a solution of the question is evident. Lambert presented us with a demonstration of this. In the general principles of morals there can be nothing uncertain, for the propositions are either utterly without meaning, or must originate solely in our rational conceptions. On the other hand,

*question* itself *is nothing*; because it does not relate to any object that can be presented to us. For this reason, we must consider all the questions raised in transcendental psychology as answerable, and as really answered; for they relate to the transcendental subject of all internal phenomena, which is not itself phenomenon, and consequently not given as an object, in which, moreover, none of the categories—and it is to them that the question is properly directed—find any conditions of its application. Here, therefore, is a case where no answer is the only proper answer. For a question regarding the constitution of a something which cannot be cogitated by any determined predicate—being completely beyond the sphere of objects and experience, is perfectly null and void.

there must be in physical science an infinite number of conjectures, which can never become certainties; because the phenomena of nature are not given as objects dependent on our conceptions. The key to the solution of such questions cannot therefore be found in our conceptions or in pure thought, but must lie without us, and for that reason is in many cases not to be discovered; and consequently a satisfactory explanation cannot be expected. The questions of transcendental analytic, which relate to the deduction of our pure cognition, are not to be regarded as of the same kind as those mentioned above; for we are not at present treating of the certainty of judgments in relation to the origin of our conceptions, but only of that certainty in relation to objects.

We cannot, therefore, escape the responsibility of at least a critical solution of the questions of reason, by complaints of the limited nature of our faculties, and the seemingly humble confession that it is beyond the power of our reason to decide, whether the world has existed from all eternity or had a beginning—whether it is infinitely extended, or enclosed within certain limits—whether anything in the world is simple, or whether everything must be capable of infinite divisibility—whether freedom can originate phenomena, or whether everything is absolutely dependent on the laws and order of nature—and, finally, whether there exists a being that is completely unconditioned and necessary, or whether the existence of everything is conditioned and consequently dependent on something external to itself, and therefore in its own nature contingent. For all these questions relate to an object, which can be given nowhere else than in thought. This object is the absolutely unconditioned totality of the synthesis of phenomena. If the conceptions in our minds do not assist us to some certain result in regard to these problems, we must not defend ourselves on the plea that the object itself remains hidden from and unknown to us. For no such thing or object can be given—it is not to be found out of the idea in our minds. We must seek the cause of our failure in our idea itself, which is an insoluble problem, and in regard to which we obstinately assume that there exists a real object corresponding and adequate to it. A clear explanation of the dialectic which lies in our conception, will very soon enable us to come to a satisfactory decision in regard to such a question.

The pretext, that we are unable to arrive at certainty in regard to these problems, may be met with this question, which requires at least a plain answer: From what source do the ideas originate, the solution of which involves you in such difficulties? Are you seeking for an explanation of certain phenomena; and do you expect these ideas to give you the principles or the rules of this explanation? Let it be granted, that all nature was laid open before you; that nothing was hid from your senses and your consciousness. Still, you could not cognize *in concreto* the object of your ideas in any experience. For what is demanded, is, not only this full and complete intuition, but also a complete synthesis and the consciousness of its absolute totality; and this is not possible by means of any empirical cognition. It follows that your question —your idea is by no means necessary for the explanation of any phenomenon; and the idea cannot have been in any sense given by the object itself. For such an object can never be presented to us, because it cannot be given by any possible experience. Whatever perceptions you may attain to, you are still surrounded by *conditions*—in space, or in time, and you cannot discover anything unconditioned; nor can you decide whether this unconditioned is to be placed in an absolute beginning of the synthesis, or in an absolute totality of the series without beginning. A whole, in the empirical signification of the term, is always merely comparative. The absolute whole of quantity (the universe), of division, of derivation, of the condition of existence, with the question—whether it is to be produced by finite or infinite synthesis, no possible experience can instruct us concerning. You will not, for example, be able to explain the phenomena of a body in the least degree better, whether you believe it to consist of simple, or of composite parts; for a simple phenomenon—and just as little an infinite series of composition—can never be presented to your perception. Phenomena require and admit of explanation, only in so far as the conditions of that explanation are given in perception; but the sum total of that which is given in phenomena, considered as an absolute whole, is itself a perception—and we cannot therefore seek for explanations of this whole beyond itself, in other perceptions. The explanation of this whole is the proper object of the transcendental problems of pure reason.

Although, therefore, the solution of these problems is unattainable through experience, we must not permit ourselves to say, that it is uncertain how the object of our inquiries is constituted. For the object is in our own mind, and cannot be discovered in experience; and we have only to take care that our thoughts are consistent with each other, and to avoid falling into the amphiboly of regarding our idea as a representation of an object empirically given, and therefore to be cognized according to the laws of experience. A dogmatical solution is therefore not only unsatisfactory, but impossible. The critical solution, which may be a perfectly certain one, does not consider the question objectively, but proceeds by inquiring into the basis of the cognition upon which the question rests.

## SECTION V

### Sceptical Exposition of the Cosmological Problems presented in the four Transcendental Ideas

WE should be quite willing to desist from the demand of a dogmatical answer to our questions, if we understood beforehand that, be the answer what it may, it would only serve to increase our ignorance, to throw us from one incomprehensibility into another, from one obscurity into another still greater, and perhaps lead us into irreconcilable contradictions. If a dogmatical affirmative or negative answer is demanded, is it at all prudent to set aside the probable grounds of a solution which lie before us, and to take into consideration what advantage we shall gain, if the answer is to favour the one side or the other? If it happens that in both cases the answer is mere nonsense, we have in this an irresistible summons to institute a critical investigation of the question, for the purpose of discovering whether it is based on a groundless presupposition, and relates to an idea, the falsity of which would be more easily exposed in its application and consequences, than in the mere representation of its content. This is the great utility of the sceptical mode of treating the questions addressed by pure reason to itself. By this method we easily rid ourselves of the confusions of dogmatism, and establish in its place a temperate criticism, which, as a genuine cathartic, will successfully remove the presumptuous notions of philosophy and their consequence —the vain pretension to universal science.

If, then, I could understand the nature of a cosmological idea, and perceive, before I entered on the discussion of the subject at all, that, whatever side of the question regarding the unconditioned of the regressive synthesis of phenomena it favoured, it must either be *too great* or *too small* for every *conception of the understanding*—I would be able to comprehend how the idea, which relates to an object of experience—an experience which must be adequate to and in accordance with a possible conception of the understanding—must be completely void and without significance, inasmuch as its object is inadequate, consider it as we may. And this is actually the case with all cosmological conceptions, which, for the reason above mentioned, involve reason, so long as it remains attached to them, in an unavoidable antinomy. For suppose:

*First*, that *the world has no beginning*—in this case it is too large for our conception; for this conception, which consists in a successive regress, cannot overtake the whole eternity that has elapsed. Grant that *it has a beginning*, it is then too small for the conception of the understanding. For, as a beginning presupposes a time preceding, it cannot be unconditioned; and the law of the empirical employment of the understanding imposes the necessity of looking for a higher condition of time; and the world is, therefore, evidently too small for this law.

The same is the case with the double answer to the question regarding the extent, in space, of the world. For, if it is *infinite* and unlimited, it must be *too large* for every possible empirical conception. If it is *finite* and limited, we have a right to ask— what determines these limits? Void space is not a self-subsistent correlate of things, and cannot be a final condition—and still less an empirical condition, forming a part of a possible experience. For how can we have any experience or perception of an absolute void? But the absolute totality of the empirical synthesis requires that the unconditioned be an empirical conception. Consequently, a finite world is *too small* for our conception.

*Second*, if every phenomenon (matter) in space consists·of an *infinite number of parts*, the regress of the division is always too great for our conception; and if the *division* of space must *cease* with some member of the division (the simple), it is too small for the idea of the unconditioned. For the member at which we have discontinued our division still admits a regress to many more parts contained in the object.

*Third*, suppose that every event in the world happens in accordance with the laws of nature; the causality of a cause must itself be an event, and necessitates a regress to a still higher cause, and consequently the unceasing prolongation of the series of conditions *a parte priori*. Operative nature is therefore too large for every conception we can form in the synthesis of cosmical events.

If we admit the existence of *spontaneously* produced events, that is, of *free* agency, we are driven, in our search for sufficient reasons, on an unavoidable law of nature, and are compelled to appeal to the empirical law of causality, and we find that any such totality of connection in our synthesis is too small for our necessary empirical conception.

*Fourthly,* if we assume the existence of an *absolutely necessary being*—whether it be the world or something in the world, or the cause of the world; we must place it in a time at an infinite distance from any given moment; for, otherwise, it must be dependent on some other and higher existence. Such an existence is, in this case, too large for our empirical conception, and unattainable by the continued regress of any synthesis.

But if we believe that everything in the world—be it condition or conditioned—is *contingent*; every given existence is too small for our conception. For in this case we are compelled to seek for some other existence upon which the former depends.

We have said that in all these cases the cosmological idea is either too great or too small for the empirical regress in a synthesis, and consequently for every possible conception of the understanding. Why did we not express ourselves in a manner exactly the reverse of this, and, instead of accusing the cosmological idea of overstepping or of falling short of its true aim—possible experience, say that, in the first case, the empirical conception is always too small for the idea, and in the second too great, and thus attach the blame of these contradictions to the empirical regress? The reason is this. Possible experience can alone give reality to our conceptions; without it a conception is merely an idea, without truth or relation to an object. Hence a possible empirical conception must be the standard by which we are to judge whether an idea is anything more than an idea and fiction of thought, or whether it relates to an object in the world. If we say of a thing that in relation to some other thing it is too large or too small, the former is considered as existing for the sake of the latter, and requiring to be adapted to it. Among the trivial subjects of discussion in the old schools of dialectics was this question: If a ball cannot pass through a hole, shall we say that the ball is too large or the hole too small? In this case it is indifferent what expression we employ; for we do not know which exists for the sake of the other. On the other hand, we cannot say—the man is too long for his coat, but—the coat is too short for the man.

We are thus led to the well-founded suspicion, that the cosmological ideas, and all the conflicting sophistical assertions connected with them, are based upon a false and fictitious conception of the mode in which the object of these ideas is presented to us; and this suspicion will probably direct us how to expose the illusion that has so long led us astray from the truth.

## Section VI

*Transcendental Idealism as the Key to the Solution of Pure Cosmological Dialectic*

In the transcendental aesthetic we proved, that everything intuited in space and time—all objects of a possible experience, are nothing but phenomena, that is, mere representations; and that these, as presented to us—as extended bodies, or as series of changes—have no self-subsistent existence apart from human thought. This doctrine I call *Transcendental Idealism.*[1] The realist in the transcendental sense regards these modifications of our sensibility—these mere representations, as things subsisting in themselves.

It would be unjust to accuse us of holding the long-decried theory of empirical idealism, which, while admitting the reality of space, denies, or at least doubts, the existence of bodies extended in it, and thus leaves us without a sufficient criterion of reality and illusion. The supporters of this theory find no difficulty in admitting the reality of the phenomena of the internal sense in time; nay, they go the length of maintaining that this internal experience is of itself a sufficient proof of the real existence of its object as a thing in itself.

Transcendental idealism allows that the objects of external intuition—as intuited in space, and all changes in time—as represented by the internal sense, are real. For, as space is the form of that intuition which we call external, and without objects in space, no empirical representation could be given us; we can and ought to regard extended bodies in it as real. The case is the same with representations in time. But time and space, with all phenomena therein, are not in themselves *things*. They are nothing but representations, and cannot exist out of and apart from the mind. Nay, the sensuous internal intuition of the mind (as the object of consciousness), the determination of which is represented by the succession of different states in time, is not the real, proper self, as it exists in itself—not the transcendental subject, but only a phenomenon, which is presented to the sensibility of this, to us, unknown being. This internal phenomenon cannot be

---

[1] I have elsewhere termed this theory *formal* idealism, to distinguish it from *material* idealism, which doubts or denies the existence of external things. To avoid ambiguity, it seems advisable in many cases to employ this term instead of that mentioned in the text.

admitted to be a self-subsisting thing; for its condition is time, and time cannot be the condition of a thing in itself. But the empirical truth of phenomena in space and time is guaranteed beyond the possibility of doubt, and sufficiently distinguished from the illusion of dreams or fancy—although both have a proper and thorough connection in an experience according to empirical laws. The objects of experience then are not things in themselves,[1] but are given only in experience, and have no existence apart from and independently of experience. That there may be inhabitants in the moon, although no one has ever observed them, must certainly be admitted; but this assertion means only, that we may in the possible progress of experience discover them at some future time. For that, which stands in connection with a perception according to the laws of the progress of experience, is real. They are therefore really existent, if they stand in empirical connection with my actual or real consciousness, although they are not in themselves real, that is, apart from the progress of experience.

There is nothing actually given—we can be conscious of nothing as real, except a perception and the empirical progression from it to other possible perceptions. For phenomena, as mere representations, are real only in perception; and perception is, in fact, nothing but the reality of an empirical representation, that is, a phenomenon. To call a phenomenon a real thing prior to perception, means either that we must meet with this phenomenon in the progress of experience, or it means nothing at all. For I can say only of a thing in itself that it exists without relation to the senses and experience. But we are speaking here merely of phenomena in space and time, both of which are determinations of sensibility, and not of things in themselves. It follows that phenomena are not things in themselves, but are mere representations, which, if not given in us—in perception, are non-existent.

The faculty of sensuous intuition is properly a receptivity—a capacity of being affected in a certain manner by representations, the relation of which to each other is a pure intuition of space and time—the pure forms of sensibility. These representations, in so far as they are connected and determinable in this relation (in space and time) according to laws of the unity of experience, are called *objects*. The non-sensuous cause of these representations is completely unknown to us, and hence cannot be intuited as an object. For such an object could not be represented either in space or in time; and without these conditions intuition or representation

[1] Dinge an sich, Sachen an sich.

is impossible. We may, at the same time, term the non sensuous cause of phenomena the transcendental object — but merely as a mental correlate to sensibility, considered as a receptivity. To this transcendental object we may attribute the whole connection and extent of our possible perceptions, and say that it is given and exists in itself prior to all experience. But the phenomena, corresponding to it, are not given as things in themselves, but in experience alone. For they are mere representations, receiving from perceptions alone significance and relation to a real object, under the condition that this or that perception—indicating an object—is in complete connection with all others in accordance with the rules of the unity of experience. Thus we can say: the things that really existed in past time, are given in the transcendental object of experience. But these are to me real objects, only in so far as I can represent to my own mind, that a regressive series of possible perceptions—following the indications of history, or the footsteps of cause and effect—in accordance with empirical laws—that, in one word, the course of the world conducts us to an elapsed series of time as the condition of the present time. This series in past time is represented as real, not in itself, but only in connection with a possible experience. Thus, when I say that certain events occurred in past time, I merely assert the possibility of prolonging the chain of experience, from the present perception, upwards to the conditions that determine it according to time.

If I represent to myself all objects existing in all space and time, I do not thereby place these in space and time prior to all experience; on the contrary, such a representation is nothing more than the notion of a possible experience, in its absolute completeness. In experience alone are those objects, which are nothing but representations, given. But, when I say, they existed prior to my experience: this means only that I must begin with the perception present to me, and follow the track indicated, until I discover them in some part or region of experience. The cause of the empirical condition of this progression—and consequently at what member therein I must stop, and at what point in the regress I am to find this member—is transcendental, and hence necessarily incognizable. But with this we have not to do; our concern is only with the law of progression in experience, in which objects, that is, phenomena, are given. It is a matter of indifference, whether I say—I may in the progress of experience discover stars, at a hundred times greater distance than the most distant of those now visible, or—stars at this distance may be met in space, although no one has, or ever will discover them.   For, if they are given as things in themselves, without any relation to possible experience, they are for me non-existent, consequently, are not objects, for they are not contained in the regressive series of experience.   But, if these phenomena must be employed in the construction or support of the cosmo-logical idea of an absolute whole—and, when we are discussing a question that oversteps the limits of possible experience, the proper distinction of the different theories of the reality of sensuous objects is of great importance, in order to avoid the illusion which must necessarily arise from the misinterpretation of our empirical conceptions.

### Section VII

*Critical Solution of the Cosmological Problem*

The antinomy of pure reason is based upon the following dialectical argument: If that which is conditioned is given, the whole series of its conditions is also given; but sensuous objects are given as conditioned; consequently . . . This syllogism, the major of which seems so natural and evident, introduces as many cosmo-logical ideas as there are different kinds of conditions in the syn-thesis of phenomena, in so far as these conditions constitute a series.   These ideas require absolute totality in the series, and thus place reason in inextricable embarrassment.   Before pro-ceeding to expose the fallacy in this dialectical argument, it will be necessary to have a correct understanding of certain conceptions that appear in it.

In the first place, the following proposition is evident, and indubitably certain: If the conditioned is given, a regress in the series of all its conditions is thereby imperatively *required*.   For the very conception of a conditioned is a conception of something related to a condition, and, if this condition is itself conditioned, to another condition—and so on through all the members of the series.   This proposition is, therefore, analytical, and has nothing to fear from transcendental criticism.   It is a logical postulate of reason: to pursue, as far as possible, the connection of a conception with its conditions.

If, in the second place, both the conditioned and the condition are things in themselves, and if the former is given, not only is the regress to the latter requisite, but the latter is really *given with* the former.   Now, as this is true of all the members of the series, the entire series of conditions, and with them the unconditioned, is at the same time given in the very fact of the conditioned, the existence of which is possible only in and through that series, being given. In this case, the synthesis of the conditioned with its condition, is a synthesis of the understanding merely, which represents things *as they are*, without regarding whether and how we can cognize them. But if I have to do with phenomena, which, in their character of mere representations, are not given, if I do not attain to a cognition of them (in other words, to themselves, for they are nothing more than empirical cognitions), I am not entitled to say: If the conditioned is given, all its conditions (as phenomena) are also given. I cannot, therefore, from the fact of a conditioned being given, infer the absolute totality of the series of its conditions. For phenomena are nothing but an empirical synthesis in apprehension or perception, and are therefore given only in it. Now, in speaking of phenomena, it does not follow, that, if the conditioned is given, the synthesis which constitutes its empirical condition is also thereby given and presupposed; such a synthesis can be established only by an actual regress in the series of conditions. But we are entitled to say in this case: that a *regress* to the conditions of a conditioned, in other words, that a continuous empirical synthesis is enjoined; that, if the conditions are not *given*, they are at least *required*; and that we are certain to discover the conditions in this regress.

We can now see that the major in the above cosmological syllogism, takes the conditioned in the transcendental signification which it has in the pure category, while the minor speaks of it in the empirical signification which it has in the category as applied to phenomena. There is, therefore, a dialectical fallacy in the syllogism—a *sophisma figurae dictionis*. But this fallacy is not a consciously devised one, but a perfectly natural illusion of the common reason of man. For, when a thing is given as conditioned, we presuppose in the major its conditions and their series, unperceived, as it were, and unseen; because this is nothing more than the logical requirement of complete and satisfactory premisses for a given conclusion. In this case, time is altogether left out in the connection of the conditioned with the condition; they are supposed to be given in themselves, and *contemporaneously*. It is, moreover, just as natural to regard phenomena (in the minor) as things in themselves and as objects presented to the pure understanding, as in the major, in which complete abstraction was made of all conditions of intuition. But it is under these conditions alone that objects are given. Now we overlooked a remarkable distinction between the conceptions. The synthesis of the conditioned with its condition, and the complete series of the latter (in the major) are not limited by time, and do not contain the conception of succession. On the contrary, the empirical synthesis, and the series of conditions in the phenomenal world—subsumed in the minor—are necessarily successive, and given in time alone. It follows that I cannot presuppose in the minor, as I did in the major, the absolute *totality* of the synthesis and of the series therein represented; for in the major all the members of the series are given as things in themselves—without any limitations or conditions of time, while in the minor they are possible only in and through a successive regress, which cannot exist, except it be actually carried into execution in the world of phenomena.

After this proof of the viciousness of the argument commonly employed in maintaining cosmological assertions, both parties may now be justly dismissed, as advancing claims without grounds or title. But the process has not been ended, by convincing them that one or both were in the wrong, and had maintained an assertion which was without valid grounds of proof. Nothing seems to be clearer than that, if one maintains: the world has a beginning, and another: the world has no beginning, one of the two must be right. But it is likewise clear, that, if the evidence on both sides is equal, it is impossible to discover on what side the truth lies; and the controversy continues, although the parties have been recommended to peace before the tribunal of reason. There remains, then, no other means of settling the question than to convince the parties, who refute each other with such conclusiveness and ability, that they are disputing about nothing, and that a transcendental illusion has been mocking them with visions of reality where there is none. This mode of adjusting a dispute which cannot be decided upon its own merits, we shall now proceed to lay before our readers.

———

Zeno of Elea, a subtle dialectician, was severely reprimanded by Plato as a sophist, who, merely from the base motive of exhibiting his skill in discussion, maintained and subverted the same proposition by arguments as powerful and convincing on the one side as on the other. He maintained, for example, that God (who was probably nothing more, in his view, than the world) is neither finite nor infinite, neither in motion nor in rest, neither similar nor dissimilar to any other thing. It seemed to those philosophers who criticized his mode of discussion, that his purpose was to deny completely both of two self-contradictory propositions

—which is absurd. But I cannot believe that there is any justice in this accusation. The first of these propositions I shall presently consider in a more detailed manner. With regard to the others, if by the word *God* he understood merely the *Universe*, his meaning must have been, that it cannot be permanently present in one place—that is, at rest, nor be capable of changing its place—that is, of moving, because all places are in the universe, and the universe itself is, therefore, in no place. Again, if the universe contains in itself everything that exists, it cannot be similar or dissimilar to any *other* thing, because there is, in fact, no *other* thing with which it can be compared. If two opposite judgments presuppose a contingent impossible, or arbitrary condition, both—in spite of their opposition (which is, however, not properly or really a contradiction)—fall away; because the condition, which ensured the validity of both, has itself disappeared.

If we say: every body has either a good or a bad smell, we have omitted a third possible judgment—it has no smell at all; and thus both conflicting statements may be false. If we say: it is either good-smelling or not good-smelling (*vel suaveolens vel non-suaveolens*), both judgments are contradictorily opposed; and the contradictory opposite of the former judgment—some bodies are not good-smelling—embraces also those bodies which have no smell at all. In the preceding pair of opposed judgments (*per disparata*), the contingent condition of the conception of body (smell) attached to both conflicting statements, instead of having been omitted in the latter, which is consequently not the contradictory opposite of the former.

If, accordingly, we say: the world is either infinite in extension, or it is not infinite (*non est infinitus*); and if the former proposition is false, its contradictory opposite—the world is not infinite, must be true. And thus I should deny the existence of an infinite, without, however, affirming the existence of a finite world. But if we construct our proposition thus—the world is either infinite or finite (non-infinite), both statements may be false. For, in this case, we consider the world as *per se* determined in regard to quantity, and while, in the one judgment, we deny its infinite and consequently, perhaps, its independent existence; in the other, we append to the world, regarded as a thing in itself, a certain determination—that of finitude; and the latter may be false as well as the former, if the world is not given as a *thing in itself*, and thus neither as finite nor as infinite in quantity. This kind of opposition I may be allowed to term *dialectical*; that of contra-dictories may be called *analytical opposition*. Thus then, of two dialectically opposed judgments both may be false, from the fact, that the one is not a mere contradictory of the other, but actually enounces more than is requisite for a full and complete contradiction.

When we regard the two propositions—the world is infinite in quantity, and, the world is finite in quantity, as contradictory opposites, we are assuming that the world—the complete series of phenomena—is a thing in itself. For it remains as a permanent quantity, whether I deny the infinite or the finite regress in the series of its phenomena. But if we dismiss this assumption—this transcendental illusion, and deny that it is a thing in itself, the contradictory opposition is metamorphosed into a merely dialectical one; and the world, as not existing in itself—independently of the regressive series of my representations, exists in like manner neither as a whole which is infinite nor as a whole which is finite in itself. The universe exists for me only in the empirical regress of the series of phenomena, and not *per se*. If, then, it is always conditioned, it is never given completely or as a whole; and it is, therefore, not an unconditioned whole, and does not exist as such, either with an infinite, or with a finite quantity.

What we have here said of the first cosmological idea—that of the absolute totality of quantity in phenomena, applies also to the others. The series of conditions is discoverable only in the regressive synthesis itself, and not in the phenomenon considered as a thing in itself—given prior to all regress. Hence I am compelled to say: the aggregate of parts in a given phenomenon is in itself neither finite nor infinite; and these parts are given only in the regressive synthesis of decomposition—a synthesis which is never given in absolute *completeness*, either as finite, or as infinite. The same is the case with the series of subordinated causes, or of the conditioned up to the unconditioned and necessary existence, which can never be regarded as in itself, and in its totality, either as finite or as infinite; because, as a series of subordinate representations, it subsists only in the dynamical regress, and cannot be regarded as existing previously to this regress, or as a self-subsistent series of things.

Thus the antinomy of pure reason in its cosmological ideas disappears. For the above demonstration has established the fact that it is merely the product of a dialectical and illusory opposition, which arises from the application of the idea of absolute totality—admissible only as a condition of things in themselves, to phenomena, which exist only in our representations, and—when constituting a series—in a successive regress. This antinomy of reason may, however, be really profitable to our speculative interests, not in the way of contributing any dogmatical addition, but as presenting to us another material support in our critical investigations. For it furnishes us with an indirect proof of the transcendental ideality of phenomena, if our minds were not completely satisfied with the direct proof set forth in the Transcendental Aesthetic. The proof would proceed in the following dilemma. If the world is a whole existing in itself, it must be either finite or infinite. But it is neither finite nor infinite—as has been shown, on the one side, by the thesis, on the other, by the antithesis. Therefore the world—the content of all phenomena —is not a whole existing in itself. It follows that phenomena are nothing, apart from our representations. And this is what we mean by transcendental ideality.

This remark is of some importance. It enables us to see that the proofs of the fourfold antinomy are not mere sophistries—are not fallacious, but grounded on the nature of reason, and valid— under the supposition that phenomena are things in themselves. The opposition of the judgments which follow makes it evident that a fallacy lay in the initial supposition, and thus helps us to discover the true constitution of objects of sense. This transcendental dialectic does not favour scepticism, although it presents us with a triumphant demonstration of the advantages of the sceptical method, the great utility of which is apparent in the antinomy, where the arguments of reason were allowed to confront each other in undiminished force. And although the result of these conflicts of reason is not what we expected—although we have obtained no positive dogmatical addition to metaphysical science, we have still reaped a great advantage in the correction of our judgments on these subjects of thought.

## Section VIII

### Regulative Principle of Pure Reason in relation to the Cosmological Ideas

The cosmological principle of totality could not give us any certain knowledge in regard to the *maximum* in the series of conditions in the world of sense, considered as a thing in itself. The actual regress in the series is the only means of approaching this maximum. This principle of pure reason, therefore, may still be considered as valid—not as an *axiom* enabling us to cogitate totality in the object as actual, but as a *problem* for the understanding, which requires it to institute and to continue, in conformity with the idea of totality in the mind, the regress in the series of the conditions of a given conditioned. For in the world of sense, that is, in space and time, every condition which we discover in our investigation of phenomena is itself conditioned; because sensuous objects are not things in themselves (in which case an absolutely unconditioned might be reached in the progress of cognition), but are merely empirical representations, the conditions of which must always be found in intuition. The principle of reason is therefore properly a mere rule—prescribing a regress in the series of conditions for given phenomena, and prohibiting any pause or rest on an absolutely unconditioned. It is, therefore, not a principle of the possibility of experience or of the empirical cognition of sensuous objects— consequently not a principle of the understanding; for every experience is confined within certain proper limits determined by the given intuition. Still less is it a *constitutive principle* of reason authorizing us to extend our conception of the sensuous world beyond all possible experience. It is merely a principle for the enlargement and extension of experience as far as is possible for human faculties. It forbids us to consider any empirical limits as absolute. It is, hence, a principle of reason, which, as a *rule*, dictates how we ought to proceed in our empirical regress, but is unable to *anticipate* or indicate prior to the empirical regress what is given in the object itself. I have termed it for this reason a *regulative* principle of reason; while the principle of the absolute totality of the series of conditions, as existing in itself and given in the object, is a constitutive cosmological principle. This distinction will at once demonstrate the falsehood of the constitutive principle, and prevent us from attributing (by a transcendental *subreptio*) objective reality to an idea, which is valid only as a rule.

In order to understand the proper meaning of this rule of pure reason, we must notice first, that it cannot tell us *what the object is*, but only *how the empirical regress is to be proceeded with* in order to attain to the complete conception of the object. If it gave us any information in respect to the former statement, it would be a constitutive principle—a principle impossible from the nature of pure reason. It will not therefore enable us to establish any such conclusions as—the series of conditions for a given conditioned is in itself finite, or, it is infinite. For, in this case, we should be cogitating in the mere idea of absolute totality, an object which is not and cannot be given in experience; inasmuch as we should be attributing a reality objective and independent of the empirical synthesis, to a series of phenomena. This idea of reason cannot then be regarded as valid—except as a rule for the regressive synthesis in the series of conditions, according to which we must proceed from the conditioned, through all intermediate and subordinate conditions, up to the unconditioned; although this goal is unattained and unattainable. For the absolutely unconditioned cannot be discovered in the sphere of experience.

We now proceed to determine clearly our notion of a synthesis which can never be complete. There are two terms commonly employed for this purpose. These terms are regarded as expressions of different and distinguishable notions, although the ground of the distinction has never been clearly exposed. The term employed by the mathematicians is *progressus in infinitum*. The philosophers prefer the expression *progressus in indefinitum*. Without detaining the reader with an examination of the reasons for such a distinction, or with remarks on the right or wrong use of the terms, I shall endeavour clearly to determine these conceptions, so far as is necessary for the purpose of this *Critique*.

We may, with propriety, say of a straight line, that it may be produced to infinity. In this case the distinction between a *progressus in infinitum* and a *progressus in indefinitum* is a mere piece of subtlety. For, although when we say, produce a straight line—it is more correct to say *in indefinitum* than *in infinitum*; because the former means, produce it as far as you *please*, the second, you *must* not cease to produce it; the expression *in infinitum* is, when we are speaking of the *power* to do it, perfectly correct, for we can always make it longer if we please—on to infinity. And this remark holds good in all cases, when we speak of a *progressus*, that is, an advancement from the condition to the conditioned; this possible advancement always proceeds to infinity. We may proceed from a given pair in the descending line of generation from father to son, and cogitate a never-ending line of descendants from it. For in such a case reason does not demand absolute totality in the series, because it does not presuppose it as a condition and as given (*datum*), but merely as conditioned, and as capable of being given (*dabile*).

Very different is the case with the problem—how far the regress, which ascends from the given conditioned to the conditions, must extend; whether I can say—it is a *regress in infinitum*, or only *in indefinitum*; and whether, for example, setting out from the human beings at present alive in the world, I may ascend in the series of their ancestors, *in infinitum*—or whether all that can be said is, that so far as I have proceeded, I have discovered no empirical ground for considering the series limited, so that I am justified, and indeed, compelled to search for ancestors still further back, although I am not obliged by the idea of reason to pre suppose them.

My answer to this question is: If the series is given in empirical intuition as a whole, the regress in the series of its internal conditions proceeds *in infinitum*; but, if only one member of the series is given, from which the regress is to proceed to absolute totality, the regress is possible only *in indefinitum*. For example, the division of a portion of matter given within certain limits—of a body, that is—proceeds *in infinitum*. For, as the condition of this whole is its part, and the condition of the part a part of the part, and so on, and as in this regress of decomposition an unconditioned indivisible member of the series of conditions is not to be found; there are no reasons or grounds in experience for stopping in the division, but, on the contrary, the more remote members of the division are actually and empirically given prior to this division. That is to say, the division proceeds to infinity. On the other hand, the series of ancestors of any given human being is not given, in its absolute totality, in any experience, and yet the regress proceeds from every genealogical member of this series to one still higher, and does not meet with any empirical limit presenting an absolutely unconditioned member of the series. But as the members of such a series are not contained in the empirical intuition of the whole, prior to the regress, this regress does not proceed to infinity, but only *in indefinitum*, that is, we are called upon to discover other and higher members, which are themselves always conditioned.

In neither case—the *regressus in infinitum*, nor the *regressus in indefinitum*, is the series of conditions to be considered as actually infinite in the object itself. This might be true of things in themselves, but it cannot be asserted of phenomena, which, as conditions of each other, are only given in the empirical regress itself. Hence, the question no longer is, What is the quantity of this series of conditions in itself—is it finite or infinite? for it is nothing in itself; but, How is the empirical regress to be commenced, and how far ought we to proceed with it? And here a signal distinction in the application of this rule becomes apparent. If the whole is given empirically, it is possible to recede in the series of its internal conditions *to infinity*. But if the whole is not given, and can only be given by and through the empirical regress, I can only say—it is *possible to infinity*,[1] to proceed to still higher conditions in the

[1] Kant's meaning is: Infinity, in the first case, is a quality, or may be predicated, of the *regress*; while in the second case, it is only to be predicated of the *possibility* of the regress.—*Tr.*

series. In the first case, I am justified in asserting that more members are empirically given in the object than I attain to in the regress (of decomposition). In the second case, I am justified only in saying, that I can always proceed further in the regress, because no member of the series is given as absolutely conditioned, and thus a higher member is possible, and an inquiry with regard to it is necessary. In the one case it is necessary to *find* other members of the series, in the other it is necessary to *inquire* for others, inasmuch as experience presents no absolute limitation of the regress. For, either you do not possess a perception which absolutely limits your empirical regress, and in this case the regress cannot be regarded as complete; or, you do possess such a limitative perception, in which case it is not a part of your series (for that which *limits* must be distinct from that which is *limited* by it), and it is incumbent on you to continue your regress up to this condition, and so on.

These remarks will be placed in their proper light by their application in the following section.


## Section IX

### *Of the Empirical Use of the Regulative Principle of Reason with regard to the Cosmological Ideas*

We have shown that no transcendental use can be made either of the conceptions of reason or of understanding. We have shown, likewise, that the demand of absolute totality in the series of conditions in the world of sense arises from a transcendental employment of reason, resting on the opinion that phenomena are to be regarded as things in themselves. It follows that we are not required to answer the question respecting the absolute quantity of a series—whether it is *in itself* limited or unlimited. We are only called upon to determine how far we must proceed in the empirical regress from condition to condition, in order to discover, in conformity with the rule of reason, a full and correct answer to the questions proposed by reason itself.

This principle of reason is hence valid only as a rule for the *extension* of a possible experience—its invalidity as a principle constitutive of phenomena in themselves having been sufficiently demonstrated. And thus, too, the antinomial conflict of reason with itself is completely put an end to; inasmuch as we have not only presented a critical solution of the fallacy lurking in the opposite statements of reason, but have shown the true meaning of the ideas which gave rise to these statements. The *dialectical* principle of reason has, therefore, been changed into a *doctrinal* principle. But in fact, if this principle, in the subjective signification which we have shown to be its only true sense, may be guaranteed as a principle of the unceasing extension of the employment of our understanding, its influence and value are just as great as if it were an axiom for the *a priori* determination of objects. For such an axiom could not exert a stronger influence on the extension and rectification of our knowledge, otherwise than by procuring for the principles of the understanding the most widely expanded employment in the field of experience.

## I

### Solution of the Cosmological Idea of the Totality of the Composition of Phenomena in the Universe

Here, as well as in the case of the other cosmological problems, the ground of the regulative principle of reason is the proposition, that in our empirical regress *no experience of an absolute limit,* and consequently no experience of a condition, which is itself *absolutely unconditioned,* is discoverable. And the truth of this proposition itself rests upon the consideration, that such an experience must represent to us phenomena as limited by nothing or the mere void, on which our continued regress by means of perception must abut—which is impossible.

Now this proposition, which declares that every condition attained in the empirical regress must itself be considered empirically conditioned, contains the rule *in terminis,* which requires me, to whatever extent I may have proceeded in the ascending series, always to look for some higher member in the series—whether this member is to become known to me through experience, or not.

Nothing further is necessary, then, for the solution of the first cosmological problem, than to decide, whether, in the regress to the unconditioned quantity of the universe (as regards space and time), this never-limited ascent ought to be called a *regressus in infinitum* or *in indefinitum.*

The general representation which we form in our minds of the series of all past states or conditions of the world, or of all the things which at present exist in it, is itself nothing more than a *possible* empirical regress, which is cogitated—although in an undetermined manner—in the mind, and which gives rise to the

conception of a series of conditions for a given object.[1]   Now I have
a conception of the universe, but not an intuition—that is, not an
intuition of it as a whole.   Thus I cannot infer the magnitude of
the regress from the quantity or magnitude of the world, and
determine the former by means of the latter; on the contrary,
I must first of all form a conception of the quantity or magnitude
of the world from the magnitude of the empirical regress.   But of
this regress I know nothing more, than that I ought to proceed
from every given member of the series of conditions to one still
higher.   But the quantity of the universe is not thereby determined, and we cannot affirm that this regress proceeds *in infinitum*.
Such an affirmation would *anticipate* the members of the series
which have not yet been reached, and represent the number of
them as beyond the grasp of any empirical synthesis; it would
consequently *determine* the cosmical quantity prior to the regress
(although only in a negative manner)—which is impossible.   For
the world is not given in its totality in any intuition: consequently,
its quantity cannot be given prior to the regress.   It follows that
we are unable to make any declaration respecting the cosmical
quantity in itself—not even that the regress in it is a regress *in
infinitum*; we must only endeavour to attain to a conception of the
quantity of the universe, in conformity with the rule which determines the empirical regress in it.   But this rule merely requires
us never to admit an absolute limit to our series—how far soever
we may have proceeded in it, but always, on the contrary, to
subordinate every phenomenon to some other as its condition,
and consequently to proceed to this higher phenomenon.   Such
a regress is, therefore, the *regressus in indefinitum*, which, as not
determining a quantity in the object, is clearly distinguishable
from the *regressus in infinitum*.

It follows from what we have said that we are not justified in
declaring the world to be infinite in space, or as regards past time.
For this conception of an infinite given quantity is empirical; but
we cannot apply the conception of an infinite quantity to the
world as an object of the senses.   I cannot say, the regress from a
given perception to everything limited either in space or time,
proceeds *in infinitum*—for this presupposes an infinite cosmical
quantity; neither can I say, it is *finite*—for an absolute limit is

[1] The cosmical series can neither be greater nor smaller than the possible
empirical regress, upon which its conception is based.   And as this regress
cannot be a determinate infinite regress, still less a determinate finite
(absolutely limited), it is evident, that we cannot regard the world as either
finite or infinite, because the regress, which gives us the representation of the
world, is neither finite nor infinite.

likewise impossible in experience. It follows that I am not entitled to make any assertion at all respecting the whole object of experience—the world of sense; I must limit my declarations to the rule, according to which experience or empirical knowledge is to be attained.

To the question, therefore, respecting the cosmical quantity, the first and negative answer is: The world has no beginning in time, and no absolute limit in space.

For, in the contrary case, it would be limited by a void time on the one hand, and by a void space on the other. Now, since the world, as a phenomenon, cannot be thus limited in itself—for a phenomenon is not a thing in itself; it must be possible for us to have a perception of this limitation by a void time and a void space. But such a perception—such an experience is impossible; because it has no content. Consequently, an absolute cosmical limit is empirically, and therefore absolutely, impossible.[1]

From this follows the *affirmative* answer: The regress in the series of phenomena—as a determination of the cosmical quantity, proceeds *in indefinitum*. This is equivalent to saying—the world of sense has no absolute quantity, but the empirical regress (through which alone the world of sense is presented to us on the side of its conditions) rests upon a rule, which requires it to proceed from every member of the series—as conditioned, to one still more remote (whether through personal experience, or by means of history, or the chain of cause and effect), and not to cease at any point in this extension of the possible empirical employment of the understanding. And this is the proper and only use which reason can make of its principles.

The above rule does not prescribe an unceasing regress in one kind of phenomena. It does not, for example, forbid us, in our ascent from an individual human being through the line of his ancestors, to expect that we shall discover at some point of the regress a primeval pair, or to admit, in the series of heavenly bodies, a sun at the farthest possible distance from some centre. All that it demands is a perpetual progress from phenomena to phenomena, even although an actual perception is not presented by them (as in the case of our perceptions being so weak, as that we

---

[1] The reader will remark that the proof presented above is very different from the dogmatical demonstration given in the antithesis of the first antinomy. In that demonstration, it was taken for granted that the world is a thing in itself—given in its totality prior to all regress, and a determined position in space and time was denied to it—if it was not considered as occupying all time and all space. Hence our conclusion differed from that given above; for we inferred in the antithesis the actual infinity of the world.

are unable to become conscious of them), since they, nevertheless, belong to possible experience.

Every beginning is in time, and all limits to extension are in space. But space and time are in the world of sense. Consequently phenomena *in the world* are conditionally limited, but *the world* itself is not limited, either conditionally or unconditionally.

For this reason, and because neither the world nor the cosmical series of conditions to a given conditioned can be *completely given*, our conception of the cosmical quantity is given only in and through the regress and not prior to it—in a collective intuition. But the regress itself is really nothing more than the *determining* of the cosmical quantity, and cannot therefore give us any *determined* conception of it—still less a conception of a quantity which is, in relation to a certain standard, infinite. The regress does not, therefore, proceed to infinity (an infinity given), but only to an indefinite extent, for the purpose of presenting to us a quantity —realized only in and through the regress itself.

## II

### *Solution of the Cosmological Idea of the Totality of the Division of a Whole given in Intuition*

When I divide a whole which is given in intuition, I proceed from a conditioned to its conditions. The division of the parts of the whole (*subdivisio* or *decompositio*) is a regress in the series of these conditions. The absolute totality of this series would be actually attained and given to the mind, if the regress could arrive at *simple* parts. But if all the parts in a continuous decomposition are themselves divisible, the division, that is to say, the regress, proceeds from the conditioned to its conditions *in infinitum*; because the conditions (the parts) are themselves contained in the conditioned, and, as the latter is given in a limited intuition, the former are all given along with it. This regress cannot, therefore, be called a *regressus in indefinitum*, as happened in the case of the preceding cosmological idea, the regress in which proceeded from the conditioned to the conditions not given contemporaneously and along with it, but discoverable only through the empirical regress. We are not, however, entitled to affirm of a whole of this kind, which is divisible *in infinitum*, that *it consists of an infinite number of parts*. For, although all the parts are contained in the intuition of the whole, the *whole division* is not contained therein. The division is contained only in the progressing decomposition—in the regress itself, which is the condition of the possibility and actuality of the series. Now, as this regress is infinite, all the members (parts) to which it attains must be contained in the given whole as an *aggregate*. But the complete *series of division* is not contained therein. For this series, being infinite in succession and always incomplete, cannot represent an infinite number of members, and still less a composition of these members into a whole.

To apply this remark to space. Every limited part of space presented to intuition is a whole, the parts of which are always spaces—to whatever extent subdivided. Every limited space is hence divisible to infinity.

Let us again apply the remark to an external phenomenon enclosed in limits, that is, a body. The divisibility of a body rests upon the divisibility of space, which is the condition of the possibility of the body as an extended whole. A body is consequently divisible to infinity, though it does not, for that reason, consist of an infinite number of parts.

It certainly seems that, as a body must be cogitated as substance in space, the law of divisibility would not be applicable to it as substance. For we may and ought to grant, in the case of space, that division or decomposition, to any extent, never can utterly annihilate composition (that is to say, the smallest part of space must still consist of spaces); otherwise space would entirely cease to exist—which is impossible. But, the assertion on the other hand, that when all composition in matter is annihilated in thought, nothing remains, does not seem to harmonize with the conception of substance, which must be properly the subject of all composition and must remain, even after the conjunction of its attributes in space—which constituted a body—is annihilated in thought. But this is not the case with substance in the phenomenal world, which is not a thing in itself cogitated by the pure category. Phenomenal substance is not an absolute subject; it is merely a permanent sensuous image, and nothing more than an intuition, in which the unconditioned is not to be found.

But, although this rule of progress to infinity is legitimate and applicable to the subdivision of a phenomenon, as a mere occupation or filling of space, it is not applicable to a whole consisting of a number of distinct parts and constituting a *quantum discretum*—that is to say, an organized body. It cannot be admitted that every part in an organized whole is itself organized, and that, in analysing it to infinity, we must always meet with organized parts; although we may allow that the parts of the matter which we decompose *in infinitum, may* be organized. For the infinity of the division of a phenomenon in space rests altogether on the fact that the divisibility of a phenomenon is given only in and through this infinity, that is, an undetermined number of parts is given, while the parts themselves are given and determined only in and through the subdivision; in a word, the infinity of the division necessarily presupposes that the whole is not already divided *in se*. Hence our division determines a number of parts in the whole—a number which extends just as far as the actual regress in the division; while, on the other hand, the very notion of a body organized to infinity represents the whole as already and in itself divided. We expect, therefore, to find in it a determinate, but, at the same time, infinite, number of parts—which is self-contradictory. For we should thus have a whole containing a series of members which could not be completed in any regress—which is infinite, and at the same time complete in an organized composite. Infinite divisibility is applicable only to a *quantum continuum*, and is based entirely on the infinite divisibility of space. But in a *quantum discretum* the multitude of parts or units is always determined, and hence always equal to some number. To what extent a body may be organized, experience alone can inform us; and although, so far as our experience of this or that body has extended, we may not have discovered any inorganic part, such parts must exist in possible experience. But how far the transcendental division of a phenomenon must extend, we cannot know from experience—it is a question which experience cannot answer; it is answered only by the principle of reason which forbids us to consider the empirical regress, in the analysis of extended body, as ever absolutely complete.

*Concluding Remark on the Solution of the Transcendental Mathematical Ideas—and Introductory to the Solution of the Dynamical Ideas*

We presented the antinomy of pure reason in a tabular form, and we endeavoured to show the ground of this self-contradiction on the part of reason, and the only means of bringing it to a conclusion—namely, by declaring both contradictory statements to be false. We represented in these antinomies the conditions of phenomena as belonging to the conditioned according to relations of space and time—which is the usual supposition of the common understanding. In this respect, all dialectical representations of totality, in the series of conditions to a given conditioned, were perfectly *homogeneous*. The condition was always a member of the series along with the conditioned, and thus the homogeneity of the whole series was assured. In this case the regress could never be cogitated as complete; or, if this was the case, a member really conditioned was falsely regarded as a primal member, conse-quently as unconditioned. In such an antinomy, therefore, we did not consider the object, that is, the conditioned, but the series of conditions belonging to the object, and the magnitude of that series. And thus arose the difficulty—a difficulty not to be settled by any decision regarding the claims of the two parties, but simply by cutting the knot—by declaring the series proposed by reason to be either *too long* or *too short* for the understanding, which could in neither case make its conceptions adequate with the ideas.

But we have overlooked, up to this point, an essential difference existing between the conceptions of the understanding which reason endeavours to raise to the rank of ideas—two of these in-dicating a *mathematical*, and two a *dynamical* synthesis of pheno-mena. Hitherto, it was not necessary to signalize this distinction; for, just as in our general representation of all transcendental ideas, we considered them under phenomenal conditions, so, in the two mathematical ideas, our discussion is concerned solely with an object in the world of phenomena. But as we are now about to proceed to the consideration of the *dynamical* conceptions of the understanding, and their adequateness with ideas, we must not lose sight of this distinction. We shall find that it opens up to us an entirely new view of the conflict in which reason is involved. For, while in the first two antinomies, both parties were *dismissed*, on the ground of having advanced statements based upon false hypotheses; in the present case the hope appears of discovering a hypothesis which may be consistent with the demands of reason, and, the judge completing the statement of the grounds of claim, which both parties had left in an unsatisfactory state, the question may be settled on its own merits, not by dismissing the claimants, but by a *comparison* of the arguments on both sides. If we consider merely their *extension*, and whether they are adequate with ideas, the series of conditions may be regarded as all homogeneous. But the conception of the understanding which lies at the basis of these ideas, contains either a *synthesis of the homogeneous* (presup-posed in every quantity—in its composition as well as in its division) or of the *heterogeneous*, which is the case in the dynamical synthesis of cause and effect, as well as of the necessary and the contingent.

Thus it happens, that in the mathematical series of phenomena no other than a *sensuous* condition is admissible—a condition which is itself a member of the series; while the dynamical series of sensuous conditions admits a heterogeneous condition, which is not a member of the series, but, as purely *intelligible*, lies out of and beyond it. And thus reason is satisfied, and an unconditioned placed at the head of the series of phenomena, without introducing confusion into or discontinuing it, contrary to the principles of the understanding.

Now, from the fact that the dynamical ideas admit a condition of phenomena which does not form a part of the series of phenomena, arises a result which we should not have expected from an antinomy. In former cases, the result was that both contradictory dialectical statements were declared to be false. In the present case, we find the conditioned in the dynamical series connected with an empirically unconditioned, but *non-sensuous* condition; and thus satisfaction is done to the *understanding* on the one hand and to the *reason* on the other.[1] While, moreover, the dialectical arguments for unconditioned totality in mere phenomena fall to the ground, *both* propositions of reason may be shown to be true in their proper signification. This could not happen in the case of the cosmological ideas which demanded a mathematically unconditioned unity; for no condition could be placed at the head of the series of phenomena, except one which was itself a phenomenon, and consequently a member of the series.

### III

*Solution of the Cosmological Idea of the Totality of the Deduction of Cosmical Events from their Causes*

There are only two modes of causality cogitable—the causality of *nature*, or of *freedom*. The first is the conjunction of a particular state with another preceding it in the world of sense, the former following the latter by virtue of a law. Now, as the causality of phenomena is subject to conditions of time, and the preceding state, if it had always existed, could not have produced an effect which would make its first appearance at a particular time, the causality of a cause must itself be an effect—must itself have *begun to be*, and therefore, according to the principle of the understanding, itself requires a cause.

[1] For the understanding cannot admit *among phenomena* a condition which is itself empirically unconditioned. But if it is possible to cogitate an *intelligible* condition—one which is not a member of the series of phenomena—for a conditioned phenomenon, without breaking the series of empirical conditions, such a condition may be admissible as *empirically unconditioned*, and the empirical regress continue regular, unceasing, and intact.

We must understand, on the contrary, by the term freedom, in the cosmological sense, a faculty of the *spontaneous* origination of a state; the causality of which, therefore, is not subordinated to another cause determining it in time.   Freedom is in this sense a pure transcendental idea, which, in the first place, contains no empirical element; the object of which, in the second place, cannot be given or determined in any experience, because it is a universal law of the very possibility of experience, that everything which happens must have a cause, that consequently the causality of a cause, being itself something that has *happened*, must also have a cause.   In this view of the case, the whole field of experience, how far soever it may extend, contains nothing that is not subject to the laws of nature.   But, as we cannot by this means attain to an absolute totality of conditions in reference to the series of causes and effects, reason creates the idea of a spontaneity, which can begin to act of itself, and without any external cause determining it to action, according to the natural law of causality.

It is especially remarkable that the practical conception of freedom is based upon the *transcendental idea*, and that the question of the possibility of the former is difficult only as it involves the consideration of the truth of the latter.   Freedom, in the *practical sense*, is the independence of the will of *coercion* by sensuous impulses. A will is *sensuous*, in so far as it is *pathologically affected* (by sensuous impulses); it is termed *animal (arbitrium brutum)*, when it is *pathologically necessitated*.   The human will is certainly an *arbitrium sensitivum*, not *brutum*, but *liberum*; because sensuousness does not necessitate its action, a faculty existing in man of self-determination, independently of all sensuous coercion.

It is plain, that, if all causality in the world of sense were natural —and natural only, every event would be determined by another according to necessary laws, and that consequently, phenomena, in so far as they determine the will, must necessitate every action as a natural effect from themselves; and thus all practical freedom would fall to the ground with the transcendental idea.   For the latter presupposes that, although a certain thing has not happened, it *ought* to have happened, and that, consequently, its phenomenal cause was not so powerful and determinative as to exclude the causality of our will—a causality capable of producing effects independently of and even in opposition to the power of natural causes, and capable, consequently, of *spontaneously* originating a series of events.

Here, too, we find it to be the case, as we generally found in the self-contradictions and perplexities of a reason which strives to pass the bounds of possible experience, that the problem is properly not *physiological*,[1] but *transcendental*. The question of the possibility of freedom does indeed concern psychology; but, as it rests upon dialectical arguments of pure reason, its solution must engage the attention of transcendental philosophy. Before attempting this solution, a task which transcendental philosophy cannot decline, it will be advisable to make a remark with regard to its procedure in the settlement of the question.

If phenomena were things in themselves, and time and space forms of the existence of things, condition and conditioned would always be members of the same series; and thus would arise in the present case the antinomy common to all transcendental ideas—that their series is either too great or too small for the understanding. The dynamical ideas, which we are about to discuss in this and the following section, possess the peculiarity of relating to an object, not considered as a quantity, but as an *existence*; and thus, in the discussion of the present question, we may make abstraction of the quantity of the series of conditions, and consider merely the dynamical relation of the condition to the conditioned. The question, then, suggests itself, whether freedom is possible; and, if it is, whether it can consist with the universality of the natural law of causality; and, consequently, whether we enounce a proper disjunctive proposition when we say—every effect must have its origin either in nature or in freedom, or whether *both* cannot exist together in the same event in different relations. The principle of an unbroken connection between all events in the phenomenal world, in accordance with the unchangeable laws of nature, is a well-established principle of transcendental analytic which admits of no exception. The question, therefore, is: Whether an effect, determined according to the laws of nature, can at the same time be produced by a free agent, or whether freedom and nature mutually exclude each other? And here, the common, but fallacious hypothesis of the *absolute reality* of phenomena manifests its injurious influence in embarrassing the procedure of reason. For if phenomena are things in themselves, freedom is impossible. In this case, nature is the complete and all-sufficient cause of every event; and condition and conditioned, cause and effect, are contained in the same series, and necessitated by the same law. If, on the contrary, phenomena are held to be, as they are in fact, nothing more than mere representations, connected with each other in accordance with empirical laws, they must have a ground which is *not* phenomenal. But the causality of

[1] Probably an error of the press, and that we should read *psychological*.

such an intelligible cause is not determined or determinable by phenomena; although its effects, as phenomena, must be determined by other phenomenal existences. This cause and its causality exist therefore out of and apart from the series of phenomena; while its effects do exist and are discoverable in the series of empirical conditions. Such an effect may therefore be considered to be free in relation to its intelligible cause, and necessary in relation to the phenomena from which it is a necessary consequence—a distinction which, stated in this perfectly general and abstract manner, must appear in the highest degree subtle and obscure. The sequel will explain. It is sufficient, at present, to remark that, as the complete and unbroken connection of phenomena is an unalterable law of nature, freedom is impossible—on the supposition that phenomena are absolutely real. Hence those philosophers who adhere to the common opinion on this subject can never succeed in reconciling the ideas of nature and freedom.

## Possibility of Freedom in Harmony with the Universal Law of Natural Necessity

That element in a sensuous object which is not itself sensuous, I may be allowed to term *intelligible*. If, accordingly, an object which must be regarded as a sensuous phenomenon possesses a faculty which is not an object of sensuous intuition, but by means of which it is capable of being the cause of phenomena, the *causality* of an object or existence of this kind may be regarded from two different points of view. It may be considered to be *intelligible*, as regards its *action*—the action of a thing which is a thing in itself, and *sensuous*, as regards its *effects*—the effects of a phenomenon belonging to the sensuous world. We should, accordingly, have to form both an empirical and an intellectual conception of the causality of such a faculty or power—both, however, having reference to the same effect. This twofold manner of cogitating a power residing in a sensuous object does not run counter to any of the conceptions which we ought to form of the world of phenomena or of a possible experience. Phenomena —not being things in themselves—must have a transcendental object as a foundation, which determines them as mere representations; and there seems to be no reason why we should not ascribe to this transcendental object, in addition to the property of self-phenomenization, a *causality* whose effects are to be met with in the world of phenomena, although it is not itself a phenomenon. But every effective cause must possess a *character*, that is to say, a law of its causality, without which it would cease to be a cause. In the above case, then, every sensuous object would possess an *empirical* character, which guaranteed that its actions, as phenomena, stand in complete and harmonious connection, conformably to unvarying natural laws, with all other phenomena, and can be deduced from these, as conditions, and that they do thus, in connection with these, constitute a series in the order of nature. This sensuous object must, in the second place, possess an *intelligible character*, which guarantees it to be the cause of those actions, as phenomena, although it is not itself a phenomenon nor subordinate to the conditions of the world of sense. The former may be termed the character of the thing as a phenomenon, the latter the character of the thing as a thing in itself.

Now this active subject would, in its character of intelligible subject, be subordinate to no conditions of time, for time is only a condition of phenomena, and not of things in themselves. No *action* would *begin* or *cease* to be in this subject; it would consequently be free from the law of all determination of time—the law of change, namely, that everything *which happens* must have a cause in the phenomena of a preceding state. In one word, the causality of the subject, in so far as it is intelligible, would not form part of the series of empirical conditions which determine and necessitate an event in the world of sense. Again, this intelligible character of a thing cannot be immediately cognized, because we can perceive nothing but phenomena, but it must be capable of being cogitated in harmony with the empirical character; for we always find ourselves compelled to place, in thought, a transcendental object at the basis of phenomena, although we can never know what this object is in itself.

In virtue of its empirical character, this subject would at the same time be subordinate to all the empirical laws of causality, and, as a phenomenon and member of the sensuous world, its effects would have to be accounted for by a reference to preceding phenomena. External phenomena must be capable of influencing it; and its actions, in accordance with natural laws, must explain to us how its empirical character, that is, the law of its causality, is to be cognized in and by means of experience. In a word, all requisites for a complete and necessary determination of these actions must be presented to us by experience.

In virtue of its intelligible character, on the other hand (although we possess only a general conception of this character), the subject must be regarded as free from all sensuous influences, and from all phenomenal determination. Moreover, as nothing *happens* in this subject—for it is a *noumenon*, and there does not consequently exist in it any change, demanding the dynamical determination of time, and for the same reason no connection with phenomena as causes—this active existence must in its actions be free from and independent of natural necessity, for this necessity exists only in the world of phenomena. It would be quite correct to say, that it originates or begins its effects in the world of sense *from itself*, although the action productive of these effects does not begin *in itself*. We should not be in this case affirming that these sensuous effects began to exist of themselves, because they are always determined by prior empirical conditions—by virtue of the empirical character, which is the phenomenon of the intelligible character—and are possible only as constituting a continuation of the series of natural causes. And thus nature and freedom, each in the complete and absolute signification of these terms, can exist, without contradiction or disagreement, in the same action.

### Exposition of the Cosmological Idea of Freedom in Harmony with the Universal Law of Natural Necessity

I have thought it advisable to lay before the reader at first merely a sketch of the solution of this transcendental problem, in order to enable him to form with greater ease a clear conception of the course which reason must adopt in the solution. I shall now proceed to exhibit the several momenta of this solution, and to consider them in their order.

The natural law, that everything which happens must have a cause, that the causality of this cause, that is, the action of the cause (which cannot always have existed, but must be itself an *event*, for it precedes in time some effect which it has originated), must have itself a phenomenal cause, by which it is determined, and, consequently, that all events are empirically determined in an order of nature—this law, I say, which lies at the foundation of the possibility of experience, and of a connected system of phenomena or *nature*, is a law of the understanding, from which no departure, and to which no exception, can be admitted. For to except even a single phenomenon from its operation, is to exclude it from the sphere of possible experience, and thus to admit it to be a mere fiction of thought or phantom of the brain.

Thus we are obliged to acknowledge the existence of a chain of causes, in which, however, *absolute totality* cannot be found. But we need not detain ourselves with this question, for it has already been sufficiently answered in our discussion of the antinomies into which reason falls, when it attempts to reach the unconditioned in the series of phenomena. If we permit ourselves to be deceived by the illusion of transcendental idealism, we shall find that neither nature nor freedom exists. Now the question is: Whether, admitting the existence of natural necessity in the world of phenomena, it is possible to consider an effect as at the same time an effect of nature and an effect of freedom—or, whether these two modes of causality are contradictory and incompatible.

No phenomenal cause can absolutely and of itself begin a series. Every action, in so far as it is productive of an event, is itself an event or occurrence, and presupposes another preceding state, in which its cause existed. Thus everything that happens is but a continuation of a series, and an absolute beginning is impossible in the sensuous world. The actions of natural causes are, accordingly, themselves effects, and presuppose causes preceding them in time. A *primal* action—an action which forms an absolute beginning, is beyond the causal power of phenomena.

Now, is it absolutely necessary that, granting that all effects are phenomena, the causality of the cause of these effects must also be a phenomenon, and belong to the empirical world? Is it not rather possible that, although every effect in the phenomenal world must be connected with an empirical cause, according to the universal law of nature, this empirical causality may be itself the effect of a non-empirical and intelligible causality—its connection with natural causes remaining nevertheless intact? Such a causality would be considered, in reference to phenomena, as the primal action of a cause, which is so far, therefore, not phenomenal, but, by reason of this faculty or power, intelligible; although it must, at the same time, as a link in the chain of nature, be regarded as belonging to the sensuous world.

A belief in the reciprocal causality of phenomena is necessary, if we are required to look for and to present the natural conditions of natural events, that is to say, their causes. This being admitted as unexceptionably valid, the requirements of the understanding, which recognizes nothing but nature in the region of phenomena, are satisfied, and our physical explanations of physical phenomena may proceed in their regular course, without hindrance and without opposition. But it is no stumbling-block in the way, even assuming the idea to be a pure fiction, to admit that there are some natural causes in the possession of a faculty which is not empirical, but intelligible, inasmuch as it is not determined to action by empirical conditions, but purely and solely upon grounds brought forward by the understanding—this action being still, when the cause is phenomenized, in perfect accordance with the laws of empirical causality. Thus the acting subject, as a *causal phenomenon*, would continue to preserve a complete connection with nature and natural conditions; and the *phenomenon* only of the subject (with all its phenomenal causality) would contain certain conditions, which, if we ascend from the empirical to the transcendental object, must necessarily be regarded as intelligible. For, if we attend, in our inquiries with regard to causes in the world of phenomena, to the directions of nature alone, we need not trouble ourselves about the relation in which the transcendental subject, which is completely unknown to us, stands to these phenomena and their connection in nature. The intelligible ground of phenomena in this subject does not concern empirical questions. It has to do only with pure thought; and, although the effects of this thought and action of the pure understanding are discoverable in phenomena, these phenomena must nevertheless be capable of a full and complete explanation, upon purely physical grounds, and in accordance with natural laws. And in this case we attend solely to their empirical, and omit all consideration of their intelligible character (which is the transcendental cause of the former), as completely unknown, except in so far as it is exhibited by the latter as its empirical symbol. Now let us apply this to experience. Man is a phenomenon of the sensuous world, and at the same time, therefore, a natural cause, the causality of which must be regulated by empirical laws. As such, he must possess an empirical character, like all other natural phenomena. We remark this empirical character in his actions, which reveal the presence of certain powers and faculties. If we consider inanimate, or merely animal nature, we can discover no reason for ascribing to ourselves any other than a faculty which is determined in a purely sensuous manner. But man, to whom nature reveals herself only through sense, cognizes himself not only by his senses, but also through pure apperception; and this in actions and internal determinations, which he cannot regard as sensuous impressions. He is thus to himself, on the one hand, a phenomenon, but on the other hand, in respect of certain faculties, a purely intelligible object—intelligible, because its action cannot be ascribed to sensuous receptivity. These faculties are understanding and reason. The latter, especially, is in a peculiar manner distinct from all empirically-conditioned faculties, for it employs ideas alone in the consideration of its objects, and by means of these determines the understanding, which then proceeds to make an empirical use of its own conceptions, which, like the ideas of reason, are pure and non-empirical.

That reason possesses the faculty of causality, or that at least we are compelled so to represent it, is evident from the *imperatives*, which in the sphere of the practical we impose on many of our executive powers. The words *I ought* express a species of necessity, and imply a connection with grounds which nature does not and cannot present to the mind of man. Understanding knows nothing in nature but that *which is*, or has been, or will be. It would be absurd to say that anything in nature *ought* to be other than it is in the relations of time in which it stands; indeed, the *ought*, when we consider merely the course of nature, has neither application nor meaning. The question, what ought to happen in the sphere of nature? is just as absurd as the question, what ought to be the properties of a circle? All that we are entitled to ask is, what takes place in nature? or, in the latter case, what *are* the properties of a circle?

But the idea of an *ought* or of duty indicates a possible action, the ground of which is a pure conception; while the ground of a merely natural action is, on the contrary, always a phenomenon. This action must certainly be possible under physical conditions, if it is prescribed by the moral imperative *ought*; but these physical or natural conditions do not concern the determination of the will itself, they relate to its effect alone, and the consequences of the effect in the world of phenomena. Whatever number of motives nature may present to my will, whatever sensuous impulses—the moral *ought* it is beyond their power to produce. They may produce a volition, which, so far from being necessary, is always conditioned—a volition to which the *ought* enunciated by reason, sets an aim and a standard, gives permission or prohibition. Be the object what it may, purely sensuous—as pleasure, or presented by pure reason—as good, reason will not yield to grounds which have an empirical origin. Reason will not follow the order of things presented by experience, but, with perfect spontaneity, rearranges them according to ideas, with which it compels empirical conditions to agree. It declares, in the name of these ideas, certain actions to be necessary which nevertheless *have not taken place*, and which perhaps never will take place; and yet presupposes that it possesses the faculty of causality in relation to these actions. For, in the absence of this supposition, it could not expect its ideas to produce certain effects in the world of experience.

Now, let us stop here, and admit it to be at least possible, that reason does stand in a really causal relation to phenomena. In this case it must—pure reason as it is—exhibit an empirical character. For every cause supposes a rule, according to which certain phenomena follow as effects from the cause, and every rule requires uniformity in these effects; and this is the proper ground of the conception of a cause—as a faculty or power. Now this conception (of a cause) may be termed the empirical character of reason; and this character is a permanent one, while the effects produced appear, in conformity with the various conditions which accompany and partly limit them, in various forms.

Thus the volition of every man has an empirical character, which is nothing more than the causality of his reason, in so far as its effects in the phenomenal world manifest the presence of a rule, according to which we are enabled to examine, in their several kinds and degrees, the actions of this causality and the rational grounds for these actions, and in this way to decide upon the subjective principles of the volition. Now we learn what this empirical character is only from phenomenal effects, and from the rule of these which is presented by experience; and for this reason all the actions of man in the world of phenomena are determined by his empirical character, and the co-operative causes of nature. If, then, we could investigate all the phenomena of human volition to their lowest foundation in the mind, there would be no action which we could not anticipate with certainty, and recognize to be absolutely necessary from its preceding conditions. So far as relates to this empirical character, therefore, there can be no freedom; and it is only in the light of this character that we can consider the human will, when we confine ourselves to simple *observation*, and, as is the case in anthropology, institute a physiological investigation of the motive causes of human actions.

But when we consider the same actions in relation to reason— not for the purpose of *explaining* their origin, that is, in relation to speculative reason—but to practical reason, as the producing cause of these actions, we shall discover a rule and an order very different from those of nature and experience. For the declaration of this mental faculty may be, that what *has* taken place and could not but take place in the course of nature, *ought not* to have taken place. Sometimes, too, we discover, or believe that we discover, that the ideas of reason did actually stand in a causal relation to certain actions of man; and that these actions have taken place because they were determined, not by empirical causes, but by the act of the will upon grounds of reason.

Now, granting that reason stands in a causal relation to phenomena; can an action of reason be called free, when we know that, sensuously—in its empirical character, it is completely determined and absolutely necessary? But this empirical character is itself determined by the intelligible character. The latter we cannot cognize; we can only indicate it by means of phenomena, which enable us to have an immediate cognition only of the empirical character.[1] An action, then, in so far as it is to be ascribed to an intelligible cause, does not result from it in accordance with empirical laws. That is to say, not the conditions of pure reason, but only their effects in the internal sense, precede the act. Pure reason, as a purely intelligible faculty, is not subject to the conditions of time. The causality of reason in its intelligible character *does not begin to be*; it does not make its appearance at a certain time, for the purpose of producing an effect. If this were not the case, the causality of reason would be subservient to the natural law of phenomena, which determines them according to time, and as a series of causes and effects in time; it would consequently cease to be freedom, and become a part of nature. We are therefore justified in saying: If reason stands in a causal relation to phenomena, it is a faculty which originates the sensuous condition of an empirical series of effects. For the condition, which resides in the reason, is non-sensuous, and therefore cannot be originated, or begin to be. And thus we find—what we could not discover in any empirical series—a *condition* of a successive series of events itself empirically unconditioned. For, in the present case, the condition stands *out of* and beyond the series of phenomena—it is intelligible, and it consequently cannot be subject to any sensuous condition, or to any time-determination by a preceding cause.

But, in another respect, the same cause belongs also to the series of phenomena. Man is himself a phenomenon. His will has an empirical character, which is the empirical cause of all his actions. There is no condition—determining man and his volition in conformity with this character—which does not itself form part of the series of effects in nature, and is subject to their law—the law according to which an empirically undetermined cause of an event in time cannot exist. For this reason no given action can have an absolute and spontaneous origination, all actions being phenomena, and belonging to the world of experience. But it cannot be said of reason, that the state in which it determines the will is always preceded by some other state determining it. For reason is not a phenomenon, and therefore not subject to sensuous

---

[1] The real morality of actions—their merit or demerit, and even that of our own conduct, is completely unknown to us. Our estimates can relate only to their empirical character. How much is the result of the action of free-will, how much is to be ascribed to nature and to blameless error, or to a happy constitution of temperament (*merito fortunae*), no one can discover, nor, for this reason, determine with perfect justice.

conditions; and, consequently, even in relation to its causality, the sequence or conditions of time do not influence reason, nor can the dynamical law of nature, which determines the sequence of time according to certain rules, be applied to it.

Reason is consequently the permanent condition of all actions of the human will. Each of these is determined in the empirical character of the man, even before it has taken place. The intelligible character, of which the former is but the sensuous schema, knows no *before* or *after*; and every action, irrespective of the time-relation in which it stands with other phenomena, is the immediate effect of the intelligible character of pure reason, which, consequently, enjoys freedom of action, and is not dynamically determined either by internal or external preceding conditions. This freedom must not be described, in a merely negative manner, as independence of empirical conditions, for in this case the faculty of reason would cease to be a cause of phenomena; but it must be regarded, positively, as a faculty which can spontaneously originate a series of events. At the same time, it must not be supposed that any beginning can take place in reason; on the contrary, reason, as the unconditioned condition of all action of the will, admits of no time-conditions, although its effect does really begin in a series of phenomena—a beginning which is not, however, absolutely primal.

I shall illustrate this regulative principle of reason by an example, from its employment in the world of experience; proved it cannot be by any amount of experience, or by any number of facts, for such arguments cannot establish the truth of transcendental propositions. Let us take a voluntary action—for example, a falsehood—by means of which a man has introduced a certain degree of confusion into the social life of humanity, which is judged according to the motives from which it originated, and the blame of which and of the evil consequences arising from it, is imputed to the offender. We at first proceed to examine the empirical character of the offence, and for this purpose we endeavour to penetrate to the sources of that character, such as a defective education, bad company, a shameless and wicked disposition, frivolity, and want of reflection—not forgetting also the occasioning causes which prevailed at the moment of the transgression. In this the procedure is exactly the same as that pursued in the investigation of the series of causes which determine a given physical effect. Now, although we believe the action to have been determined by all these circumstances, we do not the less blame the offender. We do not blame him for his unhappy disposition, nor for the circumstances which influenced him, nay, not even for his former course of life; for we presuppose that all these considerations may be set aside, that the series of preceding conditions may be regarded as having never existed, and that the action may be considered as completely unconditioned in relation to any state preceding, just as if the agent commenced with it an entirely new series of effects. Our blame of the offender is grounded upon a law of reason, which requires us to regard this faculty as a cause, which could have and ought to have otherwise determined the behaviour of the culprit, independently of all empirical conditions. This causality of reason we do not regard as a co-operating agency, but as complete in itself. It matters not whether the sensuous impulses favoured or opposed the action of this causality, the offence is estimated according to its intelligible character—the offender is decidedly worthy of blame, the moment he utters a falsehood. It follows that we regard reason, in spite of the empirical conditions of the act, as completely free, and therefore, as in the present case, culpable.

The above judgment is complete evidence that we are accustomed to think that reason is not affected by sensuous conditions, that in it no change takes place — although its phenomena, in other words, the mode in which it appears in its effects, are subject to change—that in it no preceding state determines the following, and, consequently, that it does not form a member of the series of sensuous conditions which necessitate phenomena according to natural laws. Reason is present and the same in all human actions, and at all times; but it does not itself exist in time, and therefore does not enter upon any state in which it did not formerly exist. It is, relatively to new states or conditions, *determining*, but not *determinable*. Hence we cannot ask: Why did not reason determine itself in a different manner? The question ought to be thus stated: Why did not reason employ its power of causality to determine certain *phenomena* in a different manner? But this is a question which admits of no answer. For a different intelligible character would have exhibited a different empirical character; and, when we say that, in spite of the course which his whole former life has taken, the offender could have refrained from uttering the falsehood, this means merely that the act was subject to the power and authority—permissive or prohibitive—of reason. Now, reason is not subject in its causality to any conditions of phenomena or of time; and a difference in time may produce a difference in the relation of phenomena to each other — for these are not things, and therefore not causes in themselves—but it cannot produce any difference in the relation in which the action stands to the faculty of reason.

Thus, then, in our investigation into free actions and the causal power which produced them, we arrive at an intelligible cause, beyond which, however, we cannot go; although we can recognize that it is free, that is, independent of all sensuous conditions, and that, in this way, it may be the sensuously unconditioned condition of phenomena. But for what reason the intelligible character generates such and such phenomena, and exhibits such and such an empirical character under certain circumstances, it is beyond the power of our reason to decide. The question is as much above the power and the sphere of reason as the following would be: Why does the transcendental object of our external sensuous intuition allow of no other form than that of intuition *in space*? But the problem, which we were called upon to solve, does not require us to entertain any such questions. The problem was merely this—whether freedom and natural necessity can exist without opposition in the same action. To this question we have given a sufficient answer; for we have shown that, as the former stands in a relation to a different kind of conditions from those of the latter, the law of the one does not affect the law of the other, and that, consequently, both can exist together in independence of and without interference with each other.

————

The reader must be careful to remark that my intention in the above remarks has not been to prove the *actual existence* of freedom, as a faculty in which resides the cause of certain sensuous phenomena. For, not to mention that such an argument would not have a transcendental character, nor have been limited to the discussion of pure conceptions—all attempts at inferring from experience what cannot be cogitated in accordance with its laws, must ever be unsuccessful. Nay, more, I have not even aimed at demonstrating the *possibility* of freedom; for this too would have been a vain endeavour, inasmuch as it is beyond the power of the mind to cognize the possibility of a reality or of a causal power by the aid of mere *a priori* conceptions. Freedom has been considered in the foregoing remarks only as a transcendental idea, by means of which reason aims at originating a series of conditions in the world of phenomena with the help of that which is sensuously unconditioned, involving itself, however, in an antinomy with the laws which itself prescribes for the conduct of the understanding. That this antinomy is based upon a mere illusion, and that nature and freedom are at least *not opposed*—this was the only thing in our power to prove, and the question which it was our task to solve.

## IV

### Solution of the Cosmological Idea of the Totality of the Dependence of Phenomenal Existences

In the preceding remarks, we considered the changes in the world of sense as constituting a dynamical series, in which each member is subordinated to another—as its cause. Our present purpose is to avail ourselves of this series of states or conditions as a guide to an existence which may be the highest condition of all changeable phenomena, that is, to a *necessary being*. Our endeavour is to reach, not the unconditioned causality, but the unconditioned existence, of substance. The series before us is therefore a series of conceptions, and not of intuitions (in which the one intuition is the condition of the other).

But it is evident that, as all phenomena are subject to change, and conditioned in their existence, the series of dependent existences cannot embrace an unconditioned member, the existence of which would be absolutely necessary. It follows that, if phenomena were things in themselves, and—as an immediate consequence from this supposition—condition and conditioned belonged to the same series of phenomena, the existence of a necessary being, as the condition of the existence of sensuous phenomena, would be perfectly impossible.

An important distinction, however, exists between the dynamical and the mathematical regress. The latter is engaged solely with the combination of parts into a whole, or with the division of a whole into its parts; and therefore are the conditions of its series parts of the series, and to be consequently regarded as homogeneous, and for this reason, as consisting, without exception, of phenomena. In the former regress, on the contrary, the aim of which is not to establish the possibility of an unconditioned whole consisting of given parts, or of an unconditioned part of a given whole, but to demonstrate the possibility of the deduction of a certain state from its cause, or of the contingent existence of substance from that which exists necessarily, it is not requisite that the condition should form part of an empirical series along with the conditioned.

In the case of the apparent antinomy with which we are at present dealing, there exists a way of escape from the difficulty;

for it is not impossible that both of the contradictory statements may be true in different relations. All sensuous phenomena may be contingent, and consequently possess only an empirically conditioned existence, and yet there may also exist a non-empirical condition of the whole series, or, in other words, a necessary being. For this necessary being, as an intelligible condition, would not form a member—not even the highest member—of the series; the whole world of sense would be left in its empirically determined existence uninterfered with and uninfluenced. This would also form a ground of distinction between the modes of solution employed for the third and fourth antinomies. For, while in the consideration of freedom in the former antinomy, the thing itself —the cause (*substantia phaenomenon*) was regarded as belonging to the series of conditions, and only its *causality* to the intelligible world—we are obliged in the present case to cogitate this necessary being as purely intelligible and as existing entirely apart from the world of sense (as an *ens extramundanum*); for otherwise it would be subject to the phenomenal law of contingency and dependence.

In relation to the present problem, therefore, the *regulative principle* of reason is that everything in the sensuous world possesses an empirically conditioned existence—that no property of the sensuous world possesses unconditioned necessity—that we are bound to expect, and, so far as is possible, to seek for the empirical condition of every member in the series of conditions—and that there is no sufficient reason to justify us in deducing any existence from a condition which lies out of and beyond the empirical series, or in regarding any existence as independent and self-subsistent; although this should not prevent us from recognizing the possibility of the whole series being based upon a being which is intelligible, and for this reason free from all empirical conditions.

But it has been far from my intention, in these remarks, to prove the existence of this unconditioned and necessary being, or even to evidence the possibility of a purely intelligible condition of the existence of all sensuous phenomena. As bounds were set to reason, to prevent it from leaving the guiding thread of empirical conditions, and losing itself in *transcendent* theories which are incapable of *concrete* presentation; so it was my purpose, on the other hand, to set bounds to the law of the purely empirical understanding, and to protest against any attempts on its part at deciding on the possibility of things, or declaring the existence of the intelligible to be *impossible*, merely on the ground that it is not available for the explanation and exposition of phenomena. It has been shown, at the same time, that the contingency of all the phenomena of nature and their empirical conditions is quite consistent with the arbitrary hypothesis of a necessary, although purely intelligible condition, that no real contradiction exists between them, and that, consequently, *both may be true*. The existence of such an absolutely necessary being may be impossible; but this can never be demonstrated from the universal contingency and dependence of sensuous phenomena, nor from the principle which forbids us to discontinue the series at some member of it, or to seek for its cause in some sphere of existence beyond the world of nature. Reason goes its way in the empirical world, and follows, too, its peculiar path in the sphere of the transcendental.

The sensuous world contains nothing but phenomena, which are mere representations, and always sensuously conditioned; things in themselves are not, and cannot be, objects to us. It is not to be wondered at, therefore, that we are not justified in leaping from some member of an empirical series beyond the world of sense, as if empirical representations were things in themselves, existing apart from their transcendental ground in the human mind, and the cause of whose existence may be sought out of the empirical series. This would certainly be the case with contingent *things*; but it cannot be with mere *representations* of things, the contingency of which is itself merely a phenomenon, and can relate to no other regress than that which determines phenomena, that is, the empirical. But to cogitate an intelligible ground of phenomena, as free, moreover, from the contingency of the latter, conflicts neither with the unlimited nature of the empirical regress, nor with the complete contingency of phenomena. And the demonstration of this was the only thing necessary for the solution of this apparent antinomy. For if the condition of every conditioned—as regards its existence—is sensuous, and for this reason a part of the same series, it must be itself conditioned, as was shown in the Antithesis of the fourth Antinomy. The embarrassments into which a reason, which postulates the unconditioned, necessarily falls, must, therefore, continue to exist; or the unconditioned must be placed in the sphere of the intelligible. In this way, its necessity does not require, nor does it even permit, the presence of an empirical condition: and it is, consequently, unconditionally necessary.

The empirical employment of reason is not affected by the assumption of a purely intelligible being; it continues its operations on the principle of the contingency of all phenomena, proceeding from empirical conditions to still higher and higher conditions, themselves empirical. Just as little does this regulative principle exclude the assumption of an intelligible cause, when the question regards merely the pure employment of reason—in relation to ends or aims. For, in this case, an intelligible cause signifies merely the transcendental and to us unknown ground of the possibility of sensuous phenomena, and its existence necessary and independent of all sensuous conditions, is not inconsistent with the contingency of phenomena, or with the unlimited possibility of regress which exists in the series of empirical conditions.

### Concluding Remarks on the Antinomy of Pure Reason

So long as the object of our rational conceptions is the totality of conditions in the world of phenomena, and the satisfaction, from this source, of the requirements of reason, so long are our ideas transcendental and *cosmological*. But when we set the un-conditioned—which is the aim of all our inquiries—in a sphere which lies out of the world of sense and possible experience, our ideas become *transcendent*. They are then not merely serviceable towards the completion of the exercise of reason (which remains an idea, never executed, but always to be pursued); they detach themselves completely from experience, and construct for them-selves objects, the material of which has not been presented by experience, and the objective reality of which is not based upon the completion of the empirical series, but upon pure *a priori* conceptions. The intelligible object of these transcendent ideas may be conceded, as a transcendental object. But we cannot cogitate it as a thing determinable by certain distinct predicates relating to its internal nature, for it has no connection with empirical conceptions; nor are we justified in affirming the existence of any such object. It is, consequently, a mere product of the mind alone. Of all the cosmological ideas, however, it is that occasioning the fourth antinomy which compels us to venture upon this step. For the existence of phenomena, always conditioned and never self-subsistent, requires us to look for an object different from phenomena—an intelligible object, with which all contingency must cease. But, as we have allowed ourselves to assume the existence of a self-subsistent reality out of the field of experience, and are therefore obliged to regard phenomena as merely a contin-gent mode of representing intelligible objects employed by beings which are themselves intelligences—no other course remains for us than to follow analogy, and employ the same mode in forming some conception of intelligible things, of which we have not the least knowledge, which nature taught us to use in the formation of empirical conceptions. Experience made us acquainted with the contingent. But we are at present engaged in the discussion of things which are not objects of experience; and must, therefore, deduce our knowledge of them from that which is necessary absolutely and in itself, that is, from pure conceptions. Hence the first step which we take out of the world of sense obliges us to begin our system of new cognition with the investigation of a necessary being, and to deduce from our conceptions of it, all our conceptions of intelligible things. This we propose to attempt in the following chapter.

## Chapter III—The Ideal of Pure Reason

### Section I

#### Of the Ideal in General

WE have seen that pure conceptions do not present objects to the mind, except under sensuous conditions; because the conditions of objective reality do not exist in these conceptions, which contain, in fact, nothing but the mere form of thought. They may, however, when applied to phenomena, be presented *in concreto*; for it is phenomena that present to them the materials for the formation of empirical conceptions, which are nothing more than concrete forms of the conceptions of the understanding. But *ideas* are still further removed from objective reality than *categories*; for no phenomenon can ever present them to the human mind *in concreto*. They contain a certain perfection, attainable by no possible empirical cognition; and they give to reason a systematic unity, to which the unity of experience attempts to approximate, but can never completely attain.

But still further removed than the idea from objective reality is the *Ideal*, by which term I understand the idea, not *in concreto*, but *in individuo*—as an individual thing, determinable or determined by the idea alone. The idea of humanity in its complete perfection supposes not only the advancement of all the powers and faculties, which constitute our conception of human nature, to a complete attainment of their final aims, but also everything which is requisite for the complete determination of the idea; for of all contradictory predicates, only one can conform with the idea of the perfect man. What I have termed an ideal, was in Plato's philosophy an *idea of the divine mind*—an individual object present to its pure intuition, the most perfect of every kind of possible beings, and the archetype of all phenomenal existences.

Without rising to these speculative heights, we are bound to confess that human reason contains not only ideas, but ideals, which possess, not, like those of Plato, creative, but certainly *practical* power—as regulative principles, and form the basis of the perfectibility of certain *actions*. Moral conceptions are not perfectly pure conceptions of reason, because an empirical element —of pleasure or pain—lies at the foundation of them. In relation, however, to the principle, whereby reason sets bounds to a freedom which is in itself without law, and consequently when we attend merely to their form, they may be considered as pure conceptions of reason. Virtue and wisdom in their perfect purity, are ideas. But the wise man of the Stoics is an ideal, that is to say, a human being existing only in thought, and in complete conformity with the idea of wisdom. As the idea provides a rule, so the ideal serves as an *archetype* for the perfect and complete determination of the copy. Thus the conduct of this wise and divine man serves us as a standard of action, with which we may compare and judge ourselves, which may help us to reform ourselves, although the perfection it demands can never be attained by us. Although we cannot concede objective reality to these ideals, they are not to be considered as chimeras; on the contrary, they provide reason with a standard, which enables it to estimate, by comparison, the degree of incompleteness in the objects presented to it. But to aim at realizing the ideal in an example in the world of experience —to describe, for instance, the character of the perfectly wise man in a romance, is impracticable. Nay more, there is something absurd in the attempt; and the result must be little edifying, as the natural limitations which are continually breaking in upon the perfection and completeness of the idea, destroy the illusion in the story, and throw an air of suspicion even on what is good in the idea, which hence appears fictitious and unreal.

Such is the constitution of the ideal of reason, which is always based upon determinate conceptions, and serves as a rule and a model for imitation or for criticism. Very different is the nature of the ideals of the imagination. Of these it is impossible to present an intelligible conception; they are a kind of *monogram*, drawn according to no determinate rule, and forming rather a vague picture—the production of many diverse experiences—than a determinate image. Such are the ideals which painters and physiognomists profess to have in their minds, and which can serve neither as a model for production nor as a standard for appreciation. They may be termed, though improperly, sensuous ideals, as they are declared to be models of certain possible empirical intuitions. They cannot, however, furnish rules or standards for explanation or examination.

In its ideals, reason aims at complete and perfect determination according to *a priori* rules; and hence it cogitates an object, which must be completely determinable in conformity with principles, although all empirical conditions are absent, and the conception of the object is on this account transcendent.

## SECTION II

### Of the Transcendental Ideal

#### (Prototypon Transcendentale)

EVERY conception is, in relation to that which is not contained in it, undetermined and subject to the principle of *determinability*. This principle is, that of *every two* contradictorily opposed predicates, only one can belong to a conception. It is a purely logical principle, itself based upon the principle of contradiction; inasmuch as it makes complete abstraction of the content, and attends merely to the logical form of the cognition.

But again, everything, as regards its possibility, is also subject to the principle [1] of complete determination, according to which one of *all the possible contradictory predicates* of things must belong to it. This principle is not based merely upon that of contradiction; for, in addition to the relation between two contradictory predicates, it regards everything as standing in a relation to the *sum of possibilities*, as the sum total of all predicates of things, and, while presupposing this sum as an *a priori* condition, presents to the mind everything as receiving the possibility of its individual existence from the relation it bears to, and the share it possesses in the aforesaid sum of possibilities.[2] The principle of complete determination relates therefore to the content and not to the logical form. It is the principle of the synthesis of all the predicates which are required to constitute the complete conception of a

---

[1] *Principium determinationis omnimodae.*—Tr.

[2] Thus this principle declares everything to possess a relation to a common correlate—the sum total of possibility, which, if discovered to exist in the idea of one individual thing, would establish the affinity of all possible things, from the identity of the ground of their complete determination. The *determinability* of every *conception* is subordinate to the *universality* (Allgemeinheit *universalitas*) of the principle of excluded middle; the *determination* of a *thing* to the *totality* (Allheit, *universitas*) of all possible predicates.

thing, and not a mere principle of analytical representation, which enounces that one of two contradictory predicates must belong to a conception. It contains, moreover, a transcendental presupposition—that, namely, of the material for *all possibility*, which must contain *a priori* the data for this or that *particular possibility*.

The proposition, *Everything which exists is completely determined*, means not only that one of every pair of *given* contradictory attributes, but that one of all *possible* attributes, is always predicable of the thing; in it the predicates are not merely compared logically with each other, but the thing itself is transcendentally compared with the sum total of all possible predicates. The proposition is equivalent to saying: To attain to a complete knowledge of a thing, it is necessary to possess a knowledge of everything that is possible, and to determine it thereby in a positive or negative manner. The conception of complete determination is consequently a conception which cannot be presented in its totality *in concreto*, and is therefore based upon an idea, which has its seat in the reason—the faculty which prescribes to the understanding the laws of its harmonious and perfect exercise.

Now, although this idea of the *sum total of all possibility*, in so far as it forms the condition of the complete determination of everything, is itself undetermined in relation to the predicates which may constitute this sum total, and we cogitate in it merely the sum total of all possible predicates—we nevertheless find, upon closer examination, that this idea, as a primitive conception of the mind, excludes a large number of predicates—those deduced and those irreconcilable with others, and that it is evolved as a conception completely determined *a priori*. Thus it becomes the conception of an individual object, which is completely determined by and through the mere idea, and must consequently be termed an ideal of pure reason.

When we consider all possible predicates, not merely logically, but transcendentally, that is to say, with reference to the content which may be cogitated as existing in them *a priori*, we shall find that some indicate a being, others merely a non-being. The logical negation expressed in the word *not*, does not properly belong to a conception, but only to the relation of one conception to another in a judgment, and is consequently quite insufficient to present to the mind the content of a conception. The expression *not mortal* does not indicate that a non-being is cogitated in the object; it does not concern the content at all. A transcendental negation, on the contrary, indicates non-being in itself, and is opposed to transcendental affirmation, the conception of which of itself expresses a being. Hence this affirmation indicates a reality, because in and through it objects are considered to be something —to be things; while the opposite negation, on the other hand, indicates a mere want, or privation, or absence, and, where such negations alone are attached to a representation, the non-existence of anything corresponding to the representation.

Now a negation cannot be cogitated as determined, without cogitating at the same time the opposite affirmation. The man born blind has not the least notion of darkness, because he has none of light; the vagabond knows nothing of poverty, because he has never known what it is to be in comfort;[1] the ignorant man has no conception of his ignorance, because he has no conception of knowledge. All conceptions of negatives are accordingly derived or deduced conceptions; and realities contain the *data*, and, so to speak, the material or transcendental content of the possibility and complete determination of all things.

If, therefore, a transcendental substratum lies at the foundation of the complete determination of things—a substratum which is to form the fund from which all possible predicates of things are to be supplied, this substratum cannot be anything else than the idea of a sum total of reality (*omnitudo realitatis*). In this view, negations are nothing but *limitations*—a term which could not, with propriety, be applied to them, if the unlimited (the all) did not form the true basis of our conception.

This conception of a sum total of reality is the conception of a *thing in itself*, regarded as completely determined; and the conception of an *ens realissimum* is the conception of an individual being, inasmuch as it is determined by that predicate of all possible contradictory predicates, which indicates and belongs to *being*. It is therefore a transcendental *ideal* which forms the basis of the complete determination of everything that exists, and is the highest material condition of its possibility—a condition on which must rest the cogitation of all objects with respect to their content. Nay, more, this ideal is the only proper ideal of which the human mind is capable; because in this case alone a general conception of a thing is completely determined by and through itself, and cognized as the representation of an individuum.

The logical determination of a conception is based upon a dis-

[1] The investigations and calculations of astronomers have taught us much that is wonderful; but the most important lesson we have received from them is the discovery of the abyss of our *ignorance* in relation to the universe—an ignorance, the magnitude of which reason, without the information thus derived, could never have conceived. This discovery of our deficiencies must produce a great change in the determination of the aims of human reason.

junctive syllogism, the major of which contains the logical division of the extent of a general conception, the minor limits this extent to a certain part, while the conclusion determines the conception by this part. The general conception of a reality cannot be divided *a priori*, because, without the aid of experience, we cannot know any determinate kinds of reality, standing under the former as the genus. The transcendental principle of the complete determination of all things is therefore merely the representation of the sum total of all reality; it is not a conception which is the genus of all predicates *under itself*, but one which comprehends them all *within itself*. The complete determination of a thing is consequently based upon the limitation of this *total* of reality, so much being predicated of the thing, while all that remains over is excluded—a procedure which is in exact agreement with that of the disjunctive syllogism and the determination of the object in the conclusion by one of the members of the division. It follows that reason, in laying the transcendental ideal at the foundation of its determination of all possible things, takes a course in exact analogy with that which it pursues in disjunctive syllogisms—a proposition which formed the basis of the systematic division of all transcendental ideas, according to which they are produced in complete parallelism with the three modes of syllogistic reasoning employed by the human mind.[1]

It is self-evident that reason, in cogitating the necessary complete determination of things, does not presuppose the existence of a being corresponding to its ideal, but merely the idea of the ideal—for the purpose of deducing from the unconditioned totality of complete determination, the conditioned, that is, the totality of limited things. The ideal is therefore the prototype of all things, which, as defective copies (*ectypa*), receive from it the material of their possibility, and approximate to it more or less, though it is impossible that they can ever attain to its perfection.

The possibility of things must therefore be regarded as derived—except that of the thing which contains in itself all reality, which must be considered to be primitive and original. For all negations—and they are the only predicates by means of which all other things can be distinguished from the *ens realissimum*—are mere limitations of a greater and a higher—nay, the highest reality; and they consequently presuppose this reality, and are, as regards their content, derived from it. The manifold nature of things is only an infinitely various mode of limiting the conception of the highest reality, which is their common substratum; just as all

[1] See pages 223 and 232.

figures are possible only as different modes of limiting infinite space. The object of the ideal of reason—an object existing only in reason itself—is also termed the *primal being* (*ens originarium*); as having no existence superior to him, the *supreme being* (*ens summum*); and as being the condition of all other beings, which rank under it, the *being of all beings* (*ens entium*). But none of these terms indicate the objective relation of an actually existing object to other things, but merely that of an *idea to conceptions*; and all our investigations into this subject still leave us in perfect uncertainty with regard to the existence of this being.

A primal being cannot be said to consist of many other beings with an existence which is derivative, for the latter presuppose the former, and therefore cannot be constitutive parts of it. It follows that the ideal of the primal being must be cogitated as simple.

The deduction of the possibility of all other things from this primal being cannot, strictly speaking, be considered as a *limitation*, or as a kind of *division* of its reality; for this would be regarding the primal being as a mere aggregate—which has been shown to be impossible, although it was so represented in our first rough sketch. The highest reality must be regarded rather as the *ground* than as the *sum total* of the possibility of all things, and the manifold nature of things be based, not upon the limitation of the primal being itself, but upon the complete series of effects which flow from it. And thus all our powers of sense, as well as all phenomenal reality, may be with propriety regarded as belonging to this series of effects, while they could not have formed parts of the idea, considered as an aggregate. Pursuing this track, and hypostatizing this idea, we shall find ourselves authorized to determine our notion of the Supreme Being by means of the mere conception of a highest reality, as one, simple, all-sufficient, eternal, and so on—in one word, to determine it in its unconditioned completeness by the aid of every possible predicate. The conception of such a being is the conception of *God* in its transcendental sense, and thus the ideal of pure reason is the object-matter of a transcendental *Theology*.

But, by such an employment of the transcendental idea, we should be overstepping the limits of its validity and purpose. For reason placed it, as the *conception* of all reality, at the basis of the complete determination of things, without requiring that this conception be regarded as the conception of an objective existence. Such an existence would be purely fictitious, and the hypostatizing of the content of the idea into an ideal, as an individual being, is a step perfectly unauthorized. Nay, more, we are not even called upon to assume the possibility of such an hypothesis, as none of the deductions drawn from such an ideal would affect the complete determination of things in general—for the sake of which alone is the idea necessary.

It is not sufficient to circumscribe the procedure and the dialectic of reason; we must also endeavour to discover the sources of this dialectic, that we may have it in our power to give a rational explanation of this illusion, as a phenomenon of the human mind. For the ideal, of which we are at present speaking, is based, not upon an arbitrary, but upon a natural, idea. The question hence arises: How happens it that reason regards the possibility of all things as deduced from a single possibility, that, to wit, of the highest reality, and presupposes this as existing in an individual and primal being?

The answer is ready; it is at once presented by the procedure of transcendental analytic. The possibility of sensuous objects is a relation of these objects to thought, in which something (the empirical form) may be cogitated *a priori*; while that which constitutes the matter—the reality of the phenomenon (that element which corresponds to sensation)—must be given from without, as otherwise it could not even be cogitated by, nor could its possibility be presentable to the mind. Now, a sensuous object is completely determined, when it has been compared with all phenomenal predicates, and represented by means of these either positively or negatively. But, as that which constitutes the thing itself—the real in a phenomenon, must be given, and that, in which the real of *all phenomena* is given, is experience, one, sole, and all-embracing—the material of the possibility of all sensuous objects must be presupposed as given in a whole, and it is upon the limitation of this whole that the possibility of all empirical objects, their distinction from each other and their complete determination, are based. Now, no other objects are presented to us besides sensuous objects, and these can be given only in connection with a possible experience; it follows that a thing is not an object *to us*, unless it presupposes the whole or sum total of empirical reality as the condition of its possibility. Now, a natural illusion leads us to consider this principle, which is valid only of sensuous objects, as valid with regard to things in general. And thus we are induced to hold the empirical principle of our conceptions of the possibility of things, as phenomena, by leaving out this limitative condition, to be a transcendental principle of the possibility of things in general.

We proceed afterwards to hypostatize this idea of the sum-total of all reality, by changing the *distributive* unity of the empirical exercise of the understanding into the *collective* unity of an empirical whole—a dialectical illusion, and by cogitating this whole or sum of experience as an individual thing, containing in itself all empirical reality. This individual thing or being is then, by means of the above-mentioned transcendental subreption, substituted for our notion of a thing which stands at the head of the possibility of all things, the real conditions of whose complete determination it presents.[1]

## Section III

### Of the Arguments Employed by Speculative Reason in proof of the Existence of a Supreme Being

NOTWITHSTANDING the pressing necessity which reason feels, to form some presupposition that shall serve the understanding as a proper basis for the complete determination of its conceptions, the idealistic and factitious nature of such a presupposition is too evident to allow reason for a moment to persuade itself into a belief of the objective existence of a mere creation of its own thought. But there are other considerations which compel reason to seek out some resting-place in the regress from the conditioned to the unconditioned, which is not given as an actual existence from the mere conception of it, although it alone can give completeness to the series of conditions. And this is the natural course of every human reason, even of the most uneducated, although the path at first entered it does not always continue to follow. It does not begin from conceptions, but from common experience, and requires a basis in actual existence. But this basis is insecure, unless it rests upon the immovable rock of the absolutely necessary. And this foundation is itself unworthy of trust, if it leave under and above it empty space, if it do not fill all, and leave no room for a *why* or a *wherefore*, if it be not, in one word, infinite in its reality.

---

[1] This ideal of the *ens realissimum*—although merely a mental representation—is first *objectivized*, that is, has an objective existence attributed to it, then *hypostatized*, and finally, by the natural progress of reason to the completion of unity, *personified*, as we shall show presently. For the regulative unity of experience is not based upon phenomena themselves, but upon the connection of the variety of phenomena by the *understanding* in a *consciousness*, and thus the unity of the supreme reality and the complete determinability of all things, seem to reside in a supreme understanding, and consequently, in a conscious intelligence.

If we admit the existence of some one thing, whatever it may be, we must also admit that there is something which exists *necessarily*. For what is contingent exists only under the condition of some other thing, which is its cause; and from this we must go on to conclude the existence of a cause which is not contingent, and which consequently exists necessarily and unconditionally. Such is the argument by which reason justifies its advances towards a primal being.

Now reason looks round for the conception of a being that may be admitted, without inconsistency, to be worthy of the attribute of absolute necessity, not for the purpose of inferring *a priori*, from the conception of such a being, its objective existence (for if reason allowed itself to take this course, it would not require a basis in given and actual existence, but merely the support of pure conceptions), but for the purpose of discovering, among all our conceptions of possible things, that conception which possesses no element inconsistent with the idea of absolute necessity. For that there must be some absolutely necessary existence, it regards as a truth already established. Now, if it can remove every existence incapable of supporting the attribute of absolute necessity, excepting one—this must be the absolutely necessary being, whether its necessity is comprehensible by us, that is, deducible from the conception of it alone, or not.

Now that, the conception of which contains a *therefore* to every *wherefore*, which is not defective in any respect whatever, which is all-sufficient as a condition, seems to be the being of which we can justly predicate absolute necessity—for this reason, that, possessing the conditions of all that is possible, it does not and cannot itself require any condition. And thus it satisfies, in one respect at least, the requirements of the conception of absolute necessity. In this view, it is superior to all other conceptions, which, as deficient and incomplete, do not possess the characteristic of independence of all higher conditions. It is true that we cannot infer from this that what does not contain in itself the supreme and complete condition—the condition of all other things, must possess only a conditioned existence; but as little can we assert the contrary, for this supposed being does not possess the only characteristic which can enable reason to cognize by means of an *a priori* conception the unconditioned and necessary nature of its existence.

The conception of an *ens realissimum* is that which best agrees with the conception of an unconditioned and necessary being. The former conception does not satisfy all the requirements of the latter; but we have no choice, we are obliged to adhere to it, for we find that we cannot do without the existence of a necessary being; and even although we admit it, we find it out of our power to discover in the whole sphere of possibility any being that can advance well-grounded claims to such a distinction.

The following is, therefore, the natural course of human reason. It begins by persuading itself of the existence of some necessary being. In this being it recognizes the characteristics of unconditioned existence. It then seeks the conception of that which is independent of all conditions, and finds it in that which is itself the sufficient condition of all other things—in other words, in that which contains all reality. But the unlimited all is an absolute unity, and is conceived by the mind as a being one and supreme; and thus reason concludes that the Supreme Being, as the primal basis of all things, possesses an existence which is absolutely necessary.

This conception must be regarded as in some degree satisfactory, if we admit the existence of a necessary being, and consider that there exists a necessity for a definite and final answer to these questions. In such a case, we cannot make a better choice, or rather we have no choice at all, but feel ourselves obliged to declare in favour of the absolute unity of complete reality, as the highest source of the possibility of things. But if there exists no motive for coming to a definite conclusion, and we may leave the question unanswered till we have fully weighed both sides—in other words, when we are merely called upon to decide how much we happen to know about the question, and how much we merely flatter ourselves that we know—the above conclusion does not appear to so great advantage, but, on the contrary, seems defective in the grounds upon which it is supported.

For, admitting the truth of all that has been said, that, namely, the inference from a given existence (my own, for example) to the existence of an unconditioned and necessary being is valid and unassailable; that, in the second place, we must consider a being which contains all reality, and consequently all the conditions of other things, to be absolutely unconditioned; and admitting too, that we have thus discovered the conception of a thing to which may be attributed, without inconsistency, absolute necessity—it does not follow from all this that the conception of a limited being, in which the supreme reality does not reside, is therefore incompatible with the idea of absolute necessity. For, although I do not discover the element of the unconditioned in the conception of such a being—an element which is manifestly existent in the sum total of all conditions, I am not entitled to conclude that its existence is therefore conditioned; just as I am not entitled to affirm, in a hypothetical syllogism, that where a certain condition does not exist (in the present, completeness, as far as pure conceptions are concerned), the conditioned does not exist either. On the contrary, we are free to consider all limited beings as likewise unconditionally necessary, although we are unable to infer this from the general conception which we have of them. Thus conducted, this argument is incapable of giving us the least notion of the properties of a necessary being, and must be in every respect without result.

This argument continues, however, to possess a weight and an authority, which, in spite of its objective insufficiency, it has never been divested of. For, granting that certain responsibilities lie upon us, which, as based on the ideas of reason, deserve to be respected and submitted to, although they are incapable of a real or practical application to our nature, or, in other words, would be responsibilities without motives, except upon the supposition of a Supreme Being to give effect and influence to the practical laws: in such a case we should be bound to obey our conceptions, which, although objectively insufficient, do, according to the standard of reason, preponderate over and are superior to any claims that may be advanced from any other quarter. The equilibrium of doubt would in this case be destroyed by a practical addition; indeed, Reason would be compelled to condemn herself, if she refused to comply with the demands of the judgment, no superior to which we know—however defective her understanding of the grounds of these demands might be.

This argument, although in fact transcendental, inasmuch as it rests upon the intrinsic insufficiency of the contingent, is so simple and natural, that the commonest understanding can appreciate its value. We see things around us change, arise, and pass away; they, or their condition, must therefore have a cause. The same demand must again be made of the cause itself—as a datum of experience. Now it is natural that we should place the *highest* causality just where we place *supreme* causality, in that being, which contains the conditions of all possible effects, and the conception of which is so simple as that of an all-embracing reality. This highest cause, then, we regard as absolutely necessary, because we find it absolutely necessary to rise to it, and do not discover any reason for proceeding beyond it. Thus, among all nations, through the darkest polytheism glimmer some faint sparks of monotheism, to which these idolaters have been led, not from reflection and profound thought, but by the study and natural progress of the common understanding.

There are only three modes of proving the existence of a Deity, on the grounds of speculative reason.

All the paths conducting to this end, begin either from determinate experience and the peculiar constitution of the world of sense, and rise, according to the laws of causality, from it to the highest cause existing apart from the world—or from a purely indeterminate experience, that is, some empirical existence—or abstraction is made of all experience, and the existence of a supreme cause is concluded from *a priori* conceptions alone. The first is the *physico-theological* argument, the second the *cosmological*, the third the *ontological*. More there are not, and more there cannot be.

I shall show it is as unsuccessful on the one path—the empirical, as on the other—the transcendental, and that it stretches its wings in vain, to soar beyond the world of sense by the mere might of speculative thought. As regards the order in which we must discuss those arguments, it will be exactly the reverse of that in which reason, in the progress of its development, attains to them—the order in which they are placed above. For it will be made manifest to the reader, that, although experience presents the occasion and the starting-point, it is the *transcendental idea* of reason which guides it in its pilgrimage, and is the goal of all its struggles. I shall therefore begin with an examination of the transcendental argument, and afterwards inquire, what additional strength has accrued to this mode of proof from the addition of the empirical element.

## SECTION IV

### *Of the Impossibility of an Ontological Proof of the Existence of God*

IT is evident from what has been said, that the conception of an absolutely necessary being is a mere idea, the objective reality of which is far from being established by the mere fact that it is a need of reason. On the contrary, this idea serves merely to indicate a certain unattainable perfection, and rather limits the operations than, by the presentation of new objects, extends the sphere of the understanding. But a strange anomaly meets us at the very threshold; for the inference from a given existence in general to an absolutely necessary existence, seems to be correct and unavoidable, while the conditions of the *understanding* refuse to aid us in forming any conception of such a being.

Philosophers have always talked of an *absolutely necessary* being, and have nevertheless declined to take the trouble of conceiving, whether—and how—a being of this nature is even cogitable, not to mention that its existence is actually demonstrable. A verbal definition of the conception is certainly easy enough: it is something, the non-existence of which is impossible. But does this definition throw any light upon the conditions which render it impossible to cogitate the non-existence of a thing—conditions which we wish to ascertain, that we may discover whether we think anything in the conception of such a being or not? For the mere fact that I throw away, by means of the word *Unconditioned*, all the conditions which the understanding habitually requires in order to regard anything as necessary, is very far from making clear whether by means of the conception of the unconditionally necessary I think of something, or really of nothing at all.

Nay, more, this chance-conception, now become so current, many have endeavoured to explain by examples which seemed to render any inquiries regarding its intelligibility quite needless. Every geometrical proposition—a triangle has three angles—it was said, is absolutely necessary; and thus people talked of an object which lay out of the sphere of our understanding as if it were perfectly plain what the conception of such a being meant.

All the examples adduced have been drawn, without exception, from *judgments*, and not from *things*. But the unconditioned necessity of a judgment does not form the absolute necessity of a thing. On the contrary, the absolute necessity of a judgment is only a conditioned necessity of a thing, or of the predicate in a judgment. The proposition above-mentioned does not enounce that three angles necessarily exist, but, upon condition that a triangle exists, three angles must necessarily exist—in it. And thus this logical necessity has been the source of the greatest delusions. Having formed an *a priori* conception of a thing, the content of which was made to embrace existence, we believed ourselves safe in concluding that, because existence belongs necessarily to the object of the conception (that is, under the condition of my positing this thing as given), the existence of the thing is also posited necessarily, and that it is therefore absolutely necessary—merely because its existence has been cogitated in the conception.

If, in an identical judgment, I annihilate the predicate in thought, and retain the subject, a contradiction is the result; and hence I say, the former belongs necessarily to the latter. But if I suppress both subject and predicate in thought, no contradiction arises; for there *is nothing* at all, and therefore no means of forming a contradiction. To suppose the existence of a triangle and not that of its three angles, is self-contradictory; but to suppose the non-existence of both triangle and angles is perfectly admissible. And so is it with the conception of an absolutely necessary being. Annihilate its existence in thought, and you annihilate the thing itself with all its predicates; how then can there be any room for contradiction? Externally,[1] there is nothing to give rise to a contradiction, for a thing cannot be necessary externally; nor internally, for, by the annihilation or suppression of the thing itself, its internal properties are also annihilated. God is omnipotent—that is a necessary judgment. His omnipotence cannot be denied, if the existence of a Deity is posited—the existence, that is, of an infinite being, the two conceptions being identical. But when you say, *God does not exist,* neither omnipotence nor any other predicate is affirmed; they must all disappear with the subject, and in this judgment there cannot exist the least self-contradiction.

You have thus seen, that when the predicate of a judgment is annihilated in thought along with the subject, no internal contradiction can arise, be the predicate what it may. There is no possibility of evading the conclusion—you find yourselves compelled to declare: There are certain subjects which cannot be annihilated in thought. But this is nothing more than saying: There exist subjects which are absolutely necessary—the very hypothesis which you are called upon to establish. For I find myself unable to form the slightest conception of a thing which, when annihilated in thought with all its predicates, leaves behind a contradiction; and contradiction is the only criterion of impossibility, in the sphere of pure *a priori* conceptions.

Against these general considerations, the justice of which no one can dispute, one argument is adduced, which is regarded as furnishing a satisfactory demonstration from the fact. It is affirmed, that there is one and only one conception, in which the non-being or annihilation of the object is self-contradictory, and this is the conception of an *ens realissimum.* It possesses, you say, all reality, and you feel yourselves justified in admitting the possibility of such a being. (This I am willing to grant for the present, although the existence of a conception which is not self-contradictory is far from being sufficient to prove the possibility

[1] In relation to other things.—*Tr.*

of an object.[1])  Now the notion of all reality embraces in it that of existence; the notion of existence lies, therefore, in the conception of this possible thing.  If this thing is annihilated in thought, the internal possibility of the thing is also annihilated, which is self-contradictory.

I answer: It is absurd to introduce—under whatever term disguised—into the conception of a thing, which is to be cogitated solely in reference to its possibility, the conception of its existence. If this is admitted, you will have apparently gained the day, but in reality have enounced nothing but a mere tautology.  I ask, is the proposition, *this or that thing* (which I am admitting to be possible) *exists*, an analytical or a synthetical proposition?  If the former, there is no addition made to the subject of your thought by the affirmation of its existence; but then the conception in your minds is identical with the thing itself, or you have supposed the existence of a thing to be possible, and then inferred its existence from its internal possibility—which is but a miserable tautology.  The word *reality* in the conception of the thing, and the word *existence* in the conception of the predicate, will not help you out of the difficulty.  For, supposing you were to term all positing of a thing, reality, you have thereby posited the thing with all its predicates in the conception of the subject and assumed its actual existence, and this you merely repeat in the predicate. But if you confess, as every reasonable person must, that every existential proposition is synthetical, how can it be maintained that the predicate of existence cannot be denied without contradiction?—a property which is the characteristic of analytical propositions, alone.

I should have a reasonable hope of putting an end for ever to this sophistical mode of argumentation, by a strict definition of the conception of existence, did not my own experience teach me that the illusion arising from our confounding a logical with a real predicate (a predicate which aids in the determination of a thing) resists almost all the endeavours of explanation and illustration. A *logical predicate* may be what you please, even the subject may be predicated of itself; for logic pays no regard to the content of

[1] A conception is always possible, if it is not self-contradictory.  This is the logical criterion of possibility, distinguishing the object of such a conception from the *nihil negativum*.  But it may be, notwithstanding, an empty conception, unless the objective reality of this synthesis, by which it is generated, is demonstrated; and a proof of this kind must be based upon principles of possible experience, and not upon the principle of analysis or contradiction. This remark may be serviceable as a warning against concluding, from the possibility of a conception—which is logical, the possibility of a thing—which is real.

a judgment. But the determination of a conception is a predicate, which adds to and enlarges the conception. It must not, therefore, be contained in the conception.

*Being* is evidently not a real predicate, that is, a conception of something which is added to the conception of some other thing. It is merely the positing of a thing, or of certain determinations in it. Logically, it is merely the copula of a judgment. The proposition, *God is omnipotent*, contains two conceptions, which have a certain object or content; the word *is*, is no additional predicate—it merely indicates the relation of the predicate to the subject. Now, if I take the subject (God) with all its predicates (omnipotence being one), and say: *God is*, or, *There is a God*, I add no new predicate to the conception of God, I merely posit or affirm the existence of the subject with all its predicates—I posit the *object* in relation to my *conception*. The content of both is the same; and there is no addition made to the conception, which expresses merely the possibility of the object, by my cogitating the object—in the expression, it *is*—as absolutely given or existing. Thus the real contains no more than the possible. A hundred real dollars contain no more than a hundred possible dollars. For, as the latter indicate the conception, and the former the object, on the supposition that the content of the former was greater than that of the latter, my conception would not be an expression of the whole object, and would consequently be an inadequate conception of it. But in reckoning my wealth there may be said to be more in a hundred real dollars than in a hundred possible dollars—that is, in the mere conception of them. For the real object—the dollars—is not analytically contained in my conception, but forms a synthetical addition to my conception (which is merely a determination of my mental state), although this objective reality—this existence—apart from my conceptions, does not in the least degree increase the aforesaid hundred dollars.

By whatever and by whatever number of predicates—even to the complete determination of it—I may cogitate a thing, I do not in the least augment the object of my conception by the addition of the statement, this thing exists. Otherwise, not exactly the same, but something more than what was cogitated in my conception, would exist, and I could not affirm that the exact object of my conception had real existence. If I cogitate a thing as containing all modes of reality except one, the mode of reality which is absent is not added to the conception of the thing by the affirmation that the thing exists; on the contrary, the thing exists —if it exist at all—with the same defect as that cogitated in its conception; otherwise not that which was cogitated, but something different, exists. Now, if I cogitate a being as the highest reality, without defect or imperfection, the question still remains—whether this being exists or not. For although no element is wanting in the possible real content of my conception, there is a defect in its relation to my mental state, that is, I am ignorant whether the cognition of the object indicated by the conception is possible *a posteriori*. And here the cause of the present difficulty becomes apparent. If the question regarded an object of sense merely, it would be impossible for me to confound the conception with the existence of a thing. For the conception merely enables me to cogitate an object as according with the general conditions of experience; while the existence of the object permits me to cogitate it as contained in the sphere of actual experience. At the same time, this connection with the world of experience does not in the least augment the conception, although a possible perception has been added to the experience of the mind. But if we cogitate existence by the pure category alone, it is not to be wondered at, that we should find ourselves unable to present any criterion sufficient to distinguish it from mere possibility.

Whatever be the content of our conception of an object, it is necessary to go beyond it, if we wish to predicate existence of the object. In the case of sensuous objects, this is attained by their connection according to empirical laws with some one of my perceptions; but there is no means of cognizing the existence of objects of pure thought, because it must be cognized completely *a priori*. But all our knowledge of existence (be it immediately by perception, or by inferences connecting some object with a perception) belongs entirely to the sphere of experience—which is in perfect unity with itself; and although an existence out of this sphere cannot be absolutely declared to be impossible, it is a hypothesis the truth of which we have no means of ascertaining.

The notion of a Supreme Being is in many respects a highly useful idea; but for the very reason that it is an idea, it is incapable of enlarging our cognition with regard to the existence of things. It is not even sufficient to instruct us as to the possibility of a being which we do not know to exist. The analytical criterion of possibility, which consists in the absence of contradiction in propositions, cannot be denied it. But the connection of real properties in a thing is a synthesis of the possibility of which an *a priori* judgment cannot be formed, because these realities are not presented to us specifically; and even if this were to happen, a judgment would still be impossible, because the criterion of the possibility of synthetical cognitions must be sought for in the world of experience, to which the object of an idea cannot belong. And thus the celebrated Leibnitz has utterly failed in his attempt to establish upon *a priori* grounds the possibility of this sublime ideal being.

The celebrated ontological or Cartesian argument for the existence of a Supreme Being is therefore insufficient; and we may as well hope to increase our stock of knowledge by the aid of mere ideas, as the merchant to augment his wealth by the addition of noughts to his cash-account.

## SECTION V

### *Of the Impossibility of a Cosmological Proof of the Existence of God*

IT was by no means a natural course of proceeding, but, on the contrary, an invention entirely due to the subtlety of the schools, to attempt to draw from a mere idea a proof of the existence of an object corresponding to it. Such a course would never have been pursued, were it not for that need of reason which requires it to suppose the existence of a necessary being as a basis for the empirical regress, and that, as this necessity must be unconditioned and *a priori*, reason is bound to discover a conception which shall satisfy, if possible, this requirement, and enable us to attain to the *a priori* cognition of such a being. This conception was thought to be found in the idea of an *ens realissimum*, and thus this idea was employed for the attainment of a better defined knowledge of a necessary being, of the existence of which we were convinced, or persuaded, on other grounds. Thus reason was seduced from her natural course; and, instead of concluding with the conception of an *ens realissimum*, an attempt was made to begin with it, for the purpose of inferring from it that idea of a necessary existence which it was in fact called in to complete. Thus arose that unfortunate ontological argument, which neither satisfies the healthy common sense of humanity, nor sustains the scientific examination of the philosopher.

The *cosmological proof*, which we are about to examine, retains the connection between absolute necessity and the highest reality; but, instead of reasoning from this highest reality to a necessary existence, like the preceding argument, it concludes from the given unconditioned necessity of some being its unlimited reality. The track it pursues, whether rational or sophistical, is at least natural, and not only goes far to persuade the common under-

with the credentials of pure reason, and the other with those of empiricism; while, in fact, it is only the former who has changed his dress and voice, for the purpose of passing himself off for an additional witness. That it may possess a secure foundation, it bases its conclusions upon experience, and thus appears to be completely distinct from the ontological argument, which places its confidence entirely in pure *a priori* conceptions. But this experience merely aids reason in making one step—to the existence of a necessary being. What the properties of this being are, cannot be learned from experience; and therefore reason abandons it altogether, and pursues its inquiries in the sphere of pure conceptions, for the purpose of discovering what the properties of an absolutely necessary being ought to be, that is, what among all possible things contain the conditions (*requisita*) of absolute necessity. Reason believes that it has discovered these requisites in the conception of an *ens realissimum*—and in it alone, and hence concludes: The *ens realissimum* is an absolutely necessary being. But it is evident that reason has here presupposed that the conception of an *ens realissimum* is perfectly adequate to the conception of a being of absolute necessity, that is, that we may infer the existence of the latter from that of the former—a proposition which formed the basis of the ontological argument, and which is now employed in the support of the cosmological argument, contrary to the wish and professions of its inventors. For the existence of an absolutely necessary being is given in conceptions alone. But if I say—the conception of the *ens realissimum* is a conception of this kind, and in fact the only conception which is adequate to our idea of a necessary being, I am obliged to admit, that the latter may be inferred from the former. Thus it is properly the ontological argument which figures in the cosmological, and constitutes the whole strength of the latter; while the spurious basis of experience has been of no further use than to conduct us to the conception of absolute necessity, being utterly insufficient to demonstrate the presence of this attribute in any determinate existence or thing. For when we propose to ourselves an aim of this character, we must abandon the sphere of experience, and rise to that of pure conceptions, which we examine with the purpose of discovering whether any one contains the conditions of the possibility of an absolutely necessary being. But if the possibility of such a being is thus demonstrated, its existence is also proved; for we may then assert that, of all possible beings there is one which possesses the attribute of necessity—in other words, this being possesses an absolutely necessary existence.

standing, but shows itself deserving of respect from the speculati
intellect; while it contains, at the same time, the outlines of a
the arguments employed in natural theology—arguments whic
always have been, and still will be, in use and authority. These
however adorned, and hid under whatever embellishments o
rhetoric and sentiment, are at bottom identical with the arguments
we are at present to discuss. This proof, termed by Leibnitz the
*argumentum a contingentia mundi*, I shall now lay before the reader,
and subject to a strict examination.

It is framed in the following manner: If something exists, an
absolutely necessary being must likewise exist. Now I, at least,
exist. Consequently, there exists an absolutely necessary being.
The minor contains an experience, the major reasons from a general
experience to the existence of a necessary being.[1] Thus this
argument really begins at experience, and is not completely *a
priori*, or ontological. The object of all possible experience being
the world, it is called the *cosmological* proof. It contains no
reference to any peculiar property of sensuous objects, by which
this world of sense might be distinguished from other possible
worlds; and in this respect it differs from the physico-theological
proof, which is based upon the consideration of the peculiar
constitution of our sensuous world.

The proof proceeds thus: A necessary being can be determined
only in one way, that is, it can be determined by only one of all
possible opposed predicates; consequently, it must be *completely*
determined in and by its conception. But there is only a single
conception of a thing possible, which completely determines the
thing *a priori*: that is, the conception of the *ens realissimum*.
It follows that the conception of the *ens realissimum* is the only
conception by and in which we can cogitate a necessary being.
Consequently, a Supreme Being necessarily exists.

In this cosmological argument are assembled so many sophistical
propositions, that speculative reason seems to have exerted in it
all her dialectical skill to produce a transcendental illusion of the
most extreme character. We shall postpone an investigation of
this argument for the present, and confine ourselves to exposing
the stratagem by which it imposes upon us an old argument in a
new dress, and appeals to the agreement of two witnesses, the one

[1] This inference is too well known to require more detailed discussion.
It is based upon the spurious transcendental law of causality,[2] that everything
which is *contingent* has a cause, which, if itself contingent, must also have a
cause; and so on, till the series of subordinated causes must end with an
absolutely necessary cause, without which it would not possess completenes

[2] See note on page 178.—*Tr.*

All illusions in an argument are more easily detected when they are presented in the formal manner employed by the schools, which we now proceed to do.

If the proposition: Every absolutely necessary being is likewise an *ens realissimum*, is correct (and it is this which constitutes the *nervus probandi* of the cosmological argument), it must, like all affirmative judgments, be capable of conversion—the *conversio per accidens*, at least. It follows, then, that some *entia realissima* are absolutely necessary beings. But no *ens realissimum* is in any respect different from another, and what is valid of some, is valid of all. In this present case, therefore, I may employ simple conversion,[1] and say: Every *ens realissimum* is a necessary being. But as this proposition is determined *a priori* by the conceptions contained in it, the mere conception of an *ens realissimum* must possess the additional attribute of absolute necessity. But this is exactly what was maintained in the ontological argument, and not recognized by the cosmological, although it formed the real ground of its disguised and illusory reasoning.

Thus the second mode employed by speculative reason of demonstrating the existence of a Supreme Being, is not only, like the first, illusory and inadequate, but possesses the additional blemish of an *ignoratio elenchi*—professing to conduct us by a new road to the desired goal, but bringing us back, after a short circuit, to the old path which we had deserted at its call.

I mentioned above, that this cosmological argument contains a perfect nest of dialectical assumptions, which transcendental criticism does not find it difficult to expose and to dissipate. I shall merely enumerate these, leaving it to the reader, who must by this time be well practised in such matters, to investigate the fallacies residing therein.

The following fallacies, for example, are discoverable in this mode of proof: 1. The transcendental principle: Everything that is contingent must have a cause—a principle without significance, except in the sensuous world. For the purely intellectual conception of the contingent cannot produce any synthetical proposition, like that of causality, which is itself without significance or distinguishing characteristic except in the phenomenal world. But in the present case it is employed to help us beyond the limits of its sphere. 2. From the impossibility of an infinite ascending series of causes in the world of sense a first cause is inferred; a conclusion which the principles of the employment of reason do not justify even in the sphere of experience, and still less when

---

[1] *Conversio pura seu simplex.*—Tr.

an attempt is made to pass the limits of this sphere. 3. Reason allows itself to be satisfied upon insufficient grounds, with regard to the completion of this series. It removes all conditions (without which, however, no conception of Necessity can take place); and, as after this it is beyond our power to form any other conceptions, it accepts this as a completion of the conception it wishes to form of the series. 4. The logical possibility of a conception of the total of reality (the criterion of this possibility being the absence of contradiction) is confounded with the transcendental, which requires a principle of the practicability of such a synthesis—a principle which again refers us to the world of experience. And so on.

The aim of the cosmological argument is to avoid the necessity of proving the existence of a necessary being *a priori* from mere conceptions—a proof which must be ontological, and of which we feel ourselves quite incapable. With this purpose, we reason from an actual existence—an experience in general, to an absolutely necessary condition of that existence. It is in this case unnecessary to demonstrate its possibility. For after having proved that it exists, the question regarding its possibility is superfluous. Now, when we wish to define more strictly the nature of this necessary being, we do not look out for some being the conception of which would enable us to comprehend the necessity of its being—for if we could do this, an empirical presupposition would be unnecessary; no, we try to discover merely the negative condition (*conditio sine qua non*), without which a being would not be absolutely necessary. Now this would be perfectly admissible in every sort of reasoning, from a consequence to its principle; but in the present case it unfortunately happens that the condition of absolute necessity can be discovered in but a single being, the conception of which must consequently contain all that is requisite for demonstrating the presence of absolute necessity, and thus entitle me to infer this absolute necessity *a priori*. That is, it must be possible to reason conversely, and say—the thing, to which the conception of the highest reality belongs, is absolutely necessary. But if I cannot reason thus—and I cannot, unless I believe in the sufficiency of the ontological argument—I find insurmountable obstacles in my new path, and am really no farther than the point from which I set out. The conception of a Supreme Being satisfies all questions *a priori* regarding the internal determinations of a thing, and is for this reason an ideal without equal or parallel, the general conception of it indicating it as at the same time an *ens individuum* among all possible things. But the conception does not satisfy the question regarding its existence—which was the purpose of all our inquiries; and, although the existence of a necessary being were admitted, we should find it impossible to answer the question: What of all things in the world must be regarded as such?

It is certainly allowable to *admit* the existence of an all-sufficient being—a cause of all possible effects, for the purpose of enabling reason to introduce unity into its mode and grounds of explanation with regard to phenomena. But to assert that such a being *necessarily exists*, is no longer the modest enunciation of an admissible hypothesis, but the boldest declaration of an apodeictic certainty; for the cognition of that which is absolutely necessary, must itself possess that character.

The aim of the transcendental ideal formed by the mind is, either to discover a conception which shall harmonize with the idea of absolute necessity, or a conception which shall contain that idea. If the one is possible, so is the other; for reason recognizes that alone as absolutely necessary, which is necessary from its conception.[1] But both attempts are equally beyond our power—we find it impossible to *satisfy* the understanding upon this point, and as impossible to induce it to remain at rest in relation to this incapacity.

Unconditioned necessity, which, as the ultimate support and stay of all existing things, is an indispensable requirement of the mind, is an abyss on the verge of which human reason trembles in dismay. Even the idea of eternity, terrible and sublime as it is, as depicted by Haller, does not produce upon the mental vision such a feeling of awe and terror; for, although it *measures* the duration of things, it does not *support* them. We cannot bear, nor can we rid ourselves of the thought, that a being, which we regard as the greatest of all possible existences, should *say to himself*: I am from eternity to eternity; beside me there is nothing, except that which exists by my will; *but whence then am I?* Here all sinks away from under us; and the greatest, as the smallest, perfection, hovers without stay or footing in presence of the speculative reason, which finds it as easy to part with the one as with the other.

Many physical powers, which evidence their existence by their effects, are perfectly inscrutable in their nature; they elude all our powers of observation. The transcendental object which forms the basis of phenomena, and, in connection with it, the reason why our sensibility possesses this rather than that particular kind of conditions, are and must ever remain hidden from our mental

[1] That is, which *cannot be cogitated* as other than necessary.—*Tr.*

vision; the fact is there, the reason of the fact we cannot see. But an ideal of pure reason cannot be termed mysterious or *inscrutable*, because the only credential of its reality is the need of it felt by reason, for the purpose of giving completeness to the world of synthetical unity. An ideal is not even given as a cogitable *object*, and therefore cannot be inscrutable; on the contrary, it must, as a mere idea, be based on the constitution of reason itself, and on this account must be capable of explanation and solution. For the very essence of reason consists in its ability to give an account of all our conceptions, opinions, and assertions—upon objective, or, when they happen to be illusory and fallacious, upon subjective grounds.

*Detection and Explanation of the Dialectical Illusion in all Transcendental Arguments for the Existence of a Necessary Being*

Both of the above arguments are transcendental; in other words, they do not proceed upon empirical principles. For, although the cosmological argument professed to lay a basis of experience for its edifice of reasoning, it did not ground its procedure upon the peculiar constitution of experience, but upon pure principles of reason—in relation to an existence given by empirical consciousness; utterly abandoning its guidance, however, for the purpose of supporting its assertions entirely upon pure conceptions. Now what is the cause, in these transcendental arguments, of the dialectical, but natural, illusion, which connects the conceptions of necessity and supreme reality, and hypostatizes that which cannot be anything but an idea? What is the cause of this unavoidable step on the part of reason, of admitting that some one among all existing things must be necessary, while it falls back from the assertion of the existence of such a being as from an abyss? And how does reason proceed to explain this anomaly to itself, and from the wavering condition of a timid and reluctant approbation—always again withdrawn, arrive at a calm and settled insight into its cause?

It is something very remarkable that, on the supposition that something exists, I cannot avoid the inference, that something exists necessarily. Upon this perfectly natural—but not on that account reliable—inference does the cosmological argument rest. But, let me form any conception whatever of a thing, I find that I cannot cogitate the existence of the thing as absolutely necessary, and that nothing prevents me—be the thing or being what it may—from cogitating its non-existence. I may thus be obliged to admit that all existing things have a necessary basis, while I cannot cogitate any single or individual thing as necessary. In other words, I can never *complete* the regress through the conditions of existence, without admitting the existence of a necessary being; but, on the other hand, I cannot make a *commencement* from this being.

If I must cogitate something as existing necessarily as the basis of existing things, and yet am not permitted to cogitate any individual thing as in itself necessary, the inevitable inference is, that necessity and contingency are not properties of things themselves—otherwise an internal contradiction would result; that consequently neither of these principles is objective, but that they are merely subjective principles of reason—the one requiring us to seek for a necessary ground for everything that exists, that is, to be satisfied with no other explanation than that which is complete *a priori*, the other forbidding us ever to hope for the attainment of this completeness, that is, to regard no member of the empirical world as unconditioned. In this mode of viewing them, both principles, in their purely heuristic and regulative character, and as concerning merely the formal interest of reason, are quite consistent with each other. The one says—you must philosophize upon nature, as if there existed a necessary primal basis of all existing things, solely for the purpose of introducing systematic unity into your knowledge, by pursuing an idea of this character—a foundation which is arbitrarily admitted to be ultimate; while the other warns you to consider no individual determination, concerning the existence of things, as such an ultimate foundation, that is, as absolutely necessary, but to keep the way always open for further progress in the deduction, and to treat every determination as determined by some other. But if all that we perceive must be regarded as conditionally necessary, it is impossible that anything which is empirically given should be absolutely necessary.

It follows from this, that you must accept the absolutely necessary as *out of* and beyond the world, inasmuch as it is useful only as a principle of the highest possible unity in experience, and you cannot discover any such necessary existence in the *world*, the second rule requiring you to regard all empirical causes of unity as themselves deduced.

The philosophers of antiquity regarded all the forms of nature as contingent; while matter was considered by them, in accordance with the judgment of the common reason of mankind, as primal and necessary. But if they had regarded matter, not relatively—

as the substratum of phenomena, but absolutely and *in itself*—as an independent existence, this idea of absolute necessity would have immediately disappeared. For there is nothing absolutely connecting reason with such an existence; on the contrary, it can annihilate it in thought, always and without self-contradiction. But in thought alone lay the idea of absolute necessity. A regulative principle must, therefore, have been at the foundation of this opinion. In fact, extension and impenetrability—which together constitute our conception of matter—form the supreme empirical principle of the unity of phenomena, and this principle, in so far as it is empirically unconditioned, possesses the property of a regulative principle. But, as every determination of matter which constitutes what is real in it—and consequently impenetrability—is an effect, which must have a cause, and is for this reason always derived, the notion of matter cannot harmonize with the idea of a necessary being, in its character of the principle of all derived unity. For every one of its real properties, being derived, must be only conditionally necessary, and can therefore be annihilated in thought; and thus the whole existence of matter can be so annihilated or suppressed. If this were not the case, we should have found in the world of phenomena the highest ground or condition of unity—which is impossible, according to the second regulative principle. It follows, that matter, and, in general, all that forms part of the world of sense, cannot be a necessary primal being, nor even a principle of empirical unity, but that this being or principle must have its place assigned without the world. And, in this way, we can proceed in perfect confidence to deduce the phenomena of the world and their existence from other phenomena, just as if there existed no necessary being; and we can at the same time, strive without ceasing towards the attainment of completeness for our deduction, just as if such a being—the supreme condition of all existences—were presupposed by the mind.

These remarks will have made it evident to the reader that the ideal of the Supreme Being, far from being an enouncement of the existence of a being in itself necessary, is nothing more than a *regulative principle* of reason, requiring us to regard all connection existing between phenomena as if it had its origin from an all-sufficient necessary cause, and basing upon this the rule of a systematic and necessary unity in the explanation of phenomena. We cannot, at the same time, avoid regarding, by a transcendental *subreptio*, this formal principle as constitutive, and hypostatizing this unity. Precisely similar is the case with our notion of space.

Space is the primal condition of all forms, which are properly just so many different limitations of it; and thus, although it is merely a principle of sensibility, we cannot help regarding it as an absolutely necessary and self-subsistent thing—as an object given *a priori* in itself. In the same way, it is quite natural that, as the systematic unity of nature cannot be established as a principle for the empirical employment of reason, unless it is based upon the idea of an *ens realissimum*, as the supreme cause, we should regard this idea as a real object, and this object, in its character of supreme condition, as absolutely necessary, and that in this way a *regulative* should be transformed into a *constitutive* principle. This interchange becomes evident when I regard this supreme being, which, relatively to the world, was absolutely (unconditionally) necessary, as a thing *per se*. In this case, I find it impossible to represent this necessity in or by any conception, and it exists merely in my own mind, as the formal condition of thought, but not as a material and hypostatic condition of existence.

## Section VI

### *Of the Impossibility of a Physico-Theological Proof*

If, then, neither a pure conception nor the general experience of an existing being can provide a sufficient basis for the proof of the existence of the Deity, we can make the attempt by the only other mode—that of grounding our argument upon a *determinate experience* of the phenomena of the present world, their constitution and disposition, and discover whether we can thus attain to a sound conviction of the existence of a Supreme Being. This argument we shall term the *physico-theological* argument. If it is shown to be insufficient, speculative reason cannot present us with any satisfactory proof of the existence of a being corresponding to our transcendental idea.

It is evident from the remarks that have been made in the preceding sections, that an answer to this question will be far from being difficult or unconvincing. For how can any experience be adequate with an idea? The very essence of an idea consists in the fact that no experience can ever be discovered congruent or adequate with it. The transcendental idea of a necessary and all-sufficient being is so immeasurably great, so high above all that is empirical, which is always conditioned, that we hope in vain to find materials in the sphere of experience sufficiently ample for our conception, and in vain seek the unconditioned among things that are conditioned, while examples, nay, even guidance is denied us by the laws of empirical synthesis.

If the Supreme Being forms a link in the chain of empirical conditions, it must be a member of the empirical series, and, like the lower members which it precedes, have its origin in some higher member of the series. If, on the other hand, we disengage it from the chain, and cogitate it as an intelligible being, apart from the series of natural causes—how shall reason bridge the abyss that separates the latter from the former? All laws respecting the regress from effects to causes, all synthetical additions to our knowledge relate solely to possible experience and the objects of the sensuous world, and, apart from them, are without significance.

The world around us opens before our view so magnificent a spectacle of order, variety, beauty, and conformity to ends, that whether we pursue our observations into the infinity of space in the one direction, or into its illimitable divisions in the other, whether we regard the world in its greatest or its least manifestations—even after we have attained to the highest summit of knowledge which our weak minds can reach, we find that language in the presence of wonders so inconceivable has lost its force, and number its power to reckon, nay, even thought fails to conceive adequately, and our conception of the whole dissolves into an astonishment without the power of expression—all the more eloquent that it is dumb. Everywhere around us we observe a chain of causes and effects, of means and ends, of death and birth; and, as nothing has entered of itself into the condition in which we find it, we are constantly referred to some other thing, which itself suggests the same inquiry regarding its cause, and thus the universe must sink into the abyss of nothingness, unless we admit that, besides this infinite chain of contingencies, there exists something that is primal and self-subsistent—something which, as the cause of this phenomenal world, secures its continuance and preservation.

This highest cause—what magnitude shall we attribute to it? Of the content of the world we are ignorant; still less can we estimate its magnitude by comparison with the sphere of the possible. But this supreme cause being a necessity of the human mind, what is there to prevent us from attributing to it such a degree of perfection as to place it above the sphere of *all that* is possible? This we can easily do, although only by the aid of the faint outline of an abstract conception, by representing this being to ourselves as containing in itself, as an individual substance, all possible perfection—a conception which satisfies that requirement of reason which demands parsimony in principles,[1] which is free from self-contradiction, which even contributes to the extension of the employment of reason in experience, by means of the guidance afforded by this idea to order and system, and which in no respect conflicts with any law of experience.

This argument always deserves to be mentioned with respect. It is the oldest, the clearest, and that most in conformity with the common reason of humanity. It animates the study of nature, as it itself derives its existence and draws ever new strength from that source. It introduces aims and ends into a sphere in which our observation could not of itself have discovered them, and extends our knowledge of nature, by directing our attention to a unity, the principle of which lies beyond nature. This knowledge of nature again reacts upon this idea—its cause; and thus our belief in a divine author of the universe rises to the power of an irresistible conviction.

For these reasons it would be utterly hopeless to attempt to rob this argument of the authority it has always enjoyed. The mind, unceasingly elevated by these considerations, which, although empirical, are so remarkably powerful, and continually adding to their force, will not suffer itself to be depressed by the doubts suggested by subtle speculation; it tears itself out of this state of uncertainty, the moment it casts a look upon the wondrous forms of nature and the majesty of the universe, and rises from height to height, from condition to condition, till it has elevated itself to the supreme and unconditioned author of all.

But although we have nothing to object to the reasonableness and utility of this procedure, but have rather to commend and encourage it, we cannot approve of the claims which this argument advances to demonstrative certainty and to a reception upon its own merits, apart from favour or support by other arguments. Nor can it injure the cause of morality to endeavour to lower the tone of the arrogant sophist, and to teach him that modesty and moderation which are the properties of a belief that brings calm and content into the mind, without prescribing to it an unworthy subjection. I maintain, then, that the physico-theological argument is insufficient of itself to prove the existence of a Supreme Being, that it must entrust this to the ontological argument—to which it serves merely as an introduction, and that, consequently,

---

[1] A reference to the metaphysical dogma: *Entia practer necessitatem non sunt multiplicanda*, which may also be applied to logic, by the substitution of *principia* for *entia.*—*Tr.*

this argument contains the *only possible ground of proof* (possessed by speculative reason) for the existence of this being.

The chief momenta in the physico-theological argument are as follow: 1. We observe in the world manifest signs of an arrangement full of purpose, executed with great wisdom, and existing in a whole of a content indescribably various, and of an extent without limits. 2. This arrangement of means and ends is entirely foreign to the things existing in the world—it belongs to them merely as a contingent attribute; in other words, the nature of different things could not of itself, whatever means were employed, harmoniously tend towards certain purposes, were they not chosen and directed for these purposes by a rational and disposing principle, in accordance with certain fundamental ideas. 3. There exists, therefore, a sublime and wise cause (or several), which is not merely a blind, all-powerful nature, producing the beings and events which fill the world in unconscious *fecundity*, but a *free* and intelligent cause of the world. 4. The unity of this cause may be inferred from the unity of the reciprocal relation existing between the parts of the world, as portions of an artistic edifice—an inference which all our observation favours, and all principles of analogy support.

In the above argument, it is inferred from the analogy of certain products of nature with those of human art, when it compels nature to bend herself to its purposes, as in the case of a house, a ship, or a watch, that the same kind of causality—namely, understanding and will—resides in nature. It is also declared that the internal possibility of this freely-acting nature (which is the source of all art, and perhaps also of human reason) is derivable from another and superhuman art—a conclusion which would perhaps be found incapable of standing the test of subtle transcendental criticism. But to neither of these opinions shall we at present object. We shall only remark that it must be confessed that, if we are to discuss the subject of cause at all, we cannot proceed more securely than with the guidance of the analogy subsisting between nature and such products of design—these being the only products whose causes and modes of origination are completely known to us. Reason would be unable to satisfy her own requirements, if she passed from a causality which she does know, to obscure and indemonstrable principles of explanation which she does not know.

According to the physico-theological argument, the connection and harmony existing in the world evidence the contingency of the form merely, but not of the matter, that is, of the substance of the world. To establish the truth of the latter opinion, it would be necessary to prove that all things would be in themselves incapable of this harmony and order, unless they were, even as regards their *substance*, the product of a supreme wisdom. But this would require very different grounds of proof from those presented by the analogy with human art. This proof can at most, therefore, demonstrate the existence of an *architect of the world*, whose efforts are limited by the capabilities of the material with which he works, but not of a *creator of the world*, to whom all things are subject. Thus this argument is utterly insufficient for the task before us—a demonstration of the existence of an all-sufficient being. If we wish to prove the contingency of matter, we must have recourse to a transcendental argument, which the physico-theological was constructed expressly to avoid.

We infer, from the order and design visible in the universe, as a disposition of a thoroughly contingent character, the existence of a cause *proportionate thereto*. The conception of this cause must contain certain *determinate* qualities, and it must therefore be regarded as the conception of a being which possesses all power, wisdom, and so on, in one word, all perfection—the conception, that is, of an all-sufficient being. For the predicates of *very great*, astonishing, or immeasurable power and excellence, give us no determinate conception of the thing, nor do they inform us what the thing may be in itself. They merely indicate the relation existing between the magnitude of the object and the observer, who compares it with himself and with his own power of comprehension, and are mere expressions of praise and reverence, by which the object is either magnified, or the observing subject depreciated in relation to the object. Where we have to do with the magnitude (of the perfection) of a thing, we can discover no determinate conception, except that which comprehends all possible perfection or completeness, and it is only the total (*omnitudo*) of reality which is completely determined in and through its conception alone.

Now it cannot be expected that any one will be bold enough to declare that he has a perfect insight into the relation which the magnitude of the world he contemplates, bears (in its extent as well as in its content) to omnipotence, into that of the order and design in the world to the highest wisdom, and that of the unity of the world to the absolute unity of a Supreme Being.[1] Physico-

---

[1] Kant's meaning is, that no one will be bold enough to declare that he is certain that the world could not have existed without an *omnipotent* author; that none but the *highest* wisdom could have produced the harmony and order we observe in it; and that its unity is possible only under the condition of an absolute unity.—*Tr.*

theology is therefore incapable of presenting a determinate concep-tion of a supreme cause of the world, and is therefore insufficient as a principle of theology—a theology which is itself to be the basis of religion.

The attainment of absolute totality is completely impossible on the path of empiricism. And yet this is the path pursued in the physico-theological argument. What means shall we employ to bridge the abyss?

After elevating ourselves to admiration of the magnitude of the power, wisdom, and other attributes of the author of the world, and finding we can advance no further, we leave the argument on empirical grounds, and proceed to infer the contingency of the world from the order and conformity to aims that are observable in it. From this contingency we infer, by the help of transcen-dental conceptions alone, the existence of something absolutely necessary; and, still advancing, proceed from the conception of the absolute necessity of the first cause to the completely deter-mined or determining conception thereof—the conception of an all-embracing reality. Thus the physico-theological, failing in its undertaking, recurs in its embarrassment to the cosmological argument; and, as this is merely the ontological argument in disguise, it executes its design solely by the aid of pure reason, although it at first professed to have no connection with this faculty, and to base its entire procedure upon experience alone.

The physico-theologians have therefore no reason to regard with such contempt the transcendental mode of argument, and to look down upon it, with the conceit of clear-sighted observers of nature, as the brain-cobweb of obscure speculatists. For if they reflect upon and examine their own arguments, they will find that, after following for some time the path of nature and experience, and discovering themselves no nearer their object, they suddenly leave this path and pass into the region of pure possibility, where they hope to reach upon the wings of ideas what had eluded all their empirical investigations. Gaining, as they think, a firm footing after this immense leap, they extend their determinate conception—into the possession of which they have come, they know not how—over the whole sphere of creation, and explain their ideal, which is entirely a product of pure reason, by illustrations drawn from experience—though in a degree miserably unworthy of the grandeur of the object, while they refuse to acknowledge that they have arrived at this cognition or hypothesis by a very different road from that of experience.

Thus the physico-theological is based upon the cosmological, and this upon the ontological proof of the existence of a Supreme Being; and as besides these three there is no other path open to speculative reason, the ontological proof, on the ground of pure conceptions of reason, is the only possible one, if any proof of a proposition so far transcending the empirical exercise of the understanding is possible at all.

## Section VII

### Critique of all Theology based upon Speculative Principles of Reason

If by the term *Theology* I understand the cognition of a primal being, that cognition is based either upon reason alone (*theologia rationalis*) or upon revelation (*theologia revelata*). The former cogitates its object either by means of pure transcendental conceptions, as an *ens originarium, realissimum, ens entium,* and is termed *transcendental theology*; or, by means of a conception derived from the nature of our own mind, as a supreme intelligence, and must then be entitled *natural* theology. The person who believes in a transcendental theology alone, is termed a *Deist*; he who acknowledges the possibility of a *natural* theology also, a *Theist*. The former admits that we can cognize by pure reason alone the existence of a Supreme Being, but at the same time maintains that our conception of this being is purely transcendental, and that all we can say of it is, that it possesses all reality, without being able to define it more closely. The second asserts that reason is capable of presenting us, from the analogy with nature, with a more definite conception of this being, and that its operations, as the cause of all things, are the results of intelligence and free will. The former regards the Supreme Being as the *cause of the world*— whether by the necessity of his nature, or as a free agent, is left undetermined; the latter considers this being as the *author of the world*.

Transcendental theology aims either at inferring the existence of a Supreme Being from a general experience—without any closer reference to the world to which this experience belongs, and in this case it is called *Cosmotheology*; or it endeavours to cognize the existence of such a being, through mere conceptions, without the aid of experience, and is then termed *Ontotheology*.

Natural theology infers the attributes and the existence of an author of the world, from the constitution of, the order and unity observable in, the world, in which two modes of causality must be admitted to exist—those of nature and freedom. Thus it rises from this world to a supreme intelligence, either as the principle of all natural, or of all moral order and perfection. In the former case it is termed Physico-theology, in the latter, Ethical or Moral-theology.[1]

As we are wont to understand by the term *God* not merely an eternal nature, the operations of which are insensate and blind, but a Supreme Being, who is the free and intelligent author of all things, and as it is this latter view alone that can be of interest to humanity, we might, in strict rigour, deny to the *Deist* any belief in God at all, and regard him merely as a maintainer of the existence of a primal being or thing—the supreme cause of all other things. But, as no one ought to be blamed, merely because he does not feel himself justified in maintaining a certain opinion, as if he altogether denied its truth and asserted the opposite, it is more correct—as it is less harsh—to say, the Deist believes in a God, the Theist in a *living God* (*summa intelligentia*). We shall now proceed to investigate the sources of all these attempts of reason to establish the existence of a Supreme Being.

It may be sufficient in this place to define theoretical knowledge or cognition as knowledge of that which *is*, and practical knowledge as knowledge of that which *ought to be*. In this view, the theoretical employment of reason is that by which I cognize *a priori* (as necessary) that something is, while the practical is that by which I cognize *a priori* what ought to happen. Now, if it is an indubitably certain, though at the same time an entirely conditioned truth, that something is, or ought to happen, either a certain determinate condition of this truth is absolutely necessary, or such a condition may be arbitrarily presupposed. In the former case the condition is postulated (*per thesin*), in the latter supposed (*per hypothesin*). There are certain practical laws—those of morality—which are absolutely necessary. Now, if these laws necessarily presuppose the existence of some being, as the condition of the possibility of their *obligatory* power, this being must be *postulated*, because the conditioned, from which we reason to this determinate condition, is itself cognized *a priori* as absolutely necessary. We shall at some future time show that the moral laws not merely presuppose the existence of a Supreme Being, but also, as themselves absolutely necessary in a different relation, demand or postulate it—although only from a practical point of

[1] Not theological ethics; for this science contains ethical laws, which *presuppose* the existence of a Supreme Governor of the world; while Moral-theology, on the contrary, is the expression of a conviction of the existence of a Supreme Being, founded upon ethical laws.

standing, but shows itself deserving of respect from the speculative intellect; while it contains, at the same time, the outlines of all the arguments employed in natural theology—arguments which always have been, and still will be, in use and authority. These, however adorned, and hid under whatever embellishments of rhetoric and sentiment, are at bottom identical with the arguments we are at present to discuss. This proof, termed by Leibnitz the *argumentum a contingentia mundi*, I shall now lay before the reader, and subject to a strict examination.

It is framed in the following manner: If something exists, an absolutely necessary being must likewise exist. Now I, at least, exist. Consequently, there exists an absolutely necessary being. The minor contains an experience, the major reasons from a general experience to the existence of a necessary being.[1] Thus this argument really begins at experience, and is not completely *a priori*, or ontological. The object of all possible experience being the world, it is called the *cosmological* proof. It contains no reference to any peculiar property of sensuous objects, by which this world of sense might be distinguished from other possible worlds; and in this respect it differs from the physico-theological proof, which is based upon the consideration of the peculiar constitution of our sensuous world.

The proof proceeds thus: A necessary being can be determined only in one way, that is, it can be determined by only one of all possible opposed predicates; consequently, it must be *completely* determined in and by its conception. But there is only a single conception of a thing possible, which completely determines the thing *a priori*: that is, the conception of the *ens realissimum*. It follows that the conception of the *ens realissimum* is the only conception by and in which we can cogitate a necessary being. Consequently, a Supreme Being necessarily exists.

In this cosmological argument are assembled so many sophistical propositions, that speculative reason seems to have exerted in it all her dialectical skill to produce a transcendental illusion of the most extreme character. We shall postpone an investigation of this argument for the present, and confine ourselves to exposing the stratagem by which it imposes upon us an old argument in a new dress, and appeals to the agreement of two witnesses, the one

[1] This inference is too well known to require more detailed discussion. It is based upon the spurious transcendental law of causality,[2] that everything which is *contingent* has a cause, which, if itself contingent, must also have a cause; and so on, till the series of subordinated causes must end with an absolutely necessary cause, without which it would not possess completeness.

[2] See note on page 178.—*Tr.*

with the credentials of pure reason, and the other with those of empiricism; while, in fact, it is only the former who has changed his dress and voice, for the purpose of passing himself off for an additional witness. That it may possess a secure foundation, it bases its conclusions upon experience, and thus appears to be completely distinct from the ontological argument, which places its confidence entirely in pure *a priori* conceptions. But this experience merely aids reason in making one step—to the existence of a necessary being. What the properties of this being are, cannot be learned from experience; and therefore reason abandons it altogether, and pursues its inquiries in the sphere of pure conceptions, for the purpose of discovering what the properties of an absolutely necessary being ought to be, that is, what among all possible things contain the conditions (*requisita*) of absolute necessity. Reason believes that it has discovered these requisites in the conception of an *ens realissimum*—and in it alone, and hence concludes: The *ens realissimum* is an absolutely necessary being. But it is evident that reason has here presupposed that the conception of an *ens realissimum* is perfectly adequate to the conception of a being of absolute necessity, that is, that we may infer the existence of the latter from that of the former—a proposition which formed the basis of the ontological argument, and which is now employed in the support of the cosmological argument, contrary to the wish and professions of its inventors. For the existence of an absolutely necessary being is given in conceptions alone. But if I say—the conception of the *ens realissimum* is a conception of this kind, and in fact the only conception which is adequate to our idea of a necessary being, I am obliged to admit, that the latter may be inferred from the former. Thus it is properly the ontological argument which figures in the cosmological, and constitutes the whole strength of the latter; while the spurious basis of experience has been of no further use than to conduct us to the conception of absolute necessity, being utterly insufficient to demonstrate the presence of this attribute in any determinate existence or thing. For when we propose to ourselves an aim of this character, we must abandon the sphere of experience, and rise to that of pure conceptions, which we examine with the purpose of discovering whether any one contains the conditions of the possibility of an absolutely necessary being. But if the possibility of such a being is thus demonstrated, its existence is also proved; for we may then assert that, of all possible beings there is one which possesses the attribute of necessity—in other words, this being possesses an absolutely necessary existence.

view. The discussion of this argument we postpone for the present.

When the question relates merely to that which is, not to that which ought-to be, the conditioned which is presented in experience is always cogitated as contingent. For this reason its condition cannot be regarded as absolutely necessary, but merely as relatively necessary, or rather as *needful*; the condition is in itself and *a priori* a mere arbitrary presupposition in aid of the cognition, by reason, of the conditioned. If, then, we are to possess a theoretical cognition of the absolute necessity of a thing, we cannot attain to this cognition otherwise than *a priori* by means of *conceptions*; while it is impossible in this way to cognize the existence of a cause which bears any relation to an existence given in experience.

Theoretical cognition is *speculative* when it relates to an object or certain conceptions of an object which is not given and cannot be discovered by means of experience. It is opposed to the *cognition of nature*, which concerns only those objects or predicates which can be presented in a possible experience.

The principle that everything which happens (the *empirically* contingent) must have a cause, is a principle of the cognition of nature, but not of speculative cognition. For, if we change it into an abstract principle, and deprive it of its reference to experience and the empirical, we shall find that it cannot with justice be regarded any longer as a synthetical proposition, and that it is impossible to discover any mode of transition from that which exists to something entirely different—termed cause. Nay, more, the conception of a cause—as likewise that of the contingent —loses, in this speculative mode of employing it, all significance, for its objective reality and meaning are comprehensible from experience alone.

When from the existence of the universe and the things in it the existence of a cause of the universe is inferred, reason is proceeding not in the *natural*, but in the *speculative* method. For the principle of the former enounces, not that things themselves or substances, but only that which *happens* or their *states*—as empirically contingent, have a cause: the assertion that the existence of substance itself is contingent is not justified by experience, it is the assertion of a reason employing its principles in a speculative manner. If, again, I infer from the form of the universe, from the way in which all things are connected and act and react upon each other, the existence of a cause entirely distinct from the universe—this would again be a judgment of purely speculative reason; because the object in this case—the cause—

can never be an object of possible experience. In both these cases the principle of causality, which is valid only in the field of experience—useless and even meaningless beyond this region, would be diverted from its proper destination.

Now I maintain that all attempts of reason to establish a theology by the aid of speculation alone are fruitless, that the principles of reason as applied to nature do not conduct us to any theological truths, and, consequently, that a rational theology can have no existence, unless it is founded upon the laws of morality. For all synthetical principles of the understanding are valid only as *immanent* in experience; while the cognition of a Supreme Being necessitates their being employed transcendentally, and of this the understanding is quite incapable. If the empirical law of causality is to conduct us to a Supreme Being, this Being must belong to the chain of empirical objects—in which case it would be, like all phenomena, itself conditioned. If the possibility of passing the limits of experience be admitted, by means of the dynamical law of the relation of an effect to its cause, what kind of conception shall we obtain by this procedure? Certainly not the conception of a Supreme Being, because experience never presents us with the greatest of all possible effects, and it is only an effect of this character that could witness to the existence of a corresponding cause. If, for the purpose of fully satisfying the requirements of Reason, we recognize her right to assert the existence of a perfect and absolutely necessary being, this can be admitted only from favour, and cannot be regarded as the result or irresistible demonstration. The physico-theological proof may add weight to others—if other proofs there are—by connecting speculation with experience; but in itself it rather prepares the mind for theological cognition, and gives it a right and natural direction, than establishes a sure foundation for theology.

It is now perfectly evident that transcendental questions admit only of transcendental answers—those presented *a priori* by pure conceptions without the least empirical admixture. But the question in the present case is evidently synthetical—it aims at the extension of our cognition beyond the bounds of experience—it requires an assurance respecting the existence of a being corresponding with the idea in our minds, to which no experience can ever be adequate. Now it has been abundantly proved that all *a priori* synthetical cognition is possible only as the expression of the formal conditions of a possible experience; and that the validity of all principles depends upon their immanence in the field of experience, that is, their relation to objects of empirical cognition or phenomena. Thus all transcendental procedure in reference to speculative theology is without result.

If any one prefers doubting the conclusiveness of the proofs of our Analytic to losing the persuasion of the validity of these old and time-honoured arguments, he at least cannot decline answering the question—how he can pass the limits of all possible experience by the help of mere ideas. If he talks of new arguments, or of improvements upon old arguments—I request him to spare me. There is certainly no great choice in this sphere of discussion, as all speculative arguments must at last look for support to the ontological, and I have, therefore, very little to fear from the argumentative fecundity of the dogmatical defenders of a non-sensuous reason. Without looking upon myself as a remarkably combative person, I shall not decline the challenge to detect the fallacy and destroy the pretensions of every attempt of speculative theology. And yet the hope of better fortune never deserts those who are accustomed to the dogmatical mode of procedure. I shall, therefore, restrict myself to the simple and equitable demand that such reasoners will demonstrate, from the nature of the human mind as well as from that of the other sources of knowledge, how we are to proceed to extend our cognition completely *a priori*, and to carry it to that point where experience abandons us, and no means exist of guaranteeing the objective reality of our conceptions. In whatever way the understanding may have attained to a conception, the existence of the object of the conception cannot be discovered in it by analysis, because the cognition of the *existence* of the object depends upon the object's being posited and given in itself *apart from the conception*. But it is utterly impossible to go beyond our conception, without the aid of experience—which presents to the mind nothing but phenomena, or to attain by the help of mere conceptions to a conviction of the existence of new kinds of objects or supernatural beings.

But although pure speculative reason is far from sufficient to demonstrate the existence of a Supreme Being, it is of the highest utility in *correcting* our conception of this being—on the supposition that we can attain to the cognition of it by some other means—in making it consistent with itself and with all other conceptions of intelligible objects, clearing it from all that is incompatible with the conception of an *ens summum*, and eliminating from it all limitations or admixture of empirical elements.

Transcendental theology is still therefore, notwithstanding its objective insufficiency, of importance in a negative respect; it is useful as a test of the procedure of reason when engaged with pure ideas, no other than a transcendental standard being in this case admissible. For if, from a practical point of view, the hypothesis of a Supreme and All-sufficient Being is to maintain its validity without opposition, it must be of the highest importance to define this conception in a correct and rigorous manner—as the transcendental conception of a necessary being, to eliminate all phenomenal elements (anthropomorphism in its most extended signification), and at the same time to overflow all contradictory assertions—be they *atheistic, deistic,* or *anthropomorphic.* This is of course very easy; as the same arguments which demonstrated the inability of human reason to *affirm* the existence of a Supreme Being must be alike sufficient to prove the invalidity of its denial. For it is impossible to gain from the pure speculation of reason demonstration that there exists no Supreme Being, as the ground of all that exists, or that this being possesses none of those properties which we regard as analogical with the dynamical qualities of a thinking being, or that, as the anthropomorphists would have us believe, it is subject to all the limitations which sensibility imposes upon those intelligences which exist in the world of experience.

A Supreme Being is, therefore, for the speculative reason, a mere ideal, though a *faultless* one—a conception which perfects and crowns the system of human cognition, but the objective reality of which can neither be proved nor disproved by pure reason. If this defect is ever supplied by a Moral Theology, the problematic Transcendental Theology which has preceded, will have been at least serviceable as demonstrating the mental necessity existing for the conception, by the complete determination of it which it has furnished, and the ceaseless testing of the conclusions of a reason often deceived by sense, and not always in harmony with its own ideas. The attributes of necessity, infinitude, unity, existence apart from the world (and not as a world-soul), eternity —free from conditions of time, omnipresence—free from conditions of space, omnipotence, and others, are pure transcendental predicates; and thus the accurate conception of a Supreme Being, which every theology requires, is furnished by transcendental theology alone.

## APPENDIX

### TO TRANSCENDENTAL DIALECTIC

*Of the Regulative Employment of the Ideas of Pure Reason*

THE result of all the dialectical attempts of pure reason not only confirms the truth of what we have already proved in our Transcendental Analytic, namely, that all inferences which would lead us beyond the limits of experience are fallacious and groundless, but it at the same time teaches us this important lesson, that human reason has a natural inclination to overstep these limits, and that transcendental ideas are as much the natural property of the reason as categories are of the understanding. There exists this difference, however, that while the categories never mislead us, outward objects being always in perfect harmony therewith, ideas are the parents of irresistible illusions, the severest and most subtle criticism being required to save us from the fallacies which they induce.

Whatever is grounded in the nature of our powers, will be found to be in harmony with the final purpose and proper employment of these powers, when once we have discovered their true direction and aim. We are entitled to suppose, therefore, that there exists a mode of employing transcendental ideas which is proper and *immanent*; although, when we mistake their meaning, and regard them as conceptions of actual things, their mode of application is *transcendent* and delusive. For it is not the idea itself, but only the employment of the idea in relation to possible experience, that is transcendent or immanent. An idea is employed transcendently, when it is applied to an object falsely believed to be adequate with and to correspond to it; immanently, when it is applied solely to the employment of the *understanding* in the sphere of experience. Thus all errors of *subreptio*—of misapplication, are to be ascribed to defects of judgment, and not to understanding or reason.

Reason never has an immediate relation to an object; it relates immediately to the understanding alone. It is only through the understanding that it can be employed in the field of experience. It does not *form* conceptions of objects, it merely *arranges* them and gives to them that unity which they are capable of possessing when the sphere of their application has been extended as widely as possible. Reason avails itself of the conceptions of the understanding for the sole purpose of producing totality in the different series. This totality the understanding does not concern itself with; its only occupation is the connection of experiences, by which *series* of conditions in accordance with conceptions are established. The object of reason is therefore the understanding and its proper destination. As the latter brings unity into the diversity of objects by means of its conceptions, so the former brings unity into the diversity of conceptions by means of ideas; as it sets the final aim of a collective unity to the operations of the understanding, which without this occupies itself with a distributive unity alone.

I accordingly maintain, that transcendental ideas can never be employed as constitutive ideas, that they cannot be conceptions of objects, and that, when thus considered, they assume a fallacious and dialectical character. But, on the other hand, they are capable of an admirable and indispensably necessary application to objects —as regulative ideas, directing the understanding to a certain aim, the guiding lines towards which all its laws follow, and in which they all meet in one point. This point—though a mere idea (*focus imaginarius*), that is, not a point from which the conceptions of the understanding do really proceed, for it lies beyond the sphere of possible experience—serves notwithstanding to give to these conceptions the greatest possible unity combined with the greatest possible extension. Hence arises the natural illusion which induces us to believe that these lines proceed from an object which lies out of the sphere of empirical cognition, just as objects reflected in a mirror appear to be behind it. But this illusion— which we may hinder from imposing upon us—is necessary and unavoidable, if we desire to see, not only those objects which lie before us, but those which are at a great distance behind us; that is to say, when, in the present case, we direct the aims of the understanding, beyond every given experience, towards an extension as great as can possibly be attained.

If we review our cognitions in their entire extent, we shall find that the peculiar business of reason is to arrange them into a *system*, that is to say, to give them connection according to a principle. This unity presupposes an idea—the idea of the form of a whole (of cognition), preceding the determinate cognition of the parts, and containing the conditions which determine *a priori* to every part its place and relation to the other parts of the whole system. This idea accordingly demands complete unity in the cognition of the understanding—not the unity of a contingent aggregate, but that of a system connected according to necessary laws. It cannot be affirmed with propriety that this idea is a conception of an object; it is merely a conception of the complete unity of the conceptions of objects, in so far as this unity is available to the understanding as a rule. Such conceptions of reason are not derived from nature; on the contrary, we employ them for the interrogation and investigation of nature, and regard our cognition as defective so long as it is not adequate to them. We admit that such a thing as *pure earth*, *pure water*, or *pure air*, is not to be discovered. And yet we require these conceptions (which have their origin in the reason, so far as regards their absolute purity and completeness) for the purpose of determining the share which each of these natural causes has in every phenomenon. Thus the different kinds of matter are all referred to earths—as mere weight, to salts and inflammable bodies—as pure force, and finally, to water and air—as the *vehicula* of the former, or the machines employed by them in their operations—for the purpose of explaining the chemical action and reaction of bodies in accordance with the idea of a mechanism. For, although not actually so expressed, the influence of such ideas of reason is very observable in the procedure of natural philosophers.

If reason is the faculty of deducing the particular from the general, and if the general be certain *in se* and given, it is only necessary that the *judgment* should subsume the particular under the general, the particular being thus necessarily determined. I shall term this the demonstrative or apodeictic employment of reason. If, however, the general is admitted as *problematical* only, and is a mere idea, the particular case is certain, but the universality of the rule which applies to this particular case remains a problem. Several particular cases, the certainty of which is beyond doubt, are then taken and examined, for the purpose of discovering whether the rule is applicable to them; and if it appears that all the particular cases which can be collected follow from the rule, its universality is inferred, and at the same time, all the causes which have not, or cannot be presented to our observation, are concluded to be of the same character with those which we have observed. This I shall term the hypothetical employment of the reason.

The hypothetical exercise of reason by the aid of ideas employed as problematical conceptions is properly not *constitutive*. That is to say, if we consider the subject strictly, the truth of the rule, which has been employed as an hypothesis, does not follow from the use that is made of it by reason. For how can we know all the possible cases that may arise?—some of which may, however, prove exceptions to the universality of the rule. This employment of reason is merely regulative, and its sole aim is the introduction of unity into the aggregate of our particular cognitions, and thereby the *approximating* of the rule to universality.

The object of the hypothetical employment of reason is therefore the systematic unity of cognitions; and this unity is the *criterion* of the *truth* of a rule. On the other hand, this systematic unity —as a mere idea—is in fact merely a unity *projected*, not to be regarded as given, but only in the light of a problem—a problem which serves, however, as a principle for the various and particular exercise of the understanding in experience, directs it with regard to those cases which are not presented to our observation, and introduces harmony and consistency into all its operations.

All that we can be certain of from the above considerations is, that this systematic unity is a logical principle, whose aim is to assist the understanding, where it cannot of itself attain to rules, by means of ideas, to bring all these various rules under one principle, and thus to ensure the most complete consistency and connection that can be attained. But the assertion that objects and the understanding by which they are cognized are so constituted as to be determined to systematic unity, that this may be postulated *a priori*, without any reference to the interest of reason, and that we are justified in declaring all possible cognitions—empirical and others—to possess systematic unity, and to be subject to general principles from which, notwithstanding their various character, they are all derivable—such an assertion can be founded only upon a *transcendental* principle of reason, which would render this systematic unity not subjectively and logically—in its character of a method, but objectively necessary.

We shall illustrate this by an example. The conceptions of the understanding make us acquainted, among many other kinds of unity, with that of the causality of a substance, which is termed *power*. The different phenomenal manifestations of the same substance appear at first view to be so very dissimilar, that we are inclined to assume the existence of just as many different powers as there are different effects—as, in the case of the human mind, we have feeling, consciousness, imagination, memory, wit, analysis, pleasure, desire, and so on. Now we are required by a logical maxim to reduce these differences to as small a number as possible, by comparing them and discovering the hidden identity which exists. We must inquire, for example, whether or not imagination (connected with consciousness), memory, wit, and analysis are not merely different forms of understanding and reason. The idea of a *fundamental power*, the existence of which no effort of logic can assure us of, is the problem to be solved, for the systematic representation of the existing variety of powers. The logical principle of reason requires us to produce as great a unity as is possible in the system of our cognitions; and the more the phenomena of this and the other power are found to be identical, the more probable does it become, that they are nothing but different manifestations of one and the same power, which may be called, relatively speaking, a *fundamental power*. And so with other cases.

These relatively fundamental powers must again be compared with each other, to discover, if possible, the one radical and *absolutely* fundamental power of which they are but the manifestations. But this unity is purely hypothetical. It is not maintained, that this unity does really exist, but that we must, in the interest of reason, that is, for the establishment of principles for the various rules presented by experience, try to discover and introduce it, so far as is practicable, into the sphere of our cognitions.

But the transcendental employment of the understanding would lead us to believe that this idea of a fundamental power is not problematical, but that it possesses objective reality, and thus the systematic unity of the various powers or forces in a substance is demanded by the understanding and erected into an apodeictic or necessary principle. For, without having attempted to discover the unity of the various powers existing in nature, nay, even after all our attempts have failed, we notwithstanding presuppose that it does exist, and may be, sooner or later, discovered. And this reason does, not only, as in the case above adduced, with regard to the unity of substance, but where many substances, although all to a certain extent homogeneous, are discoverable, as in the case of matter in general. Here also does reason presuppose the existence of the systematic unity of various powers—inasmuch as particular laws of nature are subordinate to general laws; and parsimony in principles is not merely an economical principle of reason, but an essential law of nature.

We cannot understand, in fact, how a logical principle of unity can of right exist, unless we presuppose a transcendental principle, by which such a systematic unity—as a property of objects themselves—is regarded as necessary *a priori*. For with what right can reason, in its logical exercise, require us to regard the variety of forces which nature displays, as in effect a disguised unity, and to deduce them from one fundamental force or power, when she is free to admit that it is just as possible that all forces should be different in kind, and that a systematic unity is not conformable to the design of nature? In this view of the case, reason would be proceeding in direct opposition to her own destination, by setting as an aim an idea which entirely conflicts with the procedure and arrangement of nature. Neither can we assert that reason has previously inferred this unity from the contingent nature of phenomena. For the law of reason which requires us to seek for this unity is a necessary law, inasmuch as without it we should not possess a faculty of reason, nor without reason a consistent and self-accordant mode of employing the understanding, nor, in the absence of this, any proper and sufficient criterion of empirical truth. In relation to this criterion, therefore, we must suppose the idea of the systematic unity of nature to possess objective validity and necessity.

We find this transcendental presupposition lurking in different forms in the principles of philosophers, although they have neither recognized it nor confessed to themselves its presence. That the diversities of individual things do not exclude identity of species, that the various species must be considered as merely different determinations of a few *genera*, and these again as divisions of still higher *races*, and so on—that, accordingly, a certain systematic unity of all possible empirical conceptions, in so far as they can be deduced from higher and more general conceptions, must be sought for, is a scholastic maxim or logical principle, without which reason could not be employed by us. For we can infer the particular from the general, only in so far as general properties of things constitute the foundation upon which the particular rest.

That the same unity exists in nature is presupposed by philosophers in the well-known scholastic maxim, which forbids us unnecessarily to augment the number of entities or principles (*entia praeter necessitatem non esse multiplicanda*). This maxim asserts that nature herself assists in the establishment of this unity of reason, and that the seemingly infinite diversity of phenomena should not deter us from the expectation of discovering beneath this diversity a unity of fundamental properties, of which the aforesaid variety is but a more or less determined form. This unity, although a mere idea, has been always pursued with so much zeal, that thinkers have found it necessary rather to moderate the desire than to encourage it. It was considered a great step when chemists were able to reduce all salts to two main genera—acids and alkalis; and they regard this difference as itself a mere variety, or different manifestation of one and the same fundamental material. The different kinds of earths (stones and even metals) chemists have endeavoured to reduce to three, and afterwards to two; but still, not content with this advance, they cannot but think that behind these diversities there lurks but one genus—nay, that even salts and earths have a common principle. It might be conjectured that this is merely an economical plan of reason, for the purpose of sparing itself trouble, and an attempt of a purely hypothetical character, which, when successful, gives an appearance of probability to the principle of explanation employed by the reason. But a selfish purpose of this kind is easily to be distinguished from the idea, according to which every one presupposes that this unity is in accordance with the laws of nature, and that reason does not in this case *request*, but *requires*, although we are quite unable to determine the proper limits of this unity.

If the diversity existing in phenomena—a diversity not of form (for in this they may be similar) but of content—were so great that the subtlest human reason could never by comparison discover in them the least similarity (which is not impossible), in this case the logical law of genera would be without foundation, the conception of a genus, nay, all general conceptions would be impossible, and the faculty of the understanding, the exercise of which is restricted to the world of conceptions, could not exist. The logical principle of genera, accordingly, if it is to be applied to nature (by which I mean objects presented to our senses), presupposes a transcendental principle. In accordance with this principle, homogeneity is necessarily presupposed in the variety of phenomena (although we are unable to determine *a priori* the degree of this homogeneity), because without it no empirical conceptions, and consequently no experience, would be possible.

The logical principle of genera, which demands identity in phenomena, is balanced by another principle—that of *species*, which requires variety and diversity in things, notwithstanding their accordance in the same genus, and directs the understanding to attend to the one no less than to the other. This principle (of the faculty of distinction) acts as a check upon the levity of the former (the faculty of wit [1]); and reason exhibits in this respect a double and conflicting interest—on the one hand the interest in the *extent* (the interest of generality) in relation to genera, on the other that of the *content* (the interest of individuality) in relation to the variety of species. In the former case, the understanding cogitates more *under* its conceptions, in the latter it cogitates more *in* them. This distinction manifests itself likewise in the habits of thought peculiar to natural philosophers, some of whom—the

[1] *Wit* is defined by Kant as the faculty which discovers the general in the particular. Vide *Anthropologie*, page 123.—*Tr.*

remarkably speculative heads—may be said to be hostile to heterogeneity in phenomena, and have their eyes always fixed on the unity of genera, while others—with a strong empirical tendency—aim unceasingly at the analysis of phenomena, and almost destroy in us the hope of ever being able to estimate the character of these according to general principles.

The latter mode of thought is evidently based upon a logical principle, the aim of which is the systematic completeness of all cognitions. This principle authorizes me, beginning at the genus, to descend to the various and diverse contained under it; and in this way extension, as in the former case unity, is assured to the system. For if we merely examine the sphere of the conception which indicates a genus, we cannot discover how far it is possible to proceed in the division of that sphere; just as it is impossible, from the consideration of the space occupied by matter, to determine how far we can proceed in the division of it. Hence every *genus* must contain different *species*, and these again different *sub-species*; and as each of the latter must itself contain a sphere (must be of a certain extent, as a *conceptus communis*), reason demands that no species or sub-species is to be considered as the lowest possible. For a species or sub-species, being always a conception, which contains only what is common to a number of different things, does not completely determine any individual thing, or relate immediately to it, and must consequently contain other conceptions, that is, other sub-species under it. This law of specification may be thus expressed: *Entium varietates non temere sunt minuendae.*

But it is easy to see that this logical law would likewise be without sense or application, were it not based upon a transcendental *law of specification*, which certainly does not require that the differences existing in phenomena should be *infinite* in number, for the logical principle, which merely maintains the *indeterminateness* of the logical sphere of a conception, in relation to its possible division, does not authorize this statement; while it does impose upon the understanding the duty of searching for sub-species to every species, and minor differences in every difference. For, were there no lower conceptions, neither could there be any higher. Now the understanding cognizes only by means of conceptions; consequently, how far soever it may proceed in division, never by mere intuition, but always by lower and lower conceptions. The cognition of phenomena in their complete determination (which is possible only by means of the understanding) requires an unceasingly continued specification of conceptions, and a progression to ever smaller differences, of which abstraction had been made in the conception of the species, and still more in that of the genus.

This law of specification cannot be deduced from experience; it can never present us with a principle of so universal an application. Empirical specification very soon stops in its distinction of diversities, and requires the guidance of the transcendental law, as a principle of the reason—a law which imposes on us the necessity of never ceasing in our search for differences, even although these may not present themselves to the senses. That absorbent earths are of different kinds, could only be discovered by obeying the anticipatory law of reason, which imposes upon the understanding the task of discovering the differences existing between these earths, and supposes that nature is richer in substances than our senses would indicate. The faculty of the understanding belongs to us just as much under the presupposition of differences in the objects of nature, as under the condition that these objects are homogeneous, because we could not possess conceptions, nor make any use of our understanding, were not the phenomena included under these conceptions in some respects dissimilar, as well as similar, in their character.

Reason thus prepares the sphere of the understanding for the operations of this faculty: 1. By the principle of the *homogeneity* of the diverse in higher genera; 2. By the principle of the *variety* of the homogeneous in lower species; and, to complete the systematic unity, it adds, 3. A law of the *affinity* of all conceptions which prescribes a continuous transition from one species to every other by the gradual increase of diversity. We may term these the principles of the *homogeneity*, the *specification*, and the *continuity* of forms. The latter results from the union of the two former, inasmuch as we regard the systematic connection as complete in thought, in the ascent to higher genera, as well as in the descent to lower species. For all diversities must be related to each other, as they all spring from one highest genus, descending through the different gradations of a more and more extended determination.

We may illustrate the systematic unity produced by the three logical principles in the following manner. Every conception may be regarded as a point, which, as the standpoint of a spectator, has a certain horizon, which may be said to enclose a number of things, that may be viewed, so to speak, from that centre. Within this horizon there must be an infinite number of other points, each of which has its own horizon, smaller and more circumscribed; in other words, every species contains sub-species, according to the principle of specification, and the logical horizon consists of smaller horizons (sub-species), but not of points (individuals), which possess no extent. But different horizons or genera, which include under them so many conceptions, may have one common horizon, from which, as from a mid-point, they may be surveyed; and we may proceed thus, till we arrive at the highest genus, or universal and true horizon, which is determined by the highest conception, and which contains under itself all differences and varieties, as genera, species, and sub-species.

To this highest standpoint I am conducted by the law of homogeneity, as to all lower and more variously-determined conceptions by the law of specification. Now as in this way there exists no void in the whole extent of all possible conceptions, and as out of the sphere of these the mind can discover nothing, there arises from the presupposition of the universal horizon above mentioned, and its complete division, the principle: *Non datur vacuum formarum.* This principle asserts that there are not different primitive and highest genera, which stand isolated, so to speak, from each other, but all the various genera are mere divisions and limitations of one highest and universal genus; and hence follows immediately the principle: *Datur continuum formarum.* This principle indicates that all differences of species limit each other, and do not admit of transition from one to another by a *saltus*, but only through smaller degrees of the difference between the one species and the other. In one word, there are no species or sub-species which (in the view of reason) are the nearest possible to each other; intermediate species or sub-species being always possible, the difference of which from each of the former is always smaller than the difference existing between these.

The first law, therefore, directs us to avoid the notion that there exist different primal genera, and enounces the fact of perfect homogeneity; the second imposes a check upon this tendency to unity and prescribes the distinction of sub-species, before proceeding to apply our general conceptions to individuals. The third unites both the former, by enouncing the fact of homogeneity as existing even in the most various diversity, by means of the gradual transition from one species to another. Thus it indicates a relationship between the different branches or species, in so far as they all spring from the same stem.

But this logical law of the *continuum specierum (formarum logicarum)* presupposes a transcendental principle (*lex continui in natura*), without which the understanding might be led into error, by following the guidance of the former, and thus perhaps pursuing a path contrary to that prescribed by nature. This law must consequently be based upon pure transcendental, and not upon empirical considerations. For, in the latter case, it would come later than the system; whereas it is really itself the parent of all that is systematic in our cognition of nature. These principles are not mere hypotheses employed for the purpose of experimenting upon nature; although when any such connection is discovered, it forms a solid ground for regarding the hypothetical unity as valid in the sphere of nature—and thus they are in this respect not without their use. But we go farther, and maintain that it is manifest that these principles of parsimony in fundamental causes, variety in effects, and affinity in phenomena, are in accordance both with reason and nature, and that they are not mere methods or plans devised for the purpose of assisting us in our observation of the external world.

But it is plain that this continuity of forms is a mere idea, to which no adequate object can be discovered in experience. And this for two reasons. First, because the species in nature are really divided, and hence form *quanta discreta*;[1] and, if the gradual progression through their affinity were continuous, the intermediate members lying between two given species must be infinite in number, which is impossible. Second, because we cannot make any determinate empirical use of this law, inasmuch as it does not present us with any criterion of affinity which could aid us in determining how far we ought to pursue the graduation of differences: it merely contains a general indication that it is our duty to seek for and, if possible, to discover them.

When we arrange these principles of systematic unity in the order conformable to their employment in experience, they will stand thus: *Variety, Affinity, Unity*, each of them, as ideas, being taken in the highest degree of their completeness. Reason presupposes the existence of cognitions of the understanding, which have a direct relation to experience, and aims at the ideal unity of these cognitions—a unity which far transcends all experience or empirical notions. The affinity of the diverse, notwithstanding the differences existing between its parts, has a relation to things, but a still closer one to the mere properties and powers of things. For example, imperfect experience may represent the orbits of the planets as circular. But we discover variations from this course, and we proceed to suppose that the planets revolve in a path which, if not a circle, is of a character very similar to it. That is to say,

[1] Not *quanta continua*, like space or a line. See page 136, et seqq.—*Tr.*

the movements of those planets which do not form a circle will approximate more or less to the properties of a circle, and probably form an ellipse. The paths of comets exhibit still greater variations, for, so far as our observation extends, they do not return upon their own course in a circle or ellipse. But we proceed to the conjecture that comets describe a parabola, a figure which is closely allied to the ellipse. In fact, a parabola is merely an ellipse, with its longer axis produced to an indefinite extent. Thus these principles conduct us to a unity in the genera of the forms of these orbits, and, proceeding farther, to a unity as regards the cause of the motions of the heavenly bodies—that is, gravitation. But we go on extending our conquests over nature, and endeavour to explain all seeming deviations from these rules, and even make additions to our system which no experience can ever substantiate—for example, the theory, in affinity with that of ellipses, of hyperbolic paths of comets, pursuing which, these bodies leave our solar system, and, passing from sun to sun, unite the most distant parts of the infinite universe, which is held together by the same moving power.

The most remarkable circumstance connected with these principles is, that they seem to be transcendental, and, although only containing ideas for the guidance of the empirical exercise of reason, and although this empirical employment stands to these ideas in an asymptotic relation alone (to use a mathematical term), that is; continually approximate, without ever being able to attain to them, they possess, notwithstanding, as *a priori* synthetical propositions, objective though undetermined validity, and are available as rules for possible experience. In the elaboration of our experience, they may also be employed with great advantage, as heuristic [1] principles. A transcendental deduction of them cannot be made; such a deduction being always impossible in the case of ideas, as has been already shown.

We distinguished, in the Transcendental Analytic, the *dynamical* principles of the understanding, which are regulative principles of *intuition*, from the mathematical, which are constitutive principles of intuition. These dynamical laws are, however, constitutive in relation to *experience*, inasmuch as they render the conceptions without which experience could not exist, possible *a priori*. But the principles of pure reason cannot be constitutive even in regard to empirical *conceptions*, because no sensuous schema corresponding to them can be discovered, and they cannot therefore have an object *in concreto*. Now, if I grant that they cannot

[1] From the Greek εὑρίσκω.

be employed in the sphere of experience, as constitutive principles, how shall I secure for them employment and objective validity as regulative principles, and in what way can they be so employed?

The understanding is the object of reason, as sensibility is the object of the understanding. The production of systematic unity in all the empirical operations of the understanding is the proper occupation of reason; just as it is the business of the understanding to connect the various content of phenomena by means of conceptions, and subject them to empirical laws. But the operations of the understanding are, without the schemata of sensibility, *undetermined*; and, in the same manner, the unity of reason is perfectly *undetermined* as regards the conditions under which, and the extent to which, the understanding ought to carry the systematic connection of its conceptions. But, although it is impossible to discover in *intuition* a schema for the complete systematic unity of all the conceptions of the understanding, there must be some *analogon* of this schema. This analogon is the idea of the *maximum* of the division and the connection of our cognition in one principle. For we may have a determinate notion of a *maximum* and an absolutely perfect, all the restrictive conditions which are connected with an indeterminate and various content having been abstracted. Thus the idea of reason is analogous with a sensuous schema, with this difference, that the application of the categories to the schema of reason does not present a cognition of any object (as is the case with the application of the categories to sensuous schemata), but merely provides us with a rule or principle for the systematic unity of the exercise of the understanding. Now, as every principle which imposes upon the exercise of the understanding *a priori* compliance with the rule of systematic unity, also relates, although only in an indirect manner, to an object of experience, the principles of pure reason will also possess objective reality and validity in relation to experience. But they will not aim at *determining* our knowledge in regard to any empirical object; they will merely indicate the procedure, following which, the empirical and determinate exercise of the understanding may be in complete harmony and connection with itself—a result which is produced by its being brought into harmony with the principle of systematic unity, so far as that is possible, and deduced from it.

I term all subjective principles, which are not derived from observation of the constitution of an object, but from the interest which Reason has in producing a certain completeness in her cognition of that object, *maxims* of reason. Thus there are maxims of speculative reason, which are based solely upon its speculative interest, although they appear to be objective principles.

When principles which are really regulative are regarded as constitutive, and employed as objective principles, contradictions must arise; but if they are considered as mere maxims, there is no room for contradictions of any kind, as they then merely indicate the different interests of reason, which occasion differences in the mode of thought. In effect, Reason has only one single interest, and the seeming contradiction existing between her maxims merely indicates a difference in, and a reciprocal limitation of, the methods by which this interest is satisfied.

This reasoner has at heart the interest of *diversity*—in accordance with the principle of specification; another, the interest of *unity*—in accordance with the principle of aggregation. Each believes that his judgment rests upon a thorough insight into the subject he is examining, and yet it has been influenced solely by a greater or less degree of adherence to some one of the two principles, neither of which is objective, but originates solely from the interest of reason, and on this account to be termed maxims rather than principles. When I observe intelligent men disputing about the distinctive characteristics of men, animals, or plants, and even of minerals, those on the one side assuming the existence of certain national characteristics, certain well-defined and hereditary distinctions of family, race, and so on, while the other side maintain that nature has endowed all races of men with the same faculties and dispositions, and that all differences are but the result of external and accidental circumstances—I have only to consider for a moment the real nature of the subject of discussion, to arrive at the conclusion that it is a subject far too deep for us to judge of, and that there is little probability of either party being able to speak from a perfect insight into and understanding of the nature of the subject itself. Both have, in reality, been struggling for the twofold interest of reason; the one maintaining the one interest, the other the other. But this difference between the maxims of diversity and unity may easily be reconciled and adjusted; although, so long as they are regarded as objective principles, they must occasion not only contradictions and polemic, but place hindrances in the way of the advancement of truth, until some means is discovered of reconciling these conflicting interests, and bringing reason into union and harmony with itself.

The same is the case with the so-called law discovered by

Leibnitz,[1] and supported with remarkable ability by Bonnet [2]—the law of the *continuous gradation* of created beings, which is nothing more than an inference from the principle of affinity; for observation and study of the order of nature could never present it to the mind as an objective truth. The steps of this ladder, as they appear in experience, are too far apart from each other, and the so-called petty differences between different kinds of animals are in nature commonly so wide separations that no confidence can be placed in such views (particularly when we reflect on the great variety of things, and the ease with which we can discover resemblances), and no faith in the laws which are said to express the aims and purposes of nature. On the other hand, the method of investigating the order of nature in the light of this principle, and the maxim which requires us to regard this order—it being still undetermined how far it extends—as really existing in nature, is beyond doubt a legitimate and excellent principle of reason—a principle which extends farther than any experience or observation of ours, and which, without giving us any positive knowledge of anything in the region of experience, guides us to the goal of systematic unity.

### Of the Ultimate End of the Natural Dialectic of Human Reason

The ideas of pure reason cannot be, of themselves and in their own nature, dialectical; it is from their misemployment alone that fallacies and illusions arise. For they originate in the nature of reason itself, and it is impossible that this supreme tribunal for all the rights and claims of speculation should be itself undeserving of confidence and promotive of error. It is to be expected, therefore, that these ideas have a genuine and legitimate aim. It is true, the mob of sophists raise against reason the cry of inconsistency and contradiction, and affect to despise the government of that faculty, because they cannot understand its constitution, while it is to its beneficial influences alone that they owe the position and the intelligence which enable them to criticize and to blame its procedure.

We cannot employ an *a priori* conception with certainty, until we have made a transcendental deduction thereof. The ideas of pure reason do not admit of the same kind of deduction as the categories. But if they are to possess the least objective validity, and to represent anything but mere creations of thought (*entia rationis ratiocinantis*), a deduction of them must be possible. This

---

[1] Leibnitz, *Nouveaux Essais*, Liv, iii. ch. 6.
[2] Bonnet, *Betrachtungen über die Natur*, pages 29–85.

deduction will complete the critical task imposed upon pure reason; and it is to this part of our labours that we now proceed.

There is a great difference between a thing's being presented to the mind as an *object in an absolute sense*, or merely as an *ideal object*. In the former case I employ my conceptions to determine the object; in the latter case nothing is present to the mind but a mere schema, which does not relate directly to an object, not even in a hypothetical sense, but which is useful only for the purpose of representing other objects to the mind, in a mediate and indirect manner, by means of their relation to the idea in the intellect. Thus I say, the conception of a supreme intelligence is a mere idea; that is to say, its objective reality does not consist in the fact that it has an immediate relation to an object (for in this sense we have no means of establishing its objective validity), it is merely a schema constructed according to the necessary conditions of the unity of reason—the schema of a thing in general, which is useful towards the production of the highest degree of systematic unity in the empirical exercise of reason, in which we deduce this or that object of experience from the imaginary object of this idea, as the ground or cause of the said object of experience. In this way, the idea is properly a heuristic, and not an ostensive conception; it does not give us any information respecting the constitution of an object, it merely indicates how, under the guidance of the idea, we ought to *investigate* the constitution and the relations of objects in the world of experience. Now, if it can be shown that the three kinds of transcendental ideas (psychological, cosmological, and theological), although not relating directly to any object nor determining it, do nevertheless, on the supposition of the existence of an *ideal object*, produce systematic unity in the laws of the empirical employment of the reason, and extend our empirical cognition, without ever being inconsistent or in opposition with it—it must be a necessary *maxim* of reason to regulate its procedure according to these ideas. And this forms the transcendental deduction of all speculative ideas, not as *constitutive* principles of the extension of our cognition beyond the limits of our experience, but as *regulative* principles of the systematic unity of empirical cognition, which is by the aid of these ideas arranged and emended within its own proper limits, to an extent unattainable by the operation of the principles of the understanding alone.

I shall make this plainer. Guided by the principles involved in these ideas, we must, in the *first* place, so connect all the phenomena, actions, and feelings of the mind, as if it were a simple substance, which, endowed with personal identity, possesses a permanent existence (in this life at least), while its states, among which those of the body are to be included as external conditions, are in continual change. *Secondly*, in cosmology, we must investigate the conditions of all natural phenomena, internal as well as external, as if they belonged to a chain infinite and without any prime or supreme member, while we do not, on this account, deny the existence of intelligible grounds of these phenomena, although we never employ them to explain phenomena, for the simple reason that they are not objects of our cognition. *Thirdly*, in the sphere of theology, we must regard the whole system of possible experience as forming an absolute, but dependent and sensuously-conditioned unity, and at the same time as based upon a sole, supreme, and all-sufficient ground existing apart from the world itself—a ground which is a self-subsistent, primeval and creative reason, in relation to which we so employ our reason in the field of experience, as if all objects drew their origin from that archetype of all reason. In other words, we ought not to deduce the internal phenomena of the mind from a simple thinking substance, but deduce them from each other under the guidance of the regulative idea of a simple being; we ought not to deduce the phenomena, order, and unity of the universe from a supreme intelligence, but merely draw from this idea of a supremely wise cause the rules which must guide reason in its connection of causes and effects.

Now there is nothing to hinder us from *admitting* these ideas to possess an objective and hyperbolic existence, except the cosmological ideas, which lead reason into an antinomy: the psychological and theological ideas are not antinomial. They contain no contradiction; and how then can any one dispute their objective reality, since he who denies it knows as little about their possibility as we who affirm? And yet, when we wish to admit the existence of a thing, it is not sufficient to convince ourselves that there is no positive obstacle in the way; for it cannot be allowable to regard mere creations of thought, which transcend, though they do not contradict, all our conceptions, as real and determinate objects, solely upon the authority of a speculative reason striving to compass its own aims. They cannot, therefore, be admitted to be real in themselves; they can only possess a comparative reality—that of a schema of the regulative principle of the systematic unity of all cognition. They are to be regarded not as actual things, but as in some measure analogous to them. We abstract from the object of the idea all the conditions which limit the exercise of our understanding, but which, on the other hand, are the sole conditions of our possessing a determinate conception of any given thing. And thus we cogitate a something, of the real nature of which we have not the least conception, but which we represent to ourselves as standing in a relation to the whole system of phenomena, analogous to that in which phenomena stand to each other.

By admitting these ideal beings, we do not really extend our cognitions beyond the objects of possible experience; we extend merely the empirical unity of our experience, by the aid of systematic unity, the schema of which is furnished by the idea, which is therefore valid—not as a constitutive, but as a regulative principle. For although we posit a thing corresponding to the idea—a something, an actual existence, we do not on that account aim at the extension of our cognition by means of transcendent conceptions. This existence is purely ideal, and not objective; it is the mere expression of the systematic unity which is to be the guide of reason in the field of experience. There are no attempts made at deciding what the ground of this unity may be, or what the real nature of this imaginary being.

Thus the transcendental and only determinate conception of God, which is presented to us by speculative reason, is in the strictest sense *deistic*. In other words, reason does not assure us of the objective validity of the conception; it merely gives us the idea of something, on which the supreme and necessary unity of all experience is based. This something we cannot, following the analogy of a real substance, cogitate otherwise than as the cause of all things operating in accordance with rational laws, if we regard it as an individual object; although we should rest contented with the idea alone as a regulative principle of reason, and make no attempt at completing the sum of the conditions imposed by thought. This attempt is, indeed, inconsistent with the grand aim of complete systematic unity in the sphere of cognition—a unity to which no bounds are set by reason.

Hence it happens that, admitting a divine being, I can have no conception of the internal possibility of its perfection, or of the necessity of its existence. The only advantage of this admission is, that it enables me to answer all other questions relating to the contingent, and to give reason the most complete satisfaction as regards the unity which it aims at attaining in the world of experience. But I cannot satisfy reason with regard to this hypothesis itself; and this proves that it is not its intelligence and insight into the subject, but its speculative interest alone which induces it to proceed from a point lying far beyond the sphere of our cognition, for the purpose of being able to consider all objects as parts of a systematic whole.

Here a distinction presents itself, in regard to the way in which we may cogitate a presupposition—a distinction which is somewhat subtle, but of great importance in transcendental philosophy I may have sufficient grounds to admit something, or the existence of something, in a relative point of view (*suppositio relativa*) without being justified in admitting it in an absolute sense (*suppositio absoluta*). This distinction is undoubtedly requisite, in the case of a regulative principle, the necessity of which we recognize, though we are ignorant of the source and cause of that necessity, and which we assume to be based upon some ultimate ground, for the purpose of being able to cogitate the universality of the principle in a more determinate way. For example, I cogitate the existence of a being corresponding to a pure transcendental idea. But I cannot admit that this being exists absolutely and in itself, because all of the conceptions, by which I can cogitate an object in a determinate manner, fall short of assuring me of its existence; nay, the conditions of the objective validity of my conceptions are excluded by the idea—by the very fact of its being an idea. The conceptions of reality, substance, causality, nay, even that of necessity in existence, have no significance out of the sphere of empirical cognition, and cannot, beyond that sphere, determine any object. They may, accordingly, be employed to explain the possibility of things in the world of sense, but they are utterly inadequate to explain the possibility of the *universe itself* considered as a whole; because in this case the ground of explanation must lie out of and beyond the world, and cannot, therefore, be an object of possible experience. Now, I may admit the existence of an incomprehensible being of this nature—the object of a mere idea, relatively to the world of sense; although I have no ground to admit its existence absolutely and in itself. For if an idea (that of a systematic and complete unity, of which I shall presently speak more particularly) lies at the foundation of the most extended empirical employment of reason, and if this idea cannot be adequately represented *in concreto*, although it is indispensably necessary for the approximation of empirical unity to the highest possible degree—I am not only authorized, but compelled to realize this idea, that is, to posit a real object corresponding thereto. But I cannot profess to know this object; it is to me merely a something, to which, as the ground of systematic unity in cognition, I attribute such properties as are analogous to the conceptions employed by the understanding in the sphere of experience. Following the analogy of the notions of reality, substance, causality, and necessity, I cogitate a being, which possesses all these attributes in the highest degree; and, as this idea is the offspring of my reason alone, I cogitate this being as *self-subsistent reason,* and as the cause of the universe operating by means of ideas of the greatest possible harmony and unity. Thus I abstract all conditions that would limit my idea, solely for the purpose of rendering systematic unity possible in the world of empirical diversity, and thus securing the widest possible extension for the exercise of reason in that sphere. This I am enabled to do, by regarding all connections and relations in the world of sense, *as if* they were the dispositions of a supreme reason, of which our reason is but a faint image. I then proceed to cogitate this Supreme Being by conceptions which have, properly, no meaning or application, except in the world of sense. But as I am authorized to employ the transcendental hypothesis of such a being in a relative respect alone, that is, as the substratum of the greatest possible unity in experience—I may attribute to a being which I regard as distinct from the world, such properties as belong solely to the sphere of sense and experience. For I do not desire, and am not justified in desiring, to cognize this object of my idea, as it exists in itself; for I possess no conceptions sufficient for this task, those of reality, substance, causality, nay, even that of necessity in existence, losing all significance, and becoming merely the signs of conceptions, without content and without applicability, when I attempt to carry them beyond the limits of the world of sense. I cogitate merely the relation of a perfectly unknown being to the greatest possible systematic unity of experience, solely for the purpose of employing it as the schema of the regulative principle which directs reason in its empirical exercise.

It is evident, at the first view, that we cannot presuppose the reality of this transcendental object, by means of the conceptions of reality, substance, causality, and so on; because these conceptions cannot be applied to anything that is distinct from the world of sense. Thus the supposition of a Supreme Being or cause is purely relative; it is cogitated only in behalf of the systematic unity of experience; such a being is but a something, of whose existence in itself we have not the least conception. Thus, too, it becomes sufficiently manifest, why we required the idea of a necessary being in relation to objects given by sense, although we can never have the least conception of this being, or of its absolute necessity.

And now we can clearly perceive the result of our transcendental dialectic, and the proper aim of the ideas of pure reason—which become dialectical solely from misunderstanding and inconsiderateness. Pure reason is, in fact, occupied with itself, and not with any object. Objects are not presented to it to be embraced in the unity of an empirical conception; it is only the cognitions of the understanding that are presented to it, for the purpose of receiving the unity of a rational conception, that is, of being connected according to a principle. The unity of reason is the unity of system; and this systematic unity is not an objective principle, extending its dominion over objects, but a subjective maxim, extending its authority over the empirical cognition of objects. The systematic connection which reason gives to the empirical employment of the understanding, not only advances the extension of that employment, but ensures its correctness, and thus the principle of a systematic unity of this nature is also objective, although only in an indefinite respect (*principium vagum*). It is not, however, a constitutive principle, determining an object to which it directly relates; it is merely a regulative principle or maxim, advancing and s'rengthening the empirical exercise of reason, by the opening up of new paths of which the understanding is ignorant, while it never conflicts with the laws of its exercise in the sphere of experience.

But reason cannot cogitate this systematic unity, without at the same time cogitating an object of the idea—an object that cannot be presented in any experience, which contains no concrete example of a complete systematic unity. This being (*ens rationis ratiocinatae*) is therefore a mere idea, and is not assumed to be a thing which is real absolutely and in itself. On the contrary, it forms merely the problematical foundation of the connection which the mind introduces among the phenomena of the sensuous world. We look upon this connection, in the light of the above-mentioned idea, as if it drew its origin from the supposed being which corresponds to the idea. And yet all we aim at is the possession of this idea as a secure foundation for the systematic unity of experience—a unity indispensable to reason, advantageous to the understanding, and promotive of the interests of empirical cognition.

We mistake the true meaning of this idea, when we regard it as an enouncement, or even as a hypothetical declaration of the existence of a real thing, which we are to regard as the origin or ground of a systematic constitution of the universe. On the contrary, it is left completely undetermined what the nature or properties of this so-called ground may be. The idea is merely to be adopted as a point of view, from which this unity, so essential to reason and so beneficial to the understanding, may be regarded as radiating. In one word, this transcendental thing is merely the schema of a regulative principle, by means of which Reason, so far as in her lies, extends the dominion of systematic unity over the whole sphere of experience.

The first object of an idea of this kind is the Ego, considered merely as a thinking nature or soul. If I wish to investigate the properties of a thinking being, I must interrogate experience. But I find that I can apply none of the categories to this object, the schema of these categories, which is the condition of their application, being given only in sensuous intuition. But I cannot thus attain to the cognition of a systematic unity of all the phenomena of the internal sense. Instead, therefore, of an empirical conception of what the soul really is, reason takes the conception of the empirical unity of all thought, and, by cogitating this unity as unconditioned and primitive, constructs the rational conception or idea of a simple substance which is in itself unchangeable, possessing personal identity, and in connection with other real things external to it; in one word, it constructs the idea of a simple self-subsistent intelligence. But the real aim of reason in this procedure is the attainment of principles of systematic unity for the explanation of the phenomena of the soul. That is, reason desires to be able to represent all the determinations of the internal sense, as existing in one subject, all powers as deduced from one fundamental power, all changes as mere varieties in the condition of a being which is permanent and always the same, and all *phenomena* in space as entirely different in their nature from the procedure of thought. Essential simplicity (with the other attributes predicated of the Ego) is regarded as the mere schema of this regulative principle; it is not assumed that it is the actual ground of the properties of the soul. For these properties may rest upon quite different grounds, of which we are completely ignorant; just as the above predicates could not give us any knowledge of the soul as it is in itself, even if we regarded them as valid in respect of it, inasmuch as they constitute a mere idea, which cannot be represented *in concreto*. Nothing but good can result from a psychological idea of this kind, if we only take proper care not to consider it as more than an idea; that is, if we regard it as valid merely in relation to the employment of reason, in the sphere of the phenomena of the soul. Under the guidance of this idea, or principle, no empirical laws of corporeal phenomena are called in to explain that which is a phenomenon of the *internal sense* alone; no windy hypotheses of the generation, annihilation, and palingenesis of souls are admitted. Thus the consideration of this object of the internal sense is kept pure, and unmixed with heterogeneous elements; while the investigation of reason aims at reducing all the grounds of explanation employed in this sphere of knowledge to a single principle. All this is best effected, nay, cannot be effected otherwise than by means of such a schema, which requires us to regard this ideal thing as an actual existence. The psychological idea is therefore meaningless and inapplicable, except as the schema of a regulative conception. For, if I ask whether the soul is not really of a spiritual nature—it is a question which has no meaning. From such a conception has been abstracted, not merely all corporeal nature, but all nature, that is, all the predicates of a possible experience; and consequently, all the conditions which enable us to cogitate an object to this conception have disappeared. But, if these conditions are absent, it is evident that the conception is meaningless.

The second regulative idea of speculative reason is the conception of the universe. For nature is properly the only object presented to us, in regard to which reason requires regulative principles. Nature is twofold—thinking and corporeal nature. To cogitate the latter in regard to its internal possibility, that is, to determine the application of the categories to it, no idea is required—no representation which transcends experience. In this sphere, therefore, an idea is impossible, sensuous intuition being our only guide; while, in the sphere of psychology, we require the fundamental idea (I), which contains *a priori* a certain form of thought, namely, the unity of the Ego. Pure reason has therefore nothing left but nature in general, and the completeness of conditions in nature in accordance with some principle. The absolute totality of the series of these conditions is an idea, which can never be fully realized in the empirical exercise of reason, while it is serviceable as a rule for the procedure of reason in relation to that totality. It requires us, in the explanation of given phenomena (in the regress or ascent in the series), to proceed as if the series were infinite in itself, that is, were prolonged *in indefinitum*; while, on the other hand, where reason is regarded as itself the determining cause (in the region of freedom), we are required to proceed as if we had not before us an object of sense, but of the pure understanding. In this latter case, the conditions do not exist in the series of phenomena, but may be placed quite out of and beyond it, and the series of conditions may be regarded as if it had an absolute beginning from an intelligible cause. All this proves that the cosmological ideas are nothing but regulative principles, and not constitutive; and that their aim is not to realize an actual totality in such series. The full discussion of this subject will be found in its proper place in the chapter on the antinomy of pure reason.

The third idea of pure reason, containing the hypothesis of a being which is valid merely as a relative hypothesis, is that of the one and all-sufficient cause of all cosmological series, in other words, the idea of God. We have not the slightest ground absolutely to admit the existence of an object corresponding to this idea; for what can empower or authorize us to affirm the existence of a being of the highest perfection—a being whose existence is absolutely necessary, merely because we possess the conception of such a being? The answer is—it is the existence of the world which renders this hypothesis necessary. But this answer makes it perfectly evident, that the idea of this being, like all other speculative ideas, is essentially nothing more than a demand upon reason that it shall regulate the connection which it and its subordinate faculties introduce into the phenomena of the world by principles of systematic unity, and consequently, that it shall regard all phenomena as originating from one all-embracing being, as the supreme and all-sufficient cause. From this it is plain that the only aim of reason in this procedure is the establishment of its own formal rule for the extension of its dominion in the world of experience; that it does not aim at an extension of its cognition *beyond the limits of experience*; and that, consequently, this idea does not contain any constitutive principle.

The highest formal unity, which is based upon ideas alone, is the unity of all things—a unity in accordance with an aim or purpose; and the speculative interest of reason renders it necessary to regard all order in the world as if it originated from the intention and design of a supreme reason. This principle unfolds to the view of reason in the sphere of experience new and enlarged prospects, and invites it to connect the phenomena of the world according to teleological laws, and in this way to attain to the highest possible degree of systematic unity. The hypothesis of a supreme intelligence, as the sole cause of the universe—an intelligence which has for us no more than an ideal existence, is accordingly always of the greatest service to reason. Thus, if we presuppose, in relation to the figure of the earth (which is round, but somewhat flattened at the poles),[1] or that of mountains or

[1] The advantages which a circular form, in the case of the earth, has over every other, are well known. But few are aware that the slight flattening at the poles, which gives it the figure of a spheroid, is the only cause which prevents the elevations of continents or even of mountains, perhaps thrown up by some internal convulsion, from continually altering the position of the

seas, wise designs on the part of an author of the universe, we cannot fail to make, by the light of this supposition, a great number of interesting discoveries. If we keep to this hypothesis, as a principle which is purely regulative, even error cannot be very detrimental. For, in this case, error can have no more serious consequences than that, where we expected to discover a teleological connection (*nexus finalis*), only a mechanical or physical connection appears. In such a case, we merely fail to find the additional form of unity we expected, but we do not lose the rational unity which the mind requires in its procedure in experience. But even a miscarriage of this sort cannot affect the law in its general and teleological relations. For although we may convict an anatomist of an error, when he connects the limb of some animal with a certain purpose; it is quite impossible to *prove* in a single case, that any arrangement of nature, be it what it may, is entirely without aim or design. And thus medical physiology, by the aid of a principle presented to it by pure reason, extends its very limited empirical knowledge of the purposes of the different parts of an organized body so far, that it may be asserted with the utmost confidence, and with the approbation of all reflecting men, that every organ or bodily part of an animal has its use and answers a certain design. Now, this is a supposition, which, if regarded as of a constitutive character, goes much farther than any experience or observation of ours can justify. Hence it is evident that it is nothing more than a regulative principle of reason, which aims at the highest degree of systematic unity, by the aid of the idea of a causality according to design in a supreme cause—a cause which it regards as the highest intelligence.

If, however, we neglect this restriction of the idea to a purely regulative influence, reason is betrayed into numerous errors. For it has then left the ground of experience, in which alone are to be found the criteria of truth, and has ventured into the region of the incomprehensible and unsearchable, on the heights of which it loses its power and collectedness, because it has completely severed its connection with experience.

The first error which arises from our employing the idea of a Supreme Being as a constitutive (in repugnance to the very nature of an idea), and not as a regulative principle, is the error of inactive

axis of the earth—and th..t to some considerable degree in a short time. The great protuberance of the earth under the Equator serves to overbalance the impetus of all other masses of earth, and thus to preserve the axis of the earth, so far as we can observe, in its present position. And yet this wise arrangement has been unthinkingly explained from the equilibrium of the formerly fluid mass.

reason (*ignava ratio* [1]). We may so term every principle which requires us to regard our investigations of nature as absolutely complete, and allows reason to cease its inquiries, as if it had fully executed its task. Thus the psychological idea of the Ego, when employed as a constitutive principle for the explanation of the phenomena of the soul, and for the extension of our knowledge regarding this subject beyond the limits of experience—even to the condition of the soul after death, is convenient enough for the purposes of pure reason, but detrimental and even ruinous to its interests in the sphere of nature and experience. The dogmatizing spiritualist explains the unchanging unity of our personality through all changes of condition from the unity of a thinking substance, the interest which we take in things and events that can happen only after our death, from a consciousness of the immaterial nature of our thinking subject, and so on. Thus he dispenses with all empirical investigations into the cause of these internal phenomena, and with all possible explanations of them upon purely natural grounds; while, at the dictation of a transcendent reason, he passes by the immanent sources of cognition in experience, greatly to his own ease and convenience, but to the sacrifice of all genuine insight and intelligence. These prejudicial consequences become still more evident, in the case of the dogmatical treatment of our idea of a Supreme Intelligence, and the theological system of nature (physico-theology) which is falsely based upon it. For, in this case, the aims which we observe in nature, and often those which we merely fancy to exist, make the investigation of causes a very easy task, by directing us to refer such and such phenomena immediately to the unsearchable will and counsel of the Supreme Wisdom, while we ought to investigate their causes in the general laws of the mechanism of matter. We are thus recommended to consider the labour of reason as ended, when we have merely dispensed with its employment, which is guided surely and safely, only by the order of nature and the series of changes in the world—which are arranged according to immanent and general laws. This error may be avoided, if we do not merely consider from the view-point of final aims certain parts of nature, such as the division and structure of a continent, the constitution and direction of certain mountain-chains, or even

---

[1] This was the term applied by the old dialecticians to a sophistical argument, which ran thus: If it is your fate to die of this disease, you will die, whether you employ a physician or not. Cicero says that this mode of reasoning has received this appellation, because, if followed, it puts an end to the employment of reason in the affairs of life. For a similar reason I have applied this designation to the sophistical argument of pure reason.

the organization existing in the vegetable and animal kingdoms, but look upon this systematic unity of nature in a perfectly *general* way, in relation to the idea of a Supreme Intelligence.   If we pursue this advice, we lay as a foundation for all investigation the conformity to aims of all phenomena of nature in accordance with universal laws, from which no particular arrangement of nature is exempt, but only cognized by us with more or less difficulty; and we possess a regulative principle of the systematic unity of a teleological connection, which we do not attempt to anticipate or predetermine.   All that we do, and ought to do, is to follow out the physico-mechanical connection in nature according to general laws, with the hope of discovering, sooner or later, the teleological connection also.   Thus, and thus only, can the principle of final unity aid in the extension of the employment of reason in the sphere of experience, without being in any case detrimental to its interests.

The second error which arises from the misconception of the principle of systematic unity is that of perverted reason (*perversa ratio, ὕστερον πρότερον rationis*).   The idea of systematic unity is available as a regulative principle in the connection of phenomena according to general natural laws; and, how far soever we have to travel upon the path of experience to discover some fact or event, this idea requires us to believe that we have approached all the more nearly to the completion of its use in the sphere of nature, although that completion can never be attained.   But this error reverses the procedure of reason.   We begin by hypostatizing the principle of systematic unity, and by giving an anthropomorphic determination to the conception of a Supreme Intelligence, and then proceed forcibly to impose aims upon nature.   Thus not only does teleology, which ought to aid in the completion of unity in accordance with general laws, operate to the destruction of its influence, but it hinders reason from attaining its proper aim, that is, the proof, upon natural grounds, of the existence of a supreme intelligent cause.   For, if we cannot presuppose supreme finality in nature *a priori*, that is, as essentially belonging to nature, how can we be directed to endeavour to discover this unity, and, rising gradually through its different degrees, to approach the supreme perfection of an author of all—a perfection which is absolutely necessary, and therefore cognizable *a priori*?   The regulative principle directs us to presuppose systematic unity absolutely, and, consequently, as following from the essential nature of things—but only as a *unity of nature*, not merely cognized empirically, but presupposed *a priori*, although only in an indeterminate manner.   But if I insist on basing nature upon the foundation of a supreme ordaining Being, the unity of nature is in effect lost. For, in this case, it is quite foreign and unessential to the nature of things, and cannot be cognized from the general laws of nature. And thus arises a vicious circular argument, what ought to have been proved having been presupposed.

To take the regulative principle of systematic unity in nature for a constitutive principle, and to hypostatize and make a cause out of that which is properly the ideal ground of the consistent and harmonious exercise of reason, involves reason in inextricable embarrassments. The investigation of nature pursues its own path under the guidance of the chain of natural causes, in accordance with the general laws of nature, and ever follows the light of the idea of an author of the universe—not for the purpose of deducing the finality, which it constantly pursues, from this Supreme Being, but to attain to the cognition of his existence from the finality which it seeks in the existence of the phenomena of nature, and, if possible, in that of all things—to cognize this being, consequently, as absolutely necessary. Whether this latter purpose succeed or not, the idea is and must always be a true one, and its employment, when merely regulative, must always be accompanied by truthful and beneficial results.

Complete unity, in conformity with aims, constitutes absolute perfection. But if we do not find this unity in the nature of the things which go to constitute the world of experience, that is, of objective cognition, consequently in the universal and necessary laws of nature, how can we infer from this unity the idea of the supreme and absolutely necessary perfection of a primal being, which is the origin of all causality? The greatest systematic unity, and consequently teleological unity, constitutes the very foundation of the possibility of the most extended employment of human reason. The idea of unity is therefore essentially and indissolubly connected with the nature of our reason. This idea is a legislative one; and hence it is very natural that we should assume the existence of a legislative reason corresponding to it, from which the systematic unity of nature—the object of the operations of reason—must be derived.

In the course of our discussion of the antinomies, we stated that it is always possible to answer all the questions which pure reason may raise; and that the plea of the limited nature of our cognition, which is unavoidable and proper in many questions regarding natural phenomena, cannot in this case be admitted, because the questions raised do not relate to the nature of things, but are necessarily originated by the nature of reason itself, and relate to its own internal constitution. We can now establish this assertion, which at first sight appeared so rash, in relation to the two questions in which reason takes the greatest interest, and thus complete our discussion of the dialectic of pure reason.

If, then, the question is asked, in relation to transcendental theology;[1] *first*, whether there is anything distinct from the world, which contains the ground of cosmical order and connection according to general laws. The answer is: *Certainly*. For the world is a sum of phenomena; there must therefore be some transcendental basis of these phenomena, that is, a basis cogitable by the pure understanding alone. If, *second*, the question is asked, whether this being is substance, whether it is of the greatest reality, whether it is necessary, and so forth. I answer that *this question is utterly without meaning*. For all the categories which aid me in forming a conception of an object, cannot be employed except in the world of sense, and are without meaning when not applied to objects of actual or possible experience. Out of this sphere, they are not properly conceptions, but the mere marks or indices of conceptions, which we may admit, although they cannot, without the help of experience, help us to understand any subject or thing. If, *third*, the question is, whether we may not cogitate this being, which is distinct from the world, in analogy with the objects of experience. The answer is *undoubtedly*, but only as an ideal, and not as a real object. That is, we must cogitate it only as an unknown substratum of the systematic unity, order, and finality of the world—a unity which reason must employ as the regulative principle of its investigation of nature. Nay, more, we may admit into the idea certain anthropomorphic elements, which are promotive of the interests of this regulative principle. For it is no more than an idea, which does not relate directly to a being distinct from the world, but to the regulative principle of the systematic unity of the world, by means, however, of a schema of this unity—the schema of a Supreme Intelligence, who is the wisely-designing author of the universe. What this basis of cosmical unity may be in itself, we know not—we cannot discover from the idea; we merely know how we ought to employ the idea of this unity, in relation to the systematic operation of reason in the sphere of experience.

[1] After what has been said of the psychological idea in the Ego and its proper employment as a regulative principle of the operations of reason, I need not enter into details regarding the transcendental illusion by which the systematic unity of all the various phenomena of the internal sense is hypostatized. The procedure is in this case very similar to that which has been discussed in our remarks on the theological ideal.

But, it will be asked again, *can* we on these grounds, admit the existence of a wise and omnipotent author of the world? *Without doubt*; and not only so, but we *must* assume the existence of such a being. But do we thus extend the limits of our knowledge beyond the field of possible experience? *By no means*. For we have merely presupposed a something, of which we have no conception, which we do not know as it is in itself; but, in relation to the systematic disposition of the universe, which we must presuppose in all our observation of nature, we have cogitated this unknown being *in analogy* with an intelligent existence (an empirical conception), that is to say, we have endowed it with those attributes, which, judging from the nature of our own reason, may contain the ground of such a systematic unity. This idea is therefore valid only relatively to the employment in experience of our reason. But if we attribute to it absolute and objective validity, we overlook the fact that it is merely an ideal being that we cogitate; and, by setting out from a basis which is not determinable by considerations drawn from experience, we place ourselves in a position which incapacitates us from applying this principle to the empirical employment of reason.

But, it will be asked further, can I make any use of this conception and hypothesis in my investigations into the world and nature? *Yes*, for this very purpose was the idea established by reason as a fundamental basis. But may I regard certain arrangements, which seemed to have been made in conformity with some fixed aim, as the arrangements of design, and look upon them as proceeding from the divine will, with the intervention, however, of certain other particular arrangements disposed to that end? Yes, you may do so; but at the same time you must regard it as indifferent, whether it is asserted that divine wisdom has disposed all things in conformity with his highest aims, or that the idea of supreme wisdom is a regulative principle in the investigation of nature, and at the same time a principle of the systematic unity of nature according to general laws, even in those cases where we are unable to discover that unity. In other words, it must be perfectly indifferent to you, whether you say, when you have discovered this unity—God has wisely willed it so, or, nature has wisely arranged this. For it was nothing but the systematic unity, which reason requires as a basis for the investigation of nature, that justified you in accepting the idea of a supreme intelligence as a schema for a regulative principle; and, the further you advance in the discovery of design and finality, the more certain the validity of your idea. But, as the whole aim of this regulative principle was the discovery of a necessary and systematic unity in nature, we have, in so far as we attain this, to attribute our success to the idea of a Supreme Being; while, at the same time, we cannot, without involving ourselves in contradictions, overlook the general laws of nature, as it was in reference to them alone that this idea was employed. We cannot, I say, overlook the general laws of nature, and regard this conformity to aims observable in nature as contingent or hyperphysical in its origin; inasmuch as there is no ground which can justify us in the admission of a being with such properties distinct from and above nature. All that we are authorized to assert is, that this idea may be employed as a principle, and that the properties of the being which is assumed to correspond to it may be regarded as systematically connected in analogy with the causal determination of phenomena.

For the same reasons we are justified in introducing into the idea of the supreme cause other anthropomorphic elements (for without these we could not predicate anything of it); we may regard it as allowable to cogitate this cause as a being with understanding, the feelings of pleasure and displeasure, and faculties of desire and will corresponding to these. At the same time, we may attribute to this being infinite perfection—a perfection which necessarily transcends that which our knowledge of the order and design in the world would authorize us to predicate of it. For the regulative law of systematic unity requires us to study nature on the supposition that systematic and final unity *in infinitum* is everywhere discoverable, even in the highest diversity. For, although we may discover little of this cosmical perfection, it belongs to the legislative prerogative of reason, to require us always to seek for and to expect it; while it must always be beneficial to institute all inquiries into nature in accordance with this principle. But it is evident that, by this idea of a supreme author of all, which I place as the foundation of all inquiries into nature, I do not mean to assert the existence of such a being, or that I have any knowledge of its existence; and, consequently, I do not really deduce anything from the existence of this being, but merely from its idea, that is to say, from the nature of things in this world, in accordance with this idea. A certain dim consciousness of the true use of this idea seems to have dictated to the philosophers of all times the moderate language used by them regarding the cause of the world. We find them employing the expressions, wisdom and care of nature, and divine wisdom, as synonymous—nay, in purely speculative discussions, preferring the former, because it does not carry the appearance of greater pretensions than such as we are entitled to make, and at the same time directs reason to its proper field of action—nature and her phenomena.

Thus, pure reason, which at first seemed to promise us nothing less than the extension of our cognition beyond the limits of experience, is found, when thoroughly examined, to contain nothing but regulative principles, the virtue and function of which is to introduce into our cognition a higher degree of unity than the understanding could of itself. These principles, by placing the goal of all our struggles at so great a distance, realize for us the most thorough connection between the different parts of our cognition, and the highest degree of systematic unity. But, on the other hand, if misunderstood and employed as constitutive principles of transcendent cognition, they become the parents of illusions and contradictions, while pretending to introduce us to new regions of knowledge.

Thus all human cognition begins with intuitions, proceeds from thence to conceptions, and ends with ideas. Although it possesses in relation to all three elements, *a priori* sources of cognition, which seemed to transcend the limits of all experience, a thorough-going criticism demonstrates, that speculative reason can never, by the aid of these elements, pass the bounds of possible experience, and that the proper destination of this highest faculty of cognition is to employ all methods, and all the principles of these methods, for the purpose of penetrating into the innermost secrets of nature, by the aid of the principles of unity (among all kinds of which teleological unity is the highest), while it ought not to attempt to soar above the sphere of experience, beyond which there lies nought for us but the void inane. The critical examination, in our Transcendental Analytic, of all the propositions which professed to extend cognition beyond the sphere of experience, completely demonstrated that they can only conduct us to a possible experience. If we were not distrustful even of the clearest abstract theorems, if we were not allured by specious and inviting prospects to escape from the constraining power of their evidence, we might spare ourselves the laborious examination of all the dialectical arguments which a transcendent reason adduces in support of its pretensions; for we should know with the most complete certainty that, however honest such professions might be, they are null and valueless, because they relate to a kind of knowledge to which no man can by any possibility attain. But, as there is no end to discussion, if we cannot discover the true cause of the illusions by which even the wisest are deceived, and as the analysis of all our transcendent cognition into its elements is of itself of no slight value as a psychological study, while it is a duty incumbent on every philosopher—it was found necessary to investigate the dialectical procedure of reason in its primary sources. And as the inferences of which this dialectic is the parent, are not only deceitful, but naturally possess a profound interest for humanity, it was advisable at the same time, to give a full account of the momenta of this dialectical procedure, and to deposit it in the archives of human reason, as a warning to all future metaphysicians to avoid these causes of speculative error.

## TRANSCENDENTAL DOCTRINE OF METHOD

IF we regard the sum of the cognition of pure speculative reason as an edifice, the idea of which, at least, exists in the human mind, it may be said that we have in the Transcendental Doctrine of Elements examined the materials and determined to what edifice these belong, and what its height and stability. We have found, indeed, that, although we had purposed to build for ourselves a tower which should reach to heaven, the supply of materials sufficed merely for a habitation, which was spacious enough for all terrestrial purposes, and high enough to enable us to survey the level plain of experience, but that the bold undertaking designed necessarily failed for want of materials—not to mention the confusion of tongues, which gave rise to endless disputes among the labourers on the plan of the edifice, and at last scattered them over all the world, each to erect a separate building for himself, according to his own plans and his own inclinations. Our present task relates not to the materials, but to the plan of an edifice; and, as we have had sufficient warning not to venture blindly upon a design which may be found to transcend our natural powers, while, at the same time, we cannot give up the intention of erecting a secure abode for the mind, we must proportion our design to the material which is presented to us, and which is, at the same time, sufficient for all our wants.

I understand, then, by the transcendental doctrine of method, the determination of the formal conditions of a complete system of pure reason. We shall accordingly have to treat of the *Discipline*, the *Canon*, the *Architectonic*, and, finally, the *History* of pure reason. This part of our *Critique* will accomplish, from the transcendental point of view, what has been usually attempted, but miserably executed, under the name of *practical logic*. It has been badly executed, I say, because general logic, not being limited to any particular kind of cognition (not even to the pure cognition of the understanding) nor to any particular objects, it cannot, without borrowing from other sciences, do more than present merely the titles or signs of *possible methods* and the technical expressions, which are employed in the systematic parts of all sciences; and thus the pupil is made acquainted with names, the meaning and application of which he is to learn only at some future time.

# CHAPTER I

## THE DISCIPLINE OF PURE REASON

NEGATIVE judgments—those which are so not merely as regards their logical form, but in respect of their content—are not commonly held in especial respect. They are, on the contrary, regarded as jealous enemies of our insatiable desire for knowledge; and it almost requires an apology to induce us to tolerate, much less to prize and to respect them.

All propositions, indeed, may be *logically* expressed in a negative form; but, in relation to the content of our cognition, the peculiar province of negative judgments is solely to *prevent error*. For this reason, too, negative propositions, which are framed for the purpose of correcting false cognitions where error is absolutely impossible, are undoubtedly true, but inane and senseless; that is, they are in reality purposeless, and for this reason often very ridiculous. Such is the proposition of the schoolman, that Alexander could not have subdued any countries without an army.

But where the limits of our possible cognition are very much contracted, the attraction to new fields of knowledge great, the illusions to which the mind is subject of the most deceptive character, and the evil consequences of error of no inconsiderable magnitude—the *negative* element in knowledge, which is useful only to guard us against error, is of far more importance than much of that positive instruction which makes additions to the sum of our knowledge. The *restraint* which is employed to repress, and finally to extirpate the constant inclination to depart from certain rules, is termed *Discipline*. It is distinguished from *culture*, which aims at the formation of a certain degree of skill, without attempting to repress or to destroy any other mental power, already existing. In the cultivation of a talent, which has given evidence of an impulse towards self-development, discipline takes a negative,[1] culture and doctrine a positive, part.

[1] I am well aware that, in the language of the schools, the term *discipline* is usually employed as synonymous with *instruction*. But there are so many cases in which it is necessary to distinguish the notion of the former, as a course of corrective training, from that of the latter, as the communication

That natural dispositions and talents (such as imagination and wit), which ask a free and unlimited development, require in many respects the corrective influence of discipline, every one will readily grant. But it may well appear strange, that reason, whose proper duty it is to prescribe rules of discipline to all the other powers of the mind, should itself require this corrective. It has, in fact, hitherto escaped this humiliation, only because, in presence of its magnificent pretensions and high position, no one could readily suspect it to be capable of substituting fancies for conceptions, and words for things.

Reason, when employed in the field of experience, does not stand in need of criticism, because its principles are subjected to the continual test of empirical observations. Nor is criticism requisite in the sphere of mathematics, where the conceptions of reason must always be presented *in concreto* in pure intuition, and baseless or arbitrary assertions are discovered without difficulty. But where reason is not held in a plain track by the influence of empirical or of pure intuition, that is, when it is employed in the transcendental sphere of pure conceptions, it stands in great need of discipline, to restrain its propensity to overstep the limits of possible experience, and to keep it from wandering into error. In fact, the utility of the philosophy of pure reason is entirely of this negative character. Particular errors may be corrected by particular animadversions, and the causes of these errors may be eradicated by criticism. But where we find, as in the case of pure reason, a complete system of illusions and fallacies, closely connected with each other and depending upon grand general principles, there seems to be required a peculiar and negative code of mental legislation, which, under the denomination of a *discipline*, and founded upon the nature of reason and the objects of its exercise, shall constitute a system of thorough examination and testing, which no fallacy will be able to withstand or escape from, under whatever disguise or concealment it may lurk.

But the reader must remark that, in this the second division of our Transcendental Critique, the discipline of pure reason is not directed to the content, but to the method of the cognition of pure reason. The former task has been completed in the Doctrine of Elements. But there is so much similarity in the mode of employing the faculty of reason, whatever be the object to which it is applied,

of knowledge, and the nature of things itself demands the appropriation of the most suitable expressions for this distinction, that it is my desire that the former term should never be employed in any other than a negative signification.

while, at the same time, its employment in the transcendental
sphere is so essentially different in kind from every other, that,
without the warning negative influence of a discipline specially
directed to that end, the errors are unavoidable which spring from
the unskilful employment of the methods which are originated by
reason but which are out of place in this sphere.

## SECTION I

### *The Discipline of Pure Reason in the Sphere of Dogmatism*

THE science of Mathematics presents the most brilliant example
of the extension of the sphere of pure reason without the aid of
experience. Examples are always contagious; and they exert an
especial influence on the same faculty, which naturally flatters
itself that it will have the same good fortune in other case as fell
to its lot in one fortunate instance. Hence pure reason hopes to
be able to extend its empire in the transcendental sphere with equal
success and security, especially when it applies the same method
which was attended with such brilliant results in the science of
Mathematics. It is, therefore, of the highest importance for us
to know, whether the method of arriving at demonstrative certainty,
which is termed *mathematical*, be identical with that by which we
endeavour to attain the same degree of certainty in philosophy,
and which is termed in that science *dogmatical*.

*Philosophical* cognition is the *cognition* of *reason* by means of
*conceptions*; mathematical cognition is cognition by means of the
*construction* of conceptions. The *construction* of a conception is
the presentation *a priori* of the intuition which corresponds to the
conception. For this purpose a *non-empirical* intuition is requisite,
which, as an intuition, is an *individual* object; while, as the construction of a conception (a general representation), it must be
seen to be universally valid for all the possible intuitions which
rank under that conception. Thus I construct a triangle, by the
presentation of the object which corresponds to this conception,
either by mere imagination—in pure intuition, or upon paper—in
empirical intuition, in both cases completely *a priori*, without
borrowing the type of that figure from any experience. The
individual figure drawn upon paper is empirical; but it serves,
notwithstanding, to indicate the conception, even in its universality, because in this empirical intuition we keep our eye merely

on the act of the construction of the conception, and pay no attention to the various modes of determining it, for example, its size, the length of its sides, the size of its angles, these not in the least affecting the essential character of the conception.

Philosophical cognition, accordingly, regards the particular only in the general; mathematical the general in the particular, nay, in the individual. This is done, however, entirely *a priori* and by means of pure reason, so that, as this individual figure is determined under certain universal conditions of construction, the object of the conception, to which this individual figure corresponds as its schema, must be cogitated as universally determined.

The essential difference of these two modes of cognition consists, therefore, in this formal quality; it does not regard the difference of the matter or objects of both. Those thinkers who aim at distinguishing philosophy from mathematics by asserting that the former has to do with *quality* merely, and the latter with *quantity*, have mistaken the effect for the cause. The reason why mathematical cognition can relate only to quantity, is to be found in its form alone. For it is the conception of quantities only that is capable of being constructed, that is, presented *a priori* in intuition; while qualities cannot be given in any other than an empirical intuition. Hence the cognition of qualities by reason is possible only through conceptions. No one can find an intuition which shall correspond to the conception of reality, except in experience; it cannot be presented to the mind *a priori*, and antecedently to the empirical consciousness of a reality. We can form an intuition, by means of the mere conception of it, of a cone, without the aid of experience; but the colour of the cone we cannot know except from experience. I cannot present an intuition of a cause, except in an example, which experience offers to me. Besides, philosophy, as well as mathematics, treats of quantities; as, for example, of totality, infinity, and so on. Mathematics, too, treats of the difference of lines and surfaces—as spaces of different quality, of the continuity of extension—as a quality thereof. But, although in such cases they have a common object, the mode in which reason considers that object is very different in philosophy from what it is in mathematics. The former confines itself to the general conceptions; the latter can do nothing with a mere conception, it hastens to intuition. In this intuition it regards the conception *in concreto*, not empirically, but in an *a priori* intuition, which it has constructed; and in which, all the results which follow from the general conditions of the construction of the conception, are in all cases valid for the object of the constructed conception.

THE DISCIPLINE OF PURE REASON 411

Suppose that the conception of a triangle is given to a philosopher, and that he is required to discover, by the philosophical method, what relation the sum of its angles bears to a right angle. He has nothing before him but the conception of a figure enclosed within three right lines, and, consequently, with the same number of angles. He may analyse the conception of a right line, of an angle, or of the number three as long as he pleases, but he will not discover any properties not contained in these conceptions. But, if this question is proposed to a geometrician, he at once begins by constructing a triangle.[1] He knows that two right angles are equal to the sum of all the contiguous angles which proceed from one point in a straight line; and he goes on to produce one side of his triangle, thus forming two adjacent angles which are together equal to two right angles. He then divides the exterior of these angles, by drawing a line parallel with the opposite side of the triangle, and immediately perceives that he has thus got an exterior adjacent angle which is equal to the interior. Proceeding in this way, through a chain of inferences, and always on the ground of intuition, he arrives at a clear and universally valid solution of the question.

But mathematics does not confine itself to the construction of quantities (*quanta*), as in the case of geometry; it occupies itself with pure quantity also (*quantitas*), as in the case of algebra, where complete abstraction is made of the properties of the object indicated by the conception of quantity. In algebra, a certain method of notation by signs is adopted, and these indicate the different possible constructions of quantities, the extraction of roots, and so on. After having thus denoted the general conception of quantities, according to their different relations, the different operations by which quantity or number is increased or diminished are presented in intuition in accordance with general rules. Thus, when one quantity is to be divided by another, the signs which denote both are placed in the form peculiar to the operation of division; and thus algebra, by means of a symbolical construction of quantity, just as geometry, with its ostensive or geometrical construction (a construction of the objects themselves), arrives at results which discursive cognition cannot hope to reach by the aid of mere conceptions.

Now, what is the cause of this difference in the fortune of the philosopher and the mathematician, the former of whom follows the path of conceptions, while the latter pursues that of intuitions,

---

[1] Either in his own mind—in pure intuition, or upon paper—in empirical intuition.—*Tr.*

which he represents, *a priori*, in correspondence with his conceptions? The cause is evident from what has been already demonstrated in the introduction to this *Critique*. We do not, in the present case, want to discover analytical propositions, which may be produced merely by analysing our conceptions—for in this the philosopher would have the advantage over his rival; we aim at the discovery of synthetical propositions—such synthetical propositions, moreover, as can be cognized *a priori*. I must not confine myself to that which I actually cogitate in my conception of a triangle, for this is nothing more than the mere definition; I must try to go beyond that, and to arrive at properties which are not contained in, although they belong to, the conception. Now, this is impossible, unless I determine the object present to my mind according to the conditions, either of empirical, or of pure intuition. In the former case, I should have an empirical proposition (arrived at by actual measurement of the angles of the triangle), which would possess neither universality nor necessity; but that would be of no value. In the latter, I proceed by geometrical construction, by means of which I collect, in a pure intuition, just as I would in an empirical intuition, all the various properties which belong to the schema of a triangle in general, and consequently to its conception, and thus construct synthetical propositions which possess the attribute of universality.

It would be vain to philosophize upon the triangle, that is, to reflect on it discursively; I should get no further than the definition with which I had been obliged to set out. There are certainly transcendental synthetical propositions which are framed by means of pure conceptions, and which form the peculiar distinction of philosophy; but these do not relate to any particular thing, but to a thing in general, and enounce the conditions under which the perception of it may become a part of possible experience. But the science of mathematics has nothing to do with such questions, nor with the question of existence in any fashion; it is concerned merely with the properties of objects in themselves, only in so far as these are connected with the conception of the objects.

In the above example, we have merely attempted to show the great difference which exists between the discursive employment of reason in the sphere of conceptions, and its intuitive exercise by means of the construction of conceptions. The question naturally arises—what is the cause which necessitates this twofold exercise of reason, and how are we to discover whether it is the philosophical or the mathematical method which reason is pursuing in an argument?

All our knowledge relates, finally, to possible intuitions, for it is these alone that present objects to the mind. An *a priori* or non-empirical conception contains either a pure intuition—and in this case it can be constructed; or it contains nothing but the synthesis of possible intuitions, which are not given *a priori*. In this latter case, it may help us to form synthetical *a priori* judgments, but only in the discursive method, by conceptions, not in the intuitive, by means of the construction of conceptions.

The only *a priori* intuition is that of the pure form of phenomena —space and time. A conception of space and time as *quanta* may be presented *a priori* in intuition, that is, constructed, either alone with their quality (figure), or as pure quantity (the mere synthesis of the homogeneous), by means of number. But the matter of phenomena, by which *things* are given in space and time, can be presented only in perception, *a posteriori*. The only conception which represents *a priori* this empirical content of phenomena, is the conception of a *thing* in general; and the *a priori* synthetical cognition of this conception can give us nothing more than the rule for the synthesis of that which may be contained in the corresponding *a posteriori* perception; it is utterly inadequate to present an *a priori* intuition of the real object, which must necessarily be empirical.

Synthetical propositions, which relate to *things* in general, an *a priori* intuition of which is impossible, are transcendental. For this reason transcendental propositions cannot be framed by means of the construction of conceptions; they are *a priori*, and based entirely on conceptions themselves. They contain merely the rule, by which we are to seek in the world of perception or experience the synthetical unity of that which cannot be intuited *a priori*. But they are incompetent to present any of the conceptions which appear in them in an *a priori* intuition; these can be given only *a posteriori*, in experience, which, however, is itself possible only through these synthetical principles.

If we are to form a synthetical judgment regarding a conception, we must go beyond it, to the intuition in which it is given. If we keep to what is contained in the conception, the judgment is merely analytical—it is merely an explanation of what we have cogitated in the conception. But I can pass from the conception to the pure or empirical intuition which corresponds to it. I can proceed to examine my conception *in concreto*, and to cognize, either *a priori* or *a posteriori*, what I find in the object of the conception. The former—*a priori* cognition—is rational-mathematical cognition by means of the construction of the conception; the latter—*a posteriori* cognition—is purely empirical cognition, which does not possess the attributes of necessity and universality. Thus I may analyse the conception I have of gold; but I gain no new information from this analysis, I merely enumerate the different properties which I had connected with the notion indicated by the word. My knowledge has gained in logical clearness and arrangement, but no addition has been made to it. But if I take the matter which is indicated by this name, and submit it to the examination of my senses, I am enabled to form several synthetical—although still empirical—propositions. The mathematical conception of a triangle I should construct, that is, present *a priori* in intuition, and in this way attain to rational-synthetical cognition. But when the transcendental conception of reality, or substance, or power is presented to my mind, I find that it does not relate to or indicate either an empirical or pure intuition, but that it indicates merely the synthesis of empirical intuitions, which cannot of course be given *a priori*. The synthesis in such a conception cannot proceed *a priori*—without the aid of experience—to the intuition which corresponds to the conception; and, for this reason, none of these conceptions can produce a determinative synthetical proposition, they can never present more than a principle of the synthesis [1] of possible empirical intuitions. A transcendental proposition is, therefore, a synthetical cognition of reason by means of pure conceptions and the discursive method, and it renders possible all synthetical unity in empirical cognition, though it cannot present us with any intuition *a priori*.

There is thus a twofold exercise of reason. Both modes have the properties of universality and an *a priori* origin in common, but are, in their procedure, of widely different character. The reason of this is, that in the world of phenomena, in which alone objects are presented to our minds, there are two main elements—the form of intuition (space and time), which can be cognized and determined completely *a priori*, and the matter or content—that which is presented in space and time, and which, consequently, contains a something—an existence corresponding to our powers of sensation. As regards the latter, which can never be given in a determinate mode except by experience, there are no *a priori* notions which

---

[1] In the case of the conception of cause, I do really go beyond the empirical conception of an event—but not to the intuition which presents this conception *in concreto*, but only to the time-conditions, which may be found in experience to correspond to the conception. My procedure is, therefore, strictly according to conceptions; I cannot in a case of this kind employ the construction of conceptions, because the conception is merely a rule for the synthesis of perceptions, which are not pure intuitions, and which, therefore, cannot be given *a priori*.

relate to it, except the undetermined conceptions of the synthesis of possible sensations, in so far as these belong (in a possible experience) to the unity of consciousness. As regards the former, we can determine our conceptions *a priori* in intuition, inasmuch as we are ourselves the creators of the objects of the conceptions in space and time—these objects being regarded simply as *quanta*. In the one case, reason proceeds according to conceptions, and can do nothing more than subject phenomena to these—which can only be determined empirically, that is, *a posteriori*—in conformity, however, with those conceptions as the rules of all empirical synthesis. In the other case, reason proceeds by the construction of conceptions; and, as these conceptions relate to an *a priori* intuition, they may be given and determined in pure intuition *a priori*, and without the aid of empirical data. The examination and consideration of everything that exists in space or time—whether it is a quantum or not, in how far the particular something (which fills space or time) is a primary substratum, or a mere determination of some other existence, whether it relates to anything else—either as cause or effect, whether its existence is isolated or in reciprocal connection with and dependence upon others, the possibility of this existence, its reality and necessity or their opposites—all these form part of the *cognition of reason* on the ground of conceptions, and this cognition is termed *philosophical*. But to determine *a priori* an intuition in space (its figure), to divide time into periods, or merely to cognize the quantity of an intuition in space and time, and to determine it by number—all this is an *operation of reason* by means of the construction of conceptions, and is called *mathematical*.

The success which attends the efforts of reason in the sphere of mathematics, naturally fosters the expectation that the same good fortune will be its lot, if it applies the mathematical method in other regions of mental endeavour besides that of quantities. Its success is thus great, because it can support all its conceptions by *a priori* intuitions, and in this way, make itself a master, as it were, over nature; while pure philosophy, with its *a priori* discursive conceptions, bungles about in the world of nature, and cannot accredit or show any *a priori* evidence of the reality of these conceptions. Masters in the science of mathematics are confident of the success of this method; indeed, it is a common persuasion, that it is capable of being applied to any subject of human thought. They have hardly ever reflected or philosophized on their favourite science—a task of great difficulty; and the specific difference between the two modes of employing the faculty of reason has never entered their thoughts. Rules current in the field of common experience, and which common sense stamps everywhere with its approval, are regarded by them as axiomatic. From what source the conceptions of space and time, with which (as the only primitive quanta) they have to deal, enter their minds, is a question which they do not trouble themselves to answer; and they think it just as unnecessary to examine into the origin of the pure conceptions of the understanding and the extent of their validity. All they have to do with them is to employ them. In all this they are perfectly right, if they do not overstep the limits of the sphere of *nature*. But they pass, unconsciously, from the world of sense to the insecure ground of pure transcendental conceptions (*instabilis tellus, innabilis unda*), where they can neither stand nor swim, and where the tracks of their footsteps are obliterated by time; while the march of mathematics is pursued on a broad and magnificent highway, which the latest posterity shall frequent without fear of danger or impediment.

As we have taken upon us the task of determining, clearly and certainly, the limits of pure reason in the sphere of transcendentalism, and as the efforts of reason in this direction are persisted in, even after the plainest and most expressive warnings, hope still beckoning us past the limits of experience into the splendours of the intellectual world—it becomes necessary to cut away the last anchor of this fallacious and fantastic hope. We shall accordingly show that the mathematical method is unattended in the sphere of philosophy by the least advantage—except, perhaps, that it more plainly exhibits its own inadequacy—that geometry and philosophy are two quite different things, although they go hand in hand in the field of natural science, and, consequently, that the procedure of the one can never be imitated by the other.

The evidence of mathematics rests upon definitions, axioms, and demonstrations. I shall be satisfied with showing that none of these forms can be employed or imitated in philosophy in the sense in which they are understood by mathematicians; and that the geometrician, if he employs his method in philosophy, will succeed only in building card-castles, while the employment of the philosophical method in mathematics can result in nothing but mere verbiage. The essential business of philosophy, indeed, is to mark out the limits of the science; and even the mathematician, unless his talent is naturally circumscribed and limited to this particular department of knowledge, cannot turn a deaf ear to the warnings of philosophy, or set himself above its direction.

1. *Of Definitions.* A *definition* is, as the term itself indicates,

the representation, upon primary grounds, of the complete conception of a thing within its own limits.[1] Accordingly, an *empirical* conception cannot be defined, it can only be *explained*. For, as there are in such a conception only a certain number of marks or signs, which denote a certain class of sensuous objects, we can never be sure that we do not cogitate under the word which indicates the same object, at one time a greater, at another a smaller number of signs. Thus, one person may cogitate in his conception of gold, in addition to its properties of weight, colour, malleability, that of resisting rust, while another person may be ignorant of this quality. We employ certain signs only so long as we require them for the sake of distinction; new observations abstract some and add new ones, so that an empirical conception never remains within permanent limits. It is, in fact, useless to define a conception of this kind. If, for example, we are speaking of water and its properties, we do not stop at what we actually think by the word *water*, but proceed to observation and experiment; and the word, with the few signs attached to it, is more properly a *designation* than a conception of the thing. A definition in this case would evidently be nothing more than a determination of the word. In the second place, no *a priori* conception, such as those of substance, cause, right, fitness, and so on, can be defined. For I can never be sure, that the clear representation of a given conception (which is given in a confused state) has been fully developed, until I know that the representation is adequate with its object. But, inasmuch as the conception, as it is presented to the mind, may contain a number of obscure representations, which we do not observe in our analysis, although we employ them in our application of the conception, I can never be sure that my analysis is complete, while examples may make this probable, although they can never demonstate the fact. Instead of the word *definition*, I should rather employ the term *exposition*— a more modest expression, which the critic may accept without surrendering his doubts as to the completeness of the analysis of any such conception. As, therefore, neither empirical nor *a priori* conceptions are capable of definition, we have to see whether the only other kind of conceptions—arbitrary conceptions—can be

---

[1] The definition must describe the conception *completely*, that is, omit none of the marks or signs of which it is composed; *within its own limits*, that is, it must be precise, and enumerate no more signs than belong to the conception; and *on primary grounds*, that is to say, the limitation of the bounds of the conception must not be deduced from other conceptions, as in this case a proof would be necessary, and the so-called definition would be incapable of taking its place at the head of all the judgments we hav • to form regarding an object.

subjected to this mental operation. Such a conception can always be defined; for I must know thoroughly what I wished to cogitate in it, as it was I who created it, and it was not given to my mind either by the nature of my understanding or by experience. At the same time, I cannot say that, by such a definition, I have defined a real object. If the conception is based upon empirical conditions, if, for example, I have a conception of a clock for a ship, this arbitrary conception does not assure me of the existence or even of the possibility of the object. My definition of such a conception would with more propriety be termed a declaration of a project than a definition of an object. There are no other conceptions which can bear definition, except those which contain an arbitrary synthesis, which can be constructed *a priori*. Consequently, the science of mathematics alone possesses definitions. For the object here thought is presented *a priori* in intuition; and thus it can never contain more or less than the conception, because the conception of the object has been given by the definition—and primarily, that is, without deriving the definition from any other source. Philosophical definitions are, therefore, merely expositions of given conceptions, while mathematical definitions are constructions of conceptions originally formed by the mind itself; the former are produced by analysis, the completeness of which is never demonstratively certain, the latter by a synthesis. In a mathematical definition the conception is *formed*, in a philosophical definition it is only *explained*. From this it follows:

(a) That we must not imitate, in philosophy, the mathematical usage of commencing with definitions—except by way of hypothesis or experiment. For, as all so-called philosophical definitions are merely analyses of given conceptions, these conceptions, although only in a confused form, must precede the analysis; and the incomplete exposition must precede the complete, so that we may be able to draw certain inferences from the characteristics which an incomplete analysis has enabled us to discover, before we attain to the complete exposition or definition of the conception. In one word, a full and clear definition ought, in philosophy, rather to form the conclusion than the commencement of our labours.[1] In

---

[1] Philosophy abounds in faulty definitions, especially such as contain some of the elements requisite to form a complete definition. If a conception could not be employed in reasoning before it had been defined, it would fare ill with all philosophical thought. But, as incompletely defined conceptions may always be employed without detriment to truth, so far as our analysis of the elements contained in them proceeds, imperfect definitions, that is, propositions which are properly not definitions, but merely approximations thereto, may be used with great advantage. In mathematics, definition

mathematics, on the contrary, we cannot have a conception prior to the definition; it is the definition which gives us the conception, and it must for this reason form the commencement of every chain of mathematical reasoning.

(b) Mathematical definitions cannot be erroneous. For the conception is given only in and through the definition, and thus it contains only what has been cogitated in the definition. But although a definition cannot be incorrect, as regards its content, an error may sometimes, although seldom, creep into the form. This error consists in a want of precision. Thus the common definition of a circle—that it is a curved line, every point in which is equally distant from another point called the centre—is faulty, from the fact that the determination indicated by the word *curved* is superfluous. For there ought to be a particular theorem, which may be easily proved from the definition, to the effect that every line, which has all its points at equal distances from another point, must be a curved line—that is, that not even the smallest part of it can be straight. Analytical definitions, on the other hand, may be erroneous in many respects, either by the introduction of signs which do not actually exist in the conception, or by wanting in that completeness which forms the essential of a definition. In the latter case, the definition is necessarily defective, because we can never be fully certain of the completeness of our analysis. For these reasons, the method of definition employed in mathematics cannot be imitated in philosophy.

2. *Of Axioms.* These, in so far as they are immediately certain, are *a priori* synthetical principles. Now, one conception cannot be connected synthetically and yet immediately with another; because, if we wish to proceed out of and beyond a conception, a third mediating cognition is necessary. And, as philosophy is a cognition of reason by the aid of conceptions alone, there is to be found in it no principle which deserves to be called an axiom. Mathematics, on the other hand, may possess axioms, because it can always connect the predicates of an object *a priori*, and without any mediating term, by means of the construction of conceptions in intuition. Such is the case with the proposition: Three points can always lie in a plane. On the other hand, no synthetical principle which is based upon conceptions, can ever be immediately certain (for example, the proposition: Everything that happens has a cause), because I require a mediating term to connect the

belongs *ad esse*, in philosophy *ad melius esse*.   It is a difficult task to construct a proper definition.   Jurists are still without a complete definition of the idea of right.

two conceptions of event and cause—namely, the condition of time-determination in an experience, and I cannot cognize any such principle immediately and from conceptions alone. Discursive principles are, accordingly, very different from intuitive principles or axioms. The former always require deduction, which in the case of the latter may be altogether dispensed with. Axioms are, for this reason, always self-evident, while philosophical principles, whatever may be the degree of certainty they possess, cannot lay any claim to such a distinction. No synthetical proposition of pure transcendental reason can be so evident, as is often rashly enough declared, as the statement, *twice two are four*. It is true that in the Analytic I introduced into the list of principles of the pure understanding, certain axioms of intuition; but the principle there discussed was not itself an axiom, but served merely to present the principle of the possibility of axioms in general, while it was really nothing more than a principle based upon conceptions. For it is one part of the duty of transcendental philosophy to establish the possibility of mathematics itself. Philosophy possesses, then, no axioms, and has no right to impose its *a priori* principles upon thought, until it has established their authority and validity by a thorough-going deduction.

3. *Of Demonstrations*. Only an apodeictic proof, based upon intuition, can be termed a demonstration. Experience teaches us what is, but it cannot convince us that it might have been otherwise. Hence a proof upon empirical grounds cannot be apodeictic. *A priori* conceptions, in discursive cognition, can never produce intuitive certainty or evidence, however certain the judgment they present may be. Mathematics alone, therefore, contains demonstrations, because it does not deduce its cognition from conceptions, but from the construction of conceptions, that is, from intuition, which can be given *a priori* in accordance with conceptions. The method of algebra, in equations, from which the correct answer is deduced by reduction, is a kind of construction —not geometrical, but by symbols—in which all conceptions, especially those of the relations of quantities, are represented in intuition by signs; and thus the conclusions in that science are secured from errors by the fact that every proof is submitted to ocular evidence. Philosophical cognition does not possess this advantage, it being required to consider the general always *in abstracto* (by means of conceptions), while mathematics can always consider it *in concreto* (in an individual intuition), and at the same time by means of *a priori* representation, whereby all errors are rendered manifest to the senses. The former—discursive proofs

—ought to be termed *acroamatic* [1] *proofs*, rather than *demonstrations*, as only words are employed in them, while demonstrations proper, as the term itself indicates, always require a reference to the intuition of the object.

It follows from all these considerations, that it is not consonant with the nature of philosophy, especially in the sphere of pure reason, to employ the dogmatical method, and to adorn itself with the titles and insignia of mathematical science. It does not belong to that order, and can only hope for a fraternal union with that science. Its attempts at mathematical evidence are vain pretensions, which can only keep it back from its true aim, which is to detect the illusory procedure of reason when transgressing its proper limits, and by fully explaining and analysing our conceptions, to conduct us from the dim regions of speculation, to the clear region of modest self-knowledge. Reason must not, therefore, in its transcendental endeavours, look forward with such confidence, as if the path it is pursuing led straight to its aim, nor reckon with such security upon its premises, as to consider it unnecessary to take a step back, or to keep a strict watch for errors, which, overlooked in the principles, may be detected in the arguments themselves—in which case it may be requisite either to determine these principles with greater strictness, or to change them entirely.

I divide all apodeictic propositions, whether demonstrable or immediately certain, into *dogmata* and *mathemata*. A direct synthetical proposition, based on conceptions, is a *dogma*; a proposition of the same kind, based on the construction of conceptions, is a *mathema*. Analytical judgments do not teach us any more about an object than what was contained in the conception we had of it; because they do not extend our cognition beyond our conception of an object, they merely elucidate the conception. They cannot therefore be with propriety termed dogmas. Of the two kinds of *a priori* synthetical propositions above mentioned, only those which are employed in philosophy can, according to the general mode of speech, bear this name; those of arithmetic or geometry would not be rightly so denominated. Thus the customary mode of speaking confirms the explanation given above, and the conclusion arrived at, that only those judgments which are based upon conceptions, not on the construction of conceptions, can be termed dogmatical.

Thus, pure reason, in the sphere of speculation, does not contain a single direct synthetical judgment based upon conceptions. By

[1] From ἀκροαματικὸι.—*Tr.*

means of ideas, it is, as we have shown, incapable of producing synthetical judgments, which are objectively valid; by means of the conceptions of the understanding, it establishes certain indubitable principles, not, however, directly on the basis of conceptions, but only indirectly by means of the relation of these conceptions to something of a purely contingent nature, namely, possible experience. When experience is presupposed, these principles are apodeictically certain, but in themselves, and directly, they cannot even be cognized *a priori*. Thus the given conceptions of *cause* and *event* will not be sufficient for the demonstration of the proposition: Every event has a cause. For this reason, it is not a dogma; although from another point of view—that of experience, it is capable of being proved to demonstration. The proper term for such a proposition is *principle*, and not *theorem* (although it does require to be proved), because it possesses the remarkable peculiarity of being the condition of the possibility of its own ground of proof, that is, experience, and of forming a necessary presupposition in all empirical observation.

If then, in the speculative sphere of pure reason, no dogmata are to be found; all *dogmatical* methods, whether borrowed from mathematics, or invented by philosophical thinkers, are alike inappropriate and inefficient. They only serve to conceal errors and fallacies, and to deceive philosophy, whose duty it is to see that reason pursues a safe and straight path. A philosophical method may, however, be *systematical*. For our reason is, subjectively considered, itself a system, and, in the sphere of mere conceptions, a system of investigation according to principles of unity, the material being supplied by experience alone. But this is not the proper place for discussing the peculiar method of transcendental philosophy, as our present task is simply to examine whether our faculties are capable of erecting an edifice on the basis of pure reason, and how far they may proceed with the materials at their command.

## SECTION II

### *The Discipline of Pure Reason in Polemics*

REASON must be subject, in all its operations, to criticism, which must always be permitted to exercise its functions without restraint; otherwise its interests are imperilled, and its influence obnoxious to suspicion. There is nothing, however useful, however sacred it may be, that can claim exemption from the searching examination of this supreme tribunal, which has no respect of persons. The very existence of reason depends upon this freedom; for the voice of reason is not that of a dictatorial and despotic power, it is rather like the vote of the citizens of a free state, every member of which must have the privilege of giving free expression to his doubts, and possess even the right of *veto*.

But while reason can never decline to submit itself to the tribunal of criticism, it has not always cause to *dread* the judgment of this court. Pure reason, however, when engaged in the sphere of dogmatism, is not so thoroughly conscious of a strict observance of its highest laws, as to appear before a higher judicial reason with perfect confidence. On the contrary, it must renounce its magnificent dogmatical pretensions in philosophy.

Very different is the case, when it has to defend itself, not before a judge, but against an equal. If dogmatical assertions are advanced on the negative side, in opposition to those made by reason on the positive side, its justification κατ' ἄνθρωπον is complete, although the proof of its propositions is κατ' ἀλήθειαν unsatisfactory.

By the polemic of pure reason I mean the defence of its propositions made by reason, in opposition to the dogmatical counter-propositions advanced by other parties. The question here is not whether its own statements may not also be false; it merely regards the fact that reason proves that the opposite cannot be established with demonstrative certainty, nor even asserted with a higher degree of probability. Reason does not hold her possessions upon sufferance; for, although she cannot show a perfectly satisfactory title to them, no one can prove that she is *not* the rightful possessor.

It is a melancholy reflection, that reason, in its highest exercise, falls into an antithetic; and that the supreme tribunal for the settlement of differences should not be at union with itself. It is true that we had to discuss the question of an apparent antithetic, but we found that it was based upon a misconception. In conformity with the common prejudice, phenomena were regarded as things in themselves, and thus an absolute completeness in their synthesis was required in the one mode or in the other (it was shown to be impossible in both); a demand entirely out of place in regard to phenomena. There was, then, no real self-contradiction of reason in the propositions—The series of phenomena *given in themselves* has an absolutely first beginning, and, This series is absolutely and *in itself* without beginning. The two propositions are perfectly consistent with each other, because phenomena as phenomena are *in themselves* nothing, and consequently the hypothesis that they are things in themselves, must lead to self-contradictory inferences.

But there are cases in which a similar misunderstanding cannot be provided against, and the dispute must remain unsettled. Take, for example, the theistic proposition: There is a Supreme Being; and on the other hand, the atheistic counter-statement: There exists no Supreme Being; or, in psychology: Everything that thinks, possesses the attribute of absolute and permanent unity, which is utterly different from the transitory unity of material phenomena; and the counter-proposition: The soul is not an immaterial unity, and its nature is transitory, like that of phenomena. The objects of these questions contain no heterogeneous or contradictory elements, for they relate to *things in themselves*, and not to phenomena. There would arise, indeed, a real contradiction, if reason came forward with a statement on the negative side of these questions alone. As regards the criticism to which the grounds of proof on the affirmative side must be subjected, it may be freely admitted, without necessitating the surrender of the affirmative propositions, which have, at least, the interest of reason in their favour—an advantage which the opposite party cannot lay claim to.

I cannot agree with the opinion of several admirable thinkers—Sulzer among the rest—that in spite of the weakness of the arguments hitherto in use, we may hope, one day, to see sufficient demonstrations of the two cardinal propositions of pure reason—the existence of a Supreme Being, and the immortality of the soul. I am certain, on the contrary, that this will never be the case. For on what ground can reason base such synthetical propositions, which do not relate to the objects of experience and their internal possibility?—But it is also demonstratively certain that no one will ever be able to maintain the contrary with the least show of probability. For, as he can attempt such a proof solely upon the basis of pure reason, he is bound to prove that a Supreme Being, and a thinking subject in the character of a pure intelligence, are *impossible*. But where will he find the knowledge which can enable him to enounce synthetical judgments in regard to things which transcend the region of experience? We may, therefore, rest assured that the opposite never will be demonstrated. We need not, then, have recourse to scholastic arguments; we may always admit the truth of those propositions which are consistent with the speculative interests of reason in the sphere of experience, and form, moreover, the only means of uniting the speculative with the practical interest. Our opponent, who must not be considered here as a critic solely, we can be ready to meet with a *non liquet* which cannot fail to disconcert him; while we cannot deny his right to a similar retort, as we have on our side the advantage of the support of the subjective maxim of reason, and can therefore look upon all his sophistical arguments with calm indifference.

From this point of view, there is properly no antithetic of pure reason. For the only arena for such a struggle would be upon the field of pure theology and psychology; but on this ground there can appear no combatant whom we need to fear. Ridicule and boasting can be his only weapons; and these may be laughed at, as mere child's play. This consideration restores to Reason her courage; for what source of confidence could be found, if she, whose vocation it is to destroy error, were at variance with herself and without any reasonable hope of ever reaching a state of permanent repose?

Everything in nature is good for some purpose. Even poisons are serviceable; they destroy the evil effects of other poisons generated in our system, and must always find a place in every complete pharmacopoeia. The objections raised against the fallacies and sophistries of speculative reason, are objections given by the nature of this reason itself, and must therefore have a destination and purpose which can only be for the good of humanity. For what purpose has Providence raised many objects, in which we have the deepest interest, so far above us, that we vainly try to cognize them with certainty, and our powers of mental vision are rather excited than satisfied by the glimpses we may chance to seize? It is very doubtful whether it is for our benefit to advance bold affirmations regarding subjects involved in such obscurity; perhaps it would even be detrimental to our best interests. But it is undoubtedly always beneficial to leave the investigating, as well as the critical reason, in perfect freedom, and permit it to take charge of its own interests, which are advanced as much by its limitation, as by its extension of its views, and which always suffer by the interference of foreign powers forcing it, against its natural tendencies, to bend to certain preconceived designs.

Allow your opponent to say what he thinks reasonable, and combat him only with the weapons of reason. Have no anxiety for the practical interests of humanity—these are never imperilled in a purely speculative dispute. Such a dispute serves merely to disclose the antinomy of reason, which, as it has its source in the nature of reason, ought to be thoroughly investigated. Reason is benefited by the examination of a subject on both sides, and its judgments are corrected by being limited. It is not the *matter* that may give occasion to dispute, but the *manner*. For it is perfectly permissible to employ, in the presence of reason, the language of a firmly-rooted *faith*, even after we have been obliged to renounce all pretensions to *knowledge*.

If we were to ask the dispassionate *David Hume*—a philosopher endowed, in a degree that few are, with a well-balanced judgment: What motive induced you to spend so much labour and thought in undermining the consoling and beneficial persuasion that reason is capable of assuring us of the existence, and presenting us with a determinate conception of a Supreme Being?—his answer would be: Nothing but the desire of teaching reason to know its own powers better, and, at the same time, a dislike of the procedure by which that faculty was compelled to support foregone conclusions, and prevented from confessing the internal weaknesses which it cannot but feel when it enters upon a rigid self-examination. If, on the other hand, we were to ask *Priestley*—a philosopher who had no taste for transcendental speculation, but was entirely devoted to the principles of *empiricism*—what his motives were for overturning those two main pillars of religion—the doctrines of the freedom of the will and the immortality of the soul (in his view the hope of a future life is but the expectation of the miracle of resurrection)—this philosopher, himself a zealous and pious teacher of religion, could give no other answer than this: I acted in the interest of reason, which always suffers, when certain objects are explained and judged by a reference to other supposed laws than those of material nature—the only laws which we know in a determinate manner. It would be unfair to decry the latter philosopher, who endeavoured to harmonize his paradoxical opinions with the interests of religion, and to undervalue an honest and reflecting man, because he finds himself at a loss the moment he has left the field of natural science. The same grace must be accorded to Hume, a man not less well-disposed, and quite as blameless in his moral character, and who pushed his abstract speculations to an extreme length, because, as he rightly believed, the object of them lies entirely beyond the bounds of natural science, and within the sphere of pure ideas.

What is to be done to provide against the danger which seems in the present case to menace the best interests of humanity? The course to be pursued in reference to this subject is a perfectly plain and natural one. Let each thinker pursue his own path; if he shows talent, if he gives evidence of profound thought, in one word, if he shows that he possesses the power of reasoning—reason is always the gainer.   If you have recourse to other means, if you attempt to coerce reason, if you raise the cry of treason to humanity, if you excite the feelings of the crowd, which can neither understand nor sympathize with such subtle speculations—you will only make yourselves ridiculous.   For the question does not concern the advantage or disadvantage which we are expected to reap from such inquiries; the question is merely, how far reason can advance in the field of speculation, apart from all kinds of interest, and whether we may depend upon the exertions of speculative reason, or must renounce all reliance on it.   Instead of joining the combatants, it is your part to be a tranquil spectator of the struggle— a laborious struggle for the parties engaged, but attended, in its progress as well as in its result, with the most advantageous consequences for the interests of thought and knowledge.   It is absurd to expect to be enlightened by Reason, and at the same time to prescribe to her what side of the question she must adopt.   Moreover, reason is sufficiently held in check by its own power, the limits imposed on it by its own nature are sufficient; it is unnecessary for you to place over it additional guards, as if its power were dangerous to the constitution of the intellectual state.   In the dialectic of reason there is no victory gained, which need in the least disturb your tranquillity.

The strife of dialectic is a necessity of reason, and we cannot but wish that it had been conducted long ere this with that perfect freedom which ought to be its essential condition.   In this case, we should have had at an earlier period a matured and profound criticism, which must have put an end to all dialectical disputes, by exposing the illusions and prejudices in which they originated.

There is in human nature an unworthy propensity—a propensity which, like everything that springs from nature, must in its final purpose be conducive to the good of humanity—to conceal our real sentiments, and to give expression only to certain received opinions, which are regarded as at once safe and promotive of the common good.   It is true, this tendency, not only to conceal our real sentiments, but to profess those which may gain us favour in the eyes of society, has not only *civilized*, but, in a certain measure, *moralized* us; as no one can break through the outward covering of respectability, honour, and morality, and thus the seemingly-good examples which we see around us, form an excellent school for moral improvement, so long as our belief in their genuineness remains unshaken.   But this disposition to represent ourselves as better than we are, and to utter opinions which are not our own, can be nothing more than a kind of *provisionary* arrangement of nature to lead us from the rudeness of an uncivilized state, and to teach us how to assume at least the appearance and *manner* of the good we see. But when true principles have been developed, and have obtained a sure foundation in our habit of thought, this conventionalism must be attacked with earnest vigour, otherwise it corrupts the heart, and checks the growth of good dispositions with the mischievous weed of fair appearances.

I am sorry to remark the same tendency to misrepresentation and hypocrisy in the sphere of speculative discussion, where there is less temptation to restrain the free expression of thought. For what can be more prejudicial to the interests of intelligence, than to falsify our real sentiments, to conceal the doubts which we feel in regard to our statements, or to maintain the validity of grounds of proof which we well know to be insufficient? So long as mere personal vanity is the source of these unworthy artifices—and this is generally the case in speculative discussions, which are mostly destitute of practical interest, and are incapable of complete demonstration—the vanity of the opposite party exaggerates as much on the other side; and thus the result is the same, although it is not brought about so soon as if the dispute had been conducted in a sincere and upright spirit. But where the mass entertains the notion that the aim of certain subtle speculators is nothing less than to shake the very foundations of public welfare and morality —it seems not only prudent, but even praiseworthy, to maintain the good cause by illusory arguments, rather than to give to our supposed opponents the advantage of lowering our declarations to the moderate tone of a merely practical conviction, and of compelling us to confess our inability to attain to apodeictic certainty in speculative subjects. But we ought to reflect that there is nothing in the world more fatal to the maintenance of a good cause than deceit, misrepresentation, and falsehood. That the strictest laws of honesty should be observed in the discussion of a purely speculative subject, is the least requirement that can be made. If we could reckon with security even upon so little, the conflict of speculative reason regarding the important questions of God, immortality, and freedom, would have been either decided long ago, or would very soon be brought to a conclusion. But, in general, the uprightness of the defence stands in an inverse ratio to the goodness of the cause; and perhaps more honesty and fairness are shown by those who deny, than by those who uphold these doctrines.

I shall persuade myself, then, that I have readers who do not wish to see a righteous cause defended by unfair arguments. Such will now recognize the fact that, according to the principles of this *Critique*, if we consider not what is, but what ought to be the case, there can be really no polemic of pure reason. For how can two persons dispute about a thing, the reality of which neither can present in actual or even in possible experience? Each adopts the plan of meditating on his idea for the purpose of drawing from the idea, if he can, what is *more than the idea*, that is, the reality of the object which it indicates. How shall they settle the dispute, since neither is able to make his assertions directly comprehensible and certain, but must restrict himself to attacking and confuting those of his opponent? All statements enounced by pure reason transcend the conditions of possible experience, beyond the sphere of which we can discover no criterion of truth, while they are at the same time framed in accordance with the laws of the understanding, which are applicable only to experience; and thus it is the fate of all such speculative discussions, that while the one party attacks the weaker side of his opponent, he infallibly lays open his own weaknesses.

The critique of pure reason may be regarded as the highest tribunal for all speculative disputes; for it is not involved in these disputes, which have an immediate relation to certain objects and not to the laws of the mind, but is instituted for the purpose of determining the rights and limits of reason.

Without the control of criticism reason is, as it were, in a state of nature, and can only establish its claims and assertions by *war*. Criticism, on the contrary, deciding all questions according to the fundamental laws of its own institution, secures to us the peace of law and order, and enables us to discuss all differences in the more tranquil manner of a legal *process*. In the former case, disputes are ended by *victory*, which both sides may claim, and which is followed by a hollow armistice; in the latter, by a *sentence*, which, as it strikes at the root of all speculative differences, ensures to all concerned a lasting peace. The endless disputes of a dogmatizing reason compel us to look for some mode of arriving at a settled decision by a critical investigation of reason itself; just as Hobbes maintains that the state of nature is a state of injustice and violence, and that we must leave it and submit ourselves to the constraint of law, which indeed limits individual freedom, but only that it may consist with the freedom of others and with the common good of all.

This freedom will, among other things, permit of our openly stating the difficulties and doubts which we are ourselves unable to solve, without being decried on that account as turbulent and dangerous citizens. This privilege forms part of the native rights of human reason, which recognizes no other judge than the universal reason of humanity; and as this reason is the source of all progress and improvement, such a privilege is to be held sacred and inviolable. It is unwise, moreover, to denounce as dangerous, any bold assertions against, or rash attacks upon, an opinion which is held by the largest and most moral class of the community; for that would be giving them an importance which they do not deserve. When I hear that the freedom of the will, the hope of a future life, and the existence of God have been overthrown by the arguments of some able writer, I feel a strong desire to read his book; for I expect that he will add to my knowledge, and impart greater clearness and distinctness to my views by the argumentative power shown in his writings. But I am perfectly certain, even before I have opened the book, that he has not succeeded in a single point, not because I believe I am in possession of irrefutable demonstrations of these important propositions, but because this transcendental critique, which has disclosed to me the power and the limits of pure reason, has fully convinced me that, as it is insufficient to establish the affirmative, it is as powerless, and even more so, to assure us of the truth of the negative answer to these questions. From what source does this free-thinker derive his knowledge that there is, for example, no Supreme Being? This proposition lies out of the field of possible experience, and, therefore, beyond the limits of human cognition. But I would not read at all the answer which the dogmatical maintainer of the good cause makes to his opponent, because I know well beforehand, that he will merely attack the fallacious grounds of his adversary, without being able to establish his own assertions. Besides, a new illusory argument, in the construction of which talent and acuteness are shown, is suggestive of new ideas and new trains of reasoning, and in this respect the old and everyday sophistries are quite useless. Again, the dogmatical opponent of religion gives employment to criticism, and enables us to test and correct its principles, while there is no occasion for anxiety in regard to the influence and results of his reasoning.

But, it will be said, must we not warn the youth entrusted to academical care against such writings, must we not preserve them from the knowledge of these dangerous assertions, until their judgment is ripened, or rather until the doctrines which we wish to inculcate are so firmly rooted in their minds as to withstand all attempts at instilling the contrary dogmas, from whatever quarter they may come?

If we are to confine ourselves to the dogmatical procedure in the sphere of pure reason, and find ourselves unable to settle such disputes otherwise than by becoming a party in them, and setting counter-assertions against the statements advanced by our opponents, there is certainly no plan more advisable *for the moment*, but, at the same time, none more absurd and inefficient *for the future*, than this retaining of the youthful mind under guardianship for a time, and thus preserving it—for so long at least—from seduction into error.   But when, at a later period, either curiosity, or the prevalent fashion of thought, places such writings in their hands, will the so-called convictions of their youth stand firm? The young thinker, who has in his armoury none but dogmatical weapons with which to resist the attacks of his opponent, and who cannot detect the latent dialectic which lies in his own opinions as well as in those of the opposite party, sees the advance of illusory arguments and grounds of proof which have the advantage of novelty, against as illusory grounds of proof destitute of this advantage, and which, perhaps, excite the suspicion that the natural credulity of his youth has been abused by his instructors.   He thinks he can find no better means of showing that he has outgrown the discipline of his minority, than by despising those well-meant warnings, and, knowing no system of thought but that of dogmatism, he drinks deep draughts of the poison that is to sap the principles in which his early years were trained.

Exactly the opposite of the system here recommended ought to be pursued in academical instruction.   This can only be effected, however, by a thorough training in the critical investigation of pure reason.   For, in order to bring the principles of this critique into exercise as soon as possible, and to demonstrate their perfect sufficiency, even in the presence of the highest degree of dialectical illusion, the student ought to examine the assertions made on both sides of speculative questions step by step, and to test them by these principles.   It cannot be a difficult task for him to show the fallacies inherent in these propositions, and thus he begins early to feel his own power of securing himself against the influence of such sophistical arguments, which must finally lose, for him, all their illusory power.   And, although the same blows which overturn the edifice of his opponent are as fatal to his own speculative structures, if such he has wished to rear; he need not feel any sorrow in regard to this seeming misfortune, as he has now before him a fair prospect into the practical region, in which he may reasonably hope to find a more secure foundation for a rational system.

There is, accordingly, no proper polemic in the sphere of pure reason. Both parties beat the air and fight with their own shadows, as they pass beyond the limits of nature, and can find no tangible point of attack—no firm footing for their dogmatical conflict. Fight as vigorously as they may, the shadows which they hew down, immediately start up again, like the heroes in Walhalla, and renew the bloodless and unceasing contest.

But neither can we admit that there is any proper sceptical employment of pure reason, such as might be based upon the principle of *neutrality* in all speculative disputes. To excite reason against itself, to place weapons in the hands of the party on the one side as well as in those of the other, and to remain an undisturbed and sarcastic spectator of the fierce struggle that ensues, seems, from the dogmatical point of view, to be a part fitting only a malevolent disposition. But, when the sophist evidences an invincible obstinacy and blindness, and a pride which no criticism can moderate, there is no other practicable course than to oppose to this pride and obstinacy similar feelings and pretensions on the other side, equally well or ill founded, so that reason, staggered by the reflections thus forced upon it, finds it necessary to moderate its confidence in such pretensions, and to listen to the advices of criticism. But we cannot stop at these doubts, much less regard the conviction of our ignorance, not only as a cure for the conceit natural to dogmatism, but as the settlement of the disputes in which reason is involved with itself. On the contrary, scepticism is merely a means of awakening reason from its dogmatic dreams, and exciting it to a more careful investigation into its own powers and pretensions. But, as scepticism appears to be the shortest road to a permanent peace in the domain of philosophy, and as it is the track pursued by the many who aim at giving a philosophical colouring to their contemptuous dislike of all inquiries of this kind, I think it necessary to present to my readers this mode of thought in its true light.

### Scepticism not a Permanent State for Human Reason

The consciousness of ignorance—unless this ignorance is recognized to be absolutely necessary—ought, instead of forming the conclusion of my inquiries, to be the strongest motive to the pursuit of them. All ignorance is either ignorance of things, or of the limits of knowledge. If my ignorance is accidental and not necessary, it must incite me, in the first case, to a *dogmatical* inquiry regarding the objects of which I am ignorant; in the second, to a *critical* investigation into the bounds of all possible knowledge.

But that my ignorance is absolutely necessary and unavoidable, and that it consequently absolves from the duty of all further investigation, is a fact which cannot be made out upon empirical grounds—from *observation*, but upon critical grounds alone, that is, by a thorough-going *investigation* into the primary sources of cognition. It follows that the determination of the bounds of reason can be made only on *a priori* grounds; while the empirical limitation of reason, which is merely an indeterminate cognition of an ignorance that can never be completely removed, can take place only *a posteriori*. In other words, our empirical knowledge is limited by that which yet remains for us to know. The former cognition of our ignorance, which is possible only on a rational basis, is a *science*; the latter is merely a *perception*, and we cannot say how far the inferences drawn from it may extend. If I regard the earth, as it really appears to my senses, as a flat surface, I am ignorant how far this surface extends. But experience teaches me that, how far soever I go, I always see before me a space in which I can proceed farther; and thus I know the limits—merely visual—of my actual knowledge of the earth, although I am ignorant of the limits of the earth itself. But if I have got so far as to know that the earth is a sphere, and that its surface is spherical, I can cognize *a priori* and determine upon principles, from my knowledge of a small part of this surface—say to the extent of a degree —the diameter and circumference of the earth; and although I am ignorant of the objects which this surface contains, I have a perfect knowledge of its limits and extent.

The sum of all the possible objects of our cognition seems to us to be a level surface, with an apparent horizon—that which forms the limit of its extent, and which has been termed by us the idea of unconditioned totality. To reach this limit by empirical means is impossible, and all attempts to determine it *a priori* according to a principle, are alike in vain. But all the questions raised by pure reason relate to that which lies beyond this horizon, or, at least, in its boundary line.

The celebrated David Hume was one of those geographers of human reason who believe that they have given a sufficient answer to all such questions, by declaring them to lie beyond the horizon of our knowledge—a horizon which, however, Hume was unable to determine. His attention especially was directed to the principle of causality; and he remarked with perfect justice, that the truth of this principle, and even the objective validity of the conception of a cause, was not commonly based upon clear insight, that is, upon *a priori* cognition. Hence he concluded that this law does not derive its authority from its universality and necessity, but merely from its general applicability in the course of experience, and a kind of subjective necessity thence arising, which he termed *habit*. From the inability of reason to establish this principle as a necessary law for the acquisition of all experience, he inferred the nullity of all the attempts of reason to pass the region of the empirical.

This procedure, of subjecting the *facta* of reason to examination, and, if necessary, to disapproval, may be termed the *censura* of reason. This *censura* must inevitably lead us to *doubts* regarding *all* transcendent employment of principles. But this is only the second step in our inquiry. The first step in regard to the subjects of pure reason, and which marks the infancy of that faculty, is that of *dogmatism*. The second, which we have just mentioned, is that of *scepticism*, and it gives evidence that our judgment has been improved by experience. But a third step is necessary—indicative of the maturity and manhood of the judgment, which now lays a firm foundation upon universal and necessary principles. This is the period of *criticism*, in which we do not examine the *facta* of reason, but reason itself, in the whole extent of its powers, and in regard to its capability of *a priori* cognition; and thus we determine not merely the empirical and ever-shifting bounds of our knowledge, but its necessary and eternal limits. We demonstrate from indubitable principles, not merely our ignorance in respect to this or that subject, but in regard to all possible questions of a certain class. Thus scepticism is a resting-place for reason, in which it may reflect on its dogmatical wanderings, and gain some knowledge of the region in which it happens to be, that it may pursue its way with greater certainty; but it cannot be its permanent dwelling-place. It must take up its abode only in the region of complete certitude, whether this relates to the cognition of objects themselves, or to the limits which bound all our cognition.

Reason is not to be considered as an indefinitely extended plane, of the bounds of which we have only a general knowledge; it ought rather to be compared to a sphere, the radius of which may be found from the curvature of its surface—that is, the nature of *a priori* synthetical propositions—and, consequently, its circumference and extent. Beyond the sphere of experience there are no objects which it can cognize; nay, even questions regarding such supposititious objects relate only to the subjective principles of a complete determination of the relations which exist between the understanding-conceptions which lie within this sphere.

We are actually in possession of *a priori* synthetical cognitions, as is proved by the existence of the principles of the understanding, which anticipate experience. If any one cannot comprehend the possibility of these principles, he may have some reason to doubt whether they are really *a priori*; but he cannot on this account declare them to be impossible, and affirm the nullity of the steps which reason may have taken under their guidance. He can only say: If we perceived their origin and their authenticity, we should be able to determine the extent and limits of reason; but, till we can do this, all propositions regarding the latter are mere random assertions. In this view, the doubt respecting all dogmatical philosophy, which proceeds without the guidance of criticism, is well grounded; but we cannot therefore deny to reason the ability to construct a sound philosophy, when the way has been prepared by a thorough critical investigation. All the conceptions produced, and all the questions raised, by pure reason, do not lie in the sphere of experience, but in that of reason itself, and hence they must be solved, and shown to be either valid or inadmissible, by that faculty. We have no right to decline the solution of such problems, on the ground that the solution can be discovered only from the nature of things, and under pretence of the limitation of human faculties, for reason is the sole creator of all these ideas, and is therefore bound either to establish their validity or to expose their illusory nature.

The polemic of scepticism is properly directed against the dogmatist, who erects a system of philosophy without having examined the fundamental objective principles on which it is based, for the purpose of evidencing the futility of his designs, and thus bringing him to a knowledge of his own powers. But, in itself, scepticism does not give us any certain information in regard to the bounds of our knowledge. All unsuccessful dogmatical attempts of reason are *facta*, which it is always useful to submit to the censure of the sceptic. But this cannot help us to any decision regarding the expectations which reason cherishes of better success in future endeavours; the investigations of scepticism cannot, therefore, settle the dispute regarding the rights and powers of human reason.

Hume is perhaps the ablest and most ingenious of all sceptical philosophers, and his writings have, undoubtedly, exerted the most powerful influence in awakening reason to a thorough investigation into its own powers. It will, therefore, well repay our labours to consider for a little the course of reasoning which he followed, and the errors into which he strayed, although setting out on the path of truth and certitude.

Hume was probably aware, although he never clearly developed the notion, that we proceed in judgments of a certain class beyond our conception of the object. I have termed this kind of judgments synthetical. As regards the manner in which I pass beyond my conception by the aid of experience, no doubts can be entertained. Experience is itself a synthesis of perceptions; and it employs perceptions to increment the conception, which I obtain by means of another perception. But we feel persuaded that we are able to proceed beyond a conception, and to extend our cognition *a priori*. We attempt this in two ways—either, through the pure understanding, in relation to that which may become an *object of experience*, or, through pure reason, in relation to such properties of things, or of the existence of things, as can never be presented in any experience. This sceptical philosopher did not distinguish these two kinds of judgments, as he ought to have done, but regarded this augmentation of conceptions, and, if we may so express ourselves, the spontaneous generation of understanding and reason, independently of the impregnation of experience, as altogether impossible. The so-called *a priori* principles of these faculties he consequently held to be invalid and imaginary, and regarded them as nothing but subjective habits of thought originating in experience, and therefore purely empirical and contingent rules, to which we attribute a spurious necessity and universality. In support of this strange assertion, he referred us to the generally acknowledged principle of the relation between cause and effect. No faculty of the mind can conduct us from the conception of a thing to the existence of something else; and hence he believed he could infer that, without experience, we possess no source from which we can augment a conception, and no ground sufficient to justify us in framing a judgment that is to extend our cognition *a priori*. That the light of the sun, which shines upon a piece of wax, at the same time melts it, while it hardens clay, no power of the understanding could infer from the conceptions which we previously possessed of these substances; much less is there any *a priori* law that could conduct us to such a conclusion, which experience alone can certify. On the other hand, we have seen in our discussion of Transcendental Logic, that, although we can never proceed *immediately* beyond the content of the conception which is given us, we can always cognize completely *a priori*—in relation, however, to a third term, namely, *possible* experience—the law of its connection with other things. For example, if I observe that a piece of wax melts, I can cognize *a priori* that there must have been something (the sun's heat) preceding, which this effect follows according to a fixed law; although, without the aid of experience, I could not cognize *a priori* and in a *determinate* manner, either the cause from the effect, or the effect from the cause. Hume was therefore wrong in inferring, from the contingency of the determination *according to law*, the contingency of *the law* itself; and the passing beyond the conception of a thing to possible experience (which is an *a priori* proceeding, constituting the objective reality of the conception), he confounded with our synthesis of objects in actual experience, which is always, of course, empirical. Thus, too, he regarded the principle of affinity, which has its seat in the understanding and indicates a necessary connection, as a mere rule of association, lying in the imitative faculty of imagination, which can present only contingent, and not objective connections.

The sceptical errors of this remarkably acute thinker arose principally from a defect, which was common to him with the dogmatists, namely, that he had never made a systematic review of all the different kinds of *a priori* synthesis performed by the understanding. Had he done so, he would have found, to take one example among many, that the *principle of permanence* was of this character, and that it, as well as the principle of causality, anticipates experience. In this way he might have been able to describe the determinate limits of the *a priori* operations of understanding and reason. But he merely declared the understanding to be limited, instead of showing what its limits were; he created a general mistrust in the power of our faculties, without giving us any determinate knowledge of the bounds of our necessary and unavoidable ignorance; he examined and condemned some of the principles of the understanding, without investigating all its powers with the completeness necessary to criticism. He denies, with truth, certain powers to the understanding, but he goes further, and declares it to be utterly inadequate to the *a priori* extension of knowledge, although he has not fully examined all the powers which reside in the faculty; and thus the fate which always overtakes scepticism meets him too. That is to say, his own declarations are doubted, for his objections were based upon *facta*, which are contingent, and not upon principles, which can alone demonstrate the necessary invalidity of all dogmatical assertions.

As Hume makes no distinction between the well-grounded claims of the understanding and the dialectical pretensions of reason, against which, however, his attacks are mainly directed, reason does not feel itself shut out from all attempts at the extension of *a priori* cognition, and hence it refuses, in spite of a few checks in this or that quarter, to relinquish such efforts. For one naturally arms oneself to resist an attack, and becomes more obstinate in the resolve to establish the claims he has advanced. But a complete review of the powers of reason, and the conviction thence arising that we are in possession of a limited field of action, while we must admit the vanity of higher claims, puts an end to all doubt and dispute, and induces reason to rest satisfied with the undisturbed possession of its limited domain.

To the uncritical dogmatist, who has not surveyed the sphere of his understanding, nor determined, in accordance with principles, the limits of possible cognition, who, consequently, is ignorant of his own powers, and believes he will discover them by the attempts he makes in the field of cognition, these attacks of scepticism are not only dangerous, but destructive. For if there is one proposition in his chain of reasoning which he cannot prove, or the fallacy in which he cannot evolve in accordance with a principle, suspicion falls on all his statements, however plausible they may appear.

And thus scepticism, the bane of dogmatical philosophy, conducts us to a sound investigation into the understanding and the reason. When we are thus far advanced, we need fear no further attacks; for the limits of our domain are clearly marked out, and we can make no claims nor become involved in any disputes regarding the region that lies beyond these limits. Thus the sceptical procedure in philosophy does not present any *solution* of the problems of reason, but it forms an excellent *exercise* for its powers, awakening its circumspection, and indicating the means whereby it may most fully establish its claims to its legitimate possessions.

## SECTION III

### *The Discipline of Pure Reason in Hypothesis*

THIS critique of reason has now taught us that all its efforts to extend the bounds of knowledge, by means of pure speculation, are utterly fruitless. So much the wider field, it may appear, lies open to hypothesis; as, where we cannot know with certainty, we are at liberty to make guesses, and to form suppositions.

Imagination may be allowed, under the strict surveillance of reason, to invent suppositions; but, these must be based on something that is perfectly certain—and that is the *possibility* of the object. If we are well assured upon this point, it is allowable to have recourse to supposition in regard to the reality of the object; but this supposition must, unless it is utterly groundless, be connected, as its ground of explanation, with that which is really given and absolutely certain. Such a supposition is termed a *hypothesis*.

It is beyond our power to form the least conception *a priori* of the possibility of dynamical connection in phenomena; and the category of the pure understanding will not enable us to excogitate any such connection, but merely helps us to understand it, when we meet with it in experience. For this reason we cannot, in accordance with the categories, imagine or invent any object or any property of an object not given, or that may not be given in experience, and employ it in a hypothesis; otherwise, we should be basing our chain of reasoning upon mere chimerical fancies, and not upon conceptions of things. Thus, we have no right to assume the existence of new powers, not existing in nature—for example, an understanding with a non-sensuous intuition, a force of attraction without contact, or some new kind of substances occupying space, and yet without the property of impenetrability; and, consequently, we cannot assume that there is any other kind of community among substances than that observable in experience, any kind of presence than that in space, or any kind of duration than that in time. In one word, the conditions of possible experience are for reason the only conditions of the possibility of things; reason cannot venture to form, independently of these conditions, any conceptions of things, because such conceptions, although not self-contradictory, are without object and without application.

The conceptions of reason are, as we have already shown, mere ideas, and do not relate to any object in any kind of experience. At the same time, they do not indicate imaginary or possible objects. They are purely problematical in their nature, and, as aids to the heuristic exercise of the faculties, form the basis of the regulative principles for the systematic employment of the understanding in the field of experience. If we leave this ground of experience, they become mere fictions of thought, the possibility of which is quite indemonstrable; and they cannot consequently be employed, as hypotheses, in the explanation of real phenomena. It is quite admissible to *cogitate* the soul as simple, for the purpose of enabling ourselves to employ the idea of a perfect and necessary unity of all the faculties of the mind as the principle of all our inquiries into its internal phenomena, although we cannot cognize this unity *in concreto*. But to *assume* that the soul is a simple substance (a transcendental conception) would be enouncing a proposition which is not only indemonstrable—as many physical hypotheses are, but a proposition which is purely arbitrary, and in the highest degree rash. The simple is never presented in experience; and, if by substance is here meant the permanent object of sensuous intuition, the possibility of a *simple phenomenon* is perfectly inconceivable. Reason affords no good grounds for admitting the existence of intelligible beings, or of intelligible properties of sensuous things, although—as we have no conception either of their possibility or of their impossibility—it will always be out of our power to affirm dogmatically that they do not exist. In the explanation of given phenomena, no other things and no other grounds of explanation can be employed, than those which stand in connection with the given phenomena according to the known laws of experience. A *transcendental hypothesis*, in which a mere idea of reason is employed to explain the phenomena of nature, would not give us any better insight into a phenomenon, as we should be trying to explain what we do not sufficiently understand from known empirical principles, by what we do not understand at all. The principles of such a hypothesis might conduce to the satisfaction of reason, but it would not assist the understanding in its application to objects. Order and conformity to aims in the sphere of nature must be themselves explained upon natural grounds and according to natural laws; and the wildest hypotheses, if they are only physical, are here more admissible than a hyperphysical hypothesis, such as that of a divine author. For such a hypothesis would introduce the principle of *ignava ratio*, which requires us to give up the search for causes that might be discovered in the course of experience, and to rest satisfied with a mere idea. As regards the absolute totality of the grounds of explanation in the series of these causes, this can be no hindrance to the understanding in the case of phenomena; because, as they are to us nothing more than phenomena, we have no right to look for anything like completeness in the synthesis of the series of their conditions.

Transcendental hypotheses are therefore inadmissible; and we cannot use the liberty of employing, in the absence of physical, hyperphysical grounds of explanation. And this for two reasons; first, because such hypotheses do not advance reason, but rather stop it in its progress; second, because this licence would render fruitless all its exertions in its own proper sphere, which is that of experience. For, when the explanation of natural phenomena happens to be difficult, we have constantly at hand a transcendental ground of explanation, which lifts us above the necessity of investigating nature; and our inquiries are brought to a close, not because we have obtained all the requisite knowledge, but because we abut upon a principle, which is incomprehensible, and which, indeed, is so far back in the track of thought, as to contain the conception of the absolutely primal being.

The next requisite for the admissibility of a hypothesis is its sufficiency. That is, it must determine *a priori* the consequences which are given in experience, and which are supposed to follow from the hypothesis itself. If we require to employ auxiliary hypotheses, the suspicion naturally arises that they are mere fictions; because the necessity for each of them requires the same justification as in the case of the original hypothesis, and thus their testimony is invalid. If we suppose the existence of an infinitely perfect cause, we possess sufficient grounds for the explanation of the conformity to aims, the order and the greatness which we observe in the universe; but we find ourselves obliged, when we observe the evil in the world and the exceptions to these laws, to employ new hypotheses in support of the original one. We employ the idea of the simple nature of the human soul as the foundation of all the theories we may form of its phenomena; but when we meet with difficulties in our way, when we observe in the soul phenomena similar to the changes which take place in matter, we require to call in new auxiliary hypotheses. These may, indeed, not be false, but we do not know them to be true, because the only witness to their certitude is the hypothesis which they themselves have been called in to explain.

We are not discussing the above-mentioned assertions regarding the immaterial unity of the soul and the existence of a Supreme Being, as dogmata, which certain philosophers profess to demonstrate *a priori*, but purely as hypotheses. In the former case, the dogmatist must take care that his arguments possess the apodeictic certainty of a demonstration. For the assertion that the reality of such ideas is *probable*, is as absurd as a proof of the probability of a proposition in geometry. Pure abstract reason, apart from all experience, can either cognize a proposition entirely *a priori*, and as necessary, or it can cognize nothing at all; and hence the judgments it enounces are never mere opinions, they are either apodeictic certainties, or declarations that nothing can be known on the subject. Opinions and probable judgments on the nature of things can only be employed to explain given phenomena, or they may relate to the effect, in accordance with empirical laws, of an actually existing cause. In other words, we must restrict the sphere of opinion to the world of experience and nature. Beyond this region *opinion* is mere invention; unless we are groping about for the truth on a path not yet fully known, and have some hopes of stumbling upon it by chance.

But, although hypotheses are inadmissible in answers to the questions of pure speculative reason, they may be employed in the defence of these answers. That is to say, hypotheses are admissible in polemic, but not in the sphere of dogmatism. By the defence of statements of this character, I do not mean an attempt at discovering new grounds for their support, but merely the refutation of the arguments of opponents. All *a priori* synthetical propositions possess the peculiarity, that, although the philosopher who maintains the reality of the ideas contained in the proposition, is not in possession of sufficient knowledge to establish the certainty of his statements, his opponent is as little able to prove the truth of the opposite. This equality of fortune does not allow the one party to be superior to the other in the sphere of speculative cognition; and it is this sphere accordingly that is the proper arena of these endless speculative conflicts. But we shall afterwards show that, in relation to its *practical exercise*, Reason has the right of admitting what, in the field of pure speculation, she would not be justified in supposing, except upon perfectly sufficient grounds; because all such suppositions destroy the necessary completeness of speculation—a condition which the practical reason, however, does not consider to be requisite. In this sphere, therefore, Reason is mistress of a possession, her title to which she does not require to prove—which, in fact, she could not do. The burden of proof accordingly rests upon the opponent. But as he has just as little knowledge regarding the subject discussed, and is as little able to prove the non-existence of the object of an idea, as the philosopher on the other side is to demonstrate its reality, it is evident that there is an advantage on the side of the philosopher who maintains his proposition as a practically necessary supposition (*melior est conditio possidentis*). For he is at liberty to employ, in self-defence, the same weapons as his opponent makes use of in attacking him; that is, he has a right to use hypotheses not for the purpose of supporting the arguments in favour of his own propositions, but to show that his opponent knows no more than himself regarding the subject under discussion, and cannot boast of any speculative advantage.

Hypotheses are, therefore, admissible in the sphere of pure reason, only as weapons for self-defence, and not as supports to dogmatical assertions. But the opposing party we must always seek for in ourselves. For speculative reason is, in the sphere of transcendentalism, dialectical *in its own nature*. The difficulties and objections we have to fear lie in ourselves. They are like old but never superannuated claims; and we must seek them out, and settle them once and for ever, if we are to expect a permanent peace. External tranquillity is hollow and unreal. The root of these contradictions, which lies in the nature of human reason, must be destroyed; and this can only be done by giving it, in the first instance, freedom to grow, nay, by nourishing it, that it may send out shoots, and thus betray its own existence. It is our duty, therefore, to try to discover new objections, to put weapons in the hands of our opponent, and to grant him the most favourable position in the arena that he can wish. We have nothing to fear from these concessions; on the contrary, we may rather hope that we shall thus make ourselves master of a possession which no one will ever venture to dispute.

The thinker requires, to be fully equipped, the hypotheses of pure reason, which, although but leaden weapons (for they have not been steeled in the armoury of experience), are as useful as any that can be employed by his opponents. If, accordingly, we have assumed, from a non-speculative point of view, the immaterial nature of the soul, and are met by the objection that experience seems to prove that the growth and decay of our mental faculties are mere modifications of the sensuous organism—we can weaken the force of this objection, by the assumption that the body is nothing but the fundamental phenomenon, to which, as a necessary condition, all sensibility, and consequently all thought, relates in the present state of our existence; and that the separation of soul and body forms the conclusion of the sensuous exercise of our power of cognition, and the beginning of the intellectual. The body would, in this view of the question, be regarded, not as the cause of thought, but merely as its restrictive condition, as promotive of the sensuous and animal, but as a hindrance to the pure and spiritual life; and the dependence of the animal life on the constitution of the body, would not prove that the *whole* life of man was also dependent on the state of the organism. We might go still farther, and discover new objections, or carry out to their extreme consequences those which have already been adduced.

Generation, in the human race as well as among the irrational animals, depends on so many accidents—of occasion, of proper sustenance, of the laws enacted by the government of a country of vice even, that it is difficult to believe in the eternal existence of a being, whose life has begun under circumstances so mean and trivial, and so entirely dependent upon our own control. As regards the continuance of the existence of the whole race, we need have no difficulties, for accident in single cases is subject to general laws; but, in the case of each individual, it would seem as if we could hardly expect so wonderful an effect from causes so insignificant. But, in answer to these objections, we may adduce the transcendental hypothesis, that all life is properly intelligible, and not subject to changes of time, and that it neither began in birth, nor will end in death. We may assume that this life is nothing more than a sensuous representation of pure spiritual life; that the whole world of sense is but an image, hovering before the faculty of cognition which we exercise in this sphere, and with no more objective reality than a dream; and that if we could intuite ourselves and other things as they really are, we should see ourselves in a world of spiritual natures, our connection with which did not begin at our birth, and will not cease with the destruction of the body. And so on.

We cannot be said to know what has been above asserted, nor do we seriously maintain the truth of these assertions; and the notions therein indicated are not even ideas of reason, they are purely *fictitious* conceptions. But this hypothetical procedure is in perfect conformity with the laws of reason. Our opponent mistakes the absence of empirical conditions for a proof of the complete impossibility of all that we have asserted; and we have to show him that he has not exhausted the whole sphere of possibility, and that he can as little compass that sphere by the laws of experience and nature, as we can lay a secure foundation for the operations of reason beyond the region of experience. Such hypothetical defences against the pretensions of an opponent must not be regarded as declarations of opinion. The philosopher abandons them, so soon as the opposite party renounces its dogmatical conceit. To maintain a simply negative position in relation to propositions which rest on an insecure foundation, well befits the moderation of a true philosopher; but to uphold the objections urged against an opponent as proofs of the opposite statement, is a proceeding just as unwarrantable and arrogant as it is to attack the position of a philosopher who advances affirmative propositions regarding such a subject.

It is evident, therefore, that hypotheses, in the speculative sphere, are valid, not as independent propositions, but only relatively to opposite transcendent assumptions. For, to make the principles of possible experience conditions of the possibility of things in general is just as transcendent a procedure as to maintain the objective reality of ideas which can be applied to no objects except such as lie without the limits of possible experience. The judgments enounced by pure reason must be necessary, or they must not be enounced at all. Reason cannot trouble herself with opinions. But the hypotheses we have been discussing are merely problematical judgments, which can neither be confuted nor proved; while, therefore, they are not personal opinions, they are indispensable as answers to objections which are liable to be raised. But we must take care to confine them to this function, and guard against any assumption on their part of absolute validity, a proceeding which would involve reason in inextricable difficulties and contradictions.

## Section IV

### The Discipline of Pure Reason in Relation to Proofs

It is a peculiarity which distinguishes the proofs of transcendental synthetical propositions from those of all other *a priori* synthetical cognitions, that reason, in the case of the former, does not apply its conceptions directly to an object, but is first obliged to prove, *a priori*, the objective validity of these conceptions and the possibility of their syntheses. This is not merely a prudential rule, it is essential to the very possibility of the proof of a transcendental proposition. If I am required to pass, *a priori*, beyond the conception of an object, I find that it is utterly impossible without the guidance of something which is not contained in the conception. In mathematics, it is *a priori* intuition that guides my synthesis; and, in this case, all our conclusions may be drawn immediately from pure intuition. In transcendental cognition, so long as we are dealing only with conceptions of the understanding, we are guided by possible experience. That is to say, a proof in the sphere of transcendental cognition does not show that the given conception (that of an event, for example) leads directly to another conception (that of a cause)—for this would be a *saltus* which nothing can justify; but it shows that experience itself, and consequently the object of experience, is impossible without the connection indicated by these conceptions. It follows that such a proof must demonstrate the possibility of arriving, synthetically and *a priori*, at a certain knowledge of things, which was not contained in our conceptions of these things. Unless we pay particular attention to this requirement, our proofs, instead of pursuing the straight path indicated by reason, follow the tortuous road of mere subjective association. The illusory conviction, which rests upon subjective causes of association, and which is considered as resulting from the perception of a real and objective natural affinity, is always open to doubt and suspicion. For this reason, all the attempts which have been made to prove the principle of sufficient reason, have, according to the universal admission of philosophers, been quite unsuccessful; and, before the appearance of transcendental criticism, it was considered better, as this principle could not be abandoned, to appeal boldly to the common sense of mankind (a proceeding which always proves that the problem, which reason ought to solve, is one in which philosophers find great difficulties), rather than attempt to discover new dogmatical proofs.

But, if the proposition to be proved is a proposition of pure reason, and if I aim at passing beyond my empirical conceptions by the aid of mere ideas, it is necessary that the proof should first show that such a step in synthesis is possible (which it is not), before it proceeds to prove the truth of the proposition itself. The so-called proof of the simple nature of the soul from the unity of apperception, is a very plausible one. But it contains no answer to the objection, that, as the notion of absolute simplicity is not a conception which is directly applicable to a perception, but is an idea which must be inferred—if at all—from observation, it is by no means evident, how the mere fact of consciousness, which is contained *in all thought*, although in so far a simple representation, can conduct me to the consciousness and cognition of a thing which is purely a thinking substance. When I represent to my mind the power of my body as in motion, my body in this thought is so far absolute unity, and my representation of it is a simple one; and hence I can indicate this representation by the motion of a point, because I have made abstraction of the size or volume of the body. But I cannot hence infer that, given merely the moving power of a body, the body may be cogitated as simple substance, merely because the representation in my mind takes no account of its content in space, and is consequently simple. The simple, in abstraction, is very different from the objectively simple; and hence the Ego, which is simple in the first sense, may, in the second sense, as indicating the soul itself, be a very complex conception, with a very various content. Thus it is evident, that in all such arguments there lurks a paralogism. We guess (for without some such surmise our suspicion would not be excited in reference to a proof of this character) at the presence of the paralogism, by keeping ever before us a criterion of the possibility of those synthetical propositions which aim at proving more than experience can teach us. This criterion is obtained from the observation that such proofs do not lead us directly from the subject of the proposition to be proved to the required predicate, but find it necessary to presuppose the possibility of extending our cognition *a priori* by means of ideas. We must, accordingly, always use the greatest caution; we require, before attempting any proof, to consider how it is possible to extend the sphere of cognition by the operations of pure reason, and from what source we are to derive knowledge, which is not obtained from the analysis of conceptions, nor relates, by anticipation, to possible experience. We shall thus spare ourselves much severe and fruitless labour, by not expecting from reason what is beyond its power, or rather by subjecting it to discipline, and teaching it to moderate its vehement desires for the extension of the sphere of cognition.

The first rule for our guidance is, therefore, not to attempt a transcendental proof, before we have considered from what source we are to derive the principles upon which the proof is to be based, and what right we have to expect that our conclusions from these principles will be veracious. If they are principles of the understanding, it is vain to expect that we should attain by their means to ideas of pure reason; for these principles are valid only in regard to objects of possible experience. If they are principles of pure reason, our labour is alike in vain. For the principles of reason, if employed as objective, are without exception dialectical, and possess no validity or truth, except as regulative principles of the systematic employment of reason in experience. But when such delusive proofs are presented to us, it is our duty to meet them with the *non liquet* of a matured judgment; and, although we are unable to expose the particular sophism upon which the proof is based, we have a right to demand a deduction of the principles employed in it; and, if these principles have their origin in pure reason alone, such a deduction is absolutely impossible. And thus it is unnecessary that we should trouble ourselves with the exposure and confutation of every sophistical illusion; we may, at once, bring all dialectic, which is inexhaustible in the production of fallacies, before the bar of critical reason, which tests the principles upon which all dialectical procedure is based. The second peculiarity of transcendental proof is, that a transcendental proposition cannot rest upon more than *a single* proof.

If I am drawing conclusions, not from conceptions, but from intuition corresponding to a conception, be it pure intuition, as in mathematics, or empirical, as in natural science, the intuition which forms the basis of my inferences, presents me with materials for many synthetical propositions, which I can connect in various modes, while, as it is allowable to proceed from different points in the intention, I can arrive by different paths at the same proposition.

But every transcendental proposition sets out from a conception, and posits the synthetical condition of the possibility of an object according to this conception. There must, therefore, be but one ground of proof, because it is the conception alone which determines the object; and thus the proof cannot contain anything more than the determination of the object according to the conception. In our Transcendental Analytic, for example, we inferred the principle: Every event has a cause, from the only condition of the objective possibility of our conception of an event. This is, that an event cannot be determined in time, and consequently cannot form a part of experience, unless it stands under this dynamical law. This is the only possible ground of proof; for our conception of an event possesses objective validity, that is, is a true conception, only because the law of causality determines an object to which it can refer. Other arguments in support of this principle have been attempted—such as that from the contingent nature of a phenomenon; but when this argument is considered, we can discover no criterion of contingency, except the fact of an event—of something *happening*, that is to say, the existence which is preceded by the non-existence of an object, and thus we fall back on the very thing to be proved. If the proposition: Every thinking being is simple, is to be proved, we keep to the conception of the Ego, which is simple, and to which all thought has a relation. The same is the case with the transcendental proof of the existence of a Deity, which is based solely upon the harmony and reciprocal fitness of the conceptions of an *ens realissimum* and a necessary being, and cannot be attempted in any other manner.

This caution serves to simplify very much the criticism of all propositions of reason. When reason employs conceptions alone, only one proof of its thesis is possible, if any. When, therefore, the dogmatist advances with ten arguments in favour of a proposition, we may be sure that not one of them is conclusive. For if he possessed one which proved the proposition he brings forward to demonstration—as must always be the case with the propositions of pure reason—what need is there for any more? His intention can only be similar to that of the advocate, who had different arguments for different judges; thus availing himself of the weakness of those who examine his arguments, who, without going into any profound investigation, adopt the view of the case which seems most probable at first sight, and decide according to it.

The third rule for the guidance of pure reason in the conduct of a proof is, that all transcendental proofs must never be *apagogic* or indirect, but always ostensive or direct. The direct or ostensive proof not only establishes the truth of the proposition to be proved, but exposes the grounds of its truth; the apagogic, on the other hand, may assure us of the truth of the proposition, but it cannot enable us to comprehend the grounds of its possibility. The latter is, accordingly, rather an auxiliary to an argument, than a strictly philosophical and rational mode of procedure. In one respect, however, they have an advantage over direct proofs, from the fact that the mode of arguing by contradiction, which they employ, renders our understanding of the question more clear, and approximates the proof to the certainty of an intuitional demonstration.

The true reason why indirect proofs are employed in different sciences is this. When the grounds upon which we seek to base a cognition are too various or too profound, we try whether or not we may not discover the truth of our cognition from its consequences. The *modus ponens* of reasoning from the truth of its inferences to the truth of a proposition, would be admissible if all the inferences that can be drawn from it are known to be true; for in this case there can be only one possible ground for these inferences, and that is the true one. But this is a quite impracticable procedure, as it surpasses all our powers to discover all the possible inferences that can be drawn from a proposition. But this mode of reasoning is employed, under favour, when we wish to prove the truth of an hypothesis; in which case we admit the truth of the conclusion—which is supported by analogy—that, if all the inferences we have drawn and examined agree with the proposition assumed, all other possible inferences will also agree with it. But, in this way, an hypothesis can never be established as a demonstrated truth. The *modus tollens* of reasoning from known inferences to the unknown proposition, is not only a rigorous, but a very easy mode of proof. For, if it can be shown that but one inference from a proposition is false, then the proposition must itself be false. Instead, then, of examining, in an ostensive argument, the whole series of the grounds on which the truth of a proposition rests, we need only take the opposite of this proposition, and if one inference from it be false, then must the opposite be itself false; and, consequently, the proposition which we wished to prove, must be true

The apagogic method of proof is admissible only in those sciences where it is impossible to mistake a subjective representation for an objective cognition. Where this is possible, it is plain that the opposite of a given proposition may contradict merely the subjective conditions of thought, and not the objective cognition; or it may happen that both propositions contradict each other only under a subjective condition, which is incorrectly considered to be objective, and, as the condition is itself false, both propositions may be false, and it will, consequently, be impossible to conclude the truth of the one from the falseness of the other.

In mathematics such subreptions are impossible; and it is in this science, accordingly, that the indirect mode of proof has its true place. In the science of nature, where all assertion is based upon empirical intuition, such subreptions may be guarded against by the repeated comparison of observations; but this mode of proof is of little value in this sphere of knowledge. But the transcendental efforts of pure reason are all made in the sphere of the subjective, which is the real medium of all dialectical illusion; and thus reason endeavours, in its premisses, to impose upon us subjective representations for objective cognitions. In the transcendental sphere of pure reason, then, and in the case of synthetical propositions, it is inadmissible to support a statement by disproving the counter-statement. For only two cases are possible; either, the counter-statement is nothing but the enouncement of the inconsistency of the opposite opinion with the subjective conditions of reason, which does not affect the real case (for example, we cannot comprehend the unconditioned necessity of the existence of a being, and hence every speculative proof of the existence of such a being must be opposed on *subjective* grounds, while the possibility of this being *in itself* cannot with justice be denied); or, both propositions, being dialectical in their nature, are based upon an impossible conception. In this latter case the rule applies—*non entis nulla sunt predicata*; that is to say, what we affirm and what we deny, respecting such an object, are equally untrue, and the apagogic mode of arriving at the truth is in this case impossible. If, for example, we presuppose that the world of sense is given *in itself* in its totality, it is false, *either* that it is infinite, *or* that it is finite and limited in space. Both are false, because the hypothesis is false. For the notion of phenomena (as mere representations) which are given *in themselves* (as objects) is self-contradictory; and the infinitude of this imaginary whole would, indeed, be unconditioned, but would be inconsistent (as everything in the phenomenal world is conditioned) with the unconditioned determination and finitude of quantities which is presupposed in our conception.

The apagogic mode of proof is the true source of those illusions which have always had so strong an attraction for the admirers of dogmatical philosophy. It may be compared to a champion, who maintains the honour and claims of the party he has adopted, by offering battle to all who doubt the validity of these claims and the purity of that honour; while nothing can be proved in this way, except the respective strength of the combatants, and the advantage, in this respect, is always on the side of the attacking party. Spectators, observing that each party is alternately conqueror and conquered, are led to regard the subject of dispute as beyond the power of man to decide upon. But such an opinion cannot be justified; and it is sufficient to apply to these reasoners the remark:

Non defensoribus istis
Tempus eget.

Each must try to establish his assertions by a transcendental deduction of the grounds of proof employed in his argument, and thus enable us to see in what way the claims of reason may be supported. If an opponent bases his assertions upon subjective grounds, he may be refuted with ease; not, however to the advantage of the dogmatist, who likewise depends upon subjective sources of cognition, and is in like manner driven into a corner by his opponent. But, if parties employ the direct method of procedure, they will soon discover the difficulty, nay, the impossibility of proving their assertions, and will be forced to appeal to prescription and precedence; or they will, by the help of criticism, discover with ease the dogmatical illusions by which they had been mocked, and compel reason to renounce its exaggerated pretensions to speculative insight, and to confine itself within the limits of its proper sphere—that of practical principles.

## CHAPTER II

### THE CANON OF PURE REASON

It is a humiliating consideration for human reason, that it is incompetent to discover truth by means of pure speculation, but, on the contrary, stands in need of discipline to check its deviations from the straight path, and to expose the illusions which it originates. But, on the other hand, this consideration ought to elevate and to give it confidence, for this discipline is exercised by itself alone, and it is subject to the censure of no other power. The bounds, moreover, which it is forced to set to its speculative exercise, form likewise a check upon the fallacious pretensions of opponents; and thus what remains of its possessions, after these exaggerated claims have been disallowed, is secure from attack or usurpation. The greatest, and perhaps the only, use of all philosophy of pure reason is, accordingly, of a purely negative character. It is not an organon for the extension, but a discipline for the determination of the limits of its exercise; and without laying claim to the discovery of new truth, it has the modest merit of guarding against error.

At the same time, there must be some source of positive cognitions which belong to the domain of pure reason, and which become the causes of error, only from our mistaking their true character, while they form the goal towards which reason continually strives. How else can we account for the inextinguishable desire in the human mind to find a firm footing in some region beyond the limits of the world of experience? It hopes to attain to the possession of a knowledge in which it has the deepest interest. It enters upon the path of pure speculation; but in vain. We have some reason, however, to expect that, in the only other way that lies open to it—the path of *practical* reason—it may meet with better success.

I understand by a canon a list of the *a priori* principles of the proper employment of certain faculties of cognition. Thus general logic, in its analytical department, is a formal canon for the faculties of understanding and reason. In the same way, Transcendental Analytic was seen to be a canon of the pure *understanding*; for it alone is competent to enounce true *a priori* synthetical cognitions. But, when no proper employment of a faculty of cognition is possible, no canon can exist. But the synthetical cognition of pure speculative *reason* is, as has been shown, completely impossible. There cannot, therefore, exist any canon for the speculative exercise of this faculty—for its speculative exercise is entirely dialectical; and consequently, transcendental logic, in this respect, is merely a discipline, and not a canon. If, then, there is any proper mode of employing the faculty of pure reason—in which case there must be a canon for this faculty—this canon will relate, not to the speculative, but to the *practical use of reason*. This canon we now proceed to investigate.

## Section I

### Of the Ultimate End of the Pure Use of Reason

There exists in the faculty of reason a natural desire to venture beyond the field of experience, to attempt to reach the utmost bounds of all cognition by the help of ideas alone, and not to rest satisfied, until it has fulfilled its course and raised the sum of its cognitions into a self-subsistent systematic whole. Is the motive for this endeavour to be found in its speculative, or in its practical interests alone?

Setting aside, at present, the results of the labours of pure reason in its speculative exercise, I shall merely inquire regarding the problems, the solution of which forms its ultimate aim—whether reached or not, and in relation to which all other aims are but partial and intermediate. These highest aims must, from the nature of reason, possess complete unity; otherwise the highest interest of humanity could not be successfully promoted.

The transcendental speculation of reason relates to three things: the freedom of the will, the immortality of the soul, and the existence of God. The speculative interest which reason has in those questions is very small; and, for its sake alone, we should not undertake the labour of transcendental investigation—a labour full of toil and ceaseless struggle. We should be loth to undertake this labour, because the discoveries we might make would not be of the smallest use in the sphere of concrete or physical investigation. We may find out that the will is free, but this knowledge only relates to the intelligible cause of our volition. As regards the phenomena or expressions of this will, that is, our actions, we are bound, in obedience to an inviolable maxim, without which reason cannot be employed in the sphere of experience, to explain these in the same way as we explain all the other phenomena of nature, that is to say, according to its unchangeable laws. We may have discovered the spirituality and immortality of the soul, but we cannot employ this knowledge to explain the phenomena of this life, nor the peculiar nature of the future, because our conception of an incorporeal nature is purely negative and does not add anything to our knowledge, and the only inferences to be drawn from it are purely fictitious. If, again, we prove the existence of a supreme intelligence, we should be able from it to make the conformity to aims existing in the arrangement of the world comprehensible; but we should not be justified in deducing from it any particular arrangement or disposition, or, inferring any, where it is not perceived. For it is a necessary rule of the speculative use of reason, that we must not overlook natural causes, or refuse to listen to the teaching of experience, for the sake of deducing what we know and perceive from something that transcends all our knowledge. In one word, these three propositions are, for the speculative reason, always transcendent, and cannot be employed as immanent principles in relation to the objects of experience; they are, consequently, of no use to us in this sphere, being but the valueless results of the severe but unprofitable efforts of reason.

If, then, the actual *cognition* of these three cardinal propositions is perfectly useless, while Reason uses her utmost endeavours to induce us to admit them, it is plain that their real value and importance relate to our *practical*, and not to our speculative interest.

I term all that is possible through free will, practical. But if the conditions of the exercise of free volition are empirical, reason can have only a regulative, and not a constitutive, influence upon it, and is serviceable merely for the introduction of unity into its empirical laws. In the moral philosophy of prudence, for example, the sole business of reason is to bring about a union of all the ends, which are aimed at by our inclinations, into one ultimate end— that of *happiness*, and to show the agreement which should exist among the means of attaining that end. In this sphere, accordingly, reason cannot present to us any other than *pragmatical* laws of free action, for our guidance towards the aims set up by the senses, and is incompetent to give us laws which are pure and determined completely *a priori*. On the other hand, pure practical laws, the ends of which have been given by reason entirely *a priori*, and which are not empirically conditioned, but are, on the contrary, absolutely imperative in their nature, would be products of pure reason. Such are the *moral* laws; and these alone belong to the sphere of the practical exercise of reason, and admit of a canon.

All the powers of reason, in the sphere of what may be termed pure philosophy, are, in fact, directed to the three above-mentioned problems alone. These again have a still higher end—the answer to the question, *what we ought to do,* if the will is free, if there is a God, and a future world. Now, as this problem relates to our conduct, in reference to the highest aim of humanity, it is evident that the ultimate intention of nature, in the constitution of our reason, has been directed to the *moral* alone.

We must take care, however, in turning our attention to an object which is foreign [1] to the sphere of transcendental philosophy, not to injure the unity of our system by digressions, nor, on the other hand, to fail in clearness, by saying too little on the new subject of discussion. I hope to avoid both extremes, by keeping as close as possible to the transcendental, and excluding all psychological, that is, empirical elements.

I have to remark, in the first place, that at present I treat of the conception of freedom in the practical sense only, and set aside the corresponding transcendental conception, which cannot be employed as a ground of explanation in the phenomenal world, but is itself a problem for pure reason. A will is purely *animal* (*arbitrium brutum*) when it is determined by sensuous impulses or instincts only, that is, when it is determined in a *pathological* manner. A will, which can be determined independently of sensuous impulses, consequently by motives presented by reason alone, is called a *free will* (*arbitrium liberum*); and everything which is connected with this free will, either as principle or consequence, is termed *practical.* The existence of practical freedom can be proved from experience alone. For the human will is not determined by that alone which immediately affects the senses; on the contrary, we have the power, by calling up the notion of what is useful or hurtful in a more distant relation, of overcoming the immediate impressions on our sensuous faculty of desire. But these considerations of what is desirable in relation to our whole state, that is, is in the end good and useful, are based entirely

---

[1] All practical conceptions relate to objects of pleasure and pain, and consequently—in an indirect manner, at least—to objects of feeling. But as feeling is not a faculty of representation, but lies out of the sphere of our powers of cognition, the elements of our judgments, in so far as they relate to pleasure or pain, that is, the elements of our practical judgments, do not belong to transcendental philosophy, which has to do with pure *a priori* cognitions alone.

upon reason. This faculty, accordingly, enounces laws, which are imperative or objective *laws of freedom*, and which tell us what *ought to take place*, thus distinguishing themselves from the *laws of nature*, which relate to that which *does take place*. The laws of freedom or of free will are hence termed practical laws.

Whether reason is not itself, in the actual delivery of these laws, determined in its turn by other influences, and whether the action which, in relation to sensuous impulses, we call free, may not, in relation to higher and more remote operative causes, really form a part of *nature*—these are questions which do not here concern us. They are purely speculative questions; and all we have to do, in the practical sphere, is to inquire into the *rule* of conduct which reason has to present. Experience demonstrates to us the existence of practical freedom as one of the causes which exist in nature, that is, it shows the causal power of reason in the determination of the will. The idea of transcendental freedom, on the contrary, requires that reason—in relation to its causal power of commencing a series of phenomena—should be independent of all sensuous determining causes; and thus it seems to be in opposition to the law of nature and to all possible experience. It therefore remains a problem for the human mind. But this problem does not concern reason in its practical use; and we have, therefore, in a canon of pure reason, to do with only two questions, which relate to the practical interest of pure reason— Is there a God? and, Is there a future life? The question of transcendental freedom is purely speculative, and we may therefore set it entirely aside when we come to treat of practical reason. Besides, we have already fully discussed this subject in the antinomy of pure reason.

## Section II

### Of the Ideal of the Summum Bonum as a Determining Ground of the Ultimate End of Pure Reason

REASON conducted us, in its speculative use, through the field of experience, and, as it can never find complete satisfaction in that sphere, from thence to speculative ideas—which, however, in the end brought us back again to experience, and thus fulfilled the purpose of reason, in a manner which, though useful, was not at all in accordance with our expectations. It now remains for us to consider whether pure reason can be employed in a practical sphere, and whether it will here conduct us to those ideas which attain the highest ends of pure reason, as we have just stated them. We shall thus ascertain whether, from the point of view of its practical interest, reason may not be able to supply us with that which, on the speculative side, it wholly denies us.

The whole interest of reason, speculative as well as practical, is centred in the three following questions:

> 1. WHAT CAN I KNOW?
> 2. WHAT OUGHT I TO DO?
> 3. WHAT MAY I HOPE?

The first question is purely speculative. We have, as I flatter myself, exhausted all the replies of which it is susceptible, and have at last found the reply with which reason must content itself, and with which it ought to be content, so long as it pays no regard to the practical. But from the two great ends to the attainment of which all these efforts of pure reason were in fact directed, we remain just as far removed as if we had consulted our ease, and declined the task at the outset. So far, then, as *knowledge* is concerned, thus much, at least, is established, that, in regard to those two problems, it lies beyond our reach.

The second question is purely practical. As such it may indeed fall within the province of pure reason, but still it is not transcendental, but moral, and consequently cannot in itself form the subject of our criticism.

The third question: If I act as I ought to do, what may I then hope?—is at once practical and theoretical. The practical forms a clue to the answer of the theoretical, and—in its highest form—speculative question. For all *hoping* has happiness for its object, and stands in precisely the same relation to the practical and the law of morality, as *knowing* to the theoretical cognition of things and the law of nature. The former arrives finally at the conclusion that *something is* (which determines the ultimate end), because *something ought to take place*; the latter, that *something is* (which operates as the highest cause), because *something does take place*.

Happiness is the satisfaction of all our desires; *extensive*, in regard to their multiplicity; *intensive*, in regard to their degree; and *protensive*, in regard to their duration. The practical law based on the motive of *happiness*, I term a pragmatical law (or prudential rule); but that law, assuming such to exist, which has no other motive than the *worthiness of being happy*, I term a moral or ethical law. The first tells us what we have to do, if we wish to become possessed of happiness; the second dictates how we ought to act, in order to deserve happiness. The first is based upon empirical principles; for it is only by experience that I can learn either what inclinations exist which desire satisfaction, or what are the natural means of satisfying them. The second takes no account of our desires or the means of satisfying them, and regards only the freedom of a rational being, and the necessary conditions under which alone this freedom can harmonize with the distribution of happiness according to principles. This second law may therefore rest upon mere ideas of pure reason, and may be cognized *a priori*.

I assume that there are pure moral laws which determine, entirely *a priori* (without regard to empirical motives, that is, to happiness), the conduct of a rational being, or in other words, the use which it makes of its freedom, and that these laws are *absolutely* imperative (not merely hypothetically, on the supposition of other empirical ends), and therefore in all respects necessary. I am warranted in assuming this, not only by the arguments of the most enlightened moralists, but by the moral judgment of every man who will make the attempt to form a distinct conception of such a law.

Pure reason, then, contains, not indeed in its speculative, but in its practical, or, more strictly, its moral use, principles of the *possibility* of *experience*, of such actions, namely, as, in accordance with ethical precepts, *might* be met with in the *history* of man. For since reason commands that such actions should take place, it must be possible for them to take place; and hence a particular kind of systematic unity—the moral, must be possible. We have found, it is true, that the systematic unity of nature could not be established according to speculative principles of reason, because, while reason possesses a causal power in relation to freedom, it has none in relation to the whole sphere of nature; and, while moral principles of reason can produce free actions, they cannot produce natural laws. It is, then, in its practical, but especially in its moral use, that the principles of pure reason possess objective reality.

I call the world *a moral world*, in so far as it may be in accordance with all the ethical laws—which, by virtue of the *freedom* of reasonable beings, it *can* be, and according to the necessary laws of *morality* it *ought to be*. But this world must be conceived only as an intelligible world, inasmuch as abstraction is therein made of all conditions (ends), and even of all impediments to morality (the weakness or pravity of human nature). So far, then, it is a mere idea—though still a practical idea—which may have, and ought to have, an influence on the world of sense, so as to bring it as far as possible into conformity with itself. The idea of a moral world has, therefore, objective reality, not as referring to an object of intelligible intuition—for of such an object we can form no conception whatever—but to the world of sense—conceived, however, as an object of pure reason in its practical use—and to a *corpus mysticum* of rational beings in it, in so far as the *liberum arbitrium* of the individual is placed, under and by virtue of moral laws, in complete systematic unity both with itself, and with the freedom of all others.

That is the answer to the first of the two questions of pure reason which relate to its practical interest: *Do that which will render thee worthy of happiness.* The second question is this: If I conduct myself so as not to be unworthy of happiness, may I hope thereby to obtain happiness? In order to arrive at the solution of this question, we must inquire whether the principles of pure reason, which prescribe *a priori* the law, necessarily also connect this hope with it.

I say, then, that just as the moral principles are necessary according to reason in its *practical* use, so it is equally necessary according to reason in its *theoretical* use, to assume that every one has ground to hope for happiness in the measure in which he has made himself worthy of it in his conduct, and that therefore the system of morality is inseparably (though only in the idea of pure reason) connected with that of happiness.

Now in an intelligible, that is, in the moral world, in the conception of which we make abstraction of all the impediments to morality (sensuous desires), such a system of happiness, connected with and proportioned to morality, may be conceived as necessary, because freedom of volition—partly incited, and partly restrained by moral laws—would be itself the cause of general happiness; and thus rational beings, under the guidance of such principles, would be themselves the authors both of their own enduring welfare and that of others. But such a system of self-rewarding morality is only an idea, the carrying out of which depends upon the condition that every one acts as he ought; in other words, that all actions of reasonable beings be such as they would be if they sprang from a Supreme Will, comprehending in, or under, itself all particular wills. But since the moral law is binding on each individual in the use of his freedom of volition, even if others should not act in conformity with this law, neither the nature of things, nor the causality of actions and their relation to morality, determine how the consequences of these actions will be related to happiness; and the necessary connection of the hope of happiness with the unceasing endeavour to become worthy of happiness, cannot be cognized by reason, if we take nature alone for our guide. This connection can be hoped for only on the assumption that the cause of nature is a supreme reason, which governs according to moral laws.

I term the idea of an intelligence in which the morally most perfect will, united with supreme blessedness, is the cause of all happiness in the world, so far as happiness stands in strict relation to morality (as the worthiness of being happy), *the Ideal of the Supreme Good*. It is only, then, in the ideal of the supreme *original* good, that pure reason can find the ground of the practically necessary connection of both elements of the highest *derivative* good, and accordingly of an intelligible, that is, *moral* world. Now since we are necessitated by reason to conceive ourselves as belonging to such a world, while the senses present to us nothing but a world of phenomena, we must assume the former as a consequence of our conduct in the world of sense (since the world of sense gives us no hint of it), and therefore as future in relation to us. Thus God and a future life are two hypotheses which, according to the principles of pure reason, are inseparable from the obligation which this reason imposes upon us.

Morality *per se* constitutes a system. But we can form no system of happiness, except in so far as it is dispensed in strict proportion to morality. But this is only possible in the intelligible world, under a wise author and ruler. Such a ruler, together with life in such a world, which we must look upon as future, reason finds itself compelled to assume; or it must regard the moral laws as idle dreams, since the necessary consequence which this same reason connects with them, must, without this hypothesis, fall to the ground. Hence also the moral laws are universally regarded as *commands*, which they could not be, did they not connect *a priori* adequate consequences with their dictates, and thus carry with them *promises* and *threats*. But this, again, they could not do, did they not reside in a necessary being, as the Supreme Good, which alone can render such a teleological unity possible.

Leibnitz termed the world, when viewed in relation to the rational beings which it contains, and the moral relations in which they stand to each other, under the government of the Supreme Good, *the kingdom of Grace*, and distinguished it from the *kingdom of Nature*, in which these rational beings live, under moral laws, indeed, but expect no other consequences from their actions than such as follow according to the course of nature in the world of sense. To view ourselves, therefore, as in the kingdom of grace, in which all happiness awaits us, except in so far as we ourselves limit our participation in it by actions which render us unworthy of happiness, is a practically necessary idea of reason.

Practical laws, in so far as they are subjective grounds of actions, that is, subjective principles, are termed *maxims*. The *judgments* of morality, in its purity and ultimate results, are framed according to *ideas*; the *observance* of its laws, according to *maxims*.

The whole course of our life must be subject to moral maxims; but this is impossible, unless with the moral law, which is a mere idea, reason connects an efficient cause which ordains to all conduct which is in conformity with the moral law an issue either in this or in another life, which is in exact conformity with our highest aims. Thus, without a God and without a world, invisible to us now, but hoped for, the glorious ideas of morality are, indeed, objects of approbation and of admiration, but cannot be the springs of purpose and action. For they do not satisfy all the aims which are natural to every rational being, and which are determined *a priori* by pure reason itself, and necessary.

Happiness alone is, in the view of reason, far from being the complete good. Reason does not approve of it (however much inclination may desire it), except as united with desert. On the other hand, morality alone, and with it, mere *desert*, is likewise far from being the complete good. To make it complete, he who conducts himself in a manner not unworthy of happiness, must be able to hope for the possession of happiness. Even reason, unbiased by private ends, or interested considerations, cannot judge otherwise, if it puts itself in the place of a being whose business it is to dispense all happiness to others. For in the practical idea both points are essentially combined, though in such a way that participation in happiness is rendered possible by the moral disposition, as its condition, and not conversely, the moral disposition by the prospect of happiness. For a disposition which should require the prospect of happiness as its necessary condition, would not be moral, and hence also would not be worthy of complete happiness—a happiness which, in the view of reason, recognizes no limitation but such as arises from our own immoral conduct.

Happiness, therefore, in exact proportion with the morality of rational beings (whereby they are made worthy of happiness), constitutes alone the supreme good of a world into which we absolutely must transport ourselves according to the commands of pure but practical reason. This world is, it is true, only an intelligible world; for of such a systematic unity of ends as it requires, the world of sense gives us no hint. Its reality can be based on nothing else but the hypothesis of a supreme original good. In it independent reason, equipped with all the sufficiency of a supreme cause, founds, maintains, and fulfils the universal order of things, with the most perfect teleological harmony, however much this order may be hidden from us in the world of sense.

This moral theology has the peculiar advantage, in contrast with speculative theology, of leading inevitably to the conception of a *sole*, *perfect*, and *rational* First Cause, whereof speculative theology does not give us any *indication* on objective grounds, far less any convincing *evidence*. For we find neither in transcendental nor in natural theology, however far reason may lead us in these, any ground to warrant us in assuming the existence of *one only* Being, which stands at the head of all natural causes, and on which these are entirely dependent. On the other hand, if we take our stand on moral unity as a necessary law of the universe, and from this point of view consider what is necessary to give this law adequate efficiency and, for us, obligatory force, we must come to the conclusion that there is one only supreme will, which comprehends all these laws in itself. For how, under different wills, should we find complete unity of ends? This will must be omnipotent, that all nature and its relation to morality in the world may be subject to it; omniscient, that it may have knowledge of the most secret feelings and their moral worth; omnipresent, that it may be at hand to supply every necessity to which the highest weal of the world may give rise; eternal, that this harmony of nature and liberty may never fail; and so on.

But this systematic unity of ends in this world of intelligences—which, as mere nature, is only a world of sense, but as a system of freedom of volition, may be termed an intelligible, that is, moral world (*regnum gratiae*)—leads inevitably also to the teleological unity of all things which constitute this great whole, according to universal natural laws—just as the unity of the former is according to universal and necessary moral laws—and unites the practical with the speculative reason. The world must be represented as having originated from an idea, if it is to harmonize with that use of reason without which we cannot even consider ourselves as worthy of reason—namely, the moral use, which rests entirely on the idea of the supreme good. Hence the investigation of nature receives a teleological direction, and becomes, in its widest extension, physico-theology. But this, taking its rise in moral order as a unity founded on the essence of freedom, and not accidentally instituted by external commands, establishes the teleological view of nature on grounds which must be inseparably connected with the internal possibility of things. This gives rise to a *transcendental theology*, which takes the ideal of the highest ontological perfection as a principle of systematic unity; and this principle connects all things according to universal and necessary natural laws, because all things have their origin in the absolute necessity of the one only Primal Being.

What *use* can we make of our understanding, even in respect of experience, if we do not propose ends to ourselves? But the highest ends are those of morality, and it is only pure reason that can give us the knowledge of these. Though supplied with these, and putting ourselves under their guidance, we can make no teleological use of the knowledge of nature, as regards *cognition*, unless nature itself has established teleological unity. For without this unity we should not even possess reason, because we should have no school for reason, and no cultivation through objects which afford the materials for its conceptions. But teleological unity is a necessary unity, and founded on the essence of the individual will itself. Hence this will, which is the condition of the application of this unity *in concreto*, must be so likewise. In this way the transcendental enlargement of our rational cognition would be, not the cause, but merely the effect of the practical teleology, which pure reason imposes upon us.

Hence, also, we find in the history of human reason that, before the moral conceptions were sufficiently purified and determined, and before men had attained to a perception of the systematic unity of ends according to these conceptions and from necessary principles, the knowledge of nature, and even a considerable amount of intellectual culture in many other sciences, could produce only rude and vague conceptions of the Deity, sometimes even admitting of an astonishing indifference with regard to this question altogether. But the more enlarged treatment of moral ideas, which was rendered necessary by the extremely pure moral law of our religion, awakened the interest, and thereby quickened the perceptions of reason in relation to this object. In this way, and without the help either of an extended acquaintance with nature, or of a reliable transcendental insight (for these have been wanting in all ages), a conception of the Divine Being was arrived at, which we now hold to be the correct one, not because speculative reason convinces us of its correctness, but because it accords with the moral principles of reason. Thus it is to pure reason, but only in its practical use, that we must ascribe the merit of having connected with our highest interest a cognition, of which mere speculation was able only to form a conjecture, but the validity of which it was unable to establish—and of having thereby rendered it, not indeed a demonstrated dogma, but a hypothesis absolutely necessary to the essential ends of reason.

But if practical reason has reached this elevation, and has attained to the conception of a sole Primal Being, as the supreme good, it must not, therefore, imagine that it has transcended the empirical conditions of its application, and risen to the immediate cognition of new objects; it must not presume to start from the conception which it has gained, and to deduce from it the moral laws themselves. For it was these very laws, the *internal* practical necessity of which led us to the hypothesis of an independent cause, or of a wise ruler of the universe, who should give them effect. Hence we are not entitled to regard them as accidental and derived from the mere will of the ruler, especially as we have no conception of such a will, except as formed in accordance with these laws. So far, then, as practical reason has the right to conduct us, we shall not look upon actions as binding on us, because they are the commands of God, but we shall regard them as divine commands, because we are internally bound by them. We shall study freedom under the teleological unity which accords with principles of reason; we shall look upon ourselves as acting in conformity with the divine will only in so far as we hold sacred the moral law which reason teaches us from the nature of actions themselves, and we shall believe that we can obey that will only by promoting the weal of the universe in ourselves and in others. Moral theology is, therefore, only of immanent use. It teaches us to fulfil our destiny here in the world, by placing ourselves in harmony with the general system of ends, and warns us against the fanaticism, nay, the crime of depriving reason of its legislative authority in the moral conduct of life, for the purpose of directly connecting this authority with the idea of the Supreme Being. For this would be, not an immanent, but a transcendent use of moral theology, and, like the transcendent use of mere speculation, would inevitably pervert and frustrate the ultimate ends of reason.

Section III

*Of Opinion, Knowledge, and Belief*

THE holding of a thing to be true, is a phenomenon in our understanding which may rest on objective grounds, but requires, also, subjective causes in the mind of the person judging. If a judgment is valid for every rational being, then its ground is objectively sufficient, and it is termed a *conviction*. If, on the other hand, it has its ground in the particular character of the subject, it is termed a *persuasion*.

Persuasion is a mere illusion, the ground of the judgment, which lies solely in the subject, being regarded as objective. Hence a judgment of this kind has only private validity—is only valid for the individual who judges, and the holding of a thing to be true in this way cannot be communicated. But truth depends upon agreement with the object, and consequently the judgments of all understandings, if true, must be in agreement with each other (*consentientia uni tertio consentiunt inter se*). Conviction may, therefore, be distinguished, from an external point of view, from persuasion, by the possibility of communicating it, and by showing its validity for the reason of every man; for in this case the presumption, at least, arises, that the agreement of all judgments with each other, in spite of the different characters of individuals, rests upon the common ground of the agreement of each with the object, and thus the correctness of the judgment is established.

Persuasion, accordingly, cannot be *subjectively* distinguished from conviction, that is, so long as the subject views its judgment simply as a phenomenon of its own mind. But if we inquire whether the grounds of our judgment, which are valid for us, produce the same effect on the reason of others as on our own, we have then the means, though only subjective means, not, indeed, of producing conviction, but of detecting the merely private validity of the judgment; in other words, of discovering that there is in it the element of mere persuasion.

If we can, in addition to this, develop the *subjective causes* of the judgment, which we have taken for its *objective grounds*, and thus explain the deceptive judgment as a phenomenon in our mind, apart altogether from the objective character of the object, we can then expose the illusion and need be no longer deceived by it, although, if its subjective cause lies in our nature, we cannot hope altogether to escape its influence.

I can only *maintain*, that is, affirm as necessarily valid for every one, that which produces conviction. Persuasion I may keep for myself, if it is agreeable to me; but I cannot, and ought not, to attempt to impose it as binding upon others.

*Holding for true*, or the subjective validity of a judgment in relation to conviction (which is, at the same time, objectively valid), has the three following degrees: *Opinion, Belief,* and *Knowledge.* Opinion is a consciously insufficient judgment, subjectively as well as objectively. Belief is subjectively sufficient, but is recognized as being objectively insufficient. Knowledge is both subjectively and objectively sufficient. Subjective sufficiency is termed *conviction* (for myself); objective sufficiency is termed *certainty* (for all). I need not dwell longer on the explanation of such simple conceptions.

I must never venture to *be of opinion*, without *knowing* something, at least, by which my judgment, in itself merely problematical, is brought into connection with the truth—which connection, although not perfect, is still something more than an arbitrary fiction. Moreover, the law of such a connection must be certain. For if, in relation to this law, I have nothing more than opinion, my judgment is but a play of the imagination, without the least relation to truth. In the judgments of pure reason, opinion has no place. For as they do not rest on empirical grounds, and as the sphere of pure reason is that of necessary truth and *a priori* cognition, the principle of connection in it requires universality and necessity, and consequently perfect certainty—otherwise we should have no guide to the truth at all. Hence it is absurd to have an opinion in pure mathematics; we must know, or abstain from forming a judgment altogether. The case is the same with the maxims of morality. For we must not hazard an action on the mere opinion that it is allowed, but we must know it to be so.

In the transcendental sphere of reason, on the other hand, the term opinion is too weak, while the word knowledge is too strong. From the merely speculative point of view, therefore, we cannot form a judgment at all. For the subjective grounds of a judgment, such as produce belief, cannot be admitted in speculative inquiries, inasmuch as they cannot stand without empirical support, and are incapable of being communicated to others in equal measure.

But it is only from the *practical* point of view that a *theoretically* insufficient judgment can be termed belief. Now the practical reference is either to *skill* or to *morality*; to the former, when the end proposed is arbitrary and accidental, to the latter, when it is absolutely necessary.

If we propose to ourselves any end whatever, the conditions of its attainment are hypothetically necessary. The necessity is subjectively, but still only comparatively, sufficient, if I am acquainted with no other conditions under which the end can be attained. On the other hand, it is sufficient, absolutely, and for every one, if I know for certain that no one can be acquainted with any other conditions, under which the attainment of the proposed end would be possible. In the former case my supposition —my judgment with regard to certain conditions, is a merely accidental belief; in the latter it is a necessary belief. The physician must pursue some course in the case of a patient who is in danger, but is ignorant of the nature of the disease. He observes the symptoms, and concludes, according to the best of his judgment, that it is a case of phthisis. His belief is, even in his own judgment, only contingent: another man might, perhaps, come nearer the truth. Such a belief, contingent indeed, but still forming the ground of the actual use of means for the attainment of certain ends, I term *pragmatical belief*.

The usual test, whether that which any one maintains is merely his persuasion, or his subjective conviction at least, that is, his firm belief, is a *bet*. It frequently happens that a man delivers his opinions with so much boldness and assurance, that he appears to be under no apprehension as to the possibility of his being in error. The offer of a bet startles him, and makes him pause. Sometimes it turns out that his persuasion may be valued at a ducat, but not at ten. For he does not hesitate, perhaps, to venture a ducat, but if it is proposed to stake ten, he immediately becomes aware of the possibility of his being mistaken—a possibility which has hitherto escaped his observation. If we imagine to ourselves that we have to stake the happiness of our whole life on the truth of any proposition, our judgment drops its air of triumph, we take the alarm, and discover the actual strength of our belief. Thus pragmatical belief has degrees, varying in proportion to the interests at stake.

Now, in cases where we cannot enter upon any course of action in reference to some object, and where, accordingly, our judgment is purely theoretical, we can still represent to ourselves, in thought, the possibility of a course of action, for which we suppose that we have sufficient grounds, if any means existed of ascertaining the truth of the matter. Thus we find in purely theoretical judgments an *analogon* of practical judgments, to which the word *belief* may properly be applied, and which we may term *doctrinal belief*. I should not hesitate to stake my all on the truth of the proposition —if there were any possibility of bringing it to the test of experience —that, at least, some one of the planets, which we see, is inhabited. Hence I say that I have not merely the opinion, but the strong belief, on the correctness of which I would stake even many of the advantages of life, that there are inhabitants in other worlds.

Now we must admit that the doctrine of the existence of God belongs to doctrinal belief. For, although in respect to the theoretical cognition of the universe I do not require to form any theory which necessarily involves this idea, as the condition of my explanation of the phenomena which the universe presents, but, on the contrary, am rather bound so to use my reason as if everything were mere nature, still teleological unity is so important a condition of the application of my reason to nature, that it is impossible for me to ignore it—especially since, in addition to these considerations, abundant examples of it are supplied by experience. But the sole condition, so far as my knowledge extends, under which this unity can be my guide in the investigation of nature, is the assumption that a supreme intelligence has ordered all things according to the wisest ends. Consequently the hypothesis of a wise author of the universe is necessary for my guidance in the investigation of nature—is the condition under which alone I can fulfil an end which is contingent indeed, but by no means unimportant. Moreover, since the result of my attempts so frequently confirms the utility of this assumption, and since nothing decisive can be adduced against it, it follows that it would be saying far too little to term my judgment, in this case, a mere opinion, and that, even in this theoretical connection, I may assert that I firmly believe in God. Still, if we use words strictly, this must not be called a practical, but a doctrinal belief, which the theology of nature (physico-theology) must also produce in my mind. In the wisdom of a Supreme Being, and in the shortness of life, so inadequate to the development of the glorious powers of human nature, we may find equally sufficient grounds for a doctrinal belief in the future life of the human soul.

The expression of belief is, in such cases, an expression of modesty from the *objective* point of view, but, at the same time, of firm confidence, from the *subjective*. If I should venture to term this merely theoretical judgment even so much as a hypothesis which I am entitled to assume; a more complete conception, with regard to another world and to the cause of the world, might then be justly required of me than I am, in reality, able to give. For, if I assume anything, even as a mere hypothesis, I must, at least, know so much of the properties of *such* a being as will enable me, not to form the *conception*, but to imagine the *existence* of it.   But the word *belief* refers only to the guidance which an idea gives me, and to its subjective influence on the conduct of my reason, which forces me to hold it fast, though I may not be in a position to give a speculative account of it.

But mere doctrinal belief is, to some extent, wanting in stability. We often quit our hold of it, in consequence of the difficulties which occur in speculation, though in the end we inevitably return to it again.

It is quite otherwise with *moral belief*.   For in this sphere action is absolutely necessary, that is, I must act in obedience to the moral law in all points.   The end is here incontrovertibly established, and there is only one condition possible, according to the best of my perception, under which this end can harmonize with all other ends, and so have practical validity—namely, the existence of a God and of a future world.   I know also, to a certainty, that no one can be acquainted with any other conditions which conduct to the same unity of ends under the moral law.   But since the moral precept is, at the same time, my maxim (as reason requires that it should be), I am irresistibly constrained to believe in the existence of God and in a future life; and I am sure that nothing can make me waver in this belief, since I should thereby overthrow my moral maxims, the renunciation of which would render me hateful in my own eyes.

Thus, while all the ambitious attempts of reason to penetrate beyond the limits of experience end in disappointment, there is still enough left to satisfy us in a practical point of view.   No one, it is true, will be able to boast that he knows that there is a God and a future life; for, if he knows this, he is just the man whom I have long wished to find.   All knowledge, regarding an object of mere reason, can be communicated; and I should thus be enabled to hope that my own knowledge would receive this wonderful extension, through the instrumentality of his instruction.   No, my conviction is not *logical*, but *moral* certainty; and since it rests on subjective grounds (of the moral sentiment), I must not even say: *It is* morally certain that there is a God, etc., but: *I am* morally certain, that is, my belief in God and in another world is so interwoven with my moral nature, that I am under as little apprehension of having the former torn from me as of losing the latter.

The only point in this argument that may appear open to suspicion, is that this rational belief presupposes the existence of moral sentiments. If we give up this assumption, and take a man who is entirely indifferent with regard to moral laws, the question which reason proposes, becomes then merely a problem for speculation, and may, indeed, be supported by strong grounds from analogy, but not by such as will compel the most obstinate scepticism to give way.[1] But in these questions no man is free from all interest. For though the want of good sentiments may place him beyond the influence of moral interests, still even in this case enough may be left to make him *fear* the existence of God and a future life. For he cannot pretend to any *certainty* of the non-existence of God and of a future life, unless—since it could only be proved by mere reason, and therefore apodeictically—he is prepared to establish the *impossibility* of both, which certainly no reasonable man would undertake to do. This would be a *negative* belief, which could not, indeed, produce morality and good sentiments, but still could produce an analogon of these, by operating as a powerful restraint on the outbreak of evil dispositions.

But, it will be said, is this all that pure reason can effect, in opening up prospects beyond the limits of experience? Nothing more than two articles of belief? Common sense could have done as much as this, without taking the philosophers to counsel in the matter!

I shall not here eulogize philosophy for the benefits which the laborious efforts of its criticism have conferred on human reason— even granting that its merit should turn out in the end to be only negative—for on this point something more will be said in the next section. But I ask, do you require that that knowledge which concerns all men, should transcend the common understanding, and should only be revealed to you by philosophers? The very circumstance which has called forth your censure, is the best confirmation of the correctness of our previous assertions, since it discloses, what could not have been foreseen, that Nature is not chargeable with any partial distribution of her gifts in those matters which concern all men without distinction, and that in respect to the essential ends of human nature, we cannot advance further with the help of the highest philosophy, than under the guidance which nature has vouchsafed to the meanest understanding.

[1] The human mind (as, I believe, every rational being must of necessity do) takes a natural interest in morality, although this interest is not undivided, and may not be practically in preponderance. If you strengthen and increase it, you will find the reason become docile, more enlightened, and more capable of uniting the speculative interest with the practical. But if you do not take care at the outset, or at least midway, to make men good, you will never force them into an honest belief.

## CHAPTER III

### THE ARCHITECTONIC OF PURE REASON

By the term *Architectonic* I mean the art of constructing a system.
Without systematic unity, our knowledge cannot become science;
it will be an aggregate, and not a system. Thus Architectonic is
the doctrine of the scientific in cognition, and therefore necessarily
forms part of our Methodology.

Reason cannot permit our knowledge to remain in an unconnected
and rhapsodistic state, but requires that the sum of our cognitions
should constitute a system. It is thus alone that they can advance
the ends of reason. By a system I mean the unity of various
cognitions under one idea. This idea is the conception—given
by reason—of the form of a whole, in so far as the conception
determines *a priori* not only the limits of its content, but the place
which each of its parts is to occupy. The scientific idea contains,
therefore, the end, and the form of the whole which is in accordance
with that end. The unity of the end, to which all the parts of the
system relate, and through which all have a relation to each other,
communicates unity to the whole system, so that the absence of
any part can be immediately detected from our knowledge of the
rest; and it determines *a priori* the limits of the system, thus
excluding all contingent or arbitrary additions. The whole is
thus an organism (*articulatio*), and not an aggregate (*coacervatio*);
it may grow from within (*per intussusceptionem*), but it cannot
increase by external additions (*per appositionem*). It is thus like
an animal body, the growth of which does not add any limb,
but, without changing their proportions, makes each in its sphere
stronger and more active.

We require, for the execution of the idea of a system, a *schema*,
that is, a content and an arrangement of parts determined *a priori*
by the principle which the aim of the system prescribes. A schema
which is not projected in accordance with an idea, that is, from
the standpoint of the highest aim of reason, but merely empirically,
in accordance with accidental aims and purposes (the number of
which cannot be predetermined), can give us nothing more than
*technical* unity. But the schema which is originated from an
idea (in which case reason presents us with aims *a priori*, and does
not look for them to experience), forms the basis of *architectonical*

unity. A science, in the proper acceptation of that term, cannot be formed *technically*, that is, from observation of the similarity existing between different objects, and the purely contingent use we make of our knowledge *in concreto* with reference to all kinds of arbitrary external aims; its constitution must be framed on architectonical principles, that is, its parts must be shown to possess an essential affinity, and be capable of being deduced from one supreme and internal aim or end, which forms the condition of the possibility of the scientific whole. The schema of a science must give *a priori* the plan of it (*monogramma*), and the division of the whole into parts, in conformity with the idea of the science; and it must also distinguish this whole from all others, according to certain understood principles.

No one will attempt to construct a science, unless he have some idea to rest on as a proper basis. But, in the elaboration of the science, he finds that the schema, nay, even the definition which he at first gave of the science, rarely corresponds with his idea; for this idea lies, like a germ, in our reason, its parts undeveloped and hid even from microscopical observation. For this reason, we ought to explain and define sciences, not according to the description which the originator gives of them, but according to the idea which we find based in reason itself, and which is suggested by the natural unity of the parts of the science already accumulated. For it will often be found, that the originator of a science, and even his latest successors, remain attached to an erroneous idea, which they cannot render clear to themselves, and that they thus fail in determining the true content, the articulation or systematic unity, and the limits of their science.

It is unfortunate that, only after having occupied ourselves for a long time in the collection of materials, under the guidance of an idea which lies undeveloped in the mind, but not according to any definite plan of arrangement—nay, only after we have spent much time and labour in the technical disposition of our materials, does it become possible to view the idea of a science in a clear light, and to project, according to architectonical principles, a plan of the whole, in accordance with the aims of reason. Systems seem, like certain worms, to be formed by a kind of *generatio aequivoca*—by the mere confluence of conceptions, and to gain completeness only with the progress of time. But the schema or germ of all lies in reason; and thus is not only every system organized according to its own idea, but all are united into one grand system of human knowledge, of which they form members. For this reason, it is possible to frame an architectonic of all human cognition, the formation of which, at the present time, considering the immense materials collected or to be found in the ruins of old systems, would not indeed be very difficult. Our purpose at present is merely to sketch the plan of the *Architectonic* of all cognition given by *pure reason*; and we begin from the point where the main root of human knowledge divides into two, one of which is *reason*. By reason I understand here the whole higher faculty of cognition, the *rational* being placed in contradistinction to the *empirical*.

If I make complete abstraction of the content of cognition, objectively considered, all cognition is, from a subjective point of view, either historical or rational. Historical cognition is *cognitio ex datis*, rational, *cognitio ex principiis*. Whatever may be the original source of a cognition, it is, in relation to the person who possesses it, merely historical, if he knows only what has been given him from another quarter, whether that knowledge was communicated by direct experience or by instruction. Thus the person who has *learned* a system of philosophy—say the Wolfian— although he has a perfect knowledge of all the principles, definitions, and arguments in that philosophy, as well as of the divisions that have been made of the system, he possesses really no more than an *historical* knowledge of the Wolfian system; he knows only what has been told him, his judgments are only those which he has received from his teachers. Dispute the validity of a definition, and he is completely at a loss to find another. He has formed his mind on another's; but the imitative faculty is not the productive. His knowledge has not been drawn from reason; and although, objectively considered, it is rational knowledge, subjectively, it is merely historical. He has learned this or that philosophy, and is merely a plaster-cast of a living man. Rational cognitions which are objective, that is, which have their source in reason, can be so termed from a subjective point of view, only when they have been drawn by the individual himself from the sources of reason, that is, from principles; and it is in this way alone that criticism, or even the rejection of what has been already learned, can spring up in the mind.

All rational cognition is, again, based either on conceptions, or on the construction of conceptions. The former is termed philosophical, the latter mathematical. I have already shown the essential difference of these two methods of cognition in the first chapter. A cognition may be objectively philosophical and subjectively historical—as is the case with the majority of scholars and those who cannot look beyond the limits of their system, and who remain in a state of pupilage all their lives. But it is remarkable that mathematical knowledge, when committed to memory, is valid, from the subjective point of view, as rational knowledge also, and that the same distinction cannot be drawn here as in the case of philosophical cognition. The reason is, that the only way of arriving at this knowledge is through the essential principles of reason, and thus it is always certain and indisputable; because reason is employed *in concreto*—but at the same time *a priori*—that is, in pure, and therefore, infallible intuition; and thus all causes of illusion and error are excluded. Of all the *a priori* sciences of reason, therefore, mathematics alone can be learned. Philosophy—unless it be in an historical manner—cannot be learned; we can at most learn to *philosophize*.

*Philosophy* is the system of all philosophical cognition. We must use this term in an objective sense, if we understand by it the archetype of all attempts at philosophizing, and the standard by which all subjective philosophies are to be judged. In this sense, philosophy is merely the idea of a possible science, which does not exist *in concreto*, but to which we endeavour in various ways to approximate, until we have discovered the right path to pursue—a path overgrown by the errors and illusions of sense—and the image we have hitherto tried to shape in vain, has become a perfect copy of the great prototype. Until that time, we cannot learn philosophy—it does not exist; if it does, where is it, who possesses it, and how shall we know it? We can only learn to philosophize, in other words, we can only exercise our powers of reasoning in accordance with general principles, retaining at the same time, the right of investigating the sources of these principles, of testing, and even of rejecting them.

Until then, our conception of philosophy is only a *scholastic conception*—a conception, that is, of a system of cognition which we are trying to elaborate into a science; all that we at present know, being the systematic unity of this cognition, and consequently the *logical* completeness of the cognition for the desired end. But there is also a *cosmical conception* (*conceptus cosmicus*) of philosophy, which has always formed the true basis of this term, especially when philosophy was personified and presented to us in the ideal of a *philosopher*. In this view, philosophy is the science of the relation of all cognition to the ultimate and essential aims of human reason (*teleologia rationis humanae*), and the philosopher is not merely an artist—who occupies himself with conceptions, but a law-giver—legislating for human reason. In this sense of the word, it would be in the highest degree arrogant to assume the title of philosopher, and to pretend that we had reached the perfection of the prototype which lies in the idea alone.

The mathematician, the natural philosopher, and the logician—how far soever the first may have advanced in rational, and the two latter in philosophical knowledge—are merely artists, engaged in the arrangement and formation of conceptions; they cannot be termed philosophers. Above them all, there is the ideal teacher, who employs them as instruments for the advancement of the essential aims of human reason. Him alone can we call philosopher; but he nowhere exists. But the idea of his legislative power resides in the mind of every man, and it alone teaches us what kind of systematic unity philosophy demands in view of the ultimate aims of reason. This idea is, therefore, a cosmical conception.[1]

In view of the complete systematic unity of reason, there can only be one ultimate end of all the operations of the mind. To this all other aims are subordinate, and nothing more than means for its attainment. This ultimate end is the destination of man, and the philosophy which relates to it is termed Moral Philosophy. The superior position occupied by moral philosophy, above all other spheres for the operations of reason, sufficiently indicates the reason why the ancients always included the idea—and in an especial manner—of Moralist in that of Philosopher. Even at the present day, we call a man who appears to have the power of self-government, even although his knowledge may be very limited, by the name of philosopher.

The legislation of human reason, or philosophy, has two objects —Nature and Freedom, and thus contains not only the laws of nature, but also those of ethics, at first in two separate systems, which, finally, merge into one grand philosophical system of cognition. The philosophy of Nature relates to that *which is*, that of Ethics to that which *ought to be*.

But all philosophy is either cognition on the basis of pure reason, or the cognition of reason on the basis of empirical principles. The former is termed pure, the latter empirical philosophy.

The philosophy of pure reason is either *propaedeutic*, that is, an inquiry into the powers of reason in regard to pure *a priori* cognition, and is termed Critical Philosophy; or it is, secondly, the system of pure reason—a science containing the systematic

---

[1] By a *cosmical conception*, I mean one in which all men necessarily take an interest; the *aim* of a science must accordingly be determined according to *scholastic* [or partial] *conceptions*, if it is regarded merely as a means to certain arbitrarily proposed ends.

presentation of the whole body of philosophical knowledge, true as well as illusory, given by pure reason, and is called Metaphysic. This name may, however, be also given to the whole system of pure philosophy, critical philosophy included, and may designate the investigation into the sources or possibility of *a priori* cognition, as well as the presentation of the *a priori* cognitions which form a system of pure philosophy—excluding, at the same time, all empirical and mathematical elements.

Metaphysic is divided into that of the *speculative* and that of the *practical* use of pure reason, and is, accordingly, either the *Metaphysic of Nature*, or the *Metaphysic of Ethics*. The former contains all the pure rational principles—based upon conceptions alone (and thus excluding mathematics)—of all *theoretical* cognition; the latter, the principles which determine and necessitate *a priori* all *action*. Now moral philosophy alone contains a code of laws—for the regulation of our actions—which are deduced from principles entirely *a priori*. Hence the Metaphysic of Ethics is the only pure moral philosophy, as it is not based upon anthropological or other empirical considerations. The metaphysic of speculative reason is what is commonly called Metaphysic in the more limited sense. But as pure Moral Philosophy properly forms a part of this system of cognition, we must allow it to retain the name of Metaphysic, although it is not requisite that we should insist on so terming it in our present discussion.

It is of the highest importance to separate those cognitions which differ from others both in kind and in origin, and to take great care that they are not confounded with those with which they are generally found connected. What the chemist does in the analysis of substances, what the mathematician in pure mathematics, is, in a still higher degree, the duty of the philosopher, that the value of each different kind of cognition, and the part it takes in the operations of the mind, may be clearly defined. Human reason has never wanted a metaphysic of some kind, since it attained the power of thought, or rather of reflection; but it has never been able to keep this sphere of thought and cognition pure from all admixture of foreign elements. The idea of a science of this kind is as old as speculation itself; and what mind does not speculate—either in the scholastic or in the popular fashion? At the same time, it must be admitted that even thinkers by profession have been unable clearly to explain the distinction between the two elements of our cognition—the one completely *a priori*, the other *a posteriori*; and hence the proper definition of a peculiar kind of cognition, and with it the just idea of a science which has so long and so deeply engaged the attention of the human mind, has never been established. When it was said— Metaphysic is the science of the first principles of human cognition, this definition did not signalize a peculiarity in kind, but only a difference in degree; these first principles were thus declared to be more general than others, but no criterion of distinction from empirical principles was given. Of these some are more general, and therefore higher, than others; and—as we cannot distinguish what is completely *a priori* from that which is known to be *a posteriori*—where shall we draw the line which is to separate the higher and so-called first principles, from the lower and subordinate principles of cognition? What would be said if we were asked to be satisfied with a division of the epochs of the world into the earlier centuries and those following them? Does the fifth, or the tenth century belong to the earlier centuries? it would be asked. In the same way I ask: Does the conception of extension belong to metaphysics? You answer, Yes. Well, that of body too? Yes. And that of a fluid body? You stop, you are unprepared to admit this; for if you do, everything will belong to metaphysics. From this it is evident that the mere degree of subordination—of the particular to the general—cannot determine the limits of a science; and that, in the present case, we must expect to find a difference in the conceptions of metaphysics both in kind and in origin. The fundamental idea of metaphysics was obscured on another side, by the fact that this kind of *a priori* cognition showed a certain similarity in character with the science of mathematics. Both have the property in common of possessing an *a priori* origin; but, in the one, our knowledge is based upon conceptions, in the other, on the construction of conceptions. Thus a decided dissimilarity between philosophical and mathematical cognition comes out—a dissimilarity which was always felt, but which could not be made distinct for want of an insight into the criteria of the difference. And thus it happened that, as philosophers themselves failed in the proper development of the idea of their science, the elaboration of the science could not proceed with a definite aim, or under trustworthy guidance. Thus, too, philosophers, ignorant of the path they ought to pursue, and always disputing with each other regarding the discoveries which each asserted he had made, brought their science into disrepute with the rest of the world, and finally, even among themselves.

All pure *a priori* cognition forms, therefore, in view of the peculiar faculty which originates it, a peculiar and distinct unity; and metaphysic is the term applied to the philosophy which attempts to represent that cognition in this systematic unity. The speculative part of metaphysic, which has especially appropriated this appellation—that which we have called the. *Metaphysic* of *Nature* —and which considers everything, as it is (not as it ought to be), by means of *a priori* conceptions, is divided in the following manner.

Metaphysic, in the more limited acceptation of the term, consists of two parts—*Transcendental Philosophy* and the *Physiology* of *pure reason.* The former presents the system of all the conceptions and principles belonging to the understanding and the reason, and which relate to objects in general, but not to any particular given objects (*Ontologia*); the latter has *nature* for its subject-matter, that is, the sum of given objects—whether given to the senses, or, if we will, to some other kind of intuition—and is accordingly *Physiology*, although only *rationalis.* But the use of the faculty of reason in this rational mode of regarding nature is either physical or hyperphysical, or, more properly speaking, *immanent* or *transcendent.* The former relates to nature, in so far as our knowledge regarding it may be applied in experience (*in concreto*); the latter to that connection of the objects of experience, which transcends all experience. *Transcendent Physiology* has, again, an *internal* and an *external* connection with its object, both, however, transcending possible experience; the former is the physiology of nature as a whole, or *transcendental cognition of the world*, the latter of the connection of the whole of nature with a being above nature, or transcendental *cognition of God*.

Immanent physiology, on the contrary, considers nature as the sum of all sensuous objects, consequently, as it is presented to us—but still according to *a priori* conditions, for it is under these alone that nature can be presented to our minds at all. The objects of immanent physiology are of two kinds: 1. Those of the external senses, or *corporeal nature*; 2. The object of the internal sense, the soul, or, in accordance with our fundamental conceptions of it, *thinking nature.* The metaphysics of corporeal nature is called *Physics*, but, as it must contain only the principles of an *a priori* cognition of nature, we must term it *rational physics.* The metaphysics of thinking nature is called *Psychology*, and for the same reason it is to be regarded as merely the *rational cognition* of the soul.

Thus the whole system of metaphysics consists of four principal parts: 1. *Ontology*; 2. *Rational Physiology*; 3. *Rational Cosmology*; and 4. *Rational Theology*. The second part—that of the rational doctrine of nature—may be subdivided into two, *physica rationalis* [1] and *psychologia rationalis*.

The fundamental idea of a philosophy of pure reason of necessity dictates this division; it is, therefore, *architectonical*—in accordance with the highest aims of reason, and not merely *technical*, or according to certain accidentally-observed similarities existing between the different parts of the whole science. For this reason, also, is the division immutable and of legislative authority. But the reader may observe in it a few points to which he ought to demur, and which may weaken his conviction of its truth and legitimacy.

In the first place, how can I desire an *a priori* cognition or metaphysic of objects, in so far as they are given *a posteriori*? and how is it possible to cognize the nature of things according to *a priori* principles, and to attain to a *rational* physiology? The answer is this. We take from experience nothing more than is requisite to present us with an object (in general) of the external, or of the internal sense; in the former case, by the mere conception of matter (impenetrable and inanimate extension), in the latter, by the conception of a thinking being—given in the internal empirical representation, *I think*. As to the rest, we must not employ in our metaphysic of these objects any empirical principles (which add to the content of our conceptions by means of experience), for the purpose of forming by their help any judgments respecting these objects.

Secondly, what place shall we assign to *empirical psychology*, which has always been considered a part of metaphysics, and from which in our time such important philosophical results have been expected, after the hope of constructing an *a priori* system of knowledge had been abandoned? I answer: It must be placed by the side of empirical physics or physics proper; that is, it must be regarded as forming a part of *applied* philosophy, the *a priori* principles of which are contained in pure philosophy, which is therefore connected, although it must not be confounded, with psychology. Empirical psychology must therefore be banished

---

[1] It must not be supposed that I mean by this appellation what is generally called *physica generalis*, and which is rather mathematics, than a philosophy of nature. For the metaphysic of nature is completely different from mathematics, nor is it so rich in results, although it is of great importance as a critical test of the application of pure understanding-cognition to nature. For want of its guidance, even mathematicians, adopting certain common notions—which are, in fact, metaphysical—have unconsciously crowded their theories of nature with hypotheses, the fallacy of which becomes evident upon the application of the principles of this metaphysic, without detriment, however, to the employment of mathematics in this sphere of cognition.

from the sphere of metaphysics, and is indeed excluded by the very idea of that science. In conformity, however, with scholastic usage, we must permit it to occupy a place in metaphysics—but only as an appendix to it. We adopt this course from motives of economy; as psychology is not as yet full enough to occupy our attention as an independent study, while it is, at the same time, of too great importance to be entirely excluded or placed where it has still less affinity than it has with the subject of metaphysics. It is a stranger who has been long a guest; and we make it welcome to stay, until it can take up a more suitable abode in a complete system of anthropology—the pendant to empirical physics.

The above is the general idea of metaphysics, which, as more was expected from it than could be looked for with justice, and as these pleasant expectations were unfortunately never realized, fell into general disrepute. Our *Critique* must have fully convinced the reader, that, although metaphysics cannot form the foundation of religion, it must always be one of its most important bulwarks, and that human reason, which naturally pursues a dialectical course, cannot do without this science, which checks its tendencies towards dialectic, and, by elevating reason to a scientific and clear self-knowledge, prevents the ravages which a lawless speculative reason would infallibly commit in the sphere of morals as well as in that of religion. We may be sure, therefore, whatever contempt may be thrown upon metaphysics by those who judge a science not by its own nature, but according to the accidental effects it may have produced, that it can never be completely abandoned, that we must always return to it as to a beloved one who has been for a time estranged, because the questions with which it is engaged relate to the highest aims of humanity, and reason must always labour either to attain to settled views in regard to these, or to destroy those which others have already established.

Metaphysic, therefore—that of nature, as well as that of ethics, but in an especial manner the criticism which forms the propaedeutic to all the operations of reason—forms properly that department of knowledge which may be termed, in the truest sense of the word, philosophy. The path which it pursues is that of science, which, when it has once been discovered, is never lost, and never misleads. Mathematics, natural science, the common experience of men, have a high value as means, for the most part, to accidental ends—but at last also, to those which are necessary and essential to the existence of humanity. But to guide them to this high goal, they require the aid of rational cognition on the basis of pure conceptions, which, be it termed as it may, is properly nothing but metaphysics.

For the same reason, metaphysics forms likewise the completion of the *culture* of human reason. In this respect, it is indispensable, setting aside altogether the influence which it exerts as a science. For its subject-matter is the elements and highest maxims of reason, which form the basis of the *possibility* of some sciences and of the *use* of all. That, as a purely speculative science, it is more useful in preventing error, than in the extension of knowledge, does not detract from its value; on the contrary, the supreme office of censor which it occupies, assures to it the highest authority and importance. This office it administers for the purpose of securing order, harmony, and well-being to science, and of directing its noble and fruitful labours to the highest possible aim—the happiness of all mankind.

## CHAPTER IV

### THE HISTORY OF PURE REASON

THIS title is placed here merely for the purpose of designating a division of the system of pure reason, of which I do not intend to treat at present. I shall content myself with casting a cursory glance, from a purely transcendental point of view—that of the nature of pure reason, on the labours of philosophers up to the present time. They have aimed at erecting an edifice of philosophy; but to my eye this edifice appears to be in a very ruinous condition.

It is very remarkable, although naturally it could not have been otherwise, that, in the infancy of philosophy, the study of the nature of God, and the constitution of a future world, formed the commencement, rather than the conclusion, as we should have it, of the speculative efforts of the human mind. However rude the religious conceptions generated by the remains of the old manners and customs of a less cultivated time, the intelligent classes were not thereby prevented from devoting themselves to free inquiry into the existence and nature of God; and they easily saw that there could be no surer way of pleasing the invisible ruler of the world, and of attaining to happiness in another world at least, than a good and honest course of life in this. Thus theology and morals formed the two chief motives, or rather the points of attraction in all abstract inquiries. But it was the former that especially occupied the attention of speculative reason, and which afterwards became so celebrated under the name of metaphysics.

I shall not at present indicate the periods of time at which the greatest changes in metaphysics took place, but shall merely give a hasty sketch of the different ideas which occasioned the most important revolutions in this sphere of thought. There are three different ends, in relation to which these revolutions have taken place.

1. *In relation to the object* of the cognition of reason, philosophers may be divided into *Sensualists* and *Intellectualists*. *Epicurus* may be regarded as the head of the former, *Plato* of the latter. The distinction here signalized, subtle as it is, dates from the earliest times, and was long maintained. The former asserted, that reality resides in sensuous objects alone, and that everything else is merely imaginary; the latter, that the senses are the parents of illusion, and that truth is to be found in the understanding alone. The former did not deny to the conceptions of the understanding a certain kind of reality; but with them it was merely *logical*, with the others it was *mystical*. The former admitted *intellectual* conceptions, but declared that sensuous objects alone possessed real existence. The latter maintained that all real objects were *intelligible*, and believed that the pure understanding possessed a faculty of *intuition* apart from sense, which, in their opinion, served only to confuse the ideas of the understanding.

2. *In relation to the origin* of the pure cognitions of reason, we find one school maintaining that they are derived entirely from experience, and another, that they have their origin in reason alone. *Aristotle* may be regarded as the head of the *Empiricists*, and *Plato* of the *Noologists*. *Locke*, the follower of Aristotle in modern times, and *Leibnitz* of Plato (although he cannot be said to have imitated him in his mysticism), have not been able to bring this question to a settled conclusion. The procedure of Epicurus in his sensual system, in which he always restricted his conclusions to the sphere of experience, was much more consequent than that of Aristotle and Locke. The latter especially, after having derived all the conceptions and principles of the mind from experience, goes so far, in the employment of these conceptions and principles, as to maintain that we can prove the existence of God and the immortality of the soul—both of them objects lying beyond the limits of possible experience—with the same force of demonstration as any mathematical proposition.

3. *In relation to method*. Method is procedure *according to*

*principles.* We may divide the methods at present employed in the field of inquiry into the *naturalistic* and the *scientific.* The *naturalist* of pure reason lays it down as his principle, that common reason, without the aid of science—which he calls sound reason, or common sense—can give a more satisfactory answer to the most important questions of metaphysics than speculation is able to do. He must maintain, therefore, that we can determine the content and circumference of the moon more certainly by the naked eye, than by the aid of mathematical reasoning. But this system is mere misology reduced to principles; and, what is the most absurd thing in this doctrine, the neglect of all scientific means is paraded as a *peculiar method* of extending our cognition. As regards those who are *naturalists* because they know no better, they are certainly not to be blamed. They follow common sense, without parading their ignorance as a method which is to teach us the wonderful secret, how we are to find the truth which lies at the bottom of the well of Democritus.

> Quod sapio satis est mihi, non ego curo
> Esse quod Arcesilas aerumnosique Solones—PERS.

is their motto, under which they may lead a pleasant and praise-worthy life, without troubling themselves with science or troubling science with them.

As regards those who wish to pursue a *scientific* method, they have now the choice of following either the *dogmatical* or the *sceptical,* while they are bound never to desert the *systematic* mode of procedure. When I mention, in relation to the former, the celebrated *Wolf,* and as regards the latter, *David Hume,* I may leave, in accordance with my present intention, all others unnamed. The *critical* path alone is still open. If my reader has been kind and patient enough to accompany me on this hitherto untravelled route, he can now judge whether, if he and others will contribute their exertions towards making this narrow foot-path a high road of thought, that, which many centuries have failed to accomplish, may not be executed before the close of the present—namely, to bring Reason to perfect contentment in regard to that which has always, but without permanent results, occupied her powers and engaged her ardent desire for knowledge.

*Everyman*
A selection of titles

*Everyman*
A selection of titles

*indicates volumes available in paperback

Complete lists of Everyman's Library and Everyman Paperbacks
are available from the Sales Department, J.M. Dent and Sons Ltd,
Aldine House, 33 Welbeck Street, London WIM 8LX.

## BIOGRAPHY

Bligh, William. *A Book of the 'Bounty'*
Boswell, James. *The Life of Samuel Johnson*
Byron, Lord. *Letters*
Cibber, Colley. *An Apology for the Life of Colley Cibber*
*De Quincey, Thomas. *Confessions of an English Opium-Eater*
Forster, John. *Life of Charles Dickens* (2 vols)
*Gaskell, Elizabeth. *The Life of Charlotte Brontë*
*Gilchrist, Alexander. *The Life of William Blake*
Houghton, Lord. *The Life and Letters of John Keats*
*Johnson, Samuel. *Lives of the English Poets: a selection*
Pepys, Samuel. *Diary* (3 vols)
Thomas, Dylan
    *Adventures in the Skin Trade*
    *Portrait of the Artist as a Young Dog*
Tolstoy. *Childhood, Boyhood and Youth*
*Vasari, Giorgio. *Lives of the Painters, Sculptors, and Architects*
    (4 vols)

## ESSAYS AND CRITICISM

Arnold, Matthew. *On the Study of Celtic Literature*
*Bacon, Francis. *Essays*
Coleridge, Samuel Taylor
    *Biographia Literaria*
    *Shakespearean Criticism* (2 vols)
Dryden, John. *Of Dramatic Poesy and other critical essays*
    (2 vols)

\*Lawrence, D.H. *Stories, Essays and Poems*
\*Milton, John. *Prose Writings*
Montaigne, Michel Eyquem de. *Essays* (3 vols)
Paine, Thomas. *The Rights of Man*
Pater, Walter. *Essays on Literature and Art*
Spencer, Herbert. *Essays on Education and Kindred Subjects*

## FICTION

---

\*American Short Stories of the Nineteenth Century
Austen, Jane
    \*Emma
    \*Mansfield Park
    \*Northanger Abbey
    \*Persuasion
    \*Pride and Prejudice
    \*Sense and Sensibility
\*Bennett, Arnold. *The Old Wives' Tale*
Boccaccio, Giovanni. *The Decameron*
Brontë, Anne
    \*Agnes Grey
    \*The Tenant of Wildfell Hall
Brontë, Charlotte
    \*Jane Eyre
    \*The Professor and Emma (a fragment)
    \*Shirley
    \*Villette
Brontë, Emily. *Wuthering Heights* and *Poems*
\*Bunyan, John. *Pilgrim's Progress*
Butler, Samuel.
    Erewhon and Erewhon Revisited
    The Way of All Flesh
Collins, Wilkie
    \*The Moonstone
    \*The Woman in White
Conrad, Joseph
    \*The Nigger of the 'Narcissus', Typhoon, Falk and other
      stories
    \*Nostromo

\*Stowe, Harriet Beecher. *Uncle Tom's Cabin*
Stevenson, R.L.
    \*Dr Jekyll and Mr Hyde, The Merry Men *and other tales*
    \*Kidnapped*
    \*The Master of Ballantrae *and* Weir of Hermiston*
    \*Treasure Island*
Swift, Jonathan
    \*Gulliver's Travels*
    \*A Tale of a Tub *and other satires*
Thackeray, W.M.
    *Henry Esmond*
    \*Vanity Fair*
Thomas, Dylan
    \*Miscellany 1*
    \*Miscellany 2*
    \*Miscellany 3*
\*Tolstoy, Leo. *Master and Man and other parables and tales*
Trollope, Anthony
    \*The Warden*
    \*Barchester Towers*
    *Dr Thorne*
    \*Framley Parsonage*
    *Small House at Allington*
    *Last Chronicle of Barset*
\*Voltaire, *Candide and other tales*
\*Wilde, Oscar. *The Picture of Dorian Gray*
Woolf, Virginia. *To the Lighthouse*


## HISTORY

---

\*The Anglo-Saxon Chronicle
Burnet, Gilbert. *History of His Own Time*
\*Crèvecoeur. *Letters from an American Farmer*
Gibbon, Edward. *The Decline and Fall of the Roman Empire*
    (6 vols)
Macaulay, T.B. *The History of England* (4 vols)
Machiavelli, Niccolò. *Florentine History*
Prescott, W.H. *History of the Conquest of Mexico*

## LEGENDS AND SAGAS

*Beowulf and Its Analogues
*Chrétien de Troyes. *Arthurian Romances*
 Egils Saga
 Holinshed, Raphael. *Chronicle*
*Layamon and Wace. *Arthurian Chronicles*
*The Mabinogion
*The Saga of Gisli
*The Saga of Grettir the Strong
 Snorri Sturluson. *Heimskringla* (3 vols)
*The Story of Burnt Njal

## POETRY AND DRAMA

*Anglo-Saxon Poetry
*American Verse of the Nineteenth Century
*Arnold, Matthew. *Selected Poems and Prose*
*Blake, William. *Selected Poems*
*Browning, Robert. *Men and Women and other poems*
 Chaucer, Geoffrey
      **Canterbury Tales*
      **Troilus and Criseyde*
*Clare, John. *Selected Poems*
*Coleridge, Samuel Taylor. *Poems*
*Elizabethan Sonnets
*English Moral Interludes
*Everyman and Medieval Miracle Plays
*Everyman's Book of Evergreen Verse
*Gay, John. *The Beggar's Opera and other eighteenth-century
      plays*
*The Golden Treasury of Longer Poems
 Goldsmith, Oliver. *Poems and Plays*
*Hardy, Thomas. *Selected Poems*
*Herbert, George. *The English Poems*
*Hopkins, Gerard Manley. *The Major Poems*
 Ibsen, Henrik
      **A Doll's House; The Wild Dick; The Lady from the Sea*
      **Hedda Gabler; The Master Builder; John Gabriel Borkman*

\*Keats, John. *Poems*
\*Langland, William. *The Vision of Piers Plowman*
  Marlowe, Christopher. *Complete Plays and Poems*
\*Milton, John. *Complete Poems*
\*Middleton, Thomas. *Three Plays*
\*Palgrave's Golden Treasury
\*Pearl, Patience, Cleanness, and Sir Gawain and the Green Knight
\*Pope, Alexander. *Collected Poems*
\*Restoration Plays
\*The Rubáiyát of Omar Khayyám and other Persian poems
\*Shelley, Percy Bysshe. *Selected Poems*
\*Six Middle English Romances
\*Spenser, Edmund. *The Faerie Queene: a selection*
  The Stuffed Owl
\*Synge, J.M. *Plays, Poems and Prose*
\*Tennyson, Alfred. *In Memoriam, Maud and other poems*
  Thomas, Dylan
        \**Collected Poems, 1934–1952*
        \**Under Milk Wood*
\*Wilde, Oscar. *Plays, Prose Writings and Poems*
\*Wordsworth, William. *Selected Poems*


## RELIGION AND PHILOSOPHY

  Aristotle. *Metaphysics*
\*Bacon, Francis. *The Advancement of Learning*
\*Berkeley, George. *Philosophical Works including the works on
        vision*
\*The Buddha's Philosophy of Man
\*Chinese Philosophy in Classical Times
\*Descartes, René. *A Discourse on Method*
\*Hindu Scriptures
  Hume, David. *A Treatise of Human Nature*
\*Kant, Immanuel. *A Critique of Pure Reason*
\*The Koran
\*Leibniz, Gottfried Wilhelm. *Philosophical Writings*
\*Locke, John. *An Essay Concerning Human Understanding
        (abridgment)*
\*Moore, Thomas. *Utopia*

Pascal, Blaise. *Pensées*
Plato. *The Trial and Death of Socrates*
*The Ramayana and Mahábhárata

## SCIENCES: POLITICAL AND GENERAL

Aristotle. *Ethics*
*Castiglione, Baldassare. *The Book of the Courtier*
*Coleridge, Samuel Taylor. *On the Constitution of the Church and State*
*Darwin, Charles. *The Origin of Species*
George, Henry. *Progress and Poverty*
Harvey, William. *The Circulation of the Blood and other writings*
*Hobbes, Thomas. *Leviathan*
*Locke, John. *Two Treatises of Government*
*Machiavelli, Niccolò. *The Prince and other political writings*
Marx, Karl. *Capital. Volume I*
*Mill, J.S. *Utilitarianism; On Liberty; Representative Government*
Owen, Robert. *A New View of Society and other writings*
*Plato. *The Republic*
*Ricardo, David. *The Principles of Political Economy and Taxation*
Rousseau, J.-J.
  *Emile*
  *The Social Contract* and *Discourses*
Smith, Adam. *The Wealth of Nations*
*Wollstonecraft, Mary. *A Vindication of the Rights of Woman*

## TRAVEL AND TOPOGRAPHY

Boswell, James. *The Journal of a Tour to the Hebrides*
*Darwin, Charles. *The Voyage of the 'Beagle'*
Giraldus Cambrensis. *Itinerary through Wales* and *Description of Wales*
Stevenson, R.L. *An Inland Voyage; Travels with a Donkey; The Silverado Squatters*
Stow, John. *The Survey of London*
*White, Gilbert. *The Natural History of Selborne*